THE SNOW TRILOGY

COLLECTOR'S EDITION

AMY M. LE

THE SNOW TRILOGY

First edition November 2021

Jacket design by Amy M. Le and Virginia McKevitt

Manufactured in the United States of America

Library of Congress Control Number: 2021914757

ISBN: 978-1-7372037-5-9 (paperback)
ISBN: 978-1-7372037-6-6 (hardback)
ISBN: 978-1-7372037-4-2 (ebook)

DEDICATION

This book is dedicated to all the refugees who risked everything for a better life and war veterans who served bravely and selflessly. To anyone who has ever felt adrift in life, may you find your tribe and hang your hat where friends, family, and food bond you together.

In memory of my mother, Snow, who sacrificed so much, this book is a tribute to her perseverance and love.

ACKNOWLEDGMENTS

Thank you to my amazing husband, Joseph Walls, and my witty son, Preston Walls, for being the best cheerleaders. To my cousin, Tri Le, you are the best brother I can ever wish to have. To my incredible family, friends, fans, and network of supporters, thank you for sharing my work, for your support, advice, stories, reviews, and encouragement.

A special thanks to my critique team "The Quixotics" (Ilene Birkwood, Keith Madsen, Frances Sonnabend, Tricia Corbett, and Mac MacCullough) for spending countless hours reading my first two books and providing invaluable feedback.

A heartfelt thanks to Alicia Dean, Ally Robertson, and Staci Mauney for your editorial scrubbing to make these pages come to life better than I could imagine.

To Estrella Sung and Virginia McKevitt, your help with my book covers was invaluable. C.M. Healy, I appreciate your guidance in launching the first novel which gave me the confidence to publish more books.

To the military veterans who shared with me their personal stories of pain and hope, I thank you sincerely for your time. My gratitude to David Cruz, Dominic Dimino, Michael Doud, Michael Harmon, Joshua McGoveran, Charles Peters, and Greg Simpson.

To my beta readers, you inspire me to write my best. Thank you, Michael Harmon, Lori Kennedy, Diana LeBeau, Brianna Neighbors, Gina Richardson, Tabitha Salom, and Lisa Schumann.

PNWA Literary Contest
2018 Finalist
One woman's extraordinary story of survival after the fall of Saigon.
SNOW
in Vietnam
A NOVEL
AMY M. LE

1 ANT SPIDERS (MAY 1973)

I never intended to marry so late. Here I am a thirty-four-year-old virgin about to marry a man I hardly know. The Paris peace treaty was signed this year and the end of the war is near. Normalcy will be restored in Việt Nam once again.

As I scrutinize myself in the mirror, I see how different I am from the other women in my hometown of Vĩnh Bình. They have long, thick black manes, straight as a runway, framing their oval faces. Then there is me, with my round face and fine head of hair, naturally speckled with cinnamon highlights left by the scorching sun. The wavy locks, tamed only by water and a barrette, are now threatening to go limp. Today, I am going for the Elizabeth Taylor look, with my pixie cut and pale skin. Most women in my town, from the young school girls to my elders, appear fragile and gaunt. Not me. Despite my small frame, my fat arms still give me away.

"Eight, what are you doing standing there?" My older sister bursts into my room, panting and looking provoked. "You and Mông Dơ can be twins." She is referring to our chicken, whose name means "Dirty Butt".

"I do not—" She never lets me finish.

Whipping me sharply around and squeezing my chubby arm, she lectures me on how to behave today. "Do not spill any tea. Bow and smile to your future in-laws and receive their gift with both hands. Under no circumstances do you show discomfort or displeasure." My sister is a bully and enjoys bossing everyone around. She is not the beauty or the brains of the family, nor is she an affectionate soul, but darn if she is not a great cook.

"Do not worry, Sister Six, I will not mess up as you did." I yank my arm away. Although I am the youngest of seven children, Eight is my name, for the parental unit is always number one. With the heat and the dread of my upcoming nuptials, I have no patience with Sister Six today.

"Do not speak until you are spoken to first. And for Heaven and Earth's sake, do something about your face!" Sister Six abruptly leaves my room.

I take a quick glance in the mirror. My skin is shiny with beads of sweat forming around my brows while the makeup is melting from the humidity. Even with all the windows open, there is no breeze. The sounds of mopeds zipping by and the familiar rasp of the old baguette lady sounding the sale of four sandwiches for twenty thousand piasters percolates through the window. From the corner of my eye, I see that Six, in her haste to exit, dropped a small photograph of my fiancé. It dances lazily to the floor, as if to convey that it, too, is in no hurry to start the day. I stare at the photo but all I can think of is Sam.

***

Two years ago in 1971, I met Sam. My niece, Tâm, who is twelve years younger than I, accompanied me on a holiday trip to the city of Tuy Hòa, northeast of Đà Lạt where I worked, some two hundred forty kilometers up the coast. We were parched from our travels and settled for some food and iced coffee with condensed milk.

"Chao Co," came a disembodied voice, gruff yet pleasant. The words were Vietnamese but the pronunciation conveyed an attempt of a three-year-old. I recognized the accent was American and pretended not to hear him, hoping he would go away. He repeated himself and I feigned interest in the live music in front by the bar, using the loud guitar chords from the band as an excuse to ignore him. I felt a reluctant tap on my shoulder.

I gazed into eyes that were pennywort green with specks of black and yellow like a ripe kiwi fruit. He was tall and his skin tan, kissed golden from the blistering sun.

"My friend and I would like to sit. May we borrow this chair?" His smile was mischievous, which made me a little nervous, but his dimple soon put me at ease. I nodded and turned my attention back to my niece. It was not long before the soldier's deep voice captivated me. Drawn in by his honeyed speech, I had to eavesdrop. My English was not bad for I had learned the language at the university.

"What do you think of her, Sky?" asked the American soldier.

"C'mon, Sam. Did you see the tits on that girl?" Sam's friend also had a deep voice but not as melodic and soothing as the green-

2

eyed soldier. I hoped they were not referring to Tâm or me.

"I prefer my women with a bigger rack, like pomelos." Sam demonstrated with his hands how big he liked them.

"Anything bigger than a mouthful is a waste in my opinion." Sky gulped down the last of his beer and ordered two more.

They watched with amusement as the owner of the watering hole pulled up a dusty canvas tarp to reveal a cooler with a big block of ice in it. He chipped a couple of big pieces into glass mugs, and in robotic synchronicity, poured two cans of warm "33" beer into their mugs. The bartender, weathered and haggard with his "555" brand cigarette dangling from his lips, adroitly handed Sky their drinks.

The two of them were quite the sight, hunched over a small table with their long legs spilling out in front of their lanky bodies like ant spiders. Sporting their M-16s, newly issued steel pot helmets and flak vests, they appeared comfortable despite the onlookers.

"Say, where are you from?" Sam took a swig of his iced beer.

"From Burien, Washington." Sky lit up a cigarette. "Born and raised in the Seattle area!"

"What?" Sam exclaimed. "Get out of here! I'm from Washington too. Bellevue, to be exact. I can't say I've been to Burien though. Pretty much stuck to the eastside."

The smell of phở brought my attention back to my table. The distinct smells of charred onions and ginger lingered in my nostrils as I took the first sip of the broth. Outside was a sweltering thirty-two degrees Celsius, but the hot soup soothed my throat.

Tâm squeezed some lime juice into her bowl. "Aunt Eight, after we eat, can we go to the beach?" I nodded as I pinched off some more basil leaves to add to my phở. "We can order more cà phê and stop to get some durian."

Again, I nodded. I was not in the mood to talk so going to the beach to relax was appealing. I was famished and debated whether to order a second bowl. The thought of gaining weight, however, quickly crushed my impulses. While my niece ordered our iced coffees, I took the opportunity to resume eavesdropping on the American GIs.

"We better get back to the truck." Sky stood up, standing almost two meters tall, and walked toward the sidewalk. "We were due back a half-hour ago."

Sam was right behind him. My eyes followed them and I was bewitched by Sam's derrière. Most Vietnamese men do not have meat on them, so to see a man with a bulging behind was hypnotizing. As he walked leisurely, the fatigues wrinkled at the base of his butt, emphasizing his muscular thighs. I was so bewitched that when he turned his head to look back at me, I was paralyzed with embarrassment.

"Cam on." He winked and gave me his thanks with a smile that showed all his perfect white teeth. *What would it be like to be courted by an American?*

The sound of a man's voice, shrieking profanities, quickly jolted me back to reality. There was a lot of commotion as bystanders rushed to the street corner. Tâm and I joined them.

There was Sky, pacing back and forth, arms raised, with his rifle hitting his leg each time he pivoted to retrace his steps. "Fuck! Damn boysans stole one of our windshield wipers and ripped off our gas can!" He nodded in the direction where the thieves made their escape. His face was redder than a lychee fruit. "And this goddamn fool was asleep behind the wheel when he should have been keeping watch!" In the driver seat sat a local boy around eleven years old. Sky continued his ranting, calling the boy worthless, saying how he should have known better than to trust the "idiot". Spit frothed at the corner of his mouth. "I paid you to watch the truck and keep it safe." His posture stiffened. He clenched his teeth and demanded his money back.

The boy was terrified of this foreigner towering over him, no doubt worried the M-16 would be pointed at him. I held my breath. I anticipated Sam would commiserate with his comrade and yell like a lunatic as well.

"Calm down." Even with his brow furrowed in displeasure, Sam remained composed. He reminded me of the actor, Clint Eastwood. "Who's to say one of these faces is an unfriendly?"

During times of war, that much was true. You could never tell the "friendlies" from the "unfriendlies". They all had the same face. While both men were temporarily distracted, the young boy took the opportunity to escape and darted down the road.

Sky roared at the boy running for his life. "Yeah, you better di di mau!"

The crowd around the two soldiers dissipated. The thrill and excitement had subsided. Yet, there I stood, motionless.

My niece startled me. "Can we go?" Tâm held our iced coffees.

"Not yet," I stalled. There was something about Sam that had me fixated.

"Excuse me, sir?" The words tumbled out of my mouth before

I realized I spoke. "You have enough gasoline?"

Sam and Sky took a couple steps closer. Tâm took a half step back, looking bewildered.

"I believe so. Thank you, er, miss…?" Sam fished for my name.

"Tuyết," I responded. "It means 'snow'. This is my niece, Tâm."

"Well shit, so there is snow in Vietnam!" Sky grinned from ear to ear.

"Tuy-yet! That sounds beautiful. I'm Corporal Sam Hammond of the U.S. Army, 180th Assault Support Helicopter Company. And this is Sergeant Skyler Herrington."

After a few pleasantries, Sky insisted they head back to base. We parted ways and I did not think I would see Sam again. Tâm and I were in Tuy Hòa for a short stay. Soon, we were expected back to Đà Lạt and back to work at the bank. Sam and Sky, the American ant spiders, had a war to win and a tunnel to infiltrate.

***

I analyze my reflection in the mirror and worry my eyes will betray my true age. The face that peers back at me can still be mistaken for a twenty-something year old. The naiveté and insecurities are still there despite my thirty-four-year-old eyes. Sister Six is right; I do look like our disheveled chicken, Dirty Butt. At least my áo dài, the traditional silk dress of Việt Nam, is not wrinkled. Sister Six insisted my dress be red and yellow, colors of our country's flag. The baguette lady makes her loop again, chirping four "bánh mì" for twenty thousand piasters, which is less than a U.S. dollar. I walk to the top of the staircase and grip the railing. It has been two years since I first met Sam and Sky at that watering hole in Tuy Hòa. There is no time to dwell on the past now. I make my descent down the stairs.

Everyone is outside. I peek into the dining room. A cloth, red as a betel nut, adorns the long dinner table. Three chairs stand on either side, like centurions waiting for instructions, or perhaps more like the Việt Cộng, waiting for their next move. The cushions are re-upholstered in yellow silk; images of dragons carved on the backs of the chairs symbolize life and prosperity. I imagine myself sitting there and blending in, becoming invisible. Out of the kitchen window, I see poor Dirty Butt confined to her dome-shaped wire cage. I, too, am soon to be caged myself.

My nephew appears and takes my hand. "They are almost

5

here." He leads me into the family room.

"Tree, wait with me." We sit together on the bench. Tree is not his real name, but we call him that because he is always climbing things. He is my eleven-year-old nephew, although he appears much younger. He is small, fast, and has a baby face. Despite his youthful appearance, he is muscular from years of running and scaling coconut trees to get away from my brother Seven's whipping. One time, I found him on top of a tall cabinet, out of his mother's reach. He squatted on top, knees and hips bent, with all his weight on the heels of his feet. What a funny sight to see him hunkered down, half crying and half taunting, while his mother jumped up and down trying to swat him with a broom handle.

From the window, I see the road leading to our home. I feel as if I am transported to another world. Sounds, smells, and colors beyond the house overwhelm me. Scooters zip by in disorderly fashion, their drivers honking at fellow riders who do not adhere to their side of the unmarked roads. Pedestrians yell as they jump out of the way to avoid getting hit while crossing to the other side. Babies are crying, no doubt hungry and uncomfortable with the heat. On typical days when there is not a wedding procession to gawk at, the view outside is drab. My neighbors, who usually wear the same boring polyester pants and tunic, in flat colors of brown or mustard yellow, now loiter around the front of their home drinking coffee or smoking a cigarette, and complain about losing a hand of cards. Today though, their animation shows off their youthful gait and toothless grins. Most flaunt their finest clothes and exchange the monochromatic for the loud, multi-colored patterns.

"Aunt Eight, let me know if you need anything." Tree is so many things I am not. He does not ask questions. He makes statements. He hates confinement; prefers the education learned on the streets to the teachings in school; he does not care much for anything except being one with nature. The boy does have a strong sense of family though and in the end, always comes home.

"I do not want to be alone. How is school?" I pat his head.

"School is for kids who do not know what they want in life."

"And you have your life figured out?"

"The American soldiers," Tree starts, "I hear them talk about their adventures. If it was not for my mom and dad, I would leave Vĩnh Bình, but someone has to take care of them."

"Yes, that is your responsibility." The faint smell of a roasted pig reminds me I have not eaten all morning. The anticipation of tasting the savory, juicy meat makes my mouth water. "Run along and fetch me some yogurt. It will be a couple of hours before we eat."

Tree quietly dismisses himself. I rarely have conversations with my nephew. Kids are here to work and do as we adults tell them to do. My interactions with Tree have been limited to fetch me this or tell your mom that. While I wait for Tree, I spy on my family standing in front of our house, looking magnificent in their tailored suits and dresses. It is the first time I smile all week.

In the distance, a procession of people from the groom's side of the family walks up the road toward us. A weathered, eighty-year-old man leads the procession. He represents the family. Next in line strides the groom's father, whom I had met once. He is still handsome for his age despite his stern and stoic appearance. I spot my future husband next. There he is, all 1.7 meters of him. He walks confidently like a dignitary, with his head held high, commanding respect, and his blue silk tunic clinging to his lean, muscular body. His legs are bowed, but on this day, it is not noticeable. The trousers underneath his ceremonial costume fit loosely and march in rhythm with his swagger. He looks sharp. Nine men, similarly dressed, follow him. Each carries a black lacquered box, adorned with a red embroidered cloth. My anxiety gets a hold of me. With each step they make, I feel a layer of independence being stripped from me.

The procession appears to go on and on. Two men carry a roasted pig hung from a spit. A group of women, young and old, cluck animatedly as they walk toward my family's house. All around the women are the "littles", each child oblivious to the etiquette preached to them minutes before the walk. At least thirty people approach the house.

A loud pop explodes through the air, followed by alternating crackles and pops in rapid succession. I smell smoke. Screams filter through the window. Dirty Butt flaps her wings, frantically squawking in protest. I stiffen and quickly drop to my knees. My headdress tumbles to the floor. I cover my face with my clammy hands as I kneel. My heart thumps loudly. I wish I had my rosary. *The Việt Cộng is raiding the village!*

"Here is your yog—" Tree's small hand wraps around my wrist. "Do not be afraid. Firecrackers were lit." He hands me my headdress and I carefully place it on my head. "You should fix your hair."

It takes a second to register I am not in danger. I hear laughter.

My future husband and his family are inside the house. I stand up with a sigh of relief and muster the strength to hold back the tears. Not today, I tell myself. There will be no crying.

"Do I look like Mông Dơ?" I take a deep breath and an exaggerated exhale. Tree's silence confirms it. "There is no time. Maybe he will call off the wedding after he sees how ruffled I look."

Tree hands me the homemade yogurt that Sister Six made. After inhaling two big spoonfuls, I step into the dining room. I am overwhelmed with all the faces looking at me, but it is my father's that makes me cringe.

Father smiles but his eyes are stern and glaring. "Mr. and Mrs. Vương, may I present to you my daughter, Tuyết."

I bow to my future in-laws and greet them. "Chào bác."

"Your daughter is lovely, Mr. Lê." My future father-in-law clasps his warm hands around mine. "She indeed is as beautiful and light-skinned as snow."

"Please, do not be so formal. Call me Sáng. We will be family soon."

"Very well, Sáng. You can call me Bình. This is my father, Ngạn, my wife, Hương, and you know our son, Tý."

"Please, sit down." My father pulls out his chair and the rest follow suit. I remain standing. Bình and Hương smile at me with kind, empathetic eyes.

Sister Six floats into the dining room with the tea tray. One look at me and her smile disappears. I sense the disapproval of my appearance. She takes her seat in the matriarch chair beside Father.

All eyes are on me as I pick up the steaming hot teapot. It is heavier than I anticipated. Sister Six brewed a large pot and must have filled it to the top. I hold my breath and slowly pour my grandfather-in-law his tea. As the eldest, he receives his tea first. *Why do the cups have to be so small?* One splash and my marriage will be doomed. Next, I pour for my father.

I draw my attention to my in-laws. They are wealthier than my family. Mrs. Hương is plump. Any woman who has such a round face clearly is not starving or working hard in the rice fields. Her skin is flawless, stretched tight from the layers of fat beneath her cheeks and neck. She has on every piece of jewelry. Jade bracelets, the shade of cilantro, decorate both wrists; matching emerald stones dangle from her long earlobes and a marquise-cut emerald, eighteen-carat gold ring, show off her pudgy ring finger. Her green silk áo dài barely hold in the rolls of fat above her pants.

Her husband is the direct opposite. Mr. Bình is not ostentatious and is quite skinny. His only accessories are his wedding band and the flesh on his face that sags loosely. It is as if all the nutrients have been siphoned by Mrs. Hương. Still, he is a handsome man. I think of my in-laws as couple number ten because he is slender like the number one and she is round like the number zero. I smile at my private joke as I carefully pour the hot artichoke tea into their cups. Not a drop escapes onto the table.

With one finger pressed onto the lid of the ceramic teapot, I continue pouring flawlessly for Sister Six and my fiancé. I feel relief. Not a single drop of tea spilled. Our marriage should be a happy and lasting one.

Tý stands up and presses his hand against the small of my back. "A toast." It is the first time we have stood this close to one another. He smells like grease, sweat, and the narcissus plant. His presence catches me off guard and surprisingly excites me. "May we be blessed with many sons!"

We all raise our teacups and sip the sweet soothing liquid. Mrs. Hương presents me with a gift. Inside the velvet box is the most exquisite twenty-four karat gold necklace I have ever seen. The chain cradles a golden phoenix with emeralds, diamonds, and rubies. "For strength and courage to always rise above." She winks at me and helps me put it on.

My wedding day goes by in a blur.

***

My wedding night is lasting forever. Tonight I lose my virtue. Other than Sam, no man has ever kissed me. As I lie here with my husband, who is grunting and fondling my body like he is prying apart a jackfruit, I recall my argument with Sister Six two winters ago.

She warned me true love did not exist. "Love is a concept for dreamers. If you do not marry soon, your shriveled prunes will do you no good."

"Sam and I are in love. He is going to marry me when his tour ends."

"You are foolish to believe your soldier will take you to America. Father will accept the first proposal he gets. You need to start a family before it is too late."

I believed arranged marriages were not for me. I was convinced life began and ended in Sam's arms. However, Sister Six was right. Love is for dreamers. I am married now.

My husband finally rolls over. "We will try again tomorrow night." His gaze wraps me in tenderness. I feel guilty for not trying to please him. In time, I know I can love him.

2 MY LITTLE DOLLY (JULY 1974)

My neighbor's rooster crows this morning like clockwork. It is 5:41 a.m. I roll over to see if Tý is still in bed, but he is not. I slide out of bed with my nightgown clinging to my sweaty thighs and swollen belly. Soon we will meet, my little dolly. I am convinced my baby will be a girl but Tý says she will be a boy. I walk down the hallway to the kitchen and pour a glass of iced coffee with condensed milk. Next to the bowl of sugar apples and soursop fruit is a note with my name on it.

"Tuyết, I hope you slept well and our son did not keep you up all night. Father needs my help this morning with the cassava crops. Do not wait for me. Belly kisses. I love you."

"How did you sleep, Aunt Eight?" Tâm's voice carries from the adjacent room.

"Like a prawn pan-fried in soy sauce." I join her on the hammock.

"That bad? This sticky heat is unbearable. Shall we go to the market and get ingredients for lunch?" Tâm grabs a basket to take to the market. "I want spring rolls."

I chuckle. "We should torture your mom by making her cook for us."

"We do that every day."

"True." I take a sip of my coffee. "No shrimp for me, though. It will make me scar. I have a feeling this baby is coming before the next sunrise."

Tâm looks at me, her mouth agape. "You are not due for another month! Besides, no shrimp during pregnancy is an old wives' tale. You are a healthy woman."

"A woman who just turned thirty-five years old."

"Well, with that face, you could still hook every creature out there, if you had not hung up your fishing net."

We laugh and link arms. "Let us go to the market," we say in unison.

As usual, the market is bustling in the city center. Vendors line the perimeters of the square, selling fabric, plastic toys, shoes, jewelry, and clothes. In the middle of the square, fishermen and their families lay out their catch from that morning. Others sell live frogs, chicken, rice mice, and snakes. We stop at the produce section. I love the kaleidoscope of vibrant colors, each fruit vying for my approval. There are durian, rambutans, longans, dragon fruits, and other exotic produce. Squatting on her haunches, an old woman picks up a large cockroach that is scurrying behind the mangosteen cart. She bites its head off and chews her prize. Crunch. I am horrified.

"You going to buy something, or stare at my mangos?" She pops the last morsel of the insect into her mouth. Tâm and I come home with more fruits than we can consume in a week.

***

"Sister Six, what is for dinner?" I saunter into the kitchen. The smell of turmeric and garlic sautéing in the frying pan beckons me.

"Crepes." Oh, how I love bánh xèo! My sister has perfected her recipe. She fries the batter so that it has a nice crunch on the outside, but still soft and savory on the inside.

"Can you make all three of mine with pork belly, onions, and bean sprouts? No shrimp. Shrimp will—"

"Make you scar. Yes, I know. You seriously want three? How are you going to fit through the door when that baby comes?"

"Make it four crepes then." I stick out my tongue. "This baby is coming today. I need my strength. Oh, and make mine extra spicy to induce labor."

Six rolls her eyes at me. She is making the sauce for the crepes, combining fish sauce with lime juice, sugar, chili, garlic, and coconut water. I try to commit to memory how to make the sauce as I enjoy my iced coffee. Strangely, I have not had any strong cravings during my pregnancy. I have been eating a lot of fruits, drinking a lot of coffee, and enjoying every spicy meal Sister Six prepares. To break up the silence, I turn on the radio.

"Richard Nixon, president of the United States of America, has been following the impeachment debate closely, but when the vote came from the House Judiciary Committee, he was nowhere near a television. Instead, he was at Red Beach in Camp Pendleton Marine Base. President Nixon was with his daughter, Tricia, and son-in-law, Edward Cox, when News Secretary, Ron

Ziegler, informed him of the vote.

"What are your thoughts on President Nixon's possible impeachment?" I strum my fingers on the table and steal a piece of the pork.

"I have more things to worry about than Nixon. Hand me the big frying pan." Sister Six pours some pig fat into the pan. "So many soldiers come here, get our women pregnant, and leave them. Half-breeds are popping out of the womb like bubbles in boiling water. Every day, there is death and we are all haunted by spirits."

"Do you remember the story of Captain Martinez?"

Captain Martinez served in the U.S. Air Force. He flew an AC-47 gunship, which was nicknamed Puff the Magic Dragon. Tâm spent a few months in Đà Nẵng where she cleaned the barracks. The men called her little mama-san and referred to her as their hooch maid. Captain Martinez once told Tâm, through a translator, that he felt the pull of nationalism and volunteered for a mission in Việt Nam. He was deployed to Đà Nẵng. At night, the Việt Cộng would launch rockets into their base, so they referred to Đà Nẵng as Rocket City.

"He was one troubled soul to have demons chasing him." Sister Six pours the crepe batter into the sizzling frying pan. The smell of lard permeates the kitchen and I am salivating.

I pop another slice of fried pork belly into my mouth. "He had an angel, not a demon. Captain Martinez was on his way to his bus pick-up after midnight for his 3 a.m. mission that morning. He was strolling and heard someone call his name. 'Captain Martinez, wait.' He stopped and looked around hoping it was his co-pilot, but it was pitch black and he did not see anyone. He shook it off and picked up his pace. Out of the corner of his eye, he saw his bus, so he started to run. He heard again the loud voice scream in his ear 'Captain Martinez, WAIT'. He stopped dead in his tracks and was paralyzed by fear. The hairs on his neck and arms stood up and he was afraid to turn around. By the time he looked up, the bus was gone. Another one finally pulled up twenty-five minutes later. The driver told him he was delayed due to engine problems and had to get another bus. Otherwise, he would have been there sooner. Three-quarter of a kilometer into the ride, Captain Martinez heard an air raid warning, followed by the sound of a humongous BOOM." I take a plate and bang it hard against the table to see Sister Six jump, hoping she will pee her pants a little.

Startled, she swears, "Mother F- I have hot grease here, Eight!"

Feeling quite pleased with myself, I continue. "He looked over his shoulder and saw flames rising one-hundred-fifty meters into the air. He thought maybe a gas truck got hit. He got to his operation and found out that boom he heard thirty minutes before was his aircraft being blown up. What had happened was the crew chief had finished fueling up. There was a loud metallic click and he ran towards the shelter as the rocket flew right into the cockpit. When it blew, it took the gas truck with it." Sister Six stares at me blankly. "So you see, Sister Six, Captain Martinez had an angel— AACCCKKKK!" I wail loudly.

Sister Six jumps. "Not funny. You about gave me a heart attack."

"No, the baby. She is coming. Oh, God."

"He cannot come yet. The crepes are not done!" Sister Six zips back and forth, flailing her arms above her head. I debate whether she resembles Dirty Butt or an orangutan.

***

I gave birth to my daughter at 11:53 p.m. on Tuesday, July 30, 1974.

"What is wrong with her?" I can see Tý in the hallway talking to the doctor.

"Mr. Vương, your wife is fine, but your baby, well, her heart does not sound normal. We need to run some tests."

"My daughter looks so frail. There is no color in her face."

"Mr. Vương, your wife is awake. Please, go see her while we tend to your baby." The doctor quickly leaves my husband.

"Tuyết, sweetheart. You are awake. How do you feel?" Tý takes hold of my hand.

"Where is our baby?" My voice is barely above a whisper. I desperately want to see her.

"You will see her soon enough."

"I told you she would be a girl."

Tý smiles at me. "You are right. I have a name picked out for her."

"I hope it is not a common name."

"Can any daughter of ours be common?"

"I like the name Tuyết Mai. She is a part of me so I like Tuyết and Mai for the beauty of the apricot blossoms."

"That is exotic. Mai also means 'tomorrow'. She is our future, and she is beautiful like her mother and the blossoms." Tý caresses my arm.

"You said you had a name picked out?"

"Yes, Thủy-Tiên."

"Water-Angel?"

"Correct, because she is an angel sent from heaven, and like water, she will bring us new life and restore hope during this time of war and drought."

"I like that. Strong like water and pious like angels." I close my eyes.

"Rest. I will be back later." Tý kisses my forehead and exits the room.

I drift off to sleep. In my dreams, I see my baby, lying limp and pale like a little dolly. She is dying.

***

The sun is shining brightly. I survey the room and take inventory of the fruits and bundles of sticky rice wrapped in plantain leaves. My stomach growls. Outside my room, the voices are muffled, but one distinct voice can be heard, drowning out the rest.

"These crepes are currently golden and fresh, and unless we see our sister right now, they are going to become old, smelly, and limp crepes, and I shall name them Doctor Vũ crepes, after you." My sister's voice can sound like television static to most people, but if you listen carefully, you can decipher the subliminal message. Sister Six and Brother Seven burst into my room.

"I would still eat the Doctor Vũ crepes," Seven says.

"They are not for you," Sister Six snaps. She rushes to my bed. "I made you some crepes, extra crispy the way you like them. No shrimp."

Never did Sister Six shine more beautifully than she does at this moment. Maybe it is her skin, moist from the tiny beads of perspiration percolating to the surface, now glistening in the sunlight. Perhaps it is her untamed hair, flowing freely over her heaving bosom, which makes her appear feral and ready to fight. My stomach rumbles in protest and reminds me, yes, Sister Six is beautiful because she is holding a plate of warm, delicious crepes.

"I am starving." I eagerly wait for Brother Seven to hand me chopsticks. "Do I get to see my baby today?" Neither of them responds. Their eyes try to convey a message of positivity and joy, as their mouth and face grimace. "Go get Doctor Vũ."

Like a lieutenant following his general's order, Brother Seven is dismissed to carry out a task. There is awkward silence as I avoid eye contact with my sister and resume eating. I am no longer hungry but I fear the wrath of Six if I push my plate aside. I have always been in competition with my sister. She is a strong matriarch, with healthy children, and a strong backbone to take charge. She is always in control and effective when conveying her suggestions. She lives in the real world while I numb my feeling of inadequacy by living in a dream state.

The door opens. Doctor Vũ and Brother Seven walk in, followed by Tâm carrying two fresh coconuts. I am happy to see my niece. One breath later, a nurse comes in, holding a small bundle wrapped in a stained white cloth. My chest feels heavy and I imagine myself being crushed, one rock at a time. My stomach is in knots. There is phlegm in my throat and I suppress the urge to vomit. The nurse gently places the small bundle into my arms. My baby feels lighter than my chicken, Dirty Butt. I cradle her. She peers back at me with her dark eyes. Her pupils, black and round, remind me of longan seeds. Her translucent skin tells me she does not belong on Earth, but on another plane of existence. Her face is round and expressionless. Her blue lips are wrinkled and puckered, like an old lady coming in for a kiss. I am overwhelmed by the exquisite beauty of her ugliness. Her breathing is weak but the rise and fall of her little chest assure me she is alive. The tears fall as I feel the imprint of my baby's love, fear, curiosity, hope, and joy. Perhaps all those emotions are what I am imprinting on her as well.

"Madame, we detect a heart murmur." Doctor Vũ is addressing me, but I only stare at him blankly. "We will want to monitor Thủy-Tiên to see if the murmur resolves itself. I must tell you though that there is a chance one of her heart chambers has a hole in it, and if the murmur is a pathological one, her condition will worsen."

"What do you mean?" I push aside my plate and sit up.

"If her respiratory rate increases, if she fails to grow at a normal rate, meaning her height and weight are stunted, if her heart rate and rhythm are abnormal, and if her energy level is low or she is always fatigued…These signs mean you must take her to the hospital right away. You will need to go to Sài Gòn or perhaps Thái Lan for the surgery to repair the hole."

"Thailand? Surgery? I cannot afford this!"

"Our hospital is not equipped to handle the situation if your baby has a pathological murmur and requires surgery. If she does not get prompt treatment, she can die. Most babies will survive and be fine though, so do not worry."

"That is enough for now." Sister Six dismisses the doctor and nurse. "Let her rest. Go find someone else's spirit to break." She scowls at them as they exit.

All I can replay in my mind are his words of 'she can die' and I sob. The waves of anxiety crash in on me and I cannot breathe. Tâm wraps her arms around me and rocks me as if I am her child, not her aunt. My brother is silent. I suspect he feels oafish finding himself in unfamiliar territory. Crying women make him nervous. He is a strong disciplinarian when it comes to his family, being the man of the household, but when it comes to his two sisters, he gives us the stage.

"This is not fair!" I scream and break free of Tâm's arms. "I have done everything right in my life. I have been good to everyone, to my parents, to my family, to my neighbors, to God! I am good to animals and I never swear! I even went to college five hours from home while you all got to stay here! Instead of marrying Sam, I get an arranged marriage to a man I do not love! And now this? The one thing I want most in my life is to have a baby of my own, who will love me and be with me. My baby is supposed to be beautiful and healthy and smart. She is meant to grow up to be successful. She is supposed to outlive me, see the world, and do better than me. She will not get that chance now! Oh, Mary, Mother of God!" I wail in anguish. My siren cry alarms Brother Seven.

Sister Six strokes my hair. "Get it out of your system. Be angry and woeful. Scream, swear, cry. Do what you need to do."

This is the first time she talks to me with such tenderness and empathy. I remind myself to remember this moment the next time her sandpaper tongue scolds me.

"Fuuccckkkk! Mother Fucker!" I let loose the kraken tongue and the swear words propel. Surprisingly, I start to feel better. "Fuck. Mother Fucker. Ass…Doctor's Ass…Vũ Crepe Fucker!" I scream some more and trip over the words.

This swearing thing is new to me. The tears marathon down my cheeks to my chin. Every breath of air I grasp sends my chest and shoulders into heavy convulsions. I cling to the hope that my dolly will be fine, that she will not need surgery, and that the murmur, whatever that is, resolves itself. Time ticks on slowly until my heaving becomes rhythmic, my tears subside, and I exhale in calm defeat.

"Are you done?" Sister Six asks. I nod, letting out a big sigh. "Feel better?" I nod again. "Good." She laughs at me. I take offense at her mockery. "That is the worse windmill swearing I have ever heard! 'Vũ Crepe Fucker'? Really?"

A smile creeps up on Tâm's and Brother Seven's face. The four of us laugh hysterically.

3 SHE-JEKYLL (APRIL 1975)

My daughter slumps against our red, vinyl chair. Propped up beside her is a tiny doll. Today Thủy-Tiên and her doll are twins, both wearing yellow onesies. Their round face and dark eyes mirror each other. I look at both angelic faces. The doll smiles at me. Her golden locks of hair peek out from under her hoodie. She looks happy and at peace. I look at Thủy-Tiên and I see a fallen angel. Her wavy black hair tussles with the crimson cushions. For the past five minutes, she has been struggling to push herself up, but her marshmallow arms fail her. At eight months old, she is barely bigger than her doll and almost as pliant. Her body falls forward and sideways.

"You can do it, my angel. Use your legs to push yourself up against the armchair." I smile encouragingly at my daughter and hope the enthusiasm in my voice serves as arms to lift her up. Thủy-Tiên's brows crinkle with anger and she rolls off the chair.

Like watching a movie in slow motion, I see her body hit the cold surface of the tiles. Her right temple ricochets off the floor and her nose smashes into the leg of the chair. Blood drips down her face and a piercing cry sends shock waves down my body.

Tý and Tree run into the room. "What happened?" They speak in unison.

"Thủy-Tiên fell off the chair." I feel disconnected from the situation.

Tý scoops up his daughter effortlessly and takes her into the kitchen. Her screams are so loud, they can split a tree.

"You look tired." As usual, Tree does not inquire, but rather, states a fact. "I will watch Thủy-Tiên while you nap."

"Wake me up if she gets too difficult for you. There is a jar of yogurt left if she gets hungry. Tell your uncle to pick me up some chicken congee and Chinese donuts. I will be hungry when I wake."

I look forward to taking a nap on my hammock underneath the coconut and banana trees. I have what Tý calls "hammock-grin" whenever I smile thinking about laying down for a nap. I walk outside to the back garden. Dirty Butt struts toward me.

"Mông Dơ, you are my best friend." I bend down and pat my chicken's head. Her beady eyes look at me blankly, but I pretend she understands. I pick her up and carry her to the outhouse with me. "Do you know what the secret to a good nap is?" I pause to give her the opportunity to answer. "Why, an empty bladder and empty bowel, of course."

I giggle as if sharing this secret with Dirty Butt makes us kindred spirits. Dirty Butt flaps her wings, perhaps in agreement, or perhaps in protest. I put her down before she uses me as a scratching post. I saunter onto the rickety boardwalk leading to the outhouse that juts three meters from the edge of the pond. The catfish swim toward the outhouse. I squat above the pond with my feet steadily balanced on top of two parallel wooden boards so as not to fall in.

The hum of Tý's scooter starts up. I recognize the rattle of the motor. "Tell your aunt I will be back in a couple hours. I have some errands to run."

"Remember the congee and donuts," Tree yells.

I hover for another minute before quickly washing myself with the bucket of water. I head to the hammock and see from the window my nephew inside the kitchen. He ladles a small amount of water over Thủy-Tiên's head and runs his fingers through her hair to spike it into a mohawk. He laughs. She looks like an emu. Fifteen minutes go by. I swing back and forth, letting the cool breeze lull me to sleep. My thoughts drift to Sam, back to December of 1971.

***

A man with a mustache appeared at the front entrance of my family's house. I did not recognize him at first. He was wearing blue jeans and a white cotton shirt that said 'God Is Our Copilot'. His eyes were covered by dark aviator sunglasses. Then he smiled and his dimple made an appearance.

"Sam!" I squealed, with a mixture of excitement and fretfulness. "What you doing here?" I wanted to run and nestle myself into his arms, but that would not have been appropriate.

"Snow, I'm on R and R!"

"What RNR?" I ushered him into the kitchen.

20

"Rest and recuperation." He flashed a smile that could make me swoon.

I returned his smile, not wanting him to suspect that his village girl did not understand the word 'recuperation'. We sat down at the kitchen table. "You stay to eat dinner? I have my sister make some rice and rabbit?"

"R and R! You are a clever woman. I am on leave for two weeks. Did you get my last letter?"

"No. Maybe I get soon. Please, stay."

We had the house to ourselves. Sister Six was playing cards with our neighbors, Tú and Vân, gambling as usual. Brother Seven was at work. Everyone else was at the market. I feared they would come home to find me alone with a man in the house.

"So, in my letter, I wrote that I was getting transferred from Tuy Hoa to Phu Cat. Also, I was eligible for R and R and wanted to see if I could visit you during my vacation. There is no one I'd rather see."

I blushed. "I will talk to my father. You maybe stay in Tâm's room. She still in Đà Nẵng. She take care of the air force camp. She not want to work at bank anymore."

"Why? Will she come home for Christmas?" Sam inquired.

"Yes, she plan come home. She can take my room with me if my father allow you to stay."

Sam cupped his hand on top of mine. "I've missed you."

Fearing Sam could feel my trembling hand beneath his warm, calloused one, I stood up and distanced myself from him. His presence in my home made me nervous.

My words petered out as I corralled the conversation back to my niece. "Tâm not happy at bank. She want to be teller, in front, talk to customers. Ice tea?" I did not let Sam answer and mechanically poured him a cup, hoping he had not noticed the drop of amber liquid that fell to the floor. "She say only pretty girls get promotion."

"Snow, I have not been able to get you out of my mind."

"I tell Tâm she have to be good with math and speak good English."

"I want to marry you when my tour is up." He took off his sunglasses and pierced me with his pleading eyes.

"I get promotion and she quit." I waited for Sam to say something.

My lips quivered. My heart pounded so hard, it tenderized my flesh. His eyes beckoned me to come to him. I wanted to feel his lips on mine and run my fingers through his hair, but I froze. To show him physical affection was not proper etiquette. I wanted to reassure Sam that I returned his amorous feelings, but that would mean cooking for him. My cooking would kill him faster than the war would.

"You will get cross-eyed if you stare any harder." Sister Six waltzed in and focused her attention on Sam as if he was on display at the curiosity shop. She shifted her gaze over to me. "He is pretty." As abruptly and quietly as she entered the room, so Sister Six left.

Sam stayed with our family the two weeks he was on rest. Tâm came home from Đà Nẵng and brought us food she snuck out of the barracks. Sister Six prepared an amazing feast for Christmas. There we were, all eleven of us sitting together. There was my father, Sister Six, her husband Thắng, my nieces Tâm and Trinh, Brother Seven, his wife Hiền, and their two sons Tree and Tuấn. The women slaved in the kitchen for days prepping our holiday feast. I was excluded from those duties.

Sister Six pushed me out of the kitchen. "Your job is to be the interpreter between Sam and the men while they eat, drink, and tell bad jokes." In other words, my presence was a hindrance, not a help.

Sam tried to help in the kitchen as well, but my father would not have it. "Daughter, tell Sam that women cook and men drink."

My father and Sam ping-ponged between Vietnamese beliefs versus Western beliefs, good beer and bad beer, and whether the *Vespa* made by *Piaggio* was worth owning.

"Mr. Sang, the *Vespa* gets incredible gas mileage," argued Sam. "It's a beautiful Italian scooter. It's fast and fun to ride. It has good storage compartments too."

"Those mopeds are too expensive and ugly. The Italians did a sexy job with the *Maserati*, the *Ferrari*, and the *Lamborghini*, even the *Ducati*, but with the *Vespa*, they got it wrong."

My father and Sam bantered back and forth until dinner was ready. The table was adorned with roasted duck, grilled pork, pickled carrots and cucumbers, mango salad, taro soup with shrimp, steamed rice, and a couple of things I did not recognize. One plate had thin strips of reddish-brownish yellow meat, while the other plate had something that reminded me of Chinese sausages.

Seeing my curious gaze on the plates, Tâm volunteered. "I got those from the air force base. They eat this every day. There was so much, I did not think they would miss a few."

Tree grabbed a strip of meat and took a bite. His eyes lit up. "This is amazing! It is crunchy and salty, but also a little chewy and tender." He grabbed three more strips and crumbled it over his bowl of rice.

Sam was amused. "He likes the bacon. It's cured meat made from pork." Sam pointed to the sausage rolls. "This here is what we call hot dogs."

My sister dipped her bacon into the taro soup. "The bacon is very fatty. Tomorrow I will fry some rice in the lard."

I fell in love with Corporal Sam Hammond that night over bacon and hot dogs.

***

Tree's voice slices into my memories of Sam. "Thủy-Tiên is throwing up."

"Did you feed her anything?" I roll out of the hammock.

"A few spoons of yogurt like you said."

I clear the vomit out of my baby's mouth with my finger. Thủy-Tiên cries and objects to me invading her tongue and gums. She throws up again and I am unsure if it is a gag reflex or normal regurgitation after eating.

"She is throwing up again?" Tý appears at the doorway and looks concerned.

"What is wrong with her? One day she is pale, the next she is blue. She cries all the time and throws up as often as she poops." I am exasperated.

Tree walks over to Tý, takes the bag from my husband's hand, and heads towards the kitchen. "This must be the congee. I will get a bowl."

"Tree, grab a towel and clean up the vomit too." My husband takes hold of my wrist. "We need to talk." Once inside our bedroom, I put my dolly on our bed. "Sweetheart, we need to leave Vĩnh Bình." I cast him a defiant look. "The Việt Cộng and northern forces have already taken control of Ban Mê Thuột, Huế, Đà Nẵng, and Nha Trang."

"No. I cannot leave my family." I notice Thủy-Tiên is trying to suck on my hairbrush. I take it from her and she cries.

Impatience simmers in Tý's eyes. "I am your family now. Pack your bags. We leave at two in the morning. And do not tell your family."

"I cannot say goodbye to them?" I hand my daughter her doll.

"You will do as I say and not question me."

My anger brews. "At least tell me where we are going."

"Sài Gòn. It will be safe there. President Thiệu is already mobilizing his forces to protect our capital and the presidential palace."

"Are you sure? And what about your parents?" I ask.

"I talked to my mother and father this afternoon." Tý's words slap me in the face.

"So you said your goodbyes to your family and I cannot say goodbye to mine?" I cannot believe the double standard.

"Pack light. One bag. We leave at 2 a.m. sharp." Tý leaves the room.

I question who this man is that I have married. My stomach turns in knots. A combination of hunger and distress descends upon me. I did not question him when we married and lived with my family instead of his. I do not question him when he disappears for hours, sometimes days at a time. And when he surprises me with money or gifts, still, I do not question my husband. Why now, do I demand answers? Suspicion gnaws at me, yet I cannot explain the root of my feelings.

Tree clears his throat before coming into my room. "I brought you the congee and Chinese donut."

"I am not hungry." I fall to the bed next to Thủy-Tiên and force myself not to cry.

***

The long bus ride from Vĩnh Bình, in the Mekong Delta, to the big city is bumpy. Every seat is occupied by a man, woman, or child, as young as one month old to as elderly as eighty-two. We arrive in District One at six o'clock in the morning. Nostalgia engulfs me. The last time I was in Sài Gòn was 1961. I was twenty-two years old, studying mathematics and English at the university. The United States of America had elected John F. Kennedy as their president, and President Ngô Đình Diệm was re-elected to power in South Việt Nam. The Americans were mass-producing military personnel and exporting them to my country. The Sài Gòn I see now is no longer the same as when I was in college. Today, I do not see many American military or government workers in the streets. They have been replaced by the Sài Gòn army. President Gerald Ford is currently America's puppet master, while President Nguyễn Văn Thiệu is ours. One thing that is unchanged between 1961 and today, April 11, 1975, is the sound of motorbikes competing with street vendors, who argue over trivial details, as they set up their booth outside the Bến Thành Market.

As the bus approaches the intersection, I see the presidential palace on the left. A few days ago, a South Vietnamese Air Force pilot dropped bombs on the palace and abandoned his cause in favor of the Việt Cộng's. Surprisingly, there is not much damage to the building. Our country's flag, yellow with three horizontal red stripes, still flies high above in the center of the building. Looking equally grand and ominous, the palace appears deserted behind the iron gates.

"Where are we going?" I ask.

"We are almost there," Tý says.

It is pointless to ask again. Thủy-Tiên sleeps soundly in my arms. I am thankful she made it through the night without any incidents. As we continue on Thống Nhất Boulevard, I see a company of Vietnamese soldiers. They walk toward the palace and grip their AK-47 rifles. One of them makes eye contact with me. I immediately shift my gaze ahead. A convoy of tanks rolls by. We pass the U.S. embassy. The building is white, big, ugly, and nondescript. Outside, posted on the gate is a sign that reads: *"PETITIONERS: Only petitions for wives and children accepted now. We will inform you when a petition for other relatives will be accepted."*

"Are we leaving our country?" I glance down at Thủy-Tiên again. Her innocence warms my heart. The thought of fleeing scares me.

Tenderness returns to Tý's face. "Sweetheart, yes. Soon. The Americans are leaving. The communists are on our doorstep. Too much blood has been shed."

I am lost for words so we ride in silence. A few minutes later, the bus stops. Tý stands up and collects our bags. I follow his lead. We walk a short distance down an alley.

"Will we be staying with your brother?" I remember Tý's younger brother lives in the city. I met him at my wedding reception.

"I have a surprise for you, Sweetheart." With a twinkle in his eye and the first charming smile he has cracked in days, Tý stops to unlock and roll up a garage door. It is empty inside except for a red scooter. "Welcome home."

"Home? I thought we were leaving the country?" I am confused.

"We are. This is a temporary home. Upstairs there is a mattress for us to sleep on and the kitchen has a few basics."

"And the *Honda*?" I point to the scooter. "How did you get your hands on one of those?"

"A friend of mine. He imports parts and assembles them here. We will not be here for long, but until then, it is yours to ride." Tý winks at me. "The woman living next to us is a good woman. I have already met her and she can watch Thủy-Tiên whenever you need."

"How did you…? When did you…? Forget it. What is her name?" I walk over to the scooter and run my fingers over the sleek body.

"Mrs. Trần. She is expecting you to introduce yourself while I go to the post office." Tý gives me a kiss on the cheek and walks out.

"Wait. You are not taking the scooter?" I ask.

"Sweetheart, these calves are not muscular from riding. I was born to run."

"You are crazy. No other man lifts weights or runs for fun, except you."

"No other man has a beautiful wife to protect as I do." He can be endearing when he wants to be. "Also, maybe if you learned how to cook, I would not be running all the time to fetch you food." He dashes out the door before I can find something to throw at him.

***

Mrs. Trần is a nice woman if you consider being tortured with a sixty-grit sheet of sandpaper on your lady parts, nice. And if pugnacious and neurotic are acceptable, then she is the epitome of a psychotic and delusional woman. She is my sister Six, cloned one too many times, and is the annoying sliver of bok choy that is stuck in my teeth, relentlessly reminding me that she is still there, regardless of how tactfully I try to circumvent her. Despite her corkscrew demeanor, she is loving and attentive to Thủy-Tiên and flutters around my little dolly like a raptor protecting her young.

"Only ugly girls have short hair." Mrs. Trần criticizes my haircut. "It is too curly like pubic hair." Mrs. Trần's need to degrade me without any filters makes me feel like my helmet is on backward. She outwits me every time when I give her tit for tat. "I hear you cannot cook either. A handsome man like your husband can do better. Must be your big chest that has him blinded."

Today I choose to bite my tongue and remind myself, not much longer. Secretly, I hope her ripe, spotted skin spontaneously combusts. "Mrs. Trần, I am riding into the Bến Thành Market. Can

I get you anything? Persimmons? Pineapples?" Mrs. Trần opens her mouth and points at her teeth. The cavern that is her mouth showcases decaying gums and rotting teeth. No doubt, it is home to a rabid bat. "I will get bananas for you then."

I kiss my baby on her forehead. One glance at Mrs. Trần and I ride off, down the alley to connect to the main street. I approach the U.S. embassy and shake my head. It is such an ugly building. The only redeeming feature on the property is the tamarind tree that stands tall and protective. I imagine how grand the building can be with a few strokes of Van Gogh's brush, as he paints the bland canvas into 'The Starry Night'. In the distance I see Tý. He stands with both hands in his pockets. He looks left and right as he negotiates when to cross. The flood of mopeds, cars, and bicycles speed by in disorderly fashion, zig-zagging around pedestrians. Most of the mopeds carry two passengers while some have pigs, ducks, or chickens strapped to the front and back, piled as high as feasible without losing balance. Tý crosses the road with ease. I plan to stop and invite him for a beer or iced coffee.

I slow down and make my way to the right side of the street. An American woman greets Tý with a hug. *Who is that?* Her fingers dovetail with his and they walk into a toy store together. I leave my shoes at the entrance, as is customary, and follow them in, careful to keep my distance. Tý and the American woman speak to the store owner.

In perfect Vietnamese, the petite woman addresses the store proprietor. "Brother Cường, will you give us a good price for this toy airplane? Our son turns five tomorrow."

"Sister Annette, consider it a gift for your son. Your husband and I have a long history together." The store owner removes the airplane from the display case and hands it to her.

She gladly accepts. "Really? You will have to tell me about it."

"Annette, another time." Tý ushers the American woman towards the exit. I quickly dash behind some big kites hanging from the ceiling. "You should get back to our son. I have business to discuss with Cường." The woman kisses Tý on the lips. "I do not like displays of affection outside of closed doors." Tý distances himself from her.

"Yes, that is the Vietnamese culture, but no one can see us except our friend Cường," she replies, again, in perfect Vietnamese. She waves to the store owner. "Thank you for the gift. Timothy will be happy with his new toy."

I am betrayed. I am angry. My knees feel weak. Who is this American woman that regards my husband with such intimacy and candor? She retrieves her shoes at the foot of the entrance and backs her scooter off the sidewalk. She is not much taller than me, perhaps one and a half meters tall. It is like discovering there is an American doppelganger version of me, except her short, wavy hair has bangs that cling to her forehead.

Tý's voice forces me to refocus. "Where is the money?" Cường hands over a child's messenger bag. Tý opens the flap and peeks inside. "If it is not all there—"

"It is all there," Cường confirms.

Tý walks out of the store. I am in disbelief at the Nixonian blow that has transpired. What lie has he been living?

I intend to find out.

***

Early the next morning, I ride to Cường's toy store. "Hello. Do you have any toy airplanes?"

"We have these two." He points to the airplanes in the glass display case behind him. I feign interest as I inspect the two models.

"How is business?" I attempt small talk to get a feel for how aggressively I should barter. He ignores my question. "How much for this one?" I intend to buy the same airplane the American woman acquired.

"One-hundred-fifty thousand piasters." He walks away from me.

"Here is eighty thousand." I put the money on the display case. I am in no mood to haggle. He is either going to take it or lose a sale. I leave the store with my purchase and ride to the Bến Thành Market to pick up pastries, barbecue pork buns, and coffee.

As soon as I get home, I hear Mrs. Trần. "Thủy-Tiên is sleeping." Mrs. Trần picks up the toy airplane. "You know you have a daughter, right?"

"Yes, Mrs. Trần." I already feel my skin pulled by her grating presence.

"My sons used to fight over toys like this airplane. I have not seen my oldest for eight years and my youngest for five years. My oldest son joined the North Vietnamese Army while my youngest joined the Republic's army. Since they were children, they always fought against each other and gave me grief, but I love my sons. Even my stupid husband…I loved him too. Now, I am an old woman, all alone."

"What happened to your husband?" My hardened heart thaws toward her. This is the first cordial conversation I have with the she-Jekyll.

"Stupidity killed him. He should have been home to celebrate Tết with me. He was out getting treats for the Lunar New Year celebration but decided to stop into work at the radio station, twenty minutes before the building exploded." Mrs. Trần slowly stands up and winces. I step toward her to assist. "Do not touch me, you stupid girl."

And there it is. Mrs. Hyde returns and casts aside the she-Jekyll. I do not understand Mrs. Trần's mood swings. I have always been taught to respect my elders and never offer an opinion. To bring honor to my parents, I had to be demurring, obedient and accommodating. Now I feel there is a Mrs. Hyde inside of me too that is begging to be let free.

"I do not understand why you hate me. I have shown you only kindness and respect. It is evident you care for my daughter and take good care of her, but, forgive me for asking, what have I done to make you bitter towards me?" I hold my breath for her reply.

"You are weak and blind. Open your eyes, you foolish girl. Your daughter is dying. Your husband is a traitor."

"What do you mean he is a traitor?"

She ignores my question. "You have everything and yet, you do not appreciate what you have. You make too many assumptions. I do not hate you, girl. I pity you, and I worry for Thủy-Tiên, to be so innocent and already cursed. There is a war going on and still, you live in a bubble." Mrs. Trần pauses and I am too stunned to speak. "I see the tears forming in your eyes. I do not give you permission to cry. One day you will be my age, and you will lose everything you hold dear, and even then, you cannot cry. You take your fears and turn them into rage. You take the energy spent on wallowing and blaze a path towards survival. In the end, you are the only person you can trust. Your tongue, not your beauty, is your greatest artillery. Say what you want. Love who you want. Take what you want. Understand?"

"I am afraid," I whisper.

At that moment, Tý walks in the door.

"Then you will teach your daughter to also live in fear." Mrs. Trần nods to Tý and takes her leave.

"What were you two talking about?" Tý sees the toy airplane and says nothing.

"I purchased a toy for Thủy-Tiên." I nod towards the airplane. "We left Vĩnh Bình so quickly, and since you only let me pack one small bag, I wanted to get her something. She misses her doll."

"Fine, but you should have bought a small ball or stuffed animal," Tý says coldly.

"Well, maybe she can play with her brother, Timothy." I brace myself for his reaction.

Tý stiffens his posture but says nothing. Instead, he grabs a bottle of alcohol from his bag and pours the clear liquid into a glass. I recognize the red label. It is *Maotai*, the official liquor the Chinese use when they want to entertain and impress distinguished guests such as foreign dignitaries. Tý hands me the glass and takes a swig from the bottle.

"That bottle costs two hundred U.S. dollars. Your parents lost their cassava farm last year from the bombs so I know their wealth is gone. How are you affording this? How did you afford the *Honda*? Did you steal all of this?"

"You are asking too many questions." Tý leans on the scooter and takes another sip from the bottle.

"I am not asking enough questions," I say.

Tý picks up the airplane. He says nothing. He sits down on the hard floor, cross-legged, and leans against the wall. "You have some nerve." He takes another drink.

"ANSWER ME!" I scream. "Who is that American woman you were with yesterday?"

"Sweetheart, you are the love of my life."

"Then who is Annette? Why was she kissing you? Why is her Vietnamese so perfect?"

"Calm down. Annette and I met a long time ago when I was in America, studying at the Milwaukee Institute of Technology. We ran into each other five years ago in Sài Gòn."

"Five years ago? Have you been together for the past five years?"

"She is a linguist and works at the embassy for the Americans as a translator. She got pregnant so we married."

I cannot believe this. "So I am your second wife and your son, Timothy, turns five today."

"You have to know, you are the love of my life."

"STOP SAYING THAT!" I shout. "Why did you marry me?"

"You were so graceful and charming. I had to make you mine."

"Are you not even going to say you are sorry? My heart already belonged to another man. I married you because you and my father made an arrangement, not because I loved you, or that I was desperate. Sam and I—"

"AND WHERE IS YOUR SAM NOW?" Tý's nostrils flare. He stands up and punches the wall. "Your soldier. Where is he now? Yes, your father told me all about your GI, how he stayed with your family for two weeks and spent Christmas with you, how he asked your father's permission to marry you after his tour ended, and how he was going to take you back to Washington state."

"Sam will always be more of a man than you. At least I was enough for him but apparently, one wife is not enough for you, is it? Any others I should know about?"

Tý lunges forward in one long stride and grips my wrist. "You were thirty-four years old with no husband and pining for a man you could never have. What man would start a family with an old virgin who burns everything she cooks? I SAVED YOU FROM YOURSELF!"

Mrs. Trần's voice creeps in my head. *I do not give you permission to cry.* I yank my arm away and free myself from his grip. "What other secrets are you keeping from me? Why did Cường give you a bag of money?" *You take your fears and turn them into rage.*

"I work for Mr. H." Tý kicks the airplane and sends it gliding across the floor. "He is one of Đại Cathay's generals."

His confession triggers my spring-loaded eyelids to open wide. "Đại was a mobster. Are you insane? You work for one of the Four Great Kings? I thought his gang disintegrated after his death in Phú Quốc?"

"No. His men still have operations underground." Ty drowns himself in more of the clear liquid.

"So you were extorting money from that store owner?"

"No. I was collecting the money from Cường, who also works for Mr. H."

"You are going to get us killed. What else?" I demand.

"You already know too much. Listen, I have exit visas for us. We leave in a week. Annette is getting us out of the country and—"

"Of course she is," I interrupt with sarcasm, "because you are her husband and we are what? The poor relatives? Does she think I am your unmarried sister, raising a child by myself? Tell me, are you the love of her life?" Mrs. Trần's message echoes in my head. *Say what you want. Take what you want. Love who you want.*

"Damn it! I have been saving my money to bribe officials to get you and Thủy-Tiên out."

"I am not going anywhere with you and I sure as hell want nothing to do with that woman."

"You are being stupid and ungrateful. Think of our daughter. It is not safe here. She will have a better chance in America, and she can get the medical attention she needs there."

I grit my teeth. "Then what? We all live together as one happy family? I am stupid to have married you, but leaving you will be the smartest thing I do." I grab the glass of *Maotai* and down half of the distilled spirit. My throat burns. I cringe at the taste but force myself to not give Tý the satisfaction of seeing me gag. I walk up the stairs to the bedroom, with my glass of *Maotai* in hand, to get away from him. His presence sickens me.

Tý follows me. "Sweetheart?"

"What?" I swivel around to face him from the top of the stairs.

Tý takes an envelope from his pocket and places it on the steps. "In one week, meet me in front of Cường's store at 8 a.m. We will be picked up and taken to the airport. Take this envelope with you and a small bag. Your and Thủy-Tiên's visas and paperwork are in the envelope. Do not be late."

"You do not understand. I am leaving you." I throw back the rest of the *Maotai*.

"And sweetheart, happy birthday."

How ironic that I share the same birthday as Timothy. I hurl my glass at Tý's head. It is too bad I miss. "A bottle of *Maotai* and exit visas...Yes. Happy birthday to me."

4 SECOND FIDDLE (APRIL 20, 1975)

A week has gone by. It is 7 a.m. A throbbing headache pulses its way from the base of my neck to my forehead and temples. I imagine the blood vessels inside my head are the Cu Chi tunnels, each harboring little Việt Cộng soldiers who pound at the walls and inflict this persistent pain. The stress of meeting Tý in an hour in front of Cường's toy store has me questioning if this is the right decision for Thủy-Tiên and me. I look at my watch. Only three minutes have gone by. I turn my attention to my sleeping baby. Her perfect little mouth quivers as if she is speaking in her dreams. Those cheeks! Oh, those perfectly round, soft, chubby little cheeks. She looks healthy and peaceful when she sleeps. Her pale skin in the morning light appears pure, as if God, Himself, was emanating His light through her wafer skin. I admire her black curly hair and the cowlick on her hairline. I caress her tiny hand. My heart swells with love and I am moved to tears. *I will always protect you, my little dolly.* I let her sleep a little longer while I gather our belongings.

From my bedroom I see Mrs. Trần sweeping the stoop that leads to the backyard of her home. She is balding. The gray wispy strands hang wildly, searching for the comfort of a bun that is not there this morning. I see her as a frail old woman, wearing her rags like a second set of skin. I hope one day her sons will come home to take care of her. I am a little sad to leave her behind. What will become of her? Her leathery feet are cracked and calloused. She shuffles around sweeping an already immaculate door front. She sets the broom aside and pulls down her pants. She is not wearing any underwear! Mrs. Trần leans forward and I can see her buttocks swaying side to side. She scowls at me for spying on her.

I dart my eyes over to Thủy-Tiên. Her small black eyes peer

intently at me. She no longer looks like the angelic sleeping baby. Her pale skin is sickly yellow; her lips purse into a sour pucker. I quickly give her the toy airplane to play with. It is now 7:28 a.m. I scoop up Thủy-Tiên and head over to Mrs. Trần's house to say goodbye.

Her door is open so I walk in and set Thủy-Tiên down on the floor. She crawls to the hammock, tugs at it, and gives me a big smile. She has hammock-grin too. I scoop her up into the hammock. She is content lying there holding her airplane while I swing her back and forth. Mrs. Trần's house smells of incense, lemongrass, and the sweet smell of overly ripe fruits. I see on her wall photos of her mother, father, mother-in-law, father-in-law, and husband. Incense burns at the "veneration of the dead" altar with an offering of cherimoya fruits and papayas. Five bowls filled with rice and grilled meats along with sets of chopsticks are also laid out. A large gold-plated figure of Buddha sits above the photos.

"Mrs. Trần?" I call out. She appears from the back room.

"Did you like the view?" She mocks me. The image of her buttocks rushes back to me.

"I came to say goodbye. I want to wish you good luck and will ask for Buddha to bestow on you peace. May you be reborn with enlightenment and good—"

"So you are leaving with him." It was a statement, not a question, and a rather bitter one.

"Yes. He is my husband and it is not safe here. Thủy-Tiên will likely need surgery and America is her best chance." I take out my handkerchief and unfold it. "I have a gift for you." I hold up the gold necklace that Tý's parents gave me on my wedding day. The ruby eyes of the phoenix pendant are especially blood-red in this light. "Tý's mother gave me this gift. She told me the phoenix is for strength and courage. I want you to have it. You need this more than I do, and if one day you find that life is too unbearable, I want you to sell it. It is worth a lot of money."

Mrs. Trần's eyes open wide. "Child, I am not worthy of such a fine gift." The tears slide down her cheek.

"I insist." I take hold of her hand and turn it palm up. I place the necklace in her small trembling hand. Despite her ratchety and abrasive personality, I understand Mrs. Trần is human after all. "Thủy-Tiên and I will always be indebted to you."

Mrs. Trần shakes her head. "Last week, I said your husband was a traitor. Let me explain." She puts the phoenix necklace into a copper coffee tin. "Tý used to serve in the South Vietnamese Army. My youngest son joined him five years ago. When your husband showed up here with you and Thủy-Tiên, living a normal civilian life, I was suspicious, because I had seen him before with an American woman and a little boy, half white, half Vietnamese. His face is square and his eyes dark, like your husband's. What am I to think, but that he is a traitor to his country, his women, and the children in his care, not to mention he abandoned my boy?"

"I see," I say coldly. I scoop up Thủy-Tiên. "I will use my documents to get to America and once I am there, I will leave my husband. I have a friend in Washington who can help me. Take care of yourself."

I return to the house, collect my bag, and put it in the compartment under the seat of my scooter. I grab the sheet off the mattress and tie a sling around my waist and shoulders. I tug at the knots to make sure they are tight and secure. "We are going for a ride, my baby. I am afraid you will have to leave your airplane, but I promise to get you a better toy."

I put Thủy-Tiên into the sling and start up the scooter. My baby cries for her airplane. Memories of Sky and Sam sweep over me. A week after Sam spent Christmas with my family and returned to base from his R and R, his letter finally arrived. I cannot believe that was over three years ago.

"My lovely Snow,

We had a barbecue last night on the base to celebrate the holidays. My new CO (Commanding Officer) sent Sky and me into Tuy Hoa city to get some ice, charcoal, and lobster if we could find any. We did. I have a ¾ ton truck assigned to me now. Sky scored some dope from a boysan for cheap. All the guys were drinking, smoking a joint, and having a good time. One guy got a little too drunk and tried to kiss us. It was actually funny. He has two women back home waiting for him. He couldn't make up his mind which one he liked better and vowed he'd marry the one who was the better kisser. I guess he thought Sky and I were his girlfriends. Snow, you will never be second fiddle to anyone.

At the barbecue, the CO gave a speech and announced we were getting transferred to Phu Cat. I'm not happy about that, because it means I will be farther away from you. I also like being on the beach. The Viet Cong don't have a navy. I'm thankful to the man upstairs for putting me on the shores of Tuy Hoa. Anyways, my extension ends soon. I'll be on the freedom bird, getting out of the army in March next year. You and I can start our life together!

Tet is two months away and we've been doing drills with our M-16s. I try to keep mine oiled and cleaned in case Charlie attacks our base. I'll be one of the guys in the foxholes for a few days during Tet. Pray for me.

I've been granted some R and R. That means rest and recuperation. There is nowhere I'd rather be than with you. If it is all right with you and your family, I would like to come for a visit. I have a question to ask you.

With love and anticipation,

Sam (December 4, 1971)

P.S. There is another guy that is DEROS'ing (going home) and he is selling me his refrigerator. I can soon put my stash of Rainier beer at arm's reach. Back home in Seattle, that's all I drink because it's brewed there in Washington State. Cold beer makes me happy, but you keep me alive."

Sam gifted me a book that Christmas, *'A Separate Reality'* by Carlos Castaneda, explaining that there was an alternate world beyond our perceived reality. He promised he would read it to me. In my bag under the seat compartment are Sam's letter, the book, two outfits each for Thủy-Tiên and me, my poncho, and the envelope containing our exit visas.

I ride through the alley and wave one last goodbye to Mrs. Trần. She waves back and gives us a sad, toothless grin. I merge onto the main road with other motorists. The sun beams down bright and hot. I squint from the glare of the light. I glance at my watch. It is five minutes to 8 a.m. I will be late. I pick up the pace. Thủy-Tiên has stopped crying. I honk my horn and speed up a little more to pass a family of three. I cannot miss the pickup in front of Cường's store. This is our chance to go to America, to start a new life. Beside me, there is another scooter. He is keeping pace with me. I slow down to let him pass but he slows down too. I speed up. He speeds up. I recognize the man as Tý's younger brother, Hải.

A boy, three years old, half black, half Vietnamese, runs out to catch his spinning top toy. Both of us swerve to avoid hitting the child. Hải falls and crashes into a tamarind tree. I feel bad, but see him get up so I keep going. Two hundred meters ahead is Cường's store. There is a silver Mercedes Sprinter van out front. I am not too late! Tý is standing on the sidewalk. He paces in circles, stops, shifts his weight to his left leg, and paces again. His blue jeans accentuate the bowness of his legs. One hand is pulling at his hair. The other hand is flailing. His head swings left, right, and left again. He is clearly agitated. I am less than one-hundred meters from the store. A slender arm extends from the van and grabs Tý's wrist. A diminutive woman steps out and pulls at him to get into the van. It is Annette. A small boy hops off the van and grabs hold of Tý's hand.

I swallow a big lump in my throat. Timothy! I let off the throttle and slow down to a stop. Other than my beating heart, the only other sound I strain to hear is the muffled cry of a desperate American woman pleading to Tý to get into the van. Annette's tiny frame is no match for him as she pushes and pulls. The veins in his forearms flare prominently; the muscles on his back and neck tense and bulge. They take turns jabbing at each other in English. Cường steps out of his store. Both Annette and Cường struggle to get my strong husband into the vehicle. I freeze and hold my breath. I am not close enough to make out all the words. They yell in unison, their voices stack on top of each other like building blocks. I notice the time. It is 8:17 a.m. In my mind's eye, I see Sam's handwritten letter. I have read that letter too many times to count. *Snow, you will never be second fiddle to anyone.* I affirm from here on out, it will be only my dolly and me. We will be second fiddle to no one. Tý hangs his head down in defeat and steps into the van. The door closes. The Sprinter van distances itself from me. Cường waves and walks back into his store.

"Sister?" Tý's brother catches up to me. The expression on his face is calm. Hải is five years younger than Tý and the same age as me. His features are softer than his brother's. Whereas Tý's face is square, chiseled and quite masculine, Hải's face is more heart-shaped, with a narrower jawline and a broad forehead.

"Hải, he is gone. He left and I let him go," I say, "I am sorry you crashed and missed the van too. I should have stopped to help you."

"I was not trying to get to the van," Hải says. "I was born here, and here is where I will die. I was told to make sure you got to the van on time."

"You were following me?"

Hải casts his eyes downward as an admission of guilt. "It does not matter now. What will you and Thủy-Tiên do now?"

"Did you know about Annette and Timothy?" I challenge him with my eyes to tell the truth.

"I am sorry, sister Two, he made me promise not to tell you."

I feel my body temperature rise. My nostrils flare. My body is rigid. I want to punch him in the face. I remember Mrs. Trần telling me that my tongue is my greatest artillery. "Fuck you for being an asshole! You and your brother are worthless pieces of shit! You both are the same with your secrets." I fire off multiple rounds of verbal ammunition. "I have nothing now. My family will probably disown me for disappearing in the middle of the night and not saying goodbye. I have no money, no dignity, and no job. I have been disgraced and have brought shame upon my father's name. What am I going to do now, you ask?" I take a breath, long enough to reload my arsenal of scathing assaults. "I am going to grow me some testicles because no man here has any! Get out of my face! I never want to see you again. Both of you are dead to me. I hate you as much as I hate him! He is a liar and you are an ugly vault of steel and ice with your cold secrets."

I hold Thủy-Tiên close and ride off. Anger courses through my veins. I have no idea where I am going. I have no idea what to do next. I tell myself not to be afraid anymore. *Stand on your own two feet. You do not need a man's love to make you feel validated.*

5 OUR PLANKTON LIFE (APRIL 21, 1975)

A rooster sounds his alarm. My weary body slithers off the mattress. I am cognizant of the little body sleeping soundly next to me. She snores softly. I rolled my scooter through the narrow alley late last night, down to this house that Tý and I shared. I had nowhere else to go. There was a light shining from Mrs. Trần's bedroom window. Her operatic sobbing encouraged me to scurry mouse-like past her gate. The poor she-Jekyll. I had ridden aimlessly all day yesterday, asking questions that had no answers. Did he and Annette leave the country already? Did I make a mistake by staying? Will he come back for us? Should I return home to see my family? How do I get a job at the embassy as a translator? Should I go back to teaching, or maybe back to the bank? Will this war ever end? Why are we not together, Sam?

I walk down the stairs to the kitchen, too tired and dazed from yesterday's events. The toy airplane sits on the floor where I had left it. A prism of emotions runs through me. Fear. Anger. Disgust. Sadness. And hunger. Is hunger an emotion? I open the cupboard doors. Empty. I pull open the drawers. Nothing but a pair of chopsticks, two rice bowls, spoons, and cups. I turn on the stove to boil some water to drink and hope I do not start a fire. I walk to my scooter and open the seat compartment. Inside is my bag, with our clothes, documents, Sam's letter, and the book, *'A Separate Reality'*. I remember the deep dimple on Sam's cheek when I tore the wrapping off the book that Christmas. My heart aches for him now.

Thủy-Tiên cries from upstairs. I make my slow climb to the bedroom. "Hush. Mama is here." She is writhing like a hungry larva. I try to cradle her back to sleep. The cries screech louder. The teardrops flood faster and bigger. "I know you are hungry. Soon you will have some water to drink." I rock side to side and bounce her up and down. "Ssshhhh." She spews curdles of white and gray matter into my hair. I take her downstairs and check on the water. It boils angrily and a couple of droplets scald my hand. The intensity of the burn makes me jump back and lose my grip on my baby. Thủy-Tiên falls to the floor. A volcanic howl erupts from her lungs. "STOP CRYING!" I slump to the floor and pick her up. "I am sorry." I hold her close.

A loud pounding snaps me out of my haze. Mrs. Trần's small palms are rat-tat-tatting loudly on my window. She disappears, but only for a moment. She is now kicking at my garage door. I open it for her.

"Give her to me," she bellows. "What the hell is going on here?"

I obediently hand over my baby and say nothing. I zombie-shuffle up the stairs. Mrs. Trần calls my name repeatedly but her voice becomes distant. The mattress is my paramour. It beckons me to lie down.

***

I open my eyes to see a gecko scurrying across the wall. *My baby! Where is she?* I run downstairs and check the kitchen. Not there. I check the bathroom. Nothing. I dash outside. No one. *How long have I been asleep?* I fly into Mrs. Trần's house. It is eerily quiet.

"Mrs. Trần?" I sprint upstairs unladylike and check the bedrooms. She has to be home. Her door was unlocked. Sanity escapes me and I peek under the bed, behind the corner television console, even inside the dirty laundry chest. I run down and out the back door to her garden of herbs. "Mrs. Trần!" I scream desperately. Right as I plunge myself down onto a bench, the bench lifts up and Mrs. Trần's bewildered face peers out at me. She emerges from the underground passageway, which is camouflaged by weeds and watermelon vines. "Mrs. Trần! Where is Thủy-Tiên?"

"She is safe, down below." She beckons me to follow.

"You have a secret room beneath your garden, under this bench?" I lift the bench up higher and slide into the hole. The cool dirt is inviting. The smell of earth, dried fish, and sweet candy flirt with my senses. We walk down a few steps, to an opening the size of eighteen square meters. The ground is flat, partially covered by a woven, straw mat. Except for a few weeds poking up through the ground, the place is immaculate. Wooden stakes, half a meter apart, line the perimeter of the room, with sandbags on the outside of the stakes. Surprisingly, it is not musty, damp or unpleasant inside.

40

"My father-in-law built this bunker during the French occupation. He was a little overzealous and built this with three rows of sandbags, all around, almost two meters high, and filled the bags with soil, rice, and whatever he could find, including packages of dried anchovies, smoked fish, and other preserved foods." Mrs. Trần points to the ceiling. "He also put sandbags on top of the boards above, so it is pretty solid. Any bag marked with a red "VN" has food hidden in it."

Thủy-Tiên sits on the floor sucking a salted cuttlefish and so preoccupied with a spool of thread, that she does not even greet me.

"VN?" I inquire.

"Ay, you are not so smart! VN for Việt Nam." She kneels down beside my daughter. "My father-in-law built this almost thirty years ago. He hated the French and fought for the Việt Minh."

At the risk of being called stupid again, I ask, "Is this bunker directly below your entire garden?"

Mrs. Trần smiles with pride. "Bigger."

"How do you get any ventilation?"

"There are two fake vents up above in case the enemies try to smoke us out, but the real vents are here." Mrs. Trần points to the openings in the opposite sides. "They lead to the outhouse and the hollow bamboo poles separating your house and mine."

"Clever. What about supplies? Water?"

Mrs. Trần lifts up the mattress of the bed to reveal sixteen wooden crates, each filled with water, dried cuttlefish, pickled mangos, pork pemmican, candied plums, tamarind, and ginger. "Enough for one lunar cycle…Longer if you cut into the bags marked VN."

"You made all these preserved foods?"

"How do you think an old woman like me survives in wartime, with no husband or sons? I make and sell all of these."

"Please teach me. I do not have any money of my own. I am too ashamed to go back home to my family."

Mrs. Trần laughs. "I cannot have you as my competition. Go home. Pride has no place when there are mouths to feed. Take your baby and go home. I will even buy you a bus ticket."

Maybe Mrs. Trần is right. I need to go home and face my family. I walk over to Thủy-Tiên and pick her up, bidding the she-Jekyll good evening. "Thank you for your offer. Instead of a bus ticket, can I please borrow some money? I want to keep the scooter and ride back to Vĩnh Bình."

"Come back this evening, around 6:30 p.m. I will give you money and some food to take with you for the journey. You can stay for dinner."

"Thank you. I will find a way to repay you. By the way, late last night, when I came home, I heard you crying. Is there anything I can do to help?"

"You were spying on me again?"

"No, I—"

Mrs. Trần laughs. "Those soap operas get me every time! In last night's episode, the village girl found out her husband loves another."

Embarrassed, I smile and leave the bunker with Thủy-Tiên.

***

At exactly 6:30 p.m. I saunter into Mrs. Trần's home. She swings carefree on her hammock and motions me to sit. "They have taken Xuân Lộc. It will only be a matter of time before they take Sài Gòn. Our country will be united."

This development makes me nervous. A part of me regrets not getting on the van with Tý. "With Xuân Lộc lost to the northern army, the highway is open and clear for them to infiltrate the capital."

We watch the news in silence on her small television while Thủy-Tiên plays with her airplane. A familiar face appears on television and I am keen to hear his message. Mrs. Trần announces our president as if I need the introduction. "Nguyễn Văn Thiệu."

We tune in to what he is saying. He recaps the development of the country under his leadership in South Việt Nam, thanks our allies for fighting against the communist aggressors, and outlines the tactics the communists used to strengthen their offensive. He tells us how he had wanted both northern and southern troops to demobilize so that North Việt Nam and South Việt Nam could govern independently. However, during the peace talks in 1972, the U.S. did not demand the north withdraw its troops from South Việt Nam, and this, President Thiệu told President Nixon and Secretary of State, Dr. Henry Kissinger, he could not support. With the United States stopping aid and withdrawing their troops, he argued that the demilitarized zone and 17th parallel be respected; otherwise, South Việt Nam would crumble. *"I regret that later on, Watergate occurred in the United States. The U.S. political situation has prevented economic aid and the continuation of the Vietnamization program as*

42

well as the program to modernize the RVN armed forces. In addition, international economic changes concerning energy and food have created difficulties and contradictions among the U.S. people." President Thiệu continues his scathing speech about the United States' trickery, broken promises, and betrayal.

Following every sentence, my heart sinks deeper into my stomach. "Maybe one Việt Nam will be a good thing. Maybe it is best that the Americans withdraw." I try to believe my words.

Mrs. Trần exhibits no emotion. "I only want my sons home."

Desperation washes over me. I must leave my country, whatever the cost. With President Thiệu resigning, there is no government to keep Sài Gòn safe. "I still have my exit documents. Come with us, Mrs. Trần. We can use that phoenix necklace I gave you and bribe the Marines to let you come with us. We can say you are my mother."

"If the war is ending, then my sons can come home. They will not need to fight anymore. I have to be here when they return."

"And what if they do not return?"

Mrs. Trần cranks her head slowly. Her body is still, her eyes cold and menacing. Chills trickle down my spine like a scampering gecko escaping danger. I am reminded of the 'The Exorcist' movie. Like projectile vomit, Mrs. Trần screeches biles of profanities at me. "You fucking stupid girl! You heartless bitch! How dare you?"

"I am sorry. I—"

"Fool!"

"I did not mean—"

"You call yourself Vietnamese? A true Vietnamese is not a deserter! A true Vietnamese fights for her country and fights for unification and fights for peace! A true Vietnamese believes that her sons, no matter what side they fight on, will come home, because they are strong in their convictions and brave in their hearts! How dare you suggest they are dead?" Mrs. Trần's whole body convulses as she barks at me. The she-Jekyll extends her bony finger at me and nods toward the door. The hostile rage in her eyes warns me not to come back.

I regret speaking so brazenly to her, but surely, she comprehends the tectonic landscape is shifting? That the seismic waves of change will soon disrupt our plankton life? "If you change your mind—"

"Get out! Leave! Take your daughter and get the fuck out of my country!" Mrs. Trần picks up her slipper and hurls the rubber shoe at me. It smacks my ear and brushes against Thủy-Tiên's head on the way to the floor. It startles Thủy-Tiên but she does not cry.

A flicker of compunction crosses Mrs. Trần's face, and I grasp the opportunity to speak my mind. "I feel sorry for you, that this war has turned your heart bitter. You talk about courage and conviction, peace and unification, but you have not reconciled your own fears. You once told me I was weak and blind, that you pitied me. It is you who is weak and blind." Mrs. Trần collapses to the floor on her knees. I want to hoist her up and shake the frail woman before me. "Open your eyes. Even if both of your sons make it home, do you think life will be glorious with sunshine and coconut trees? One war ends and another begins. That is the only thing our country knows. You say I am a deserter? If I have to run to feel safe, to find freedom, shit, to feel full instead of hungry, then yes, I am the poster child of a deserter!"

"Stop! No more!" Mrs. Trần pleads. "Get out of my house, you insolent cunt! I curse the day you came here!"

"I will pray for you. I do hope that both of your sons come home safely, that they can shed the terrors and whatever price they paid in the rice paddies. I hope you do not have to live the rest of your life alone, that the moonlight does not haunt you, and that the sunlight does not beat you with regrets. I hope you can forgive yourself over your husband's death. I hope that in the end, you will not find yourself all alone with nothing but your money and your bitter pride." Mrs. Trần sobs uncontrollably. Tension loosens its grip on my heart and my voice softens. "I am afraid too." I kneel down and wrap one arm around her shoulders, squeezing her tight. Mrs. Trần does not resist. I try to comfort her. "We are not that different from one another. We are both dreamers. But I am beginning to see the reality before us. Your sons may be coming home for their own funeral."

6 THE FALL (APRIL 29-30, 1975)

A week has passed since President Thiệu resigned and left for Taiwan. He handed the presidency over to Vice President Trần Văn Hương. In a broadcast on Saigon Television, President Hương promised his army that he would stand by them if they still wanted to fight. He declared that if the Republic of Việt Nam ceased to exist, then his pile of dry bones will lay beside the bones of his fellow soldiers. Well, after one week, he resigned, and yesterday, General Dương Văn Minh was sworn in as president of South Việt Nam. President Minh has called for a cease-fire and asked all Americans to leave within twenty-four hours. This past week has been chaotic as many of my neighbors and fellow countrymen abruptly abandoned their homes and journeyed to the port city of Vũng Tàu, planning to climb aboard any vessel they can find to leave Việt Nam and be rescued by the U.S. Thousands of desperate people rushed to Tân Sơn Nhất airport to get out. The North Vietnamese Army fired rockets at the airport early this morning, destroying the runways and forcing a closure. Sài Gòn is surrounded. There is no way out.

"Are you sure you do not want to go with us?" I ask Mrs. Trần. She and I have made our peace.

"My sons will be home soon." She remains adamant about staying.

I admire her optimism. "Good luck to you."

She contently sits on the mattress inside her bunker. As I lift the garden bench to exit the bunker, Mrs. Trần's amplified version of the national anthem of South Việt Nam gives me goosebumps.

I wrap Thủy-Tiên tight around me and make my way to the U.S. Embassy. Outside on the streets of Sài Gòn, there are trash and debris everywhere. Anarchy is upon us. People are looting stores and commissaries. Babies are crying. Parents cling tightly to their children. The elderly look confused. Dogs run in every direction seeking shelter or morsels of food. In the distance the explosive sounds of M-16s firing and the pulsating rotors of the helicopters crisscrossing over the city, gives me vertigo. A massive crowd is outside the embassy gates. Everyone is screaming and waving papers, pressing against the wall or climbing it. The moment I get off my scooter and grab my bag, someone runs off with my scooter in the opposite direction. I want to chase after the thief but getting into the embassy is of higher priority.

I run toward the embassy gate. "I have papers!" I wave my exit documents and visas. I shove my way through the crowd, past flying elbows, spit, and men blowing snot rockets out of their nostrils. With one hand, I cover Thủy-Tiên's head, and with the other, I shove people aside, ducking under arms, squeezing through gaps between sweaty bodies. The forceful shouts and desperate cries of men, women, and children, compete to be heard, while the U.S. Marines on the other side of the gate are overwhelmed and exasperated. Thủy-Tiên cries out. I recognize her cry of pain. I glance down to see blood streaming down her nose.

I think of Mrs. Trần, still sitting in her bunker, singing our national anthem.

"Oh citizens! Our country has reached the day of liberation. Of one heart we go forth, sacrificing ourselves with no regrets. For the future of the people, advance into battle. Let us make this land eternally strong. Should our bodies be left on the battlefields, the nation will be avenged with our crimson blood. In troublesome times, the Race will be rescued. We the People remain resolute in our hearts and minds. Courageously we will fight such that everywhere, the Glory of the Vietnamese forever resounds! Oh citizens! Hasten to offer yourselves under the flag! Oh citizens! Hasten to defend this land. Escape from destruction, and bask our Race in glory. Make its name shine, forever worthy of our race."

With the song in my head, I press on. "Sir! I have visas! I have my baby." One of the soldiers makes eye contact with me. He sees the blood on my baby's face. I plead with my eyes. "My husband inside." I lie.

He signals to another soldier, nods, and together, they open the gate a sliver, to let me through. A thunderous roar of protest whips through the air. The two soldiers lash back. A piercing pain shoots through my lower back and legs. Everyone is scratching, shoving, and hitting one another as they force their way through and tailgate behind me. With them comes the revolting smell of urine, cigarette smoke, and halitosis. The horrid stench of fear emanating through their pores send me into dry heaves. I see the Marines hitting people with the butt of their rifles, smashing fingers, and yelling words that fall on deaf ears. I feel relief to be inside the gates.

"Your baby is bleeding." Cường, the toy store owner who sold me the airplane, stands before me. He is skinnier than I remember. His eyes are red as if he had been crying. He lifts Thủy-Tiên's chin up with his right index finger and examines the cut. "It is a surface wound. It looks like she got scratched at the base of her nose."

He takes a handkerchief from his pocket, wipes away the blood, and applies pressure to stop the ooze. Even though the handkerchief is soiled like it has seen the inside of a hog stall, I do not protest. At least it is a familiar face.

"Thank you," I say.

"I am Cường." He does not remember me.

"Tuyết, and this is my daughter, Thuỷ-Tiên."

"She is so cute. How old is she?" he asks.

"Nine months."

"Is that so? She is so small. I thought she was six months old. Where is her father?"

I try to decipher whether he is serious or not. "We have met before. I came into your store and purchased a toy airplane. You know my husband, Tý." Cường's eyes widen. "Remember Tý? He has an American wife named Annette? He works with you for Mr. H?" His lips twitch as if they are trying to formulate the right words to say. "Đại Cathay's general?"

"I know who Mr. H is," he says emphatically.

The helicopters flying above seduce Cường's attention away from me. He says nothing more. Only the chuk-chuk sounds of the Huey blades drown out his silence.

The smell of urine invades my nose and I feel the wetness of my baby's legs soak into my shirt. Thủy-Tiên pees unabashed. I search for a wash station. Thousands of hysterical people try scaling the embassy gates, their arms flailing, mouths moving, while others who have made it inside the gates, sit in the courtyard clutching their bag or each other.

I notice the swimming pool and dash in that direction. "I will be right back." I strip off Thủy-Tiên's pants and soak it in the pool.

"Let me help you." Cường kneels beside me. He reaches for

Thủy-Tiên, who immediately is entertained by the strip of hair over Cường's upper lip. She pets his mustache.

With Thủy-Tiên's pants now smelling like chlorine, I lay it on the concrete to dry, and splash the water onto my shirt to rinse off the urine. The cool water feels good on my skin. I cup the water into my hands and splash it onto my face. The memory of my childhood washes over me, when I used to stand in the alley, naked, and let the monsoon rain pummel my skin. The rainy season always breathes life into my spirit. I have the urge to dive in and go for a swim. I reach for Thủy-Tiên, but she rejects me. Cường lets out a laugh. I miss the sound of a masculine laugh.

"You have made a new friend." I welcome him holding the little sack of rice. She gets heavy after a while. "People are climbing up to the roof and getting airlifted out. We should get in line."

"Yes, grab your things." Cường picks up Thủy-Tiên's pants and together we walk toward the end of the long line. "That is all you have?" Cường points to my bag.

"I still have my watch and my wedding ring," I say sadly.

"And a nice jade bracelet." He points at my wrist.

"Yes, I bought this three years ago as a birthday present to myself."

We wait in line for hours. Everyone's bag is inspected and documents checked. The smell of smoke permeates the air as embassy employees burn documents from the rooftop. It takes me back to being in the kitchen with Sister Six. How I miss our banter. How I miss food. My stomach rumbles obscenely. I imagine there is a loud, hungry critter inside my body, gnawing away my stomach lining and gobbling up my intestines. I am embarrassed for each loud, gurgling sound.

Cường rummages through his knapsack and hands me something wrapped in banana leaves. "Try not to eat it all at once."

I peel away the banana leaves clumsily. The smell of coconut milk makes my mouth salivate. Thủy-Tiên stares at it, ready to pounce on it if I do not feed her now. I pick off a corner of the sticky rice and give it to her. She practically bites my fingers off. The sweet taste of grilled, soft bananas inside the crunchy, chewy, sticky rice sends my taste buds to nirvana. I close my eyes and savor the first bite.

A U.S. Marine inspects my documents and waves me to the side of the building. I am instructed to wait. I step aside and wait for Cường. The marine reviews the visa, assesses Cường, hesitates, and then examines the visa again. He waves one of his comrades over for a second opinion, a tall African-American soldier with the most beautiful, flawless black skin I have ever seen. If my skin is as white as snow, his is as dark as the purest, roasted coffee bean. The coffee-bean soldier inspects the documents and smiles.

"What do you think, Bryant?" the Marine asks his comrade.

"Let him in, David." He waves Cường through.

Together we head to the building and stand by one of the pillars. Hours pass. Waves of people hustle and rush into the helicopters. A tamarind tree in the courtyard is taken down to make room for more helicopters to land. Papers fly everywhere into the parking lot of the embassy as helicopters land and take off. The three of us receive no signal that it is our turn. Still, I am hopeful. We are inside the embassy gates while many are still outside, clamoring to be let in. The primal sounds of the helicopters break the tedium of the day and numb my restless mind.

Day turns to night. The banana dessert that Cường gave me is long gone. Thủy-Tiên rests her head on Cường's knapsack. I yawn.

"Close your eyes and sleep. I will wake you when it is time." He beckons me to him and offers his thigh as a pillow. I obediently lie down, heedless of the fact that Cường and I are still strangers, thrown together during this harrowing circumstance. The thumping sound of the helicopter lulls me to sleep.

***

Cường walks toward me. "My leg was asleep and I needed to relieve myself. You and Thuỷ-Tiên were working hard bulldozing something. Was it the Berlin wall or the Great Wall of China?"

"We were snoring that loud?" I ask. "What time is it?"

"You are the one with the watch."

"It is almost four in the morning!" I scan the area. There are still a few hundred of us waiting. Everyone appears hopeful, defeated, or weary.

"It has been awhile since a helicopter came by," Cường says matter-of-factly. "We need to prepare ourselves. No one but the Việt Cộng is coming for us."

"What?" I shriek. "But we have visas. They cannot leave us!" Fear delivers a hammering blow to my gut. "You are wrong! The Americans will come back and get all of us out!" *Please come back.*

Hours pass. Still, we wait. The orange haze of dawn illuminates the sky. I am restless and realize there will be no rescue. The light of sunrise is the blanket of death. It brings news that hell on Earth is

49

here.

"I looted the embassy!" Cường holds up plastic bags full of pilfered items. Engrossed in my own sense of doom, I did not notice he disappeared the past hour. Other people perk up and come to check out what he has in the bags. They all talk animatedly and sprint to the embassy doors. "I found these garbage bags and a lot of useful things. I have candy and this camera. I found some sweaters and shoes and some sandwiches. I even found this!" He holds up a bottle containing yellow liquid. The label says 'GALLIANO'.

Horrified, I ask, "Is that urine?"

Cường laughs. "No, it is liquor, but if it was pee, it smells sweet!"

All around us, people run out of the embassy building carrying everything from typewriters to boxes of knick-knacks. Most return multiple times to grab more stuff. They pile their loot onto chairs and wheel them out. I give in and join them. I intend to take everything I can carry. *Those damn Americans owe me!*

With Thủy-Tiên strapped to me, I push my chair outside of the compound, feeling exhilarated with my two trashcans filled with Western medicine, coffee, snacks, a pretty silk scarf, toilet paper, and office supplies. Those who are outside of the gates storm in. There are no soldiers to stop them. Everyone is running, yelling, grabbing anything and everything worth selling, trading, or keeping. As I roll my office chair full of stuff toward our temporary house in the alley, I brace myself for the sarcasm that will surely be dished out by Mrs. Trần.

"Where are you going?" Cường strolls up beside me.

In the midst of my shopping spree, I forgot about him. "I am going to check on my neighbor. You are welcome to accompany us."

Together we walk down the street, me pushing a chair and he carrying trash bags full of stuff. The roads are crowded. Bombs go off in the distance. Smoke roils the skyline above the jagged rooftops and around the buildings, while people walk in every direction, holding on to their loot.

Then the tanks roll by.

The uniforms are of the North Vietnamese Army. This can mean only one thing. It is the fall of my beloved capital.

Communism wins.

My legs give way and I collapse to the ground. My body

trembles, weakened by the sight. I command the tears to pull back but they seize control. Everything unravels before me.

Someone screams. "It is over! They are going to kill us!"

All around me, the people are polarized in their cheers and cries. Some people run in fear. Some embrace each other and shake enthusiastically the hands of the North Vietnamese Army. Soldiers with the People's Army strip off their clothes, helmet, boots, and gear. They desert their belongings and walk in their underwear, head hanging down in defeat. Sympathizers from balconies throw them clothes so they can blend in with society. Hopelessness seizes my throat and metastasizes into my bones, piercing deeper with each flick of the wrist as soldiers wave the Communist flag, red with a yellow star, victoriously. I mourn the fall of Sài Gòn.

Cường lifts me to my feet and walks me to a nearby shop. There is music flowing out of the storefront. A family of three gathers around the radio, along with one American man who is a reporter with the *Associated Press.*

Music is interrupted by a news broadcast. *"This is General Dương Văn Minh. I ask that the ARVN drop their weapons and surrender unconditionally to the National Liberation Front."*

Another tank rolls by with eight people sitting on top, wearing civilian clothes and waving the yellow-starred flag. A few Việt Cộng female fighters walk alongside the tank. They smile, wave, and cheer. One of them points to the American reporter sitting with us. "Go home!"

My mouth agape, I am overwhelmed with so many emotions, it is hard to describe. There is singing now on the radio.

"Hello, Sài Gòn. It took thirty years to have today. We sing this victorious song. The sounds of our victorious song will echo in every street and district... We sing in the name of him, Hồ Chí Minh forever, Hồ Chí Minh forever...Hello Sài Gòn. In the North, Central and South, in one house of Việt Nam, together we sing our victorious song."

7 A BITTER MELON DAY (MAY 1975)

The quiet is deafening. I walk slowly down the stairs, leaving my sleeping daughter to her dreams. I get to the kitchen and nearly trip over Cường. He sleeps soundly, sprawling on the floor, with one arm across his garbage bag of loot. My eyes trace his left arm, from his shoulder down to the dirt under his long, jagged fingernails. He has a wedding band! I never noticed that before. His other hand is tucked underneath his trousers. *So, you are right-handed.*

I take a few minutes to scrutinize this dirty specimen before me, from his oily hair to the stubbles on his face and neck. His mouth is wide open and his teeth are crooked and yellow, probably from nicotine, coffee, or both. For a Vietnamese man, he is hairy, with untamed eyebrows and "peek-a-boo" nostril hairs that come out with every exhale, and disappears with every inhale. His shirt is unbuttoned all the way. There are scars on his body. *Did the mafia put those there?*

I give Cường a gentle kick in the ribs. His right hand comes out of his pants and waves in the air, before falling onto his stomach. He still sleeps. I kick him again, harder, with my lead leg, but still, he does not respond. I sit down cross-legged and rifle through one of his bags, curious to see what other items he took from the embassy yesterday. I see the yellow *'Galliano'* liquor and open the cap to see what it smells like. It definitely does not smell like pee. The sweet smell of vanilla, cinnamon, anise, and other flavors bewitch me to take a swig of the enticing yellow nectar. It is so good. I take a couple more swigs.

Inside the bag, I spy a wrapped sandwich. My eyes open wide and my mouth twitches with excitement. Yes, it is a stale ham and cheese sandwich! The lettuce is wilted and the creamy sauce has a pungent vinegar smell, but I take a large bite and pulverize it with childish delight. I wash my sandwich down with another sweet gulp of '*Galliano*'. I jump up, sandwich in hand, and run up the stairs, two steps at a time, eager to share with my baby. Aw, still asleep. I strum her lower lip a few times like a guitar chord, listening to the blips as her lower lip springs up and smacks her upper lip. She does not stir or make a sound. I lift her arms up and release, allowing them to thump against the mattress. Still, she does not object.

I let out a giggle and scoop her up to hug her tightly. "Let us go pay a visit to our old neighbor next door." I head outside into the alley. There are five people outside, setting up shop like it is business as usual. I give a couple courtesy knocks on the door and enter the familiar house. "Mrs. Trần? It is me, Tuyết, and Thủy-Tiên."

I am greeted with "What are you doing back here?"

I leap forward to hug her with my free arm. "You are all right!"

"Of course I am!" My she-Jekyll dismisses my concern. "You have tried twice to leave this country and yet you are still here! Shit, if the Americans do not want you, I sure as hell do not either!"

"Yesterday we had a country. Today, Sài Gòn is no more, and there is no South Việt Nam, no president, and no U.S. embassy." My eyes glisten but instead of crying, I laugh. "I will tell you what we do have though. We have a stale sandwich, a wonderful drink called *Galliano*, and a half-naked man on my floor next door!" I roar with laughter at the absurdity.

"Child, are you drunk or just stupid crazy?"

"Yes!" I shout.

"Hello?" A male voice speaks from the doorway. There is a soldier standing at the entrance, dressed in his faded, dark green North Vietnamese Army uniform. He holds a basket of fruits and a bag of rice. The stranger has Mrs. Trần's face, and although he is young, his face is weathered, making him look much older than he probably is. The stranger runs past me and picks up Mrs. Trần. He swings her around while she kisses every inch of his face.

Mrs. Trần lets out a shrill cry. "My son! You are home!" She kisses her son's hands, puts them to her cheeks, and weeps uncontrollably.

"Mother! I am home. The war is over. I will never leave you and Father again! I promise!"

Mrs. Trần howls louder. "Your father is dead, son."

The soldier drops to the floor like a puppet without strings. "What?" He buries his face into his mother's hip and clutches her waist. I stand here bearing witness to this difficult reunion. The louder he weeps, the harder it is for me to hold it together. With tears still meandering down his tired face, the man-child looks up at his mother's puffy face. "Where is Lopsided?"

Mrs. Trần cups her trembling hands around her son's face. "I have not seen your little brother for five years now! He joined the South Vietnamese Army."

"How could you have let him, Mother?"

She has no words of comfort for him, no answers to ease his sorrow. Together, they surrender to sadness and sob like angry babies. The two of them cling to each other and let the past unbearable years avalanche down their shoulders.

I hold Thủy-Tiên a little closer and walk out the front door. I am now sober and somber. *So, this is you oldest son who left eight years ago to fight for the other side.*

***

The journey back to Vĩnh Bình is an interesting one. I never imagined myself straddling a motorbike behind a man other than my husband. Yet here I am with my arms wrapped around a man I barely know, cruising these one-hundred kilometers through provinces, past hamlets and decaying, fallen bodies, with one-hundred thirty-one more kilometers to go. Towns on either side of us are destroyed, deserted, or teetering on the edge of extinction, on their way to becoming a distant memory.

"Sister Two, we will need to fuel up soon," yells Hải, my brother-in-law.

I nod. Hải's long hair tickles my forehead as it flutters with the breeze. To a casual observer, we are a family riding into town, with our daughter wedged between us. None of us have a helmet on, which I am glad is still not required by the new government. It would be nice to have a hat though. It is a hot, sunny day. I am grateful for my facemask, to shield against dust and bugs. For the past couple of hours, I felt free riding along the stretch of concrete and past the red, sandy desert.

"We have to stop." Hải slows down. There is a line of motorists being questioned by the police.

My heartbeat changes tempo and goes from a waltz to a swing dance. "This is new. Security checkpoint?" My body is tense, my posture straight, and my stare grim. After twenty minutes of waiting in the stale, humid heat, it is our turn.

"Hello, friends." The policeman greets us. He looks small and

54

green in his olive-colored uniform and matching hat. "What are your names?"

Hải introduces us to the police. "I am Vương Văn Hải. This is my wife, Vương Ngọc Tuyết, and our daughter, Vương Ngọc Thủy-Tiên."

I cringe, not because it is customary in Việt Nam to provide our surname first, followed by middle name, then given name, but because he lied so matter-of-factly that I am his wife and Thủy-Tiên our daughter.

"Registration for the bike." The policeman's face becomes serious and he glares at Hải.

"We do not have any paperwork." Hải's storytelling is impressive. "Our home was destroyed. The damn American helicopters literally blew away our belongings. We do not have much left."

"Where did you come from and where are you going?" The policeman smirks at me with eyes of lust, then suspicion. "Take off your facemask." I obey.

"We left District One in Sài Gòn—"

"Hồ Chí Minh City." He corrects my "husband".

"Yes, sorry, Hồ Chí Minh City. Long live Uncle Hồ."

The policeman smiles. I find him repulsive. The pimples on his face are ripe for the picking, and with his green uniform, he resembles a bitter melon. However, since he is small and thin, I decide he can also pass as a diseased okra.

Hải continues. "We are on our way to see our family in the Vĩnh Bình province."

"How much gold are you carrying?"

"We do not have any gold bars, only enough money to get to our family."

"How much?" His eyes narrow and his lips tighten. If he scowls any harder, I fear all his pimples will burst like fireworks. I wish I had my facemask on.

"Twelve," Hải answers.

"Twelve thousand piasters?" The bitter melon man laughs. "Good luck, friend. You will need it. You still have another three or four hours' journey. You can travel farther with an American dollar than twelve thousand piasters!"

"Then may we be blessed by the good Buddha to find a U.S. dollar along the way." Hải plays along mirthfully.

"Get off." The policeman walks around the motorbike,

pausing at various spots to inspect closely. He runs his fingers along the back of the seat and traces the letter "M" on the *Minsk*. "A Russian *Minsk*. Good motorbike." He rummages inside the storage compartment and confiscates our small watermelon. He points to my bag. I reluctantly hand it over. Inside is Sam's book with his letter tucked between the pages. I can tell he is suspicious because it is written in English.

"I was a teacher." I try to stay composed while I lie to his face. "This book was a tool I used to teach my students about..." I look at the cover with the image of a man who has a ball of light for a head. "...about a man who clears his mind to embrace new teachings. I can use it to evangelize those who oppose reunification."

The guard hands me the book but holds onto my satchel. "You are free to pass after you pay the toll."

"How much is the toll?" asks Hải.

The bitter melon man stretches out his hand. "Today, it will cost you twelve thousand piasters and your wife's bracelet." Hải takes the money from his shirt pocket and hands it over. I struggle to slide the solid jade bracelet off my wrist. Admittedly, I have no plans to give it up since I purchased it as a birthday present for myself. The policeman loses patience with me and confiscates my watch instead. "Maybe if you find that U.S. dollar, you can get your wife proper traditional clothes, not the vulgar Western garb she has on now."

We finally clear the inspection point. I am frustrated. "Now what? We do not have any money to fuel up."

Hải pulls from his socks a stack of cash. "Five hundred thousand."

I squeal with delight and impetuously kiss Hải on the neck for his cleverness. Immediately I am flushed with embarrassment. For the next hour of our journey we ride in silence, except for the occasional "are you doing all right?" and "I have to pee". Along the way, we see many police officers, stopping people indiscriminately, motorists and pedestrians, young and old, to ask questions about their business.

It will take us six hours to go from Sài Gòn to Vĩnh Bình with all the checkpoints. Riding on the motorcycle with Hải gives me a lot of solitude and time to reflect. Naturally, it is the memory of Sam that occupies my thoughts.

8 LET GO

Three years ago, in April 1972, I purchased a jade bracelet for myself as an early birthday present. As I exited the store, two Americans were walking toward me, one in uniform and one in civilian clothes.

"Hello, Snow!" Sergeant Skyler Herrington had a mischievous smile on his face.

"Hello, Sky! Hi Sam!" I was so excited to see them both. "Sky, why you not in uniform?"

Before Sky could respond, Sam lifted me up and kissed me. It happened so fast, I had no time to object. I was of course embarrassed by the public display of affection. I dared not make eye contact with any of the locals who were no doubt gawking in disbelief.

"Sky is on R and R and is accompanying me so that he can witness this." Sam took a hold of my hands and got down on one knee. "My lovely Snow, will you be my wife and make me the happiest man in the world?"

"My father give you blessing?"

"Of course he did," answered Sky, "and if you say yes, damn it, you will make him the happiest son-of-a-bitch!"

Even with Sam on one knee, I was not that much taller than him. "Sam Hammond—" I started.

"Wait!" Sky punched Sam on the shoulder. "The ring, man, you can't forget the damn ring!"

"Oh, bloody hell." Sam pulled out of his pocket a red velvet box with the words *"Tiệm Vàng Hạnh Phúc"* embossed on the top, meaning Happiness Jewelry Store. Inside was an eighteen-carat gold ring with a large oval-cut emerald, accented with tiny diamonds cascading around the center stone. It took my breath away.

"Oh, Sam! I make you happiest son-of-a-bitch!" I squealed.

The three of us laughed and took turns hugging each other. Sam was so elated, he hugged Sky twice. The three of us talked animatedly as we walked home, my arm linked with Sam's.

"My tour is over," Sam explained. "I was given special permission to come collect you. We only have two days to get married and then you'll be flying home to the states with me."

"I'm the best man," Sky proudly declared.

"The ceremony needs to be small and inconspicuous," Sam says.

"What that mean?" I asked.

"Discreet," Sky answered.

"Private," Sam added. "We do not want to draw any attention. There have been too many air strikes and raids recently."

"More than usual." Sky stopped to tie his shoelace. "The less attention we draw, the less likely fucking Charlie will crash the party."

On the walk home, we wanted to buy some coconut water to quench our thirst. Sam was the first to spot a beverage stand. "Over there."

There was a woman and her daughter standing on the side of the street, waving us over. As we approached, the young girl stepped from behind the cart and held high above her head a grenade. The intensity in her eyes assured us she was ready to use it.

"Fuck." Sky grabbed my arm and swung me behind him. He pulled out a .45-caliber pistol and held it steady.

Sam immediately swung his M-16 up and aimed his rifle right at the girl's head. The mother screamed and grabbed her *Mosin-Nagant* rifle and fired at us. Her first shot was too high and went over our heads. Sam pulled the trigger but the rifle jammed on him. The mother fired a second shot that hit Sam in the throat and he crumpled to the ground.

"Sam!" I leapt to aid him. Sky squeezed my arm so hard, I hissed in pain. "Let go!" Sky clenched tighter. Two more shots ricocheted through the air and then there was silence. The woman and her daughter fell to the ground. Sky loosened his grip. I ripped my arm from his talons and knelt beside Sam. The tears rained down my eyes and blurred my vision. I kept wiping them away but the waterworks were turned on. Sam's eyes rolled back a couple of times. The more he tried to focus on me and talk, the louder he gurgled as his blood geysered from his neck and the drool slid down his chin. "Do something, Sky. Save him!"

Skyler stood towering above Sam, motionless and devoid of any expression. He kept blinking away his tears and was paralyzed by grief and shock. Sam took his last breaths and then was gone.

***

"We have another hour to go before we arrive at your father's house." Hải's voice brings my thoughts back to reality. "I need to pee." We stop on the side of the road for Hải to relieve himself. "Were you crying?"

I do not want to admit I was thinking of Sam. "Mrs. Trần is on my mind."

"You have to let go, Sister Two," Hải says. "There is nothing you can do about it."

"Stop calling me 'Sister Two'. In my mind and in my heart, I am no longer your big brother's wife. You can call me Tuyết like everyone else."

"That will take me some time, but if that is your wish…"

"It is. And you must promise me that if your brother contacts you, you will not tell him where I am or anything about me – or his daughter. Never. Understand?"

"Why?"

"Because I need to let go of my past. I need to survive and take care of my baby. The last thing I need is to lament his departure. Besides, you owe me for keeping a secret from me. He was already married and you did not tell me."

Hải's eyes plead me to forgive him. We get back on the *Minsk* and ride the last stretch of the journey home. My memories ping-pong between wretched Mrs. Trần and Sam.

***

On the evening of May first, the day after the war ended, Cường and I stepped out of the house to find Mrs. Trần and her son sitting on their front steps.

"I will sell your loot for you," Cường said to me. "You know where to find me." He nodded at Mrs. Trần and her son, before walking down the alley toward his toy store, carrying the garbage bags of loot.

"You trade your husband for that one," Mrs. Trần noted sarcastically, shaking her head. "You need to upgrade, not downgrade. My son, Minh-Hoàng, would be the best upgrade."

I gave Mrs. Trần's son a weak smile, leery of his gaze on Thủy-Tiên and me. He was a communist and I did not trust him. His stare burned into me as if he was committing to memory everything

59

about me, from my mannerisms to the way my body moved, from how I smelled, to how I spoke.

Mrs. Trần broke Minh-Hoàng's stare by springing to her feet like an agile gibbon and sounding her vocal alarm. "Oh! I cannot believe it! Ay!"

Confusion quickly sidestepped to clarity. Mrs. Trần ran down the alley with Minh-Hoàng right behind her. Both of them yelling, "Lopsided!"

A man with one leg shorter than the other quickened his pace and ran into the open arms of Mrs. Trần and Minh-Hoàng. The three of them embraced and jumped for joy, laughing and crying, talking animatedly over each other, and patting one another on the shoulders. The lopsided younger brother looked savage, like a wounded dog fighting to stay alive. It brought me to tears witnessing such a reunion. *Your sons came home after all.*

That night, Mrs. Trần invited Thủy-Tiên and me to dinner, to celebrate her sons returning from war. I had never seen her so happy, so motherly and kind, telling jokes and laughing genuinely. She was affectionate, even towards me. During that first couple of hours, any animosity I had toward Minh-Hoàng or pity I felt for Lopsided, evaporated with the steamy broth of our egg noodle soup.

Urgent knocks at the door interrupted our lively dinner.

Minh-Hoàng opened the door to find two government officials standing outside. They did not wait for an invitation, but rather, crossed the threshold until they were both inside.

"We are here for Trần Trinh Huy," said the one with a mustache.

"What is your business with my brother?" asked Minh-Hoàng.

"Your brother served the South Vietnamese Army and wrote some propaganda for the enemy. He is to report to a re-education camp for reform and retraining, to get on board with the new government."

"For how long?" asked Minh-Hoàng.

"Two weeks."

"Well, he is not here."

"Your brother is standing next to your mother. If you interfere, we will be forced to arrest you."

Lopsided spoke up. "It is all right, Brother Two. I will go with them. It is only for two weeks, and I will see you and Mother again soon." He kissed Mrs. Trần's cheek. "You waited five years for this day. I will be home soon and then you will not be able to get rid of me so easily. By this time next year, you will be trying to marry me off to some poor village girl and be embarrassed by my dancing skills at my wedding."

Mrs. Trần gave her son a brave, reassuring smile. She held her youngest son tight before finally letting go. Her hands trembled as she tried to choke back the tears.

The two men left with Lopsided in their custody. The door closed behind them. The sound of silence haunted us all that night.

***

The sputtering sounds of the *Minsk* snaps me back to the present.

"What is wrong?" I ask Hải. "Are we out of fuel?"

Hai pulls over to the side of the road to check. "There is still fuel in the tank but we are low. Let me check the sparkplugs."

Hải turns the petrol filter switch to "reserve". He examines the tubes, blows on it, and checks the carburetor, the filter, the sparkplugs, and other things that I do not understand. I watch him troubleshoot the problem and feel a small attraction to him, impressed that he knows what he is doing. Hải attempts to kick start the motor a few times, but nothing happens.

"Can you fix it?" I worry we will be stuck on the side of the road.

"Yes," answers Hải, "but I have no tools. We have to walk the rest of the way. It will take us an hour."

His news exasperates me. In Việt Nam, everyone would rather ride their scooter down to the next block than walk. It is faster, easier, and cooler because the heat can be unforgiving. I dread seeing my father, who will likely scold me for leaving in the middle of the night with Tý and Thủy-Tiên, without so much as a note or a goodbye. I cringe because I know Sister Six will pinch or slap me, to inflict physical pain equal to the emotional pain I caused her. Brother Seven will probably ignore me. His silence will be worse than his yelling. I sigh. The whole family will be shocked to see me returning, not with my husband, but with my husband's younger brother. They will jump to conclusions and will have already made up their mind that I have brought scandal and dishonor to the family. I will have to let go and trust God will give me the strength to endure.

9 MOOR PHEEN AY (MAY-JULY 1975)

Hải, Thủy-Tiên, and I walk up the path to my father's house. It is dusk when we arrive. We are greeted by warbling sounds coming from the side of the house.

"Mông Dơ!" I run to Dirty Butt. She waddles a dance around my feet and flaps her wings, chirping animatedly. I scoop her up and give my best friend a squeeze. "You are alive, you resilient dirty thing!" I laugh and give her another squeeze as I nuzzle my cheek into her feathers. Dirty Butt lets out a sharp peep in protest.

My family runs out, with Tree leading the way, followed by my niece, Tâm, and the two youngest, Trinh and Tuấn. We hug and rejoice. Through tears of happiness I see Sister Six, Brother Seven, their spouses, and my father. I walk to them, respectfully, and know that as my elders, I cannot expect them to come to me.

"Father," I begin, "I ask for your forgiveness. I must have scared you when I left without any warning and did not try to contact you the past few weeks."

My father raises his hand to quiet me. I lower my head, ready to accept the harsh words that will rain down on me. He takes a step closer. My body seizes up and my buttocks involuntarily tense, like muscle memory from all the times I was spanked and whipped as a child. My father wraps his arms around me and squeezes. He weeps uncontrollably. I feel the weight of his body slumping against me, so I wrap my arms around him to hold him up. I do not recall a time when I have received such affection and love from my father.

And then I feel a sharp pain on my forearm. Someone pinches me hard.

"You are a big shit to disappear all this time without telling anyone, especially me! Now, you come home, expecting us to receive you with open arms?" My sister glares at me with arms folded. I can almost see the smoke coming out of her lady-dragon nostrils. They flare with seething anger. "You had us worried and going insane, speculating what happened!"

Sister Six slaps my arm a couple of times and throws a jab at my shoulder. I wince but absorb her punch. My only assurance comes from understanding that the harder she hits, the more she loves and misses me. My brother-in-law and sister-in-law take their turn hugging me. We are not an affectionate family, but on this night, we make an exception.

Brother Seven wraps one arm around my shoulder. "I see you came home with Hải. Where is Tý?"

"Why not go inside the house and talk about this," Sister Six suggests. "People might be spying on us. You all must be hungry."

"And tired. My feet hurt and I am sure Hải's arms are sore from holding Thủy-Tiên." I nod towards Hải. "We have been walking the past hour."

Tree takes my hand. "I will rub your feet."

I sit down and prop my feet up on his lap. "You are a good boy."

Tâm takes Thủy-Tiên upstairs and puts her to bed. On the way here, my poor daughter cried so much, she passed out from exhaustion. Sister Six warms up some congee and sprinkles pork floss onto the rice porridge. Both Hải and I do not wait for an invitation to eat. We dig into the hot congee and shovel a big spoonful into our mouth. In between swallows, I recap how Tý insisted we leave right away, how he secured temporary housing for us in District One, and how he had documents for us to leave the country. I tell them all about Mrs. Trần and her sons. I explain the reason I was not with Tý was that I found out he had an American wife and son, and that Tý worked for the mob. They are all shocked and angry. I recount how I got through the embassy gates but the helicopters never came for us and how Cường and I stole bags of stuff from the American embassy.

"Aiyah, how did you end up coming back here with Hải?" my sister-in-law asks.

"My brother told me where their temporary house was and wanted me to make sure they got on the van," Hải says, "but when they did not go, I offered to escort them home."

"You are welcome to stay with us as long as you want," my father says. "We do not have much, but we are happy to share what we do have."

"Thank you, Uncle." Hải bows to Father.

"So much has already changed since the Việt Cộng took over," Brother Seven chimes in. "Many of our neighbors have left and some abandoned their homes to escape on the open seas. Others were lucky enough to fly out with the Americans."

"Yes," Sister Six says, "and some of them got arrested and taken to re-education camps, like Lopsided, whom you mentioned, or they were transferred to a new economic zone to farm the land."

"Yesterday," Tâm adds, "Grandfather had me burn all our western clothes and our books. All we have are our pajamas and some traditional áo dài dresses."

My father clenches his fist. "I am not going to give them the satisfaction of taking our belongings and then fining us for such possessions."

"Or worse, imprisoning us," my sister-in-law, Hiền, adds. "They want to destroy all remnants of the bourgeois culture. Aiyah, they are coming into homes and seizing valuables. It is only a matter of time before they come here and take all our food and money."

"My friend's mother was asked to spy on her neighbors in the village," Tâm says, "and to report any peculiar behaviors or suspicious actions against the government. In return, they would reward her with food and money."

"We must be proactive," Hải says. "We need to combine our money and gold, hide anything valuable, maybe sell some of it if we need to, and live conservatively." Everyone nods in agreement. "And no one better be pregnant."

"What does being pregnant have anything to do with this?" my brother-in-law asks.

"Oh, believe me, there is no more bang in my firecracker," Sister Six admits dryly.

"There is no fuse left in my firecracker, either," Hiền offers.

I chime in. "I am thirty-six now, and there is not enough powder—"

"No, no. Have you all not heard? There is a new family law that is going to take effect soon, requiring abortion," Hải says.

"Why?" we all ask in disbelief.

"I am guessing the government wants to make sure no more half-breeds are born." Hải takes a second helping of the congee and pork floss. Everyone starts talking over one another saying "this cannot be" and "how can they do this?"

"Good thing I did not lie with a Westerner!" Tâm proclaims.

"I would kill you if you got pregnant out of wedlock," Sister Six threatens.

"But what if you are already pregnant in your second or third trimester?" my almost thirteen-year-old nephew asks.

"Tree?" Brother Seven is unsure what to make of his son's question.

I, too, am suspicious of my nephew. He never asks questions, only offers statements as his own truths.

"Relax! I did not get anyone pregnant! I was only asking!" Tree responds.

"I do not know," Hải answers.

"Those bitter melon men are unpredictable," I say. "Who knows what they will do. We need to do as they say and tread carefully."

"Who are the 'bitter melon men'?" Hiền asks.

"That is what I call all the North Vietnamese government officials," I answer. "On the way here, we had to go through security checkpoints and one of the policemen who inspected us had big pimples all over his face, and because he was wearing a green uniform, he looked like a bitter melon." Tree laughs. "He took my watch!"

"I am tired." Father rises from his chair. "I am going to retire for the night. I am happy you are home. Everyone get some sleep."

We bid him goodnight and stay up talking for another hour before finally succumbing to sleep.

∗∗∗

My daughter turns one year old today, July 30, 1975. In my country, many babies die before reaching the first anniversary of their birth. For this reason, to make it to one year is a big relief for the parents and is a special milestone to be celebrated.

We have been at my father's house now for three months. The government has since changed the country's currency and replaced the piaster with the dong. I barely recognize my hometown these days. Neighbors, who were once friendly with one another, now spy on each other. The only ones we trust are our neighbors, Tú and Vân, who play cards with Sister Six.

The government incentivizes us to report suspicious activity. One family was rewarded with twice the rice and meat ration for the month because they reported overhearing another family make covert plans to flee the country. Another family was accused of harboring an uncle who served in the South Vietnamese Army and aided both the Americans and members of the old regime. The uncle was arrested and that family had their monthly monetary allowance cut in half. The couple who reported this received the other half of the monthly allowance. In a nearby village, a daughter returned home from Sài Gòn with a swollen belly and was forced to have an abortion. The mother claimed it was swollen from malnutrition, but I heard the unborn fetus was mỹ lai đen, meaning black half-breed. The daughter committed suicide and her parents were sent away to some rural, remote area.

"Spying on the neighbors?" Hải walks toward me. Dirty Butt keeps pace behind him, looking gaunt but still spirited.

I bend down to stroke my chicken's head. "I have known most of my neighbors since childhood and now, many of them are gone."

"Yes, it is distressing," Hải comments. "At least your family is together."

"I have you to thank for bringing us home safely." I smile warmly at him.

"Changing the subject… Thủy-Tiên turns one today," Hải says. "We should celebrate. We have to allow ourselves some joy."

"If we celebrate, our spying neighbors will wonder how we afford it, and then report to the communist cadres that we must be doing something illegal."

"And they would be right." Hải chuckles. "Come with me."

I pick up Dirty Butt and carry her with me to the trees by the family outhouse and pond. My nephew slides down from the mango tree and startles me. Dirty Butt is not happy about the intrusion. She hops out of my arm, flaps her wings and squawks away.

Tree and Hải walk to the other side of the pond while I follow. We stop at the stalls where my father keeps our pigs. We used to have four pigs, but now there are only two. My father sold one to make some money to survive and slaughtered another so that he could feed our family. We were forbidden to give any of the animals a name, but when I started referring to our chicken as 'Dirty Butt', my sister tattled. Father got upset. "It is a chicken, not a pet! Now I cannot kill it."

"We have something to show you in the bunker," Tree says.

We walk down into the bunker and immediately I am reminded of Mrs. Trần. My father's bunker is bigger than hers. It needs to be, to fit all members of our family. It is constructed like hers, except there are no sandbags marked with the letters "VN" on them. Mrs. Trần's voice rings clearly in my head. "Ay, you are not so smart! VN for Việt Nam." I wish our bags had preserved foods. What I would not give for some smoked fish and rice right now!

"I remember when I was as young as six years old," Tree says, "I would be so fascinated with the hospital."

"The one near our house?" I ask.

Tree nods. "I would walk home from school and hear all the ambulance sirens, and then see them dump all the bodies into piles behind the hospital."

"Your grandfather was head of the school then." I reminisce with Tree. "I remember the terrible smells blanketing the air from the piles of rotting flesh."

"It still lingers." Tree looks down at his feet before continuing. "I was never afraid. I do not know why, but it fascinated me to see those decomposing bodies. It may be morbid, but I was drawn to it."

"You were always a curious child, examining things." A few seconds go by before I pipe up again. "Remember when you would always stop at that café by the hospital and bring home an iced coffee with condensed milk for me?"

"I bet you would be in heaven if you could have one of those coffees now."

"Yes, I would probably sell you off for a year's worth of indentured servitude, if I could have a taste of that coffee!"

Tree glares at me. I add a wink to lighten the mood and put him at ease.

"So, Tuyết," Hải says, "Tree found something near the hospital."

Tree pulls something out from his shorts pocket. I notice the small hole near his crotch and the thread fraying at the seams. I will have to ask Hiền to sew that up later. I read out loud the big block letters on the glass bottle. "Moor pheen ay."

"I think it is pronounced 'moor pheen'," Hải says. "It is a strong painkiller."

"This small bottle of Western medicine will sell fast on the black market," Tree says.

"How much do you think we can sell it for?" I inspect the bottle.

"Three million," Tree responds confidently.

My eyes open wide. My heart races fast and I am excited. "The government only gives each household two-hundred-thousand a month. With our combined households, we get six-hundred-thousand each month." I do some quick calculations in my head. "That is five months of government subsidy for our family in this little bottle of magic!"

"You did that math in your head so quickly!" exclaims Hải.

"I used to be a math teacher before I worked at the bank," I say proudly. "This is a day for celebration after all." I clasp my hands together and jump up and down.

"Tomorrow, I will go into the market and sell the morphine," Tree declares.

"Be careful you do not get caught by the cadres or any of our neighbors," I caution him.

"I am twelve," he retorts, "no one pays attention to me."

"Maybe there are more painkillers at the hospital." I am excited at the possibility.

"No. It has been completely looted." Tree extinguishes my hope.

"There was medicine in the loot that I took from the embassy. I gave my stuff to Cường and asked him to sell all of it for me. I do not remember what kind of medicine, but maybe there were other painkillers. We need to make a trip to Sài Gòn so I can collect."

***

Tree comes into my bedroom, his eyes wide with excitement. "Meet us in the bunker after lunch."

After a small lunch of boiled cassava root dipped in sugar, the family retires to their bedroom for a nap, while Tâm washes the pot and plates. I sneak off to the bunker, anxious to learn how much money Tree got for the morphine.

"Did anyone see you go into the bunker?" Hải asks.

"No. They are all going to take their nap. Tâm is washing the dishes and then she was going to patch the holes in Tree's shorts," I respond.

Tree sits down on the small chair in the bunker and reaches into his pocket. "I went to the market and asked around to see where I could buy Western medicine. I found a lady who took me into her fabric shop and she showed me her medicine supply. She had a lot but I do not know what they all were."

"So, did she buy what you had to sell?" I ask.

Tree smiles at me and leaves me in a moment of suspense, before responding, "Yes." He dangles a red pouch in front of me.

"For Heaven and Earth's sake, spit it out! How much?"

"She offered me two million—" Tree says.

"That is not enough!" I exclaim.

Hải pipes up. "Let him finish."

"I told her my family would beat me if I did not get at least four million for the morphine." Tree hands me the pouch. "She laughed at me and waved me off, but I lied and told her the man three stores down offered me three million. Then I left her shop. She chased after me a minute later and offered me three million five hundred. I told her it was better to have a beating on a full stomach than an empty one, and accepted her offer."

The biggest grin spreads across my face and I laugh. "Tree, you are a clever scoundrel." I open the silk clutch, embroidered with a mai flower on the front. Inside were thin, rectangular, gold bars, with the words *Kim Thành* embossed on them.

"Since the government froze everyone's bank accounts last month and any currency that was not exchanged became useless, we are buying gold bullions."

"Tuyết, you and I should go and buy some more gold leaves. We need to turn cash into gold quickly, before they change currency again," Hải urges.

"Yes, with all this gold and the government subsidy, our family of twelve can live conservatively for a year, without raising suspicion." I smile at him. He smiles back. Why have I never noticed how attractive he is?

We celebrate Thủy-Tiên's first birthday by getting her ears pierced.

10 RAGAMUFFIN CHIC (AUGUST 1976)

I wake to the sound of heavy rainfall pounding against my window. It is only 4 a.m. My two-year-old sleeps beside me. Her breathing is labored and irregular. Her skin is dark and bruised-looking. I wonder if my drinking coffee during pregnancy caused her heart to tear. Every morning, I fear I will wake up to a lifeless child. I imagine what our life would be like if Thủy-Tiên and I went to America with Tý. My daughter would have received the medical care she needed to repair her heart.

I change the story in my mind and imagine myself married to Sam. I can picture us living in his hometown of Bellevue, Washington, and I would be chasing after two beautiful Amerasian kids, with another one on the way. We would have many children, and I would call them Two, Three, Four, Five…

It has been four years since Sam's death. For so long, I carry in my heart the sound of Sam's laughter, deep and beautiful, except for when he is in an absolute uproar and no sound escapes his open mouth. His head would tilt back, his eyes in tears, his hands slapping his knees, and his mouth agape… and for a few seconds, he would laugh in silence, until he caught his breath, and let out a lion's roar. How I miss his laugh. How I miss his dimple and his kiwi-colored eyes. I wish I had a photo of Sam so that I can remember every detail of his face. At least I still have the book and his letter.

I twirl my wedding ring around. It is time to take it off. It has been one year and four months since that day Tý and Annette pulled away from Cường's store. I walk to my dresser and pull open the last drawer. It creaks and wobbles in protest, like a piglet separated from the comfort of its mother's body. I pull out from the bottom of the pile my old, black pajama pants with the big elastic waist. It is the first and only pair of pants I ever attempted to sew. Brother Seven's wife tried to teach me a few years ago but gave up.

"The waist is crooked!" Hiền had said.

"Sister Seven, you told me to zig zag the stitching!" I barked.

"Instead you zig-zagged your pants. One pant leg is wider than the other and this one is also noticeably shorter. Aiyah, Sister, the elastic at the waist is all wrong, too. And why do you have three different colors of thread?"

"I broke the black thread and then could not get another through the eye of the needle, so I started over with the red thread, but when that one broke—"

"Aiyah, you cannot pull so hard! And you are supposed to lick the end to smooth the fibers out before you thread the needle!"

"Well, if you were not so cheap and purchased stronger thread, they would not be breaking!"

"Aiyah, you are hopeless. A woman who cannot cook or sew! Let us hope you are the last of your kind!"

She made me put it on and do a fashion show for the whole family. Sister Six laughed so hard, she fell off her chair and split the seams under her right armpit, pointing as she fell. "Poor little sister, let me give you a piaster for those exquisite pants! I must have them for fashion week in Paris! Monsieur and Mademoiselle, may I proudly present this year's theme, Ragamuffin Chic!"

Now, the only thing these pants are good for is hiding precious mementos in the elastic waistband. I strip the pants inside out and search for the small hole in the waist. I find the opening and drop my wedding band into it. Clink. I remember what else is in there. My heart beats fast as my fingers work, inch by inch, to guide the small object through the length of the waist until a portion of it peeks through the hole.

In the palm of my hand lies the oval-cut emerald ring that Sam gave me, with its glorious tiny diamonds surrounding the center stone. I put it on and feel the eighteen-carat gold wrap itself around my left ring finger and imagine Sam's arms wrapped around me.

Muffled voices come from downstairs. The women are awake. I put Sam's ring back into the waistband and tuck the pants back in the bottom drawer. I join my family in the kitchen.

"I wish it would end." Hiền sits at the table twirling a chopstick.

"You wish what would end?" I ask.

"The monsoon season," Hiền responds. "Aiyah, we have two more months of rain. I cannot wait for the mid-autumn festival in a few weeks."

"I miss the old days when our husbands would let us sit with them at the table and drink all day long!" Sister Six chimes in.

"Yes, and after you nhậu all day long, I remember us kids having to clean up all the beer cans you adults threw under the table!" Tâm exclaims. "I am glad I am not a child anymore!"

"And then we would play tứ sắc all night long, and you would always lose, Sister Six." I poke her ribs playfully.

Sister Six slaps my hand away. "Because I would be drunk by then! I cannot distinguish one card from another after half a dozen beers!"

"Aiyah, do not make excuses. You are always bad at gambling. We can see right through you." Hiền points the chopstick at her. "When you lie, your left eye flutters like this." She demonstrates her left eye going into seizures.

"And when you have a good hand, you pass gas!" I form my right hand into a fake gun and aim at Tâm's shoulder. I let out two fart pops. "Bang. Bang."

Tâm pretends to fall over dead. "That, dear Mom, is how lethal your farts are when you are winning tứ sắc." Tâm blows my sister a kiss. We all laugh.

Sister Six grumbles, "I cannot help it if I get relaxed and gassy when I am excited." We laugh harder. "Keep laughing but remember who cooks for this family. You want to eat, do you not?" Sister Six threatens us with a pouty glare.

"What is so funny that you all are laughing so hard this early in the morning?" Brother Seven stands at the bottom of the staircase, dressed in his usual faded black slacks and white cotton shirt, with yellow armpit stains, ready for work. *Now that is ragamuffin chic.* "What do we have to eat?"

"Not much," Sister Six responds. "We ran out of all the gold bouillons two months ago and everything costs four times more than they used to!"

"Well, what can we sell?" he asks.

"We do not have anything else to sell."

"Look again. By tomorrow morning, I want everyone, including the children, to bring me one item we can sell."

"Aiyah, Husband, there is nothing, unless you want to sell our children!" Sister Seven protests.

"We can sell my jade bracelet," I say reluctantly. "Brother Seven, I want to go with you today. I need to see Cường and finally collect on the sale of my loot from the embassy. Our family needs the money. I also want to check in with Mrs. Trần and see how she is doing, if there is time."

"I am a truck driver, not a bus driver or your personal chauffeur. It is a long, uncomfortable six hours to Sài Gòn. It is too much of a trip for you and Thủy-Tiên."

"I will entertain her." Tree stands on the last step of the stairs in his underwear scratching his stomach. He lets out a big yawn.

"It is settled then," I say.

***

Brother Seven and I ride out at 5:30 a.m. We share a sweet potato for breakfast and save the other two for lunch and the ride back.

"Do you like being a truck driver?" I attempt to fill the silence.

"So far, it is not bad. There are worse things than driving twelve hours each day, seven days straight."

"Brother, each day, you leave before 6 a.m., get to the brewery by 12 p.m., and spend two hours eating, napping, and reloading the truck. You get home by 8 p.m., tend to the needs of your family, get five hours of sleep, and then do it all over again, with no rest. What can be worse than that?"

"For one, getting home past the 9 p.m. curfew and getting harassed by the police. And for another, listening to my wife nag for twelve hours. 'Aiyah, Husband, go help your son, Tuấn, with his bath.' Or, 'Aiyah, Tree climbed up the roof again and you need to get him down.' 'Aiyah, aiyah, aiyah.' I am one 'aiyah' away from going insane."

I chuckle. "Brother, you act stern, but I know you love her."

"I like driving despite the relentless schedule. The bitter melon men, as you call them, do not give me any trouble at the checkpoints, especially when they see I am transporting beer."

"Speaking of beer, can we can get some for the mid-autumn moon festival?" I ask.

"It depends if you get money from Cường. Do you think he sold your embassy loot and pocketed the money?"

"We will see. I want to believe that his moral compass is pointed in the right direction, but then again, he does work for the mob."

"Speaking of mob, has Tý written?"

73

"No."

"Is there something between you and Hải? I see how he looks at you."

"He is nothing like his brother. He is a good, selfless man, and the best ally we have. I owe Hải so much." I sigh. "I know he is in love with me. A woman knows these things, but I am still a married woman, raising a child who will grow up never knowing her father. At least I hope she will grow to be an adult. I hear in America, the streets are paved with gold. People have money and fancy cars. They have the best education and world-class doctors who can determine what is wrong with Thủy-Tiên's heart and fix it."

"You missed two opportunities to go to America and you are going to try again?" my brother asks.

"I missed three opportunities if you count my plans of marrying Sam and moving to Washington."

"I am sorry about Sam. I will help you escape if you promise to take Tree with you."

"It is too dangerous. I cannot be responsible for him. He is just a boy," I protest.

"He is almost fourteen years old. It will be he who will take responsibility for you. He can protect you, and take care of Thủy-Tiên." My brother's eyes tear up. "His chances for a happy and safe life are greater in America than here, and it is worth the risk."

"I will think about it," I promise pensively.

***

I leave my shoes at the entrance and walk into the toy store. Behind the showcase is a weathered-looking man slumped over his stool, removing a kite from its cellophane wrap. My heart sinks. Time has aged him and he is thinner than a year ago.

"Cường?" I ask.

Cường looks up and gives me a blank stare. For a moment, I see the anguish on his face, but a flicker of life ignites in his eyes. He recognizes me.

"Tuyết!" He stands up and waves me to sit with him on the adjacent chair. "What brings you back here?"

"It has been a long time and it is presumptuous for me to ask, but I am hoping to collect my share of the money, from the sale of the stuff I got at the U.S. embassy." I hold my breath for Cường to respond, expecting him to tell me he does not have it.

"I was able to sell most of your belongings. I wrote an inventory of everything, including the chair and two trashcans. Let me get the list." Cường disappears in the back room for a few minutes and returns with a notebook. He squats back down on the stool and thumbs through the pages, stopping on a page that is written in blue ink instead of black ink. "Here, take a look." He hands me the booklet.

I scan the list. "You only got three-hundred-thousand for all this?" I am disappointed.

Cường nods. That is not much more than what the government gives each family each month. What is that in U.S. currency? Ten dollars?

"Tuyết, I sold what I could to those northerners relocating down here to Sài Gòn, I mean, Hồ Chí Minh City, and those guys are tough to bargain with."

"Tell me, do you remember if there was any Western medicine like morphine in my bag?"

"What is morphine?"

"It is an expensive painkiller and we can get a lot of money for it on the black market. My nephew found a bottle and Tý's brother, Hải, knew exactly what it was. We were able to sell it for three and a half million back home!"

Cường's eyes widen. "Maybe Vĩnh Bình is a better market for the Western drugs than they are here?"

"Maybe," I speculate. "The demand in my hometown is higher than the supply. We are in dire need of food and supplies. The Việt Cộng cut off a lot of our food supply and is forcing families to hand over everything, especially our rice crops. People are starving and resorting to stealing, lying, cheating – anything to survive and be in good favor with the new government."

"It is madness here, too. It is a daily struggle and I am hustling to take care of my sick relatives and aging parents. My wife, she could not take it anymore and took her life last year. She poisoned herself."

Cường becomes quiet. I am lost for words, unsure of how to comfort this man who is neither family nor friend. Instead, we share a moment of silence in her memory. Abruptly, Cường rushes to the back room and disappears for a couple minutes. He rummages through paper and plastic and shoves a chair aside. He comes back with a box.

"We found abandoned pallets of stuff at the port in Vũng Tàu, including this *Bayer*' bottle. Of course, we hauled everything we could grab, and came back several times. So many people had the same idea. We had to fight them off at the docks to claim the pallets that we have. So, do you know what this *Bayer* is used for?"

"No, but I will ask Tý's brother, Hải," I answer. "There is a great demand for Western medicine in my hometown. Why not let me help you sell some of it there? Everything costs four to ten times as much as they used to and with such a short supply of medicine and other necessities, people are willing to spend money on the care they need. There are still people with money. We need to find them."

"That is fine, but we split the sale 70/30."

"What?" I shriek. "No. Equal partners, Cường. You may be the supplier but I am the one taking all the risk and doing the footwork. I have to travel twelve hours round trip each time and smother those bastards at the security checkpoints with my charm."

"Here is the deal. Take this box of *Bayer* back to Vĩnh Bình and let us see how fast you can sell it all, and how much money you can get for it. If you can get five-hundred-thousand đồng for it within a week, we will be equal partners."

"I will see you in three days with at least five hundred," I say confidently. "Now, where is my three-hundred-thousand đồng?" *What am I getting myself into?*

11 MOONCAKE TO FREEDOM (SEPTEMBER 1976)

It is the eve of the mid-Autumn moon festival. Brother Seven received some beer as payment for his driving, so we will be enjoying that tonight. Sister Six, Tâm, and Hiền are in the kitchen preparing for the celebratory dinner. While meats and rice are scarce, there are some fish and potatoes at our disposal. Tonight's dinner will be steamed fish, lightly salted in a pan of water, with boiled potatoes, lightly sweetened. Tree climbed our fruit trees this morning and plucked some coconuts and unripe mangos, which we will dip in fish sauce and sugar. I wish we had pea vines to stir-fry. My body is craving leafy vegetables.

"You are not helping them prepare dinner?" Hải sits down beside me on the bench in our front lanai.

"I am banned from the kitchen." I lean down and pet Dirty Butt.

Hải laughs. "Will you be going to Sài Gòn tomorrow to see Cường or Mrs. Trần?"

"No. I have been selling those drugs for two weeks now and have not been able to save nearly enough money to buy a boat or hire a captain. Cường is taking sixty percent of what I sell. I still need to save enough for Tree. My brother wants me to take him with me."

"What about your wedding ring? You still have that?"

"I do, but that will not be enough. Are you sure you do not want to go, too?"

"No, I have told you once before. I was born here, and here is where I will die."

"Well, at this rate, it will take me at least another year to have enough money to not only pay for all three of us but to afford some gold bars in reserve for when we make it to America."

It makes me sad to be leaving everyone and everything behind. "There are families pooling money together and planning their escape together." Hải lights up a cigarette.

"Yes, I know of four other families right now, willing to risk everything to leave."

Hải sits down on the stone bench outside our front porch. He rests his elbows onto his knees. "There is something I have always wanted to tell you." He makes eye contact with me and lets out a deep sigh. "Before you leave the country, I have to confess I have loved you since the day of your wedding tea ceremony."

"Hải—"

"Please, let me finish. It has taken me a long time to have enough courage to tell you. I hope you can forgive me for being so bold. I know we can never marry, but we can still have a life together. I will take care of—"

"That will never be acceptable to my family." I interrupt again.

"Stay here with me, with your family. Together, we will survive through this."

"I do not want to survive, Hải, I want to live. Thủy-Tiên needs medical care and she cannot get good medical attention here."

"Do you have any feelings for me?" It is an honest question from Hải, but one I struggle to answer. Admitting that I feel something for him would betray the light I hold for Sam and the marriage vows I gave to Tý.

"Your silence says it all," Hải says with sadness in his eyes.

"It is not that simple," I protest. "Having feelings for one another is not enough. My daughter comes first now. What kind of life will we have, if we cannot live as husband and wife, to yearn for one another, but not be able to show any affection or be accepted as a couple?"

"We can love each other behind closed doors and from afar. Side by side, I will be with you until the day I die. There are worse things than being loved. Let me love you."

"I cannot dishonor my father's house and bring more shame to the family. We invited you into this house and treat you like family. What would happen if we loved each other behind closed doors and my family finds out?"

Hải says nothing. I want to give him a tender squeeze on the arm but hold back. Instead, I leave him and go into the house to insist helping with dinner.

***

"Aiyah, Eight, no! You do not peel a mango that way! You will cut yourself. And all this meat still left on the skin! That is wasteful!" After this reprimand, Hiền grabs the mango from my hand. She scrapes the mango flesh off the strips of skin with her lower teeth and chews on the crunchy, unripe fruit. She peels the skin slowly to make sure I see the action. "See? Like this." She hands me the knife and a fresh mango.

An hour later, we all sit around the outdoor table. Brother Seven proudly opens a can of beer for each adult. He puts an unopened one in front of Tree. We all laugh and cheer.

My father stands up and raises his *Tiger* beer in the air. "Family, tonight we celebrate. There is no seat for Doubt or Fear at this feast tonight. We have many blessings, despite all the pains. Let me celebrate each one of you. First, to my son, Seven! You have always been the quiet one, but when you speak, the birds stop to listen. You have grown up to make this old man proud because your quiet resolve has seen this family through tough times. Your commitment has never faltered. Cheers!" Father takes a swig of his warm beer.

We all yell cheers, "Vô!" and take a drink.

Father raises his beer to Tree. "My grandson, you are like your father, sure of yourself, committed to your family, and resourceful…although, it would have been nice if you found us ice for the beers!" We all laugh. "I have witnessed your athleticism, your tenacity, and your grit over the years and I believe that without you, there would not be enough food on the table. Tonight, we toast you."

We all yell, "Vô!" and take a drink. My nephew is all smiles. He grimaces as he drinks his beer but is happy to be treated like an adult tonight. Father goes around the table and addresses each family member.

"Hải, you brought my daughter and granddaughter home safely to us. I am in your debt. You have proven to be a sound thinker and I know where your heart and loyalty lies. You have good intentions and genuinely care for my family. Cheers to you."

We all take our third gulp of beer and cheer, "Vô".

I am already feeling the effects of my *Heineken* beer, or "ken" as we like to call it. I make eye contact with Hải. He smiles. I remember our conversation earlier and his declaration of love for me. I pretend to fuss over Thủy-Tiên, who sits patiently on my lap.

My father addresses the children, Tuấn and Trinh, thanking them for being good kids and for picking up all the beer cans later, to which we all giggle, yell "vô" and take a drink. I pace myself and take a tiny sip. My stomach gurgles and I wish Father would hurry up. He says something nice to Sister Six's husband, something about his ability to stay calm, and to Brother Seven's wife, about her sewing. I drown out his speech and focus on my impatient stomach. I say "vô" on cue and drink on autopilot.

"Father, the fish and potatoes are colder than our beer," warns Sister Six.

"Six, you are a better cook than your mother ever was, and even though our food is getting cold, it will still taste like a masterpiece," Father compliments. "You nourish our spirit and give our body strength. Vô!"

"Vô!" we all parrot.

"And to my youngest child, although not a child anymore!" Father glances at me, then to Thủy-Tiên. He will likely struggle to find something nice to say. I must be a disappointment to him – the only child to turn away from Buddhism towards Catholicism, the only one to fall in love with an American GI, the only child to marry late and not be able to hold onto her husband, the only one who cannot cook or sew or do anything domesticated like a good wife can.

My body involuntarily tenses and I catch myself holding my breath. "Father, we should eat. Sister Six prepared a nice meal for us and we should not let it—"

"Tuyết," my father says, "let me finish." Everyone is quiet. Did anyone else notice he called me Snow and not Eight? Why is he being so formal? "From the day you were born, you gave me grief." *Fantastic. Here we go.* "I was always worried that your beauty and charm were the only things you had going for you. The world fell at your feet and people fussed over you every day of your life. But, Eight…" My father's lips quiver and his eyes brim with tears. "Child, you boldly left home to get a uni education—"

"Father, the university took me away from home, where I should have been, to care for you and Mother—"

"Stop interrupting me, Eight," my father says softly. "You learned English and became a math teacher, and then earned your promotion at the bank. You are raising my granddaughter on your own without a husband, and I see the courage in how you fight for her. You know what you want and are not afraid to take chances. In this old man's eyes, I see defiance and quiet strength, not carelessness or weakness. Cheers to you."

I am speechless but Dirty Butt comes to my rescue, strutting to the beer cans at Brother Seven's feet. She clucks loudly and provides comic relief.

Everyone yells, "Vô!"

Tree takes a sip of his beer and reaches down to pet Dirty Butt's head. "Mông Dơ is ready to party."

Father invites everyone to eat and we voraciously dig into the steamed fish and potatoes. I finish my two "ken" beers and am drunk.

***

It is nearly 3 a.m. and I cannot sleep. Conversations from the evening replay in my head. It took three beers for little Tree to get drunk. I was impressed my nephew had such tolerance. We ate everything and picked at the fish until there was nothing on the bones. Everyone offered the last potato to Father, but secretly, we probably all wanted it. The coconut and mangos had never tasted more divine. Hải and I shared one coconut and he made sure I got most of it. A couple of times our hands touched or his calves grazed against my leg, but I did not pull away from him. And once, when I stood behind him to clear the plates from the table, my breasts brushed against his shoulder. An electrifying sensation coursed through my body and I was curious what it would feel like to have his mouth on them.

Still feeling a little lightheaded from the two beers I had earlier, I seek Hải out. A quick glance at Thủy-Tiên assures me she is in deep slumber. I tiptoe to Hải's room, which was once Tree's room. They were sharing the bedroom until Tree volunteered last week to sleep in the bunker, and give each other their own space. I pass Sister Six's bedroom. She is snoring loud tonight. I turn the knob slowly to Hải's bedroom and walk in, careful not to make a sound. The cool tiles feel refreshing on my bare feet. Hải's window is wide open and the temperature is pleasant. It is raining again. I stand at the foot of his bed and negotiate whether I should leave. It takes a minute for my eyes to adjust to the new darkness of the room and I can make out the outline of Hải's body. His breathing is slow and deep. He rolls over. His eyes are open.

Without a word, I unbutton my shirt slowly with trembling hands and let the shirt fall to the floor. I slip off my pants and stand before him in my underwear, feeling vulnerable and thankful for the darkness that blankets my imperfections. Hải lifts up his bedsheet and I walk toward him, my heart beating fast. I slide underneath the

81

sheet as his arms wrap around my waist, and we kiss with passion. The masculine scent of beer on his breath and grease on his skin, from all the years of tinkering with cars, scooters, and motorbikes, draws me in. I cannot get enough of him as he tightens his grip on my hips and pulls me to him. Tonight, I feel free and let my body surrender to his touch.

After our lovemaking, Hải gets out of bed and walks to the dresser. "I have something for you." The silhouette of his naked body is beautiful with the moonlight on him. He sits on the bed and hands me a round pastry. "It is not a mid-Autumn festival without a mooncake."

My heart swells with excitement as I clasp my hands together with glee. "Is the filling bean or lotus seed paste?" I hope it is the latter. I cannot wait to sink my teeth into this delicious, thick and rich dessert.

"Lotus seed." Hải offers me the first bite. "Too bad we do not have tea to go with it."

Without shame, I take a big morsel. "It is so sweet and dense and decadent and…Wait. How did you get this?"

Hải laughs. He carefully breaks the mooncake in half so as to not break the salted egg yolk inside. It is a perfect yellowish-orange orb, round like the autumn moon. He places the yolk gently into the palm of my hand. I lift it to my mouth. "Do not eat it yet!" I stop and notice a small hole in it. How strange. Hải grabs my other hand and leads me to the window. "Look at the moon. One day, you will be looking at this same moon, but from a window in America."

I want to pop the creamy yolk into my mouth. "We can be looking at this same moon together someday, in America, if you come with us."

Hải shakes his head no. "I cannot go with you."

We stand in silence, admiring the night sky. The light of the moon illuminates our bare skin. I feel such peace and happiness but have not forgotten the yolk in my hand. I want to eat it.

Sensing my eagerness, Hải chuckles. "Go ahead and break the yolk open." I pinch the yolk with my fingers and with a light squeeze, it crumbles apart in my hand. There is a small capsule inside. "This is your mooncake to freedom. Open the capsule."

I give Hải pieces of the broken yolk and open the capsule carefully. There is a small scroll. I read the message out loud. "Rooster, 29, cyclo, bananas." I do not understand its meaning.

"On the twenty-ninth of October, when you hear the rooster

crow in the morning, be ready. There will be a cyclo passing by with a bunch of bananas on it. You and Thủy-Tiên are to get in it and pretend you are going to the market. Instead, you will be taken to a secret meeting place by the river. There will be a boat to take you out to sea. I am sorry but I did not have enough to pay for Tree, and you cannot afford to wait. There may not be a better opportunity any time soon."

I am speechless. Is this happening? How did he arrange this? I lean into him and wrap my arms around his neck, kissing him fervently at first, and then caressing his mouth gently with my tongue. I ease down to his neck, to the base of his throat, and slide my lips over his clavicle. Hải exhales and pulls me close, guiding me to the floor. My legs open willingly for him and I let out a moan of pleasure as I feel him ease inside of me. Soon the sun will rise and deliver another day of challenges, but right now, there is only Hải and my mooncake to freedom.

12 THE TAXI PEDDLER (OCTOBER 1976)

The rooster crows the day I leave Việt Nam on the twenty-ninth of October in 1976. It is the year of the mighty dragon. I must be fearless like the dragon so that we can get to America safely. My family is still asleep although Brother Seven is stirring to get ready for work. Same routine every day for my poor brother. He will be furious when he discovers that I am gone and did not take Tree with me. I will miss Sister Six, despite her nagging and opinionated comments. Alas, I do not have time right now to dwell on what or who I am leaving behind. I have been consumed the past month with sadness, fear, excitement, anxiety, and a mix of a hundred different emotions. It is now time to look forward.

"Are you ready?" Hải stands behind me, cigarette in hand.

"I am ready," I say. "I have in my bag an extra change of clothes, some money that you gave me, some dried fruits, sugar cane, and the fried bananas Sister Six made last night. She will be mad when she finds out I took them." Hải walks with me to the end of the alley. He says nothing. "I also have my wedding ring and will sell that if I have to."

He caresses Thủy-Tiên's cheeks. "Be a good girl for your mother. No crying. You must be quiet and brave, and when you make it to America, get a good education. Take care of your heart so it beats strong and do not give your heart to anyone unless he can make your heart beat stronger. Understand?" My little dolly reaches for Hải, but he does not pick her up.

"Hải, I have gone over the plan a dozen times in my head, but when I get to the fisherman's boat, what happens next?"

He reaches for my hand but then stops, probably because someone may be spying. "The monsoon season is over. You should have calm waters for the journey." His eyes tell me to stay as he searches for the right words, but instead, he abruptly walks briskly back to the house.

I want to chase after Hải but a man's cough distracts me. "Miss, do you need a xích lô to the market this morning?" The cyclo has arrived, with bananas in the front carriage. I hop onto the bicycle taxi before I lose my courage, and with Thủy-Tiên on my lap, we ride away towards the town center. "Hold your tears."

He weaves through pedestrian traffic, choosing the alleys instead of the main roads. He stops a couple of times to sell bananas. My peddler has bouts of coughing during our fifteen-minute ride. At one point, he has a harsh coughing spell and swerves too far to the right, hitting a chili plant on the ground. We arrive at the market, now coming to life as people begin setting up for the day. He stops in front of a tailor shop.

I hop off and thank him. "Cảm ơn bạn."

"Take these and go into the shop." My taxi peddler hands me a bunch of bananas.

I leave my shoes outside on the stoop and step inside. Samples of fabric hang from the ceiling, vibrant colors of red, gold, blue and green, in a variety of designs. There are two mannequins dressed in festive wedding attire. The garments remind me of my wedding day. There is a doorway to a back room, with a lime-green curtain covering the entrance.

"Hello?" I inquire.

A young woman steps from behind the curtain and beckons me to follow her to the back room. "If anyone asks, your name is Thu."

"That is perfect since it means Autumn," I respond.

"Put these clothes on for you and your daughter." She hands me brown polyester pajamas with green paisley patterns on them. Thủy-Tiên receives a pale yellow sundress and bonnet. "With these clothes, no one will recognize you. Listen carefully, Thu. My husband is going to take you on foot to a nearby village. A casual observer will see the three of you as a poor family heading to the river to catch a fish. And walk with a limp with your head down. Understand?"

I nod. "Thank you, friend. I will not forget your kindness."

While we dress, the young woman leaves to retrieve my shoes. We exit through the back door and my "husband" waves me to follow him.

"Head down and limp," the seamstress whispers.

I immediately shift my weight over to my left leg and limp behind my guide. It dawns on me that he is the same man as the taxi peddler, only he is wearing different clothes with holes in them.

"You and your wife are so kind." I struggle to keep pace with him carrying Thủy-Tiên. "If there is anything I can do to repay you, please let me know. I will make good on my debt once I make it to America." Pretending to have an impaired leg is not an easy facade to maintain when you have to walk nearly two kilometers.

My companion slows down. "Let me carry the child." He takes Thủy-Tiên from my arms before I give him consent.

"What is your name?" I ask.

My companion coughs and spits out phlegm. He stops to hunch over and put his left hand on his knee. His breathing is laborious and he is now wheezing. I worry he will drop Thủy-Tiên. "Call me Husband." He stands up and we resume walking. "Your brother-in-law, Hải, is a good, honest man. He used to fix our scooters. We met many years ago in Thái Lan when the tuk-tuk I was riding broke down. It turned out to be bad, watered-down fuel. We crossed paths again a year later and have been friends since then." My "husband" stops to cough again. More sputum is expelled from his mouth.

"You are sick. Do you smoke?" I ask.

"No. It is probably the bad air quality and the fumes left from the airplanes, all the chemicals the Americans sprayed." He clears his throat, spits again, and then launches a gelatinous, sticky substance from his left nostril.

"I used to sell western medicine," I say. "That is how my family has been able to survive. I wish I had some to give you, but if you make it to Sài Gòn, there is a man who can get some for you. His name is Cường and he owns a toy shop near the old U.S. embassy."

"I will remember that."

We walk in silence for a while, stopping frequently when my companion has his fits of coughing or has to pee in the bushes. My limping does not help our pace either. It takes us an hour to walk almost two kilometers to the village.

There is smoke rising from the shanties. The village is on fire.

***

As we approach the village, I smell gasoline, incense, and pineapples. Strangely, the scent takes me back to my home the night my mother died of cancer. My siblings and I were all lighting incense at the altar, asking our ancestors to receive our mother, and burning joss paper so that her spirit can have money in the afterlife. Many of the offerings were Mother's favorite foods, such as pineapples, sugar apples, duck noodle soup, escargot grilled in lemongrass, and coconut-mango sticky rice. The scene now before me is grim.

The villagers are dressed in rags, their clothes held together by pineapple or banana leaf fibers. Most of them are barefoot. Their homes are small, thatched huts or cottages with leaky roofs due to the heavy rainfalls. There is a small grave site near a grove of jackfruit trees, the tombs and markers knocked down by either the force of the monsoons or maybe by the communists so that families cannot mourn the dead. The Vietnamese believe desecration of graves will anger the spirits and bring harm to the living. I can only hope the destruction was done by natural causes and not by humans. Children huddle beside their parents, scratching their tender young flesh at what appears to be scabies, their skin raw and red from the rash caused by tiny mites burrowed into their bodies. There is laughter mixed in with the screaming and crying.

I see a woman on her knees, her hands clasped together in prayer, as she begs a man in uniform. "Please, have mercy and spare this old lady. I will have nothing if you burn down my home."

The officer laughs. "You remind me of my grandmother."

"Then take pity on this old grandmother as you would of your own," she beseeches.

"My grandmother was a cruel woman and stingy as hell. I bet you are like her." He mocks her and lifts up his torch.

"Stop!" I scream and run to the old woman, forgetting my limp.

My "husband" whispers, "Are you crazy?"

I kneel down in front of her, shield her from any blow the officer may strike, and wince as I prepare for a beating. "Where is your respect for your elders? This woman is not your grandmother. If you are going to harass anyone, why must it be someone feeble, who has nothing, and is not worth your energy?"

I see a glimpse of abhorrence in the officer's eyes before I feel the hard brunt of his torch handle, first in my right temple, then again in my throat. The sharp pain in the jugular notch of my neck drowns out the pain on my head. I gasp for air and cough. I reach for the old woman to stand up but she runs away. The officer kicks me in the stomach. "You look more beautiful on your knees." I crumble to the ground. Pain shoots up my spine.

I see "Husband" hand Thủy-Tiên to a teenage girl and rush to my side. Two more cadres stride up to join the party. One of them, a young man probably not more than twenty years old, drags a young woman behind him by the hair. "You found yourself a pretty one." The woman with him screams and kicks, her body writhes in pain, her shirt unbuttoned down to her navel. Around her breasts are teeth marks. My heart sinks into my stomach.

"A little older, but definitely pretty," my aggressor responds. "Maybe she can teach me a thing or two."

The three officers laugh. My taxi peddler finds his voice and points to the young man that is clutching the girl's hair in his fist. "You look familiar. You are Giáp's nephew."

The smile on the young officer's face disappears. "Who are you?"

"I am a man who peddles bananas on the streets and make my living transporting people around on my bicycle," my "husband" says. He coughs a couple times before continuing. "This is my wife, Thu. In another life, I was a physician, Doctor Phạm Văn Minh. Are you not the nephew of the great General Võ Nguyên Giáp, military commander of The People's Army?"

"Speak carefully. My uncle is the Minister of National Defense and now Deputy Prime Minister for the Socialist Republic," the young assailant warns.

"Yes," my new friend, Doctor Minh, acknowledges, "your uncle was once my father's history teacher as well as a patient of mine. I was one of his physicians who treated him when he needed medical attention. Your uncle is in my debt, and I ask that you show the people of this village mercy, as an honorable act of repaying your uncle's debt."

"These villagers must be tormented and taught a lesson," the young cadre responds. "They have been harboring war criminals and helping them leave the country."

"I believe they all have learned their lesson, and if you show us all mercy now, we will tell our children about this day, how three kind officers protected us from our own demise." Minh coughs again and chokes on his saliva. He regains his composure and continues. "These villagers were wrong to help the war criminals, however, please, let my wife, my child, and I pass unharmed. We were heading to the river to catch some fish, and are not a part of this deception."

"Is that so? Then go to the river and catch us three fish. Your wife and child stay here. When you come back, she will cook us a meal, and then we will be on our way."

Panic courses through my veins. Me? Cook a meal? I plead to Minh with my eyes not to leave us. He nods and hacks some more. "Let me bring my wife to the river. It will be easier to catch fish with two people so that you all can be feasting sooner."

The third officer finally speaks up. "Let them go. We will keep their child until they return."

"Our child is only two years old. She needs her mother," Minh says, coughing again and clutching his chest. "I give you my word, we will return. My wife is the best cook in our province. You will not be disappointed."

Again, panic strikes me.

"Enough. I have no more patience with you," the young cadre says. "Your wife and child stay here. I promise them no harm, but you have one hour to bring back three fish."

I encourage Minh to leave. "Return hastily with three of the mightiest fish you can catch. We will be safe, as he promises."

Minh runs through the brush towards the river, bending over once to cough and catch his breath. I pray he will return within an hour. Three hours ago, he was a taxi peddler to me, selling bananas and taking me to his wife's tailor shop. Now, he is my pretend husband, a doctor, a fisherman, and hopefully, a hero.

I walk over to the teenage girl holding Thủy-Tiên and take my daughter from her. The three officers ignore me. They light up their cigarette and talk about their favorite Vietnamese or French cuisines. The young cadre that was holding the village girl's hair releases his grip on her ebony locks. He gives her a kick in the butt and tells her to fetch him something to drink. She runs toward the graveyard, her hands clutching her shirt close. I follow for a short distance but then the young girl runs into a dilapidated shed. I head to the cemetery instead.

I sit down on the bench with Thủy-Tiên and share one of Sister Six's fried bananas with her. I try to read some of the headstones, but most are broken. I am content to not be bothered and allow myself to relax. The throbbing pain in my throat and stomach subsides, and it is nearly an hour that passes before the sounds of footsteps disturb my tranquility. My pulse quickens as my heart pounds hard behind the inner chamber of my chest. Is Minh back?

I prepare a warm smile to greet whoever is behind me. My smile fades into shock. I catch my breath. "Minh-Hoàng." It is Mrs. Trần's oldest son.

13 THE CLEVER PHOENIX (OCTOBER 1976)

Minh-Hoàng stands before me with intensity in his eyes. It has been over a year, since last May, that I was silently interrogated by his eyes. Today is no different.

He surveys me up and down, stopping briefly at my breasts, before finally focusing on my temple. "You are hurt. Let me see."

"I am fine." I tilt my head to the side so he can examine my injury. "How is your brother, Huy? And your mom?"

"Lopsided was taken to a re-education camp as you know. He was transferred a couple times. My mother and I visited him once before he was transferred." Minh-Hoàng falls quiet.

"Surely he is out now, perhaps married with a family of his own?" I inquire. "If I remember correctly, he was only going to be at the facility for two weeks."

"Two weeks became two months," Minh-Hoàng says matter-of-factly, "and now, we are heading on two years. I do not know which camp he is at, or if he is even alive."

"Did you try to get him out? You have connections—"

"Of course I tried!" he says curtly. "He is my brother. You have no idea how much he suffered and how terrible he was treated." Minh-Hoàng sits down on the bench and rests his head on his hands. I feel sorry for him.

"How is your mom handling this?" I am worried Mrs. Trần's heart is broken once again.

"I feel her spirit slipping away, day by day. She begs me to do something, but what can I do? I have no influence with anyone in control of the camps. I feel so helpless while my brother is forced to do hard labor. He is being starved with a small bowl of rice and a cup of water each day, and confined to a metal box no bigger than two meters high and wide."

We sit quietly for a few minutes. I have no words to comfort him and although afraid to say something that will offend him, I speak anyways. "Why are you here with those men? They terrorized those people in this hamlet, innocent people, young and old."

"Innocent?" he asks. "Are you innocent?" I dare not respond. "I am guessing you and your daughter were heading to this village to seek refuge, before meeting up with a fishing crew or someone at the river. No doubt you paid some people nicely for the voyage to the Philippines or somewhere. I guarantee you the boat is long gone or already caught. I will take you both back home to your family."

"I cannot leave without my friend, Doctor Phạm Văn Minh. Your men sent him off to the river to catch some fish for lunch. It has been over an hour but he should be returning soon."

"You are naïve. Your companion is long gone. Why would he return for you when he can escape and hide? Maybe he is on that boat already and out to sea."

The thought of abandonment and betrayal is daunting. A wave of emotions sweeps over me, changing from sadness to anger to fear and finally, joy. Maybe Minh managed to get home.

"You are not going to arrest me?" I ask with trepidation.

Minh-Hoàng laughs. "My mother would skin me alive if I let any harm come to you. She adores you."

My eyes open wide. Surely he is not referring to cranky, old Mrs. Trần, the she-Jekyll, the woman with a razor-sharp tongue and a personality coarser than a sixty-grit sheet of sandpaper?

"I am not ready to go home. I want to go to Sài Gòn to see your mother."

"It is Uncle Hồ's city now," he reminds me, "but yes, I can take you. It is a long journey. Do you want to rest tonight and leave in the morning?"

"No, I would like to see your mother tonight. Maybe I can bring her some comfort."

"How will you return to your province?" he asks.

"I have a friend who can take me," I lie, referring to Cường.

***

The ride back to Sài Gòn in Minh-Hoàng's *Kaiser-Jeep M715* is an uncomfortable one. The utility truck only seats two, with a large battery box between the two seats. The cargo bed is austere with space for only the wheel wells and some provisions. Thủy-Tiên sits on my lap for the duration of the trip and my legs are sore. Luckily, the journey is faster and easier when you are sitting next to a communist. We drive through every security checkpoint with ease. Minh-Hoàng flashes his military credentials and receives a nod to proceed.

"Thủy-Tiên is hungry. Are you?" I offer snacks to Minh-Hoàng to be polite. "I have some dried fruits, sugar cane, and bananas in my bag."

He takes a handful of dried tamarind and pops them in his mouth, one by one, chewing and sucking on each piece slowly so as to savor the taste, before spitting the seed out. "My mother is the master of dried foods."

"I know. She showed me the bunker. I would give anything for some iced coffee with condensed milk to go with these fruits."

"There is a nice café not far from here. We can stop."

"It is too much trouble and I do not have enough money to spare."

"What about your monthly stipend?" he asks.

"I am not eligible to receive the two-hundred-thousand đồng a month. Only the heads of households get a monthly allowance and because I am a woman with no husband—"

Minh-Hoàng arches his eyebrow. "How have you been managing?"

I cannot confess to peddling western medicine on the black market. "I am living with my father under his stipend."

"You should get your own monthly allowance. You have a daughter to feed and clothe. You need to register under your maiden name, with a different address apart from your father's."

"So if I had registered under my family name as Lê Ngọc Tuyết, instead of Vương Ngọc Tuyết, I could have received money?" I am now worried that I may have shared too much with this communist, even if he is Mrs. Trần's son.

"You will begin receiving the monthly stipend. I will take care of it," he says. What ulterior motives does he have? What does he want in return?

I thank him and switch topics to something I feel is safe to discuss. "What is your mother's name? I always call her Mrs. Trần, but she never shared with me her first name."

"Diệp," he answers. "She hates her name. She said when Lopsided and I were born, she wanted to make sure our names had powerful meanings."

"So she named you the clever phoenix and your brother radiance."

"Yes, but we have yet to live up to our names," Minh-Hoàng says.

"I disagree," I offer. "You were clever enough to stay alive for eight years and return home, and Huy, well, it is clear he brought light and sunshine to your mother's life."

Minh-Hoàng pulls the truck over and kills the engine. "We are here. This café makes the strongest coffee."

Minh-Hoàng orders me a café au lait with a spoon of condensed milk. He insists I have it hot instead of my usual iced coffee with two spoons of condensed milk. Otherwise, how can I truly appreciate the coffee this café has to offer? I am not disappointed. I sip slowly and enjoy every trickle of liquid down my throat. This is so divine.

***

By 7 p.m. we drive through the streets of District One in Sài Gòn. The Bến Thành Market remains the same. Thống Nhất Boulevard, which once ran in front of the Independence Palace, has now been renamed to Lê Duẩn Street, after the Communist Party's General Secretary, who took over power after Hồ Chí Minh's death. The Independence Palace, now called the Reunification Palace, still looks the same except gone is the yellow flag with three red stripes. Here to stay is the red Republic of Việt Nam flag with a yellow star in the middle.

I am unexpectedly nervous to see Mrs. Trần again. Will she receive me with open arms, like a lost daughter who has returned, or will she have a snarky comment to belittle me for once again failing to leave this country? We walk through the familiar alley and step into Mrs. Trần's house. It is immaculate. Not a speck of dust or a fly buzzing by. Thủy-Tiên walks immediately over to the hammock and tries to crawl in by herself. It is quiet in the house. The air is stale. I was hoping to be greeted by smells of curry or caramelized sugar, hoping that she may have prepared dinner. There is no sign of Mrs. Trần. Minh-Hoàng checks upstairs while I walk outside to the back garden. I peek around and do not see any trace of her.

A gut-wrenching scream comes from upstairs. I run back inside the house and up the two flights of stairs to the top floor. I check the rooms but see no one. The cry comes again and I fly up to the landing of the roof. Clothes hang on a rod across the rooftop. I see the bottom of Minh-Hoàng's shoes and rush to his side, pushing away pants and sheets hanging on the clothesline. His deep, throaty

94

gurgle evolves into a maniacal roar, like an insane man throwing a tantrum. He is kneeling on the ground, cupping Mrs. Trần's face in one hand and supporting her lifeless body in his other arm. His jerky movements go from shaking her body to stroking her head, back to cupping her face and then slapping her cheeks.

"Má! Má ơi!" Minh-Hoàng sobs, saying "Mother! Oh, Mother!" over and over again. He cradles her and rocks back and forth. "Mother! Oh, Mother!"

I kneel down next to Mrs. Trần and lift her limp hand. It is cold and clammy. I feel a faint heartbeat on her wrist. I wish Dr. Phạm, my taxi peddler friend, is here. He would know what to do. Mrs. Trần's body convulses. She gasps for air and her eyes pop open. I see the pupils constrict before her eyes roll up and back. She goes into cardiac arrest and seizes again. I search for clues as to what happened. I see a bottle with a chloroquine label. Would malaria pills have this effect on her?

"She poisoned herself with these pills," I say to a grief-stricken Minh-Hoàng.

He hysterically asks over and over again why she left him. "Má! Tại sao Má bỏ con?"

I run down the stairs and out the front doors. "I need a doctor!" I pound my small fist on the door across from Mrs. Trần's house. "Please, someone, help." No one answers. I dash over to the next house and rap hard on the window. "Please help. My aunt is dying. I need a doctor."

A woman opens her window. "Take her to the hospital."

"Do you have a car? Please, we only have a jeep that seats two people and there is no space in the back large enough for—"

I am cut off by the window slamming shut in my face. I am shocked but have no time to argue. Minh-Hoàng's shrill cry has me darting back inside the house as quickly as I can. Thủy-Tiên is by the hammock, oblivious to what is happening right now, and still trying to climb into the hammock.

Minh-Hoàng carries his small, lifeless mother down the stairs. Tears rain down his face. "Why?" I half expect her to answer as if this is a cruel joke she is playing. "She is gone. She has left me. I am all alone now." His knees buckle beneath him and he kneels to the floor. Minh-Hoàng bends his head down in sorrow.

My heart is heavy. My monsoon tears begin where Minh-Hoàng's ends. "I will call the temple for a monk."

14 STARTING OVER (NOVEMBER 1976)

Minh-Hoàng had a beautiful tomb built above ground for his mother three days after her death. She now rests in the backyard, in her garden of herbs, watermelons, and narcissus flowers. The tomb sits atop five levels of ceramic and stones, to ensure the water level never rises high enough during the monsoon season to flood it. It is a richly decorated tomb in colors of mauve and yellow. Erected at the foot of the tomb, on either corner, sits a tiger statue, to guard and protect her spirit. In the center of the headstone, there is a personalized painting, glazed in ceramic tiles, of Mrs. Trần's face. The inscription underneath reads:

Trần Bích Diệp

July 20, 1914 – October 29, 1976

Here lies a Wood Tiger of Việt Nam, mother to many, wife to one, and slave to none.

I can only imagine how much this cost to build. The funeral is somber, despite the food, drinks, music, and incense to celebrate Mrs. Trần's life. At her altar, joss money is burned to prepare her for the afterlife, the rebirth. Some of her favorite foods are offered, including some dried, preserved goods. There are nineteen people attending the ceremony, most of us wearing our white mourning robes and white bandanas or pointed hoods. White represents the ashes of the dead. Minh-Hoàng wants to keep it small and intimate since elaborate funerals are discouraged under the new communist rule. I could not help but secretly wonder if she had many friends or family members left. Surprisingly, Cường is here to pay his respects, even though he only met her once.

"Your mother was born the month and year of the wood tiger. My daughter is a wood tiger as well," I say to Minh-Hoàng, who is standing next to Cường.

Neither man says a word to each other, but both look relieved to see me. I hand Minh-Hoàng an envelope of money, as is the custom in Vietnamese culture for weddings and funerals, to help the family with expenses. It is most of the money I have from Hải for my escape.

"Thank you. Yes," Minh-Hoàng responds, "and like the tiger zodiac, she was independent, courageous, and confident."

"And like the wood element, she had a lot of leadership capabilities that strengthened her resolve," I add.

"I only met her once," Cường chimes in, "but she scared me."

Minh-Hoàng and I laugh.

"She scared me too," I agree.

"Try being her son," Minh-Hoàng says. "She used to beat Lopsided and me daily when we were kids. It did not stop until we left home to join the army."

"Well, tigers are known to be fierce and short-tempered," I say.

"And arrogant," Minh-Hoàng adds. "Everything always had to be the best with her, always perfect, always spotless."

Cường and I nod. Not one of us knows what to say next as we have nothing in common. Perhaps the only common thread that weaves through all of us is the one of committing illegal acts to stay alive. I never believed I would stand next to a known communist enemy and feel compassion for him. I never imagined I would stand next to a gangster whom the mob still puppeteers and trust him with my livelihood. What a great team we would make.

"What is next for you?" Cường asks me.

"I still have to find a cure for Thủy-Tiên and I am not going to find it here. Something is wrong with her heart," I say.

"If it is money you need," Minh-Hoàng offers, "I can help you. I told you I would take care of your stipend."

"And I can continue to help you as well," Cường adds.

Minh-Hoàng gives Cường a curious glance. "What do you mean?" Cường and I both bite our tongue, fearing the truth will put us both in prison. "Spit it out or else I will be forced to investigate and things will not turn out good for you both. Tell me the truth and maybe I can help or protect you."

We both continue to hold our tongue. Minh-Hoàng is agitated. Finally, I speak up. "Cường has been—"

Cường grabs me by the arm and leads me to the other side of the garden, not offering an excuse or apology to Minh-Hoàng for being abrupt. "What are you doing? Are you crazy?" Cường is seething with anger. "You cannot tell him I have been supplying you contraband drugs and that you had been selling them in the black market."

"First of all," I say, "they are not drugs that have been imported or exported illegally. They are western medicines that have been abandoned by the United States."

"It does not matter. What we are doing is not legal and we will be punished if caught. We cannot trust him."

"Then let us test him. Let me see if he is a man true to his words. Let me see if he gets me that monthly stipend."

"And then what?" Cường is still unsure.

"Let me do something illegal in front of him and make sure he sees me. We will see what he does. If he protects me and does not have me arrested, then we can trust him."

"And if you get arrested?" Cường asks.

"I will have Thủy-Tiên with me. He will not arrest me. He once told me that his mother would skin him alive if he let any harm be done to me. I believe him and I believe that he will continue to honor his mother's wishes because he loves her."

"How do you know she even said that or if she even meant it?" Cường asks. "Or if he will even hold himself accountable now that his mother is not here to beat him?"

"Well, she can still haunt him. Cường, you were not there when he found his mother. She had a broken heart and she ended the pain by overdosing on malaria pills. He cried like a tormented child. His mother was his everything. He may be a communist, but he has his convictions and his loyalties, the greatest of all were to his mother."

Cường consents. "All right, but what if he arrests me instead? I am your supplier."

"Then you tell him one of Đại Cathay's generals will come after him. Who cares if that is true or not? The threat will be real enough."

In the few days that followed, I received my two-hundred-thousand đồng stipend that Minh-Hoàng promised. He completed the application using my maiden name and the address next to his home, where Tý and I lived briefly. Thủy-Tiên and I have been staying at that house the past week since it is an abandoned home.

"Are you going to go home, back to your family?" Minh-Hoàng asks.

"Yes, but first I need to say goodbye to Cường." I sip my iced coffee. "Their coffee is not strong, but the aroma is enticing." The little café in the city center is not busy this morning. There are not enough patrons who can afford such luxuries. I cannot either, even with the small stipend I received.

"They probably diluted it with extra water to make the supply stretch," Minh-Hoàng says. "Are you going to tell me how Cường has been helping you?"

"Last year, Cường helped me sell some things I took from the U.S. embassy after the Americans abandoned it and went home. He also gave me a steep discount on a toy for Thủy-Tiên when I did not have much money. He helps when he can."

"Is he family?" Minh-Hoàng leans in and looks directly into my eyes.

"No. He was a friend of my husband's." I hold his gaze to prove I have nothing to hide.

"Why was he so nervous or upset at my mother's funeral?"

"He was not sure how you would react to us stealing from the embassy. Maybe he was a little embarrassed, also, because you might think we have a relationship."

"Do you? A married man helping another married woman, even if she is separated from her husband, only means he has feelings for her."

"Cường is a hard-working man who makes next to nothing selling toys to take care of his sick relatives and aging parents. His wife committed suicide two or three years ago. She poisoned herself."

Minh-Hoàng's eyes mist up. "I feel the pain he must still feel."

"Maybe you and Cường can be friends," I say optimistically. "The American War is over. We are one country now but we still have many enemies. The Cambodians, Laotians, and the Chinese, they all want control of our land and our waters. Life will continue to be oppressive. Our people are poor and starving, or disabled and unable to work. The government controls everything, from our food supply to the media. You may not feel the same hopelessness I feel, but you cannot deny we are not in prosperous economic times right now."

"It will get better. Why do you want to leave when your family is here and you can get medical help for your daughter here or in Thái Lan?"

"The mortality rate for children under five years old is the highest it has ever been here. I believe Thủy-Tiên will have a better chance of survival where there are better medicine and easier access to those medicines. Thái Lan is too expensive and I do not trust them, even though our two countries have established diplomatic relations. I hear people talking all the time about the Thai pirates stealing and raping women. Besides, where are all our doctors? Most of them have died, fled, or are detained in re-education camps. The ones we have left have lost their practice, lost their hospital, are in hiding or lost their will."

"I disagree with you," Minh-Hoàng says, "but do what you want." I can tell he is annoyed and getting defensive. I do not care.

"It would be helpful if there is a way I can go about my business without any trouble or detainment at the checkpoints. I want to get home as quickly as possible without any searches. Do you have the ability to help with this?"

"Give me a day or two. I will see what I can do, then you can go home."

"Thank you," I say, "and also for the coffee. I need to say goodbye to Cường now."

Minh-Hoàng nods and I take my leave with my daughter in tow. I can feel Minh-Hoàng's eyes on me as I walk away. I sway my hips a bit more to accentuate my curves, hoping my little strut will encourage him to try hard for my security clearance at the checkpoints.

***

I meet Cường at his toy store. Thủy-Tiên's eyes open wide. All the crinkly cellophane wrappers tempt her to touch them; all the colorful toys beg her for attention. She teeters as she runs from one doll to another before getting distracted by a stuffed animal or a plastic toy figure. I let her enjoy this moment and play with the toys. I see Cường finishing up with a customer and patiently wait for him to complete the sale.

"Business must be good," I say after the customer leaves.

Cường laughs. "One customer does not mean business is good."

"I had coffee with Minh-Hoàng," I report. "He got me the stipend like he promised, and he is working to ensure I have no problems with the security checkpoints to Vĩnh Bình."

"What about the checkpoints back to here?" Cường asks.

"I assume that clearance getting home would be the same as getting back to Sài Gòn."

"I hope you are right. Now we need to do the ultimate test." Cường hands me a small olive green nylon pouch with a U.S. medical department insignia on the front of the cover flap. "You have to do something illegal right before his eyes to see if he will turn the other way or arrest you."

"So what do you have for me today?" I open the snap and pull out a green plastic box. Inside are medical supplies - an assortment of dressings and bandages, a bottle of iodine water purification tablets, a bottle of disinfectant, a container of foot powder, lip balm, and some tablets, probably painkillers. "I am not going to be able to sell these items individually."

"I have five more of those bags, three *Zippo* lighters, 48 tablets of codeine, and six pills of *Dexedrine*," Cường adds.

"What do the codeine and *Dexedrine* do?"

"Codeine is for pain but I am not sure about the *Dexedrine*."

I close the snap on the plastic box and put it back into the nylon pouch. "I will be leaving either tomorrow or the following day, depending on when Minh-Hoàng gets me the license to go through the checkpoints. I hope to return in one or two weeks with your share of the money."

I scoop up Thủy-Tiên, who taps excitedly on the glass of the display case. I see the same airplane model that we had to leave behind in the old house next to Mrs. Trần's house, now Minh-Hoàng's house. Sadly, the abandoned house was robbed and everything was taken.

"Take the airplane." Cường hands it to Thủy-Tiên. "You can pay me later."

"This time, it is fifty-fifty split." I leave before he argues with me.

✳✳✳

Starting over is not an easy thing to do, but this time, I feel better equipped to handle what may be coming around the river bend. I recognize now that I do not have control of anything, and for this reason, I feel prepared for everything. My escape now seems light years away. Starting over means back to selling and saving, being patient until I have more than enough money to ensure safe passage, negotiating power, and a new start in America. It means I must take charge of my own departure and not rely on Hải or anyone to do it for me. And it means making my own allies, using and beguiling my enemies, and, like Mrs. Trần once said to me, letting my tongue be my greatest artillery.

Thủy-Tiên and I walk next door to see Minh-Hoàng. I hope he has good news for me. We find him in the garden, sitting on the bench above the bunker. "I was talking to my mother."

"I can feel her presence," I say.

"Do you believe in ghosts?" he asks.

"Yes, I had been taunted by one, a long time ago when I was at uni," I say. "I was pushed off my hammock one night when nobody was around. Another time, I woke up to sounds of people walking. There was no one there but all the slippers in the house were moving."

"My mother once told me a story about how, in a village near Cần Thơ, the sound of a woman crying by the Hậu River can be heard right before dawn breaks. Many people have heard her crying, even my mother, so she claimed. The local people were told by a fortune teller to dig up an unmarked grave near the river and bury the woman in a separate grave. At first, people dismissed the fortune teller as crazy, but after many reports of hearing the woman's cry, they dug up the grave. They found four skeletons in one grave, one of which was a woman's. They removed her bones and gave her a separate resting place. The locals said the crying stopped."

"Is your mother haunting you?" I sit down beside him and let my daughter explore.

"More like nagging me," he answers. "She wants to make sure I help you succeed in leaving, even though it is against what I think you should do. She wants the best for Thủy-Tiên."

"You should listen to her. She can still whip you."

Minh-Hoàng smiles. "Yes."

I change the subject. "Do you have an update for me?"

"I do." He springs to his feet and picks Thủy-Tiên up. "Join me for dinner and I will tell you. I am a good cook." I agree to have dinner with him and we walk back into the house to the kitchen. "You will have to earn your dinner tonight and help me cook."

My eyes open wide in protest. "What are we cooking?"

Minh-Hoàng laughs at me. "Eel congee soup with perilla leaves. You better learn now before Thủy-Tiên finds out her mother is a fraud." *Damn Mrs. Trần! This is your doing!* I wish I had not agreed to dinner. "I also have some coconuts. We can drink the juice and eat the young coconut meat to finish the palate."

The live eels squirm about in the plastic colander. They are a little longer than half a meter and quite dark, a mixture of green and black. Their skin is shiny and slimy.

I am nauseated. "I can help make the congee and wash the perilla, but I am not touching those eels."

"You are not going to trick me into believing you are sick and unable to help me cook." My host does not let me off the hook. "You are going to learn everything from beginning to end. If you want to survive on your own and take care of your daughter in the new land, you need to be self-sufficient and not rely on anyone."

I concede, only because he is right. Minh-Hoàng guides me through the process of killing the eels, cleaning them, preparing the grill in the makeshift fire pit, and cooking them.

"I thought I was helping you cook, not doing everything myself," I say sarcastically.

"How else can you take all the pride when I tell you it is delicious?" Minh-Hoàng asks. "While the eels are cooking, we will cook the rice and prepare the perilla."

"You mean, I will cook and prepare. There is no 'we' is there?" I ask.

"See? You are already learning and proud of yourself." He hands me a bowl.

"You smile more than your mom ever did." I scoop two cups of rice into the bowl and wash the rice. I drain the water and repeat until the water runs clear. "You are different from your mom."

"You are wrong. I am very much my mother's son." Minh-Hoàng puts the rice into a pot and cooks it over an open flame. "Lopsided was more like my father. My mother loved them both and showed them affection. As the oldest son, I was always on the receiving end of her vexations. At times I resented her, but I loved and respected her too. She made me resilient so that I could endure anything, and always rise up to adversities. Lopsided was weak – too much love – and look where it got him. Same with my father."

"Receiving love does not make you grow up to be weak." I take a wooden spoon and stir the rice so it does not stick to the pot. "People need affection. Love is stronger than hate."

"Is it?" Minh-Hoàng washes the perilla leaves. "Thirty years of war for our country, from the Japanese to the French to the Americans, all because hate is stronger than love. And it is not over yet. Another war with Cambodia and China is coming."

"Another reason for me to leave with Thủy-Tiên. If her failing health does not kill her first, the war with Kampuchea or China will," I affirm. "Now would be a good time for you to tell me about tomorrow. Will we be able to get home and through all the security checkpoints without any harassment?"

"Yes, but I will fill in the details over dinner." Minh-Hoàng instructs me on how to flavor the rice congee soup. He then hands me a coconut and demonstrates how to break open one without any tools. "Do not cheat by using a knife."

I mimic his actions, first by pounding the bottom of the coconut repeatedly against a big boulder. My arms feel the fatigue of repetition and absorb the shock from each knock on the rock. I then use a small, sharp rock to carve into the husk and strip away the outer layer with my hands. With the coconut first between my thighs and then later between my feet, I use all the muscles I can muster to peel the outer layer. I am sweating now. My wrist is sore. My thighs are bruised. It takes Minh-Hoàng less than thirty minutes to crack it open but takes me forty-five minutes to free the coconut from its outer casing. Minh-Hoàng tends to the eel and congee while I continue working on the coconut.

I pound the coconut against the big boulder, rotating it as I go, swearing under my breath and ready to hurl it at Minh-Hoàng's head. Finally, it cracks open big enough for me to pry it apart. The coconut oil glistens beautifully and I am overwhelmed with pride and joy. I scream with triumphant delight and take a big bite of the coconut flesh. Finally, we are ready to eat.

"Save the fibers. I can use them to make a broom or a bed for myself," he advises. "Also, we are going to eat outside with my mother in her garden."

We serve up some grilled eel, congee, perilla leaves and coconut for Mrs. Trần as an offering to let her know she is still with us. We light some incense and say a prayer, before sitting down on the ground to eat. Thủy-Tiên sits contentedly next to me, picking at the eel and slurping a spoonful of congee. She puts a purple perilla leaf in her mouth, only to pucker up at the bitterness of the herb. She spits it out and cries. Minh-Hoàng and I laugh.

"Tomorrow, when you pass the first checkpoint, hand the guard this paper." Minh-Hoàng hands me a license to transport dried goods for non-commercial sale. "Do not lose it and make sure you get it back every time."

"And what dried goods will I be transporting?" I ask.

"My mother's stock of dried fish, shrimp, squid, and whatever else she has. I will give you some. Have the supply on you at all times. Do not sell or consume them. If you get searched, show them your bag of goods. This will allow you to come and go with minimal detainment. You have to get a new license every year."

"Thank you. I am so grateful," I say sincerely. "I am even thankful to have cooked this meal for you."

"You will never starve if you can open a coconut." The clever phoenix winks and digs in to the food we prepared together. It is delicious.

15 OUR TRUE SELF (NOVEMBER 1976)

In the morning, Thủy-Tiên and I stop by Minh-Hoàng's house to say farewell, and to also test his trustworthiness. I have to do something illegal in front of him and see how he reacts. I find Minh-Hoàng sitting at the kitchen table clipping his toenails in his underwear and no shirt. He shows no indication of embarrassment or vulnerability when I approach. I notice the scars on his body and conjure up possible atrocities that were inflicted upon him. I wonder if they are from Mrs. Trần's beatings or from the war.

"From the war." Minh-Hoàng reads my thoughts. "You are here to say goodbye."

"Yes, and to also present you with something." I open my bag and take out some codeine tablets. I hand them to Minh-Hoàng. His brows furrow. I cannot decipher whether he is angry or worried. "Codeine to treat pain."

"I know what it is." He looks angry now. I am nervous he will take away my papers, have me arrested, and hold me hostage here.

"You look like you are always in pain and by the looks of your scars, I am betting you still have residual pain. These can help."

"My pain is not physical, and if my face displeases you, do not worry. You will not have to see me again after today."

"That is not what I mean." I wonder why he is cranky today. "I want to do a kindness for you since you have done so much for me."

His face softens. "Where did you get these?"

"I cannot tell you. Are you going to have me arrested?" I am scared of what he might say.

Minh-Hoàng stands up and walks over to his grandparents' alter. He takes out a canister from beneath the altar table. I recognize the copper coffee tin. He opens the can and takes out the phoenix necklace. "My mother told me you gave this to her right before your first attempt to leave with your husband. She said it was the greatest gift she ever received because it came with such sacrifice and was given to her so selflessly." Minh-Hoàng stares at me. I avoid his glare, partly because he is in his underwear. "This is why my mother loved you and why she made me promise to always take care of you. I am paying her debt to you." He hands me the necklace that Tý's parents gave me on my wedding day. It makes me happy to be reunited with it. "I am not going to arrest you, but I owe you nothing more."

I take the necklace and hide it in my scarf, then tie the scarf around my waist like a sash. I leave Minh-Hoàng the same way I found him, sitting by the table cutting his nails.

***

Thủy-Tiên and I board the first bus departing from Hồ Chí Minh City to Vĩnh Bình early this morning. In my bag is the loot Cường gave me, hiding underneath Minh-Hoàng's dried goods that were given to me last night after the eel dinner. I take a seat twelve rows behind the driver, anticipating if a guard boards the bus, I will have time to dispose of the bag. By sitting on the same side as the driver, I will not get singled out first, since inspectors tend to scan from left to right.

I observe out the window as others board the bus. It is going to be a long ride and a full one at that. With stops at security checkpoints and bathroom breaks, I estimate it will take eight hours to get to Vĩnh Bình, by around 3 p.m. The stink of the dried squid, shrimp, and other preserves, combined with the stench of people who have not bathed in days, compel me to sit with the window open. An elderly woman and her husband sit down behind me. The man takes off his shoes and gets comfortable.

"Put your shoes back on or else I will vomit," warns his wife.

"No," the husband simply responds.

I collect Thủy-Tiên and my bag and sit a few more rows back. The bus pulls away from the station nearly thirty minutes late, but at last, we are on the road. Along the way, we pick up more passengers and drop off some. Thủy-Tiên plays with her airplane like a good girl and lets me rest my eyes for a few minutes at a time. We drive through the first inspection point without any incident, and again, no trouble at the second station. At every hour, we are given a twenty-minute bathroom break. Thủy-Tiên and I take the opportunity to snack on some French bread or our left-over congee. Outside, the hills and the roads blend into each other. The red-orange mud and dirt in the countryside near the coast make me yearn for the sandy river beaches in Cần Thơ. Sprinkled along the journey on the side of the roads are carts selling bread, beverages, fruits, or cheap toys. Every once in a while, the bus slows down to let a herd of water buffalos or cows pass. The roads are bumpy but the ride is fairly comfortable. Surprisingly, we make it all the way to Vĩnh Bình without any trouble.

It is almost 4 p.m. when I step off the bus. I walk through the market and make a detour before heading home. I have unfinished business to resolve first.

***

I step into the familiar tailor shop with the same lime-green curtain covering the doorway to the back room. The same samples of fabric hang from the ceiling, in colors of red, gold, blue and green. The two mannequins, however, are not wearing the same festive wedding attire. Instead, they are wearing identical yellow silk pants and the traditional red áo dài, with a yellow star in the center – the flag of the new Việt Nam.

"Can I help you?" A woman's voice calls out.

I see the same woman who gave me the brown garb with green paisley patterns. She is shocked to see me. From behind the green curtains, her husband steps out.

Now it is me who is shocked. "Doctor Minh." My taxi peddler is alive and well.

"Please let me explain," he says. "Come. Let us speak in the back room." I follow him and his wife behind the curtains. Behind their shop is where they live and where Thủy-Tiên and I had changed into our peasant clothes. There is a small kitchenette, a card table and four chairs, a tiny television, and not much more. Dr. Minh pulls a chair out and sits at the card table. "Allow me to first properly introduce ourselves. This is Thủy, my wife. And my name is not Phạm Văn Minh. I was a practicing doctor, that much was true, but my real name is Nguyễn Văn Đức. We are happy to see you are safe as well."

I glance at his wife, who winks at me. How strange. She smiles and I smile back. "Đức, your name suits you. You are a morally good man." I compliment the doctor. "And Thủy, you are a skilled seamstress. The clothes you provided fit perfectly. I would love to learn how to sew from you one day."

"Of course." Thủy winks. "Can I hold your daughter? She is so

108

cute.”

"She is a frail and sick child as you can see.” I put Thủy-Tiên down off my lap and she immediately walks over to Thủy. "She usually does not like to be held by anyone.”

Thủy is delighted and giggles. "She likes me.” Another wink from her left eye. Funny how I did not notice that the first time we met.

"We never had children,” says Đức, "but we adore them. They are little adults in training and are a direct reflection of us. They are a product of how we treat them, educate them and love them. It is a shame we never had children to help with the business.”

"Yes, but it is also a blessing that you do not have extra hungry mouths to feed,” I say. "Đức, tell me what happened after you left the village.”

"I did not make it to the river. Instead, I changed my mind and ran back to see Thủy,” he says. "Together, we went into the market and while she created a diversion, I stole three fish and ran back to the village, as fast as I could, hoping I would not be too late. So you see, I am not that virtuous, as my name implies. I robbed someone of their fish and their family went hungry that night.”

"We could never leave a young mother and her child in the clutches of the communists!” Thủy exclaims. "My husband did pay the debt and left some money anonymously for the family that we stole from.”

"I came back to the burned village, but it was too late. You were with a different officer, in the burial grounds, and he was taking you somewhere in his jeep,” Đức says. "The other three officers let me go and had one of the village girls cook up the fish.”

I notice Thủy handing Thủy-Tiên a pair of chopsticks and a pan to bang on. Her left eye twitches again. She is sitting on the floor now with my daughter, playing drums and clapping. She would have made a great mother.

"Since you did not return in an hour, I did not know if you deserted us, if you left on the boat, if you got caught or stepped on a mine… I was hoping in the end that you returned to your wife. I ended up leaving with that officer to return to Sài Gòn.”

"He did not hurt you, did he?” Thủy asks. The poor woman. Her left eye keeps twitching.

"No. I actually knew his mother. He mentioned his mother was not well and I asked him to take me to her.”

"That was honorable but also dangerous,” says Đức. "He is a

communist."

"Yes, but a communist I trust, as much as anyone can trust one, and we both have an understanding. It is good to have your enemy close."

"Yes any leverage is a good one to hang on to," agrees Đức.

"I came back here to explain what happened, in case your husband did not make it back to you." I touch Thủy's arm. "He acted brave and nobly."

Thủy's eyes light up. She places her hand gently on top of her husband's. It is obvious they love each other and contrary to cultural norms, they show affection freely.

"I have to ask, Thủy, what is causing your eye to twitch like that?"

Minh answers before Thủy can respond. "It is tetany. It is due to alkalosis, where her alkaline level is at 7.45 and her body cannot absorb calcium, so the facial nerve on her left is doing cartwheels from the mineral deficiency." I nod my head but do not understand a word he says. Sensing this, Đức rephrases. "Basically, her blood ph level is too high. Stress is the cause of her tetany. It is not permanent and can be remedied."

"I am relieved to hear that," I say. Husband and wife look at each other and smile as if they have a hidden secret they are not sharing. "Since you are a doctor, I have a question for you. Can a person overdose on malaria pills and die from it?"

"It depends on the type of antimalarial drugs one takes," answers Đức. "Do you know what kind?"

"Chloroquine," I answer.

Đức's eyes open wide. He leans back in his chair, stretches out his legs, and folds his arms across his chest. "Chloroquine is a synthetic quinoline derivative and extremely toxic if overdosed. It can cause blindness, heart failure, coma, and death."

"The woman I visited in Sài Gòn was that communist officer's mother and I believe she overdosed on it."

"Intentionally or accidentally?" asks Thủy.

"I believe she committed suicide to end her suffering." I shift my posture and pivot closer to Đức. "Have you heard of the drug *Dexedrine?*"

"Yes," he answers confidently, "it is a stimulant and it helps you stay awake. Do you have any?"

I rummage through my bag and dig to the bottom, underneath the dried foods and medical supply bags. I pull out a small envelope. "There are six tablets in there."

The doctor examines the pills. "These are amphetamines. The U.S. military used them to stay awake for long missions or extended combat operations. The Americans gave these to our soldiers fighting in the south too. I have treated men with extremely high levels of *Dexedrine* in their system. My patients always described the feelings of euphoria and invincibility, and having endless energy."

"That sounds amazing. Is it dangerous? Addicting?" I ask.

"No. Whereas we smoke cigarettes to calm down and relax, these pills help us stay awake and have energy," Đức replies.

I have trouble believing that it is not addicting but I trust him.

"How much are you selling them for?" asks Thủy. "We want to buy them."

"All six tablets?" I ask in disbelief.

"All of them," confirms Đức.

"I will sell them to you at a discount. Sixty for all of them."

Thủy lifts up her tunic and pulls out sixty-thousand đồng from her money belt. She hands the money to me. "What else do you have?"

"I want to build my practice again," says Đức. "We have been helping families leave the country and organizing escape routes. We have a cousin who made it to Australia and he wrote to us about his experience. The money from our operation is good but risky, and I want to help again through medicine."

"Do you mind me asking how much you charge for helping people escape?" I ask.

Thủy's left eye twitches a couple of times. They hesitate to disclose the amount.

"It depends on what the family can afford," Thủy finally answers.

"How much did my brother-in-law pay you for my arrangements?"

Again, they both are quiet. I wait patiently for one of them to answer. Finally, Thủy breaks. "Fifty million đồng for you both."

I am speechless but recover quickly from the shock. "I want to propose we go into business together. I can help supply you with more medicine and supplies as you build up your practice again if you can help me get out of this country. It will take me some time to save enough money, but my daughter is sick and I have to get out of here."

"What is wrong with her?" Thủy asks.

"I think she has a hole in her heart or a heart murmur."

"I am not a cardiologist," Đức says, "but I can listen to her heart as soon as I get my hands on a stethoscope. You have yourself a deal."

We spend the next ten minutes finalizing the sale of five first aid kits, all forty-eight codeine tablets, and one *Zippo* lighter. As I stand up to leave, something dawns on me. "Đức, you have not coughed once since I arrived here. You must be feeling better."

"My friend," he replies with a smile, "that was all an act, like your limp was an act, and like Thủy's eye twitching is an act."

She gives me an exaggerated wink and laughs. "We pretend to be people we are not so that when the communists interrogate others, they will come intending to arrest someone who does not exist."

"Also," adds Đức, "the ones who are weak or crippled usually receive mercy or leniency, and we find people are more willing to help us when we are not fully able-bodied."

Thủy takes my hand into hers and leans forward. "Not to mention, people ignore you if you withdraw to the background and make yourself look ugly and poor. If you look poor, the communists will not seize your property, your food, your animals, or your business. They will skip past to the next place. Only to those we trust do we show our true self."

16 HOME AGAIN (NOVEMBER 1976)

On the walk home to my father's house from the market, I give a lot of appreciation to what my new friends Thủy and Đức said. It is a wonder that people are not who they appear to be anymore and everyone has secrets they hold deep in their hearts. I yearn for the days of my childhood and my university days. I was young and happy living in my little bubble. People were always nice to me. Neighbors did not spy on one another. We could leave the doors unlocked and never fear of being robbed. We had visitors all the time and we shared food with one another. I had many friends. I remember walking to school with them, as well as with Sister Six and Brother Seven, and their friends. We all would run home together for lunch and a nap, then return to school for another few hours. After school, we would go swimming or fishing or cheer for Brother Seven when he fought his crickets. Then we would go home to help around the house before studying and doing homework. I had two best friends, both of them named Hồng. To distinguish them apart, I called one of them Baby Hồng, because she complained about everything, and the other one Fat Hồng, because she had a sweet tooth and was always eating. Now, not only have I lost most of my friends but also my country. I am reminded that I have no husband, no home of my own, no scooter, and no respectable job. I have lost the freedom to go as I please from the city to the countryside unless I have permission or a license, and when I get home, I may not even have my family.

My heart aches for Sam and I long to hear his voice. It has been a lifetime ago since I felt alive, in love, and happy. My only happiness now is through Thủy-Tiên, and if I were to lose my daughter too, I would not be able to live another day. I stroll through the familiar streets of my hometown, in no hurry to get home and realize how much the landscape has changed. I round the corner and see a scuffle between a boy, around sixteen years old, and a couple of police officers. There is shouting between the two officers and the young boy, who resists arrest and tries to run away. His mother is on the ground crying, begging for mercy and apologizing for her son's stupidity. The father tries to pull his son into the house, yelling that they cannot take his son. One of the police officers hits the father and kicks him while the other officer runs after the boy. I hold onto Thủy-Tiên a little tighter and walk slowly.

There are a few spectators, cognizant to keep their distance and not get involved. Others run into their homes, while some check the scene from their window. I ask a bystander nearby, "Do you know what is happening?"

"The boy was caught handing out anti-communist leaflets and ridiculing Hồ Chí Minh," he responds. "The police are probably going to send him to jail for six months, maybe more."

I continue walking slowly and head down a different alley. It takes me another twenty minutes to get to my father's house. I stand at the beginning of the long walkway and remember the last time I stood here; I was waiting for my taxi peddler, for Đức. I take a deep breath and walk toward the door, afraid of what calamity awaits.

***

The smell of burnt rice assaults my nose and I run to the kitchen. To my dismay, rice is scattered all over the floor. A small pot lies on its side on the ground. I notice the house is stripped of adornments. Furniture is missing. It is disturbingly bare.

I take notice of Dirty Butt's loud, frantic clucking and am appalled with the scene before me. My family is chasing after my chicken. Everyone is yelling for my father to catch her. I see a meat cleaver in his right hand and rush out to the backyard. Poor Thủy-Tiên bobs up and down on my hip while I run outside.

"Stop!" I scream. "Do not touch Mông Dơ!"

My family freezes. Bewildered eyes reflect my own disbelief.

Sister Six is the first to speak. "What are you doing here?"

"You should have not come back!" My father lunges forward.

"Aiyah, grab the chicken!" Hiền snatches the meat cleaver from my father. "She is getting away."

"You are not going to kill my Mông Dơ." I chase after Hiền. "She is family."

114

"Daughter, she is a chicken." My father blocks me from catching Hiền. "Why did you have to go and give her a name? We are starving here!"

"Father, I have money. I will buy Mông Dơ from you. No one is to touch her."

"Look around you," my father beckons. "What do you see?"

I pause and survey our backyard. The bunker has not changed. The pond and the outhouse appear the same. I scan up at the fruit trees and notice not one tree has any fruit. It dawns on me that our pigs are also gone. Every face staring at me is sad and desperate. Father's expression makes him look haggard, old and defeated. Even Sister Six's determined spirit has left, leaving behind a hollow woman.

"What happened here?" I am afraid of the answer.

"The Việt Cộng came through a couple of days ago," says Hải. "They took everything -our rice, our pigs, even our potatoes and herbs. They made Tree climb up and get all the fruits." Hải points to the barren trees. I am in shock that there is not one coconut or banana left.

"And somehow Mông Dơ managed to escape their clutches?" I ask in disbelief.

"They tried," Tree says, "but she is a clever one. They tried to shoot her when they could not catch her. She must have superpowers. They finally left and said they would leave her for all ten of us to fight over…well, nine of us."

Everyone's head bends down, their crestfallen faces say it all. I take a quick survey and realize who is missing. "Tâm! Where is she?"

Sister Six bursts into tears. Her husband holds her tight and little Trinh clings to her parents. She cries too seeing her mother cry.

"They took her," was all Brother Seven could manage to say.

I put Thủy-Tiên down and cover my mouth in horror. The floodgates open and all the tears of past rainy seasons unleash with madness. I cover my eyes and fall onto my knees. Not my niece, my sweet niece, my Tâm…my heart. Her face and her smile flash before me in my mind. I can see us walking arm in arm to the market as we had done so many mornings in the past. I can see us laughing, drinking our coffees, and trying to outwit each other with our clever jokes and innuendos. I clutch my heart. I fear deep in the core of my being that I will never see my beautiful niece again, and even if by some divine miracle we do see each other again, she will not be the same innocent and good-humored young woman I know.

"You must have had a long journey today," says Hải. "Get some rest and we will talk later this evening. We can all catch up."

I surrender to Hải's arms as he lifts me to my feet. Hiền leads me back to the house through the kitchen while Tree takes Thủy-Tiên by the hand and walks with her.

I shout over my shoulder, "Do not touch my chicken." I let sleep sweep over my fatigued body and carry me into the dark recess of my mind.

***

Sister Six and Brother Seven are arguing. I rise from the bed and walk into the kitchen. I must have slept a long time. It is dark outside and the crickets are singing.

"We have to find her." Sister Six pounds her fist on the kitchen table.

"You have to let her go," urges Brother Seven.

"How can you say that? What if it was one of your sons? Would you give up so easily?"

My poor family, all huddled together in the kitchen. My father and Hải lean against the kitchen counter, while Brother Seven stands over his wife, who is sitting on the floor, cross-legged with their son, Tuấn. Sister Six, her husband, and their daughter, Trinh, sit at the table.

Tree is holding Thủy-Tiên on his lap and is the first to notice me. "You are awake."

Seeing Sister Six's eyes swollen from crying and her nose red and dry, makes me want to hug her. "Sister, I agree with you. We cannot give up. We have to find Tâm." I try to give her hope but am unconvinced myself. She could already be dead by now. "Tell me what happened."

My brother-in-law kick starts the story. "Two days ago they came into town, asking every family questions about what our trade is, how much money we have to declare, who lives in this house. They went through the house, took everything of value, which was not much since we sold everything of value."

"They acted sweet but we suspected what they were up to," says Hải. "They asked us about our political views and whom we prayed to. Of course, we parroted what we read in their newspapers and that pleased them."

"They questioned Tâm about her profession," Hiền chimes in, "and she made the mistake of saying she worked as a maid in one of the U.S. Air Force barracks. Aiyah, stupid girl."

Sister Six shoots a scathing glare at Hiền. "They did not like that answer and accused her of betraying the government."

Hải squeezes Sister Six's forearm. "Those Việt Cộngs accused her of not supporting the Party and arrested her."

"We were all scared and did not dare to fight them," says Tree.

Sister Six busts into tears. I cannot help my tears of sorrow either, tears of longing for my niece. I rush to her side.

"What are you doing back here, Tuyết?" asks Hải. "I told the family about our clandestine plan to get you and Thủy-Tiên out of the country. Why are you back?"

I sigh and tell them all about the taxi peddler and his wife, and how Doctor Pham Văn Minh was actually Doctor Nguyễn Văn Đức, incognito. I told them of the burning village and the assault that took place there, to which Hải was concerned about my treatment. I told them about Mrs. Trần's suicide and got a little emotional. As much of a thorn as she was in my life, she was also a mother figure, and a wood tiger that I came to understand and respect. When I got to the part about Cường and Minh-Hoàng helping me, voices erupted with disapproval and concern.

"Aiyah, sister, you cannot trust either of them," warns Hiền.

"That is too dangerous," says my father.

"You were so stupid," adds Brother Seven.

Only Sister Six defends me. "You always had beauty and now, it is good to see your brain finally catching up." Even in her pain, our grieving matriarch is strong and defiant, swimming against the current. "This is a good thing for all of us. She has a communist in the palm of her hands, not to mention a mob boss' puppet working alongside her. Can you all not see? Cường is motivated by money and greed and has her taking all the risks to sell Western medicine for him. Without her, he would have to face his boss. And Minh-Hoàng? Well, he is either in love with her or is using her as a pawn in some crazy scheme of his. Either way, Eight, you have to continue playing their game, and never let them know you are anything other than a pretty and naïve woman who was betrayed by her husband and must care for a sick child. Men like to rescue women and be in control."

"You are playing a dangerous game," says Hải.

I defend myself. "I am not playing a twisted game. I am in this for survival and freedom."

"You are going to bring suffering to us all," says Hiền. "They will find out and will come for you. They will burn our house or seize the property. They are already starving us out and controlling everyone. Aiyah, you should not have come back and endangered us all."

"Quiet, Wife," orders my brother. "How can you say that?"

"Brother, she is afraid, and I understand, but this is what they want. They want to divide families, make us spy on each other and our neighbors, and rival one another. They pretend to be nice and helpful, and yet, they restrict us to our hamlets, make our currency obsolete, take away our food, burn our villages, and steal our livelihood. We are not liberated as one country under one flag. We are the conquered people in a land that is no longer ours."

"How can we live like this much longer?" My father's stomach rumbles.

"When was the last time you ate, Father?" I ask.

"Two days ago." Father rubs his belly. "I am tempted to catch the catfish we have in the pond and cook those up to eat."

"You cannot!" I exclaim, mortified. "Those fish catch the feces from our outhouse."

"I am an old, hungry man. I am not too proud to do that to feed my children and grandchildren. Or maybe we sell the catfish and buy some food?"

I remember the dried foods I have in my bag that Minh-Hoàng gave me. Surely I can spare some to feed my family? "Father, you have your retirement money from your days of teaching, plus the monthly government subsidy, yes?"

"Yes, but they took everything. We have to start over. Besides, if I spend it freely, the communists will say we have plenty and restrict us further, but if we do not spend it for fear of suspicion, then we starve."

"We cannot win," says Hải, "but maybe if we spend it on things we can plant and grow or raise, we can avoid scrutiny."

"Yes, we have to try," I say, "and Brother Seven, you still have your truck driving and monthly subsidy, right? Sister Six, you have your family subsidy, too?" They both nod. "We will be conservative and discreet on how we spend and rotate who goes to the market each day to buy or sell on the free market. No one will be targeted or reported. Until we get paid, I have the money I received from selling to the good doctor and his wife."

"I have my subsidy too," says Hải.

"And I now have my own as well." I notice Hải shifts his weight and runs his fingers through his hair, feeling uneasy.

"Like it or not, at least Minh-Hoàng got Eight her monthly allowance and safe passage from Sài Gòn to home," reminds Sister Six.

"Tomorrow, we will start again. For now, we eat." I take out the bags of dried food Minh-Hoàng gave me and toss them on the kitchen table.

All eyes light up seeing the edible pile of gold and new hope is restored in their faces. I will have to buy more or have Sister Six preserve some to replenish the supply. We tear open the dried shrimp and cuttlefish, pop open the jar of pickled mangos, and divide the candied plums, tamarind, and ginger amongst us. All of us dig in. I am happy to be home again with my family, but tonight when I go to sleep, thoughts of my niece will disrupt my slumber. I will pray for her.

***

I cannot sleep. Tâm's face haunts me. To settle my restlessness, I stroll outside to get some air. I now have doubts about leaving Việt Nam. I am in the twilight of my life. Staying here means a decline in quality of life, but how can I leave my family, when they are in so much pain and distress? Losing Tâm changes everything.

"This is my favorite time of day when the light from the sky glows softly and the sun is about to rise. It is peaceful." Sister Six catches up with me.

"Sister—"

She cuts me off like she usually does. "After Brother Two and all our other siblings died, it was my burden to take care of you, of Seven, and our parents. After I got married and had children, I never had any time for myself. The only peace I found was at dawn."

"You have sacrificed so much," I say, "and I admire how strong you are, how independent and self-sufficient you are."

"A part of me has always been jealous of you," my sister confesses. Alarmed, I ask her why. "You are the youngest and therefore the most loved, most cherished, and definitely, the most spoiled. You can do no wrong. I never got the love and attention that you got as a little girl. Mother and Father showed me no leniency. I always had to make sacrifices, taking the smallest portion of food or the burnt food, accepting the imperfect clothes that

Mother made, being dutiful around the house…I have lived a rigid life and as a result, have cast my shadow onto my children. They are timid rule followers, all because I did not teach them to live freely."

"You were always tough on me, but I always felt your love, and after Mother died, and Father was a wreck, it was you who kept the household together. You are the woman I want to emulate."

My sister stops and squeezes my hand. "Do not underestimate your own inner strength and your resolve to find a better life. I am glad you are not rigid like me. You are adaptable and this skill will serve you well when you leave this communist hell we are in."

A rooster crows and a few dogs bark in the distance. Morning crests above the jagged rooftops. I wrap my arm around Sister Six's shoulder. "You are a good wife and a wonderful mother. And, lucky for you, my favorite sister."

She slaps my butt cheeks. "I am your only sister."

The village comes to life. Neighbors switch on their lights, open their windows, or start up their scooters. Somewhere nearby, a man is choking on his own spit as he clears his throat.

"I do not want to see our family go hungry." I pull my sister's arm and head back to the house. "I will plan on going back and forth between Sài Gòn and Vĩnh Bình for as long as it takes, to sell medicine and save money until our family has enough to sustain a comfortable life. Brother Seven wants me to take Tree to America with me, so I need to save enough money for all three of us to go."

"This is going to take you years, not months."

"Hải paid fifty million đồng for us, so I imagine it will take another twenty-five million to pay for Tree, plus have some money for emergency use. There is still a matter of finding a boat and a captain."

"This is too dangerous. What if you get arrested? I lost Tâm. I cannot lose you too."

I hold my sister's hand in mine, giving it a reassuring squeeze. "A moment ago you told me not to underestimate my inner strength and that I had the determination to get out of this communist hell."

"I know," she says. "Make sure you do it right this time. You keep leaving and then coming back like the ocean waves. Each time you do this, you strip more sand from me."

"Sister, you have more grit than anyone. A tsunami can come and try to strip away all of Việt Nam, but it will find itself absorbed by you."

My sister scowls at me. Dirty Butt warbles by and roosts in the grass on the side of the house. I notice her hackle feathers are wet. *What mischief have you gotten yourself into?*

17 SURRENDER TO SORROW (DECEMBER 1977)

Today is Christmas Eve, 1977. I wake up to the sound of my nephew screaming and my sister-in-law swearing. "Aiyah, what the fuck is wrong with our son?"

"We need to get Tuấn to a doctor," demands my brother. "Tree, go wake up Aunt Eight."

"I am awake." I walk over to my little nephew. "Doctor Nguyễn Văn Đức can help."

"My brother complains about stomach pains and has diarrhea," says Tree.

"He is going to throw up." I curl my fingers to catch the vomit.

My little nephew scratches his legs and buttocks and cries.

"We can all go," says Brother Seven, "since I do not have to work today or tomorrow."

On our walk to Đức's and Thủy's house, we make a quick stop at the market to buy some guavas and a papaya. We arrive at the tailor shop and leave our shoes at the stoop.

Tree gets excited. "Aunt Eight, this is the fabric store where I sold the morphine two years ago!"

"Are you sure?" I ask. He nods.

"Aiyah, this is a nice shop. I wish I could sew as skillfully as the seamstress here!" Sister Seven kicks off her shoes and rushes to the mannequins. She is distracted by their clothes and the fabrics hanging from the ceiling. She walks over to the fabric samples folded neatly on the shelves along the walls and runs her fingers over them.

"Thank you for the compliment." Thủy steps out from behind the green curtains. "Sister Tuyết, what brings you to the shop? An áo dài?"

"Aunt Eight, that is the woman I sold the morphine to!"

exclaims Tree.

"I recognize you." Thủy rests her hand on Tree's shoulder.

"You purchased morphine from me a long time ago," says Tree.

"Yes, I remember!" exclaims Thủy. "Unbelievable!"

"Hello, Sister Thủy," I say. "It is good to see you. What a strange twist of fate!"

"Indeed!" she responds.

"My family and I are here to see your husband. Is Đức available?"

"Yes, he will be here soon," Thủy says. "He is out pedaling his cycle around town, selling bananas."

I nod and make the introductions. "This is my sister-in-law, Hiền, and my brother, Seven, and their two sons, Tree and Tuấn."

Hiền quickly drowns Thủy with compliments. "Aiyah, Sister Thủy, you have such beautiful attention to detail. The patterns align so perfectly; the dress drapes flawlessly on these mannequins. And the seams are so even around the bust area. And the thread! Aiyah, the thread that you used for these are the perfect color and thickness!"

Thủy laughs at Hiền's enthusiasm. "You have an eye for sewing. You must be a great seamstress as well."

"I sew, yes, but not like you," Hiền says. "I am too frugal to buy quality thread and do not have the creative patience. You, however, aiyah, can fashion a runway in Paris!"

"My wife is the best designer." Đức parks his cyclo and joins us in the shop. Husband and wife smile at each other adoringly. It makes the rest of us embarrassed to see such open affection and love. I introduce Đức to my family and explain the purpose of our visit. We follow him into the back room, to the small kitchen.

"Tuấn, how old are you?" asks Doctor Đức.

"Yes, Doctor, I am eight years old," responds my nephew respectfully.

"And tell me, what have you been experiencing?"

"Sometimes I feel dizzy and want to throw up, but I cannot."

"Anything else?" asks Doctor Đức.

"Yes, Doctor, my butt itches all the time," Tuấn answers.

Tree adds, "And he complains about his stomach hurting."

"Hmm." Đức waves my brother to follow him. "With your permission, I will examine him in the back room."

Brother Seven disappears with Đức and Tuấn behind a door.

Hiền and Thủy patty-cake back and forth over áo dài designs, fashion styles, fabric textures and types of thread. I listen patiently, yearning to understand exactly what are silk threads, metallic threads, cotton threads, and wool threads, and how they differ from nylon or rayon threads, bobbin threads and designer threads mixed with different types of other threads. My head is spinning and I find it humorous the two women can banter so animatedly about fibers. Poor Tree. He is sitting next to me as stone-faced as I am.

Finally, the back door opens and Đức, Brother Seven, and Tuấn walk out.

"Aiyah, what is it? You all look like you have seen a ghost." Hiền clutches her chest.

Brother Seven's face is stark. "Our son has pinworms living inside his rectum. He may also have tapeworms."

Hiền spits out a distressed aiyah.

Đức gets right to the point. "Either the boy ate something that was contaminated and not fully cooked, or he came in contact with feces that had eggs or larvae in it. Luckily there is no infection around the anus."

"What can we do, Doctor?" asks Hiền.

"You can start by making sure your son washes his hands well with soap and water after every bowel movement, and you should keep his fingernails trimmed. Eggs can get under his nails and spread to anything he touches."

"Are there any medicine or remedies to treat the worms?" I ask.

"There are anti-parasite medicines he can take, but unfortunately, we have none. Any of you can be infected as well and not show any symptoms."

"My poor son! Aiyah, if we have no medicine, then what do we do?" asks Hiền.

"Go home and clean the whole house and wash his bed linens. Clean all his toys and pretty much anything he regularly comes in contact with. Pinworms can survive for three days without a host. Keep an eye on him and bring him back if he has any big changes in his eating habits, if his vision changes, if you find any lumps on his skin, or if he has seizures. Those are signs of eggs entering his bloodstream and hatching in his tissues."

"Tapeworms usually leave your body on their own," says Tree.

"They can, but the eggs can remain. Always wash your hands after going to the bathroom or handling food. Cook everything well, keep clothes and linens clean and take baths regularly. Garlic and coconut oil is helpful for treating this, so use the coconut oil as a topical remedy around the affected area. You can crush the garlic with the oil and apply it together. I recommend he eats minced garlic or drinks it with some tea or water as well, to remove the yeast and kill the parasite. You may want to try eating a lot of carrots, papaya seeds, and cloves, too. It can help flush the worms out."

We all thank Đức and Thủy for their time. As payment, Tree presents them with the guavas and papayas we purchased at the market. I give Đức some money as well.

We spend Christmas Eve and Christmas Day cleaning the house from top to bottom. No one dares to speak of the worms and I suspect we all are a little worried we might be infected too.

18 A FORGOTTEN RAG DOLL (FEBRUARY 1978)

The Lunar New Year is here. Today is February 2, 1978. It is the lucky year of the horse. To welcome good fortune and health for this zodiac sign, families and businesses in our village decorate their establishments in colors of yellow and green. Those who can afford to, have fresh jasmine or calla lily flowers on the altars. The sweet aroma of these flowers can be intoxicating and when I get a whiff of one of these, it brings me so much joy and fond memories of happier times. I remember when I was a little girl; I would get new clothes and receive red envelopes with money in them from my elders. We would eat, pay tribute to our ancestors, set off firecrackers, enjoy the dragon dances, and play games. Our family celebrated for three days. There was to be no arguing and no cleaning, otherwise, bad luck could enter our home and stay for the whole year. My favorite game to play as a child was "Bầu Cua Tôm Cá", which means "Gourd Crab Shrimp Fish". It is a traditional Vietnamese gambling game using three dice. Each side of the dice shows a picture of a gourd, crab, shrimp, fish, rooster or deer. The game board has six squares; each square has a picture of one of the animals. Growing up, my siblings and I would use our new year's money to place bets. We put our money on the animals of choice and held our breath as the three dice were rolled. If the animal we bet on appeared, we got paid up to three times our bet. Sister Six usually lost and Mother usually won.

There will be no celebrations this lunar year. I have spent the last year going back and forth between Sài Gòn and Vĩnh Bình, sometimes via bus, sometimes hitching a ride with Brother Seven, to sell whatever Cường gives me – alcohol, cigarettes, writing paper, typewriters. Most recently, it is opium and marijuana. My license for selling dried goods expired a few months ago and Minh-Hoàng helped me renew it. My family has been able to stay out of trouble with the communist government and we have been lucky to keep our house. Still, no news of my niece Tâm and we still speculate each day what happened to her. Minh-Hoàng tried to help but he hit a dead end trying to find her. My fear is that she is dead. I lay awake at night imagining horrible things that may have happened to her. Was she raped? Was she beaten to death? Is she in some prison, being tortured and starved? Is she someone's sex slave? Was she forced to clear minefields and got herself blown to pieces of decomposing flesh?

In the mornings, the first thing I do when I wake is check on Thủy-Tiên. I am always afraid I will find her not breathing. She continues to get weaker with every passing year. Her breathing gets more labored. She will be four years old this July, but has not gained much weight and has barely grown since the year before. Sometimes her complexion is pale and other times, blue, especially around her lips. In the past six months, she has had a lot of fevers and does not have much interest in eating. Today, her belly is a little swollen and she is unusually tired. I take her to see Doctor Đức.

Đức takes out his stethoscope and listens to Thủy-Tiên's heart. He has her take deep breaths as he checks her chest and back. "No change since the last time you brought her to me. I still hear some fluttering when I listen to her heart." I stare intently at his face, trying to read his expressions. "With her existing heart murmur, I would say there is a problem with a heart valve or she may have a hole between the two chambers that is pumping blood in and out of her heart."

I cannot help it. The tears escape and slide down my face. "Is she going to die?"

"If she has a serious congenital murmur or an infection in the heart, and does not get surgery, she may not live past her fifth birthday. Without being able to see her heart, I am not certain what we are dealing with, but then again, I am not a cardiologist."

"I have been praying every night for her to get better," I say. "It is a miracle she is still alive."

"She is a fighter, like her mother. How are you holding up?" Đức's question was an invitation to release all my stress.

My mouth erupts and an avalanche of anxiety spills out onto his empathetic ears. "I am so lost. Every day I put my life and my family's life at risk selling illegal items on the free market, and I am only halfway where I need to be in order to leave this country; this motherland that was once our home is now a prison! My daughter is dying. My family is starving. Oh God! I would rather die than live in this communist wasteland! Everything is so expensive and the government controls it all! We cannot buy anything without a ticket. People cannot even go eat at a restaurant without a ticket. It makes no sense! My family has been planting vegetables, but it has been difficult feeding eleven mouths. The soil does not have any time to rest between harvests and our crops have been meager this past year! After my nephew recovered from the worms and expelled everything from his body, my father became ill. We tried everything for him, from drinking Chinese herbs to cupping therapy and skin coining, inhaling vapors or rubbing ointment all over his aching body, but still, he has headaches and colds that last longer and occur more frequently! We still do not know what happened to my niece and my poor sister floats through the house like a ghost. I would give anything for her to snap back to her usual self and say something condescending to me, but it is like she has gone mute. There is no life in her eyes! What if she commits suicide like Mrs. Trần?”

I sob uncontrollably. I try to talk some more and tell Đức how it is unfair that I do not have Sam, how I hate my husband for his deception, and how I am living in sin with Hải. Thankfully, I am not making any sense to him. The more I try to compose myself, the more I trip over my words. Each time I gasp for air, I skip around in my thoughts and I speak in broken sentences. I try to tell Đức that I am approaching thirty-nine years old and am too young to be having a meltdown or some mid-life crisis, but here I am, beaten and ready to die to make it all go away.

“Not yet,” Đức says. “It is not your time to die. You, a Catholic, should know that suicide is not an option. Life can be cruel, but you have to accept what has happened. There are many aspects of your life that you still control.”

I surrender to sorrow and weep. Fatigue sweeps over me and I sit in Đức’s kitchen, slumped over like a forgotten rag doll, in my patchwork clothing made of spare scraps of cloth, my unruly hair, my stained face, and floppy body.

“I want to give Thủy-Tiên the life that I dreamt of for myself but did not get.”

“It is good to keep things in perspective and remind yourself what you are fighting for. Everyone has a different fight,” says Đức.

“What is your fight?” I ask.

"It is to help you, and other families like yours, find their purpose."

"You are a good man." I wipe my tears. "How many families have you helped?"

"Too many to count and many more still to come," Đức responds. "I am still working different channels to get a boat and a captain for you when you are ready. As more people leave, it is getting more expensive to bribe the right people. The risks are greater with people leaving, so desperate, they are willing to gamble with their lives out at sea. Last week I helped a family of thirteen. They had been saving for two years to buy a boat. They had a family friend who was going to captain the boat but he backed out the night of their departure, too afraid to escape. So, they took their chances and went anyways. I hope they make it."

"Me too." I hand Đức some money. "Thank you for examining Thủy-Tiên. I need to go home now and check on my sister and my father."

19 FISH AND SNAKE (SEPTEMBER 1978)

I sense Hải's presence behind me as I brush my hair. His arms wrap around my waist so I put the brush down. Neither of us speaks for a while. I see my father step out of the outhouse from behind the banyan tree.

"Is he…?" I ask.

"He sure is!" confirms Hải.

We both run outside. Hải grabs a towel on the way out.

"Father!" I call out to him. "You forgot your underwear."

Father notices his nakedness and places his hands on his butt cheeks. "So, I did!"

Hải wraps the towel around my father's waist. "Come, Uncle, let me help you find something to wear."

The two of them disappear into the house. I walk over to my favorite hammock and lay down, swinging it with my left leg. It makes me sad to see my father's memory deteriorating and his health declining. This man who used to be so vibrant and strong, who used to spank his children when we did something bad, can now hardly take care of himself.

"What is making you frown?" Hải returns with some peanuts to share. My brother accompanies him.

"Father." I crack open the shell and pop a peanut in my mouth. "Most parents beat their children with a belt or bamboo or rattan, but not Father. His favorite weapon was a dried, bull's penis."

Brother Seven chuckles. "That thing was a half meter long and flexible despite how hard it was. You girls were lucky, though. He never used it on you, just the boys."

"True," I acknowledge. "Mother used a wooden spoon."

"Remember that time you slipped a frying pan down your

pants, hoping she would not notice? You thought you were being so clever, kneeling there straight as a pool cue, anticipating the punishment that was to be ramrodded down your backside."

I laugh. "How old was I, do you remember?"

"You were around Tuấn's age, seven or eight," answers Brother Seven.

"So what happened?" asks Hải.

"She was a little bit of a tomboy when she was younger," says Brother Seven, "and she loved tagging along with me and my friends after school. One day, I was going to fight one of my crickets but when I opened the matchbox, he jumped out and escaped. We forfeited and returned home. On the way home, there was a crowd of people yelling and getting all excited about something. She convinced me to take her over to check it out. There was a fish fight going on, so I placed a bet, and she was right beside me, placing a bet herself! It took over three hours for the fish to kill the other."

"We lost track of time and were late getting home to do our chores." I continue Brother Seven's story. "Mother yelled at me for betting and acting unladylike. I lost all of my money from the Lunar New Year on that stupid fish. And because I was not home to do my chores, my punishment was to kneel on my knees and face the corner of the wall for an hour, before accepting my spankings."

"You got off easy that day." Sister Six joins us. She takes a peanut and throws it in the air. Instead of catching it in her mouth, it bounces off her chin and falls to the ground. "Eight convinced me to get her a frying pan from the kitchen and I was shocked when she stuck it down her pants." She goes to retrieve her peanut but Dirty Butt darts from behind a bush and steals it from her.

"So you were going to shield your rear with the frying pan?" Hải roars with laughter. "You did not think your mother would notice?"

"I was seven years old. I was so scared!" I say.

"Of course Mother noticed the pan right away," says Brother Seven. "She could not contain her amusement and laughed so hard. She called every family member into the room to see, and we all laughed and mocked poor little Eight, kneeling there, facing the wall, with a round pan and the handle sticking out of her pants."

"We laughed until we cried and our stomach ached." Sister Six throws another peanut in the air and catches it in her mouth. "My dear sister achieved for the first time something that none of us ever achieved. She did not get a spanking that night."

"No," I add, "but I had to kneel for another half hour and go to bed without dinner."

"I miss those days." Sister Six's eyes mist up.

"Me too," I say. "I would give anything to have Mother here, even if it was to spank me."

"I miss her voice and how she used to sing to us," says Brother Seven.

As if on cue, the three of us sing together Mother's favorite song, "Sài Gòn Đẹp Lắm", meaning "Saigon So Beautiful":

"In the land where the sun does not fade. Far away where the silk dresses flow. People come here to connect and delight. Sài Gòn so beautiful. Oh Sài Gòn! Oh Sài Gòn! Horses and cars like water on streets. People run, they say hello and greet. The city welcomes me to join the fun. Sài Gòn so beautiful. Oh Sài Gòn! Oh Sài Gòn! Lá la la lá la. Lá la la lá la. Laughing with the wind and drinking with joy. Lá la la lá la. Lá la la lá la. Life is beautiful like poetry."

"You should not sing so loud." Tree walks over to us, holding both Tuấn's and Thủy-Tiên's hand. "We might get in trouble."

Sister Seven and Brother Six are right behind them. They finish the song quietly. *"A love that is worth singing about; Let love remember the distant past. May today's brightness never fade in me. Sài Gòn so beautiful. Oh Sài Gòn! Oh Sài Gòn!"*

***

The seasons pass like a child's merry-go-round, spinning faster and faster until events become a blur. I, however, remain constant. Daily routines and familiar things continue to happen and sometimes, it is like déjà vu, but there is always some element that is a little different than the last time. The monsoon season is here again.

Hải breathes softly next to me while outside, the wind shrieks and the rain marches fanatically sideways. A small gecko scurries through a crack in the wall. The world around me is unraveling at the seams. The house is slowly rotting and the trees and vegetation outside are not thriving. Maybe that is my imagination, but the outside walls are collapsing in and my world is getting smaller.

My mind is awake so I get up and go shower in the rain before the first rooster sings. The clay floor leading to the back courtyard cools my feet. I strip off my clothes, down to my underwear, and let the raindrops fervently kiss my face and body, like a lover savoring an approaching climax. I cannot get enough of Mother Nature's tears. I cup the water from the cistern in my hands. The cool water trickles down my throat. I drink more water to appease the hunger, but I might as well be pouring salt into the sea, knowing it is useless, for no amount of water can make me satisfied.

A light illuminates one of the bedrooms a couple houses over. I grab my clothes and go inside to dress. Somewhere there must be a typhoon as the downpour is relentless. I step outside, onto the front steps of the house, and see a small shadow. The dark movement gets closer and I squint to decipher who the intruder is at this hour.

"Tree?" I call out. "Is that you?"

"Yes."

"Where have you been?"

"Fishing." He grins from ear to ear. "When it rains like this the fish wash up onto the fields." He approaches closer and I see in one hand a thick stick and in the other hand, a pillowcase slung over his shoulder.

"How many did you get?" I ask excitedly.

"One for each of us, plus a snake." He triumphantly raises his club in the air.

We spend the day cleaning and gutting the fish. Sister Six prepares the snake and steams two of the fish in soy sauce, ginger and onions for dinner tonight. The rest will be salted and preserved over the next two to three weeks. Because tonight is a special meal, the family waits for Brother Seven to come home from work, so we can all eat together.

One of our neighbors unexpectedly drops in for a visit. "We can smell the ginger and onions from our house." He stands before us, barefoot, bunions on his feet, wearing a brown tunic and faded black trousers that are a little too short for him. He is dark-skinned. His hair is long and unwashed. I notice his hands are calloused and cracked, his fingernails untrimmed and dirty. The memory of my nephew's worm incident flashes across my mind. I remember cleaning his bedsheets and scrubbing his fingers while he cried. It makes me shudder.

My brother-in-law greets him. "Brother Tú, come in." The two men shake hands. "Tree caught us some fish and a snake early this morning out in the fields."

"I see the women are busy preparing a feast for tonight." Tú smiles and I notice he is missing a few teeth. The ones remaining are stained with nicotine.

"Yes, it has been a long time since we have eaten meat," says

Brother Six.

"We are in the same situation, becoming vegetarian by necessity, not by choice," says Tú.

"You must come for dinner this evening, and of course, bring your wife and son," invites Brother Six.

"We would be honored. We have a special bottle of rice wine that I made and can bring over. Maybe we can play cards as well."

The two men shake hands and our neighbor walks home. The second he is no longer in sight, Sister Six scolds her husband. "What are you doing inviting three more mouths to feed?"

Brother Six defends himself. "They are our friends. You used to play cards with his wife every week. It is our obligation to help others when we can. Besides, it will bring good karma back to us."

"God would want us to be kind to our neighbors, but your wife has a point." I rip the innards of the fish out with my bare hands. A small piece of it flies upward and hits Sister Six on the face, narrowly missing her eye. She flinches and I laugh.

"Aiyah, they can go and catch their own fish," says Hiền. "They have a son that is Tree's age. That boy is so lazy, though, not good like my son."

Father wakes up from his nap and joins us women and my brother-in-law in the kitchen. "Where did all these fish come from?" It is the second time he has asked us today.

"Father, Tree caught them early this morning in the fields," I answer.

"Oh, that is my good grandson," he says and heads to the outhouse.

"Aiyah, he is getting so forgetful these days," says Hiền.

We all nod and continue with cooking, cleaning, and preserving the fish.

***

Our neighbors announce themselves at our doorstep before walking in. Tú is more presentable now than he was a few hours ago. I am relieved to see he clipped his fingernails and washed up. His wife, Vân, is pretty, even without makeup. Behind them is their fifteen-year-old son. He is the same age as Tree, but that is where the similarities end. The boy before me has always been immature and disrespectful. His parents come from a line of poor, uneducated families, where school takes a backseat to farming and selling food at the market. This boy is attractive, though, I will admit. It is probably the only redeeming feature I can pick out.

Because he is their only child and the only son, he has been coddled and spoiled all his life. Without any siblings to rival him and no other relatives around to discipline the boy, he is lost.

My brother-in-law welcomes them. "Brother Tú, Sister Vân, please, come in."

My nephews, Tree and Tuấn, and my niece, Trinh, all run out, line up, and greet our neighbors. "Welcome, Uncle Tú. Welcome, Aunt Vân."

Our neighbors pat each one of them on the head. The three of them leave the adults and go back to finish their chores. Tree sweeps the floor, Tuấn sets the table, and little Trinh resumes plucking gray hairs from her grandfather's head.

"Brother Thắng, as promised, I brought the rice wine." Tú hands the bottle to my brother-in-law.

"Your son has grown since a couple of months ago!" Thắng exclaims. "I cannot believe how much he has grown in such a short amount of time!"

"Lộc, say hello to everyone," his mother nudges. I can see she is embarrassed by his rude manner. Lộc bows. "They cannot hear you. Speak up. Be courteous and address everyone. They are so gracious to invite us to dinner tonight, on the eve of the mid-autumn festival."

Lộc bows to each of us. "Hello, Aunt Eight. Hello, Uncle Six. Hello, Aunt Six. Hello, Uncle Seven. Hello, Uncle Hải. Hello, Aunt Seven."

"Good, now go find the elder of the house and pay your respects," Lộc's mother commands him.

"Tell our father it is time to eat and bring him out to the courtyard to join us," I call after Lộc. The boy does not acknowledge me and continues through the house.

We all walk out to the courtyard. Our table tonight is the floor. Sheets of newspaper are laid out below our feet; they stand in for a tablecloth and rest underneath teacups, bowls, and chopsticks. The courtyard is illuminated tonight by the full moon above and two lanterns on either side of our "table".

"Look at this feast." My father enters the courtyard with Tree and Lộc. We all bow and say our greetings to Father. "Who prepared this meal?"

Thắng answers, "Your daughter, Six, prepared the meal, as always, but of course, we all helped."

"Where did we get the snake and the fish?" Father asks, again.

"Father, Tree caught them early this morning," I answer patiently, "out in the fields. The fish washed ashore from the heavy rainfall and a nearby tropical storm. The river flooded the neighboring rice fields."

"What a good grandson." He pats Tree on the shoulder. "Sit. Eat."

We all sit down on the floor, cross-legged, around the newspaper table. The women choose to sit together on the far end. I notice there is one extra place setting between my sister and brother-in-law. I understand it is reserved for Tâm.

Sister Six prepared a fine meal. At either end of the table is a platter with one steamed fish, covered in soy sauce, julienned ginger, and chopped green onions. Working from the outside edge inward, there are large bowls of rice and soup on either side, then a plate of sweet potatoes, and in the center, is the snake, flavored with salt and fine chili powder, sautéed in coconut oil, and garnished with minced coriander from the garden.

Tú pours rice wine into each of our teacups. He notices the extra place setting and pours some of the wine into the cup, for Tâm. The children fill their tea cup with rainwater from one of the cisterns. We wait until Father has the first bite before we all eagerly dig in, picking morsels of food, family-style, with our chopsticks. Each of us takes a small serving to be polite but Lộc helps himself to a large serving of everything. I pretend not to notice. The men talk about how Tree caught the snake this morning before switching topics to the process of making rice wine. They applaud Tú for being able to make it without detection from the police since it is now illegal to produce alcohol without a license.

On our end of the table, Vân starts up a conversation with us women. "I have never prepared snake before. Sister Six, how do you do it?"

Sister Six slurps a mouthful of soup from her bowl and swallows quickly. "You first have to make sure the snake is dead." We all laugh. "And when you cut the head off, you have to cut at least this much below the head to remove the venom glands." Sister Six shows Vân her middle finger indicating the full length of her finger as the measurement to use. I smile, understanding well that my sister is not happy our neighbors are here, intruding on our family life, eating our food, and possibly spying on us for the government. I learned from Sam many years ago that the middle finger is the symbol to go "fuck off".

My sister continues. "You have to bury the head, otherwise, it can still bite you and kill you." My sister narrows her eyes and shows her fangs, and slithers her face inches from Vân's, making the frightened woman jump and gasp. I am enjoying this interaction between my neighbor and my wonderful sister.

"Then you rip the skin off, like tearing off filthy, smelly, sweat-soaked socks from your feet. You start from where the head was severed, and you pull and tug hard until you strip it clean." Sister Six demonstrates with exaggerated gusto by pulling an imaginary sock from her foot, which is now straight up in the air at a forty-five-degree angle to her hip. I almost spit out my potato from trying not to laugh. She looks ridiculous with her left leg still crossed and her right leg in the air.

"Aiyah, Sister, put your leg down," orders Hiền, "before all the bats fly out of your cave."

I choke on my potato.

"Do you feed the snakeskin to your livestock?" asks Vân.

"No." Sister Six's eyes roll back and she laughs. "The snake is a symbol of rebirth and healing. You save the skin for medicinal purposes, not for feeding your chickens!"

The poor woman casts her eyes downward as if embarrassed. It is apparent she is from a lower class of less educated people than my family.

"Sister, you will spoil Sister Vân's appetite." I try to be polite and rescue her.

"Nonsense. Next, you put your hands into the belly of the beast and shovel out the innards like this." My sister cups her hand into a bowl and scoops imaginary guts. Her nose wrinkles. "The smell is foul, especially if you cut too deep into the stomach." Our guest's eyes open wide and she covers her mouth. Her face is frozen with disgust. I can tell Sister Six is relishing the moment. "It takes a long time for rigor mortis to set in so the fresh kill will writhe and twitch for hours." My sister thrashes about like a demon-possessed woman. "The heart still pumps in the headless snake, and—"

"Enough, Sister," Hiền pleads.

"Fine." Sister Six takes a bite of the snake. She and I exchange a secret glance and a mischievous smile. Tonight's dinner has been entertaining.

Father stands up to loosen his pants. "I am so full. I need to unbutton to make room for more food." He pulls down his pants to his knees.

Hải jumps up. "Uncle, how about we have you change into loose pants with an elastic waist?"

"Good idea." Father goes with Hải inside the house.

As soon as they are out of sight, I address Hiền and Sister Six. "What is it with Father lately, not wanting to wear pants?"

Hiền shrugs. "He is going senile."

The rest of our evening is cordial and light. The rice wine helps to keep us loose. The alcohol reminds me of the mid-autumn festival two years ago when Hải gave me a mooncake.

20 FURY (SEPTEMBER 1978)

A series of loud knocks rap at the door. I run to the foyer and see Sister Six beat me to it. She opens the door and stumbles backward as three cadres enter the house.

"Who is the head of the household here?" The oldest one asks.

"Our father." Sister Six's voice is barely audible. Her lips quiver.

"We must speak to him."

I walk to Father's room to fetch him. I return to see our whole household has gathered by Sister Six. I see the fear in my sister's face and am guessing she is reliving the day Tâm was taken. This is the first time I have seen her so afraid.

"Elder, we received a tip that your family has stolen government property," the oldest cadre accuses. "We will search your house now and take back what is rightfully the property of the Socialist Republic of Việt Nam."

"My family is innocent," answers Father. "You will find nothing stolen here."

The three officials disperse to different areas of the house. They leave every room in disarray like a tornado had ransacked the area.

"Here!" yells one of the cadres. We all run outside to the back of the house and into the garden. He holds a jar that contains brine and snakeskin. "I also found the fish." He points to the nine fish soaking in saltwater.

"We caught those during the rainstorm when the fish washed onto the fields from the river." I cannot believe they are accusing us of stealing. "And my nephew caught that snake. We did not steal anything."

"You took these from the field without the government's

permission." The oldest cadre collects our fish and the jar. "Everything belongs to the government."

"Please, we are under the protection of one of your cadres, Trần Minh-Hoàng." I lie and hope that in a sea of communist officials, Minh-Hoàng's name will mean something to these men. "I ask that you please spare our family by leaving us at least a couple of fish. We have young children who are hungry."

"That name means nothing to me," says the oldest cadre.

"I served with him in the army," says the young cadre holding the jar with the snakeskin. "If she says they are under his care, I believe her."

"What is your relation to Minh-Hoàng?" the oldest one asks me.

Again, I lie. "I was his mother's caretaker. Mrs. Trần loved me like a daughter."

The oldest cadre gives me a lurking grin. I smirk back but feel violated with his eyes piercing through my clothes. The cadre takes a step towards me but I stand firm, ready to challenge him.

Hải quickly steps in front of me. "You have what you came here for. Take the fish and the snakeskin and go." My father stands defiantly beside Hải. His scowl challenges the cadre.

"Step aside, old man." The cadre pushes my father to the ground. Father loses his balance and crashes to the floor. He lands on his hip and braces his fall with his elbow. He winces.

I immediately kneel down to tend to him. "Father, are you hurt?"

The cadre advances forward to grab my arm and roughly pull me to my feet. Hải punches the cadre in the face and chaos erupts. Sister Six and I help Father up but Hải falls back. He slams into me with such force that I crumble to the floor, taking Father with me. Father cries out in pain. His head hits the ground. In the middle of this scuffle, Dirty Butt squawks in protest and runs to the back of the banyan tree.

One of the other cadres, the ugliest one, chases after her. "They have a chicken!"

Sister Six tends to Father while I chase after the third cadre. "You leave my chicken in peace or else I will feed you to her for dinner!" I threaten.

A gunshot fires and I halt in my tracks. A hushed groan escapes my throat. The children cry out in fear. Hiền cries one of her "aiyahs".

The young cadre who found the fish and snakeskin waves his pistol in the air. "Stop where you are and kneel with your hands behind your back!"

We all do as we are told.

"You are all stupid to first steal from the government and then dare to challenge us," says the oldest cadre. "We can fine you and take away your government subsidy. How would you like that? Or we can take your house, and declare it a meeting house for us. How does that sound? Maybe, we arrest you all and separate you so that you will never see each other again. We can put the children in orphanages, or send them to rural areas to farm the land." The cadre continues his speech, threatening us with torture and even death.

With our heads bent down and our eyes focused on the floor, we have no choice but to listen. Hiền whimpers softly inside the house. Somehow, it is not fear but rage that bubbles to the surface. The longer the cadre talks, the more it fuels my anger. He finally stops talking and rounds us up in the courtyard. We huddle in silence, waiting for our sentence. I cannot help but be suspicious of our neighbors. Perhaps they were spies and reported us. Who else could it be?

"Because this is the year of the horse, and I was born under this sign, I will show you compassion. You can keep your house for now." He pauses to let the weight of his message sink in. "We are taking everything else you own, including one member of this family. I will let you determine who will get arrested today."

Cries of protest escape from each of us. This cannot be happening! One of the cadres, the ugly one, ties us up with rope. We sit helpless as they haul away the salted fish, the snakeskin in brine, and my beloved Dirty Butt. My heart anchors into my stomach knowing the fate that awaits her. They remove our hammocks, rip up our plants, and take our clothes hanging on the clothesline. They take our pots and pans, our cooking and eating utensils, even our mattress and the bicycles. We are scared and deeply dejected.

"Have you decided who is leaving with us today?" asks the oldest cadre. We can no more choose than pierce a dagger into each other's heart. It is a cruel demand.

Father stands up. "Arrest me. I am old and have lived a long life."

"No, that is not happening," I say. "Take me."

"I will not let you sacrifice yourself," says Sister Six. "You have a daughter."

"Take me," says Hải. "I am the one who punched you."

"No!" I search for Hải's hands. "There has to be another way."

"There is no other way." A tear hangs on to the corner of Hải's eye.

I mouth the words "I love you" and lean in to rest my head on his shoulder. My tears stain his shirt.

"It has been decided then," says the cadre. "Come."

"No!" I refuse to let go of Hải's hands. He pulls Hải to his feet but my grip tightens around Hải's wrist. "No!" I scream again. The cadre pries our hands apart and kicks me in the ribs. I claw at his legs and try to trip him. He escorts Hải into the house. I struggle to stand up with my hands tied behind my back and run after them. "No! Please! No!"

Outside the front of our house, I see our belongings loaded onto a truck. They even take the Buddha on our ancestors' altar. I run to Hải and beg them not to take him. The young cadre shoves Hải into the truck. The ugly cadre pushes me to the ground. They all jump in the truck and start up the engine.

I scream at the top of my lungs with the fury of a deranged lunatic. "Fuck you all to hell! I curse each of you a life of misery and pain! I will conjure up the dead to haunt and possess you, and torture you until the day you meet Satan!"

The truck speeds away and I chase after it. I see Hải's head bobbing up and down. We lock eyes and for one second, time freezes. Then, the truck screeches around the corner and is gone. I fall to the ground and succumb to grief. My world shatters.

***

"How is my father doing?" I ask Đức.

The good doctor shakes his head. "There is a severe hematoma on his thigh."

"What does that mean, exactly?" I bite my lower lip.

"He has a big bruise where he fell. The swelling and pain should go away in a few weeks. The best thing he can do is rest, keep his leg elevated, and apply ice or anything cold on it. Hopefully, it will not clot as the blockage can cut off blood flow and cause major damage."

"And his elbow? His head? What about his hips?"

"His elbow is scraped. He is lucky he did not break his hips. It will be tender for a while but he is not complaining, so that is reassuring. His head is where I have the most concern. There is a

142

big bump there. It is possible he has a contusion or even a concussion."

"Meaning what, exactly?" I pace back and forth. "I am sorry, but I do not understand all the medical terms and how serious they are or what complications can arise."

"No need to apologize," says Đức, "but keep vigilant over the next few days. If he complains of persistent headaches, dizziness, or blurred vision, or if you notice his speech is slurred and he is confused or has trouble remembering things, they can be signs that there is bleeding in his head, in which case, the blood can fill his brain and suffocate the brain tissue."

"Thank you for coming." I walk Doctor Đức out the door. He pedals off on his cyclo. I run back into the house and grab Sister Six by the arm. "We are going over there now!"

"I am coming with you," insists Brother Thắng. The three of us storm into the house located behind ours.

"Where are you?" I yell out to our neighbors. "You cannot hide from us!"
"Brother Tú, Sister Vân," my brother-in-law calls out.

"My parents are not home." The expression on Lộc's face says it all. I lunge at him and grab him by the ear. The boy wails in pain and slaps my hand away.

Sister Six holds me back before I can sink my nails into his flesh. "He is only fifteen."

"We cannot make assumptions and false accusations," says Brother Thắng.

"How can you both be so calm and rational?" I demand. "It is obvious he is the traitor."

"What are you talking about?" Lộc looks past me to avoid eye contact.

"Do not play games with me, you liar." I am seething with so much anger that my voice shakes and my hands tremble.

"Did you tell anyone about our dinner together?" asks my brother-in-law.

"No," Lộc stammers.

"You are deceitful," I tell him.

My sister advances over to the boy. He steps back until he is pinned against the wall. Sister Six's breathing matches his, breath for breath. She stares at him. Her eyes take hold of his. They are nearly the same height. I wait to see what she will do next. Sister Six clocks her head side to side. Tick tock. Her eyes hold the boy prisoner. A smirk crosses her lips and then she blows hard into his open eyes. "Confess, or else I will see to it that they come knocking on your door next."

Lộc yells in shock and pain. "I told my friend; that is all. I was jealous. Please, I meant no harm. He must have repeated it—"

"Or maybe your friend is a communist!" I scream. "Your mouth caused my family to lose everything! They came and took all our possessions, even our furniture! We are eating and sleeping on the floor. My father is badly hurt and has to SLEEP ON THE FUCKING FLOOR!" I pound my fist on the wall next to his head. "They arrested Uncle Hải. Your mouth cost our family so much, you stupid boy."

Exasperated, we depart our neighbor's house and leave Lộc to his misery. There is nothing we can do or say to undo the damage that has already taken place.

A new dawn scatters across the sky. To stay warm, I wear several layers of clothes. At least the cadres left us some clothes and a few miscellaneous things that were not worth their time or could not fit into the truck. Not surprisingly, they did not take my crooked pants with the uneven pant legs. I check the elastic waist and am relieved Sam's emerald and diamond ring is still there, along with the phoenix necklace. I take off my wedding ring and put it in the elastic waistband as well. It is too painful to love. A rooster announces the rising sun and the pangs of guilt amplify my longing to hold Dirty Butt. My poor little chicken. Of all the chicks, there was something about her that stole my heart. I gave her more love than any chicken has ever known and saved her from an early death. In the end, I could not save her from fate; instead, I prolonged the inevitable.

I enter my father's room to check on him. His leg is propped up on Tree, who sleeps on his side to keep his grandfather's leg as high as it can be. Lying on either side of Father are little Trinh and Tuấn. Their little bodies give off enough heat to keep Father warm. Even Thủy-Tiên wanted to do her part and keep Grandfather warm. She lies by his head, curled into a ball; her little butt pressed against his temple. My heart swells with so much love for them. My thoughts meander to Tâm and I let the tears stream down my face. I let out a long sigh and walk outside.

"You are awake," I say to Sister Six.

"I told you this was my favorite time of day," she says. "The only time I have to myself before the rest of the world wakes. Sometimes, it is also my least favorite time of the day. I have only my opinions to keep me company, and right now, my opinion is that life is bleak."

"I need to go to the city today and get more things from Cường," I say. "This will be my last run. I am going to say my goodbyes to him and to Minh-Hoàng, and once I sell the last of this supply, I should have enough to leave."

"I wish I could leave with you," my sister says, "but I have to stay and take care of Father." This is the first I have heard of her wanting to leave.

"Let Brother Seven and Hiền take care of Father. Come with me," I say.

"Brother Seven can barely take care of himself and his family. With his truck driving schedule, he is never home. And we both know our sister-in-law does not have the backbone to do this all by herself."

"Hiền would rise to the occasion if she had to," I say, "but you are probably right, our sister-in-law would not be able to handle the stress for long before she goes crazy."

"I have to stay, in case Tâm comes back one day."

"Maybe when I get to America and settle in, get a job, I can send home some money. And when Tâm comes home one day, I can sponsor the whole famil—"

"That would be a dream come true. I fear it is getting more dangerous every day to live here," Sister Six says. "Ever since the Khmer Rouge slaughtered our people in Ba Chúc five months ago, it will be a matter of time before our military counterstrikes with a massacre of their own."

"All our country knows is war," I say.

"Are you taking the bus into Sài Gòn, or—"

"Catching a ride," I say. "Can you watch Thủy-Tiên for me?"

***

We ride in silence into the city. Brother Seven and I do not have much to say this morning. We approach the last checkpoint before entering Sài Gòn. Brother Seven shows the guard his papers. The uniformed officer checks the truck before handing the documents back to him. We pull away from the gate.

"Stop!" The guard's face reappears in front of us.

My brother steps on the brakes. "Is there a problem?"

"Who is the woman with you? What is her business?"

"I sell dried goods," I say. "Squid, shrimp, mushrooms...fruits."

He glares at me. "I was speaking to him, not you. Know your place."

146

Brother Seven mirrors my response. "My companion sells dried squid, shrimp—"

"Shut up." The guard nods to me. "Show me your license." I hand him my papers. "This license expires today. Where is your new one?"

"I am heading home now to District One to pick it up." I force myself to show composure and hope he believes my lie. How did I forget it was expiring?

"Show me your product," he barks.

Sensing my panic, Brother Seven answers, "She sold the last of it in the last village."

The guard is satisfied with Brother Seven's response and waives us through. We both let out a sigh of relief. The cadres who arrested Hải had also taken all my dried foods. I have been so preoccupied with everything that I overlooked this detail.

***

I step into the familiar toy store and see Cường faithfully perched on his stool, waiting for a customer. He smiles but I do not smile back.

"What is wrong?" he asks. I pile it on thick, starting with the snake dinner, climaxing with Hải's arrest, and finishing with my father's condition. "Such bad luck. What about the money from the last supply I gave you?"

"I have your share." I hand him the gold bar. "I had them hidden in our bunker. This is my last supply run. I will steal a boat if I have to, but I must leave soon. I cannot wait another year."

Cường disappears momentarily behind the store and comes back with a bag. "It may take you a while to sell them."

Seeing the contents, my body temperature rises. "How the hell am I going to sell these? You seriously want me to sell these rhinoceros horns?"

"You say this is your last run, why not make it a big one? There is a high demand for these."

"African rhinoceros parts have been banned since last year," I remind him.

"Horns sold in our country have not been prohibited yet. International commercial trade of African horns has been banned but these are Asian horns and they are stronger," argues Cường.

"My journey with you ends here. I am not going to sell these."

"Do not be a fool. You can sell these for eight hundred U.S. dollars per kilogram. With your share, you can easily set your family

147

up comfortably before you leave. Not to mention, these horns have medicinal powers and can help your father's ailments." Cường can be convincing. He hands me the bag. Maybe he is right. If I can sell these by Christmas, I can be out of the country before New Year's Day.

"Thank you, Cường, for everything. Take care of yourself," I say. "And so you know, there are no medicinal powers in any of the rhinoceros horns." I walk out of his store empty-handed.

***

My walk to Minh-Hoàng's house is bittersweet. This city that is so much a part of my heart and mind will never be the same. The sunlight does not shine the same. The trees no longer present themselves as strong and wise. The shops have lost their appeal. I am a small child in this familiar, yet strange, city. Gone are the happy days when I was a university student here. Will Sài Gòn ever reclaim her glory again? If I ever return, will this city welcome me back? Or am I dead to her now? Are we both lost to each other? Goodbye, beautiful Sài Gòn. I will never forget you.

I knock on Minh-Hoàng's door. No one answers. I call out his name but hear nothing. I peek in the window and see no one. I walk to the back of the house and see him sitting next to his mother's tomb. There are cans of "333 Premium" beer, once named "33" beer until the communists took over, lying all over the garden.

"You are drunk," I say to him.

"I am lonely…and drunk." Minh-Hoàng takes a big gulp of beer.

"Come into the shade." I reach for his arm.

He slaps my hand away. "Why are you here?"

"I came to ask for your help."

"Favors. All you ask are favors. Never show gratitude. You give me nothing in return."

"I am sorry. I have asked a lot of you, especially with trying to find my niece."

"What do you want now?" Minh-Hoàng wobbles back and forth and takes another swig of his beer. He tosses it carelessly on Mrs. Trần's tomb and pops open another can. "I have given you money, and food, and a permit…" He hiccups. "…to come and go as you please."

"I need some more of your mother's dried squid and shrimp, or anything you can spare. I promise this is the last thing I ask of

148

you. My permit expires today and I will not be renewing it."

Minh-Hoàng stands up and meanders toward me. "Why not be…why will you renew…not renewing it?" He slurs his words. His breath is foul with the smell of cigarettes and beer. Beads of sweat pour profusely down his neck. Has he even bathed these past few days?

"My father is ill and requires my full devotion to his care," I say. "I plan to stay in Vĩnh Bình for as long as he needs me."

"Why does everyone leave me?" He yells and spits droplets of beer on my face. "All I ever wanted from you is respect and gratitude."

I take a step back. Minh-Hoàng wraps one arm around my waist and pulls me close. The beer in his left hand sloshes out onto the ground. I push his chest but he holds me tighter. His lips press hard against mine and his wet, clumsy tongue thrusts deep into my mouth. I choke and slap him hard on the face. The sting of his hand cuts across my cheek. I am stunned for a moment. He takes the opportunity to grab my hair and pull my head back. He groans and kisses my neck. His hot breath on my ear and the urgency of his desire make me want to throw up. He drops his beer and with his free hand, fondles my breast.

My heart races fast and I am frightened. "Stop!" I cry out. I push harder against his body but that only excites him more. Minh-Hoàng tugs at my shirt. *Oh God, this cannot be happening!* I stomp on his bare toes.

Minh-Hoàng shrieks in pain. "Mother Fucker! You bitch!"

I run but a tightness digs into my stomach and holds me hostage. Minh-Hoàng's talons seize hold of my pants and jolt me back. My body slams into his. The hardness of his penis against the small of my back disgusts me. He picks me up around the waist and carries me inside the house. I kick and scream and throw my head back to thrust a blow to his head. It does not faze him. He throws me to the floor and straddles himself on top of me. The full weight of his body bearing down on my abdomen and hips hurt my ego more than my physical being.

"Minh-Hoàng, please, stop!" I try to reason with him. "This is your mother's house. You are dishonoring her if you continue."

He laughs. "This is my house now and she is dead."

He rips open my shirt and slides both sides of my bra straps down, exposing my flesh to his hungry eyes. I say a prayer for God to give me strength. Instead, He sends me a loud, thunderous explosion. Outside, women and children scream. The house shakes and the windows rattle. A vase falls over and shatters to the floor. I grab a fragment and dig it deep into Minh-Hoàng's throat. He howls in pain and rolls over. His erection quickly deflates. I spring to my feet and give him a powerful kick to his testicles before running out the door.

Outside is chaos. A nearby building is ablaze with fire and smoke. Ash is falling from the sky. I run in the opposite direction of the building. I am afraid that if I look back, I will see Minh-Hoàng chasing me. I clutch my shirt tight with one hand and catch a falling ash with the other. I do not stop until I see Brother Seven.

22 FATHER (SEPTEMBER 1978)

The long ride back to Vĩnh Bình is bumpy and loud. Without any dried merchandise to sell or a renewed license to show, Brother Seven agrees to hide me in the back of the truck behind the hundreds of cases of beer. We arrive back home shortly after 8 p.m. Brother Seven quickly unloads half of the beer until he sees my anxious face. I jump out of the truck and run frantically to the outhouse. My bladder burns like it is on fire and going to burst. I squat down with my feet planted on the slats and wait for relief. It takes some time before I can pee.

I walk inside and see my family's defeated faces.

"I am hungry," says Trinh.

"I want food," says Thủy-Tiên.

"Me too," says Tuấn. "When can we eat?"

My sister shakes her head.

I usher the children to the cistern. "Fill your stomachs with water and go to bed. We will have food tomorrow morning."

My daughter, niece, and nephew do as they are told, but complain the entire time, until they lie down next to Father in his room.

"How is Father doing?" I ask.

"Aiyah, Sister, he has been sleeping all day," says Hiền. "He woke up a couple of times and stayed awake to talk a little bit, but then he fell asleep again to the sound of his stomach crying out for food."

"Brother Seven, you get some sleep. You have to drive again tomorrow morning," I say. He slithers off to the bedroom. "Brother Six, can you load the cases of beer back onto the truck? Brother Seven has to deliver them to Phú Quốc tomorrow." My brother-in-law nods. "Sister Hiền, please keep an eye on the

151

children and Father." I toss Sister Six a bucket. She does not even try to catch it. "And you, dear sister, are going to catch lizards. Fill a spray bottle with cold water. If you see one, spray it to slow it down and trap it with a bucket. With luck, you will catch some and fry them up to eat."

"Why do I have to catch geckos?" She picks up the bucket. "What about the money you saved up from selling your medicines? Why not use some of it to buy food?"

"I have not had the chance to convert it to gold bullions yet. It would be too suspicious if we went to market with large bills."

"Fine. What are you and Tree going to do while I catch chameleons and geckos?"

"We are going to get us a bird," I say. "Tree, grab your slingshots. It might rain later tonight, in which case, we will see if we can catch some frogs too."

My sister grumbles. "Who made you boss?"

***

Tree and I return to the house at midnight. We did not take down a bird although there were a few perched on some trees. They taunted us before flying off. We did catch four nocturnal frogs that came out thanks to the rainfall. Tree captured three and I caught my first one.

"Do you think Aunt Six caught any lizards?" I ask Tree.

"No," he responds.

"I do not either. Good job tonight. Get some sleep."

Tree walks off and I head to Father's room. Thủy-Tiên, Trinh, Tuấn, and Father are all sleeping soundly. I walk to my room and put on two layers of clothes to keep warm through the night. I lay down on the cold, hard floor, exhausted. The memory of Minh-Hoàng forcing himself on me earlier today has me crying quietly in my room. This is a burden I will carry alone.

***

Brother Seven's truck is not outside. My guess is he left for Phú Quốc hours ago. I remember the frogs that Tree and I caught last night and walk over to check on them. They are still moving in the bag. Father will be pleased.

I enter Father's room to wake up the children and him. I sit on the floor and scoop Thủy-Tiên onto my lap. Her eyes open and she smiles at me. I poke at my niece and nephew. They grumble and plead to be left alone. I tickle them and before long, their giggles fill the room.

152

"Time to wake Grandfather up," I say. "Do you think he is ticklish?" All three of them nod and wiggle their fingers across Father's feet, neck and ears. It does not work. "Try again, maybe his ribs." The four of us tickle, poke and scratch at Father's ribs, but he does not stir. I fear something is wrong. "Father?" I touch his hand and it is cool. "No, no, no, no." I notice his mottled skin appears marbled in hues of red, purple and blue. "You cannot be dead!" I yell at his lifeless body. I search for a pulse and find none. "Father, wake up!" I shake his shoulders. "Father! Wake up! Wake up!"

I throw myself over his torso and once again, surrender to the pain.

***

Although the tears did not make a public appearance with my taciturn sister, I believe inside, her heart is breaking into a million pieces. She is exhausted from staying up the past two days cooking to cater the funeral service herself.

"I am going to prepare everything that Father likes," she says, "the way he liked them, and I do not want any help."

If doing everything herself will keep her distracted so that she does not have time to cry, I support her wishes. Brother Seven and my brother-in-law, Thắng, handle the tomb arrangements. My sister-in-law, Hiền, calls for a monk to chant and say prayers. Tree helps me notify extended relatives and trusted friends in our hamlet, while I write letters to those who live too far to come.

Today, my brother's sunken eyes, weary movements, and gaunt figure make him age ten years older. Brother Seven is taking it the hardest, perhaps because he has loved Father longer than any of us. Thủy-Tiên is the only one here with dry eyes. She does not quite understand what is happening and what death means. Her face shows curiosity. One day, she will understand the pain of losing a parent. For now, I am thankful she is innocent and not burdened with sadness.

We lay Father to rest in a tomb next to Mother. Most of the money I saved up from selling on the black market went to building the tomb and paying for the funeral service. Like Minh-Hoàng's service for his mother, Father's service is also simple, with only a handful of people in attendance, including our neighbors, Tú and Vân, who came to pay their respects.

Sister Six still holds a grudge. "They came to eat free food."

"Bite your tongue," I say. "Today is already a sad day, and we are here to honor and celebrate Father."

"Who invited them?" Sister Six asks but does not expect an answer. "I cannot believe they had the audacity to come to the funeral."

"Sister, it takes bravery to come and pay their respects, especially since their son brought shame and embarrassment to them. They can barely look at our family because their son's carelessness cost us so much."

"They are misers," she continues. "They never share anything with us and Vân rarely loses at cards. I know she cheats."

"They are poor. Let forgiveness enter your heart before you turn into a chicory root."

"Why are you not bitter?" she asks.

"I am, but not at them," I say. It is the Communist Party and people like the bitter melon man who has me all twisted inside.

23 THIS IS IT (JANUARY 1979)

Hiền hands me a letter. "Hurry and open it." I stare at the envelope. "Aiyah, open it!" It is from a prison. "Read it out loud."

My hands tremble as I hold the unopened letter addressed to me. For the past three months, I questioned whether Hải was still alive. I sit down and open the letter.

"My lovely Tuyết," I read, "I hope this letter finds its way to you. I am taking a big risk to smuggle this out. I am being held at the Thủ Đức prison in Bình Thuận Province."

"That is one-hundred-forty kilometers north of Sài Gòn," says Hiền.

"I am told I will be here for three to five years as punishment for hitting a police officer," I continue reading, "and I hope I survive that long. The conditions here are deplorable. My small cell is shared with many others. It is humid and putrid here and there is urine on the walls. Water leaks down from the ceiling and it is uncomfortable to sleep. I am either too hot during the day or too cold at night. My body aches from the hard physical labor they force on us prisoners. Every night we have to sit and listen to their teachings and give confessions. We only get a little bit of rice to eat each day and I am hungry all the time. Anything that moves becomes food if I can catch it. When we see a dog or a cat, we all howl and salivate, wishing we could catch it. If you get this letter, maybe you can send me some food. There are all kinds of people here, men and women, from religious and political leaders to artists and scholars. I keep hoping I will see Tâm amongst the women prisoners here but am disappointed every time. My memory of you and the script I write in my mind's eye of our future together help me persevere. Do not try to visit me. It is too far of a journey and will only make us both sad. Remember the mooncake to freedom and let that be your focus. Freedom. Do not underestimate yourself and the power of the human spirit. Please send my love to your family. I dream of the day I can see you and TT again. With love from your greatest admirer…faithfully and forever yours, Hải."

My sister-in-law cries. "At least he is alive."

"Yes." The energy drains from my body. Tears of guilt threaten to roll. "We should send him a few things."

"Should we send him something of Father's?" asks Hiền.

"Hải would like that. I am going to the market. We can include some food for him. Can you see what is left of Father's belongings and find the thickest sweater, comfortable pants, and a pair of shoes? Father still has a pair of those plastic shoes for wearing in the rain and mud."

Hiền nods and scurries off on her mission. I am relieved to have a moment of silence to myself. I reread Hải's letter. This time, the tears flow freely.

***

I walk slowly to the market with my old school satchel slung over my shoulders. Hải's letter is tucked safely inside along with all my valuables. Five meters in front of me is a jewelry store. As I approach the store, a beggar tugs at my arm. I am alarmed by his touch and jump aside with a gasp. The condition of his skin is appalling. Mosquito bites cover his body from head to toe. Fresh claw marks scorch the areas where he scratched himself hoping for relief but only feeling fire. He is sunburned and his flesh raw.

He clasps his hands together in prayer. "Sister, please, can you spare some food? I have not eaten for days. They took everything from me."

Begging is now forbidden and helping a beggar is against government policy. I notice a few eyes on me, including the jewelry store owner. I take a deep breath and ignore the man. I keep walking but he keeps begging. I shove him away. "I am so sorry, Brother."

I step inside the jewelry store. The owner approaches me. "You did the right thing. If you help him, you would be helping a parasite."

I open my mouth to respond but am interrupted by the loudspeaker. "Citizens, today we celebrate! Two weeks ago, our military forces marched into Kampuchea and took down the Khmer Rouge army. They were no match for our mighty forces and today marks the first day of our occupation and reign. The war is

156

over."

The jewelry store owner and I are speechless. Cheers erupt in the market and people disperse to run home to their families.

"We must cheer," says the jeweler, "otherwise they will arrest us for not being patriotic."

She and I jump up and down and hug each other. It is the strangest feeling to pretend to be loyal and nationalistic and to share enthusiastic cheers with a stranger. I am a live puppet in my own country. A few firecrackers set off in the square. Some people shake hands and talk wildly about the news, while others continue their business. I recognize the fake smiles on their faces. They are smiles of pain and suffering.

I take out of the satchel my wedding ring and the phoenix necklace. "I would like to sell these."

"This is exquisite." The jeweler perks up as she examines the necklace. "Where did you have this made?"

"It was a gift on my wedding day."

"And is this your wedding ring?"

"Yes. My husband died over three years ago." I watch her weigh the wedding ring and hope my sad story appeals to her maternal heart. "I need to sell these so I can feed my children."

"You are lucky they did not find these and confiscate them. Concealing things is considered unpatriotic and can get you arrested." I say nothing. "I will give you twenty million for both."

"The necklace alone is worth over twenty million đồng," I say matter-of-factly.

"Wake up, my friend," she says. "People are not exactly buying a lot of luxuries right now."

I counter. "Twenty-five million for both the necklace and ring. Our war with Kampuchea ended. Prosperous times are coming. I can sell these tomorrow and get my asking price without any negotiations, or I can sell them to you right now, and you will be the only jeweler with this unique and sought-after necklace."

The jeweler hesitates. "We meet in the middle."

I have hooked her. "I am firm on twenty-five million. In the days to come, you can sell this necklace for over twenty million and the ring for another ten million."

"No, twenty-two and a half is my final offer." She is stubborn.

"Fine," I say. I see her shoulders relax and a smile creeps up her face. "I will take my jewelry to another shop tomorrow." Her smile disappears. I gather up my necklace and ring, wrap them up slowly in my handkerchief to give her a chance to stop me, and place them back into the satchel. "I am sorry we could not come to an agreement." I turn to leave.

"Fine. Stay. I will give you twenty-five million for both."

"In gold coins, please." I smile sweetly at her.

She hands me twenty grams of gold and the remainder in paper money. I use the cash to buy a few dried fish to send to Hải. Before walking to Thủy's and Đức's tailor shop, I walk past the beggar and "accidentally" drop one of the dried fish at his feet. I walk a few paces and glance over my shoulder. The beggar drops to his knees and picks up the fish.

"Arrêt." A police officer approaches me and demands I stop. My legs tense up and I halt in mid-stride. "Show me your hands." I spread out my fingers, palms facing up. My heart is clapping frantically. I remain unemotional and refuse to meet his gaze directly, lest he feels challenged. "Turn your hands over." I do as I am told. He takes out nail clippers from his back pocket. Grabbing hold of my left hand, he trims my fingernails, then does the same with my right hand. "Coquetry is prohibited." He lets me off with a warning and walks off.

I let out a big sigh of relief. *Thank you, Lord.*

***

Inside the familiar tailor shop, Thủy greets me warmly. "Come in. How have you been?"

"I have been slowly picking up the pieces." I make myself comfortable in the back room. "This whole country is under constant surveillance. There are suspicion and hypocrisy around every corner. I am so sick of it."

"With the news of us defeating Pol Pot's army and stripping the Khmer Rouge's reign in Kampuchea, peace is imminent," believes Đức.

"There will never be peace until we are free from the communist regime," says Thủy.

"I believe that to be true as well," I say, "and that is why I plan to leave soon. I received a letter from Hải. He is in a prison north of Sài Gòn. I came into the market to buy some dried fish so we can send them to him."

Đức hands me a bag of fried banana chips from the cupboard. "Send him these too, from us. You should send them quickly. I hear they transfer the prisoners around every few months so the prisoners cannot form friendships. The guards fear the bond would lead to uprisings. This also prevents the family from keeping track

158

of their relative and hence, cannot send them aide. The prisoners become weak and completely dependent on the guards. They do as they are told out of fear."

"I cannot believe the world we live in, here in our own country." I take the gold coins out of my satchel and hand them to Đức. "This should be enough. How soon can I leave?"

"The Lunar New Year falls on January twenty-eight this year," Đức says. "There is a group scheduled to leave that night from Ba Động Beach. Do you want to join them?"

"Yes, the sooner the better."

"Perfect," Thủy chimes in. "Soon it will be the year of the goat. People will be wearing lucky colors of red, purple, and green. While celebrations are taking place, you all can slip out. Make sure you wear layers in these colors to blend in."

"Normally, we would advise you to wear old, dirty clothes to look poor and ordinary," says Đức, "but because of the celebrations, even the poor will be wearing their best clothes."

"I do not have any nice clothes or clothes in those colors," I say, "but maybe I can find something that belongs to my sister."

Thủy springs to her feet and walks briskly to her mannequins. She removes the green silk tunic from one of them and hands it to me. "Take this. We are family now. Do you have black pants to compliment the tunic?"

I nod. "Thank you."

"New Years is two weeks away," says Đức. "That will give me time to finalize some details and secure your seats. I will pedal to your house on the morning of January twenty-six. You can buy some bananas from me. I will place a message inside one of them for you."

"Be ready," says Thủy. "This is it."

"There will be other families joining yours so you will not be alone," says Đức.

"Remember to wear layers and bring only a small bag, like this satchel is perfect." Thủy points to my bag.

"Pack some food that does not spoil, like nuts and dried fruits," says Đức.

"Yes," says Thủy, "but also bring some things to quench your thirst, like cucumbers, lemons, and coconut water."

"And bring matches or a lighter," says Đức. "Fire and water will be your most prized possessions."

We finish our conversation with hugs and tears. I rush home,

anxious to put my plans in motion to leave this country once and
for all.

<h1 style="text-align:center">24 THE LOTUS FLOWER (JANUARY 1979)</h1>

Out in the courtyard, I survey my surroundings. The banyan tree stands big and bold. I remember how Tree loved to climb up on it and take naps. The stillness of the pond and the outhouse reminds me of Father standing there without his underwear. A big lump forms in my throat. My chest caves from the weight of these memories. Way in the back is the bunker, where Tree told me about selling morphine on the black market. It reminds me also of Mrs. Trần and her bunker. I hope my niece is out there somewhere, alive and safe, and that she will return home one day. I sit down cross-legged and remember Sister Six's snake dinner. A smile escapes my lips recalling her demonstration to Vân how to strip the skin from a snake, with her leg in the air. My thoughts sweep over to Cường. I am in his debt and will be forever grateful to him for getting me this far.

Brother Seven steps into the courtyard. I see from his red eyes that he has not stopped crying. His presence adds another few pounds of brick onto my crushed heart. His tears race faster down his face. I stand up to hug him.
He weeps like a child in my arms. "I want you to stay."

My sister, hearing our cries, comes out to the courtyard. Then my brother-in-law comes, and finally, my sister-in-law. Their hugs become layers of concrete that crush my body and suffocate my desire to leave. My family gathers around me. I am afraid to say the words goodbye, for fear it would be too final.

Tree comes into the courtyard. "No crying. It is New Year's!"

Brother Thắng puts on a brave face. "These are tears of joy."

Brother Seven straightens up. "You are right." He puts his hand on his son's shoulder. "Go collect extra sets of clothes. You are going to escort your aunt and Thủy-Tiên to the shores of Ba

Động beach and then help them to Bạc Liêu Province."

Tree does not move. "Today is Sunday and it is almost 9 a.m. It is bad luck to travel on New Year's Day."

"Who told you that?" snaps Sister Six.

"Do as you are told." Brother Seven puts on his stern face. "You will be back soon." As soon as Tree leaves, he cries again.

"You have to tell him," I urge. "This is his chance to say goodbye."

"If I tell him, he will not go," says Brother Seven. "No, he needs to go to America. There is no life for him here. And he can help you."

Tree comes back with a plastic bag and shoves his clothes into the bag. "I am ready."

Sister Seven hugs her son close. "Be careful and stay safe. Keep alert and protect your aunt and little cousin."

"I will be back soon, Mother," says Tree.

"Aiyah, I know. I will miss you. I am being a silly woman." Hiền hugs him again and runs into the house to conceal the torrential downpour brimming in her eyes.

Tree points to the front door. "Doctor Đức is here."

I put on my straw hat and hug my family one last time. It takes all my will not to cry and abandon my plans to leave. Thủy-Tiên kisses her aunts and uncles and hugs her cousins, Trinh and Tuấn. The three of us climb into the cyclo and wave our goodbyes.

"I do not understand why everyone is so sad," says Tree. "I am only escorting you to Bạc Liêu to help you settle in, and then I will return in one, maybe two, weeks."

"This is the first time you have been away from home," I say. "It is natural for your parents to worry."

"I am sixteen years old now, not four like Thủy-Tiên."

"One day when you are a father, you will understand what it is like to worry about your children."

"They are worried about you too and you are almost forty years old. You are going to another village for a teaching job and it does not even start until next week. They act as if they will never see us again."

Đức joins our conversation as he pedals his cyclo through the town to the other side of the market. "It proves that no matter how old you get, family always worry about family."

"Is it bad luck to travel on New Year's Day?" I am nervous and excited at the same time. "I know it is bad luck to argue or work or do housecleaning—"

"It should be a day for resting and spending time with family," reminds Tree. "We should be eating, drinking, gambling, and celebrating, so yes, traveling is a bad idea. I do not understand why we did not delay your travels until after all the celebrations."

"When will we get there?" asks Thủy-Tiên.

"It will take us a couple of hours to get to the beach," I say.

"I am hungry," my daughter declares.

Đức stops pedaling and reaches into his basket. "Have some deliciously dried bananas."

Thủy-Tiên eagerly takes the bananas. "Thank you, Uncle Đức."

Tree offers to pedal. "Let me know when you get tired."

"We can switch in twenty or thirty minutes," says Đức. "I will escort you to the Quan Chánh Bố canal."

We ride through several hamlets. Tree and Đức switch every few miles. Thủy-Tiên and I remain in the buggy. I offer to pedal but Đức says people will be suspicious seeing a woman dressed in a nice silk tunic transferring two men and a child. We continue through the countryside. Every home is different as we ride through the dirt roads. The poor live next to the rich. Thatched roof homes made of bamboo, banana leaves, straw, clay, or palm stand beside three-story homes built from brick, tile, wood, or stone. Some homes are modestly decorated for the Lunar New Year while others are lavishly adorned with banners, flowers, lucky red envelopes, and firecrackers. Despite the economic differences from one house to the next, all of them have hammocks outside or on the balconies.

"Múa Lân!" Thủy-Tiên squeals excitedly and points ahead.

"Yes, my dolly, a dragon dance," I say.

There is a large celebration commencing at this hamlet. The beat of the drums resonates through the streets into the cheering crowd. There are two sets of dragon costumes, one in red, and the other in green, with men underneath the shiny dragon cloth tapping their feet and marching to the beats. A cymbal chimes and the dancers holding the head of the dragons jump into the air to stand on the shoulder of the man behind him. The dragons pretend to grab the lucky red envelop hanging from the storefronts. I see a hand extend from one of the dragon's mouth and snatch the envelope. Firecrackers pop nonstop leaving a trail of red paper confetti. Smoke rises and swirls around the dancers. A person dressed as the happy Buddha with an oversized paper mâché mask prances around the dragons and wiggles his butt to the crowd.

Everyone laughs. It is nice to hear genuine laughter in the streets again. The dragons bow to the store owner with gratitude and the happy Buddha waves his fan to cool off the store owners. The people chuckle and cheer. They clap with enthusiasm. Three young men carry colorful red, green, and purple flags that represent their school. They march on to the next business for more New Year's envelopes.

Thủy-Tiên tugs at my shirt. "Do I get a red money envelope?"

Đức comes to the rescue. "If you be a good girl, tomorrow, you will get many red envelopes with a lot of money in them."

My daughter is reassured by his promise. "I will be good."

"Another thirty minutes and we will arrive at the canal," says Đức. "There will be someone to take you across so you can continue your journey."

I nod and continue viewing the scenery. In the distance, there is a large, two-level wood house on stilts with a palm-leaf roof and a fish pond. The pond is covered with aquatic plants, including bright lotus blossoms, in ombre colors of pink and yellow. It looks peaceful.

"Those sun-kissed water lilies are so pretty," says Tree.

"The spirits are with us, Tree," I say. "This is a good sign that we are seeing these blooms."

"There is so much mystery around these flowers," says Đức. "Their roots live in the mud underneath murky water and every night, they submerge to rest, awakening every morning to re-bloom. Yet, there is no mud or any residue on the petals."

"It is a symbol of rebirth and is truly miraculous," I say.

"I feel spiritual right now," says Tree.

"You should. It is not every day that we get to experience such beauty." I squeeze his hand. "This flower can live in such filthy conditions, surrounded by grime and pesky bugs, but every morning, it wakes and revives unscathed, to grace mankind with its purity."

"The lotus flower is resilient and has a strong will to live. A lotus seed can survive hundreds of years without water," adds Đức.

"I feel like we are lotus flowers," says Tree. "We are still here despite living in murky waters."

"Yes, but some of us are prettier than others." I give my daughter a gentle pinch on the cheeks. "The prettiest one being Thủy-Tiên."

Her smile brightens my world. We ride the rest of the way in silence. With every full rotation of the tires, I am closer to the dreadful goodbye to Đức and to my country.

25 VIỆT NAM ECLIPSES (JANUARY 1979)

The Quan Chánh Bố canal was dug in the 1800s and now connects to the Hậu River. It flows along Highway fifty-three and spills into the East Việt Nam Sea. It can support vessels carrying up to ten-thousand tons of cargo. I sense crossing the channel of water will be the easiest part of our journey.

Đức makes an abrupt stop at the end of the provincial road. "This is where my journey ends and yours begins." I hop off the buggy and adjust my hat. My black pants and green tunic stick to me from the humidity. Đức leans close and whispers in my ear. "Things will get difficult, and when they do, remind yourself that the struggle here in Việt Nam eclipses any adversity you will face on your search for freedom in America. This will all be worth it."

I nod. "Take care of yourself. Send my love to your wife. Thank you for everything."

Tree offers his back to Thủy-Tiên who monkey jumps happily onto him and wraps her arms and legs around her cousin. He collects his plastic bag of clothes and my satchel.

Đức pats Tree on the arm and hands him a red envelope. "Happy New Year."

Tree receives the envelope with two hands. "Thank you, Uncle. May the new year bring you good health, prosperity, and great purpose."

Thủy-Tiên slides off Tree's back and jumps up and down excitedly. "I wish you love and happiness."

Đức laughs and bends down on one knee. "Very good." He hands Thủy-Tiên a red envelope. She opens it and proudly shows me her money. He hugs the three of us and pedals back down the same road. We watch until he is out of sight.

Tree taps my shoulder. "Here comes our guide."

I see an old, weathered-looking man walking towards us. He is barefoot. He slows down and nods at us. "The road conditions are terrible with cracks and potholes." He searches my face for a response.

"And no bridges so we must go around."

He gives me a toothless grin. "Follow me."

Tree raises his eyebrows. "That made no sense."

"Do not worry," I say. "He spoke in code to make sure we were his guests. My response assured him we were."

"He should have said, 'Hello, I am your liaison. Are you Tuyết?'"

I smile at my nephew. Poor thing has no idea. After tonight, he will no longer be a citizen of Việt Nam. We follow quietly behind our guide. For an old man, he scurries quickly and with agility, easily jumping over fallen trees, stepping over big rocks, and dodging intrusive brush. I keep alert, watchful for any police and being mindful of where I step, in case there are snakes. We walk along the channel and cut through a jungle. Tree and I alternate carrying Thủy-Tiên on our back.

"Is it much farther?" I ask.

The old man points to a river. "We cross there."

"Where is the boat? Is there a canoe?"

"No, we cross over on that." The old man points to a fallen acacia tree, less than a meter wide and twenty-one meters long. "I will go first." He steps up onto the fallen tree and spreads his arms out for balance. With his toes gripping the bark, the old man walks slowly across.

Immediately my pulse quickens. "You and Thủy-Tiên go next. Do not be afraid. Go slow and be careful." The river is wide and the stream is steady, but the tree is narrow.

"I am not afraid," answers Thủy-Tiên. "We are going on an adventure. If I am a good girl, I will get more envelopes tomorrow."

"Hold on tight and be still, like a statue, otherwise, you will fall into cold water."

Tree takes off his shoes, puts them in the plastic bag, and steps up onto the acacia. He steadies himself and once balanced, he takes his first step with Thủy-Tiên clinging to his neck. He is ten paces behind our guide.

I take off my shoes and put them in my satchel. I sling it over my shoulder like a cross-body bag. I take a deep breath and do a quick Trinitarian sign of the cross on my forehead, chest, and shoulders. Our guide is almost all the way across. My nephew and daughter are not too far behind him. I step up slowly and take a moment to get familiar with the texture of the tree. It is dry and rough at the base. Step by calculated step, I inch across the narrow beam of wood, praying there are no rot or ants on the tree. I concentrate on my movements for fear of losing my balance. The sap sticks to my toes and gives me some security I will not fall. The smell of the tannins from the remaining leaves is pungent. Below me, the river rushes past. I blink a few times to maintain depth perception and not let the moving rapids become a blur. I am almost halfway to the other side.

A vibration under my feet signals to me that they have made it to the end and jumped off. I continue to focus and am now shuffling my feet instead of picking them up one in front of the other. I see some moth larvae squirming in one of the divots of the tree and scrunch my face in disgust. Taking another deep breath, I shuffle along and quickly erase the image of those translucent yellow grubs.

I hear Tree encouraging me. "You are almost at the end."

"Almost to the end, Mama." Thủy-Tiên's voice comforts me.

"Another six or seven meters," says the old guide. "Nice and steady."

I continue to glide my feet across the tree, but a piercing pain shoots up my toe. I scream in agony. I lose my balance and struggle to regain composure, but gravity takes control. I give in to the pull of the water.

"Mama!" Thủy-Tiên shrieks.

I fall in with great force. The cold river stabs me with its icy fingers. The current is deceptively fast. I gasp for air and try to swim to the bank of the river but the water sweeps me down before I can close the distance. My straw hat floats away. The old man, Tree, and Thủy-Tiên run with me downstream.

"Get on your back and keep your feet and head above water," yells the old man. "Look downstream and stay calm." I do as he tells me although the shock of the cold rapids impairs my motor functions. "Breathe, and try not to swallow too much water." *Old man, of course I am not trying to swallow the whole river!* "There is a calm area coming up. When you get there, turn over and swim over here, diagonally, and not against the current."

The rapids ease up and I realize I am in calmer waters. I flip over and swim diagonally downstream. Tree holds out a long branch for me to grab. Together, all three of them pull me up. Thủy-Tiên flings her arms around my neck and squeezes tight. Little tears slide down her cheeks.

I cough from her choking me. "I am sorry I scared you, my little dolly." I hug and kiss my daughter. "I am safe now."

An acacia thorn is burrowed deep inside my big toe. The throbbing causes me to wince. Tree kneels down and without warning, removes the thorn. I screech, more from surprise than from the discomfort.

"Can you walk?" The old man extends his hand to assist.

"Yes." I hobble along taking great care not to put any weight on the injured toe. I am distraught that Sam's book, as well as his letter and Hải's letter, are wet inside my satchel. We walk for forty-five minutes before coming to a clearing. By now, my clothes are almost dry. The village is small with only a dozen or so huts.

Our guide takes us into one of the homes made of leaves and straws. "This is my wife. You can call her Aunt Five."

An old woman greets us warmly with hugs. "Sit. Eat. You can rest for a few hours." She hands us a small bowl of porridge salted with fish sauce.

I bow to Aunt Five and wish her happy new year. Right away, I like her. We make small talk while we eat. Honestly, we are all too tired to have meaningful conversations with our kind hosts. Aunt Five wraps my big toe with strips of cloth and puts a fresh sock over my foot. I am grateful to her for nursing me.

The old man hands me a towel. "Change into something less festive after you eat."

Tree leans in close to me. "They took us in the wrong direction."

I hesitate before telling him the truth. "We are not going to Bạc Liêu."

"But your teaching job is in the Bạc Liêu province."

"There is no teaching job," I say. "We all lied to you."

My nephew's face becomes pale. He stares through me like a ghost. He stands up and walks out the door.

"Let me talk to the boy," says Uncle Five.

I stand up and walk over to the entryway to eavesdrop on their conversation. I hear a match strike and then an exhale. The smell of cigarette smoke permeates the air and wafts through the open doorway. A second match strikes and then a dry cough from Tree. He is smoking!

Aunt Five shakes her head. "Let them be."

I remain with my ear pressed against the straws that are humbly holding the roof up over our heads. Thủy-Tiên is content slurping the porridge and keeping the old woman company.

Tree takes another amateur puff and coughs again. "I want to go back."

"You cannot go back," says Uncle Five. "Your aunt and little cousin need you. It is not safe for them to travel alone."

"My family needs me," says Tree. "I know the way back to the river. I can cross it and find my way back home."

"If your parents told you, would you have gone?"

"Of course not," Tree answers. "I am going to be seventeen years old this year. I stopped going to school when I was thirteen and we lost our country. There is nothing for me in America. I cannot even speak the language and it will be too difficult to learn."

"You will find your purpose there," says Uncle Five. "Right now, your purpose is to grow up and be a man, to escort your aunt safely to a new home abroad. They cannot do this without you."

"It all makes sense now why everyone was crying when we left." The sadness is unmistakable in my nephew's voice. He takes another drag from the cigarette and does not cough this time. "I wish I had the chance to say goodbye."

"One day, you will get the chance to say 'hello' and they will be ecstatic that you made it." They finish smoking their cigarettes and come back into the house.

"Tree," I say, "your father insisted that I take you. He wants you to have a better life."

"I understand," Tree says, "but I thought you did not have enough money yet, after paying for Grandfather's funeral."

"I sold my wedding ring and the necklace I got on my wedding day. Do you remember the phoenix necklace?"

Tree nods, and for the next couple of hours, he is lost in his own thoughts.

It is almost 3 p.m. Aunt Five has already retired to her hammock for a nap. The wait for another escort to guide us to the beach makes the time drag on. I put on a fresh romper for Thủy-Tiên while she sleeps. Her belly is full of porridge and she is not disturbed by my intrusion. I undress and change out of my silk tunic and trousers. I put on the crooked black pants that I sewed myself, with the elastic waist hiding the only jewelry I have left…Sam's emerald and diamond ring. I look ragamuffin chic, all right, with my zigzag pants and pajama top. Tree changes into a different pair of shorts and an avocado-green cotton shirt.

Uncle Five springs out of his hammock. I am again amazed at how nimble he is for such an old man. He peeks outside. "It is time." He walks over to the round dining table and shows me a small bottle. "This is my last one and there is half left, but you will need this for your daughter. It is medicine made from valerian root and will help her calm down and sleep if she gets anxious."

"Uncle Five, I do not have any money—"

"Your money is no good here." He puts the bottle in my pocket. "You should go to the toilet. You have a long journey ahead of you."

Tree steps outside and finds a secluded spot to urinate. There is no outhouse so I, too, find a hidden area to squat down in. I am definitely in the rural countryside.

Back inside the hut, I lift Thủy-Tiên up into my arms. She remains asleep and is dead weight like a sack of rice. A young man around thirty years old appears at the doorway. He is covered in dirt and his pants are wet from the knees down.

"This is my son, Slanty-Eyes," says Uncle Five. "He will take you to Ba Động beach."

"This is my nephew, Tree, and—" I start to introduce my family.

"He is hard of hearing," says Uncle Five. "He lost his hearing a long time ago when a bomb blew close to him out in the rice paddies. He has a sixth sense, though, and is extremely alert. Of our thirteen children, he is the only one left."

"Oh, I am so sorry," I say. "Can he read my lips?"

"Most of the time. Ever since the police confiscated our writing paper, we have been getting by with gestures or writing with animal blood. Do not bother talking to him. He speaks but chooses not to."

Slanty-Eyes beckons us to follow him. We bid farewell and leave the abode. Again on foot, we traipse through the dense terrain. Our journey is short. We make it to the Hậu River where a woven basket canoe awaits. The canoe seats six people and has a wood canopy partially covering it. We climb in. Slanty-Eyes points to the canopy and gestures us to hide underneath. I am glad Thủy-Tiên is asleep during this transition.

Slanty-Eyes pushes the canoe into the river and climbs in. He rows in silence. I cannot see anything from my crouched position underneath the wood canopy but can hear the sounds of the paddle rubbing against the canoe each time our escort rows. The riverboat glides smoothly and effortlessly. I close my eyes and listen. I hear Tree breathing and the crinkle of his plastic bag when he shifts his weight. I hear the delightful soft buzz of Thủy-Tiên's snores while she slumbers soundly. Boat engines rumble by, a little too close to our canoe for my comfort. I eavesdrop on a conversation nearby from some people on a fishing boat. It sounds like they did not catch much this morning. Slanty-Eyes rows the boat for what amounts to forever. Occasionally, he rests his arms, but not for long before he resumes again.

"My foot is asleep." Tree shifts and tries to get comfortable.

"Mine too, and I have a cramp in my left leg." I reposition as well.

Slanty-Eyes' face conveys the message clearly: Be quiet.

Two hours pass. Thủy-Tiên stirs and opens her eyes. "I am thirsty."

"You will have to wait." I tell her we are playing a game and challenge her to be as quiet and immobile as a pangolin. The game interests her for only five minutes.

Tree tries to distract her. "Can you guess how many fingers I am showing behind my back?"

"Five!" She shows her hand with all five fingers spread apart.

"Shhh." Slanty-Eyes scowls at Thủy-Tiên.

She scowls back and mimics him. "Shhh."

He bribes her silence with a tamarind candy. Day gives way to night. We have been on the water for nearly four hours. My body aches. I am tired, thirsty, and hungry. We finally slow down and Slanty-Eyes gives us the signal that it is safe to come out. We climb out of the canoe and stretch our whole body. I survey our surroundings and see only water all around us. The soft haze of the moon illuminates the shimmering river. In a faraway place, the crackle of firecrackers, the blare of music, and the talent of someone singing resonates in the air. People are celebrating the year of the goat. Once again, we are asked to follow Slanty-Eyes. He takes us through a path with brush and trees on both side, and soft dirt beneath our feet. We come to a small clearing and I see fifteen people sitting around. Our guide bows to me and motions us to sit with the rest of the group. He pats Thủy-Tiên on the head, smiles, and disappears. *Where the hell are we?*

***

I study the woman sitting next to me. She is younger than me and Chinese. Her long hair is tangled and matted. Her eyes are closed, her lips open, and her head shakes side to side. She moans in distress. She takes out a menthol ointment and rubs it on her temples. She swipes some more cream from the tiny container and lathers it on her lower abdomen.

"Would you be willing to share that *Tiger Balm*?" I ask.

She opens her eyes and hands over the analgesic ointment. "What is your ailment?"

"My toe is throbbing and my legs are cramping. Yours?"

"I am a week away from having my monthly cycle. I suffer from cramps and headaches right before my period."

I rub the menthol on my calves and hand it back to her. "Do you know where we are?"

"We are at some peninsula," she responds.

"How long have you been waiting?"

"My brother and I have been here for an hour, maybe more. Every twenty or thirty minutes, more people come, in pairs or groups of three and four. Small groups mean less risk of getting caught. They come from different directions and are escorted by different people. When we arrived, there were already eight people here, including a one-year-old baby."

"Where is your brother?" I ask.

She lifts up her bony finger and points. "The one without a shirt is my little brother, Tùng, and I am Hồng-Mai." Her brother stands wearing shorts and sandals, with his shirt tucked behind his back like a tail. He is talking to another man.

"I am traveling with my nephew, Tree, and my daughter, Thủy-Tiên," I say. "My name is Tuyết."

"My youngest sister and her husband left a year ago and made it to Australia. That is where we want to go. Our parents did not join us. What is your story?"

"It is a long one," I say. "Who is the man your brother is talking to?"

"He is the co-sponsor of this operation. My brother is coming back this way. He will tell us." My new friend Hồng-Mai introduces us to her brother.

Tùng sits down with us and reports his findings. "That man I was talking to is Sơn. He and his friend are the ones who organized this escape."

"Where is his friend?" I ask.

"At home apparently," answers Tùng. "He is waiting for everyone to arrive here before heading out to meet us. Sơn said he is expecting twenty-five more people and does not expect his partner to show up until after midnight."

"That is over three hours from now!" exclaims Hồng-Mai. "He is probably celebrating the new year getting drunk!"

"He better not," says Tùng, "he is the captain of our boat."

"Your sister is probably right," I say. "He is probably spending all the money we paid him on eating and drinking, or gambling."

More time elapses and more people arrive, from different directions like Hồng-Mai said. Night brings with it mosquitos and other creatures. The collective sound of thousands of mosquitos buzzing around my head is deafening. Tree grabs a handful of mosquitos in the dark. He clenches his hand into a fist and crushes them. The pesky insects appear in droves. There is nothing we can do to escape them.

Our group has grown in size to thirty people. One would think we were all mental patients as we flail our arms and swat at the mosquitos, or slap each other to crush the ones that have landed to drain our blood. There are five children in our group…six if you count Tree. The youngest is only two months old while the other children are younger than my daughter. The poor babes cry out and their parents try to hush them. Thủy-Tiên is not immune to the blood-suckers either. Her skin is on fire each time she scratches herself. I take out the valerian root medicine that Uncle Five gave me and give Thủy-Tiên a sip, hoping it will put her to sleep and ease her suffering. Her tender flesh is inflamed and red from the allergic reaction to all the bites.

Mothers and fathers smother their babies' mouth to muffle the cries, for fear of being heard by the maritime police. This only makes them more delirious. I walk to each family with a child and offer a sip of the medicine. Every parent consents. We are all desperate for them to be quiet.

It takes another half hour for the cries to die down. The valerian root goes into effect and the children finally find relief in sleep. I hold my four-year-old and rock her back and forth. The mosquitos are still relentless but I barely feel them now. Tree still expends all his energy trying to mass murder them, one fistful at a time.

The loud rat-tat-tat sound of an AK-47 fires nearby and stuns everyone motionless. Tùng whispers, "Get down! If they see us, they will kill us all!" People scramble to hide and lie down.

"Where are they?" a voice yells out in the dark.

A woman moans, her voice barely audible. "I do not know."

A flashlight illuminates enough light for me to make out the silhouettes of two men, one woman, and a small child.

"Kneel." One of the men hit the woman on the head with the butt of the rifle. She yelps and falls to the ground like a beaten dog.

"Mama!" yells the child.

"On your knees, boy! Hands behind your head. Both of you!" The man with the flashlight shoves the child to the ground.

"Open your mouth." It is too dark to determine which one of the men is talking. The man with the flashlight crumples up something and shoves it into the woman's mouth. She cries and resists, thrusting her head side to side.

"You want to leave this country? You love money and those westerners that much? Here, eat these bills. This is the price you will pay. This is what it will cost you and your son."

The other man with a shrill voice screams, "Chew, old hag. I want to see you swallow every đồng!"

The boy cries uncontrollably and the woman gags on the

money. Rounds of bullets pelt the woman's body and pummel the boy's head. They both slump to the ground, dead.

"Throw them in the water. We will go back and question the captain where they are hiding."

I am paralyzed by what I witnessed. An eerie silence blankets the forest for a brief second until the thunderous taunts of mosquitos slap me back to reality.

***

We sit together in silence and wait. A few more people arrive and I count a total of thirty-six adults, five children, and one teenager. Forty-two. How many more will show up? It has been two hours since the incident with the woman and her son being murdered at close range.

Distressed and fearful, I lean on Tree. "How are you?"

"Itchy," he answers.

"Are you afraid?" I ask.

"No. I miss home, though." Tree scratches his calves.

"Me too."

Just when I relax a little, searchlights now illuminate the darkness. I hold my breath pondering if there are more people joining our party, or more police searching with the thirst for blood.

"Lay down!" says Sơn, the co-sponsor of this trip and leader in our group.

We wait quietly. Only the thick swarm of mosquitos and our loud beating hearts give us comfort that we are still alive. The searchlights scan the area for nearly an hour. Hồng-Mai pants and resists the urge to cry out in agony from the pain of her cramps. If she is in this much pain now, I cannot imagine the misery she will face when her menstrual cycle flows. The voices coming from the boat are loud and clear. They are close. Despite the size of the peninsula, they search exactly in the general area. I assume they beat the information out of the captain of our boat, who foolishly waited at home to join us after everyone has arrived. My thoughts circle back to the woman and boy who were killed hours ago. Were they the captain's wife and son? Were they unfortunate souls who paid a high price to escape with the rest of us? It makes me sad. What if it were us who got caught and killed? I shudder.

"I do not see anything," says one of the maritime policemen.

"That bastard lied to us," says another policeman.

"He is a dead man. Let us go back to his house."

"After we kill him, I need a few beers. It is Lunar New Year."

176

"I am ready to get drunk."

The searchlights get dimmer and the sound of the boat's engine becomes distant. We all stand up and breathe a sigh of relief.

Sơn motions everyone to gather around him. "We were supposed to have forty-six people in our group, but we have lost our captain and two of our passengers."

"I counted forty-two people earlier," I say. "Where is the last person?"

"We cannot wait for the last person," says one of the men in the group. "We need to leave now before the police return." I cannot get a good glimpse at him in the dark from the other side of the circle. His voice, however, is distinct, with a northern accent, and quite deep.

"The last person is the one who will be bringing our boat before dawn," says Sơn. "Is there anyone here who can operate a fishing boat for us and take us out to sea?"

No one speaks up.

"What about the person delivering the boat at dawn?" asks Tùng.

"He is too young and inexperienced," answers Sơn.

The same man with the deep northern accent speaks up. "I have navigated rivers most of my life but never out in the ocean."

"You are our best chance then," says Sơn. "What is your name?"

"Nguyễn Minh-Tú," he responds.

"Listen, everyone," says Sơn. "Brother Minh-Tú will steer and operate the boat for us. You all have come this far. Now you must choose to put your trust in Minh-Tú or to stay here."

"If we stay, how do we get back to shore from the peninsula?" asks a voice in the dark.

"If you stay, you are on your own and will have to find a way back."

"What about our money that we paid you?" asks a woman in our group.

"The money is gone. Your money paid for the boat, the guides who led you here, the fuel, the food and shelter in the villages, and for the boat captain and me."

The group erupts with everyone talking over each other. Some want to press on, others want to turn back. Many are afraid and unsure.

I grow impatient with the squabble. "Listen, Brothers and

Sisters. We all took the same risks and have sacrificed greatly to get to this point. There were never any guarantees. If you choose this direction," I point to the shores of Ba Động Beach, "you will be choosing to suffer for the rest of your life, however long that may be, and if you choose that direction," I point to the sea, "then you have a chance of living, a chance for freedom."

"She is right. I will give you five minutes to decide," says Sơn. "Those who wish to go can stand next to me. Those who wish to stay can stand next to that banana tree."

We deliberate amongst our families and travel companions. Slowly, people make their decision. Many walk toward Sơn to stand with him, including Hồng-Mai and her brother, Tùng. Our new boat captain, Minh-Tú, crosses the circle to stand beside Sơn. I hold Thủy-Tiên's hand and join them. No one is standing beside the banana tree.

My nephew stops and glances at the tree, then at me. I plead with my eyes for him to come with us, but he is motionless. I realize he cannot see my face so I walk to him. "Tree, we need you to come with us."

"But my parents and my little brother are in that direction." Tree points to the beach.

I try to reason with him. "This is what your parents wanted. If anything happens to you on the way back, we may never know, and your parents will never forgive me."

"I know how to navigate through the streets and the jungles, Aunt Eight, and I know how to survive and stay out of trouble."

"You are so smart and resourceful. Unlike me, you know what to do when you find that bottle of morphine and you know how to hunt for snakes and fish during the monsoon. Please, help us get to America, and after we get there, I will do everything I can to get you reunited with your family."

Tree weighs his options. He is clearly conflicted. He finally picks Thủy-Tiên up and walks toward the group standing by Sơn. I let out a private sigh of relief.

27 NESTLINGS AND FLEDGLINGS

At 4 a.m. the chug of a small boat announces its arrival at the peninsula. I hold my breath, fearful the police are back for another early morning search.

"The boat is here." Sơn whistles. "Minh-Tú and Tùng, help me carry these canisters of gasoline."

The three men swoop down to grab the fuel containers and hustle to the boat. The rest of us follow. I am exhausted from staying awake all night, but manage to run to the boat. What a vision the pastel green shrimp trawler makes with its blue hull and the numbers '93752' painted in dark red. The beautiful sun, large and brazen, glows in the distance and kisses our little blue boat with its golden rays. It is not larger than ten meters long from bow to stern, and with forty-three people fighting for space; it is going to be an uncomfortable voyage. Still, the wait is finally over and we are about to embark on the greatest escape of our life. Inside the boat is a teenage boy. He maneuvers as close to shore as possible and waves us in.

Thủy-Tiên tugs at my shirt. "Mama, do I get my red envelopes?"

"There are no red envelopes." I grab hold of her hand. She pulls her hand away and stands still. The excitement and eagerness in her face drains and her eyes mist up. I notice the large welts on her skin from the mosquito bites and the blood on her neck where her nails furiously dug for relief. My face softens. I gently take hold of her little hand. "You have been a good girl and you deserve something better than red envelopes." The wetness around her eyes recedes. She searches my face for clues as to what can possibly be better than a lot of money envelopes. "Come with me and I will show you a secret."

With excitement, Thủy-Tiên laces her fingers through mine and walks with me through the elephant grass. We come to a spot far enough to not be seen, but close enough that I can hear the group.

"First, we need to pee before we get on the boat," I say. "Do you have to pee?"

My daughter nods and squats down to relieve herself. I join her. Her face squints. The sun is rising and shining brightly into her eyes. Thủy-Tiên grunts and I realize she is doing more than peeing. I find a couple of large banana leaves. I strip some of the fibers off and tell her to wipe her bottom.

"My butt is still dirty," she says.

"Take off your pants. We can wash our hands and your butt in the water, and while you are doing that, I will show you the secret." I inch around the elastic waist of my pants in search for Sam's ring. I feel the hardness of the gems and squeeze it toward the small opening in the front by my belly button. Thủy-Tiên's face is all smiles when she sees the emerald poking through my pants. "This is our little secret. This ring is worth millions of red envelopes and it is yours to keep when we get to America. And you cannot tell anybody, not even the animals or the plants. They will all get jealous and steal your ring."

"How can plants steal my ring?" she asks.

"The plants have snakes and birds living among them and they might overhear you telling them your secret."

She nods and promises not to tell a single soul.

"Aunt Eight, we are leaving!" yells Tree.

Thủy-Tiên and I run and climb in to the crowded boat. I step on at least one person's hand. People curse at me. An elderly man gives me a dirty look but he has such an endearing face that I forgive him.

I make my way to the rear to join Tree. "Did I miss anything?"

"We filled the motor with fuel and refilled the canisters with water." Tree scoots over an inch for me to squeeze down beside him.

Minh-Tú fires up the engine and pulls away from the peninsula. We all cheer. There is no turning back now. All forty-three of us are in this together.

***

The sunrise is breathtaking and with the soft breeze caressing my hair, my energy is restored and my hope renewed.

Our leader stands up and makes a speech. "Everyone, I need your attention. We still have to clear the border so I need everyone to cram below and hide. Only Brother Minh-Tú and I will be visible as if we are heading out to fish. Right now, it is 5 a.m. and we should clear in thirty or forty minutes. We will let you know when it is safe to come up."

"Do you know where you are going?" someone asks.

"We have a compass and the stars to navigate us. The plan is to steer towards the Philippines and stay away from the Gulf of Thailand. There have been stories of Thai pirates stealing from refugees like ourselves, or raping women and kidnapping people to sell into slavery."

Women gasp and Hồng-Mai speaks up. "How fast can we make it to the Philippines?"

"Do we have enough fuel to cross the South China Sea?" asks Tùng.

"What happens after we get to the Philippines?" another person asks.

"Everyone, please," says Sơn, "I do not have all the answers, but—"

"But you are our guide!" says one person.

"We paid you a lot of money!" cries out another angry person.

"Turn back!" demands another.

Sơn remains calm. "I know you are all scared and you have questions, but right now, I need everyone to go below the cabin. Stay hidden and quiet. If we are spotted, we will die."

"Once we clear the border, we can figure things out," I say.

"Right," says Sơn. "The police have no problems shooting without asking questions."

Begrudgingly, people squeeze down below to the hull and the engine compartment. We all sit with our knees up and arms wrapped around our legs. Thủy-Tiên sits next to me with her legs bent too. Parents hold their babies the best they can and fight for space to make sure no elbows or knees bump into their baby's head. The air is stifling below. The residual smell of fish and shrimp suffocates me. I cannot see anything other than the tired and nervous faces of those around me. The boat skates across the water for fifteen minutes. Other than the rumble of the engine and an occasional cough, all is quiet.

"Shit!" exclaims Minh-Tú. Pop. Pop. Pop. Rat-tat-tat-tat.

"Speed up," exclaims Sơn. Rat-tat-tat. "Keep going! Do not

stop!"

The children scream. Hồng-Mai yelps and purses her lips tight. She closes her eyes and covers her ears. I am reminded of the "three wise monkeys" statue that Tâm purchased at the Bến Thành Market. The figurine represents "Speak No Evil, Hear No Evil, and See No Evil". Thủy-Tiên hunkers close to me and leans into my arm. I wrap my arm around her and squeeze. The unmistakable sound of AK-47s firing at us has everybody tense. The foul smell of people's breath assaults my nose as the screams of panic penetrate the dank and musty cabin. I catch a whiff of gasoline brewing in the still air. The boat is going fast and the ride is choppy. One of the elders in our group is seasick. Not a second later, vomit permeates from her mouth. She tries to hold it back and swallow it, but liquid oozes from her lips. Her vomiting sparks a chain reaction.

I challenge Tree to be strong. "This is not permission for you to throw up too."

The stink is so rancid that I find it hard to keep it together. I plug my nose. Smell no evil. The faster our boat goes, the bumpier the ride. A mixture of tears, saliva, and sweat are added to the mixture. The stench is unbearable.

The boat finally slows down and eases into a steady purr.

"It is safe now," says Sơn.

We all clamor over each other and climb out of the filth to breathe in the fresh air. Men leapfrog over women. The strong shove aside the weak. The biggest amongst us step on the smallest of us. We are desperate for relief and pure oxygen.

"We made it." Minh-Tú slaps Sơn on the shoulder.

Cheers ripple across our little boat and despite the turmoil we experienced, everyone is in good spirits.

Sơn steps onto a wooden crate. "Listen, everyone. By tomorrow, with some luck, we will come across a ship that will rescue us and take us to safety."

"That is true," says Tùng. "My sister and her family made it safely to Australia last year. They wrote to us and told us about a ship that was circling the international waters rescuing our fellow countrymen."

"Yes," pipes in Hồng-Mai, "we will be rescued by humanitarian organizations."

"Even if that is true, we need to conserve our energy, our water, and our food," declares Sơn. "I have on the boat some jicama that we all can share today. I wish I had more but I had to travel light to avoid suspicion. Each person gets one-fourth of a jicama. There is also a little bit of rice and I have enough rice balls for everyone. Also, each person can have one capful of water per day from this fuel canister."

"That is not enough," yells out a man by the cabin.

"You were told to bring provisions for yourself as well," answers Sơn firmly.

"What about the extra jicama?" I ask. "You were expecting forty-six people but since we lost our captain and the police murdered that woman and her son…"

Sơn frowns at me. "I will distribute with discretion." He passes out the already-peeled and quartered jicamas to each one of us, including the children. Some of the people who do not have children argue that the kids should share since they do not eat as much, but Sơn disagrees. "Every person here paid the same amount of money, regardless of age, profession, or connections. If you are Chinese, Cambodian, Vietnamese or Laotian…It does not matter."

With our hands outstretched to receive food and water, we are helpless baby birds. Those without their shirts on, like Tùng, are like hungry, featherless nestlings, while the rest of us are fledglings. The water makes its way to me, finally, and I pour a capful for Thủy-Tiên to drink.

"I want more, Mama," she says. "I am thirsty." I pour another capful and give it to her.

"Wait!" The teenager who had navigated the boat to the peninsula this morning stands up. "She gave her daughter two capfuls of water!"

All eyes are on me. One hand pulls the canister of water away from me. Another person shoves me and yells, "I get two capfuls, then!"

"We all should get two a day!" cries out another voice. "One is not enough."

"She should not get any water tomorrow," yells someone behind me.

"Quiet!" I scream. "I am giving my daughter my share! I was not planning on taking any! You all shut the hell up!" I point at the person who shoved me. "If you touch me again like that or my family, I will shove you over this boat myself." To my accuser, I ask, "What is your name?" He looks at me defiantly and does not respond. "Where are your manners, boy? Have you lost your respect for your elders as well as your tongue?" Still, he does not answer me but rather, shoots a scathing sneer in my direction. I am embarrassing him. "Fine, I will call you 'Snitch'. If you were my son or nephew, I would spank you until your ass is as red as the rising sun." I hand the water can to Tree and sit back down. I am so upset, I am shaking.

***

Hours pass and we see nothing for miles in every direction. The scorching sun is slow-roasting us for a scavenger's feast. If only I had my straw hat. There are no other boats in sight, nor land or skyline to speak of. There is nothing to do but torture oneself with narrations of what will happen to the family left behind. My emotions scatter through the prism of the rolling saltwater. The waves beckon me to remember the peaceful, fun times of my youth spent with friends and family on the beach. I remember holding my daughter in my arms when she was a baby. She was so alien yet so magnificent. And then there was Sam, with his dimple and green eyes, that beautiful smile with those gorgeous white teeth and full lips.

I see a water snake swim by and think of my dear sister, who always made sure I ate well, from the crepes to the field snake, from the fried bananas to the coconut mango sticky rice. Her love surpassed all boundaries and she showed it through food. I was such an ungrateful and selfish brat to her all my life. I cannot help but feel responsible somehow for my family's suffering, with Father's death, Hải's punishment, Tâm's arrest…even my failed marriage to Tý.

Darkness falls upon us as the night chill sets in. Stars raid the sky and the blackness of the sea pollutes my emotions, turning them from remorse to emptiness and despair. What if this is all for nothing and we die right here, right now? What if we are not rescued tomorrow but must endure days or weeks wandering hopelessly in this vast shimmer? I close my eyes and pray, tuning in to God's voice. Only the sounds of eerie silence echoes back. Too tired, weak and hungry, I invite sleep to come, but even that is too much to ask.

The longest ten minutes go by. Tree breaks the strange quietness by peeing over the side of the boat. One by one, people pop up to relieve themselves into the sea. Grunts, groans, and farts orchestrate our movements. At least we are still alive.

And then the climactic ending to our symphony…The engine sputters.

Hồng-Mai lets out a sharp, screeching sound. Tùng rushes to his sister's side. "What is the matter?"

"My cramps are getting worse." She takes out the *Tiger Balm* salve and spreads it on her stomach.

"Rub it on your feet. Your feet have more pores and the menthol will absorb faster," I say. "A doctor once told me that."

The smell of menthol, eucalyptus and wintergreen oils remind me of my injured toe. I remove my sock and the bandage to inspect it. My big toe is white and wrinkled but is otherwise fine. The engine sputters again. Minh-Tú takes the key out of the ignition and disappears to pour the last canister of fuel into the boat. It roars back to life and we continue our journey toward the Philippines.

Snitch perks up like a meerkat. "A ship!"

My eyes follow in the direction where his finger is pointing. I stand up and wave my arms wildly. Sơn climbs onto the cabin top and waves our old Vietnamese flag. Tree takes off his shirt and joins Sơn. He ties the shirt sleeves around the bottom end of the flagpole, sets it on fire, and waves it in the air. He jumps up and down to get their attention. All able-bodied passengers on our boat are now on their feet, hollering, waving and jumping to flag the other boat's attention. It is unclear to me whether the boat is getting closer to us or farther away. A couple people whistle while others bang loudly against the boat to amplify our SOS. Minh-Tú blares our boat's horn repeatedly to signal our distress. It is no use. We might as well have been debating with Slanty-Eyes over some political issue because our pleas fell on deaf ears. The ship gets smaller and disappears off the face of the Earth.

Our forlorn efforts go unnoticed. I sit down and open my satchel. I take out Sam's book and the letters.

Tree stops me from opening them. "Stop torturing yourself. You always cry when you read their letters. Uncle Hải and Sam are gone. You need to let them go."

The ink on the airmail paper is smeared from me falling into the river. The thin sheets are warped and crunchy. The pages of the book are bent and the cover does not close all the way. I put them away and soothe my disappointment with some cucumbers that Sister Six packed.

I hand Thủy-Tiên a small cucumber. "If you chew slowly, you will trick your stomach into thinking you have a lot of food and it will feel full. It is a trick that your grandfather taught me."

We munch on our cucumbers slowly to savor the taste and prolong the supply. Tree stops eating and gives his piece to Thủy-Tiên. "I miss Grandfather."

"You are a lot like him in that you are resourceful," I say. "Before he was the principal of your school, he taught French. We lived on his pension. He raised seven children on his pension!"

"I remember my mom used to hand out money in the morning before school. I would buy pastries and treats, and Grandfather always asked me what I bought at the school."

"His favorite was the bánh bao chỉ," we say in unison.

Tree laughs. "I would give anything to have a taste of that glutinous rice mochi, filled with sweet mung bean paste and rolled in shredded coconut!"

"Your aunt Six makes the best desserts. She needs to write her recipes down. In Đà Lạt, where I taught mathematics, she would sometimes visit me and bring her latest experiments. My favorite was the yogurt. It was the right balance of sweet and tangy."

"Tell me about my other aunts and uncles," says Tree. "I do not remember them."

"Uncle Two died during the revolution against the French. Uncle Three was drafted to the military and died in the early part of the American War. Aunt Four and Uncle Five were twins and they died from pneumonia."

"A lot of deaths in our family," says Tree. "I remember when I was younger, like eight or nine years old, I saw oxcarts full of dead bodies behind the hospital by our house. The swollen bodies would be washed and dressed right there outside in the back and sometimes, they could not get to the bodies fast enough. More and more bodies got dumped, some without heads, most missing a limb. Days would go by and their flesh would smell ripe and the rot attracted all sorts of insects and rodents. It did not scare me though. I was curious and fascinated."

"That explains why you always ran toward the hospital when you heard the sirens!"

"I especially liked the interesting smell of dead bodies combined with the aroma of the coffee from the café across the road."

"You are a strange human being," I say. "The war was not so long ago yet I have managed to suppress its gravity. There was a time when we all ran to the bunker and hid when there was fighting or gunshots or bombings. The sounds of those AK-47s and M-16s were like a thousand bubble wraps popping at once."

"I liked the American GIs though," says Tree. "They are funny. One time, it was raining and I was kicking the soccer ball around in the house. I heard some yelling outside and was amused to see a group of soldiers running and jumping on each other, yelling and chasing after a man that had a ball. They were covered in mud and looked crazy tackling each other over a small ball."

Tree and I continue reminiscing about life in our home country. We talk for hours and enjoy our rice that has been hand-packed into small balls. Before long, omnipresent clouds roll across the sky and the sun runs off to hide. Our little boat prepares to host the uninvited guests. Thunder and lightning burst onto the scene. A few people seek shelter under the deck and some, including Tree and me, pull a tarp over our head. The rain pelts it's vengeance onto the plastic cover and gives us front row tickets to the loudest concert we have ever attended. Sơn opens the gas containers to catch the rain. We are all wet and cold. Our small boat is tossed around like an egg and us its yolk.

Below deck, people are thrown side to side, getting seasick and throwing up. I grab hold of Thủy-Tiên and tightly cling to the cleats bolted to the boat's toe rail. Relentlessly, the storm continues all through the night, and I take advantage of the rain to pee my pants where I sit.

***

Day three. Sơn does a head count to make sure we did not lose anyone during the storm. "All forty-three of us are still here. The rain last night spared us and replenished our water supply."

"We barely survived!" says a woman sitting behind Sơn. I notice her belly is swollen and realize she is pregnant. "You said we would be rescued after a day, but we have only seen one boat!"

"We are all going to starve to death and die out here," says a man next to her.

"You were instructed to pack some food," says Sơn. "I provided you with water, rice, and jicamas. After the water is gone, we are all on our own."

"We ate what we brought already," says the man. "My wife is six months pregnant."

"She can drink some water and take what she needs, but it is not my fault you did not bring enough food or paced yourselves, and it certainly is not my fault that you risked your wife's and unborn child's life!" says Sơn.

The man lunges at Sơn and takes a swing at his face. Sơn falls back and gets entangled with other people's arms and legs. The two of them try to throw punches but are too weak to cause any damage. It becomes a shoving and blaming contest.

Despite the distraction, I catch Snitch taking big gulps of water from the canister. "You are drinking all the water!" Others do the same and pass the three canisters around to their family members.

"Give me that," demands the pregnant woman. Her husband grabs one of the canisters and trips over a toddler.

I try to subdue the situation before it gets out of control. "Stop! Everyone, we are wasting our energy fighting. We came here together and we will either die together or survive together. I propose we combine whatever food or drinks we have and share equally amongst ourselves, as we did with the jicamas and the rice."

"Who made you the boss?" yells a man behind me.

"That is a good idea," says the pregnant woman.

Snitch sneers at the pregnant woman. "Of course you would say that, but what do you have to contribute?"

"Do you speak to your family this way?" I ask the boy. "We have to take care of each other. Right now, we are each other's family. We have a pregnant woman who needs our strength. We have a boy," and I point at Snitch, "who is traveling alone without his family and he risked his life to bring us this boat. I have a sick daughter who needs medical attention for her heart. We all are running away from the same thing and we all have the same dreams of freedom."

"Sister Tuyết is right," says Hồng-Mai. "We are in this together. My brother and I do not have much, but we will share with our new family what we have." She takes out the *Tiger Balm* ointment, sanitary napkins, two mangos, a small knife, some dried, shredded squid, and a small loaf of stale bread, and places the items on her lap.

"Hồng-Mai, thank you," I say. "My family is adding to this community pile a jar of sliced lemons soaked in water and sugar, what is left of the valerian root medicine, a bag of peanuts, dried bananas, coconut meat, coconut water, and glow sticks."

"I have some jackfruit, two cans of beer, a bottle of cognac, and a bottle of *Malathion*." Minh-Tú shrugs. "This is my suicide kit."

I stare at him in disbelief. "What is *Malathion*?"

"Insecticide," he answers.

"Keep that poison away from my daughter." I place a protective hand on Thủy-Tiên.

"We can put everything, except for the pesticide, in here." Sơn hands Hồng-Mai a burgundy duffel bag. "I have a few pieces of the jicama to add. Since this was Sister Tuyết's idea, she can be in charge of distribution."

The bag gets passed around and everyone contributes what they have. The husband and wife who are expecting a baby throw money into the bag.

"Since we are now family, we should all introduce ourselves." Tùng's optimism and energy is infectious. "I can start."

The rest of the day we share our stories and introduce ourselves. I learn that Snitch's real name is Thành and that he is thirteen years old. His family committed suicide a year after the fall of Sài Gòn by poisoning themselves, but he survived. To stay alive, he did odd jobs for Sơn, who lived in the same hamlet.

Sơn was in the army and after the war ended, he reported to the police station to serve his mandatory few weeks of re-education. However, he was there for over a year. After he got out, he and his friend, who was going to captain this boat before he got caught, attempted to leave the country five times. They first had a raft but that quickly fell apart. They tried stealing an old woman's boat but she caught them and her husband tried to shoot them. Other attempts were made but they all failed for one reason or another.

I learn that the pregnant woman's name is Tiền and that the baby is due end of April. Her husband's name is Trương, and he hopes their first baby is a boy. They used to have a large rice production company but the government seized their property and sent them packing to one of the new economic zones.

Hồng-Mai and Tùng are Chinese. They left their parents behind to join their sister and her family in Australia, with the hopes of sponsoring their parents over later.

Minh-Tú was a farmer and a fisherman. He and his wife had eleven children. He and his three sons were arrested and spent two years in a re-education camp, because they provided food and shelter to the South Vietnamese army. His sons died in the prisons and he was released because he was so close to death, the guards were convinced he was going to die anyway. He recovered but discovered his wife and daughters replaced him with another man. He is on this journey alone, adrift with a broken heart.

Everyone's story is unique yet heartrending. To lighten the mood, we sing some songs, recite poems, tell jokes, and even re-enact some scenes from a famous Chinese movie. By nightfall, we brace ourselves for another storm, but it does not come.

"We are out of fuel." I open my eyes and see Minh-Tú.

"How long have we been drifting?" I ask.

"I am not sure," he answers. "It must have happened during the night when we were all sleeping. I have no idea where we are."

"I thought Snitch, I mean Thành, was helping you navigate."

"He was, but he fell asleep."

Tree lifts up one of the fuel containers and surveys what is inside. "Everyone is going to panic once they wake up and realize what is happening." He tilts the container back and sucks out what is left of the contents.

"I thought they were all empty," I say.

Tree cringes and chokes. "They are, but there was a sliver of water floating above the oil."

"You drank the gasoline?" I ask in shock.

"Aunt Eight, I am so parched and dehydrated. I checked the bag and all the coconut water and lemons were gone – rinds, seeds, everything. Even the beer cans are empty. The only thing left is the cognac."

"Nothing else?" asks Sơn.

"Only things we cannot eat, like the money that aunt Tiền and uncle Trương threw in, the feminine napkins, medicine…The only things that can be consumed are the cognac and sunflower seeds. Someone stole the rest of the jicama."

I throw a suspicious glance at Snitch.

"If we are going to die out here, it is better to die drunk than die back home from starvation, malnutrition and under communist control," says Minh-Tú.

"If we see any fishing boats, maybe we can buy some fish with the money and the cognac. Thủy-Tiên received forty thousand đồng in her red envelope from Doctor Đức. How much did he give you?" I ask Tree.

"One-hundred," says Tree.

"Wake everybody up and we will distribute the last of the sunflower seeds," says Sơn.

***

We drift aimlessly all day with the heat of the sun beating down with such malice and contempt. Many of the elderly, the women, and the children take refuge down below to escape the intensity of the rays. It is not any better down there with the rancid smells of urine, vomit, and bad body odor. Hour by hour, we get weaker and more delirious. I see Tree scoop up some ocean water to drink. I try to tell him it will make it worse, but I am too late.

Another day makes an encore. We have been on the run for five nights and four days, battling everything from the mosquitos on the peninsula to the storm at sea, and now, the cruelest punisher of all, nothingness. We are all too ill from the big waves, the hot days and cold nights. Those below deck vomit and pee where they sit and pass out from the stale air and foul smells. I sit here contemplating if I should eat the money that is in the red envelopes. Will that help the hunger pains subside? I pray for some rain but none comes. We are in dire straits. Thủy-Tiên sleeps beside me with the green silk tunic covering her head.

"Boat," whispers Tree. He points.

I sit up and sure enough, there is a boat. We siphon the last ounce of energy left and try to get the boat's attention. It turns and heads toward us, getting bigger and bigger. I am ecstatic.

After ten minutes, the elation is replaced with fear. Two vessels, both with Thai flags, pull up and tether our boat to theirs. I count seven dark-skinned, shirtless men, armed with knives, hammers, and rifles. Five of them board our boat while the other two stay with their vessel. Their sinister faces are premonitions of what is to come. The women on our boat yell and scream in fear. Some of them try to make themselves hideous by tousling their hair and rubbing grease on their face or vomit on their body. Like me, they have heard stories of girls getting brutally raped or kidnapped by the Thai pirates. They continue to be assaulted by gangs of fishermen, even after the girls hemorrhage out and die. Others get sold into slavery or deposited onto a deserted island, only to be repeatedly violated at the mercy of these men's whims.

One of the pirates, the shortest one with curly hair, wearing a

192

sarong and a headband, speaks to his crew. I am guessing he is the operator behind this. I cannot understand anything he says. Stricken with fear and wasted from lack of food, we all stand or sit in our place, immobile. I wrap my protective talons around Thủy-Tiên and avoid eye contact.

The same pirate speaks to us in English. "Men over here. Women over there."

They separate us, even the babies and children. The leader rummages through our belongings and searches the boat for valuables, finding gold, jewelry, money and the bottle of cognac. Two of the pirates stand guard in front of our men, threatening them with guns and machetes. The other two pirates walk to our group of women and hold us hostage. There are fifteen of us women, ranging from twenty-three years old to seventy years old, a two-month-old infant, and my daughter, age four. The pirate with the curly hair lifts my chin with his knife to get a good look at my face. He smiles at me before diverting his attention to Tiền, the woman who is six months pregnant. His eyes scan down to her swollen belly before diverting his attention to a young mother holding her two-month-old daughter. He grabs her wrist and drags her toward his boat. She cries out and resists. The rest of us try to protect her and pull her back, but his companions punch us in the face and hit us with hammers. The young woman's husband screams for mercy and begs them to leave his wife alone. He receives a blow to the head with the butt of a rifle for his outcry. They throw him overboard. One of the pirates uses a pole to jab him and keep him submerged. The pirate laughs like it is a game. The young woman is lifted up onto one of the vessels. She kicks and screams while still holding her baby tight. Four more women get separated from us and taken aboard the other boats. The rest of us are forced below deck with the hatch locked. The anguished screams of women getting raped, while the baby cries and the pirates cheer, haunt me. Sơn, Minh-Tú, Tree, and Tùng try to break open the hatch.

An hour goes by and the cries have stopped. There is splashing in the water and moments later, the engines fire up and the two boats drive off. I am stunned. I close my eyes and pray, letting the tears escape. I smell something burning and realize our boat is on fire. There is panic below deck and screams coming from both inside the boat and outside in the water. The men take turns trying to force the hatch open and finally are able to break free. We clamber out and work together to smother the fire.

I grab one of the fuel canisters to fill it up with water and spot the five women in the ocean. "Tree, Snitch, help them into the boat!"

As the women are being pulled into the boat, the rest of us fill up the three canisters and douse the fire. We stomp on the flames and beat it back with our shirts. Finally, the fire is extinguished.

We all weep, relieved that the boat is still intact. I stumble to the women who were raped. All of them are shaking. One of them is hysterical. I realize her baby is not with her. I rush to the port and starboard of the boat. My eyes dart side to side, far and near, praying for a miracle. I run to the stern, and the miracle I was hoping for appeared. The young husband treads closer to the boat and in his arm is his infant daughter. His face shows pain and exhaustion. I take the baby from him. As soon as the baby is in my arms, the young man slips underneath the water. Tree dives in and lifts him back up to keep his head above water. Sơn and Minh-Tú pull him into the boat and lend a hand to my nephew.

All forty-three of us are alive and back on the boat…Safe for now.

The young husband and wife with their two-month-old daughter are now safe, but brewing underneath their tears of relief is pain. This experience will surely leave them scarred for the rest of their lives. I pray it will not tear their family apart.

I notice there are red whip lashes on the young husband's leg. "What is your name again?"

The young husband is barely audible. "Tú."

"I had a neighbor also named Tú," I share.

"My wife's name is Thảo and our daughter is Mỹ-Linh."

"I am Tuyết," I say. "You are in pain."

"There were some jellyfish in the water," Tú responds. "My leg is tingling and itchy. There is intense pain all over the area I got stung."

"Hopefully the burning sensation will go away in a few hours. As soon as we find land, we will see if that can get treated."

"Can you check on my wife? She will not talk to me or acknowledge my existence." Tú breaks down and sobs. "I could not protect them."

"Give her time. She went through something horrific. You saved your daughter and kept yourself alive for your family. You are a hero in my opinion." I make my way to the five who were victimized.

Hồng-Mai and some of the elders tend to the traumatized women. They are shivering but not because it is cold. Nothing can make things right or better. I am afraid to touch them and comfort them as they may find my presence repulsive. I cannot give them water or even cognac to soothe them. I sit in front of Thảo. She clutches her daughter so tight that the baby cries.

"Sister Thảo, let me take care of Mỹ-Linh," I say. "She is

crying because you are crushing her and she cannot breathe."

Thảo loosens her grip but does not voluntarily hand the baby over to me. I gently ease my arms around Mỹ-Linh and slowly pull her into my lap. Thảo does not object. I rock the baby and hush her until she is calm. If only the heavens could open up right now and send milk down to our little blue boat.

We drift aimlessly for hours and I stare into the vast distance, dazed by the cruel and perilous events of today. I realize that if our boat was attacked by Thai fishermen then we are no longer heading east toward the Philippines. Without fuel to steer the trawler, we have drifted south near the Gulf of Thailand. This could mean more pirate attacks. We are like fish in a barrel for these pirates to do as they please without any consequences, without any police to patrol the area and protect us.

Tree states the obvious to me. "We cannot go back to Việt Nam and we are not heading towards the Philippines." My nephew sits down next to me with Thủy-Tiên in his arms. "If we are lucky, we will end up in Malaysia." My daughter leans over to kiss me on the cheek and then kisses the baby's head. What an empathetic and tender child. I lean down to kiss her on the head.

"Tree, eventually we will see land and when we do, we need to get Uncle Tú medicine for his stings and these women examined," I say. "I will need your help."

"I know," he responds.

Thảo sits completely still, her eyes closed. The faint rise and fall of her chest reassure me she is sleeping. I lean against Tree, back to back, and drift off to sleep to pass the time.

I dream that my stomach has come to life and is eating itself. I become an emaciated zombie with a hole in my lower torso. My hunger for meat has me tearing into my boat companions' flesh, biting down to the layer of fat. I relish the taste and am hungry for more. I see a four-year-old girl, her skin is smooth and white, her arms plump and juicy. She screams from my first bite.

"Wake up." Tree shakes me vigorously.

I open my eyes. Thủy-Tiên is screaming. Tú, Sơn, and Minh-Tú peer over the side of the boat. They are in a panic. The rest of the crew is powerless to do anything. Mỹ-Linh is not in my arms and Thảo is not sitting in front of me. I lean over the boat. There is only darkness in the water. Tú jumps into the ocean and dives down, in desperate search for his wife and daughter.

"Someone go with him!" I urge. "He was stung by jellyfish

earlier. He will not last long in the freezing water."

No one jumps in to brave a rescue. There are many creatures lurking beneath the calm darkness of the sea. Before I can plead my case to Tree, my nephew takes off his shoes and simply says, "I know."

"Take this with you." I take out a *Cyalume* light stick from the duffel bag. I tear the wrapper away, bend the tube until it snaps, and then shake the stick until it illuminates. "Cường gave me these military glow sticks to sell and I ended up keeping them for myself."

"It looks like a giant firefly." Tree dives into the menacing abyss. He disappears for a couple minutes at a time before coming up for air.

Sơn and Minh-Tú jump in as well. I give them both a glow stick. The three of them are now searching for Thảo, Tú and their daughter Mỹ-Linh. Their heads bob up like musical notes but never in sync. As soon as one disappears, another one reappears.

"Watch Thủy-Tiên." I hand over my satchel to Snitch. "I am going to help. They are getting tired."

"It is no use," he protests. "They are gone."

"We have to try." I jump into the cold water with another glow stick.

The view under the water is incredible. Below I see some exotic aquatic life, mostly different varieties of coral, fish of all sizes, an eel and some starfish. I keep hoping I will find Thảo and her husband, Tú, and their baby, Mỹ-Linh, but my gut tells me Thành is right. Their bodies have probably been claimed by the sea. Their spirits will never embrace peace. A breathtaking blue glow in the water catches my attention and seduces me to come closer. Someone touch my arm. Tree points up toward the surface. We swim up and catch our breath.

"Did you find them?" I cling to the side of the boat.

Tree shakes his head. "We should not venture farther."

I nod in agreement. We climb back into the boat where Sơn and Minh-Tú are already waiting.

"What should we do now?" asks Sơn. "Three people in our group committed suicide. Should we say a prayer?"

"We all should pay our respects silently." I shiver and wrap my arms around myself. "When we reach land, I want to have a veneration service in their memory."

"Did you see the stretch of blue lights glowing in the distance?" Tree asks. "It is so beautiful."

"Yes. The last time I saw the sea sparkle like that was when I was in Hạ Long Bay," I say.

"You saw bioluminescence?" Minh-Tú jumps with excitement. "We are close to land!"

"What makes you think that?" I ask.

"Every time I witness these blue lights, the view is always from a coast," he answers.

"Well, since you have only navigated rivers, never oceans, of course you would only see them from shore," I say.

Minh-Tú sits down and ponders what I said. We all settle into our spot and try to get some sleep. It is hard to reconcile straight when you are hungry, cold, and tired. Some of the people on the boat have not stirred since the pirate attack earlier today. They are too weak, too famished, or too seasick. Left with only my self-sabotaging thoughts to keep me company, I ask God how much longer we will drift. Will it be days or weeks? How many more pirate attacks can our group take? Will we survive another one? I imagine Thủy-Tiên dying in my arms in the middle of nowhere, below the deceptively peaceful sky, and above the mighty waves of this ocean. How much longer will her heart beat before it, too, gives up on life? I remember my crazy dream of resorting to cannibalism to stay alive. Who would I eat first? Or perhaps I would be somebody's supper? I am getting delirious. I close my eyes and try to conjure an image of Sam's face. That was a lifetime ago.

"I see trees," says Snitch.

"Me too," says Tree.

I open my eyes and see silhouettes far away, poking out from the horizon.

"Land!" cries out Sơn.

"We should drop our anchor," suggests Minh-Tú. "Get a good night's rest and then, in the morning, figure out how to safely get to shore."

***

The sun's warm glow rouses me awake. I stand up to stretch and am greeted by stark, unapologetic stares from eight sets of black eyes. Dark-skinned men sitting in kayaks and canoes with fishing nets greet me with curiosity. They smile and wave. I conclude they are non-threatening.

"Hello," I say in Vietnamese. "We need help getting to shore. Can you help us?"

Some of them speak but I do not understand them. I repeat

198

myself in English, but they once again respond in their native tongue. None of them understand me.

Minh-Tú tries to communicate to the fishermen that we want to get to shore. He points at our boat and then points to the shore. Sơn joins in the charade. He points to them and mimics them pulling a rope. I put my hands together and wave it side to side, to imitate a fish swimming.

"Ya, ya," says one of them.

"I think they finally understand our gestures." I breathe a sigh of relief and jump with jubilation. I pick Thủy-Tiên up and wrap my arms around Tree's shoulder. The soft breeze of the early morning caresses the hair tendrils away from my ears and the warmth of the sun kisses my face. It is good to be alive. Sơn pulls up the anchor and Minh-Tú throws down our ropes to the fishermen.

"Are we in America?" asks Thủy-Tiên.

"No, my dolly, we are in Indonesia. See the flag on that man's kayak?" I point to the last green boat leaving the coast. "These men are helping us to shore. They are pulling us in slowly so we do not crash into the big reefs. If we approach too fast, the reef below can split our boat." I point down to the water, as smooth and clear as glass, so she can see.

"Those are so big, like the size of a house," she says.

"The water is still quite deep and we are still far from shore. You can stand here but hold my hand or Brother Tree's. I do not have the energy to swim right now if you fall in."

The islanders work their magic, pulling and guiding our small boat towards the shoreline. We weave around the reefs and Minh-Tú expertly and patiently maneuvers the trawler over and around large rocks. We get as close to shore as possible to disembark. Those who have energy to swim jump off and do so. Those who do not know how to swim or are too weak, hold onto a plank of wood and are pulled by a fellow swimmer. I lift Thủy-Tiên onto my hip. I make eye contact with one of the fishermen. I point to my daughter, then to his canoe, hoping he understands my request for a ride.

He nods. "Ya."

I ease my daughter down. She dangles from my arms while the fisherman lifts up his arms to receive her.

"Stop!" A uniformed official approaches us in a canoe, taxied by another fisherman. He speaks authoritatively in English through a megaphone. "You cannot stay on this island."

I hoist my daughter back into the boat. Those of us on the boat who understand English are up in arms and visibly upset. The hell we have been through is unexpectedly extended, making previous moments of mercy only teasers.

Hồng-Mai joins me by my side. "What is he saying?" I translate for her and watch the blood drain from her face.

"This island only has four hundred people and is not a refugee camp," the official says. "You need to go to the bigger island, another six hours journey." He points to the sea behind us, but to no defining direction. "You cannot stay here. We can provide you some fuel and sustenance before helping you back out to sea."

The official ignores our pleas. He speaks to the fishermen in their native tongue and one by one, the canoes leave. The men head out to sea to resume their fishing plans for the morning. Twenty minutes later, a small boat comes to retrieve us. It makes multiple trips to bring all forty of us to shore. At last, I am sitting on a beach, thankful to be on land, and am elated for the hospitality, despite the temporary extension. Shortly afterwards, food, water, and fuel are brought to us. Men dressed in olive green uniforms hand out bowls of rice, canned sardines, fresh mangosteens, sugar apples, and passion fruit.

I go straight for the water. "This is the sweetest, most divine water I have ever drunk." The cold liquid trickles down my throat but does not satiate the thirst.

Thủy-Tiên buries her face in the cup and asks for more water. We turn our attention to the food and dive in with our fingers, picking up every morsel like wild island monkeys. I try to savor each bite and eat like a lady, but after the first two pinches of rice and sardines, I give in to the animalistic hunger. *Forget it.* I scarf the food down.

After our thirst is quenched and our bellies satisfied, we sit and socialize with each other like civilized and polite members of the extended family. I laugh with Thủy-Tiên, Tree, Minh-Tú, Sơn, Snitch, Hồng-Mai and Tùng. The stress from being out at sea for five days evaporates through my pores. Even my big toe that was injured by the acacia thorn is unburdened and feeling nourished. The four women who were raped by pirates show some signs of renewed life and hope. They eat and speak with Trương and his pregnant wife, Tiền. The group relaxes and takes full advantage of the hospitality for a few hours.

Later in the afternoon, a boat approaches. It is a wood boat similar to ours, but much bigger. The official tells us it is time to leave. And with one sweep of his arm and a flick of his wrist, he rewinds our journey. Once more, we load onto a small boat and are taken back to our trawler. Three trips back and forth before we are all onboard the tiny boat that represents both freedom and a death sentence. We load the canister of fuel, a jug of water, and some plain, cooked rice that was donated to us by the Indonesian officials, onto our boat. As the big boat pulls our smaller boat out to sea, I notice the officials have quickly disappeared. The beach clears and is deserted. Empty, like we were never there. Funny thing about human existence - One day we exist in this world. We breathe, we laugh, and we love. We experience hardships, we go to work, and we enjoy our time with friends, family, and other passions. And then, our bodies slow down. We age, we die, and then we are invisible to those who loved us and talked to us every day. The farther I get from the sandy shores, the more distant and withdrawn my spirit becomes, and the stress of life reenters the pores of my skin.

The larger boat picks up speed and causes big waves that jostle our little boat. It thrashes up and down uncontrollably. We are air-born for a few seconds before crashing down on the hard surface of the sea. Over and over we helplessly bob up and down, powerless to change our fate. People are getting seasick now and some are throwing up the food they ate. We yell out and ask them to slow down but the people on the mightier boat cannot hear us, nor can they understand us.

"Our boat is getting battered." Sơn can no longer handle the bumpy ride and cuts the ropes. The large boat slows down and circles back to us. Sơn waves this appreciation. "We can go alone from here."

The captain of the mightier boat points in the distance. "Galang". The big boat returns to its point of origin and is soon a speck on the horizon.

Minh-Tú steers our boat slowly. "It is another six hours before we get to Galang Island and that is assuming we are heading in the right direction."

"Now that we have seen land and been on one of the Riau islands, I do not want to risk our lives back out at sea," says Sơn.

"There is no guarantee that we will not be boarded by pirates again or that our engine will not fail on us," I say.

"We will surely die out there if Galang does not receive us or if we are not rescued by another boat along the way," says Tùng.

Hồng-Mai whispers to me. "My menstrual cycle started. All the jumping waves unplugged the dam."

I address Sơn and Minh-Tú. "We have to return to the island and beg for temporary asylum. The Indonesians will have to figure out what to do with us."

Sơn agrees. "We will keep sight of the island and circle slowly around. We can wait until nightfall and make our way back undetected."

"I will not take us far," says Minh-Tú. "We are already vulnerable this far out."

The stars get brighter and the moon relieves the sun from duty. Under cover of night, our boat heads back to the island.

"I have seared into my memory how to get us back and mapped out in my mind how to navigate around the reefs to get close to shore." Minh-Tú puts his hands on his waist.

"We should burn our boat and force them to let us stay," says Sơn. "That will buy us some time."

"Anything is better than staying out here another night," adds Snitch.

Hồng-Mai scoots over to me. "The blood flow is getting heavier. I fear it will soak through my pants."

I hand her a pair of socks. "Tuck this in your underwear to absorb the blood. You can wash your handkerchief and let it dry to reuse."

"Now?" she asks.

"No. Wait until we get to shore, otherwise we will become dinner for the sharks."

Sơn interrupts our conversation. "When we get close enough, the last person off the boat needs to set it on fire."

Minh-Tú volunteers. "I will do it."

I remind myself of Dr. Đức's message, that no matter how difficult things get, the struggle back home eclipses any adversity I will face on my journey for freedom in America. This will all be worth it.

Sơn surveys our group. "Who cannot swim?"

Three adults raise their hand plus one four-year-old child…mine.

I kneel down and hug my daughter. "Little dolly, we will use a plank of wood from the hatch for you. You can sit on it, and I will push you to shore."

"What about the babies?" asks one of the mothers on board. "How do we get the babies to shore?"

"We will get the boat as close as possible and hopefully if the water is shallow, you can walk to shore with your baby in your arms," answers Sơn.

"But what if it is too deep?" she asks.

"We can use the planks of wood and set the children on top, and push them to shore as we swim beside it. Do not worry, we are all here to help one another," I say.

"But I cannot swim and I am too big to sit on a piece of wood." An elderly man, wafer thin and weighing only forty-five kilograms at most, voices his concern.

"If you cannot swim, find a partner who can. Then hold on tight to their neck," says Sơn.

"But try not to strangle them or you both will drown," warns Minh-Tú.

The non-swimmers plead with fellow passengers and try to convince others to give them a ride on his or her water-taxi backs. They finally sort it out and we approach the shore feeling assured on what to do. That is, until we are greeted by AK-47s.

Warning shots fire near our boat. Bullets plunge into the water around us and whiz by our heads. I cover Thủy-Tiên's head and duck down. People take cover where they can - below deck, behind the engine compartment, inside the cabin, or flat on the deck. Some of us have nowhere to go so we lie on top of other people and pile up two or three people high. The bullets hit our boat. Splinters of wood shatter and separate from the deck and prow. I cover my head and yell Tree's name.

He answers back. "I would gladly trade these bullets for mosquitos!"

A couple of people who are sitting on the roof of the cabin get hit from stray bullets that ricochet off the stern. Our boat crashes into a big rock and a loud noise ripples through the dark. The impediment to the forward momentum of our boat thrusts everyone forward. Screams of fright bring shivers up and down my body and raise the hairs on my neck. Terror crosses Thủy-Tiên's face and I hug her close. A bullet grazes Minh-Tú's ear. He groans and hunkers down.

"There is an oil leak," someone yells out.

"The boat is broken," yells Sơn. "Everyone jump off and swim!"

More bullets blaze by. I scramble to get the wood from the hatch and grab it. A woman tries to pry it from my hands. It is fight or flight time. I step on her foot and tear the plank of wood from her grip. She cries out. I throw the piece of wood into the water, swoop Thủy-Tiên up in one arm, and jump. I aim for the driftwood and grab it. Thủy-Tiên climbs on. She sits cross-legged and bends down to hold onto the sides. Her left cheek rests on the wet surface. Her eyes seize mine.

"Keep your eyes on Mama, and do not let go," I say. She nods.

Others jump in, one by one or in pairs. A bright light illuminates the dark sky. Our little fishing boat is ablaze. Red and orange flames dance sacrificially upward while below in the sea, heads of black hair bob up and down. Cries blend in with the sounds of AK-47s ripping through the night. I weep for the little trawler, sad that it is dying a slow, painful death, yet grateful that it got us this far.

The shooting stops. I swim to shore, pushing the plank of wood, while Tree swims on the other side of us.

A man howls in pain. "I stepped on a damn sea urchin." He wades to shore, wincing and hobbling as he goes.

The Indonesian military waits for us on the beach. Their leader speaks to us in English. "My name is Abu and I am in charge here. Kneel with your hands behind your back." His men force us all on our knees. No one in the group dares to speak. The injured stifle their pain. "Who set the boat on fire?" We are all mute. Abu asks again and once more, we choke back our fears. He bends down and thrusts his face inches from Minh-Tú's. "Was it you?"

Minh-Tú says nothing. Abu kneels down to Sơn's level and asks Sơn the same question, but Sơn shakes his head. The commander goes down the line and stops in front of the poor man who stepped on a sea urchin. He tries to intimidate the man by staring into his eyes, challenging him to confess. The man whimpers in pain.

Frustrated, the commander orders his men to incentivize us. The cadres attack the men in our group with kicks to the face, punches to the body, or rifle butts to the head. Young or old, every man is beaten. They spare the women and children, including Tree and Snitch. The men do not fight back. I am afraid for their life. Still, no one speaks up.

Abu calls for a halt. "I have shown you nothing but hospitality. We showed you how to get to the nearest refugee camp but instead, you spit at our help. Your defiance deserves punishment. Let us see how long you survive on your own here without our help."

The military leaves us. I let out a big sigh, thankful they are gone. I stand up and mourn our pathetic little boat, still on fire and putting on a show for the waxing crescent in the sky. Below our feet, the sand is speckled with blood from the beatings and bullet wounds. Above us, the bright stars are like a million alien eyes peeking through peepholes of a black curtain; they witness our sad scene. Thủy-Tiên holds my hand. Together we witness our boat burning in the distance. I shall never forget this picture.

"We should find a place to sleep." Tree digs a sandpit and fills it with branches, leaves, and whatever he can find in the brush, including a dirty, torn, plastic poncho and a pair of mismatched flip-flops. Hồng-Mai and her brother settle in next to us.

"How is your stomach?" I ask Hồng-Mai.

"I almost forgot about my cramps from this ordeal," she answers.

"I forgot my satchel on the boat." I am miserable that Sam's book, his letter, and Hải's letter are gone forever.

"What was in it?"

"A book and some letters." I roll over and turn my back to her. "Get some sleep."

"Going to sleep in wet clothes while your uterus bleeds out is no fun."

I turn back over and face her. "On the hopeful side, maybe your menstruation will turn the sea red and Moses will appear to lead us to the Promised Land." I joke wryly, but she gives me a curious expression.

I tell her the biblical story of Moses leading the Israelites out of slavery by parting the Red Sea with his staff, how the Egyptians all drowned, and how they came to the land of Canaan safely, as God promised.

"Buddha teaches us to have perseverance. Only then can we overcome our obstacles," says Hồng-Mai, "although, I am willing to believe in your God if it means by tomorrow we are delivered to the promised land."

We chat some more until our eyelids anchor us into slumber. The boat people of trawler 93752 finally surrender to sleep.

***

As exhausted as I am, I am restless most of the night. I flounder around, trying to steal heat from Thủy-Tiên's little body or Tree's. My dreams race back to distant memories and catalog all my experiences, from the zenith of my happiness to the nadir of my miseries, and everything in between. My university days were when I was happiest, studying with my friends, going to the cafes or the beach, daydreaming about my future spouse that I had yet to find.

A rustling sound brings me back to consciousness. I blink a couple times to let my eyes adjust to the darkness. I see four men from the Indonesian military snooping around our sleeping bodies searching for valuables. One of them finds nothing and walks toward Hồng-Mai and me. I close my eyes and pretend to sleep.

Hồng-Mai cries out. "No!" I open my eyes to see her gripping the waist of her pants while the cadre is tugging at them. Hồng-Mai sees that I am awake and begs me to help. "Sister, please tell him not to hurt me."

I cannot pretend I am asleep anymore and must do something. I see Mrs. Trần in my mind's eye and she reminds me that my tongue is my greatest artillery. "This woman on her monthly cycle."

My English startles the cadre. He stops. His face leaves me breathless. I want to hate him but he is the most handsome Asian man I have ever seen. There is something exotic and masculine about his symmetrical features. His face is perfectly shaped by a strong, defined jawline and the bridge of his nose is high and strong. Even his ears are perfect in size and shape and stick out the right amount, level with his almond-shaped eyes. He regards me inquisitively, as if I am familiar to him, like a long-lost lover. What captivates me most are his full lips and the thick strands of blue-black hair on his head. The character lines on his face do not make him appear old, but rather, distinguished and mature. He is beautiful.

He breaks the gaze and speaks. "She is hiding something in her clothes." He tries to lift up her shirt so that he can pull down her pants. "She is hiding gold."

Hồng-Mai cries out in protest.

"Gold take by Thai pirates," I say. "The boat and sea take everything. We have nothing."

"You are lying," he says. "She is hiding something. They are always hiding something."

"Not her. You only find blood." The man continues to tug at Hồng-Mai's pants. "What will your leader, Abu, say tomorrow when he find out?"

The man pauses. "You will not tell him anything."

I notice the name stitched on his uniform and address him boldly. "No, Ommo, I will not tell if you take your friends and leave now."

I hold my breath and tense my muscles firm. I challenge him with my eyes. My heart is pounding fast. I am afraid of what he might do next, but I channel all the strength of Mrs. Trần and Sister Six into my psyche. I imagine them with me and together, we are an army ready for battle.

He relents and stands up to leave. He waves his men to go with him. He is taller than the other three men. His physique is lean and even under the dull glow of the moon and stars, I can see the muscles pressed against his cotton shirt and the tattoo peeking out from the short sleeves. I wait for them to disappear out of sight and then let out a long sigh of relief. Hồng-Mai hugs me. We both tremble.

***

In the early morning, I see some of the Indonesian fishermen paddle out with their kayaks and canoes. What a sight we must be to them, vagabonds loitering on the beach with nowhere to go and nothing to do. Thủy-Tiên, Hồng-Mai, and her brother Tùng, are still asleep. Tree, however, is missing. I panic and stand up to see if he is with any of the others. I see Snitch stand up and stretch. My excitement sinks realizing that he is not Tree. I am distraught and count to see if anyone is missing. Thirty-nine people are accounted for and Tree is the only one missing.

"Have you seen my nephew?" I ask the man who stepped on a sea urchin last night. He shakes his head.

I ask several others who are nearby and awake but they have not seen Tree. I gently nudge Tùng and Hồng-Mai to wake up.

"I will go find him." Tùng takes off along the stretch of sand and asks anyone who is awake, including a couple of fishermen getting ready to head out in their woven boats. He cuts through the brush and disappears.

Thirty minutes pass and I see men appear from behind the dense brush. The Indonesian military are back. I recognize one of the men, but it is not Tùng or my nephew. It is Ommo from last night.

The commanding officer, Abu, addresses our group. "Who speaks English?"

I wait for someone to volunteer, but none of the men speak up after their beating last night. None of the women dare to speak, unsure of what will happen to them if they do confess.

I catch Ommo gawking at me. He knows I speak English and am afraid he will say something. However, informing on me would also blow his cover to the commander. Ommo leans in and whispers in Abu's ear.

Abu nods. "I need a translator so if you speak English, raise your hand, and I promise no harm will come to you."

Sơn raises his hand and so does the injured sea-urchin man. I raise my hand as well. Abu waves us over. I ask Hồng-Mai to keep an eye on Thủy-Tiên. The three of us walk over to Abu and his legion of men.

"What is your name?" Abu asks the injured man.

"Biện," he answers.

"Why are you limping?"

"I step on sea urchin last night," Biện answers.

"I overheard a rumor this morning that some of my men visited your group late last night," says Abu. "Is this true?"

Biện shakes his head. "I no see no one."

"What about you?" Abu questions Sơn.

He shakes his head. "No, sir, I sleeping. I see nothing."

Abu steps close to me. "And you? Did you see any of my men here last night?"

"No, sir Abu. It was peaceful night," I respond.

"You can tell the truth," he urges. "You will not be harmed."

"If I tell you, will you give my people some rice?" I ask.

Ommo pleads with his eyes not to say anything. I ignore him.

"What is your name?" Abu asks.

"Snow," I say. "Do we agree?"

"Snow, I promise to extend to your people the same hospitality as before if you tell me everything truthfully."

"Same hospitality as before?" I inquire. "Do you mean AK-47 hospitality or rice and sardines hospitality?"

Abu laughs. "You are a smart woman. I will have to keep my eyes on you. I promise you rice and sardines."

"That is good." I give him a sweet smile, still not trusting that he is a man of his word. "Last night, I hear sounds from the bushes and trees. I was scared."

A glimpse of nervousness comes from Ommo.

"Well, who was it? Can you point to identify them? Are any of those men here right now?"

"No. I only see saltwater crocodile come out of bushes and monkeys in trees."

"That is all?" Abu asks.

"Bats too," I say, "but that is all."

He drops the inquiry and calls out some orders to his men. They disperse. "My men will bring back some food," says Abu. "Ommo and Gus will stay here to make sure there is no trouble."

"Thank you sir Abu." I walk back to where Hồng-Mai and Thủy-Tiên are sitting.

Hồng-Mai leaps up and grabs a hold of my wrist. "What did he say?" I replay the conversation. Hồng-Mai is not happy with how I handled the situation. "Why did you not tell him what his men did? Why did you protect them?" She wants the four men punished.

"What is more important? For their commander to punish them or for us to eat and survive another day?" I pick up Thủy-Tiên and put her in my lap. "They did not harm us last night and they could have. They were only after gold. Because of what I did, we all get a meal and now Ommo and his bandits owe me. You see? I have a little leverage now."

"Use your leverage wisely then," Hồng-Mai says.

"I am worried about Tree. Where the hell is he?" The question barely escapes my lips when I see in the distance my nephew running towards the group wearing his underwear and carrying a bucket.

Thủy-Tiên is excited to see him. "Brother Tree!" She hops out of my lap to meet up with him. The two of them talk animatedly as he shows her what is in the bucket. She claps her hands and skips in the sand back to Hồng-Mai and me.

Tree stands before me dripping wet. I stand up and grab him by his right ear and pull him aside a couple meters. "Where did you go? I was so worried. You were gone a long time. What were you doing?"

Tree flinches. "You are hurting me."

"Do not interrupt." I pinch his arm. "You are my responsibility. You cannot leave without telling me where you are going."

"I did not want to wake you."

I slap his shoulder. "I said do not interrupt me. What if something happened to you? What if when you came back we were gone?"

"Where would you go?

I punch him in the arm. "If you interrupt me again, Tree, I would be justified to give you a beating."

"You are turning into Aunt Six."

I spank my nephew. Tree opens his mouth to say something but I give him the meanest, most serious expression I can, and he closes his mouth. "You better have a good explanation for disappearing. Brother Tùng went searching for you and he has not come back yet. What if something happens to him? How would you feel? You scared us. I have enough worries and after everything that we have been through, I cannot take any more. Never do that again. Do you understand?" Tree says nothing. "You can answer now."

"Yes, I understand and I am sorry. It will not happen again," he says. "Look what I have in the bucket!"

We walk back to where Hồng-Mai and Thủy-Tiên are squatting. I peer inside the bucket to see two coconuts and ten crabs.

"Can we keep them Mama?" asks Thủy-Tiên. "So pretty. We can give them names."

"They are food," I say. "We cannot give them names. It would not be right to eat our pets."

"But you gave your chicken a name!" Thủy-Tiên scrunches her face up to cry.

"Let her keep one, Aunt Eight." Tree pats her head. "There are many more I can catch. This morning I woke up early because I could not sleep. I planned on being back before you woke up. I found some coconut trees way down there and climbed one. Then I got hot and went for a swim to cool off. There were blue crabs everywhere! If you go down the beach far enough, there are villagers living by the beach. I asked one of them if I can borrow their pot and some matches to cook these in exchange for some crabs. I gave them the female crabs and they invited me back when we are ready to cook them."

I grab Tree and give him an affectionate slap on the head. "So you speak Indonesian now? You are forgiven. Thủy-Tiên, you can pick one for a pet and give him a name."

My dolly selects the largest male crab in the bucket, twenty-two centimeters wide. His brilliant blue markings have elements of purple in them near the claws and his white spots resemble large swirls of condensed milk. He is missing one of the back paddle legs.

"I am going to name him King," she says.

"Make sure you keep King in the water otherwise he will die," I say to my daughter.

"I am going to swim out and grab what is left of our trawler. There are some pieces of wood we can burn after they dry up." Tree wades into the water and swims out to our boat. There is not much left of trawler 93752. The once pastel green boat with its pretty blue hull and number painted in deep red now resembles a large lump of black coal floating in the water.

"We should have a veneration ceremony tonight for Brother Tú, Sister Thảo, and their baby, Mỹ-Linh," I say to Hồng-Mai. She agrees.

"You have upgraded from sardines to blue swimmer crabs." A distinct voice interrupts us. I find Ommo's presence unnerving.

Hồng-Mai takes her leave, muttering something about finding her brother. I find myself paralyzed by his Adonis face and have trouble grasping for words.

He stands with his arms crossed in his camel-colored uniform and black beret. His rifle hangs loosely at his side. The veins on his forearm protrude and disappear under the sleeves. His aviator sunglasses hide his eyes and I cannot decipher his mood. I have no desire to engage so I am quiet.

"Why did you not tell my commander what happened last night?" Ommo breaks the silence.

"I tell him I see saltwater crocodile come from bushes—"

"Yes, and monkeys and bats," finishes Ommo. "Am I the crocodile and my friends the monkeys and bats?" I ignore his question and pretend I am concerned for Tree swimming out to sea. I step aside to get a view of my nephew. "Is this your daughter?" Still, I say nothing to him. I pick Thủy-Tiên up and walk toward the water. She protests and runs back to King, her pet crab. Ommo walks with me. "I want to thank you, Snow, for not saying anything. I did not mean to scare you or your friend. We were looking for valuables."

"In her vagina?" I snap. "You try to pull her pants and rape her."

"What? No!" Ommo defends himself. "We always have boat people like you wash up on our shores like beached baby seals. They hide jewelry and gold in their clothes, sewn inside the pockets or tucked in the hem."

"You take advantage of helpless people. Hit them on head with guns and kick us."

"I do what my commanding officer orders me to do. I am trying to tell you I am sorry and grateful for your silence. Do not disrespect me in front of others or I will be forced to put you in your place."

I bite my tongue and wait for Tree to swim back. He carries a few planks of wood with him. I walk with my nephew back to where Thủy-Tiên is squatting with the bucket of crabs and coconuts. Ommo joins his companion, Gus, and leaves us alone.

Within the hour, the military returns. Coincidentally, so does Hồng-Mai with her brother. As promised, Abu and his men hand out rice, sardines, water, and fruits for us to enjoy. The subject of conversation this morning amongst the group is not how wonderful the food is, but how I negotiated the meal for everyone. People come by to chat and say thank you. They drool over the blue crabs and coconuts that Tree collected.

The rest of the day is uneventful. The military leaves us and tells us we are on our own until they arrange for us to get off the island. The group works together to prepare a memorial service. Tree and Tùng go for a swim in search of more crabs and take their catch to a villager's home to cook. I show Sơn and Minh-Tú how to open the coconuts, drawing from my lesson from Minh-Hoàng. The three of us take turns pounding the coconuts against rocks and strip the fibers. Others collect branches, litter and anything they can find to build a bonfire.

The evening breeze rolls in. We honor the family that died at sea by sitting around the bonfire, saying prayers and chants, sharing stories of family honor and bond, eating morsels of the ten blue crabs that Tree and Tùng caught this afternoon. A few local Indonesians join us and share their picnic food with us. A man with a hat sits down beside me underneath the palm tree and plays a musical instrument for the group. I have never seen this type of instrument before. The closest instrument I can think of is a guitar crossed with a violin, but this one only has two strings that run from the two tuning picks down to the bottom of the instrument. He stands the instrument up and strokes the two strings with a bow, pressing his fingers at various intervals on the strings. The melody is nice and soothing. He finishes and we all clap. Thủy-Tiên is especially fascinated by this new toy. She glides her fingers over the strings. The man hands her the bow and she slides it across the instrument. It screeches and we all laugh.

"Your daughter can use some lessons." His voice screeches over me like the bow. I recognize the voice and my body immediately becomes tense. I get a good look at the islander sitting beside me and recognize those almond-shaped eyes.

"What you doing here?" I ask Ommo. "You check on baby

seals in distress?"

"I like to come down to the beach and play my rebab whenever I feel sad or lonely. It calms me and lifts the stress."

"Why you have to come to my beach?" I feel hostile and territorial.

He chuckles. "Your beach is a thousand meters from my mother's house and this island is small, so there is only one. You chose the nicest part of the beach to burn your boat."

"We not set boat on fire. Your bullets hit our boat and the oil leak—"

"It does not matter." Ommo dismisses my rantings. It only irritates me more. "What matters is I have not learned of your daughter's name yet." I glance across to Hồng-Mai, who shoots me a warning look. "I already know yours, which I have to say, I have never seen snow in Indonesia before. Now I have."

His comments make me miss Skyler Herrington. "Aw, so there is snow in Vietnam!" he had said.

I hesitate but answer him. "My daughter name is Dolly."

"Dolly huh? Pretty, like her mother," Ommo responds.

I blush and change the subject. "Tell me about your instrument."

"This rebab was my father's. It is made from a sapodilla tree."

"Sapodillas? The fruit is so sweet, like candy on a tree," I comment.

"This was handmade by my father. It is one string that starts from the highest tuning pick, goes down the body and then back up again. The bow is from horse hair. There are two essential scales when you play gamelan music, slendro and pélog. You hold the bow with your right hand and pull the hairs tight with the third finger, like this." Ommo demonstrates the proper way of holding the bow. He plays another melody for the group. They clap for him and demand for more. If only they realize this is the same man who tried to steal their valuables while we slept and who abused our men when we washed up on shore. I remember him mistreating my new family and it makes me mad. I shoot up and grab hold of Thủy-Tiên's hand to take her back to our sleeping area on the beach.

"I want to stay." Thủy-Tiên emphatically sits down and crosses her arms. She throws me a pout and casts her resentful eyes.

"No, it is time to sleep." I wrap both arms tightly around her arms and thighs like a straitjacket and jerk her up off the ground. I am embarrassed by her defiance. I leave the circle without saying goodbye or giving Ommo another thought.

***

For the next twelve days, the beach is our home. Every day, we eat blue crabs and coconut. Tree goes out every morning and evening for a swim and catches crabs for us to eat. He feels for them with his feet and pries them up out of their safe, sandy haven. Sometimes he sees them skipping sideways along the shallow surface and pins them down with his feet. He has gotten good at catching them, filling a five-gallon bucket in ninety minutes. We use the saltwater to boil the crabs and borrow cooking supplies from the natives nearby. Thủy-Tiên's pet, King, died on the second day. King's death hit her hard and so begins the lessons of loss, mourning, and healing. She is on her fifth pet crab, named King the Fifth.

Every day I search for coconuts that have fallen from the tree and spend hours trying to pry one open. My arms are getting strong. I am sick of eating crabs and coconuts. Sometimes arguments break out amongst our group over who sees the coconut first. We share our food with the elders but tell everyone else they are on their own. Tree and Snitch have become good friends. I treat Snitch like my own nephew, bossing him around and telling him to find sticks for fire or fetch some matches from locals who take pity on us. He never complains. The Indonesian military has not come back to check on us and true to his word, Abu and his men have not given us any more food or support. Some days, I think they have forgotten us, but then Ommo shows up, always in the evening, and I believe he is their spy.

Today, he comes to the beach carrying a bag slung over his shoulders. "I have a gift for you."

"Why you keep coming here?" I ask.

"You are still mad?" He smiles and dumps out the contents of the bag onto the sand.

"Sapodillas!" I exclaim.

"I had to wait ten days for them to ripen. They are from my mother's tree."

A few people gather around us. Ommo takes out a knife and cuts the fruit in half. He hands Thủy-Tiên and me the fruit. He then cuts up the rest into small slices and hands everyone in our group a piece.

I bite into the flesh of the sapodilla and savor the delicious meat. "Why you being so nice?" I am in heaven. "You here five times now, always in the evening."

"You have been counting," he says. "You must miss me when I do not come." I dismiss his narcissist remark. "I have two more presents for you." He hands me two ponchos. "It is supposed to rain late tonight."

"Last time you bring us blanket. Before that you bring tarp. Other time you come and play your rebab. Does your commander send you to spy on us?" I find Ommo annoying, like he is trying to buy my forgiveness.

"Why should I tell you? You never told me why you did not tell my commander about that night."

If he did not bring us much needed things or was not so distracting to look at, I would despise him. "You said two presents. These two ponchos our presents or is there more?"

He laughs at me. "You are greedy." I take another bite of my fruit to avoid saying something he might not like. "Tomorrow afternoon there will be a Norwegian ship coming at one o'clock to take this group to the island of Galang. They have rescued others out at sea who have left Vietnam and are transporting them to the refugee camp. Abu has arranged for them to come here and take you to Galang, where you will stay until you get relocated to a country willing to sponsor your family."

I cannot believe the news and jump up and down with happiness. Biện, the man who stepped on the sea urchin but has since recovered from the pain, walks over to ask why I am so happy. I tell him the good news and tell him to spread the word.

"I see you will not miss me," says Ommo.

"I not know you well to miss you, but thank you for being kind to my family," I say sincerely.

"You are welcome. Stay dry tonight and be careful of the crocodiles, monkeys, and bats," says Ommo.

"And snakes," I say. "Many snakes here."

Ommo laughs. "And snakes." He leaves without saying goodbye.

I catch up to him and gently touch his forearm. "Ommo, take care yourself. If you see more helpless baby seals beached here, do not steal their hope. Please give them hope, like you did for me today."

Ommo nods. "Take care of yourself and Dolly."

***

Today there will be a ship to take us to a refugee camp. It will mean one step closer to getting my family to America. I wake earlier

217

than usual this morning and join Tree for a swim while others sleep. I wade out to the warm water and immerse my body under the gentle waves. These same waves once rocked our little boat so violently, it made us throw up, and brought us pirates that changed some of our lives. These harsh waves claimed the life of three of our boat members. How many countless more? These waves that could not quench our thirst when we were dehydrated or feed us fish when we were starving. Today I elect to forgive these waves.

Tree and I enjoy the peaceful morning. We splash around and try to outswim each other, playing games to see who can swim faster or submerge further and longer. He teaches me to spot for blue swimmer crabs and how to catch them. We have a contest to see who can catch the most. Of course, he wins. Together we fill the five-gallon bucket with crabs in an hour, with me catching fourteen of the sixty blue swimmers. We get out of the water and spot a bask of crocodiles sleeping with their mouth open to release the heat. Tree and I stay clear of them and walk back to the group with our catch. I cannot wait to leave this little island.

This morning will be our last crab and coconut feast on the beach. I am grateful that we did not starve the past two weeks, but am sick of the same meal every day and cannot wait for rice, meat or fish. I daydream about fried frog legs and the crepes that Sister Six makes, only this time, with lots of shrimp and pork. By 1:15 p.m., the group stands clustered together on the beach. There is a lot of excitement this morning. The big Norwegian ship is here and larger than I imagined, at around fifty or sixty meters. It waits for us far in the distance and drops down smaller boats into the water to retrieve us. Group by group, we are ferried to the glorious vessel while the Indonesian military supervises. I find myself searching for Ommo but he is not here today.

Alongside the massive steel cargo ship, we are hoisted up with ropes and nets. Sơn, Tùng, Minh-Tú, Biện and other men climb the ladder. A man throws a large canvas bag down to me and directs me to put Thủy-Tiên in it. My four-year-old is hoisted up into the boat. Her body bangs against the ship a few times on the way to the top. My arms are raised in case I have to catch her. Thủy-Tiên is trusting in what is happening at the moment. *My brave girl.* Tree and Snitch climb the rope and I follow behind them. Hồng-Mai and others wait for the net.

I grab hold of Tree's arm. He pulls me in. I survey the deck and see there are already four hundred other refugees onboard, all rescued at sea. I am so elated and speechless. It is heaven on water! Announcements come over the speakers, first in English, then in Vietnamese, that we are all going to the island of Pulau Galang. We all cheer. Volunteer firefighters, doctors, nurses, and counselors walk to our group and offer assistance. They give us fresh water and a bowl of noodles. A young woman with blonde hair and blue eyes, wearing a knitted Marius sweater around her shoulders, hands Tree and me a metal utensil with a long handle and four sharp, narrow tines that curves upward at the end.

"It is a type of cutlery, called a fork," she says. "You spear the food and put it in your mouth." I find her accent darling and sing-song-like with the different inflections. I especially like the way she pronounces the word "food". Although her mouth is stiff and her lips tense, her eyes shine. I can listen to her all day.

"I want chopsticks. I am not putting these sharp spikes into my mouth," says Tree.

She finds Tree's appalled expression amusing and laughs. "We use it like this." I find her charming and her pronunciation of "we" as "vee" endearing. She takes Tree's fork, stabs the noodles, spins it in circles until a layer of noodles is wrapped around the utensil, and hands it back to him. "Linguine with herring." I give it a try and take a bite of the noodles. It is delightful. She points to the front of the boat. "Over there, we have clothes that have been donated by various charitable organizations. Take what you need."

I realize we are safe and with tears of joy in my eyes, I hug Tree. "We are not going to die."

Tree's face lights up. "No, and we are no longer government property."

After eating, I take Thủy-Tiên over to the pile of clothes. She selects a white cotton shirt with a print of *Raggedy Ann and Raggedy Andy* on it, and another black shirt that says *"Barbie"* on it in pink lettering. We pick a pair of shorts to go with them. A yellow shirt with a pretty woman on the front of it catches Thủy-Tiên's eyes but it is too big for her. She insists I wear it. The woman on the t-shirt has long black hair. She is wearing a bathing suit in colors of red, yellow and blue. Her bikini bottom has white stars on it. Below her picture are the words *"Wonder Woman"*. I take the shirt because the colors remind me of Việt Nam's flag but also the American flag. A purple blouse catches my eye and I take that one as well to compliment the jeans and polyester pants I have slung over the crook of my elbow.

With our new clothes in hand, I take Thủy-Tiên to the washing station and wait in line. Soon it is our turn. I rinse her down with water and wash her hair and body before scrubbing myself clean. I feel human again. I put on my clean yellow Wonder Woman shirt and slip on the same crooked black pants I had sewn years ago, afraid of losing the emerald engagement ring that Sam gave me. I search for it in the elastic waist and smile knowing the ring is still there. Sam, my first love. I promise myself to never sell his ring. I smile again and imagine myself as ragamuffin chic with my bright yellow shirt and crooked black pajama pants. Or should I say, refugee chic, since I am now a refugee? I imagine myself walking the runway in Paris wearing my uneven pants, one pant leg wider and shorter than the other, stitched together with three different colors of thread. I giggle out loud imagining Sister Six's shocked face to see my horrible pants make it to fashion week. I spend the next few hours enjoying the boat ride, embracing the breeze on my face, and watching the sea come to life with fish jumping out of the water. Thủy-Tiên makes friends with some of the other children on the ship. They run around making up games and laugh with childhood innocence. I make small talk with some of the families sitting around me. Before long, we arrive at the harbor and get ready to disembark on the gangplank.

Who should be waiting for us at the dock but Ommo?

Uniformed men stand to attention and wait for all four-hundred forty of us refugees to get off the Norwegian vessel. I catch a glimpse of the pretty blonde woman who taught us how to use a fork and wave to her. The Indonesian military search everyone's bags and take what they want. An uneasy feeling settles in my chest. I want to run back to the ship and be a stowaway, maybe end up in Norway. Now, the idea of waiting at the refugee camp until sponsorship to America feels like an impossible dream. Ommo, Gus, and a few other soldiers ask the group questions and separate us into clusters.

Ommo points at me and waves me over. "Your name please."

"You know my name," I say.

"I need your full name," he demands in a serious tone.

"Lê Ngọc Tuyết." I give him my maiden name. "Surname Lê. First name Tuyết."

"I thought it was Snow?"

"Tuyết means 'snow'."

"Spell your name." I spell my full name for him. "How many are in your group?"

"Three," I respond.

"Spell their names for me." I comply with his request. "I thought your daughter's name is Dolly?"

"It is a nickname I call her, just like Tree is my nephew's nickname. Why you separate people in groups, Ommo? I do not—"

"What are their ages and relationship to you?"

"My daughter is four-years-old and my nephew is sixteen." Ommo annoys me. He is the eyelash adhered to my eyeball, the loose insole in my shoe, the run in my pantyhose. I want to crumple him up like paper and toss him in a trashcan.

"Are you the head of the family?"

"Yes. You cannot separate—"

"Your birthdate and theirs?" He cuts me off again.

"July 30, 1974, and December 16, 1962. My birthday April 13, 1939."

"Please take your family and sit over there in group A. You will be given instructions."

"Ommo, there is another boy, Thành. He travel same in our boat but he have no family. I want him with my family."

"He will be in group D with the unaccompanied minors."

There are a lot of children sitting in Group D and more joining them. Children as young as eight or nine years old wait to discover their fate. They are with other children and teenagers. Somehow, they got separated from their family. I need to work on getting Snitch to join us or at least be with Sơn. I do not want him alone.

Tree, Thủy-Tiên and I sit down on the dirt and rocks with the rest of the families classified as Group A. I am disheartened when my group is called to be transported to the camp. There are still hundreds of people being interviewed and every face appears the same. The boat people of trawler 93752 have been separated and are lost in the crowd of black hair and polyester clothes.

The bus ride to the camp is a loud one. People talk over each other, making plans to write to their family back home or ask for money from relatives who have settled in other countries. Some are nervous and fear they will never receive sponsorship. Others are excited to be on land and dream of endless possibilities for the bright future ahead. I am vexed about what this camp means for my family. I am hopeful it is a bridge to a better life and the chance to forget the recent past.

There is a longing in me to return to the old Việt Nam. I miss my country that is lost forever. I miss my family whom I may never see again, at least, not until it is safe to return. I am nothing more than a homeless person stuck between yesterday and tomorrow and two countries that do not want me.

I see mangos growing on the island and wild monkeys swinging on the trees. If I allow the green foliage to blend together into a blur, maybe I can convince myself that I am in a rural jungle near Vĩnh Bình. Perhaps on the other side is a nice beach, with a bustling market nearby, and if I try, I can convince myself that my family is sitting around the table playing tứ sắc, the Chinese four-colors card game. I envision Sister Six cooking bò lúc lắc, a French-inspired Vietnamese cuisine of cubed beef marinated in sesame oil, garlic, oyster sauce, soy sauce, salt, and sugar, then sautéed and enjoyed with a salad tossed in a lime vinaigrette dressing. I yearn for a different life, one that has Tâm, Hải and Sam in it.

The bus stops and I exit with the rest of the passengers. Tree and Thủy-Tiên get off before me. A big sign "Welcome to Pulau Galang" stands prominently.

A man with a large mole between his eyebrows strides to the front of the covered shelter where we congregate. He carries a megaphone and is wearing brown-tinted sunglasses, large like aviator goggles. His bell-bottom pants are too short for him and his shirt is a bit tight. "Hello, friends. My name is Don. I am a representative with the office of the *United Nations High Commissioner for Refugees.* Welcome to Pulau Galang." A young Vietnamese woman with long black hair, wearing a floral dress, lifts up her megaphone to translate his message. "The UNHCR is here to help you with resettlement into a participating country or repatriation if you voluntarily would like to return to your country." Don pauses so the woman can translate. "Everyone here has been assigned to Group A because you are traveling with your family and have a small child. We currently have two thousand refugees in the camp and hundreds more coming each day." He pauses for the translator. "Unfortunately, we do not have enough barracks for everyone so we will assign by lottery. You will be reassigned into a barrack as soon as a family vacates. Until then, you will need to find a spot anywhere within the camp borders to call home. We have minimal supplies available and more will be received next week. If your family's name is not called for an assigned barrack, please make use of the tents and tarps provided by the *American Red Cross.*"

The longer the representative speaks, the more desperate I feel. It dawns on me that I am essentially in prison. The camp border is outlined with barbed wire. Indonesian soldiers and guards dressed in green or tan uniforms stand by, on alert to pounce and maintain order if they need to. As far as I can see, there is no running water or sanitation system. I see a well and am suspicious it has contaminated water in it. Beyond the barracks is a small hill with rows and rows of dilapidated structures and makeshift shelters. There are huts put together using tarps, weathered pieces of wood, blankets, palm or bamboo leaves, corroded aluminum, or rusty tin parts.

Clothes hang on ropes or drape over partitions to dry. There are so many people loitering around, so bored that they find chewing on their nails entertaining. Some are asleep on a hammock with their arm draped over their eyes to shield the glare of the sun. I see mothers tending to their babies, all of whom are either topless or bottomless.

"Aunt Eight, he called your name." Tree taps my hand. "We are in barrack two."

I am relieved our family has a room rather than a tent to sleep in. Tree, Thủy-Tiên and I receive a welcome kit that includes soap, utensils, towels, and a kerosene stove. We report to our assigned barrack with the clothes on our backs and whatever articles we selected on the Norwegian ship.

Each barrack has a row of five living quarters on top and five open spaces below. The barrack is held together with bent nails and crooked boards affixed to some rotting wood. There are five sets of stairs leading to the door of each living quarter. Down below, the open space is bare, with three walls and no door. In the corner are a pot, a few cooking utensils, a plastic water basin, some plates, bowls, cups, and cutlery. I suspect these items were left by previous inhabitants. I walk the ten steps up the stairs to the second level and stand at the platform. I take a deep breath and open the door.

I am greeted by hot, stale air, with a hint of dust and mold permeating my senses. The room is roughly twenty square meters and other than the wood platforms with mattresses on them, it too is bare. There are six pads to sleep on, three on the floor and three on the wood shelves. The thin mattress pads are lumpy and stained. A thin blanket sits on each. Only two have pillows and one pad actually has a sunken box spring. Tree claims one of the beds on top with the box spring. It is closest to the window shutters.

"Alô?" A young Vietnamese woman greets us from the doorway with her husband and their twin daughters.

"Hello." I nod to the family. "Is your family assigned to this room as well?"

"Yes," she answers. "I believe we are sharing. My name is Mai. This is my husband, Khải, and our daughters, Mỹ-Kiều and Mỹ-Loan."

"Your daughters are so lovely. How do you tell them apart?" I ask.

"We can see their differences," says Khải, "but others can tell them apart by their ears. Mỹ-Loan is the older one by two minutes and she has her ears pierced."

"Yes, I see," I say. "Mỹ-Loan, how old are you and your sister?"

"Yes, Auntie, we are eleven and will turn twelve next month," answers Mỹ-Loan politely.

I introduce myself and the family and tell them to call me Eight. We spend the rest of the day getting acquainted with each other and the families in the other rooms. I learn that Mai and her family have been at the camp a month. They stayed in a tent at first. I understand the Red Cross, the Indonesian Red Crescent Society, and other world relief organizations keep the camp operational, offering services in health, education, and social welfare. The UNHCR manages the resettlement programs but it is the Indonesian government that implements them. The military guards the camp and limits people entering or leaving. Many of them can be bribed and a lot of the single women who have relationships with them find their application for resettlement approved much faster than others. And if you have a large family, you can expect to live in the camp for a long time before your whole family gets sponsored.

One of my neighbors, Bảo, was a successful business owner and is a highly educated man. He speaks good English, French, Mandarin Chinese, and Vietnamese. He and his large family of thirteen have been in the camp for a year. Like many others, after the war ended, his family's rice plantation, cars, and scooters were seized by the government. He risked arrest many times by purchasing food in his town and reselling them in Sài Gòn for ten times the price. His family was starving. The communists transported all the rice from the south to the north to feed their people. He saved enough money to buy a boat thirteen meters long for nine taels of gold. He even spent three million đồng on fishing nets to pretend he was a fisherman, but their boat captain ended up changing his mind and staying back. Luckily they had no problems getting past the border. They were in international waters for seven days with only a toy compass and a letter from a friend that detailed the navigation route. Eighty-eight people were in the boat in the beginning. They survived on raw squid and fish that flew onto the boat during the tempest rainfall. Everyone was miserable and cold. Politeness and social order quickly vanished as everyone fought for space. They were attacked by pirates four times and nine people were murdered. Eventually, they were rescued by a Dutch merchant ship that hoisted them up onto the boat with a suspended gangplank. I conclude that we both knew Dr. Đức and his wife as they helped both our families escape.

"You have a higher power protecting you to be so fortunate to have a barrack already," says Bảo. "I hear the UNHCR is building two hundred barracks on Galang to accommodate twenty-thousand people, and there will be a hospital, administrative offices, and community facilities."

"I hope they build bathrooms with running water so we can take showers," I say.

"I would like to see a church or a pagoda. There are many monks, nuns, and priests here," says Bảo, "but each day I drift further from spirituality."

"I hope your family gets sponsored quickly."

"I have a large family so it will be some time before someone pays for all of us. We can separate and go at different times or places, but I insist we stay together."

Mai and Khải grab a chair and join Bảo and me.

"How do things operate around here?" I ask.

Khải lights up a cigarette and exhales before answering. "If you are hungry, there are some basic items that are provided to us, such as rice, canned fish, salt, sugar and cooking oil."

Mai provides additional insight. "Rice is brought in every week or two but there is never enough. It will last your family two days. Sometimes there are meat or fresh vegetables. Many of us try to grow our own vegetables."

Bảo surrenders to the temptation of Khải's cigarette and bums one from him. "You will find that life here is monotonous and the only thing to do while you wait for your application to get approved is to sleep and garden, but the soil here is hard and dry." Bảo takes a deep drag of the nicotine and exhales. "There is no running water so we rely on catching the rain. One other thing. My advice to you, when you are cooking your rice, is to fill the kerosene half way. Otherwise, it will expand and leak out. If you need help getting the wicks started and lighting the burner, I can show you. It is a little fickle."

"Thank you. Tell me, Brother Bảo, how do I apply for resettlement? Is there an interview process?" I ask.

"There are announcements daily over the loudspeakers. Your family will be called to the interview office. It will take some time before you learn of your status. They will announce the names of people accepted to leave but then you have to wait again for the country to make arrangements to receive you. There is a lot of paperwork and travel planning, medical inspections and shots…Hundreds of people arrive here each day, more than the number of people leaving. You will see. Life here is hard."

"Where did you get your mosquito net?" I ask.

"You can ask the guards to get you things but they will expect you to pay three times the cost. Each family receives a monthly subsistence allowance from the UNHCR for necessities. If you have family who can send you money, I suggest you write them. You can have my net after I leave, if you need it."

I chat with Bảo, Mai and Khải for another fifteen minutes. They are full of information but Bảo is the storyteller.

34 A TORNADO

It has been two weeks since we arrived at the camp. Time drifts slowly here. Bảo was right, life is hard on Galang. There is no clean water. On the weekends the guards let us go to the beach to swim, bathe, and do laundry. Our daily menu consists of sardines or tiny dried shrimp stir-fried in soy sauce, and a cup of rice to cook. It is never enough and we are always hungry. The whole camp is rat and snake-infested. I fight to keep our rice and food supplies sealed. At night there are swarms of mosquitos and without a net to ward them off, we become a buffet feast for them. The worst part is the stench. The crowded shanty town of poorly-constructed barracks and makeshift tents is nothing more than a large pot of rotting flesh, urine, and feces. Many people have scabies or are sick with malaria or some ailment. Every day people die as more become ill. There are as many births as there are deaths here.

Thủy-Tiên passes her time playing made-up games with children nearby. Her favorite one is dropping the handkerchief on top of another child's head and then having that child chase and catch her before she runs a full circle around their group of friends and sits down in the empty seat at the circle. Tree passes time by climbing like a monkey over the fence and disappearing for hours at a time. At night or in the early morning, he hops out of his top bunk, slithers through the window, and scales down the railings. He says he is fishing and hunting for wild boar, but sometimes he comes back smelling like alcohol, which is illegal to have in the camp. Christmas and Lunar New Year are the only two holidays in which it is permissible to imbibe. I ask him about his disappearances and he dismisses me like a nosy neighbor. He is growing distant from me, becoming disrespectful, and either angry or sad all the time. In not so many words, he is telling me he yearns to return to Việt Nam and resents his elders for forcing him to leave. This morning I lay awake on my mattress and read the carvings on the walls. There are names and dates scratched on them from previous tenants. I resist the urge to carve my name because years from now, what will it matter? Who will see it? Who will care?

"Shit!" Tree scrambles off his mattress and jumps down.

"What is the matter?" I leap up to see what is wrong.

"This is disgusting!" Tree pulls back his thin mattress to expose the sunken box spring. Crawling out of the cracks of the walls and covering his bed are hundreds of tiny rice-size bed bugs. Tree scratches his back frantically. I lift up his shirt and see red welts covering his entire back where the bloodsuckers dined. Tree flips the bed to the floor and we both get to work stomping on them. Our roommates join the blitzkrieg.

Thủy-Tiên wakes up from the ruckus. "Black pepper?" She mistakes the dead bugs for ground pepper.

"I cannot stand it here!" Tree screams. "How much longer are we staying in this hell?"

Before I can answer, he sprints out of the door and down the stairs. Mỹ-Loan and Mỹ-Kiều run after Tree but cannot keep pace with him. They abandon their quest and return back to the barrack.

Mai tries to comfort me. "Give him time. Both of our families have a good chance of getting sponsored soon. We are a small family with young children."

"Mai," I say, "I had my interview with the administration office to see if we are eligible for refugee status and can be resettled. I told the authorities I wanted to go to America and they asked if I had friends or family there. The only person I know is my friend, Sergeant Skyler Herrington, who served in the U.S. Army. He was born and raised in the Seattle area."

"Maybe the UNHCR will track him down. Maybe he can sponsor your family." Mai shakes the dust from her blanket out the window.

"I hope so. I wrote to my family back home. Thủy-Tiên's dad wrote to them and they included his letter in their mail to me. He is in South Carolina but will soon be moving to a town called Houston in the state of Texas. He is doing well. He will be working under a division manager for some company, managing one-hundred-fifty employees, but his goal is to open his own machine shop."

"You belong in Houston, not Seattle." Mai's husband, Khải,

restores Tree's mattress to the top bunk.

"He is married to an American woman and they now have two sons."

"You should write to your husband and ask him to send you money," says Mai.

"I do not want him to know where we are," I say. "We each have chosen different paths and it is best we live separate lives."

"Do you think that is fair to Thủy-Tiên?" Mai gives me something to think about.

"And how are your family doing?" asks Khải.

"My sister is paranoid with the government. She calls them all Việt Cộngs and does not dare venture outside after 8 p.m. curfew. There are always people patrolling the streets and the perimeters of the towns, waiting to catch you doing something illegal. People's crops and livestock are still being seized. My sister has had some luck selling cakes and pastries so she is starting her food business. My sister-in-law is learning to perfect her sewing skills and wants to be a seamstress with her own tailor shop someday. My brother is still driving a truck each day and my brother-in-law is trying to get his hands on a chicken and a rooster. He wants to raise and sell them or fight them. They are doing anything they can to live."

"My family back home is struggling as well. They eat rice soup and sweet potatoes every day, once a day," says Khải.

"Yes, my family does not have enough money to buy anything and depend on what they can grow or raise," says Mai.

We watch the twins teach Thủy-Tiên how to play a game with chopsticks. They toss a small ball in the air and pick up as many chopsticks as they can before the ball drops.

"We should go to the beach for a swim and let our daughters play," I suggest.

"Yes, I can use the distraction. Let me grab our laundry," Mai says.

***

Bảo's family joins us for the afternoon. We walk the one and a half kilometers to the beach. There are a lot of people frolicking on the sandy shore today. Families, teenagers, and small children take advantage of the sand to exfoliate their skin and run into the crashing waves to wash themselves clean. Several children are standing naked in the shallow banks of the beach, splashing each other gleefully. A woman shrieks in the distant shoreline. A handful of people run to her and gather around to see what is going on.

Curiosity beckons me to follow.

A young woman's body has drifted to the coastline. Her waterlogged body shows signs of severe maceration. Her skin and nails are detached and most of her hair has separated from her head. There is a dead crayfish entangled in her hair. The palms of her hands and soles of her feet are wrinkled. The body is green and black. Her eyes have been picked over by birds or sea creatures and what is left cannot be distinguished. And yet, I recognize her clothes. It is Thảo's body, the young mother who was brutally raped by the pirates and who took her and her baby's life at sea. My heart shatters into a thousand pieces but my tears do not flow. My heart grows cold and my anger rises. It is a perfect recipe for a tornado of emotions as I flash back to the Thai men dragging the women to their boats to violate them and toss them into the sea like a used tissue. The face of Tý and Minh-Hoàng form a funnel cloud in my mind. It swirls angrily and collects the faces of all the bitter melon men and pirates who harmed my friends and family and caused destruction along the way.

The Indonesian Navy arrives to take the body away. They load Thảo into a car with a red cross symbol on the side door. Everyone is asked to return to the camp.

***

I replay over and over Thảo's body washing to shore and I cannot sleep. I quietly get out of bed and notice Tree is not in his. My little dolly is sound asleep. I walk down the stairs and stand outside. Next door Bảo and his wife are having sex. I brave the walk alone and resolve ten minutes away from my daughter should be fine, since Mai and Khải are here.

I walk toward the perimeter of the camp until I can make out the outlines of the barbed wire fence. There are two people smoking and drinking but I cannot make out their faces.

"What barrack are you in?" asks the smaller of the two shadowy figures.

"The second one," says the taller figure.

I recognize their voices and crouch down to stay hidden.

"I am in sixty-eight, near the guards' barrack," says Snitch. "There are one-hundred-twenty of us unaccompanied minors crammed in there. One man is living with us to take care of us. He is nice. Have you been on the outskirts of the camp?"

"Fuck, Thành, I go anywhere I want on this Shit Island," says Tree. "This camp is sitting in the middle of a cleared forest. The

231

harbor is five kilometers from camp. I am guessing there are ten thousand people here."

I am appalled he is using foul language and smoking. This is a new side to him that I do not like. Where is my caring, loyal and resourceful nephew I helped raise?

"Have you heard about Hồng-Mai or seen her brother?" asks Snitch.

"Fuck, it is terrible what happened." Tree takes a drag of his cigarette and chases it with some beer.

"I have not run into any of the other people from our boat, have you? There must be a hundred barracks here."

"Sơn and Minh-Tú are in barrack fifty-eight, I think. Have you been sponsored yet?"

Snitch takes the last gulp of his beer and throws the can on the ground. "Germany is taking a lot of the unaccompanied minors. I am going on the next boat."

"Shit, send me a letter when you get to Germany so we can keep in touch. Otherwise, I will not fucking recognize you when you call my name with a German accent."

The two boys laugh.

"I heard every week a ship comes to take people to Australia or Germany or America," says Snitch.

"My aunt wants to go to America. I want to volunteer for repatriation, but I am a minor under her care so I am fucking stuck. I miss our country even if it is infested with Uncle Hồ's legion of Cộng Sản."

"Why would you want to run back to Hồ's legion of communists?"

Tree laughs. "The rice is better there."

"There is a rich Chinese woman who is selling jasmine rice that her family sends here. You should get some. It is the same quality we are used to. Meet me here tomorrow at noon and I will take you to her."

"Shit, that rice better be good," says Tree. "It is almost 3 a.m. The guards should be having wet dreams by now. I am going to get us more cigarettes and with some luck, more alcohol."

The two boys part ways. I am scared he will get caught and beaten. Tomorrow I will have to beat him first.

***

The announcement comes over the loudspeakers. "Lê Ngọc Tuyết, you and your family are to report to the administration office in fifteen minutes. I repeat. Lê Ngọc Tuyết, please bring your family to the office in fifteen minutes."

My heart races. There can be only two reasons why I am being called. Either Tree got into trouble or we are going to America. I grab Thủy-Tiên's hand and run to the office. It is raining heavily today. The dirt walkways are muddy. There is standing water and large puddles to slow us down. I pray Tree also heard the announcement and will meet us there. On the way, I notice a woman smiling brightly at me. Her mouth showcases her wide row of white teeth and a wider row of gums above them. She points to her handwritten sign, advertising a cup of jasmine rice for four hundred thousand đồng or two hundred fifty rupiahs. She must be off her hammock to charge that extortionary price.

We burst into the refugee camp office and startle the people in there. I announce myself. A woman hands me an envelope and directs me to the resettlement processing center. We run to the UNHCR center drenched in rain and breathing heavily. I sweep my hair out of my face and recognize the three people sitting at the table in front of me. The first person is Don, the UNHCR representative who welcomed us to Galang. The mole between his eyebrows appears darker and larger than I remember. Next to him is the Vietnamese woman who translates for him. She wears a name tag that says "Mary". The third person, to my surprise, is Ommo. The same Adonis face I remember, but softer and kinder today. He waves to Thủy-Tiên and she waves back.

"Mama," my daughter says excitedly, "it is the man who plays that instrument."

I nod to her and we take a seat. The third seat is empty and I desperately pray Tree will show up. I hand Don the envelope.

"Where is your nephew?" Don opens the envelop and reviews the documents.

"He coming," I say nervously in English.

"We have reviewed your application," says Mary. "Your first choice is the United States, second is Canada, and third Sweden. We are happy to inform you that you have been approved for resettlement in Sweden."

"Oh, I am happy," I respond. "I pick Sweden because my friend, Minh-Tú, you know him? He say there is Swedish embassy in Hà Nội and he hear they help bring my family in Việt Nam to reunite with us."

"I cannot confirm that Sweden can help your relatives back in

Vietnam emigrate to Sweden." Don hands the documents over to Mary for further review. "Let's worry about your family first."

"Your nephew needs to be here. We need to do a complete medical examination and give you some vaccinations," says Mary. "We need to prepare travel arrangements and visas."

I hope Ommo is not the one doing the medical assessments. He notices my eyes on him and smiles. *Why are you so handsome when you smile?*

"Yes, you need to be immunized against smallpox, hepatitis, tuberculosis, tetanus and a couple other diseases," says Don.

"But if your nephew does not arrive for this appointment, your application will be recycled back into the waiting pile." Mary flips open an ink pad. There are two stamps in front of her. One says "APPROVED" and the other one says "REJECTED".

I panic. I do not want to stay at this camp longer than I have to. Being here for two weeks is nothing compared to others who have been here months. Tree has never failed me. I am hopeful he will come any minute now.

"If Sweden does not work out, we have an opportunity for you while you wait for a sponsorship." Don slides me a folder. "We need volunteers to teach English to refugees who have been approved for resettlement. While they wait for the transfer, they will be learning English and basic cultural information about their host country. We chose you because your application indicates you used to teach math and your English is good. You and your daughter would be living in staff housing. Your nephew can live in the unaccompanied minor barrack until your departure. And Ommo here is assisting the camp commanding officer. He will help you—"

"No," I say.

"No?" Ommo's kind face now grows cold and upset.

"My English not so good and my nephew cannot separate with me," I say. "He will come."

"If he is not here in five minutes, we will have to reject your placement with Sweden," says Mary. "You can appeal."

We sit in awkward silence. I avoid eye contact with Ommo but Thủy-Tiên is enamored with him. She waves to him and asks him in Vietnamese where his rebab instrument is.

After five minutes, Don stands up. "We cannot wait any longer."

"Please, two more minutes. He will come," I plead.

"I am sorry. We have another family to meet with." Don hands me the folder on the table. "Consider teaching while you wait."

"I will escort them back." Ommo grabs a large umbrella and ushers me out the door. "It is raining hard outside." The warmth of his hand on my back comforts me but the hurried push of his fingers contradicts this security. I sense his impatience to leave the processing center and cannot understand why he is upset. I would rather slither in the mud than walk with him back to the barrack and listen to his reprimands.

35 TREE

Ommo and I walk down the row of vendors in zone two of the camp with Thủy-Tiên wanting to hold his hand not mine. On either side, there are people selling various items in the stands. There is even a café under a blue tarp and a small restaurant nearby. Some of the strangers stare at us inquisitively, while others, judgmentally. I am paranoid they will spread rumors that I am sleeping with this man to get special treatment. I pause to smell the coffee beans and close my eyes to enjoy the aroma.

"Would you like a cup of coffee?" asks Ommo.

"No," I lie.

"Sit. I want coffee." Ommo orders two cups of coffee and warm tea for my daughter. "Why do you hate me so much?"

"I no hate—"

"I have been trying to make things right with you ever since we met and I apologized for hitting your boat mates. I was following Abu's orders. I played music for you—"

"Not for me, for—"

"No, for you, Snow, and I brought you sapodilla fruit from my mother's tree. I pulled favors to get your family into a barrack and got your application processed with priority."

I am stunned and speechless. He is exasperated with me. He throws his hand in the air as if to say "I give up" and rubs his palms on his knees.

Our drinks arrive. I take a sip of the hot coffee. If only every moment in life is like the first sip. "Thank you."

Ommo relaxes his shoulders. "You are welcome."

"I need to find my nephew."

"I will help."

"I wish to see my friends too. Do you know where they are?" I ask.

He takes out a pen and small pad of paper from his shirt pocket. "Write down their names and I will find them." I write down Hồng-Mai's and Tùng's name, as well as Sơn's and Minh-Tú's. "I need more than their first names. I need surnames. There are thousands of people here with the same names."

"I sorry. I have only first names. Maybe you check names of everyone arrive to Galang on same day as me."

Ommo sighs. "I will see what I can do." He abruptly whips his head around and addresses curtly the two women working the coffee stand. He says something to them in Indonesian and they stop speaking to each other.

"They are spreading rumors about us," he says.

"What they say?" I am upset.

"They think we are lovers." He winks at me.

I blush and divert my attention to Thủy-Tiên. We spend the next ten minutes enjoying our beverages and talking about my daughter's health and what heart surgery would mean for her. Ommo escorts us back to the barrack via a longer route. He walks leisurely and is in no hurry to get out of the mud and rain. We arrive at my barrack the same time as Tree.

I lunge for my nephew to grab his ear. I am furious he has been out all night and caused us to miss the opportunity to go to Sweden. Before I can yell at him, he collapses to the ground.

Ommo carries Tree into our room and places him on my mattress. "He is burning up."

I grab a towel and run down the stairs to the drum of fresh rainwater. With the towel soaked in cold water, I run back and apply it to Tree's face and neck. "We need a doctor and medicine."

Thủy-Tiên, Mai, Khải, and the twins stand by helplessly.

"There are none that will come to you," Ommo says. "If he had a minor illness and the strength to stand in line, he can visit the Red Cross tent for treatment."

"He cannot die." I am terrified. "So many people get bury here and their site have no sign. No dignity for them."

"He will not die." Ommo places a reassuring hand on mine.

Tree is conscious and shivers. "I am cold."

I wipe the moisture off his face. I do not know if the beads are from his sweat or the rain.

Ommo offers a diagnosis. "It is possible he was bitten by a snake in the forest or ate something bad." Tree writhes in discomfort and it reminds me of Tuấn, when he had pinworms in his body. "Try to keep him cool and as comfortable as possible. I have to report to work after my lunch break." Ommo reluctantly leaves our side with the promise to return later with medicine for Tree's fever.

***

My defiant nephew has been sick for over a month but he is getting stronger. Headaches and abdominal pains are frequent visitors, so is vomiting and diarrhea. Khải helps Tree downstairs whenever my nephew needs to throw up or have a bowel movement. Sometimes, they are not fast enough or Tree is not strong enough so Mai helps me clean up. I pray several times a day.

Dear Lord, in Your light I entrust You with our lives. Please Heavenly Father, wrap Your protective arms around Tree and place Your healing hands on him. Keep us safe from harm and deliver us to freedom. Please also bless the friends and families in our lives. In Thy holy name I pray, Amen.

I have learned that Tree has been infected with malaria. Sometimes his body will convulse and he passes out from exhaustion. I feed him water with a spoon to keep him hydrated and sleep next to him to try to keep him warm. All day and night I keep vigil and have no energy for myself. I give Tree the malaria pills that the Red Cross gave us. The pills bring back haunting memories of Mrs. Trần overdosing on chloroquine. My roommates are a blessing and help with Thủy-Tiên. They take her with them to the dining hall to eat and bring back food. They help her go to the bathroom and take her to the beach for bathing and distractions. The twins have become her older sisters and play with her. They cleverly take stones they find and scrape the edges on the cement to smooth the surface into round balls and shoot them like marbles. With the subsistence allowance from the UNHCR and through Ommo's kindness, I am able to buy two mosquito nets.

Ommo and I have become friends this past month. The twins and Thủy-Tiên adore him. He brings them a treat when he visits or plays marbles with them and talks to them like little adults. I want to trust him but my experience with Minh-Hoàng reminds me to never let my guard down. I want to love him but every man I try to love ends up gone from my life. Mai is smitten with him and says he looks like a movie star. Khải is not happy when Ommo visits, mainly out of jealousy, but he tolerates him, probably because Ommo is in a position to make life either comfortable or difficult for us.

238

"I have some news for you today," says Ommo. "Can we talk outside, the two of us?"

I leave Thủy-Tiên with the twins and Tree with Mai and Khải. We walk outside towards the church that the other refugees are erecting from supplies provided by humanitarian organizations. The sun shines brightly so we find a tree to sit down against.

"I have made contact with your four friends," Ommo says.

"That is wonderful. I want to see them," I say.

"I informed Sơn and Minh-Tú you were in barrack two and they will visit."

"Thank you. What about Tùng and his sister?"

"I do not have good news about Hồng-Mai. Last month she was raped while heading to the toilet. She cannot identify her assailant. It could have been a guard or a refugee at the camp. Her brother is quite distraught."

The shock of this news shakes my core. I can only imagine the pain and shame Hồng-Mai is going through and how alone she must feel. I burst into tears.

Ommo wraps his arms around me. "You need to go see them today. Her brother is beside himself with worry and cannot comfort her. She will not talk to him or let him touch her. She will not eat or bathe."

I give in to his comforting embrace. "Take me to her. We go now."

"The police are investigating the incident. I requested a caseworker and a legal officer—"

"Now, Ommo. We go now. I need to see her."

***

Hồng-Mai's face is barely recognizable. She lies on the clay floor in a trancelike state of mind. She is emaciated and smells bad. I suspect it has been a couple of weeks since she last bathed. She exhales. The foulness of her breath makes me cringe.

Tùng also looks lethargic. "I am weary of living." Tùng drops his head into his hands. "I am going insane here."

"Your sister needs you to help her get through this." I gently touch his hand. "We need to be strong for her and I will be strong for you."

"We do not want to suffer anymore." Tùng grabs hold of my hands and squeezes. His tight grip of desperation cuts off my circulation.

I notice my fingers turning red and try to extract them from his grip. "Everyone here is in their own tormented hellhole, but if you wait a little longer, you will find light again."

Tùng sobs. "There is too much darkness to find light." He leaves his bamboo hut to cry alone. Ommo exits to follow him and leaves me with Hồng-Mai.

I slowly caress Hồng-Mai's head. "We will get justice for you and destroy the man who did this to you. Do not be ashamed." I remove the strands of hair from her face. "You did not cause this. Let me be your strength, Hồng-Mai. Lean on me. You are not going through this alone. I am here with you. Do you understand me? We will take it one day at a time. Together." Hồng-Mai clings to me and cries uncontrollably. The tighter she squeezes, the tighter I squeeze back. "Be strong and persevere. Is that not what Buddha teaches you?" I rub her back and soothe her as if she were a child. "Negative thoughts will lead to more suffering. I will find some incense to burn. We will ask a monk or a nun to chant for you to purify your mind and meditate with you, so you can find enlightenment." I lift her face up so she can see mine. "Hồng-Mai, remember, it is wrong to take a life, so eradicate those poisonous ideas."

Hồng-Mai weeps louder. I hold her tight and rock her. Together we share her sorrow.

***

A week has passed. Tree's energy is rising to the peak of his recovery and he wants to go for a swim. I am comforted by his enthusiasm and appetite. Even Hồng-Mai appears to be healing although the emotional scar will always be with her. I help her bathe daily by wiping her down with a wet washcloth and scrub her scalp and hair with a bar of soap before rinsing it. Today, I leave Hồng-Mai for a couple hours to sit with my nephew on the beach and enjoy a bowl of rice and pâté while Thủy-Tiên slurps on her porridge.

"I am sorry for disrespecting you and ruining our chance of leaving here to go to Sweden," says Tree.

"All is forgiven. I understand how much you miss home. You are becoming a man and you were dealing with everything the best way you could. I have put a lot of pressure and demands on you and that is a heavy burden of responsibilities."

"I enjoy being helpful. It makes me feel worthy, but I miss my parents and my little brother."

"I strongly believe we will go to America one day," I say. "I hope we can sponsor them."

"Are you sure that is still what you want? I mean, you can have a life here."

"In the camp?"

Tree laughs. "No, I mean with Ommo. He likes you and you like him too but will not admit it."

"I hung my fishing net a long time ago, Tree. I do not want a man to complicate my life. You and Thủy-Tiên are my life now. You both come first."

"More refugees arrive every day and live in makeshift houses. It will be only a matter of time before they build a second camp and we take over this island. Ommo can take you away from all this"

"It is turning into a tent island for sure. There are rice bags and tarps hung everywhere for shade, and fishing line or rope to hang clothes. Ommo is a convenient solution but it would not be right to take advantage of him. And I am not in love with him."

"In time you can love him. He is a good man in the wrong uniform. He serves Indonesia but his heart serves you. I am sure of it."

I laugh. "Tree, you are a romantic. Come, we need to swim."

The three of us splash around in the water for the next hour to forget our problems. Thủy-Tiên finds a crawfish and wants to keep him as a pet. She is mad and pouts when I tell her no.

Sơn and Minh-Tú stroll up to the barrack and call out my name. I poke my head out of the window. Their faces greet me with impatient grins.

"A reunion with my brothers." I fly down the stairs. We keep our formal custom by shaking hands but if there were no eyes around, I am sure we would have hugged like relatives. We sit on the stools outside and catch up.

"Thành got resettled in Germany," says Sơn. "Did anyone get a sponsorship yet?"

"I am happy for Snitch," I say. "We got approved for Sweden but Tree missed the interview and health inspection so we are now waiting again."

"I was sick with Malaria." Tree reminds me.

"There was a lady near my barrack who failed her resettlement interview. She wanted to die when they rejected her application," says Minh-Tú in his thick northern accent.

"She can appeal." I pick up a stick and draw figures of us in the dirt.

Sơn kneels on the ground and uses his finger to give my stick figures hair. "She has three options – appeal, get sent back to Việt Nam or die here."

"If she was pretty or had money, she would have received approval," says Minh-Tú. "There are twice as many men than women here and all the pretty single ones are having relationships with the guards to get their resettlement approved."

Minh-Tú's comment makes me uneasy. It was because of Ommo that I was assigned a barrack upon arrival and because of him that my application for resettlement was processed so quickly.

"I hear the price to bribe the papas is one thousand U.S.

dollars if you want a ticket out of here." Sơn now adds shoes to our stick figures in the dirt.

"This makes me wish I was a rich, pretty young girl." Minh-Tú laughs at his own comment.

"What is a papa?" I ask.

"That is what they call the Indonesian officials," says Sơn.

"Why?"

Sơn shrugs his shoulders. He and Tree focus on drawing a family portrait of us.

"I do not ask questions either," says Minh-Tú. "I am sticking to myself and cultivating a garden to grow squash and chilies. A friend of mine sent me some clothes and I traded them for supplies with another refugee in the camp."

"I want to run a coffee shack," says Sơn. "A relative sent me money so I plan to build a coffee stand to pass the time. My coffee stand will be the only one with music. There is someone who is selling his *Sony CF-210L* portable stereo cassette recorder."

"Fancy. I will be your biggest customer," I say. "The administration offered me a teaching opportunity. I would be teaching English to prepare people for resettlement, but I declined."

"Why?" asks Minh-Tú. "You would be great at it and I would be your worst student." We laugh together at his confession.

"What if I get sponsored soon and have to leave before I make any traction teaching you to say 'Hello, my name is'?" I giggle, happy to be sitting with my honorary brothers, talking about whatever subject the breeze brings.

"At least I would have learned something when I get to Canada or Australia." Minh-Tú beams.

"I bet you will end up in Australia," says Sơn. "There is less red tape and a shorter waiting period."

"But Australia only takes professionals with special skills," proclaims Minh-Tú. "I am a farmer and a fisherman."

"Yes and I was in the army and then an unsuccessful thief trying to steal boats to leave our country," says Sơn.

"Denmark and Switzerland would take you both. They take refugees with special needs," I joke. We all laugh. I wish we had some fried squid and *Heineken* beer right now to ăn nhậu, the pastime of socially eating and drinking with friends.

"Have you seen any of the others who were in our boat since we landed on Galang?" Minh-Tú takes my stick and draws a frame around the family portrait.

"Whatever happened to Biện, the man who stepped on the sea urchin?" asks Sơn.

Minh-Tú and I shrug our shoulders. I tell them about Hồng-Mai and Tùng. We agree to visit them. Perhaps the reunion will do them good and they will not feel alone having friends who care about them. The boat people of trawler 93752 are my new family and I am excited to reconnect.

Tree and Thủy-Tiên join us on the walk. We stroll past the coffee stand that Ommo took me to in the rain. The same two women who were talking rumors about Ommo and I being lovers give me disapproving glares. Am I the camp slut to them? I try not to be disturbed by what they may or may not be thinking about me.

We pass a merchandise stand selling daily sundries. One of them is pushy trying to sell me a sun umbrella. On our walk to Tùng's and Hồng-Mai's hut, we talk about the police brutality Sơn witnessed when some of the refugees staged a hunger strike to protest the unfair treatment here. The military came in with tear gas and dogs. Those protestors were arrested and thrown in jail. He claims the military wants to make life unbearable here so that we want to return to Việt Nam.

Tree shares what he does at night, sneaking out of the camp and running through the forest to get to the beach so he can swim and fish.

"You will be beaten if you get caught," cautions Minh-Tú. "They only let us go on the weekends."

"Why you cannot be like the other kids, Tree, I do not understand. There are safer ways to pass the boredom, like painting one of the shacks or playing soccer or making paper boats to float," I say.

"I am not a kid and I like to sleep and swim," answers Tree. "That is it."

Sơn and Minh-Tú share with us how they survived in the re-education camps. Minh-Tú ate mice, crickets, and frogs raw, and rotten vegetables, spoiled rice, and wild bananas. He got so constipated from the tannins in the bananas and developed dysentery. He almost died. Sơn said leeches feasted on the prisoners and some snakes and lice shared the prison space. Many died from diseases like beriberi and malaria and illnesses like tetanus. Minh-Tú says every week prisoners had to stand naked in their cell while the guards hosed them down with water. Sơn shares how he once caused problems by speaking negatively to the guards. They beat him, twisted his arms and stepped on his head.

"Life in prison was debilitating and tragic," says Sơn.

My thoughts skip to Hải sitting in prison and rotting there because he tried to protect me. Then there is my sweet niece, Tâm, and I worry about her sufferings too. My good spirits become eclipsed by the gloom.

We arrive at Tùng's and Hồng-Mai's hut. We step inside and receive greetings from angry swarms of flies. The odor cripples me and I gasp at the sight of Tùng and Hồng-Mai lying on the cold clay floor, their fingers laced together, with a bottle of *Malathion* between them.

Minh-Tú picks up the bottle of insecticide. "I thought this went down with the boat."

I fall to my knees and wail out the feelings of anger, hurt, betrayal and deep sadness in the loss of my fellow brother and sister. "Why did you do this? Why?" I pound my fists against both of the lifeless bodies before me. I am angry that others did not even care to check on them and that the smell of their death melted in with the sour smells of the camp.

Sơn tries to pull me away and Tree shields Thủy-Tiên from the scene. I cannot take any more deaths. I have to leave this terrible place.

37 GOODBYE GALANG (FEBRUARY 1980)

Life in the camp this past year has been a struggle. I can almost
equate it to the Stockholm syndrome. I have become accustomed to
the daily grind and the routine of accommodating more refugees
each day. Usually, the refugees are ferried from Malaysia, Thailand,
or Singapore, but not too long ago, there was a boat from Việt
Nam that washed directly onto the shores of Galang Island. I can
coexist with the Indonesian military and have learned that not
everyone is bad.

Thủy-Tiên is now five years old and Tree is seventeen. In two
months, I will turn forty-one. Today is Lunar New Year, February
16, 1980. It is the year of the monkey.

Earlier today I visited Hồng-Mai's and Tùng's grave and prayed
they found enlightenment in another consciousness. Many of the
graves are unmarked but theirs is not. We used scraps of wood
from the church that was being built and Tree nailed them together
into a Buddhist swastika. We painted it red and staked the symbol
into the mound of dirt. Minh-Tú planted a chili plant at the base of
the marker so sometimes I take chili to the barrack to spice up a
meal.

Refugees continue to come and go and when there is a group
leaving the camp, there are always people to wish them well at the
harbor. Bảo's departure was bittersweet. His family all got
sponsorships, but unfortunately, got split up and went to different
countries. He was so insistent about keeping them together.
Indonesia continues to take volunteers who wish to repatriate back
to their country of origin. A second camp will be built several miles
from this first campsite and will be opened next year, mid-1981.
People who get accepted for resettlement will transfer to the second
campsite while they wait three months for all the arrangements to

be made. If I am not sponsored by next year, there is a good chance my family will move to the second site. English and cultural orientation classes will be mandatory there and I intend to volunteer for the *Save the Children* organization to help teach English in the camp schools. I get a t-shirt if I do. Through donations from various organizations, my wardrobe has expanded to more than a *Wonder Woman* shirt, a purple blouse, and my ragamuffin chic pants. There is an American man named Gaylord Barr who served in the *Peace Corps* in Morocco and will soon come to Galang. He is going to interview and select volunteers to teach English as a second language to those resettling. He is from Washington State, like Sam and Skyler. Hopefully, my English is good enough and he will select me as one of the teachers.

Social networks have developed here but also rivalries and disputes. Life here is generally mundane and bearable. Sometimes it is even fun. The camp now has many more facilities than when we first arrived. There is running water but we are only allowed to run water an hour each day. A few showers and toilets have been installed and in addition to the camp administration office, Indonesian Red Cross hospital and UNHCR offices, there is a youth center, sports center, and music center, places of worship, a post office, and a cinema that shows Chinese movies dubbed in Vietnamese.

We plan to be entertained by one of the Chinese movies in the cinema today and then celebrate the New Year with some beer and tea in the youth center.

"Aunt Eight, her lips look blue to me," says Tree.

I kneel down and take a hold of Thủy-Tiên's hands in mine. "Is it hard to breathe?" My dolly nods. Her lips are indeed blue and so are her fingertips.

"We should take her to the PMI," says Tree.

"No hospital!" Thủy-Tiên sits down in protest. "I want to see the movie."

"She looks tired and her fingers are swollen," says Tree.

"You enjoy the movie, Tree. I will take her to the PMI."

"No!" Thủy-Tiên punches the ground with her tiny fists. "No Red Cross! No hospital!" She works herself up into a tantrum and instantly turns on the water faucet. Tears pour from her eyes and her face is flushed pink. I pick her up and she fights me. "No PMI!" Her writhing body makes it difficult to hold her. I lose my grip and Thủy-Tiên falls to the ground. She runs from me. "I want to see the movie!”

I grab her wrist and drag her in the opposite direction of the cinema. My daughter stomps on my foot and slaps me in the face. I am surprised that for a sick little girl, she is quite strong. Tree tries to pick her up but with her kicking and punching, he loses balance. They both fall to the ground. Together we drag her away as people gawk. We barely walk two hundred meters before her body goes limp. Thủy-Tiên passes out from the exertion.

The line at the Indonesian Red Cross, known officially as *Palang Merah Indonesia*, is long. There are pregnant women and people with toothaches, snake bites, fevers, and all kinds of illnesses.

I am impatient to stand in line and run to the front. “Please help. She sick. Not breathing!”

Tree is right behind me. People grumble, swear, and push us as we rush past but I do not care. One of the nurses points to a room and tells me to wait. A man standing in line curses at the nurse and argues he has been standing in line for an hour with a deep cut in his arm. I lean close to my daughter’s face and can feel the faint exhale from her nostrils.

Minutes later a doctor comes into the room. He listens to her heart. “Her heartbeat is faint and I can hear clearly a swooshing sound. It is erratic. She definitely has a hole in her heart.”

“Will she live?” I ask fearfully.

“Sometimes the problems will resolve on their own,” says the doctor.

“She have this since she born,” I say.

“Then she will likely need surgery to patch the hole. The blood between the two chambers of her heart is mixing and if left untreated she will have heart failure.”

Tree is worried. “What is he saying? Her color is worse.”

“There is not much we can do for her, except let her rest and monitor her the next few days,” says the doctor.

“No surgery here?” I ask in a panic.

“This is a basic hospital. I am sorry.”

“She cannot die here!” I scream. I grab his shirt and beg him to save her.

***

Two days go by and Thủy-Tiên’s health has improved slightly. My daughter’s tiny frail body is motionless but she is sleeping peacefully. Sometimes she wakes up and asks for water.

Ommo comes to visit. "Has there been any change?"

I nod. "She better. I was scared to bury her here."

He caresses my cheek. "Snow, marry me. Let me take you all out of here. You can finally say goodbye to the camp."

"I want to leave Galang, but…" I am conflicted, torn between wanting to say yes because it would mean we would be taken care of, and saying no because I am not in love with him.

"I know you do not care for me the way I care for you," says Ommo. "But I can make you happy and take care of you, Dolly, and Tree. Please say yes."

His handsome face draws me to touch him. For the first time, I feel the velvet softness of his skin. Ommo puts his hand over mine. The warmth of his fingers radiates through mine. His eyes hold me captive. He leans in and I can smell his minty breath. Our lips touch and I find myself responding to his sweet kiss.

"Yes," I whisper.

***

This morning my name is called over the loudspeaker. Tree carries Thủy-Tiên on his back and we run to the United Nations resettlement processing center.

"Ommo knows how to work his magic," says Tree. "I cannot believe we are leaving this refugee camp."

"We have been here for a year. Can you believe it? Soon we will say goodbye to the Galang camp."

"We aimed for America and we could have landed in Sweden, but here we are, about to permanently call Indonesia our home." Tree gallops like an excited horse and my dolly loves the ride.

"God works in mysterious ways." I slow down to a walk to catch my breath. "Soon I will marry Ommo and we will be much closer to our family and you can return when it is safe to do so."

We check into the office to receive papers from the refugee task force then head to the UNHCR office.

"Hello, Don." I greet the UNHCR representative, who is sitting in the same seat as the last time I was here. I notice the mole between his eyebrows is definitely larger.

"You have all members of your family with you this time." Don shakes my hand. His excitement mirrors my own.

"Yes. We are very excited." I sit down and hand Don my papers. I steal a glance at Ommo, sitting in the third seat, looking very dapper in his uniform. There is a radiant glow coming from his eyes and his smile.

In the middle seat is a man I do not recognize. His name tag says "Joseph". *What happened to the translator, Mary?*

Don picks up on my curiosity and queues the introduction. "This is Joseph. He is a VOLAG representative."

Ommo arches his eyebrow and delivers a questioning glance at Joseph. "What do you mean VOLAG? You are not the translator?"

Joseph snickers. "Of course not. We all know she does not need a translator." Joseph dismisses Ommo and turns his full attention to me. "Hello, Ms. Le. I am with a private voluntary agency and I am extremely pleased to inform you that you have been accepted to resettle in the U.S."

"What do you mean?" Ommo stands up and glares at Joseph and Don. If shuriken stares could penetrate through the skin, Don's and Joseph's arteries would be shredded open right now. That radiance I saw earlier from Ommo has been ignited by a flame that is going to explode.

I am thankful I am not on the receiving end of Ommo's fury. "We go to America?" I divert Ommo's attention away from them.

"Yes, Ms. Le." Joseph is not intimidated by Ommo towering over him. "My job is to provide placement services for you and your family in the United States. There is a church in Seattle, Washington…well, Kent, Washington actually, that has accepted sponsorship of your family. We received a letter from—"

Ommo pounds his fist on the table, making everyone jump. "No, this meeting is to inform her that she is no longer a refugee and—"

"I am sorry but it has already been arranged." Joseph lowers his voice an octave. He rotates his body a few degrees towards me, as if to send Ommo a message that he does not appreciate Ommo infringing upon his business. "Your family leaves in two days."

Ommo kicks back his chair. He clenches his fist but refrains from showing his rage. "What are her options here? She can decline and not accept your services, right?" He sits down and pleads with his eyes for me to reject the placement.

Tree grabs my hand. "What is happening? Why is Ommo so upset? Are we not permitted to stay in Indonesia?" My nephew who never asks questions is now asking all of them at once.

My head is spinning. I am elated about the news yet devastated for Ommo and me. I was mentally prepared to marry him and start a new life with him. I even imagined Ommo playing his rebab for Thủy-Tiên before bedtime. I was getting used to the idea of having a husband and convinced myself I could love Ommo enough to be happy with him.

Joseph ignores Ommo's tantrum and talks to me. "Ms. Le, we received a letter from Skyler Herrington. He is a member of a Presbyterian church in Kent. The church has raised enough money to sponsor your family of three to the United States. I have been working with him and the church to ensure they assist you with housing, community integration, and job placement. They will be there at the airport to receive you in Seattle."

Don stands up, walks around the table, and leans on the edge of it. He is directly in front of my chair. "You can, of course, reject the placement, but your application would not be recycled back into the resettlement process. Your family will be sent back to Vietnam."

"Snow." Ommo intercepts Don's speech. "We are going to marry and start a life together here. Tell them."

Don does not give me time to think. "We need to do a health inspection and give you all the necessary vaccinations today. Your travel arrangements are being processed. In two days, there will be a boat at the harbor to take you and others who have been approved for resettlement to Singapore. It is a five-hour boat ride."

Tree stands up. "He said Singapore. Are we going to Singapore? I do not want to go to Singapore."

I ignore Tree. "Tell me more, Mr. Don." I find it difficult to meet Ommo's eyes. His heart must be breaking and desperate for reassurance that I will choose him over America. I cannot give him the comfort he seeks. My head and my heart are not in agreement.

"You will be in Singapore for two weeks before flying to Hong Kong, then Japan, and finally, to Seattle."

My nephew is now livid. "Hong Kong? What is in Hong Kong? What is happening? Tell me!" I let the news sink in and then tell Tree. "We are staying here." Tree crosses his arms defiantly across his chest. "You accepted Ommo's proposal! Thủy-Tiên is so fragile she might not make the trip. If we stay in Indonesia, we can be closer to our family. We cannot go to America. Either you reject the placement and we get sent back home or you marry Ommo."

I try to calm him down. "Tree—"

"You can go! I am staying." Tree imitates Ommo's actions and kicks his chair back. "I can live with the unaccompanied minors and volunteer for repatriation."

As if Don can understand Tree, he says, "Your nephew cannot stay here by himself. Either you all go or you all stay, or return to Vietnam."

"We never go back to communist country," I say.

Tree stomps toward the exit door. I stand up and block him from leaving. He challenges my authority and pushes me aside. In one quick advance, Ommo slams the door shut and tells Tree not to disrespect or hurt me, but of course, my nephew does not understand English. Ommo restrains Tree and forcefully pushes him back into his seat. I am determined not to let Tree ruin my chances for America. I reach out and take hold of Ommo's hand.

He gently extricates himself from my grip. "There is nothing to say, Snow. Your eyes cannot betray your heart and I already know your decision."

"You are being selfish." Tree's voice is cold. He crosses his arms and looks at me with so much hatred. "You are breaking two hearts if you take us to America."

"This escape was never about your heart or Ommo's. It was about Thủy-Tiên's. I am sorry you feel this way. My heart is broken too, but I am not the selfish one here. My decision to flee our country was not made lightly but I never misrepresented my intentions to go to America." I swallow the lump in my throat and force back the tears. "Mr. Don, Mr. Joseph…I accept the placement to Seattle."

Ommo shuffles over to Thủy-Tiên and lifts her up into his strong arms. "I will escort them to their medical examination and make sure they receive their immunization."

"It is settled then." Don claps his hand together. "The church was adamant that we processed quickly."

Joseph shakes my hand. "Congratulations. I wish you a safe journey. I will be in touch to assist you once you're in Seattle."

Tree does not make it easy for the nurse to check his head for lice, get a blood sample, or give him vaccinations. A physician is called in to finish the medical evaluation and Ommo prevents Tree from leaving the examination room.

"I am not going to beg you to stay." Ommo pins Tree down with the weight of his body. "But please think about the uncertainty that awaits you in America. If you stay here with me, you will be safe. You do not have to work, or if you want, you can teach again. I will make sure your daughter gets help from the best doctor, whether it is in Thailand or Singapore, or here in Indonesia. And Tree can go to school…be close to his parents and return when the conflict is over."

I feel so conflicted right now. One moment I am sure I need to stay and the next, I am determined to leave. "I care for you. I know you be good husband to me. I understand your heart, Ommo. It loves my daughter and nephew very much. But I risk everything to go to America. Now I have chance. My friend Skyler will help us."

"I love you. I want to spend the rest of my life taking care of you. Just give it some more thought."

I nod. Tree springs up and bolts out the door.

***

Wednesday morning I wake up early to the sounds of laughter outside the barrack. I open the shutters and appreciate the view of so many familiar faces. I wave to them. "I will be down shortly." I check to see if Tree is in his bed and am thankful he did not run off in the middle of the night. His eyes are red from crying all night. He jumps off the top bunk, shoves our clothes into a plastic bag, and storms out of the room without saying a word to anyone. I hand Mai my mosquito nets. "I know Bảo gave you his when he left, but you can have ours too. Maybe you will want to sell them."

Mai, Khải, and the twins hug Thủy-Tiên and me, but we save our tearful goodbyes for later. We walk down the stairs and into a crowd of cheers and applause. Sơn, Minh-Tú, and all who are left from trawler 93572, including Biện, are here. Even Tiền and her husband, Trương, came with their daughter, who is now ten months old. Together we walk to the entrance gate of the camp where a large group is already waiting to leave. The school shut down today and there are students and teachers congratulating those of us who are leaving. Personnel from UNHCR, the Red Cross, Red Crescent Society, and other humanitarian organizations wish us the best. There is a lot of excitement today but also sadness to be leaving this camp that has become a home. The military is here to escort us to the harbor. I scan the area but Ommo is nowhere to be found.

The walk to the harbor is leisurely and will take us two hours. There are thirty of us leaving today. I assign Tree the task of walking with Thủy-Tiên and the twins, Mỹ-Kiều and Mỹ-Loan. Perhaps the responsibility will prevent him from running away. I keep searching to catch a glimpse of Ommo but instead I catch sightings of monkeys in the trees and faces of strangers dressed in tan uniforms.

To keep my mind off of Ommo, I chat with Tiền and her husband, Trương. "I cannot believe a year ago, you were pregnant and our lives were so bleak. Now you have a daughter and next month you are going to America."

253

"It was not long ago that we were fighting over drinking water and I was throwing punches at Sơn." Trương chuckles at the memory.

Hearing his name, Sơn joins the conversation. "I told you all to bring your own provisions. At least I brought jicamas." We laugh now looking back on how we behaved.

Tiền can hardly contain her excitement. "Life is full of surprises. My cousin left in '75 and was at a refugee center in Fort Chaffee, Arkansas for a while before she resettled in Oklahoma City. She is sponsoring us to Oklahoma with the help of a Catholic parish."

Trương hands their daughter over to his wife. "Your turn to hold her."

"No, let me hold her." I fight over their daughter. "She is deliciously chubby. You gave her the perfect name. It is very suitable."

"We thought naming her after the empress, Nam Phương, would be perfect," Trương declares proudly. "She will be the bridge between East and West."

"Tell me more about Oklahoma," I say to Tiền and Trương. "What did your cousin say in her letters?"

"Not much, other than it is fairly inexpensive to live there. She opened a restaurant and it is starting to do well. There are many refugees settling there. We are going to help with the restaurant and eventually, we want to open our own grocery store," says Tiền.

"She also said," adds Trương, "those streets are not paved in gold there. Maybe they are in Seattle, but not Oklahoma City. What was the street she mentioned? Classic? Claston?"

Tiền corrects her husband. "Classen."

I chat some more with my friends on our walk to the harbor and divide my time between them. Son and Minh-Tú are still waiting for sponsorship but California and Texas are looking promising. Mai, Khải, and the twins have been approved for resettlement in Canada, but they will be in Galang for another three months while arrangements are made. As for Biện, he has his heart set on Australia.

We finally arrive at the jetty and wait on the dock. The military inspects our bags once again and I notice a few of them take liberties to pocket what they want. My nephew stands solemnly holding Thủy-Tiên's hand. He has barely spoken to me the past two days.

I wrap my arms around Tree. He resists at first. I persist and hold him tighter. "Let me hug you." He eventually gives in. I feel his muscles relax. He weeps. "I love you so much. When we left Vĩnh Bình, I told myself I had to be strong and brave for all of us. When your father asked me to take you with me, I was so scared. I thought, I can barely take care of myself. When Uncle Tý left, I did not know how I was going to take care of Thủy-Tiên. And you know what? You were my partner all along. I drew my strength and my courage from you. You were the one who taught me to take risks. We have come so far and survived so much together. This is another new beginning for us. It is not the end."

Tree squeezes his arms around me and lets go of all the emotions he had bottled up inside. His body shakes and I let him cry until there are no tears left. We stand together with the others who are departing Galang today. There are a lot of hugging, kissing, and handshakes taking place. Displays of yin and yang sentiments pour from everyone, with tears of joy and tears of sadness. Even some of the guards who have built friendships with us are emotional.

A large blue and white ferry boat arrive. The crowd cheers and I am overwhelmed with jubilation. I give Mai and her family another hug and let the tears flow freely. Sơn and Minh-Tú cannot hold back their tears either. One of Abu's men, Gus, announces through a megaphone that we can begin loading. Tree, Thủy-Tiên, and I stand in line with our papers and belongings. To commemorate the day, I wear my *Wonder Woman* shirt. The line moves and we step onto the plank. I turn to wave goodbye. The roar of the crowd gets louder. And then, I see him.

Ommo smiles and waves. I break free from the line and run to him. My handsome, beautiful, kind Adonis. Ommo pushes through the crowd to meet me. He pulls me close and holds me. I stand in his embrace and breathe in his scent.

He kisses my head and hugs me tighter. "The boat is not going to wait for you."

"It will," I say with confidence.

"Write to me. Send pictures." Ommo kisses my forehead. "Come back and visit."

"I will."

Ommo leans down and grazes his lips against mine. His minty breath consumes me and I pull him down to my hungry mouth. I have no cares that people are watching and gasping. I have to take a piece of him with me.

A gentle breeze blows and I reluctantly let go of him. We run together to the plank so that Ommo can say his goodbyes to Tree and Dolly.

I board the ferry boat with my family and the others. As we pull away from the island of Galang, I blow Ommo a kiss. There is only one word to describe this exhilaration. Euphoria.

THE END

Thủy-Tiên aka Dolly (Vietnam, 1974)

HONORABLE MENTION
A war refugee's story of rebuilding and thriving.
SNOW in Seattle
A NOVEL
AMY M. LE

1. ATRIAL SEPTAL DEFECT (AUGUST 1980)

Her face, both lionhearted and bitter, represents the willful baby I fought to keep alive and the hardened woman she may one day become. My daughter rests on the hospital bed with her small fingers squeezing the bedrails. Her eyes cast shurikens at the medical staff as if they are samurais coming for her. Ready for battle, Dolly accepts her fate and acknowledges that her chest will be cut open to fix the defect in her heart.

The fear inside me is parasitic. One would think the origin of the infestation came when Sài Gòn fell and communism blanketed Việt Nam. Perhaps it derived from abandonment and betrayal by my husband who left us in 1975. Or maybe the fear stemmed from the difficulties of escaping my country and facing uncertainties with forty-two other boat refugees on trawler 93752. I am certain my fears began the day I became a mother. That fear has evolved and today, it has a name: atrial septal defect.

"Snow, please step aside and let them do their job." Sky Herrington laces his calloused fingers through mine and leads me to the black upholstered chair with the yellow and red tribal designs. On the wall are pictures of Chief Seattle and David Swinson "Doc" Maynard. Their black eyes drill holes into my heart. They understand about uncertainties.

I watch helplessly as the nurses at Seattle Children's Hospital wheel my six-year-old, my little dolly, into surgery. She gives me a brave smile and waves. My nephew, Tree, stands by the window. His stare is vacant. A tear belies his strength. I ache to comfort him and erase his worries as I did when he was a child. A hug and the promise of some banana and coconut pudding was all it took back then to bring a smile to his face. He is seventeen years old now. My touch repels him and his recoil daggers my spirit. I have only Sky to comfort me.

Sergeant Skyler Herrington, my old friend who was in the US Army, who did everything he could to deliver my freedom but also nothing to save the love of my life. At only thirty-six years old, his vibrant youth has been replaced by careworn senescence. The last time I saw him was eight years ago, in my hometown of Vĩnh Bình, where he stood shell-shocked over Sam's lifeless body. Sam, the soldier I was going to marry…the man who still haunts me when I close my eyes. The Việt Nam War took its toll on all of us, but perhaps in some ways, it robbed Sky of more than his peace of mind; it siphoned the essence of him, the embodiment of everything Skyler.

Still, a part of me resents him for not doing more. More of what, I cannot say. Just more. Can I forgive him for Sam's death?

"Aunt Eight," Tree says, "Thủy-Tiên is not going to make it." My nephew does not turn around to address me. He stares at a photo of the Space Needle and Seattle skyline.

"We did not come all this way for her to die." I want to shove my nephew up against the wall and slap some sense into him. How dare he inflict his doubt on me? Of course, my daughter will make it through open-heart surgery. She's stubborn and resilient. I know Tree is still angry with me for bringing him here to America. I want to punch something.

"I have never seen her skin so blue. And her fingernails…They were black." Tree looks directly at me and challenges me to acknowledge the possible truth that my daughter may die. What if I never hear her laugh again? Never feel her soft, sticky hands holding my own? Never soak up her kisses or melt into her arms?

Sky looks at me questioningly. He does not understand Vietnamese. I give him an unnerving smile. He stands up and mutters, "I'll get us coffee," and strides off quickly. I want to shake him, too, but I remain calm.

How did I get here, to this space where I hate the world and resent those closest to me?

Five months ago I stood on a boat that was docked at Galang Island in Indonesia, saying goodbye to the refugee camp that was home to Tree, Thủy-Tiên, and me…and saying goodbye to my friend, Ommo. To him, I was the woman he loved and wanted to marry, but to me, Ommo was my ticket out of the refugee camp. That was, until Skyler successfully sponsored us to the United States.

The five-hour ferry trip from the Galang camp to Singapore went by quickly, and the two weeks we spent in the Sembawang camp were amazing. As a response to the humanitarian crisis following the end of the Việt Nam War, the British army barracks at 25 Hawkins Road were converted to a Vietnamese refugee camp by the United Nations High Commissioner for Refugees. It was a small transit camp that housed only 150 people; the revolving door of refugees that came through was high.

Everyone there had been accepted for resettlement and was waiting for the next leg of their bon voyage. It was paradise to me with its simple, but clean, accommodations. Each day food was brought to us, and I felt like royalty. The library that became my reading room was painted a happy yellow, and the schoolroom where I tried sewing again was always filled with laughter. Thủy-Tiên and I spent our days playing badminton while Tree explored the area. He often wandered off for hours but always stayed within the confines of our five-star prison.

The number of women and children combined equaled the number of men. I never felt afraid of rape, torture, or murder by the camp leaders, volunteers, or military officials. What a difference between 25 Hawkins Road and the Galang Refugee Camp.

Our sponsorship to America by the Presbyterian Church in Kent, Washington, was surreal. Before long, we flew from Singapore to Hong Kong, then to Japan, and finally to the United States on a Pan American transatlantic flight. I'll never forget my first Boeing 747 experience.

To say the plane was big was an understatement; it was nicknamed the "jumbo jet" for a reason with its gargantuan double-decker body, a spiral staircase leading to the upper seating section, ten doors of entry, wide aisles with a cabin that was eight feet high and twenty feet wide, and rows of nine seats across. It was like flying inside a blue whale, only it was two-and-a-half times bigger. We sat in the bubble of the jetliner and enjoyed Western cowboy movies. Seeing Clint Eastwood on the screen made my heart ache for Sam. It was the closest I had felt to him in a long time.

"Aunt Eight, America is so rich." Tree settled comfortably

in the leather seat and admired the spacious airplane. "I cannot wait to see the streets paved in gold and the big houses."

"We are going to a place in King County, and I bet a place with the word 'king' in it has to be majestic." I was as excited as my nephew.

"Will there be a lot of food and sweets for me to eat?" my little dolly asked. I nodded.

"I hope they have all the bacon we can eat." Tree's eyes lit up.

I was reminded of the Christmas dinner we had so long ago with my family when I fell in love with Corporal Sam Hammond over bacon and hot dogs, items my niece, Tâm, stole from the air force base where she had worked.

We thought of America as grand, wealthy, and beautiful but quickly became disillusioned as we saw how dreary, underdeveloped, and sparse it was. We arrived at Seattle-Tacoma International Airport on a cold, rainy day. It was March 20, 1980, on the eve of spring, yet the chilling fifty-degree temperature made us all shiver in our tropical clothes.

"It is colder here than Đà Lạt," Tree commented. He referred to the central highlands region of Việt Nam where the mild climate vastly differs from the rest of the tropical country.

The three of us deplaned and were ushered through a long walkway before spilling out into a room of pale, white faces, all crowded together with cheers and smiles. People held signs that read "Welcome to America!" and "We love you LE family!" A dull headache formed as my pulse quickened. It was quite overwhelming to see fifty strangers jumping up and down, eager to shake our hands, give us hugs, pat our backs, and thrust flowers or stuffed animals in our arms. Thủy-Tiên whimpered but did not cry. Tree basked in the love and energy of the welcoming committee and unabashedly accepted their gifts.

The first face I recognized was Joseph's, our VOLAG representative, there to assist with the settlement. He was shorter than I expected at 1.7 meters tall; when we met at the UNHCR office on Galang Island, he was sitting behind a desk. Still, five feet, ten inches tall is bigger than the average Vietnamese man.

Joseph pushed his way toward me, a big grin on his face. "Ms. Le, it is good to see you again. Welcome to Seattle." He extended his hand, and I warmly accepted it. "There are a lot of people anxious to meet you. Are you tired?"

"No, but very cold," I said, "but also so happy to be here finally to America."

A very tall, balding man with silver wisps of hair and a full white beard strode up to us. He was wide-chested and heavyset, in his late fifties and full of muscle. The sheer brown and cream striped polyester shirt he wore clung to his skin and accentuated his protruding nipples. His expression was full of mirth, revealing a big smile, two dimples, and shimmers of pure joy in his eyes. He held in his left hand a petite woman's hand. She stood a foot shorter than he did, her hair curly, peppered with blue and white highlights. Her glasses were askew as she fought to keep up and not get knocked down by others. Her crooked smile revealed crooked teeth, but there was no mistaking the merriment on her face. Right next to her was her replica, except she wore makeup, a string of pearls, high-heel shoes, and no glasses. Looking at the two sisters was like looking at Elizabeth Taylor and Joan Collins. I thought I was among movie stars.

Joseph piped up with the introductions. "Ms. Le, this is Mr. Theodore Vanzwol, his wife Catherine, and her sister, Katrina Cunningham. They are your primary sponsors. They were not only huge financial donors, but they fought tirelessly alongside Skyler Herrington and the church to bring your family here as quickly as possible. Katrina is Skyler's mother, and as you can see, she and Catherine are twins. You will stay with Theodore and Catherine in Kent until we get you settled into your apartment."

Theodore could not contain his excitement. He ignored my hand and went in for a tight hug. "Toots and I couldn't be more thrilled." He shook Tree's hand and patted him hard on the shoulder. Tree fell forward but quickly regained his balance. He towered over us at six feet, four inches tall. "You can call me Teddy. Only I get to call the wife Toots, though." He jabbed Tree in the ribs with his elbow and expelled a hearty laugh. Teddy swung Thủy-Tiên up in his right arm and gave her a loud peck on the cheek. I was afraid he'd break all her bones. She squealed like a piglet. I was not sure if it was fear, pain, or delight she was expressing, but then she laughed when he poked her in the stomach.

We next said hello to Pastor George of the First Evangelical Presbyterian Church and his family. He was handsome, unusually tan with dark, feathered hair and a square face. Unlike Teddy, he was quite reserved and formal. He stood a couple of feet away, bowing his head before offering a handshake. His wife, Dawn, was equally matched in looks with her feathered blonde hair and flawless makeup. Their three girls were attractive as well in their Sunday dresses, with their porcelain white skin, sparkling hazel eyes, and silky hair.

"Snow!" A voice I hadn't heard since April of 1972 sang out loud. The crowd swayed left and right as Skyler emerged from the thicket of people.

"Sky!" I yelled. We embraced, and I did not want to let go. It felt for a moment like I was holding Sam in my arms again.

"You're a sight for sore eyes."

"What you mean?" I asked.

"It means I am happy to see you." Sky squeezed my hand. "I see you've met my mom, aunt, and uncle-in-law."

Katrina took hold of my hand and cupped it in her warm, soft ones. "Well, actually, I was waiting for my turn to welcome them to Seattle." Sky's mother was beautiful and glamorous. I did not see much of Sky's features in her and wondered why their last names were different, why Sky was so tall and she so small, and why they both looked sad despite their smiles. In time, I would understand.

Sky squeezes my hand and brings me back to the present. He smiles at me. "A penny for your thoughts." I hold out my hand, and Sky laughs. "It's an old English expression. You don't actually get a penny."

"I have much to learn with expressions," I say. "When we first land in Seattle, meeting your mom, Teddy, and Catherine. I so happy."

"That was the first time I met Dolly. I'm sorry. I still have a hard time pronouncing your daughter's name. Twee Tin, is it?"

I laugh at Sky's attempt. "Yes, that good. I maybe give her American name. Easier to say."

Sky chuckles. "You always refer to her as your little dolly so, in my mind, she's Dolly…but Le, not Parton, without the big boobs. Shit, who knows, she might be the Asian version of Dolly Parton, with big knockers like yours—"

"Sky, I not understand what you saying."

"Never mind. I'm just gonna shut up now." Sky scratches his head and stands up. "Here, drink more of your coffee before it gets cold."

I take a sip of my lukewarm coffee and cringe. "This like water but dirty. I miss the Vietnamese coffee, so strong with condensed milk back home." I remember a time when I would have given anything for a cup of coffee. The war seems so long ago. "It been six hours. You think surgery go well?"

"Seattle Children's has the best cardiologists and surgeons. Don't worry," Sky says.

I nod and turn my attention to Tree, just in time to see him pick his nose and wipe his finger on the chair. He looks at his fingernails and inspects the dirt lodged underneath. He is a mess. He needs a haircut. I will have to see if I can borrow Catherine's scissors when we are back at home.

He will be eighteen in four months. The Vanzwols tell me I need to register him and Thủy-Tiên for school this summer; she will start first grade at Springbrook Elementary. As for Tree, he is too old for high school, but we will try enrolling him just the same.

"What took you all so long?" Sky asks.

Teddy, Catherine, and Katrina rush into the waiting room. Katrina looks beautiful and graceful as usual, but I notice the bags under her eyes. She hugs her son. "Sorry, sweets, traffic was bad, and your father was giving me lip again. I finally had to hang up."

I wonder what Katrina means by "giving me lip." Maybe they were too busy kissing and "hanging up" means a handjob. These Americans must have no discretion at all with their intimate side of life. Public displays of affection are inappropriate in Việt Nam.

"Parking was a bear." Catherine walks toward me and hugs me. "Sorry we are late. By the time we got off work, we had to rush home, feed Biscuit, and let him out to potty. How are you holding up?"

"I tired," I answer. "In my country, we eat dogs to stay alive."

I must have said something strange because everyone except Tree, who does not understand English, freezes, and stares at me. They are all mute, expressionless.

Sky is the first to break the awkward silence. "Dolly has been with the sawbones for six hours now."

"Well, we brought pizza and sodas." Teddy strides over to Tree and offers him the first slice. "I know how teenage boys can eat. You must be famished." Tree looks at the cardboard box and crinkles his nose. Teddy laughs. "Here, like this." He picks up a slice with his hand, folds it in half lengthwise, and takes a bite. "I love me a good anchovy and pineapple pizza. Extra pineapples, light on the parmesan."

The smell is unpleasant, but Tree takes a slice to be polite. Upon biting into the doughy pie, his frown dissipates. Tree bobs his head up and down and grins as he takes a larger bite before swallowing the first one.

"Atta boy." Teddy slaps Tree hard on the knee. "You'll be bulking up and taking girls away from their daddies in no time." He roars in jest. The two of them sit content, chewing their fishy cuisine.

I opt for the "volcano" pizza which has ham, pineapples, jalapeños, and extra mozzarella cheese.

"Why pizza call 'volcano'?" I ask, to no one in particular. "Because Mount Saint Helens blow up and lost the…oh, how you call red sauce from its mountain hole?"

"You mean when she erupted, and lava and ash spewed everywhere?" Katrina asks.

"I can't believe that was just three months ago," Catherine says.

"I can't get over the huge cloud and the destruction," Teddy says. "I doubt the forest will ever recover. You know, Snow, the day you arrived in Seattle, on March 20, there was a magnitude 4.2 earthquake. I think our cheering when your plane landed caused it." Teddy winks. "Then in May, a bigger earthquake, magnitude 5.1, I think, hit and that broke the camel's back. Helen popped her cherry." Teddy laughs and the sound rumbles down the hall. "Now, that's a knee slapper!" Teddy slaps Tree's knee.

Catherine shoots Teddy a look that makes him close his mouth. I understand only half of what they are saying. Poor Tree does not understand a word, so he sits and smiles when others smile.

"It's so sad how many lives were lost, properties destroyed, vegetation wiped out, and all the animals that died," Sky says.

"Hey, let's change the subject," Teddy says. "I got some Seahawks tickets this season. Want to go?"

"Duh," Sky replies. "Is the Kingdome indestructible? Does Largent pee standing up?"

"So that's a maybe?" Teddy says with a twinkle in his eye.

Sky throws a crumpled napkin at him. "Fuck, yeah I want to go…As sure as it rains in Seattle. The SuperSonics just won the NBA Championships. It'll be the Hawks' turn to clench the Lombardi trophy this season. I can feel it in my bones."

I listen to my hosts talk passionately and loudly about

American football for thirty minutes. Their conversations stack over one another. As soon as one person barely finishes talking, someone else steamrolls over with an opinion. They never did answer my question of why the pizza was called the "volcano."

Dr. Hall enters the waiting room. His presence blankets the air like a cloud of smoke, and just like that, all talk comes to a halt as if a referee blew his whistle. I hold my breath. "I have an update on the surgery." His face is stolid.

I walk into Thủy-Tiên's room at the hospital. The sun shines brightly through the window and the warm glow of the light wraps its rays around her face. She is my angel. My eyes mist up seeing her small body connected to all the monitors with tubes and wires. I sit beside her bed and caress her cheeks. Her eyelids spring open but quickly close again. She smiles.

I flip her upper and lower lip like a light switch and listen to the blip sounds as her lips smack into each other. She laughs.

"I know you are awake," I say. "I saw your eyes open. You cannot trick me."

"Mama," she says weakly.

"You are as tough as Aunt Six's callouses," I say. "Our family back home would be so proud of you for being a brave and strong girl."

"How do you know?"

"Because they love you," I say.

"Do I have a new heart?"

"Better than a new heart. You have the same one God gave you when you were born, but the doctors patched it up—"

"I want a new one," Thủy-Tiên says, and the tears threaten to jump, "because the one God gave me had a hole in it."

"Yes, but your old heart stores all the love that Aunt Six, Uncle Seven, and cousin Tâm gave to you."

"And Daddy's love too?"

The mention of Tý startles me. She cannot possibly remember him. She was nine months old when Sài Gòn fell. "Yes, your Daddy too."

"Then I will keep the same heart."

The door swings in, and an entourage of people walk in

slowly and quietly. Behind them is Dr. Hall, the amazing surgeon who brought us this miracle. I leap up and scurry past Sky and the others.

"Dr. Hall," I say and take hold of his wrist, "thank you very much. You save my daughter. She awake, and she look not sick anymore."

"I couldn't have asked for a stronger patient or a smoother surgery." Dr. Hall pulls the hospital gown down to inspect his work. I am in awe of the six-inch cut down the center of her chest, from the base of her throat to a couple of inches above her belly button. The staples in her chest make her look vulnerable. "Looking good." He checks my daughter's temperature and listens to her heart. "We will remove the sutures in a few days, and soon, you can go home." Dr. Hall jots down some notes. "The incision should heal nicely, but it will be at least a month before she feels better."

Tree climbs into the bed with Thủy-Tiên and holds her hand. He whispers something in her ear and she giggles.

"She will start school in a few weeks," Catherine says.

"She is going to need her rest and to take it easy," Dr. Hall advises. "Delay her start until October. I'll give you a note to give to the school. It'll be six months before her heart can handle anything strenuous, so limit the exercise and play."

"We'll take good care of her, Doc," Teddy says, "and make sure she eats a lot of burgers and steaks to regain her strength."

"But no shrimp," I say. "Shrimp make her scar."

"You'll want to check the incision daily. If you notice any swelling, redness, or drainage, these can be signs of infection. You'll get a chart to take home to track her progress and check for signs of fatigue, chest pains, and such. The nurse will give you more instructions when you check out along with some dermal adhesive and dressings."

"Don't worry," Sky says.

"Yes, we'll take good care of Dolly," Katrina adds.

"Dinner should be here soon," Dr. Hall says. "I'll check back tomorrow."

Shortly after Dr. Hall leaves, a tray of food is brought in. Thủy-Tiên eyes the food suspiciously. There are noodles covered in red lumpy sauce, a green gelatinous cube, a bowl of mushy fruit, milk, and a green soda can.

Tree picks up her fork, a utensil he is familiar with after he was introduced to it on the Norwegian ship several months ago. He stabs the noodles, twirls it around the tines of the cutlery, and feeds it to her. Her eyes light up.

"She likes the spaghetti," Catherine says. "I'll make you some when you get home."

"Toots is a great cook," Teddy says. "Where do you think my year-round winter coat comes from?" He pats his belly and laughs. He playfully pats Catherine on the buttocks and leans down for a kiss.

"Oh, stop," Catherine gushes, "you burly beast. Underneath that sexy winter coat is a whole lot of iron."

Teddy flexes his muscles, and biceps emerge like mountains on his arms. He urges Tree to feel them. "You and me, we're gonna work out together. Put some iron on your bones, fatten you up."

We watch Thủy-Tiên eat and observe her facial expressions. She tries the bowl of fruit and spits it out.

"I guess she doesn't like the fruit cocktail," Catherine says. "I don't blame her. Fresh is best."

My daughter washes the taste out with the milk. She swallows it and puts it back down. "This milk is bad. It is not sweet."

I translate for the others. "In our country, milk is sweet with sugar."

"Not here in the States, although we Americans do have a sweet tooth," Sky says. "Maybe she'll like the Jell-O." He points to the gelatinous cube.

"We call that *thạch rau câu*," I say, "but ours is thick and many layers. My favorite with coffee and coconut." Sky, Teddy, Catherine, and Katrina try to pronounce the words, and I laugh at their accent, especially with the word *thạch*.

"Here, wash it down with some soda." Katrina pops the soda can and pours the fizzy, clear liquid into a glass. She hands it to Thủy-Tiên. "7-Up."

My daughter takes a small sip, then a bigger gulp. She chugs the whole glass and asks for more. "Seven up!"

"Hell, she just said her first English words," Sky says proudly.

###

December 16, 1965. That is the birthdate I put on Tree's high school enrollment application. I tell the school he is younger than he is to give him a chance for a free education. With no official paperwork to prove his birth date and legal name, all lost after the communist party took over in Việt Nam, my nephew is now known as Lê Minh Trí and is fourteen again.

"I do not want to go to school," Tree says. "I have not been in a classroom since I was thirteen, and I'll be eighteen in a few months."

"If anyone asks, you are fourteen, turning fifteen in December. The war robbed you of your schooling," I say. "This is your chance to start over and get an education…learn English."

"Being life-smart is better than school-smart."

"You need to balance. Education leads to success. Besides, here, you do not need to work the streets to sell drugs or catch fish to eat or climb trees to survive. America is rich and friendly."

"I cannot learn if I do not understand English." Tree turns his head to look at me.

"Sit still," I command. I stop cutting his hair for a moment and put the scissors down on Catherine's spinning wheel. "At least try. We have the opportunity to succeed. It is what your parents want for you. Otherwise, they would not have made me take you to America."

I hear the floor squeak and see Catherine walk down the stairs to the furnished basement. She shuffles over to us in her furry slippers. Even in her frumpy, pale pink bathrobe and no makeup, she is a pretty woman. She hands me a cup of coffee. "How's it going?"

"Almost done," I say. "Tree ready for school tomorrow." I pick up the scissors and resume cutting my nephew's hair.

"Oh dear," Catherine gasps. "Snow, his hair is very…layered."

I step back to see. His hair is jagged and uneven. The look on my face is enough to send Tree flying into the bathroom to take a look.

A loud groan escapes Tree's throat. He stomps out of the bathroom and stands with his hands on his waist. I have a flashback to when he was three years old and his mother, Hiền, gave him a buzzed haircut.

"Aiyah, he is so cute, like a baby monk," Hiền had said. We had a good laugh about it then. I dare not laugh about his hair now.

"Let me try," Catherine says. She motions for Tree to sit back in the chair. She picks up the scissors and then puts it back down again. "The first lesson of the day. Different scissors have different purposes. There are specific scissors for food, for gardening, for paper…What you have here are pinking shears. You use this on fabric and the zig-zag edges keep the cloth from raveling."

"Raveling?" I ask.

"Yes, it means fraying or coming apart."

Catherine tries to fix Tree's hair. The more she tries to even it out, the more hair drops to the floor. In the end, she cannot fix the haircut. Tree will have to start school with a shaved head.

###

We have been staying with the Vanzwols for six months. While Teddy is at work at Boeing, Catherine occupies herself with spinning wool, knitting, gardening, and cooking. In these past few months, I have learned how to cook spaghetti, sew a pillowcase, and start a garden. On Fridays we clean the house together in case we have visitors but mainly so that Teddy can relax after a long week at work. We often bundle up and take walks to get fresh air and help Dolly get stronger. We have been teaching my daughter basic English so that she will be prepared on her first day of school. Tree has gone to school each day for nearly a month. When he gets off the school bus, Catherine always has a glass of milk and a sandwich waiting for him, usually bologna and mayonnaise or peanut butter and jelly. The milk makes his stomach hurt. We both crave rice, but we do not complain. It is nice not to feel hungry. Sometimes, though, I feel like we are a novelty to Catherine and Teddy, like exotic pets that they do not know what to feed.

Tree is having a hard time adjusting at school with his limited knowledge of the American language, culture, and education system.

Most of the time when I ask him how his day was, he simply answers, "Fine," and heads to his room. When I ask him what he has learned, he answers, "Nothing," and slams the door. His only real joy is bonding with Teddy over food, exercise, or American football.

Occasionally, I get more than one-word answers if I press a little harder and ask the right questions. This morning over breakfast, I take the opportunity. "Tell me what your initial reaction was on the first day at Kent-Meridian."

Tree chomps on his cereal and swallows before answering. "I was shocked."

"How so?" I ask.

271

"Everyone is white. There are no Asians or Mexicans or Blacks. Back home I saw so many but not here."

"Well," I say, "back home there was a war, so you saw soldiers from all parts of the world."

"Do you know how stupid I feel being almost eighteen years old and pretending to be fourteen, in a classroom of immature kids?"

"What about your ESL class?" I ask. "There must be other students you can connect with who are learning English as their second language."

Tree shakes his head. "I sit in the ESL class for an hour with four other kids. There is one boy from India, two kids from Saudi Arabia, and a girl who I think is Vietnamese, but her accent is so thick, and she squeaks like a mouse. I cannot understand her, much less hear her. We all look like mute, dumb, rejected orphans."

"It will get better. Do not give up. You were thirteen when you dropped out of school. This is your chance to start over."

Tree sighs with exasperation. "I have to catch my bus." He shoves the last bit of cereal into his mouth, brings his bowl to the sink, and exits out the front door without saying goodbye. I turn my attention to Dolly, whom I can count on to talk to me.

"Are you excited about your first day at Springbrook Elementary?" I ask my daughter.

"Yes. I will have new friends," Thủy-Tiên says as she devours her Lucky Charms cereal. "Why do I have to tell everyone my name is Dolly Le?"

"It will be easier for them to say 'Dolly' than 'Thủy-Tiên.' It is a cute nickname, and before you know it, everyone will want to be your friend because you are so special, like a doll from an exotic land far away."

"If they make fun of me, I am going to smash them," Dolly says as she grinds her right fist into the palm of her left hand.

Catherine drives us to the school, and the three of us walk hand in hand into the school's administration office. The single-story brick building is deceptively large inside. The office is as big as my father's house back in our hometown of Vĩnh Bình. There are papers everywhere and children's artwork on the walls. A loud bell rings, and children scurry in different directions. It reminds me of the many times the sirens sounded back home, alerting us that the Việt Cộng was raiding the village or a missile strike was taking place nearby. My family would run and hide in our bunker.

A voice comes over the intercom. "Good morning, Dolphins. This is Principal Jenkins. Please stand for the Pledge of Allegiance."

I watch as the office staff rise to their feet and turn to the American flag hanging in the northeast corner. They all put their right hand over their heart and deliver the same words. It brings me back to when the North Vietnamese Army announced their victory over the Khmer Rouge army, and we were forced to cheer to show allegiance to the Northern military forces.

Catherine pledges her allegiance to the flag of the United States of America. When they are done with the recitation, the principal resumes with announcements while Catherine gets my daughter checked in.

I feel Thủy-Tiên's small hand tremble in mine. "I want to go home." She pouts and looks down.

"I know you are afraid," I say and squeeze her hand. "First grade is going to be fun. You are about to start a new adventure."

Her lips quiver, and her skin turns pink. Her eyes puff up, and she wails, "Do not make me go!"

The tear gates open. She wraps her arms around my thigh and squeezes hard. I bend down. She flings her arms around my neck, constricting me like a boa, and hisses at me for being mean, for making her go to school. I try to pry her off.

"No!" she screams.

"You have to go to school," Catherine says. Her words fall on deaf ears. My daughter does not understand. She cries torrential tears. Her voice cracks like thunder and pierces through the principal's voice over the intercom. I remember the last time she had a hysterical fit; it was at the Galang Refugee Camp right before she fainted from getting so worked up. I fear she might pass out again from the exhaustion. I imagine her chest bursting and her heart gushing blood like a geyser out of the hole Dr. Hall patched.

The front desk administrator tempts my daughter with a Tootsie Pop candy. Thủy-Tiên slaps the lollipop away. It drops to the ground and skids a foot away.

"It's best if you all leave now," the administrator says. "The longer you stay and prolong this, the harder it will be for Dolly to adjust."

"She afraid," I say.

"I know," the school administrator acknowledges. She looks at me sympathetically. "We will make sure she has a buddy to help her."

I try to soothe my child. "This nice lady is going to take you to your classroom so you can meet your teacher. You have a friend who is excited to meet you." She gives me a despairing look, but I give her a brave smile. "I cannot wait to hear about your day later."

Thủy-Tiên calms down enough for me to free myself from her bear-trap grip. The administrator quickly takes hold of my daughter's hand. She leads her out of the office and down the hall, dragging my daughter like a ball and chain. One last look to see my child's face—her eyes drill holes into my heart. They turn the corner, and I hear the cries start up again.

I leave the school with Catherine and feel a hundred pounds heavier.

###

The telephone rings. Catherine and Teddy's four-year-old Cairn Terrier, Biscuit, looks at me as if to ask, "Are you going to answer that?"

With Catherine out visiting a friend and Teddy at work, I am home alone. After three rings, I lift the receiver from the yellow phone on the wall. "Alô?"

"Hello. This is Abigail from Kent-Meridian High School. May I speak to Tree's guardian?"

"I am his aunt, Snow," I respond. "How I help you?"

"Your nephew has not been in school the past two days," Abigail says, "and as a matter of fact, he has missed a total of ten days since school started. His absences, excused or not, can result in suspension and failing his classes. I am calling to check if he is okay and when we can expect him at school. If he is ill, we need a note from his doctor." Abigail is speaking so rapidly I do not understand everything she says. I do not know how to respond. "Hello? Mrs. Le, are you still there?"

I am concerned he has not been in school. Every morning Catherine and I see him onto the school bus. There must be a mistake.

"Thank you," I say. "I make sure he go. Bye-bye." I hang up the phone even though Abigail is still talking.

###

Catherine has set a lovely table for dinner. Tonight she prepares a feast of roast beef, mashed potatoes, roasted beets, and

274

corn on the cob. The kitchen is filled with aromas of garlic, butter, caramelized meat, and fresh herbs. My mouth waters.

"I made strawberry rhubarb pie for dessert," Catherine says. "And this is what we call charcuterie." She glides her hand over the platter filled with colorful, edible snacks. There is an assortment of meats, cheeses, crackers, and things I do not recognize. America truly is the land of rich abundance and gluttony.

"We have this in Việt Nam, from the French," I say. "We have pâté, fruits, baguettes, and ham."

"I bet you are an amazing cook. You will have to teach me your favorite dishes."

I shake my head. "No, Catherine, I terrible, but I maybe try make rice and eel for you and Teddy one day. My sister, she good cook. Anything she know how to make."

Mentioning Sister Six makes me sad. A knot forms in my throat, and my eyes glisten with wetness. I turn away so Teddy and Catherine do not see me. But nothing escapes Tree, always observing and taking in his surroundings, never forgetting where he is, constantly ingraining in his memory bank other people's actions, remembering what has to be done.

I scowl at him, partly for witnessing my secret tears, but mostly for skipping school. I know your secret, too, dear nephew. I have yet to punish him. Anger swells inside me, but I suppress the feeling. I turn my attention back to Catherine, who is still chattering on about the charcuterie.

"These are rosemary crackers. I like to put orange marmalade and brie cheese on mine. This is foie gras, along with salami, chocolate-covered almonds, grapes, bleu and gouda cheese, and osetra caviar…very special caviar for this special occasion."

Teddy throws a grape in the air and catches it in his mouth. "But you'll have to wait until dessert for your surprise. It's wonderful to have your family here. Toots and I are excited about this cultural exchange."

While we wait for the roast to cook, we nibble on the snacks. Tree contents himself with talking to Thủy-Tiên and eating the crackers and foie gras. He follows Catherine's lead and spreads marmalade and brie onto a cracker to give to Thủy-Tiên. He scoops a large heaping of caviar onto a piece of salami and shoves it in his mouth. My nephew smiles, nods, and gives two thumbs up.

"Oh dear," Catherine whispers.

Teddy laughs. "The boy has a fine palate!"

"And expensive taste buds," Catherine says. "That was a hundred-dollar morsel he just popped in his mouth."

I translate for Tree. His face quickly changes from pleasure to guilt.

Teddy spoons a big amount of fish roe onto a slice of salami and puts it in his mouth. He winks at Tree as he chews. "Enjoy, son. Tonight we dine like kings. But only I get to sleep with the queen." He laughs at his joke and pinches Catherine on her butt.

"Teddy, stop," Catherine protests. "You're embarrassing them."

"One hundred dollar," I say. "More than my family make in one month."

"Really? And what about during the French occupation of Vietnam?" Catherine leans in. I can tell she is intrigued. I think she is well-intentioned and genuinely wants to know about our life and our history. Still, at times, I wish in my heart I could be rude and not answer. These memories should sink to the bottom of the sea. These sad, tragic stories belong to the dead. They should not have a place in the hearts of the living.

"The French occupy Việt Nam for long time. Under their rule, they turn Sài Gòn into a dizzy city. They call Sài Gòn 'Pearl of the Orient.' My family do not like the French much."

"But the French influenced a lot of your culture," Catherine says.

"Yes, that true. My favorite is French coffee. Việt Nam have perfect climate for coffee. I enjoy mine with ice and condensed milk," I say.

"You know, Sky's father is half French, half British."

The timer on the oven beeps. Catherine sticks a thermometer in the meat. "Roast is done." She takes it out of the oven. "We'll let it rest for a bit."

Why should it rest when it is already dead? I wonder.

"You know, speaking of coffee, I like mine mixed with hot milk for a café au lait," Catherine says.

"And I like mine the color of Tree's hair," Teddy pipes in. "Black!" He ruffles Tree's hair and gives him a jab on the arm. Tree rubs his arm and grins. "Although," Teddy continues, "I do like a good affogato."

I do not know what an affogato is, so I continue sharing my thoughts on the occupation. "The French tax my people big, force us do hard labor on coffee plantations, and make us sick on opium. They make us fight their wars. In my village, my oldest brother die during revolution against French. And Dolly grandmother on her father side raped by French soldier. Dolly father watch it happen when he was little boy. We are peaceful people, but too many years of war make us bitter and no trust of outsiders. My country is small, but we have longest coast. Make it good for fishing and import or export. That why so many want to rule us. The Việt Nam War, which we call American War, change my people. The country is together, but the people are divide and nobody trust anymore. I pray for peace."

"It is good that the country is unified. It will make it stronger in the long run," Teddy says. "War is a terrible thing, but good can come out of it too."

"In time, things will get better, and I should hope you will be able to go back to your country," Catherine says, "and see your family again."

"I hope you right," I say. "I miss my country."

Teddy pops a large crumble of moldy cheese in his mouth. "Dolly, do you like cheese?" He gives my daughter a piece.

She immediately spits it out and shows great disdain for the violation of her taste buds. "Stinky!" Her face turns red. "Like poop."

"We not digest well the cheese and milk," I explain.

Teddy roars with amusement. "I don't think it's a matter of being lactose intolerant. I think Dolly hasn't developed a taste for bleu cheese yet." Teddy turns to Tree. "Here, give it a try."

My nephew reluctantly takes a piece. "Very pungent and salty." We all laugh watching his face morph into an expression of disgust. He swallows the cheese anyway.

"Teddy, you like smelly foods," I say. "We have a lot in my country, like fish sauce, dried squid, and shrimp paste. My favorite is *sầu riêng*, a fruit. On outside the skin is sharp but inside, so creamy and sweet. Very stinky."

"Dinner is ready," Catherine says. She puts the roast on the table. "Shall we pray?"

We all gather around the table, bow our heads, and clasp our hands together.

Teddy speaks. "Dear Lord God and Heavenly Father, we thank you for this time of togetherness. We feel your blessing with this wonderful meal that Toots prepared for us, so lovingly, to feed our bodies and nurture our souls. Thank you for Snow, Tree, and Dolly, for bringing them to safety and enriching our lives with their presence. In thy holy name…Oh, wait. I pray I get a chance to try this stinky, creamy fruit called 'so run' that Snow talked about. The stinkier the better. In thy holy name we pray. Amen."

I laugh at Teddy's mention of the stinky durian fruit.

Teddy carves the roast while Catherine passes the plates of food around for us to serve. We spend the next hour engaging in lively conversation. Tree tries to learn some English words and phrases with Teddy's encouragement. My daughter repeatedly asks for refills on her 7-Up. The meal is so delicious; I cannot stop eating even after I am full. I wonder what my family is eating back home, if they are eating anything at all. I can hear my sister-in-law, Hiền, say, "Aiyah, you do not peel the mango that way," and I can see Brother Seven roll his eyes. I think about my niece, Tâm. Oh, my heart, are you still alive? I imagine her eating her vomit in prison for that false sense of nourishment. I think about my brother-in-law, Hải, and whether he ever received the food we snuck into the reeducation camp. My thoughts turn to Mrs. Trần's son, Lopsided, and hope he is in eternal enlightenment with his parents, suffering no more. Waves of faces come crashing in as I remember the ones lost at sea, the tragedy that struck my boat mates on trawler 93752, and the pain of losing friends at the refugee camp. Angry thoughts rush back over my husband's betrayal. I yearn to speak to my mother and father once more. I want to feel Sister Six's stinging insults and squeeze her so hard she lets out a fart. I half laugh and half cry thinking of her facial expressions. My thoughts turn to Ommo, to Minh-Hoàng, to my beloved Sam.

I taste the salty moisture on my lips. It tastes like the South China Sea.

"Snow?" Catherine reaches for my hand. "Are you all right? Are you crying?"

"Yes," I whisper. "I so happy." I lie. I want to scream, pull at my hair, and curl up into a ball. Poor Biscuit is under the table begging for scraps of food, and for one fleeting moment, I want to kick the dog to leave me alone. Instead, I smile to contain my sadness and feelings of guilt.

"Well, we are happy too," Teddy says. "So, Tree, how was school?"

I swallow my pain and resume my role as a translator.

"Hard," Tree says. "I do not understand anything."

"Give it time," Teddy says. "We are here to help. Just ask."

"I like the music class and the sports class," Tree says. "My teachers are patient."

"That's wonderful," Catherine says. "Have you made any friends?"

"I have a girlfriend," Tree says.

I stare at him in disbelief and sit in silence. Catherine asks me to translate, but I ignore her. I cannot listen to his lies any longer. I bolt up out of my chair and grab him by the ear. He howls in pain. Catherine gasps and covers her mouth with her hand. Teddy stands up. Thủy-Tiên whimpers.

"What girlfriend? The squeaky mouse? You have missed ten days of school," I shout. "What have you been doing? Where have you been going? How can you sit here and lie to us?"

"You do not understand, Aunt Eight," Tree yells back. "I am stupid. I cannot learn."

"You have not tried," I scream back.

"I am not you. I will never learn English. I have no friends. People laugh at me and point. I tell them 'đụ má mày,' but they do not even understand when I swear at them. I hate it here! You should have never brought me. You should have let me go back." Tree briskly walks out of the dining room. He stomps his feet as he exits.

I follow him to the staircase. "I cannot help you if you do not tell me. By keeping my eyes blindfolded, you only serve to tie my hands."

"How can you help? Will you go to every class with me? Follow me around like a damn Việt Cộng? I am sure I will make many friends with my aunt as my shadow," Tree remarks sarcastically.

I want to slap my nephew for his disrespect and sarcasm. It hurts me knowing he is in pain, and I do not know what to do.

"Go to your room," I say with exasperation. "We will talk later."

Tree storms to his room and slams the door shut. From the dining room, I hear Thủy-Tiên cry.

I return to the table. "I sorry, Catherine, Teddy. Tree no go to school for ten days. I mad at him. He lying to us."

"Oh dear," Catherine says. "This must be so hard for him being in a foreign country and starting over."

"I'm afraid to ask how Dolly's first day of school was," Teddy says between mouthfuls of beets.

We finish our dinner quickly and quietly. I help Catherine clear the table and wash the dishes while Teddy reads Dolly a book about a flying boy in green tights who never grows up.

"Do you want dessert?" Catherine asks.

"No, thank you," I say. "I have no room in stomach."

"Do you want to know your surprise?"

"Maybe tomorrow. Tonight, I too sad to be happy."

Catherine rubs my shoulder. "Get some rest."

I nod and walk into the family room. My daughter is curled up on the recliner with Teddy. She fights to keep her eyes open.

Teddy closes the book and sings. "You are my sunshine, my only sunshine. You make me happy when skies are gray. You'll never know dear, how much I love you. Please don't take my sunshine away."

3. THE SURPRISE (NOVEMBER 1980)

Teddy and Catherine rise particularly early on this Sunday morning. I hear their movements downstairs. The smell of coffee brewing in the kitchen beckons me to roll out of bed. Outside the skies are overcast, and the dew of the autumn morning makes me hesitant to face another disillusioned day. The entire landscape is blanketed in a blue-gray haze. A row of pyramidalis trees line the property and are perfectly hedged to give the Vanzwol property privacy. Their backyard oasis is a swirl of blues, oranges, reds, and yellows as if an artist used his fingers to create his oil painting masterpiece. The bouquets of hydrangeas are mesmerizing, and the fall harvest leaves on the trees glow like fire. In the distance, a wisp of light makes the water fountain coruscate. The only sign of life outside is a ladybug clinging to the vastness of my window.

"I feel the same as you, lady beetle. So small in this big world," I say. "At least you can fly away with no worries. You do not suffocate from loss like me."

"Snow, are you awake?" Catherine calls from the bottom of the staircase.

"Yes, I awake," I respond.

"Good. We are going to the nine o'clock service this morning. Pastor George is making an announcement to the congregation, and you will want to be there."

I nudge my daughter awake. "Time to get your church dress on."

I lift her onto her knees and slip the pink, ruffled dress over her head. She slumps side to side like an intoxicated invalid. Her eyes remain closed as she slips her small arms through the puffy sleeves. Her curls tickle my arm. I work to pull her cotton tights up her legs.

Thủy-Tiên straightens her legs and stiffens her body. She makes me work hard to dress her. "Pretend I am a big rock, Mama." She giggles.

I play along with her game. "Dear Lord, help me move this heavy rock off the bed so I can get it to church." I pretend I cannot lift her. "Oh, what is that you say? If I tickle her, the rock will be easier to move?"

My daughter squirms to the other side of her bed and springs out from the covers. "Try to catch me." She laughs and protects her body from my wriggly fingers. She shrieks hysterically when I lunge at her.

I give her half a dozen kisses. "Brush your teeth and meet me downstairs."

I check Tree's bedroom. He is not in bed. I clutch my chest. My heart jolts into action. I run downstairs. My thoughts jump to memories of the refugee camp. Why did you run away? I find Catherine in the kitchen. "Catherine!"

She takes a small step backward and leans against the stove. Her mouth agape, she quickly puts the coffee pot down. "What is the matter? Is Dolly all right?"

Teddy and Tree appear from the dining room. I exhale with relief. "Dolly okay." My nephew's smile reassures me I have not lost him. "I…Do you have pantyhose I borrow?"

"Your nylons run off with my socks again?" Teddy winks and laughs.

"Oh, Teddy," Catherine says. She rises to her tippy-toes and kisses him. "Snow, what do you think of Tree's suit? Doesn't he look handsome?"

I nod. "It so perfect." My nephew looks very grown-up in his cobalt blue pants and matching jacket. I beam with pride and wish Brother Seven and Hiền could see their son now.

###

Pastor George greets us at the entrance of his First Evangelical Presbyterian Church. "Welcome. Good morning." His dark, feathered hair is shorter since I last saw him, making his face look more square and chiseled. He shakes my hand. "Cold hands but warm heart. Glad you can join us, Snow."

Pastor George's wife, Dawn, wraps her arms around me and squeezes. She is deceptively strong despite her thin frame and bony arms. Her blonde hair looks darker today, like it had been soaked in molasses. Perhaps it is the November dampness that has turned her golden streaks to ashy caramel. She appears prettier and younger each time I see her.

"Your hair so pretty," I say. "It darker."

"Yes, well, the summer sun gave me highlights, but now autumn has set in," Dawn says. "Your hair is getting long. It is lovely."

I smile and thank her. Dawn's three daughters walk over to us. The oldest, Olivia, takes hold of my daughter's hand. She is twelve years old and a replica of her father. Although pretty, the squareness of her features makes her look oddly masculine. She is my favorite of the three with her sweet and calm demeanor, her love and respect for all beings, and her mature sensibility in handling distracted children. "Dolly, are you ready for Sunday school?"

Thủy-Tiên looks at me. "What did she say?"

I nod my approval. "Go with Olivia. She is going to take you to school."

"School again?" Thủy-Tiên shakes her head. "No."

Pastor George's middle child, Opal, leans down. Her hazel eyes look straight into my daughter's umber ones. "There'll be cookies and milk after worship." Her bribery does not work.

Thủy-Tiên scrunches her face and sticks out her tongue. "No milk."

Opal folds her arms. "Well, I tried." She turns and strides into the church. It is difficult to get close to Opal. She is a willful child who can be controlling and demanding when anyone disagrees with her or challenges her authority. In some ways, Opal reminds me of a ten-year-old version of Sister Six.

"She always looks mad. If she smiles, her face will crack," Thủy-Tiên says. My daughter believes Opal's face is broken and is dialed into the "grumpy" setting one-hundred percent of the time.

The pastor's youngest daughter, Ocean, is the prettiest, with tight flaxen curls, pearly skin, and inquisitive eyes. At age seven, she already knows how to turn on her charm. She takes hold of my daughter's hand and simply says, "7-Up."

The two of them walk off together toward Sunday school. Although Ocean is only a year older than Thủy-Tiên, she is almost a head taller. These Americans are so tall. What do they eat?

"Skyler, Katrina," Dawn says. "We're so glad to have you both today."

I turn to see Sky and his mom hugging Dawn. The mother and son duo look like they walked straight out of a glamorous movie set and into the foyer of God's house. Katrina is stylish in her houndstooth dress and trench coat. Poor Catherine looks so plain and homely next to her twin.

Sky walks over to Tree. "You sure clean up nice." He shakes my nephew's hand and comments on his hair. "Buzzcut, huh? It suits you."

"Well, apparently there was a mishap with pinking shears," Teddy says. The two of them laugh.

Catherine links her arm with mine and leads me to the front pew. Katrina walks with us. The men follow. How strange.

"In Việt Nam," I say, "the man is number one. Woman follow man."

"Oh, honey," Katrina says, "you'll soon learn that in the States, women come first."

"Hallelujah," Catherine says. "We let them think they are first, but we women are really in charge."

"Amen," Katrina says. "They are all big babies who need mothering. They couldn't find their ass unless we handed it to them."

The three of us laugh at our little secret. I feel a kindred spirit with these sisters.

The organ music plays, and Pastor George walks to the pulpit. My chest swells, and I am overcome with peace and grace. The choir sings, and the energy in the chapel is electric.

Following a scripture reading, Pastor George gives a powerful, emotionally charged homily about giving our anxieties to God. He is so passionate about addressing the assembly, his body shakes, and tears stream down his face. "Proverbs 12:25. What do you think he means when he says that an anxious heart weighs a man down, but a loving word lifts him up? Friends, many of our soldiers came back from the Vietnam War with a heavy heart and a burdened soul. We didn't see what their eyes saw. We don't know what it's like to fire an M-16 and instantly extinguish a life. Nor have we piloted a helicopter over the jungles of a foreign land, searching for our prisoners of war. We didn't breathe in the toxic gas, step on landmines, carry our fallen friends to safety, or watch helplessly as civilians died before our eyes. Our veterans have. And they came home to a seditious country, plagued with civil unrest and shame. They came home with missing limbs, with anxieties and fears and nightmares. Friends, they carry this deep in their hearts, and it is our job, yours, and yours, and yours…” Pastor George points at members of the congregation, including Katrina. “And mine…each and every one of us has a responsibility to help alleviate the anxiety in their hearts, to lessen the burden, to help wipe the tears. And all it takes, my friends, is kindness. But to help others, we need to also help ourselves. I want you to unload your anxieties on God. I want you to love and be loved. Only when we are free can we begin to free others. Brothers and sisters, we have many veterans here in our house this morning who are hurting. Let us show them kindness and help them give their anxieties to God.”

I glance over at Sky. His sorrow, unharnessed, bursts through his eyes, and the tears flow unabashed. His wails resonate within the church walls and crash between the ceiling and floor. Katrina stands sobbing quietly next to her son. My tears escape, too, thinking how hard it must be for Sky to carry the burden of witnessing Sam die before his eyes and feeling powerless to save him. My hardened heart relinquishes the blame I hold over Sky. I reach over and squeeze his hand.

Pastor George continues. “First book of Peter, chapter five, verse seven. ‘Cast all your anxiety on him because he cares for you.’ Philippians chapter four, verses six and seven. ‘Do not be anxious about anything, but in everything by prayer and petition, with thanksgiving, present your requests to God. And the peace of God, which transcends all understanding, will guard your hearts and your minds in Christ Jesus.’ Friends, turn to one another, and give thanks for one another.”

“Peace be with you,” Catherine says to me.

“And also with you,” I reply. I turn to each person around me and say, “Peace be with you.” I take hold of Sky’s hand, and he pulls me in for a hug. “Peace be with you, Sky. There nothing we can do to save Sam. I forgive you, and I sorry.”

As I hold Sky, I feel the tension in his body release. “I am sorry too. I let you down.” He hugs me tighter, and together we exhale.

The choir sings “Praise the Lord,” and we join in as the collection plate is passed.

Pastor George closes the service with some blessings and an announcement. The children are brought in from Sunday school, and all line up in front. Tree taps my shoulder and points to Thủy-Tiên, who stands next to Ocean and Olivia. My daughter tugs at her dress and scratches her thigh. The tights must be itchy on her. She fidgets and looks for me. It does not take long before she spots me in the front row. I wave to her. She waves back and gives me a "thumbs up" sign. She is catching on fast with the American culture.

Pastor George blesses the children and says a prayer. Each child sits down cross-legged and waits to be dismissed.

"Before we end service today, I have a special announcement," Pastor George says. "Snow, Tree, and Dolly…Can you please stand and come up here?"

Katrina and Catherine urge me to stand up. I hear Teddy say, "Stand up, son."

We both walk to the front. Pastor George and Dawn receive us on stage while Olivia, Opal, and Ocean escort Thủy-Tiên up to join us. I look out at the congregants, to the field of white faces. All eyes are on us. Most are smiling as if they are in on the secret surprise. A few are scowling and look away when our eyes lock. I feel uneasy being in the spotlight. I believe in their good intentions but feel like a charity case. I know it is because of their tithing and fundraising that my family is here, and it is by their generous grace that we have the necessities of food, shelter, and clothing. Yet I cannot help but feel guilty for being here while many other refugees have perished or suffered. I look at the warm, encouraging smiles from Teddy, Sky, Katrina, and Catherine and wish they were Vietnamese. I do not see one person with the same skin color as mine or anyone remotely Asian-looking. I feel small, alone, and sad. Right now, more than anything, I yearn to be with my family as we were many ocean waves ago, eating Vietnamese cuisine, sharing stories, and teasing one another mercilessly.

"Last year you all answered God's call," Pastor George says, "and together we raised enough money to sponsor this family to the United States. In March we were there to greet them at the airport and welcome them to Seattle. Now, as you know, the Vanzwols, Ms. Katrina Cunningham, and Sky Herrington have been shepherding them in their day-to-day living, and they've been doing a splendid job helping Snow, Tree, and Dolly get acclimated. Today we reach another milestone as we give them wings to establish a new life here on their own."

The assembly claps. At the end of the long, carpeted aisle, I see Joseph, our VOLAG representative, walk toward me. His face lights up, and he quickens his pace to the front of the church.

Pastor George turns to us. "Snow, it is with great joy that your family here at First Evangelical Presbyterian Church presents you and your family with this gift."

Joseph extends his arm and sets a pair of brass keys into my hand. "Welcome home, Snow. We found your family an apartment of your own."

I look at Joseph, confused.

Joseph laughs. "These are the keys to your home. Just in time for Thanksgiving. How about that?"

My legs tremble. It hits me what he is saying, what the keys represent. I cover my mouth as the tears surge down my face. "Gia đình của mình có một ngôi nhà!" I scream in Vietnamese. Tree and Thủy-Tiên jump at the news. Arms fly all around me as they hug and rejoice. I realize the congregation looks confused. "Our family have house!" I yell in English. Cheers erupt, and congratulatory handshakes are exchanged.

"Do you want to go see it?" Joseph asks.

I nod and beam with happiness.

Katrina, Sky, and I follow behind Joseph's car, a beautiful glacier blue 1975 Buick LeSabre convertible with white interior, wood trim, and chrome accents. Tree rides shotgun in the front with Joseph, and although it is the start of November, they have the top down and the heat blasting high.

We cruise down to the East Hill-Meridian side of Kent and pull into an apartment complex along 108th Avenue Southeast. The sign out front reads Homestead Apartments. Teddy and Catherine pull into the parking spot next to us.

Thủy-Tiên is the first to jump out of the car. "Hurry. I want to see our new home."

There are three brown two-story apartment buildings in the complex, each separated by sidewalks that lead to a backyard area. The buildings look new, and each section has a letter of the alphabet nailed to the cedar boards.

Joseph points to the building marked H. "That one is yours, on top. The corner units are usually a little bigger, so I think you'll like it. These apartments were built in 1977, just three years ago. In the back is a grass area for the neighborhood kids to play, and in the center is a courtyard for basketball and hopscotch or four-square. There is a community clubhouse, too, that you can reserve for parties. Are you ready to see the inside?"

I am already ahead of him, bounding up the stairs, anxious to insert the key and turn the lock.

Thủy-Tiên counts the steps to the top. "Thirteen."

I cross the threshold and breathe in the fresh scent of pine and lemon. There are two doors to the right of the hallway and one door on the left. As if reading my mind, Joseph says, "There are two bedrooms and one bathroom. And over this way, there are two hallway closets."

Tree goes into the first bedroom closest to the entrance door. "This one's mine."

Thủy-Tiên runs into the other room. "And this one is mine, but you can share with me, Mama."

"Take off your shoes," I command. "Where are your manners?"

They both shuffle out of their shoes and run to the living room. I am still in disbelief. The light from the windows warm my skin, and I dig my nyloned feet into the soft, shag carpet. In the living room, a sliding glass door opens out to a deck with a storage closet to the left. Down below, I see the sloping grass area for the children to play, and on the far side of the fence, there is another apartment complex.

"The adjacent apartments are the Cascade Apartments," Joseph notes. "You can cut through those apartments to get to Dolly's school. Springbrook is a mile away and an easy walk through Cascade. You'll love the walk. There's a property next to the school that has horses, and they love to graze next to the fence where the children walk."

"There are a few community colleges nearby if you want to take classes," Catherine adds. "I think some vocational training for you and English language training for Tree would be a good start."

"Back home, I was math teacher and also bank teller," I say. "Maybe I get job like that here."

"That's splendid," Catherine says. "I don't see why not."

"You are very close to Safeway when you need groceries," Katrina says. "It's just at the corner. There will also be a new convenience store down the road on the same side of the street as your apartment. Otherwise, you can cross the street to the 7-Eleven."

A loud whistle skewers my ear, and outside I hear a man yell in a deep, growly voice, "Melissa."

We all scramble out to the deck to see what is happening. The sharp, shrill whistle sounds again, and the same rough, masculine voice yells, this time with more authority. "Get your butt in here now!" The voice comes from the building to my right, around the corner.

I catch a glimpse of a man with long black hair that hangs down to the middle of his back. It looks coarse. He wears black shorts and a dirty, white tank top. His legs are thick and so are his arms. A large black and gray suncatcher tattoo covers his neck. His skin tone is dark, almost red-brown. He walks inside his apartment from the deck before I can see his face.

A moment later, two girls appear from behind the community building and run toward us. They both have long blonde hair that sticks to their faces from sweat. The smaller of the two children look up at us long enough for me to see her green eyes and freckles. My guess is she is six or seven years old. The other child is older, perhaps nine or ten. The freckled blonde waves to Thủy-Tiên.

"Come on, Jen," she says to the older girl. Both girls run off and disappear between the two buildings.

"Well, I hope that doesn't become a regular occurrence," Sky remarks. "That's kind of annoying."

"Are they going to be safe here?" Teddy asks. "Maybe you all should just live with us forever."

The thought of living with Teddy and Catherine forever does not appeal to me at all. "Thank you, Teddy, but we cannot trouble you more. Joseph, please, how we can pay for this?"

"Your first year of rent will be taken care of. Homestead Apartments is low-income housing that the government subsidizes. With your permanent-resident alien status, you are eligible for public assistance to help you transition to independence and citizenship. You are very fortunate. Katrina and Sky are covering the difference in rent, and the Vanzwols have hosted you for eight months, which is seven more than what was initially planned. Even the church has gone above and beyond. Members of the community are stopping by shortly to deliver some furniture and food for your fridge and pantry."

I am speechless and ashamed of my thoughts earlier of feeling like a charity case. Once again, my eyes mist up. "Oh, thank you. Thank you all. Thank you so much!" I hug everyone and tell Tree and Thủy-Tiên to show their gratitude.

"I get to teach you and Tree how to drive," Sky declares.

"Yeah, he picked the short straw," Teddy exclaims. He playfully punches Sky in the arm.

"Short straw?" I ask.

"It's a thing we do to decide who has to do an unwanted task," Catherine says. "We didn't actually draw straws though."

We all chat a little bit more about logistics, such as how I receive my welfare benefits, how often I have to check in with the Department of Social and Health Services, and how the food bank operates. I also learn about dialing 9-1-1 for emergency help and a book called the *Yellow Pages* that lists every telephone number to all the businesses nearby.

"It looks like the pastor and his entourage are here," Katrina says. "I'm going to bid you farewell and stay out of their hair. See you all in a few days for Thanksgiving. Joseph, you are welcome to join us."

"I came with Mom," Sky says, "so she's my ride. I'll check in on you later, Snow, and we'll have our first driving lesson after Thanksgiving."

"Smart idea," Teddy says. "You'll want some of that turkey and cranberry relish in case it's your last meal."

Catherine elbows Teddy in the ribs. "Always the jokester."

They say their goodbyes to us and greet Pastor George and his crew of three men on the way out the door. I send Tree down to help unload the truck and bring up furniture and supplies. After an hour of going up and down a flight of thirteen steps, we finally bring in the last box.

Pastor George stands before me, panting and sweating. "I'm not as young as I used to be."

We both share a chuckle. He helps himself to a glass of water from the kitchen faucet. It still amazes me how easy it is to get access to clean, drinkable water here in America. And Western toilets are my favorite invention. Where our waste goes after flushing is a mystery to me. It beats squatting over rickety bamboo boards over a pond of fish, hoping you do not fall in and that no one disturbs you while you're in the outhouse. This truly is the land of technology and riches.

"Pastor, the sermon today very good," I say. "Make me cry."

"I'm glad you received the message," Pastor George replies. "What are your anxieties?"

I sit down on my previously-owned sofa donated to us by a church member. I pat the fuzzy velour cushion and invite the pastor to sit down. I am undecided on whether I love it or find it hideous. The design is a bit busy. The fabric has repeating images of a rustic barn with red and gold daisies around it and pheasants peering at the barn from between the flowers. The dark wood accents on the arms and legs have rust-orange markings on them like it has been scratched and dented one too many times from being moved. I do like the smell of it, with its hints of peppermint and sticky-sweet mothballs.

"I have many anxieties," I start, "but today, I let go of the one I hold in my heart for Sky. Many years I hold anger and cannot forgive him. I forgive him now."

"That is good. Love and forgiveness are what he needs, but it is what you need as well. It is important to love and forgive yourself."

"Yes. When my Sam die, my heart die too. It freeze and turn to stone. Sky with me when Sam die, and I think he freeze too. I did not know I was mad all this time. I too busy running from the Việt Cộng and keep us alive. Now, no more running, and I realize many emotions. I feel bad I hate Sergeant Skyler for so long."

"My dear Snow, such is life. When you stop, everything comes crashing. God gave you the grit and tenacity to make it this far. He will give you the strength to get to the finish line. Giving your anxieties to Him is the first step. Learning to love and forgive, not only yourself but others are the next step."

"Thank you for everything."

"You're welcome. Come talk to me at any time. Dawn and I are here for you and your family. You're stuck with us like this barn is stuck to this couch."

4. THANKSGIVING 1980

Today is Tuesday, November 25. Tree, Thủy-Tiên, and I spend the
day getting settled into our new apartment. Outside the rain comes
down steadily but not pounding hard like in Việt Nam, where the
streets boil from the pummeling water droplets. My daughter is in
charge of sorting all the clothes into piles for each of us, then
folding or hanging them in their respective bedrooms. I empty the
boxes filled with kitchen items and put them where they belong,
while Tree hangs our framed art pieces and decorates the home.

"Where do you want to hang the cross and this picture of
Jesus?" Tree asks as he takes a voracious bite of an apple.

"Above the television," I respond.

He walks over to our previously-owned RCA color TV in
its wooden box and powers up the console. "I wish there were
more than six channels...four, five, seven, nine, eleven, and
thirteen. That is it." He turns the dial a full rotation.

"We are lucky to have a television," I remind him.

He goes through all the channels again and stops at channel
four. A familiar, funky tune catches my attention.

"Oh, yes," I say excitedly.

Thủy-Tiên runs out of the bedroom into the living room.
She recognizes the tune as we have watched the show many times
with Teddy and Catherine.

"Come knock the door," she sings.

Tree echoes the same verse. We all hold our hands out like
we are holding a microphone.

"We wait on you," she sings.

Tree and I chime in. "We wait on you...Where kisses hers
and his and hers, three company too."

"It is eight o'clock," I say. "We will watch this show and then get ready for bed. School tomorrow, then Thanksgiving the next day."

The three of us huddle around the television set and watch the Downhill Chaser episode of *Three's Company*. It is the happiest period we have had together in a long time as we laugh at the slapstick comedy.

###

We carpool with Catherine and Teddy to Katrina's house. As we pull off the main road, we are welcomed by umbrageous pink dogwood trees that line both sides of the six-hundred-feet driveway. Teddy slows the car as we approach the immaculately landscaped circular drive. An asymmetrical, mid-century home sprawling across the high-noon sky comes into view. Unlike Teddy and Catherine's multi-level home, Katrina's is a custom ranch with a low-pitched gable roof that extends out to give the front entryway shelter. Bright hanging baskets with blooms of fiery orange and crimson red adorn the wide hanging eaves. The home is nestled six hundred fifteen feet from the road, surrounded by twenty acres of lush woods, blackberry thickets, a greenhouse, a barn, stable, and a large, fenced, round pen, about one-hundred feet in diameter—big enough to train two horses in the bullring at the same time.

Katrina opens the door before we have a chance to knock. "Come in! Happy Thanksgiving!" She is dressed in classic black slacks, a cream-colored V-neck sweater, and black Mary Jane pumps. How polished and regal she looks.

"For you," I say and hand her a floral bouquet.

Sky is a couple of steps behind her. He wears an apron with an image of a big turkey on it. He looks funny since the entire apron is brown with ruffles around the trim in alternate colors of red, yellow, and orange. In the center of his chest is the face of a turkey. He holds a drink and greets us. "What would you like to drink? We have eggnog, virgin or spiked, your choice…and wine, regular or mulled. There's also hot buttered rum, champagne, and of course, 7-Up."

Inside, the smell of cinnamon and chocolate tantalizes my senses. Catherine and Teddy hand over their homemade honey rolls, cranberry-orange relish, and pumpkin pie. They head straight into the living room. I kick off my shoes, eager to see the house.

"Keep them on," Katrina says. "We keep our shoes on here."

293

"In my country, it bad to wear shoes inside. We do everything on the floor. Eat, sleep, prepare our food, play…"

Sky takes our coats. "Is that why? All this time, I never knew. That makes sense though. It's as if you're walking on someone's bed or dining table with your dirty street shoes." He disappears down the hallway for a couple of minutes and reappears with a wrapped gift. He hands it to Thủy-Tiên. "I hear you've been a good girl, Dolly."

My daughter nods and accepts the gift with both hands.

"Say 'thank you,'" I remind her.

She tears open the present, and a big smile spreads across her face. "Thank you!" The box contains a pink Barbie wardrobe closet, one Barbie doll, and a few accessories, such as tiny pink shoes, sunglasses, a purse, and a suitcase. The closet has three outfits including an evening gown. "Pretty." My daughter strokes the long blonde hair.

"Good heavens," Catherine says. "That should entertain Dolly for a while."

"A dolly for Dolly," Teddy says.

My daughter sits down on the floor and looks at Teddy. "Mr. Van, you play."

Teddy sits down in a procession of three steps: first kneeling on both knees while his hand uses the coffee table for support, then leaning sideways onto his hip before finally swinging his legs around to sit cross-legged. "Sky, get your dear old uncle a drink, will ya?"

Sky comes into the living room. "Here you go."

With his eyes still on my daughter and his arm outstretched to receive his drink, Teddy grabs what Sky hands him—only it isn't a cocktail. "What the—?" He looks at his hand to find a Ken doll. We all laugh. In Sky's other hand is the cup of hot buttered rum for Teddy. "That's more like it!"

Tree sits down and plays with them. Katrina hands him four plastic horses. "You can play with these. I've had these since I was a kid. This one," Katrina points to the gold horse with a flaxen mane and tail, "is my favorite. My first horse was a palomino named Butterscotch."

"Pal-oh-mee-no?" Tree asks.

"Yes, that's right. And this one here is a Cleveland Bay."

"Clee-lun-bay."

Katrina smiles. "A great uncle of mine gave me this one on my fourteenth birthday. This one here is an Arabian."

"Uh-rab-un."

"See how its tail is up? That's partly because of their breeding but also because they have fewer vertebrae than most horses. And because of their compact bodies, it's more comfortable for them to hold their tail up, especially when they canter." Katrina points to the fourth horse, a spotted white and brown one. "This is a paint. Tree, I think your first English words will be equine ones!"

Sky takes my elbow and leads me to the sliding glass door. "Want a nickel tour of the place?" I do not understand what he means. He must have sensed this or read the confused expression on my face as he explains. "It's another idiom of ours…an expression meaning a quick look. Back in the old days, people paid five cents for a guided exhibit."

We walk into the open kitchen, and the aroma of a roasting turkey invites us to peek in the oven. Sky turns on the oven light. "Another half-hour and the turkey will be done. It'll have to rest for a bit before I carve it."

"Sky, you cook?" I ask, impressed to know a man is not afraid of the kitchen.

"I'm no cook like Aunt Catherine, but I'm not bad. I had a lot of practice growing up." The corners of Sky's mouth lift into a smile, but he looks sad. Perhaps I am imagining it, but I sense a memory has emerged that he would rather forget.

"The kitchen so big," I exclaim, "and bright." The big windows let in a lot of natural light while the white walls give the room an airy feel. On the walls are three art pieces from the 1950s, replicas of Pablo Picasso's *Women of Algiers* series.

We walk into the dining room next. There is an accent wall painted in teal with a graphic wall hanging in geometrically opposed shapes of squares and circles in colors of orange, brown, green, and bright blue. It is very eclectic.

"I made that in art school," Sky says. "I hate it, but Mom loves it."

"I think it wonderful, like splashes of life," I say. "You see?"

"What do you mean?"

"The blue for sky, the brown for earth, green for life, and orange for sun. See? You have talent too."

"I never looked at it that way. My dad is the one with artistic talent." That sad expression appears again on Sky's face. He is quiet for a moment, and in the few seconds of awkward silence, I study his eyes. They look at me but do not truly see me. He looks distant and lost. I want to ask him what is wrong but dare not intrude. I touch his arm, worried that the wetness on his lower lashes will develop into thick tears. Sky clears his throat. "Anyways, my grandfather was also very talented. He built this teak table for my parents as a wedding gift. It seats six but expands to accommodate ten people. Maybe Grandpapa hoped there'd be more grandkids."

"The table lovely," I say.

The centerpiece on the table is a gorgeous floral arrangement dominated by orange gerbera daisies. In front of every chair, resting on red placemats, are crystal wine glasses, fine china plates, silver flatware, cloth napkins, and hand-blown water tumblers in swirls of tangerine and avocado. The table is set for eight tonight. How odd as there are only seven of us. Maybe it is a place setting to honor a dead relative. The memory of my niece, Tâm, surfaces. Now it is my turn to feel sad.

"We have more guest coming?" I ask.

"There is a chance my dad might show up," Sky answers dryly. "Let me show you the rest of the house."

Sky leads me into the bedrooms and bathrooms. Each of the three bedrooms proudly displays some kind of abstract art on the textured wallpaper, and every bathroom has a sunburst mirror in either a rustic mahogany finish or brushed silver lines. My favorite room in the house is the reading nook. Books huddle cozily together from floor to ceiling; their spines beckon me to touch them; the pages vie for my readership. The plant-based motifs of floral slate wallpaper and block-print ferns on the throw pillows give the room a private, treasured sanctuary feel. One day I hope to have a nook such as this.

Back in the living room, everyone is drinking, chatting, and munching on appetizers. Teddy has given up on the Ken doll and is now fiddling with a glass of wine. Tree sits soaking in his surroundings and straining to catch a word he understands.

Katrina holds court and tells us about her new horse. "I just got him this past Saturday. He's a quarter horse, four years old, and just a hair over fifteen hands. Isn't he beautiful?"

Sky points to the window, and my gaze follows his finger. I catch a glimpse of the magnificent animal standing in his pen. He is a tincture of black, like sable, with a small strip of white between his eyes.

"What his name?" I ask.

"Blazing Six Guns," Katrina answers. Her face lights up, and she shifts back and forth in her blue velvet egg chair. "He's named after a western comic anthology." She speaks of her horse with wildfire energy, and I find her enthusiasm so infectious that it almost makes me want to own a horse of my own. The memory of my pet chicken, however, tugs at my heart and reminds me that the joy of owning an animal is too fleeting. "There I was at the Enumclaw auction. Mind you, I had no business being there if it weren't for that handsome Judd. He's the auctioneer. There's just something about a cowboy in ripped jeans. Oh, Lord, have mercy." Katrina fans her heart with her hand. "I tell you what, whatever he's selling, I'm buying. Next thing I knew, I was raising my paddle willy-nilly and lo and behold, Judd looked me dead in the eyes and said, 'yours,' and I nearly fell off my rocker."

I have never seen Katrina so animated. I want to hear more about cowboy Judd, but the oven timer rings.

"Oh good. I'm starving." Catherine makes her way to the kitchen before we all can stand up. "That turkey's been resting for four hours in the oven. I say we carve her up and let her rest in our bellies."

Sky tends to the turkey while we women bring food to the table. Tree fills everyone's tumbler with water and helps Thủy-Tiên pour her soda. Teddy follows with a decanter of wine and opens another bottle to let it breathe.

"Snow," Catherine says, as she lowers the oven temperature to 140 degrees, "why don't you put the pies in the oven to keep them warm?"

I look at the four pies on the counter. Catherine made the pumpkin pie, but I wonder about the other three. "Sky, you make pies?"

"Yes," he answers, as he carves the turkey and puts it on a large blue and gold platter. "There's chocolate bourbon pecan pie, apple cinnamon pie, and pear and almond cream tart."

"I think I will like all," I say. "This platter so pretty."

"Augarten porcelain from Vienna. This platter has been handed down in my family from generation to generation to the first-born. My dad gave this to me right before I joined the army. He told me I had to come back alive if I wanted to claim this heirloom."

"And you hand to your child one day," I comment. "What if you have twins?"

Sky pauses to think for a second. He shrugs. "Ask me again when I have twins. I first have to find a woman who'll want to marry me. You want to marry me, Snow?" He smiles, and I realize he is being playful.

"When you learn Vietnamese, maybe I marry you," I tease.

"Well, when you can drive a stick shift and your feet touch the pedals, maybe I'll marry *you*."

We laugh and join the family in the dining room, already salivating over the feast. Teddy takes hold of my hand and bows his head. I reach for Thủy-Tiên's hand on the other side of me and close my eyes.

Teddy's rich baritone voice soothes me as he says a prayer. "Oh gracious God, thank you for the blessings of this feast, so lovingly prepared by Skyler and Catherine. Even Katrina's salad is a blessing, but Lord, you know me. I'm a meat and potatoes kind of guy." A few chuckles overlap the prayer. "Gracious Father, please kindly withhold pie from whoever just kicked me. We thank you for our health, our home, our family and friends, especially those present today and gathered around this table. In your name we pray. Amen."

And just like that, we go from holding hands to grabbing plates of food and everyone asking to pass the gravy. What took two days to prepare only takes us thirty minutes to consume.

"Round two," Teddy declares. "Pass me the stuffing, won't you?"

Amid our chatter, we do not notice the looming figure in the foyer until a loud *pop* ricochets off our ears and into our chests.

Sky jumps up, startled and programmed to fight. His fists clench, knuckles white. His eyes are wild with rage. Like a caged animal whose iron gates spring open, he lunges toward the man in the hallway. I wrap my arms around Thủy-Tiên and duck in fear. My heart pumps fast. For a millisecond I think about running to my bunker for safety.

A throaty laugh and then a gasp. "Sorry I'm late, but I brought some Perrier-Jouët!" The man stands with a bottle of champagne in the air.

"Damn it, Dad!" Sky screams. "You're always one for piss-poor timing."

Katrina walks over to her husband and son. She looks calm on the surface, but her pursed lips betray her cool exterior. "Let's not ruin Thanksgiving."

Skyler's father sits down at the table. A wisp of sweet musk and menthol flirts with my senses. He interrogates me with his intense gaze. I cringe as the joyous mood of the room evaporates. I imagine lurking behind those dark pupils is a communist countryman eager to drag me home to the jungles of Việt Nam. He says nothing but nods politely. Bald and clean-shaven, the only things on his head are the pair of dark caterpillar eyebrows clinging to his face. There is arrogance in the way he sits and places the dinner napkin on his lap. His movements are fluidic, even poetic, but the graceful way in which he moves makes the hair on my arms rise. The devil himself has floated in for dinner and is now sitting across from me. He is dressed from top to bottom in black, from his turtleneck sweater and blazer to his pants and loafers. Hard. Strong. Beautiful…just like the black opal that is nestled in the tungsten carbide band he wears on his pinky finger.

He pours himself a glass of the Cuvee. "Jean-Adrien. And you are?"

"Snow," I half-whisper.

The presence of Jean-Adrien rattles my core yet kindles warmth between my legs. I dare not make eye contact for the rest of the evening.

5. THE OOPSIES (NOVEMBER 1980)

Sky opens the door to his old Lincoln Town Car. "Ready? Thought I'd teach you in my old college car first. After you get your driver's license, we'll advance to a stick shift. Everyone should know how to drive a manual."

Tree, Dolly, and I slide into the vehicle. The smell of the leather seats combined with the pine air freshener hanging from the rearview mirror washes over my anxiety and restores my excitement.

Sky drives us to Hazen High School. "They have a large parking lot. Plenty of room for oopsies."

"Oopsies?" I ask.

"You know, accidents and mistakes." Sky grins. "You and Tree can give it a go without worrying about hitting anything…or anyone."

Tree leans forward from the backseat of the old Lincoln sedan. "Can I go first?" He has a big smile on his face.

I volunteer my nephew, as he is eager to drive. It is nice to see his face light up with such enthusiasm. "Tree go first. I never drive car before, only my scooter back in Việt Nam. My brother, Seven, he truck driver, but he never teach me."

"It's never too late to learn." Sky puts the car in park and turns off the engine. I slide out of the passenger seat and sit in the back with Dolly. "Okay, Tree, before you turn on the ignition, you need to adjust your seat and all your mirrors." I translate every step of the way. Sky goes over which pedal is the brake and which one is the accelerator. We learn the basic anatomy of the car, its quirks, and what every knob, lever, handle, and letter mean. Finally, Sky permits Tree to put the car in reverse. "Seatbelt on. Then, nice and easy, take your foot off the brake and push down on the gas."

Tree drives us around the parking lot and around to the back of the school. He practices stopping and starting, going forward and reverse, using his turn signal to go left or right. Sky even encourages Tree to accelerate and stop the car using the emergency brake. Dolly and I slosh around in the back seat at every turn as Tree negotiates each corner, going around and around the building. My daughter's eyes and mouth are wide open, but she claps her approval whenever Tree makes a sharp turn. I hold tightly to the grab handle and breathe out an "oh Jesus" while Sky growls a "yee-haw."

"This is so fun," Tree declares. He steps on the accelerator again, pumping the brakes only for the speed bumps. Nausea is permeating out of my stomach and making its way up my esophagus.

Sky punches the roof of his car a couple of times and sticks his head out the window. "Waa hoo!"

After thirty minutes of driving around the parking lot, Tree takes the car to a hard stop. Our heads jerk forward. "Can I take it out on the road?"

I take a hard swallow of my saliva.

"Yes, let's go," Dolly squeals.

Sky lets Tree drive around the neighborhood a few blocks, careful to stay within the residential speed limit. The last lesson is parallel parking.

"Okay, Tree, pull alongside this parked car. Good. Now, put it in reverse and slowly back up until the front of our car is by the driver's side door of that car." My nephew handles the car with confidence. "Turn your wheel softly to the right and let the car roll back nice and slow. Good. Now turn it to the left, nice and easy, and slide straight back."

It takes Tree three tries to park the car five inches from the curb of the sidewalk.

"Well done!" Sky whips his head around and winks at me. "Snow, you ready?"

Tree tosses the keys back to me.

"No," I say but get out of the car anyway. I manage to suppress the gopher knot bubbling up my throat.

"Mama's turn," Dolly says. "You can do it. And then it will be my turn."

I laugh. "When you can reach the pedals and see over the dash, we will teach you." I get in the driver's seat and start the engine.

"Adjust your seat, and check your mirrors," Sky says. "Seatbelt."

I turn on the blinker and slowly pull out to the street. I cruise at fifteen miles per hour and keep alert. My eyes dart left and right. I rotate my gaze to the front and rear. Before long, I relax my grip on the steering wheel and enjoy the drive.

"The speed limit is twenty-five miles per hour," Sky says. I step on the gas and take the car to thirty. "Slow down, Snow. You'll get a ticket."

The road unexpectedly curves to the left. I take the sharp turn, oversteering enough to drift a little bit. I glance at the speedometer. It reads thirty-five. I self-correct and jerk the wheel to the right to straighten out.

My daughter claps her hands. "This is fun!"

"Stop!" Sky points to the red, octagonal sign. His sudden scream and jerky movements cause panic. I step down on the gas for a half-second, then slam my foot onto the brakes. We all lunge forward. The screech of the tires beckons pedestrians to stop and stare.

"Oopsies," I say.

Sky pulls the e-brake. "Let's have you practice in the parking lot."

Back at Homestead Apartments, Sky promises to take us out again for another driving lesson. "We'll keep practicing until you're ready to take the test."

"Sky, you stay for dinner?" I ask.

"Sure," he answers. "You've never cooked for me before."

We head up the stairs together, and on the last step, a high-pitched whistle wedges itself between the damp air and the caws of the crows.

"Melissa! Dinner!" The same jagged, macho voice yells from the other side of my corner unit.

The blonde girl with freckles runs past us. She stops and waves at Dolly. "Want to play?"

Two more children appear below. I recognize the other blonde girl, Jen, but to my surprise, they are with an Asian boy around the same age. I am guessing seven or eight years old.

My daughter waves to them and gives me a pleading look.

I nod. "But play in the back where I can see you."

Dolly bounds down the stairs. "Hi."

Melissa lifts her head, closes her eyes, and yells at the sky. "I'm not hungry, Tony! One more hour? Please?"

A woman's voice responds. "Fine."

I address the boy in my native tongue. "Are you Vietnamese?" He nods. "And do you live here?" He points to the apartment unit across from mine. "So we are neighbors. Do you live with your parents? Do you have any brothers or sisters?"

"It is just my mom and me," the boy answers.

"C'mon," Jen commands. "I have to be home before dark."

The four of them walk off and disappear around the corner.

"If only I could make friends that easy." Tree opens the apartment door, saunters straight to his bedroom, and closes the door.

From the sliding glass door of my deck, I see Dolly and her new friends playing foursquare. Sky is in my kitchen rifling through the cupboards and taking inventory of what is in the refrigerator. "I should have brought leftovers from Thanksgiving."

"You cooking for us?" I ask.

"Sure." He pulls out the chicken drumsticks. "You can keep an eye on Dolly while I make us some fried chicken. Do you have any stock?"

"What you need sock for?" I ask.

Sky laughs. "Stock, not sock." He opens the last drawer. "Oh good, you have chicken broth. I'm thinking some dirty rice and greens on the side should do it."

"You wash rice," I say, "so not dirty." I glance down at the courtyard. The children jump rope now. The Vietnamese boy and Dolly laugh hysterically over something funny. I smile to see pure joy in her face. This was the dream for us in America.

"Sky, tell me about your life. Tell me what happen after you come back fromViệt Nam." I sit down at the table and notice a small cockroach crawling out from behind the refrigerator. Not long ago I was so hungry I would have dived for the insect.

Sky stops and turns to me. "I just want to forget. Can't we talk about something else? Anything, just not that." Sky clenches his teeth.

"I want to know. You not want to know about me after war? After Sam?"

Sky blinks rapidly to will the tears away. He lowers his head and is silent. I hold my breath. His voice is a half octave lower when he speaks again. "I've spent the past eight years trying to forget, to move on."

"That something we never can forget." I pull on Sky's hand. "Sit."

"Damn it, I said I don't want to talk about it." He pulls his hand away but sits down next to me. He slumps forward. "Do we have to do this now?"

"I talk. You listen." I hope that by sharing my story, Sky will open up and share too. "One year after Sam die, I meet Dolly father, Tý. He was teacher from Sài Gòn. He transfer to my village to teach. My father was head of school. He arrange my marriage."

"Was he good to you?" Sky places his hand on mine. His face softens. "Please tell me he gave you and Dolly a good life."

"He good in beginning, but he tell many lies. He already have first wife. American. Her name Annette. And they have son. When Sài Gòn fall, he leave with Annette and son to America."

"What? That bastard." Sky's face is hard again. He scowls and exhales a heavy sigh. "Do you know where he is now?"

"Yes, but it not matter now. He have his life. I have my life."

"But, Snow, he needs to be a man and take care of his family."

"No." I shake my head vigorously. "I take care myself. I do not need him. After communists take over, my family starve. My father die. We lose everything. The Việt Cộng arrest Tâm—"

"Your niece? But why didn't you tell me all this in your letters when you were at Galang?"

"I no trust military at refugee camp. I afraid they read letters. I afraid they not mail to you."

"What about Ommo?" Sky asks. "Weren't you going to marry him?" Just hearing his name makes me more sad. I crushed his heart. I owe him a letter. I owe Sister Six and Brother Seven a letter as well.

"Yes, Ommo is good, but he in past. I not in love with him. I make decision come here. Cannot go back." I look out the window to check on my daughter. The children stand in a circle with two kids and bounce an orange ball to one another. "I want to live in present. I want to look to future."

"I am tired of living within my memories," Sky says. "It's torture. I feel suffocated. The screams of the dying play over and over like a damn broken record."

"Who we can trust if we cannot trust ourself?" I ask.

"Exactly," Sky says.

"The only man I trust is Tý brother, Hải. The Việt Cộng take him away too. I not know if Tâm or Hải still alive in prison camps. So many time, I try escape my country. So many time, Dolly, Tree, and me could die." My voice trembles and cracks. I am fired up now with emotions. I push through the tears and swallow the knot in my throat. "I almost lose Dolly at refugee camp. You save her. You sponsor us to Seattle. You are good man."

"I had to find a way to bring you here. Sam would have wanted that. He was a brother to me. I failed him. I failed my country. I wasn't going to fail you too. I just couldn't." Sam stands up and walks to the window. I cannot see his face, but I suspect he is holding back the tears. His voice shakes to a whisper. "I am not a good man."

"The war not your fault," I say.

"My life has been a failure. You don't know about all the things I have done."

"The war feel a lifetime away. In a place ocean apart. War make all people criminal, even children. Good people turn bad to survive. Like me."

"What could you have possibly done?" Sky questions tersely. "You are as pure as your name implies. Who did you kill? Who did you have to fuck to forget?" He pounds his fist on the window. It rattles loudly. His body shakes. "You have no idea what it was like to come back here, not as a hero, but as the foul heathen who should have died in Nam." Sky is yelling now. "This damn country…this goddamn country. I fought for this country, and it turned its back on me when I got home. Instead of peace signs, I got the middle finger. This ungrateful society that we live in. I was so confused and fucked up in the head. I still am. Not once did I get a thank you. Not once did I hear 'glad you made it home safely.' 'Baby-killer.' That's what I heard. 'Rapist.' I've been spat on, kicked, harassed, fired at, cursed. Yeah, I'm a loser. Thirty-four years old and still living with my mom because I can't hold down a job. People I grew up with turned away like they didn't know me." Sky cranks his head and looks over his shoulder. "We lost the war. You don't get the red carpet and fireworks when you come home. You don't get a welcome reception. No. You get the devil's asshole. Piss and vinegar. Fire and ice. I wasn't returning home. I returned to an institution where a death penalty would have been more humane than a life sentence."

"Sky—"

"You wanted to know what happened after I got back. Well, I'm telling you. I got back to Seattle and developed symptoms of malaria. Did the VA take care of me? No. They denied me health care because I didn't have symptoms in Nam. They pushed me out faster than Charlie taking a shit. I tried to cash in my education benefits and go to college. My GI benefits were worthless! My entire payout was a hundred-fifty dollars when the cost was three hundred dollars per credit. *Per credit*, Snow! Yeah, as soon as I applied for jobs and they found out I was a Vietnam veteran, they treated me like a ticking time bomb."

"But Katrina and Jean-Adrien—"

"What about them? My dad is a son of a bitch. Don't let his money and looks and charms fool you. My mom fell for it, and we're all paying the price. Time and time again my dad has failed me, for as long as I can remember. And my mom is the bigger fool for staying married to him."

"Why?" I ask. "What happen?"

"Hell if I know why she stays. He's a cheat and a womanizer. He travels around the globe, flexes his big shot architect muscles, smiles, and people just fall at his feet. Take our house, for example. He built it to buy our love, but he was never around. Where the hell was he when I was six years old? When I fell off my bike and scraped my knee? He was MIA. When I needed a man to talk to, he was screwing his coworker. Where was he when I was…when I needed…" Sky's words trail off. I wait for him to continue, but he does not.

"Need what?"

"His protection," Sky whispers. I barely hear him. "I needed him to protect me." The tears burst from Sky's eyes. Wetness covers his mouth and nose. He wipes them away with the back of his hand like a toddler drying his tears.

"Protect from what, Sky?"

"My uncle." The anguish in his cries sounds like cats mating. He crumples to the floor with a haggard howl. The wailing gets louder, more jagged. He is reduced to a vulnerable, scared child, not the sarcastic, confident soldier I once knew.

I am shocked. "You mean Teddy?"

Sky shakes his head and wails louder.

Tree flings his bedroom door open and appears in the hallway, a grim expression on his face. I shake my head as if to say *not now*. He retraces his steps back to his room and quietly closes the door.

If not Teddy, then who?

###

I did not see Sky at church. He did not come to give Tree and me another driving lesson. When I call, Katrina says he is not home. For days, I wonder who had hurt Sky. Whatever accident or mistake took place, it is clear the incident still haunts him.

Christmas is not far away. Teddy and Catherine have been busy with their families. While Tree and Dolly are at school, I occupy myself by watching television and spying on my neighbor. The Vietnamese woman next door has been elusive. I have caught a few glimpses of her from my bedroom window, but we have not met. I know her name, though, having overheard voices two nights ago. Someone had knocked on their door, and when it opened, I heard a woman say, "Hi, Yip." I wonder if her name is Diệp. In Vietnamese, if the letter D does not have a straight line across it, the letter sounds like the English letter Y. Hearing her name makes me sad for old Mrs. Trần, who is probably haunting all of Hồ Chí Minh City. Tomorrow I will visit Diệp and introduce myself. It will be nice to have another female to banter with in Vietnamese like the old days back home.

I turn on the television and flip the channels. Every channel is the news. I turn past channel two but something catches my eyes. I turn the knob back. Although the channel does not come in clear and the sound is distorted, there is no mistaking the face reporting the news is that of an Asian woman. I cannot see her full name but can make out the word "Chung." To my surprise, she is Chinese. I am more fascinated by the features of her face than what she is saying. Her teeth are perfect and her lipstick a vibrant shade of red. Her sultry voice and how she moves her head are graceful. Her skin is smooth and flawless, her nose high and regal, her bone structure immaculate. She is on screen for only a minute before the camera switches to footage of another Asian woman.

I gasp. Yoko Ono! The news is talking about Yoko Ono and John Lennon. I strain to listen, but the report is unclear. Words of *dead* and *age forty* assault my ears. I change the channel to find better reception.

"We interrupt this program to bring you a special report from NBC news. Late last night, former Beatles member, John Lennon, died at St. Luke's-Roosevelt Hospital from gunshot wounds to the chest. One police officer says they are treating this case as seriously as the assassination of John F. Kennedy. New

York City's Chief of Detectives, James T. Sullivan, surveyed the scene and interviewed the witnesses, as well as the officers who responded to the call. The gunman has been identified as Mark David Chapman from Hawaii, whom one witness said had been lurking outside Lennon's New York City apartment. Another witness said she saw Chapman approach Lennon for an autograph yesterday morning. Lennon and his wife, Yoko Ono, were on their way back from the studio late last night, where they were recording a track for their new album 'Double Fantasy.' When their limo pulled up to the Dakotas building on the Upper West Side, a gunman came from the shadows and fired several shots at close range. Four bullets entered Lennon's chest, of which three exited through the back. Police confirmed the weapon was a thirty-eight caliber Charter Arms pistol. Lennon was still alive and conscious when they arrived on the scene but was pronounced dead around eleven-thirty eastern time. At one-fifteen this morning, a mortuary division vehicle left the Roosevelt Hospital with Lennon's body. Yoko returned to the residence where a crowd of about four hundred people had already gathered around Seventy-Second Street and Central Park West to hold a vigil and mourn the singer. We will bring you more news as it breaks."

My heart cracks in two. I clutch my heart and cover my mouth to muffle my cries. I imagine being in Yoko's spirit. I understand the irreparable pain her entire being is suffering right now. That despairing feeling of being alone and lost, that horrible feeling of guilt and helplessness because someone took your lover's life, robbing you both of happiness. I cry for her. I cry for John Lennon. And I cry for my Sam.

6. FULL CIRCLE (DECEMBER 1980)

Dolly sings as she soaks in the bubble bath and plays with her Barbie doll. "Jesus loves me, this I know, for the Bible tells me so. Little ones to him belong. They are weak but he is strong."

I kneel on the floor beside her and gently massage the shampoo into her hair. Her hair is fine like mine, but much shorter. "Did you learn that in Sunday school?" She nods, then coughs. I feel her forehead. It is a little warm. "Do you feel sick?"

"Sometimes it is hard to breathe," she says.

"Dr. Hall said it would be six months after surgery before you felt better." I look at the long scar down the center of her chest. "Does it hurt anywhere?"

"Sometimes my stomach hurts. After I go poop, it feels better. My poop is runny."

"Mama will ask our neighbor next door if she has any tiger balm we can borrow."

"Hùng's mom?" Dolly asks.

"Oh, is that your friend's name? Hùng?"

"Yes. He says it means hero. What does my name mean?"

"Thủy-Tiên means water angel. It is also the name of a flower."

"Hùng's mom is Mrs. Diệp."

"And their last name?"

"Trần."

I sit back on my haunches. I find it strange that my neighbor next door has the same name as the she-Jekyll who lived next to us in Sài Gòn. Even in Seattle, I cannot escape Mrs. Trần. Full circle.

"What a coincidence," I say, more to myself than to Thủy-Tiên. "What about Mrs. Diệp's husband?"

"Dead."

Interesting…so was Mrs. Trần's husband back home. Now, if Mrs. Diệp also has two sons, of which one is a communist, then it can only mean one thing—Mrs. Trần is here to haunt me.

"I think you should grow your hair out long," I suggest, changing the subject.

"No. I like it short."

"But you look like a boy."

"Boys do not wear dresses," she says. "I do. And I look dangerous with short hair."

I make the mistake of laughing. My daughter glares at me.

"All right, keep your short hair. Before you were born, I had a short pixie haircut like Elizabeth Taylor."

"Who?" My daughter dismisses her question and tells me about other lessons she is learning in Bible classes. "I learned about the Trinity. God, Jesus, and the Holy Ghost. I think Olivia is like God and Ocean is like Jesus. But Opal, she is the ghost for sure. She is scary."

I chuckle. "Pastor George and Mrs. Dawn might have something to say about that. What makes you think Olivia and Ocean are like God and Jesus?" I am curious to know how her little mind works.

"In the beginning, there was God," she says, "and he is wise and knows everything. Olivia is the oldest and smart. She knows everything. She is a good reader and loves all animals. Ocean is my best friend. She is like Jesus because she loves me."

"And you think Opal is scary like a ghost?"

"She is mean and bossy. I do not like her, even when she smiles or laughs."

"When the Bible talks about the trinity, it is referring to God being the Father, the Son, and the Holy Spirit. The word 'holy' means good or divine. A holy ghost is a good ghost."

My daughter puts her doll down and takes my face between her wet, wrinkly hands. She looks at me squarely in the eyes. "Then Opal is the devil."

"Stop this nonsense." I am taken aback that she should feel this way. "Opal is ten years old and the middle child. She has to work twice as hard to outshine her older and younger sisters. You should be happy you are the only child and get all the love."

"Do you like Opal?" Dolly asks.

Indeed, she is not my favorite out of the three girls, but in many ways, Opal is like my sister; she speaks her mind, calls things as she sees them without sugar-coating anything, and does not care what others think.

I reach under the water to pull the plug and drain the bathwater. "I like Opal. She reminds me of your Aunt Six. People like Opal make the best kind of friends because they will always tell the truth and not lie to you. You will see. I am going to set you and Opal up for a playdate."

"No!" Dolly slams the palm of her hands down on the water. "Only Ocean. I want to play with Ocean." Her outburst takes me by surprise.

Thick, round tears make their appearance behind Dolly's curtain of lashes. They race down her cheeks and pause at her chin before leaping into the water. I hoist Dolly out of the tub. She arches her back and kicks the tub. We both fall back onto the linoleum floor. She runs out of the bathroom, naked and dripping wet, into the bedroom. She slams the door shut. I hear pounding on the wall and drawers slamming shut. A loud thud assaults the floor. I am guessing she has thrown a book or toy. She wails louder. I peek into the room to make sure she is all right and am greeted with an angry stare. My daughter is acting like a spoiled, entitled child.

I do not give in to her tantrum. "I am giving you a warning. Behave or get a spanking." I close the door and walk into the kitchen to make some tea.

###

Another cold morning. The drizzle outside dampens my mood. I yearn for sunshine and tropical heat. Dolly appears in the kitchen wearing a long periwinkle dress with tiny white dots. She has done a wonderful job dressing herself this morning with white tights and white, polyurethane, double strap Mary Jane shoes. Her expressive face, however, does not match her beautiful dress. She scowls at me, no doubt still upset about the playdate.

"You know the rules," I say. "No shoes in the house."

"We are not in Vietnam anymore," Dolly reminds me. "We are in America. I hate your stupid rules."

"Listen, child—" I say.

"And I want a different name. I hate Dolly. The kids call me names."

"What do they call you?" I ask.

"Dolly Parton and Dolly Pop-Up." My daughter crosses her arms across her chest. "And Dolly Hand Truck! I hate it here. Why can't we go back and live with Ommo or back to Vietnam and stay with Uncle Seven?"

Tree puts down his Cap'n Crunch cereal. He lifts Thủy-Tiên onto his lap. Her beady eyes cast suspicion. Her claws are ready to pinch him.

"You look like a princess to me," Tree says. "Do you know how many princesses there were in Vietnam?" Dolly shakes her head. "A lot. And do you know how many princesses there are here?" Again she shakes her head. "None. Here, you are special. They do not know it yet, but they will. Why not go with your real name? Thủy-Tiên is a beautiful name and it means 'water angel'."

"I want to be called Nancy. I told a girl at school my real name and she laughed and called me 'Tiny Tim'. Stupid girl."

Tree and I look at each other, speechless. I hear a horn honk outside.

"They're here," I say. "We will talk about this after church."

The three of us gather outside, and as I turn the key to lock the apartment, I hear a gasp from Tree and a scream from Dolly. My gaze shifts in time to see my little girl tumble down the last ten steps and lie crumpled on the cold, wet cement. We all rush to her.

"Tiên!" I yell. There is a tinge of blood on her lips.

Teddy kneels next to her. "We don't want to lift her in case she broke something."

"Oh dear," Catherine exclaims. "Did she trip on her dress? What happened?"

"Can you sit up?" Tree asks. "Where does it hurt?"

My daughter sits up and points to her abdomen. She yelps.

"We go to hospital," I say.

Teddy gently lifts Dolly into his arms. "Toots, open the car door." He eases my daughter into the back seat of his Nova. She winces and sobs. The drive to Seattle Children's Hospital is thwarted by road closures, detours, and traffic.

"Faster, Teddy," I urge.

"There is construction everywhere," Catherine notes. "I-5 is gridlocked. Do you think there is an accident ahead?"

"Let's get on the viaduct and cut over." Teddy exits the freeway. We head north on the SR-99 corridor and travel on the elevated freeway above downtown Seattle. Despite our present situation, the drive along the waterfront is still breathtaking as we pass the piers, cruise terminal, and port marina.

"If the clouds burn off," Tree says, "I bet we can see Mount Rainier looming over the lake." I nod in agreement. "It would be wonderful to see the snow."

I rub my daughter's arm for reassurance. "We are almost there."

We cannot get there fast enough. The surface streets are riddled with one-way roads and plagued with red traffic lights.

"We should have called the ambulance," Catherine mumbles.

We arrive at the emergency entrance. The doors open, and a rush of odors attack my nose. The smell of disinfectants wafts through the air and dances with the scent of diapers. I can taste the baby powder and antiseptic.

Teddy and Catherine do all the talking. Tree and I stand helpless but vigilant. An orderly wheels Thủy-Tiên down the hallway for X-rays. We follow and are instructed to wait in a different room. I cannot lose you.

###

A Bangladeshi woman with an olive green hijab walks into the waiting room. Her silk headdress accentuates the brightness of her green eyes, and the gold caduceus dangling from her necklace rivals for attention with her nose piercing. "I am Dr. Khan. Are you Dolly's mother?"

"Yes," I say. "I am Snow."

"The good news is she did not break anything from the fall," Dr. Khan states. "However, we did find something concerning."

"What is it?" Catherine asks. "What's wrong? Is it her heart?"

Teddy rubs his weary eyes. "Dr. Hall was the surgeon who operated on her. Four months ago. Here, at Children's."

"It is not her heart," Dr. Khan continues. "You are from Vietnam?" I nod. "And you are new immigrants? War refugees?" Again, I nod affirmatively. "That explains it."

"Oh, for Pete's sake, what is it already?" Teddy rubs his bald head and narrows his eyes. I wonder who this Pete person is.

Dr. Khan looks at the documents in her folder. A frown settles on her face. "There is a parasite living inside your daughter…intestinal worms."

The mention of worms brings me back to when my nephew, Tuấn, had pinworms in his rectum. I shudder at the memory of having to clean the house thoroughly, of washing all the sheets and clothes, and my nephew screaming in pain as Brother Seven scrubbed his son's body raw.

"Who knows how long she's had them," Catherine says. The blood drains from her face, turning her flushed cheeks white.

I translate to Tree what is going on. A strange sound escapes his lips. He half laughs and half groans. "We made a full circle, Aunt Eight."

Dr. Khan speaks again. "Roundworms can live inside the small intestine for a couple of years and grow to a foot long. It is a vicious cycle. Health conditions worsen once you're infected. It wreaks havoc on your immune system, which can be fatal. This is my fifth case of helminths since Washington started resettling refugees five years ago."

"Did she show any symptoms, Snow?" Catherine asks. "Actually, what are the symptoms?"

"Fever, coughing, rash—"

"Dolly have all them, but she alway sick since she born," I say.

Dr. Khan looks at me sympathetically. "Because of the micro-nutrient deficiency caused by the worms, the infected person can lose concentration, suffer abdominal pain, and be anemic. In children, it can stunt their growth because nourishment is siphoned from the host. There are a lot of adverse effects if left untreated, causing liver and bladder failure, lung disease—"

"Okay, but you can treat it, right?" Teddy asks.

"We are going to do some more scans to make sure the parasite hasn't gotten into her brain or spine, and take a stool sample to test for the presence of eggs…but yes, it can be treated with anthelmintic such as mebendazole."

All these years, I believed my daughter was frail, small, and sick because of her heart, but in truth, she was battling more than a heart murmur…she was sharing what little food she had with damn worms. I want nothing more than to hold her, comfort her, and protect her. My poor baby.

###

The phone rings.

"Alô?" I answer.

"You were not at church." It is Sky. "Everything okay?"

"You not talk to Teddy or Catherine?" I ask.

314

"No, I've been out of town," Sky says, "and came back Saturday night. I didn't see you at church. Mom hasn't heard from anyone either."

"We at hospital—"

"Oh my God. Which one? I'll come now."

"No, we home now." I give Sky an account of what happened and how Dolly is on medication so her body can expel the parasite and kill any eggs that may be in her system.

"That poor girl has been through so much," Sky says. "How are you holding up?"

"I good, I think."

"Listen, Snow, I owe you an apology." I wait for Sky to continue, but there is only silence, then a sigh. "I need to explain some things about my past. Are you coming to Christmas Eve dinner?"

"Yes."

"Good. We'll talk then. See you Wednesday."

We say our goodbyes, and I resume my chores. I gather up the dirty clothes in the hall closet, grab the laundry detergent and money, and check on my nephew.

"Tree?" I call from the other side of his closed bedroom door. No answer. I open the door. My nephew sleeps. My daughter is curled next to him. His room smells like damp, sweaty socks. It is dark with the curtains closed. Black fluorescent lights illuminate the large, velvet posters of menacing cobras and evil dragons on his walls, pinned on either side of his bed. Teddy had taken us to an outdoor flea market a couple of weeks ago on Aurora Avenue, and Tree had to have them. I gather up his dirty clothes and put them in the large trash bag.

It is partly sunny outside, but the chill nips at my nose. I walk down the steps and around the corner to building F. Hauling my garbage bag of soiled socks, stained shirts, and thricely worn pants, I make the short trek to the community laundry room. Thoughts of Cường carrying his bags of loot out of the US Embassy the morning Sài Gòn fell makes me smile and ache for home. I dream of the day I am reunited with my family.

Inside the laundry room, it is nice and warm. A man transfers wet clothes into a dryer. He looks familiar. Two boys help him, one dark-skinned teenager, about Tree's age, and a young boy of elementary age with a milky-white complexion. I cannot help but stare. The man reminds me of someone.

"Can I help you?" The gentleman starts the dryer, and all three of them approach me.

"I…sorry. How I wash?" I ask.

He lifts the lid to one of the machines. "You'll probably need to do two loads." I dump my bag into the machine, but he stops me. "Whoa. Maybe you should separate them into dark and light." I stare at him blankly. "Let me help you. Do you mind?"

I shake my head. I watch as the stranger sorts my clothes and loads two machines, separating the white clothes from the black ones. I blush each time he touches my delicates.

"The colored items go with the blacks," the man says.

After sorting the items, I see that the white pile is very small and only fills the machine a third of the way. It seems wasteful to have the washer so empty.

"Fifty cents to wash and a dollar to dry," the stranger says.

I put the quarters in the machines. It pains me to spend four quarters for both machines when I can shove all the clothes in one load.

The man fills the tray with laundry soap. He closes the lids and presses the different buttons. "It takes thirty minutes to wash and an hour to dry."

"Thank you," I say. "My name Snow. You movie star?"

"Me?" He laughs. "No, but people tell me I look like the younger version of Philip Drummond from *Diff'rent Strokes.*"

"Oh, yes. I watch show. You look like rich man on television."

"Pretty much, down to the adopted kids too. These are my boys, Jason and Ricky. And I'm Donald." I smile at the boys. Jason is the younger child, pale and knock-kneed. His shaggy blond hair could use a good washing. His face is dirty and his eyes dull. He lowers his eyes. "Jason's my shy one."

Ricky is a big boy, both tall and burly. His dark complexion is coated with pubescent acne and stubble on his face. "Hi…Hi, I'm…I'm Rick…Ricky…Hi."

"Ricky stutters, as you can see, but he is not shy," Donald says. "He wants to be an entertainer one day."

Donald and I get acquainted while I wait for my clothes to wash. I learn he moved into Homestead Apartments three weeks ago. His wife passed from Parkinson's disease. He and his boys left Oregon to get a fresh start and away from the painful memories. I share bits of my story and we agree to get our families together after Christmas.

After the laundry is done, I stuff everything back into the garbage bag and walk home. My neighbor is walking up the stairs, carrying a plastic bag. She wears rainbow-colored suspenders to hold up her pants which are two inches too short above her ankles. Her polka-dot turtleneck sweater has a hole on the right shoulder. I imagine a gecko poking its head through and making an escape.

"Chị Diệp?" I call out to her.

She stops and adjusts her glasses. "Chị Tuyết?"

"Yes," I say. "I think your son and my daughter—"

"Yes, they are friends. Nancy is cute."

"Her name is—"

"She is much darker than you. You know, I thought she was a boy at first."

"She looks like her fath—"

"Our kids play well together. I see them play with the other children here. Your daughter is good at basketball and throwing the football."

"Really?" I ask.

"That is why I thought she was a boy…and her short hair…and her dark skin. She does not look Vietnamese."

"She is one hundred percent—"

"So I am just getting home from Safeway."

"Did you—"

"Walk?" Diệp nods. "Yes. Would you like to join us for dinner tonight?"

"I would love—"

"Splendid. Come over at seven." Diệp pats me on the arm. "I look forward to getting to know you, Sister Tuyết."

"Me too," I say. "What can I bring to—"

"Nonsense, just you and Nancy and your nephew." Diệp bounds up the stairs. I follow behind her. She smiles and enters her apartment, closing the door as I nod farewell to her. What an odd woman. Her appearance is youthful, perhaps in her late twenties, but the eyes behind her glasses reflect the eyes of a grandmother who has experienced much. Perhaps she has secrets like me. I wonder if my forty-year-old eyes look old.

My exchange with Diệp was brief, but I feel devoid of energy. She did most of the talking, and yet I feel exhausted. Small doses…I can only handle Diệp in small fractions of time and space.

Diệp's apartment has the same floorplan as mine, only flipped. The pungent smells of fish sauce and Chinese herbal medicine greet me. It smells like Việt Nam. Incense burns in the corner, and I detect a faint hint of menthol. It makes me homesick.

In one corner of the kitchen are bags of dog food and canned cat food. There are pictures of the Virgin Mary and Jesus on the wall, a cross above the sliding glass door, and statues of Happy Buddha, female Buddha, and serenity Buddha on a bookcase.

Thủy-Tiên and Hùng sit on the floor and play together. They both pretend the green GI Joe action figures are waging war against each other, using the matchbox cars as shields.

I pause a moment to take in the scene before me. Diệp's apartment does not have the luxuries of a sofa or TV. She has one hammock, a few folding chairs, and a glass table. While the décor is of muted colors, mostly gray and burnt sienna, Diệp's outfit is rather eclectic. The décolletage of her vibrant rainbow-colored bathing suit leaves little to the imagination, while her bright turquoise spandex pants accentuate every lumpy, subcutaneous fat deposit on her thighs and butt. A green sweatband hugs her head while neon orange leg warmers cover her calves.

"Do you like my hot socks?" Diệp asks. "I noticed you looking at them. I got them at the Goodwill store for ninety-nine cents."

"Yes," I say. "You are very colorful. Do you need help?"

"No. Sit. Where is your nephew?" she asks.

"He is coming," I say. "He is cutting up apples and—"

"I told you not to bring anything."

"Do you have a dog or a cat?" I ask.

"No. Why do you ask?"

"I noticed your bags of dog food and the cans of cat food."

Diệp grins. She wipes her hands on the kitchen towel and saunters over to the corner. She picks up the canned cat food and hands it to me. "I got these on sale. Nineteen cents. There is an aisle at Safeway that has all flavors of cat and dog food."

"Yes, but if you do not have any pets—" It then dawns on me.

"No, silly woman. This is food made of cats and dogs, like back home, but ready-to-eat."

I swallow hard. I recognize the pet food only because Teddy and Catherine feed their Cairn Terrier, Biscuit, this stuff. I mull over how to tell her delicately. Luckily, I do not have to.

Tree lets himself into the apartment. He places the plate of apples and grapes onto the table and grabs the can of cat food from my hand. "You have a cat."

"No," Diệp says, "I was just telling your aunt it is made of cat."

"No, Cô Diệp. This is food *for* cats." Tree points to the bags of dog food. "And those are food *for* dogs. Not for people."

"That is right," I say and point to the ingredients. "See here? The ingredients say chicken, meat by-products, guar gum…no mention of cat."

Diệp's eyes open wide. "What am I going to do with all this food?"

"Tell me we are not having this for dinner," Tree says.

I give him a disapproving look to remind him of manners.

"Mama!" Thủy-Tiên abandons her play and runs to me. She fans her mouth. "Hot." She sticks out her tongue. I see nothing. Tears bead up and make her eyes sparkle. "It burns!"

"What happened?" I ask. Neither she nor Hùng confesses.

"Do we need to go to the hospital again?" Tree asks.

Timidly, Hùng hands me a small bottle with green liquid in it. The label is printed in Chinese, but I recognize what it is. "She swallowed a drop of this menthol." It is a medicated oil, an external analgesic manufactured in Singapore by Eagle Brand. It's a cure-all for muscle aches, itchiness from mosquito bites, headaches, stomach pains, and congestion.

"Why would you drink this?" I ask.

Diệp hands Thủy-Tiên a glass of tap water. "Drink up. You will be fine."

My daughter drinks the whole glass. "He dared me." She points at Hùng. "So I did."

"That was a stupid thing to do," I yell at my daughter, who is holding her throat like she is going to die. She gags and stifles her tears.

Diệp stomps off to the bedroom and returns with a paddle. Her son darts behind me for protection.

"Chị Diệp, that is not necessary." I urge her to put the paddle away. "This is not a spanking offense. They are just being children."

"I think we need to try dinner another time," Diệp says. "I am sorry, Chị Tuyết. Have a good night."

Tree, Dolly, and I leave the apartment, and as we close the door, we hear Hùng cry for mercy and forgiveness as the paddle thuds against his body. "Mother, I will not do that again!"

"At least we are not eating dog food for dinner," Tree says.

"Or cat food," I say.

"I wanted to prove to him I was tough," Dolly says.

7. CHRISTMAS EVE 1980

Katrina's house is a magical adventure park, inviting us in with Christmas lights and garlands strung throughout the property, both inside and out. Smells of pine and caramelized sugar beckon me to take off my coat and stay. A Christmas vinyl spins on the turntable with The Jackson 5 group harmonizing to "I Saw Mommy Kissing Santa Claus." Potted poinsettias in colors of red, white, and pink adorn every room in the house. Hanging on the fireplace mantle are large, furry socks in alternating colors of red and green. In the corner is a twelve-foot, frosted tree, decorated with ornaments, tinsel, and lights. On top of the tree is a beautiful angel, and below are piles of boxes wrapped in shiny paper and hugged with ribbons or bows.

Dolly's eyes are wide with wonder and excitement. Katrina takes my daughter's hand and leads her into the family room. "Dolly, honey, I thought you could help string some popcorn and cranberries for the birds."

"Ocean!" my daughter calls out.

"Dolly! Come sit with me," Ocean says. "Opal, move over." My daughter and Ocean hug. Ocean shows Dolly how to thread the puffy kernels. They alternate the popcorn with raw cranberries, making an edible garland. Olivia puts together a gingerbread house, and Opal cuts paper snowflakes. All four girls are in festive spirits, chatting animatedly about Disney princesses and the gifts they asked for from Santa.

A merry-go-round of "Merry Christmases" passes from everyone's lips to receptive ears. I give Pastor George and Dawn hugs. Tree joins them on the sofa to watch TV and help himself to the bowl of popcorn. I follow Katrina, Teddy, and Catherine into the kitchen.

Perching on the counter stool, I watch Katrina navigate through the kitchen and hope to learn the art of cooking through osmosis. Like a lost tourist, she fumbles her way around, opening cupboards, rifling through the spice rack, opening the fridge, and finally throwing her hands up in defeat.

"Where in the world is the balsamic glaze? Maybe there's some in the garage. Be right back."

Meanwhile, Teddy and Catherine maneuver around each other in the kitchen like two birds during a mating ritual. "Santa Claus Is Comin' To Town" blasts from the record player. Teddy wiggles his hips and swivels his legs like he is crushing a bug underneath his shoes.

"Motown with me, Toots." He swings her around, and she laughs.

"Why, Mr. Vanzwol, I do declare. I knew there was a lot of gospel and soul in you, but you might be too R&B for me."

"I'm channeling my inner Stevie Wonder," Teddy says. "You like my groove?"

"Oh yes," Catherine says in between breaths. "It's a heatwave." The two of them laugh as one lovebird. "Come on, Snow!"

With a little pressing, I agree and hop off the stool to synchronize my dance moves with theirs.

"What's this?" Katrina asks. "A dance party without me?" She stands behind the counter with a bottle of balsamic in her hand.

The four of us dance and giggle, embracing the magic of the holidays. Seeing Teddy and Catherine in love after thirty years of marriage gives me hope that it is possible for me too. Teddy surprises me by swinging me around and dipping me. I am filled with love for these people who, nine months ago, were strangers but have now become family.

"Where Sky?" I ask.

"He'll be here shortly," Katrina answers. "He's picking his dad up from the airport."

"Oh, Jean-Adrien coming tonight?" I ask. The thought of sharing Christmas Eve with him makes me nervous. I remember his steely eyes were cold at Thanksgiving, yet his gaze made me flush with desire. He exudes strength, power, money, and charm. I can understand how Katrina got swept away by his current and why other women threw themselves into his arms. His good looks and pocketbook are abyssal.

"Yes," Katrina breathes, "it's going to be a full house tonight."

"Our daughters are coming," Catherine says.

"You'll get to meet Frances and Penny," Teddy says. "Plus their husbands."

"Penny and Todd are expecting their first child," Catherine says. "They live in Oregon. Frances and Frank have two little boys, Jacob and John. They're driving in from Wenatchee."

Over the next thirty minutes, guests trickle in. I meet the family and feel overwhelmed with the buzzing conversations crisscrossing from room to room. I cannot keep up with their talk, so I seek out the children, but they have their own game of hide and seek. I sit with Tree.

"How are you feeling?" I ask my nephew. "Hungry?"

Tree nods. "I am always hungry, but I eat a lot, too, so I do not have to talk much."

"He who eats a lot talks the least," I say. "I wonder how our family back home is doing."

"I think they are fifteen hours ahead, so it is already Christmas there," Tree says. "I miss them. Have you written to them?"

"Yes," I say, "but have not mailed it yet."

"Good, I want to add my letter before you send it."

"I need to find a job and make money to send home," I say. "I keep praying every day for a job."

"How are you looking for work?" Tree asks.

"Our apartment building has a board in the laundry room that has announcements," I say. "I saw a 'help wanted' post for a babysitter."

Tree grimaces. "Aunt Eight, you can do better. You have a university degree, and you worked at a bank. You also taught math, and your English is good. You need to talk to everyone here, and maybe they can give you a job."

"You are right," I say, "but I feel we already ask so much of them."

"What does Katrina do?" Tree asks. "She is rich. Maybe she can give you a job."

"I do not know what she does. Sky is in between jobs right now, and Catherine is a housewife. Teddy is a big engineer boss at Boeing. The company makes airplanes, like the one we flew in on. Pastor George and Dawn have the church."

"What about Katrina's husband?"

"Jean-Adrien is an architect," I say, "and a very successful one. He travels a lot and built this house. He is coming tonight."

"Ho, ho, ho!" comes a voice from behind me.

"Sky!" I am startled to have him so close to me all of a sudden.

He sits down with Tree and me. "I need a drink. Twenty minutes in the car with my dad is more than I can take."

"It good to see you," I say. I reach over and pat his hand. "Merry Christmas."

"Merry Christmas, Snow. Merry Christmas, Tree."

The three of us stand up and join the family in the kitchen and dining room. I see Jean-Adrien standing with Katrina, his arm around her waist. The two of them laugh and look happy.

Sky hands me a wine glass. "Look at her, still looking at him with puppy-love eyes." He pours me some merlot from the decanter. "After dinner, let's talk privately in the reading nook. I owe you an explanation…and an apology."

The pace of the evening picks up with Sky's presence at the dinner party. He does not leave my side and is attentive to me, making sure I am comfortable until it is time for us to sit down and eat. I allow myself to enjoy the occasion despite the guilt gnawing at my conscience thinking of my family in Việt Nam.

With Teddy and Catherine's children and grandchildren present, nineteen of us are gathered tonight. Pastor George says grace before we all swarm around the food. I learn the menu tonight consists of prime rib, bone-in ham, butternut squash, smashed garlic and thyme potatoes, bacon-wrapped dates, buttery rolls, sweet potato fries, Portobello mushrooms, creamed spinach, and balsamic roasted vegetables.

Sky leans in and whispers into my ear. "Do you know the seven deadly sins?" I shake my head. "There's envy, gluttony, greed, pride, lust, sloth, and wrath." Sky explains what each means.

"What sin belong to you?" I ask.

"All of them," he answers and winks. "Let's play a game. Let's guess who here has committed these sins."

"Okay, how about lust?" I ask.

Sky rolls his eyes. "Easy. My dad. How about gluttony?"

I imitate Sky and roll my eyes. "Easy. Me."

Sky laughs. "And greed?"

I scan the room and point to Dolly, who is trading her roasted vegetables for Tree's bacon-wrapped dates and sweet potato fries. We laugh.

"Envy?" I ask and keep the game going. "I think Catherine. She envy your mom."

Sky disagrees. "I think it's the other way around. My mom envies Aunt Catherine. She wants the kind of marriage that Catherine and Teddy have."

"But maybe Catherine wish she have fortune with nice clothes, big house—" I argue.

"If anything, I think Catherine has pride. There is nothing my aunt cannot do that she does not do well. She's managed to raise her children, learned to spin wool, knit, sew, and crochet. She has her garden, cooks like a master chef, keeps Teddy happy…"

"Maybe you right," I acknowledge. "Sloth?"

Sky drums his fingers on his thigh. "Hmmm. Teddy for sure. He may be big and manly, but he looks like Santa Claus. He can stand to shed some pounds."

"Teddy work hard. He not lazy. I think Tree is sloth. He sleep all day."

"Okay, I agree. What about wrath?"

We say "Opal" in unison and burst out laughing. Opal must have heard her name because she looks straight at us and narrows her eyes. We both smile at her but she does not relent.

Sky and I grab a slice of warm apple pie and some Asbach brandy before heading to the reading nook. I sink into the green upholstered chair and feel the billowy softness of the cushions. I admire the floor-to-ceiling bookshelves, full of literary wonder and richness of adventure.

Sky pulls out a gift-wrapped book from the top shelf and hands it to me. "For you."

I tear open the shiny foil and am speechless. As I run my fingers delicately over the words, I can think of only one person: Sam. I hug the book and inhale the faint smell of vanilla coming from the pages. "How you know?" I ask as one tear escapes the corner of my eye. "I lost book. This Sam give to me. It burn with shrimp boat when I go Indonesia."

Sky flips open the cover of Carlos Castaneda's book *A Separate Reality* and points to the photograph lying loosely between the first two pages. It is a picture of Sam and Sky in their army fatigues, posing with their M-16s on the beach. A tear falls down my cheek and blazes a trail for more to follow. I finally have a picture of my Sam.

"That Christmas he spent with you and your family when he was on R and R was the happiest he had ever been," Sky says. "He told me he gave you this book. Told me he was going to marry you and that he'd read it to you each night."

"Yes," I say, "and he say this book about different visions of life. What look real may not be real."

Sky nods. "Nam was terrible for us all. It was a quicksand war. Sam and I used to daydream all the time. We'd be on our cots in the barrack and think about our favorite foods or in the foxhole talking about what we'd do once we got back home. Hell, even when we were sitting on the crapper, we'd talk about girls, and I'd say, in a separate reality, I'd be married to both Heather Locklear and Ann Margret." A sad smile graces his lips. He takes a swallow of his German cuvee, aged twenty-one years, and pours a second helping. "Sam would always say his reality was you."

"We can still have the reality we want," I say. "We can still have love and freedom, but different vision of it."

"Different version?" Sky asks. "Yes, I suppose. I'm sorry, Snow, for my outcry at your home. I hope I didn't scare you. I'm just so angry all the time. It's like, what's the point of living. You know?"

"You not scare me," I say. "I have many worry. For you, for my family, for finding job. You can talk to me and tell me everything. We help each other."

"I need help, Snow. I was already a broken man before I went into the military. My uncle…" Sky trails off and purses his lips. He takes another gulp of the brandy and stands up. His head lowers, his shoulders slump, and his body trembles. I sit patiently waiting for him to continue, fearing if I say anything, he will dismiss his pain and leave the room. Sky turns his back to me and leans against the back of the chair. "I was sexually abused by my dad's brother, Uncle Dawson, when I was eight years old. I kept that secret for years." When I say nothing, Sky turns around to check and see if I am still here. "My dad was never around. Too busy building his career, whoring his way across the globe, while my mom sat at home pining for a husband who made up for lost time with expensive gifts and cheap promises. She knows of his affairs and still, she loves him, or the idea of him. Uncle Dawson was around when Dad wasn't. He was the only man in our life at the time. Thank God Aunt Catherine married Uncle Teddy. I stayed with them every chance I got. Aunt Catherine is like a mom to me. You know, after I was drafted and before I left for Nam, I told my parents what happened with Uncle Dawson. Mom slapped me, and Dad laughed."

Sky's story claws at my heart and kicks me in the throat. "I sorry this happen to you. You not tell Teddy or Catherine?"

"I was too scared," Sky says. "Uncle Dawson said I had to keep it a secret, that no one would believe me if I told them. He said he'd just deny it and claim I was making up stories for attention. He made me think my parents would divorce if they knew what a bad boy I had been. At the time, that scared me tremendously."

"Where Uncle Dawson now?" I ask.

"Rotting in hell, I hope." Sky curls and uncurls his fingers. His tight fist presses down on the table until his knuckles turn red. "He died in a car accident. Drove drunk and bowled down a family of four."

I am unsure what to say but keep talking, trusting the right words will drip out. "Remember Pastor George? He say we must give anxiety to God. You keep big secret. It too much. That why you broken. Your secret like a monster, a tumor. It grow too big for you and rip you apart."

"But how do I let it go?" Sky asks. "I thought joining the military and being a world away from here was going to bury my problems, not add to them."

"You tell your story," I say. "You forgive yourself, and you forgive your parents…your uncle too. Then," I place my palm on Sky's chest, "you make room in your heart for what make you happy."

"But how? Don't you think I've tried to forget?"

"Not forget, Skyler…forgive." I take hold of Sky's hand and give it a hard squeeze. "It what we both must do."

"You know, after our driving lesson, I went to Massachusetts for a meditation retreat. My mom suggested I go clear my head."

"Maybe I meditate too," I say. "I try yoga. It nice."

"There's a meditation retreat in California I wouldn't mind trying. You can come with me."

"Maybe. I need job and I have Dolly," I say. "I watch yoga on TV. I learn down dog to cobra and child pose."

"I have no idea what that means, but okay." Sky gives me a soft hug. "Let's get our shit together for Sam. He'd want us to be happy."

I hand Sky his brandy, and we lift our glasses. "For Sam."

The church is bursting with members this morning. Outside the air is wet, and the clouds are ombre shades of gray. A loud rumble of thunder ripples across the evergreens, and with one crack of God's whip, a bolt of lightning pierces the sky, signaling the start of the race. Everyone runs into the house of our Lord like there is a free television inside and takes shelter from the rain. Teddy drops us off at the entrance and circles the grounds for a parking space.

Pastor George and Dawn greet each one of us with cheer as we rush in like good Christians on Christmas morning. Dolly runs off to Sunday school. She knows the routine now. Frances and Frank, together with their two little boys, Jacob and John, are already seated in the church. They will drive back to Wenatchee following the service.

A very pregnant Penny waddles toward Catherine. "Hi, Mom." She points to her husband, who stands and waves at us from the fourth row. "Todd and I saved everyone a seat."

I follow them to the front and sit next to Tree and Catherine. We wait for Teddy. The room is filled with radiant energy. A choir of large poinsettias, dressed in delicate robes of crimson and white, stand in front of the podium with their green foliage outstretched, welcoming us to service. White lights are strung around the pew; they glow and give off God's love. On either side of the room is an artificial tree, adorned with shiny ornaments and more lights. The fragrance of citrus fruits seduces me to sniff the air around me. I pinpoint it to the wood benches. I imagine this is what heaven is like—bright, warm, peaceful, and lemon-scented.

The time is 9:05 a.m. Teddy taps Tree's shoulder. We stand up and let him slide in beside Catherine. He is drenched from the rain, and beads of water trickle down from his shiny head into the thick forest that is his beard.

The children file into the room. There are whispers of confusion among the congregation. My eyes instinctually search for my daughter. She is the second to last in the line. Dolly looks so out of place being the only brown child in the group, but she certainly does not look like she feels out of place. My daughter smiles and fidgets with her dress. She looks for me, and we lock eyes. I wink. Her smile gets bigger.

The children sing, "He's got the whole world in his hands," as they sway back and forth and do hand gestures to the lyrics, raising their arms above their heads and forming an O to symbolize the world. I watch with delight as Dolly cradles her arms and rocks side to side while singing, "He's got the little bitty babies in his hands." They sing two more songs and then settle on the floor in the front. I beam with happiness and pride.

Pastor George addresses the congregation. "Merry Christmas." We all echo "Merry Christmas" back. "We started this morning off a little unorthodox, didn't we?" The audience chuckles. Tree and I do not understand, so we look at each other and shrug. "Well, today is not a typical day. It's not every day our Savior is born. Today we celebrate the Son of God."

I look around the church to see if I can spot Katrina and Sky but do not see them. Pastor George continues his message, opening with Hebrews 4:16. I partially listen, too distracted by Sky and Katrina's absence at church. I keep looking for them and wonder if Jean-Adrien's visit has anything to do with them not being here today.

"When we seek his grace and mercy," Pastor George cries out, "we must do so with confidence. In times of need, that is when we must approach God's throne boldly and ask our Father to help us. What happens if we keep quiet? If we absorb all the pain and hardship ourselves? If we internalize the fear, the guilt, the sadness…when we bear our burden alone, it becomes a poison. It eats away our joy. It robs us of our mental, spiritual, and physical health. It devours our soul and paralyzes us so that we are held hostage in our solitude."

"Amen," the congregation responds.

"When we show our vulnerability and confide in him our woes," Pastor George continues, "our God can take away our paralysis. Be it financial or health, be it cultural or spiritual…whatever is holding you back from living your life in his glory, turn it over to him, and trust that he will lift your burden. Join me in reading a passage from Mark, chapter two, verses one through twelve."

I follow Teddy's lead and open the Bible to page 1074. The house reads in unison about Jesus not only healing a paralytic man but also washing away his sins.

Pastor George closes his Bible. He takes off his reading glasses and looks straight at me. His gaze is intentional. "Your sins are forgiven."

Through Pastor George, God speaks to me. The angels and Sam and all my friends and family…they speak to me. They forgive me.

Without warning, I burst into uncontrollable tears. I am saved. Pages and pages of images fly through my thoughts. I see Sam's eyes roll back as I cradle him in my arms, his blood drenching the sleeves of my tunic. I see my father, cold and still, dead from the trauma he suffered. Sister Six's face flashes in front of me. I imagine a look of terror in her sunken eyes as her daughter is taken from her. I see Hồng-Mai's face, gaunt and painted with tear tracks, as she was raped…as she took her own life. I could not save any of them. I only saved myself. I left them all behind. So many lives lost or ruined. This burden has been with me for too long.

I can hear the screams of the women at sea as the Thai pirates violated them. Even more deafening are the silent cries of those who gave up and slipped away, letting earth and sea claim them. Maybe if I were a better wife, I could have held on to my husband. Maybe if I had fought harder, I could have saved Hải from torture and starvation. I should have tried. I could have tried. Why did I not do better?

The sadness and guilt are too much to bear. I climb over Tree and run out of the church. The doors feel heavier than usual, but I manage to push one open. I repeat to myself: I am forgiven. I am forgiven.

Outside, rain hammers the pavement. The roar of thunder urges me to stay indoors, but I see the outline of a man emerging from the parked cars. I run to him. The sting of every raindrop pricks my skin, needle and threading every memory into my body, telling me I can never forget, but that I can forgive. I am forgiven.

"Snow," Sky breathes. He takes me into his arms and holds me. I cling to him tighter and tighter, wanting to dissolve into him so that I no longer exist. I sob uncontrollably. I have been an imposter this whole time, pretending I am strong. The paper-thin veil drops. I am exposed, vulnerable, and fragile.

Sky picks me up and carries me to his car. Inside the safety of his 280ZX, I let it all go.

8. EAST IS NOT WEST (JANUARY 1981)

Some days, it is easier to pretend I do not speak or understand English than to engage in meaningless conversations with children who only value their point of view.

Dolly's friends, Melissa and Jen, sit at my table and help themselves to a bowl of rice. While my daughter dribbles soy sauce over her steamed jasmine rice, Melissa pours cold, bland milk into her bowl, and Jen sprinkles three spoons of sugar on top of hers. I cringe watching the kids shovel the white kernels into their mouths. What is it with Americans and their dairy and sugar?

Jen, the oldest of the three girls, has no problem taking charge. "We should have a slumber party at my house this weekend." Dolly and Melissa nod in agreement. She mother hens the other two, and they eagerly lap up her praise and opinions.

"What slumber party?" I ask.

"It's when everyone sleeps over at someone's house," Jen says, "and we stay up late playing and talking."

"And play dress up," Melissa chimes in, "and we can do each other's hair and paint our nails and put on makeup."

"And eat junk food and watch scary movies," Jen adds.

"Dolly cannot slumber party," I say. "She sleep at home. She only six year old. When she in college or marry, she sleep away from home."

Jen frowns at me. "She goes by Nancy now. And I am eight. My mom let me have slumber parties since I was four."

I am not going to let this child intimidate me or challenge my authority. "You call her Dolly or Thủy-Tiên, or Tiên, but never Nancy." I cross my arms and narrow my eyes. "And no slumber party. We not do that in Việt Nam."

"We are not in Vietnam," Dolly says defiantly, "and my name is Nancy."

I do not appreciate her tone. If I dared to disrespect my parents and talk back to them, I would have gotten spankings or kneeling time on the tile floors and would have been staring at the corner of a wall for an hour.

I scowl at my daughter. "Why Nancy?"

Dolly rolls her eyes at me. "Nancy is our new president."

"What?" I ask.

Jen sprinkles more sugar on her rice and says, with her mouth full, "Actually, she is the first lady. Ronald Reagan is our president. It's all over TV."

"Don't you know anything, Mama?" Dolly asks.

I do not know if it is the American culture or the influence of Melissa and Jen, but I will not tolerate the insolence. "Girls, time go home."

"But we are still eating," Melissa states.

"Home, now." I point to the door.

Both girls put on their shoes, wave, and say, "Bye, Nancy."

Thủy-Tiên stands on top of her chair and screams "why?" at me in Vietnamese. "Tại sao? Tại sao?" She stomps her foot and throws her spoon across the kitchen.

This temper of hers can only be from her father, I conclude.

I walk to the hall closet and pick up Tree's size ten sneakers. Thủy-Tiên sees the shoe and runs, but in our small apartment, there is nowhere to hide. I have her cornered.

In my calmest voice, I speak to her in Vietnamese. "East is not West. Do you understand what that means?"

She shakes her head no. The tears stream down her face.

"How we lived our life in Việt Nam is not how we will live our lives in America. Everything on the outside is different—how we dress, what we eat, where we live…even the name we are called, but everything on the inside, under the surface, must never change. That means our values, our beliefs, and our identity. You will respect your elders. You will respect our traditions. You will never roll your eyes or scream at me. Do you understand?"

"Okay," she mumbles.

"Not 'okay.' 'Yes, Mama.'"

"Yes, Mama," she whispers.

"Ask for forgiveness, and I will not spank you," I say.

"Con xin lỗi Mẹ."

The apartment smells like home as I add curry, lemongrass, and coconut milk to the chicken. I let the food simmer and join Tree and Dolly on the velour couch. On the television screen, a man welcomes everyone to the historic first inauguration, under the west front terrace of our nation's capitol. A decorated marine by the name of Michael Ryan steps to the podium and operatically sings.

"We are supposed to stand," Tree says.

I take hold of Tree and Dolly's hands and together we stand.

"Is he the president?" Dolly asks.

"Of course not," Tree says. "Presidents do not sing and presidents are supposed to be old."

The soldier finishes his song, a short verse of "America the Beautiful."

"Please be seated," the man on television says. So we sit.

A reverend of a Presbyterian church is introduced, and we are asked to stand again. Before long, Governor Ronald Reagan and his wife, Nancy, dressed meticulously in red, step up to the podium. We watch as he takes his oath and is sworn in as the fortieth President of the United States. I am mesmerized with the lovely couple and can feel the love Nancy has for her husband as well as the adoration he has for her. That is the kind of marriage I hope for Tree and Thủy-Tiên as well as for me one day.

"Is he our president?" Dolly asks. "I like his hair."

I am so engrossed in his speech and his mention of Arlington National Cemetery, I forget there is curry on the stove. His mention of rice paddies and jungles of Việt Nam catch my attention, and the tears flow seeing the white grave markers. I dismiss the aroma of burnt meat, and instead, hug my daughter and nephew. President Reagan tears up as he concludes his speech. "We are Americans. God bless you and thank you."

A sudden, jarring succession of beeps pierces our ear canals. Startled, I curse out, "Má mày!" The sound of the alarm and the smell of smoke wafting past my nostrils triggers a flashback to the sirens in my province of Vĩnh Bình. I beg for mercy. "Mother Mary, please do not let us die!"

Dolly squats down and covers her ears. "Make it stop!"

I squat down and wrap one protective arm around her. Tree jumps up from the couch, but I pull him down onto the floor. "Lay down! We are under attack! The Việt Cộng are here!"

Tree pulls away from me despite my plea. He runs into the kitchen and turns off the stove. My nephew removes the pot of curry from the electric burner, but the alarm continues to wail. He runs from room to room, cursing, "Đụ má mày."

"Stop!" I order. "What are you looking for? Get down!"

"Aunt Eight, it is a stupid smoke detector or something. It is not an air raid. Help me find it so we can turn it off!"

I ease back into reality and run to the deck. I open the sliding glass door and look outside. All is calm. There are no pulsating chuk-chuk sounds of helicopter rotors, no pops of M-16s or rat-tat-tats of AK-47s. The air is still and moist but not humid like the streets of Việt Nam.

The three of us look for the source of the beeps.

Dolly points to the ceiling. "Is that it?"

Tree drags a chair to the smoke detector and steps up. He searches for a switch. He pulls on the cover and rips out the batteries. The beeps stop. It is quiet once again. I let out a sigh of relief and look at Tree. He smiles at me.

Dolly hops onto my lap and takes my face in her small hands. "Can I have a dollar?"

I smile at her. "What for?"

"I found the alarm."

"Fine." I stroke her hair. "Thank you."

"Mama, you have some gray hair. Can I pluck them for twenty-five cents? Each?"

I laugh. "Each? I will pay you fifty cents for an hour of head scratches, massages, and gray hair plucking…but if you pull any black ones out, you pay me."

She gives two seconds of serious thought. "I charge five cents for every gray. I have fast fingers." She wriggles them as proof.

It amuses me that at age six, she is already hustling to make money. I agree to her terms. "You are just like your father."

"No," Tree says. "She is just like you."

A loud knock at the door disrupts our moment and kick-starts my heart. "Who can that be?" The knock comes again, urgent and louder.

"Are you there?" It is my neighbor, Diệp. "Chị Tuyết, ơi!"

"Ơi," I call back.

Tree lets her into the apartment. "Alô, Cô Diệp."

"Are you all right? I heard the alarm." Diệp and her son, Hùng, barge in. Both of them wear sweatbands on their foreheads, shorts that go to their knees, white socks pulled over their calves, and brown, oversized rain boots. I think of Sister Six's definition of *ragamuffin chic*. "Ơi, you found the smoke detector. It is so sensitive. Next time, open the doors and windows and wave a towel below it." She demonstrates by vigorously waving an invisible towel overhead and thrusting her whole body back and forth. "The 'eeeek, eeeek' will stop. The first time it happened to me, I wet my underwear and smashed the smoke alarm with a frying pan."

Tree stands behind our neighbors and tries to suppress his laughter. I force my composure as well.

"I burned the curry," I say. "What are you wearing?"

Diệp lifts her leg and curls her back like she is a dog about to mark his territory. She points to her man-boots. "You like them? I got these boots from the dumpster. Somebody threw these perfectly good shoes away! If you want, you can have his." She points to her son. "Hùng, give Cô Tuyết your boots."

"No, I have a pair of rain boots the church gave me." I lie. "But maybe Tree wants them?"

My poor nephew is put on the spot. Tree furrows his eyebrows and shakes his head vehemently but quickly smiles when Diệp insists he takes the hideous boots. He enthusiastically accepts. She is pleased.

"If your curry cannot be saved, come over for dinner. We have plenty." Seeing Tree and me look at each other hesitantly, she adds, "It is not dog food."

We all burst out laughing, and I heartily accept her invitation.

###

Inside her apartment, the pungent smell of fish sauce assaults my nose, but it is balanced with the aroma of pan-fried garlic, green onions, and scallions. Despite it being forty-three degrees outside, she has all the windows open to air out the smell. I watch as she lifts the lid of the clay pot with one hand and dips a pair of chopsticks into the sauce with the other.

Diệp licks the chopstick and nods. "Perfect."

"You need to teach me how to make the braised catfish," I say.

She waves me over. "Come have a taste."

I must admit, Diệp is a good cook. "Your *cá kho tộ* is delicious! My Sister Six is the best cook. This tastes exactly like her recipe." I admire the caramelized, golden color of the fish steaks and the vibrant hue of the green onions. My stomach rumbles.

"There is a small grocery store in Seattle east of I-5 in Little Saigon. It's the Mekong store." Diệp sprinkles ground black pepper on the catfish and turns off the stove. "I hear that later this year there is going to be another market opening called Việt Wah. I spoke to the owner, Đức. He came here in 1976."

I call Tree and Thủy-Tiên into the kitchen to help set the table and bring food out. My neighbor hands them sets of chopsticks, soup spoons, and bowls. There are only four chairs but five of us.

Diệp and her son, Hùng, bring out the catfish and winter melon soup. I grab the pot of rice and a plate of fried eggplant.

"Do you want me to feed you, or do you want to eat at the table and stand?" I ask my daughter.

"I want to eat with you," Dolly replies. Standing at the table between Hùng and me, Dolly is the same height as I am seated.

Tree searches for an extra plate in the kitchen. "We need something for the bones." He finds a small saucer in the dish rack.

Diệp invites me to eat. "Mời ăn, Chị Tuyết."

I give her my thanks. "Cám ơn."

I remind Dolly she needs to invite her elders to eat, as is customary in our culture.

She lets out an exaggerated sigh. "Why do I have to do that? We do not do that at Mr. and Mrs. Van's house or Aunt Katrina's house."

"They are not Vietnamese. We all are," I remind her. "We may be living among Westerners, but we must never give up our roots."

Dolly rolls her eyes. She starts with the hostess, then me. "Mời Cô Diệp. Mời Mẹ."

"Do not roll your eyes. I have told you this before. If you disrespect me again, you will eat pea vines for the rest of the week," I say.

My daughter apologizes and extends the invitation to Tree and Hùng. Diệp's son picks up his chopsticks and shovels rice into his mouth.

Diệp slaps her son behind the head. "Your turn."

After the formality of the kids inviting elders to eat, we dive in family style with our spoons and chopsticks; no one cares to use separate serving utensils for the food.

"Cô Diệp," Tree says with his mouth full of rice, "thank you for dinner. You must have owned a restaurant back home."

"No, we did not have a restaurant," she says, "but my mother was a good cook. I learned from her." Diệp's eyes mist up with the mention of her mother.

A small lump forms in my throat as I briefly recall my mother's face and the lovely smile she wore. I shove the memory aside. "What province are you from? Did you come here by boat like us?"

Diệp adds more catfish to Tree's bowl. She licks her lips and opens her mouth to speak, but nothing comes out. She shakes her head and stops chewing. She does not look at me. A lonesome teardrop splatters on the table. Diệp wipes her left eye but another droplet of water escapes. "Mỹ Lai."

She whispers the words so quietly I am not sure I hear her correctly. "Mỹ Lai?" I ask. "In the Quảng Ngãi province?"

She nods. Her shoulders shake. The massacre that took place there in 1968 was unspeakable.

I place my hand on her shoulder. "I am sorry."

Diệp looks at me. Her lips quiver. Her hand trembles as she puts her chopsticks down.

"Why are you sad, Auntie?" Dolly asks. "I thought 'mỹ lai' means half Vietnamese and half American."

"No, that is the name of the village my mom is from," Hùng says.

"Tree, take the children to our apartment," I say. "I want to talk to Cô Diệp alone."

My daughter protests. "I am not done eating."

"Take your bowl of rice and go," I order. "Both of you, go with brother Tree."

Tree loads up their bowls of rice with fish, eggplant, and soup and ushers the kids out the door. My daughter complains her rice is now soggy from the soup. Once the door closes, I turn my attention back to Diệp.

###

Tears run freely down her face. I sit in silence with my hand on hers. Patiently, I wait as her emotions run their course, from quiet mist to flowing sobs, onto jagged, thunderous cries and wails

337

of anger. Diệp leans into me, and I soothe her until she is quiet once more.

She sits up and takes a deep breath. Diệp closes her eyes and exhales. "The helicopters flew in early that morning. It was March 16, 1968…a date I will never forget. I was around Tree's age, just seventeen. When the shooting started, everyone ran. I was on my way to the market but had turned back to fetch more money. When the helicopters landed, all these men in fatigues and M-16s spilled out. I ran as fast as I could to my house, but then a heavy body fell on me. He had been shot from a distance and was dead before he fell, his eyes wide open in terror. I heard the people screaming, their pleading voices screeching like wild cats. I wanted to run to my family, but I was frozen in fear, so I stayed down in the field and pretended I was dead. Another corpse fell on me. I could see between their bodies the soldiers rounding up people and shooting their rifles indiscriminately. It was horrible, all the shooting and stabbing…raping. Hours went by before it was over, and I lay there for a long time after they left. I felt like a coward. I saw one man with his scalp removed and a boy with his hand cut off. There was blood everywhere. I went crazy trying to make sense of it. Why? We were not armed. We were not Việt Cộng or sympathizers. What did we do? We were just trying to live day by day. I hated the Americans. That hate consumed me for years. It was like a meat cleaver chopping my heart into pieces. I lost my mother and father, my brothers and little sisters. I should not be alive, but I am because I was a coward, pretending to be dead while my village was getting burned down and my family and friends killed."

I pat her knee. "You did what you had to. You were smart to play dead. I do not think you acted cowardly. I believe the heavens have a plan for you."

"Do you know what it is like to live while the people you love die? It is like a ratchet around your entire body that tightens every time you let joy into your life. The guilt brings you back so you cannot let go."

I nod in agreement. "For me, guilt is the giant boulder at the end of a noose around my neck. Learning to love and forgive ourselves is hard. My mom told me a woman's fate is to suffer. I hope we were spared so that we can end that cycle of suffering."

"I am glad I have a boy." Diệp smiles. "The misery will skip a generation, but you have a daughter. Her fate will bring her sorrow too."

"We all suffer to some degree. It is part of the journey to self-love and self-worth. Do you still hate the Americans?"

Diệp shakes her head. "I came to realize that it was not hate I felt for those soldiers. I think the heart can learn to love again. I love Americans now. Life is defined by the heart. If the heart dies, you die. Do you agree?" My neighbor does not give me a chance to answer. "I think fear is more poisonous than hate. I feared the Americans more than I hated them. Fear lives in the mind, and the mind does not know how to be strong. The mind is weak, unlike the heart."

"You need both a strong mind and heart to have a healthy life," I say. "Thủy-Tiên's mind is stronger than her heart, but I think it is more balanced now. She had a hole in her heart when she was born and had open-heart surgery last August."

"Look at us, single women raising our children alone in a foreign country. I do not recognize my life. I always envisioned marrying a handsome man from my village, and we would have ten children, a field of water buffalos, and all the mangos and rice we could eat!" Diệp cracks a smile. "And I would grow old to raise a few dozen grandchildren."

"You can still have a version of that dream, minus the buffalos." I chuckle. "It is ironic that you feared the Americans and yet ended up here. I think fate brought us together. You could have gone to Australia or somewhere else, but you ended up in Seattle."

"This was not fate, Sister. This was by design. Tell me, if a pack of street dogs attacked you, would you not be afraid of all dogs?"

"Yes, I think that is to be expected," I say.

"Exactly, but I was not going to live the next sixty years of my life mottled by fear. We live and struggle and fight for our children, do we not? I chose America so that I could face my fears and not let them steal more of my life."

"See? That kind of thought is an emblem of bravery not an insignia of cowardice."

Diệp rubs her eyes and grinds the salty tears into her crow's feet. She licks her dry, cracked lips, and looks out the window. "I know not all Americans are bad. I am learning to forgive what happened so I can move on with my life and learn to be happy with the family that I have. My son has been a blessing."

"Hùng is a good boy," I assure her. "I feel the same about Thủy-Tiên or Dolly…or Nancy. I do not even know what to call her! She is all I have. Each time I think I am going to lose her, her heart beats on. Tree is a teenager, and he has a wandering spirit. He will leave me soon. That is what boys do."

Diệp drapes a few rogue strands of hair behind her ear and looks at me. "I am too hard on my son sometimes. It is because I love him so much. Our children will have a good life. They will have the freedom to choose who they love and marry and get a good education and job."

"I think it is our motherly duty to suffer so that our children do not. We are paying the price to lessen their debt."

"Where is Thủy-Tiên's father?" Diệp asks.

The memory of Tý disappearing into the Mercedes sprinter van and leaving us behind haunts me more than I care to admit. "He left Việt Nam in 1975 right before we lost Sài Gòn. He lives in Texas now. We did not make it out until 1979. It feels like a lifetime ago. What about Hùng's father?"

"I met Duy in 1972. We loved each other right away and had a small wedding. It happened so fast. A year later, Hùng was born. We left in July 1979 and drifted in the ocean for seven days before a German ship found us and dumped us on Kuku Island in Indonesia. I was seven months pregnant with our fourth child. I lost her a month after she was born. Hùng is my only child who survived. A month later, my husband fell ill and died. One day, I want to have my ashes brought to Kuku."

"I am sorry. I cannot imagine how devastating that was for you. What was it like on Kuku?" I ask. "We were on Galang, and it was terrible at first."

"Kuku was a small, remote island. There were fifty-three people on our boat. Our engine died, so we drifted aimlessly. We lived like savages, fighting over morsels of food that we scavenged and climbing trees to get bananas. That first week, it rained so hard. We had no shelter, so we took the beating. The jungle was thick with flies and mosquitos everywhere. There was no toilet, so we just pooped wherever, which made problems worse with the flies. We made huts from bamboo and plastic, whatever we could find, and lived on the beach until one day a helicopter flew over us and dropped parcels of canned food and supplies. It had a big red cross on it and the letters U and N."

"You must have been so relieved," I comment.

"Yes, we thought we were saved. A week later, a ship called *World Vision* came and brought us dried foods, fish, and potatoes. I boiled the fish in seawater. It was sandy and salty with a lot of bones, but Hùng and I devoured it."

"What did the Indonesian government do?" I ask.

"They were so overwhelmed. They erected a camp for us refugees, but before long, more and more boat people were tossed onto camp Kuku's shores…hundreds of them, two or three times a week. It soon was very crowded. I would wait until nightfall to go to the toilet. Eventually, we got organized and dug holes a couple of kilometers away from camp. The women would go in groups, and we all shared this one poncho for modesty. Some of the men just did their business in the ocean. More and more boats came, from Save the Children or UNHCR, and delivered food and supplies. We ate a lot of cabbage and canned tuna or sardines, but we were always hungry. One time, a group of us caught a stray cat and ate it. You know the saying, '*ăn thịt mèo nghèo ba năm*'?"

"Yes, eat cat meat and you will be poor for three years. My mother used to say, '*tránh xui xẻo, không ăn thịt mèo.*'"

"Yes, avoid bad luck, do not eat cat meat. Well, we were too hungry to care."

"Now I understand why you purchased dog food and canned cat food," I tease.

My neighbor laughs. "You will never let me forget, will you?"

"We are sisters now, and as your big sister, I have the duty of chastising you."

"You know, despite the hardships, there were a few fond memories on camp Kuku. One time, another refugee boat washed on the shore, and Hùng rushed to me, so excited to show me what he had found on the boat. His little hands flowered open, and there were tiny kernels of rice that he had picked off the floorboards. Time went by so slowly then. We swam a lot to exhaust the daylight. The coral reef was pretty, and there were so many colorful fish. It was a magical dream world beneath the water."

"We spent a lot of time in the water as well," I say. "Above the water lived weariness and disease…diarrhea…malaria…It was better to spend our days in the water catching crabs."

"Look at us, talking like old women. I am not even thirty years old yet," Diệp says.

"I will be forty one years old this April," I say dryly.

"What?" Diệp slaps my thigh playfully. "You look my age. We need to find you a husband. I will be your matchmaker. I know this doctor…"

9. ONE CHANCE (AUGUST 1981)

Dear Sister Six, Brother Seven, and Family,

I have been in America for over a year now. So much to tell you all, I do not know where to begin. More and more Vietnamese refugees are coming here. We are like an army of ants storming to take over the American picnic tables. Tree dropped out of high school and found a temporary job as a school janitor. He spends his time removing gum from under the classroom tables and restores the rooms each night for summer classes. It pains me to see his mind and talent go to waste. He turned eighteen in December but looks fifteen like his documents state. Here in America, you are entitled to do whatever you want after you turn eighteen and are treated like an adult. He has been hanging out with other refugees. He does not have a car or scooter, not even a bicycle, so he walks everywhere. I see buses here, but we do not know how to ride them or how much it costs. He has been staying at other people's homes, moving from one couch to another like a homeless vagabond. I have no way to contact him. He calls home and checks in every once in a while. Most of the time he plays soccer with other refugee kids and loiters with new friends. I do not understand why their parents allow him to stay with them.

Thủy-Tiên is doing well in school and making friends. We speak two languages at home. I speak in Vietnamese, and she answers in English. I am afraid she will forget her native tongue. I think she is having an identity issue. A couple of months ago, she wanted to be called Nancy, but now she wants to be Kristine or Christie…She has not decided yet. I have one chance to raise her right, and I worry I will ruin her doing it alone. There are moments when I do not recognize her. Her body is frail but her spirit is strong and defiant. She questions me, challenges my patience, and talks back to me. Many of the children here are not afraid to be disobedient. They are not dutiful and accepting of authority. Thủy-Tiên is like a sword. Only time will tell if she will save me or kill me.

I hope to find a job soon so I can send money home to you. The government welfare system here is good. Every month I get food coupons from an organization called DSHS. They give us cash and medical assistance and my apartment is subsidized. It is nice, but we now share our home with cockroaches. Some are as big as my toenail. When I turn on the kitchen light, they scatter as fast as we all used to every time you, Sister Six, farted. I miss those funny days. I do not miss eating cockroaches to stay alive though.

My neighbor, Diệp, has been teaching me how to cook a few simple meals, and I am learning to make a variety of sandwiches at Green River Community College. They have classes for everything. I took some English and computer drafting classes at ITT Technical Institute. Thủy-Tiên wants to eat only American food, like cereal, peanut butter and jelly sandwiches, and pancakes with syrup. Her favorite is macaroni and cheese. We do not have these foods back home so I cannot explain what they are. Basically, anything with sugar, starch, and no vegetables is edible to Thủy-Tiên. I miss your cooking and I am desperately in need of a good bánh mì. The baguettes here have too much dough filling.

My sponsors continue to be a big part of our lives. We go to church every Sunday. I have a driver's license now and can drive but no car. I rely on Mr. and Mrs. Van. Sometimes Katrina or Sky takes us. After I get a job, I will save some money to buy a car. People do not ride scooters here. The streets are wide and organized with lines, signs, and lights. It is not crowded at all like back home. Animals here are spoiled pets not to be eaten. The Vanzwol family has a dog named Biscuit. He is smart. They talk to him like he is a child and give him human food. Such waste! They let Biscuit sleep on the bed with them and he has domain over the house and furniture. It amazes me how much the people here kiss their animals and take them to places! It makes me miss Dirty Butt, that poor chicken.

Please write and give me news about our family. Any word from Hải or Tâm? Has Tý written? Hiền, I hope you will achieve your dream of opening a fabric and tailoring shop one day. I am getting better at sewing, and my stitching is straight. You would be proud of me. Tell Tuấn and Trinh Auntie Eight misses them.

All my love,
Snow

###

While my daughter plays outside with Melissa, Jen, and Hùng, I cut up the sweet potatoes, lemongrass, and chicken to make curry for dinner. It is the one meal I have perfected and have been cooking at least once every couple of weeks.

It is quiet in the apartment without Tree to talk to. I turn on the television and listen to KING-5 News.

"In April 1975, with the collapse of the South Vietnamese and Cambodian governments, over one hundred forty thousand refugees were evacuated and resettled in the US under the Indo-Chinese refugee program. Now, six years later, the exodus from Vietnam hasn't let up. Many state and local organizations, voluntary agencies like IRC, the International Rescue Committee, wonder if the waves of boat people will ever cease. Even private citizens like Nathaniel Knobb are scratching their heads and pushing back."

I turn down the stove to let the curry simmer and pay close attention to the news. A local reporter interviews a Seattle resident.

"These gooks are leaching off the system. We spend hundreds of millions of dollars helping them with education and public assistance. Our hard-earned tax dollars support them while our citizens struggle," Nathaniel says. "We need to shut our doors and not let any more of them in. Hell, we should send some of them back."

The reporter turns to the camera and says, "Refugee task forces have undertaken massive humanitarian efforts to get refugees resettled and integrated into society as quickly as possible. There are those like Seattle native, Jean Dragseth, who welcome the Vietnamese and appreciate the cultural richness of their presence."

"They are here to stay, and we need to embrace them," Jean says. "They have to overcome so many obstacles to be self-sufficient again. I cannot imagine losing my home and having to start over, adjusting to new customs, dealing with language barriers and employment issues. The American thing to do is to help them."

The reporter continues. "Earlier today I sat down with sisters, Phuong and Van Nguyen, who were among the first wave of refugees to arrive in the United States in April 1975. They were brought to Travis Air Force Base in California because refugee reception centers had not yet been established. In June of that year, they were resettled in Washington State through the efforts of the VOLAGs."

"When we arrived," Phương says in Vietnamese, "we were provided one month of financial assistance to help transition into the community. We were so happy to receive five hundred dollars, but we discovered that five hundred does not stretch far in the United States."

Phương's older sister, Vân, agrees. "Our VOLAG representative directed us to apply for state welfare. In Việt Nam, I was a pharmacist, but now, I clean rooms at a motel. My sister cleans tables at a diner. Our English skills are not very good. I want to practice pharmaceuticals again, but there are different requirements here to practice."

"In 1975," the reporter says, "Washington State received three percent of the total refugees who resettled in the US. The unemployment rate back then was nine percent. Today, with the Iran-Iraq War raging on, Americans are once again up in arms as the unemployment rate rises to an all-time high of ten percent. People are worried."

I am worried also. I must find a job. I turn the TV off and walk back to the kitchen to check on the curry. I hear sounds of laughter and look out the window. My daughter jumps rope with her friends. Donald, the man I met at the laundromat, is also outside playing basketball with his adopted sons, Jason and Ricky.

"Alô, Donald," I call out.

Donald dribbles the orange ball and launches it into the basket. He stops to wave. "We never did get together after Christmas, did we? And here we are the middle of summer already."

"You join us for dinner tonight?" I ask.

"Another time," Donald says. "The boys and I need to finish packing. We're taking a road trip and doing some camping before school starts up. Ricky has been accepted into WSU."

The words "camping" and "WSU" are foreign to me, but I smile and nod anyway. "Have safe trip. I see you next time."

Ricky waves to me. "Hi…hi. Hi, Snow. I'm…going…to Wazzu."

"Washington State University, also known as Wazzu," Donald explains, "for the sheer reputation of being a party zoo."

"Oh, Ricky become animal doctor," I say. "Very good."

"No, actually, well…nevermind." Donald pats Ricky's head. "Who knows, maybe he will become an entertaining animal doctor one—"

"Mama, can Melissa and Jen sleep over?" My daughter cuts Donald off and yells to me in English.

"No," I respond in Vietnamese. "Time to come in and take a bath. Dinner will be ready soon."

"What is for dinner?" Dolly asks.

"Chicken curry."

"Again?" She pouts. "Can we eat at Hùng's house? They are having egg rolls."

"No," I say. "Come in now."

My daughter thrusts the jump rope on the ground and says goodbye to her friends. She stomps her feet as she walks to our apartment. Moments later, I hear the door open and slam shut. She emphatically kicks her shoes off and drags her feet to the bathtub. I pretend not to notice her dramatic entry.

She turns on the water and screams. "I hate curry!" She stands before me in her underwear, arms crossed, and lips quivering. "I am going to live with Brother Tree in California."

"Really?" I call her bluff. "After your bath, we can call him. If he says yes, I will pack your clothes and put you on an airplane."

Forty minutes later, Dolly emerges from the bathroom, wrinkled and wet. She hastily dresses and slumps in front of the bowl of curry. My daughter slowly draws the spoon to her lips. She takes a bite and gags. My patience wears thin. I do not find her defiance amusing. She takes another bite and coughs, heaving and spraying yellow sauce all over the table. I stare at her, secretly wanting to shove the food in her mouth.

"Not too long ago, we were starving and living in a jungle," I remind her. "And you almost died. You had a hole in your heart, you had worms in your gut, and you were bony thin. Now, eat your dinner and be thankful you have food."

"It looks like poop," she says. "And it tastes like vomit. And it stinks like farts."

"If you do not want to eat it tonight, you do not have to," I say.

Her eyes light up, and instantly, the tears that threatened to drop vanish behind her lids. "Can I have cereal?"

"No. Go to bed."

Dolly bangs the spoon down and storms into the bedroom. She shuts the door but opens it to shut it again with a loud thud.

In the morning for breakfast, a cold bowl of curry awaits her.

###

Sky darts around the car with an athletic gait. He opens my door, bows, and takes my hand. He leads me into the seafood restaurant.

The beautiful hostess greets us. "Welcome to Ray's Boathouse. Reservation for two?"

"Three, actually," Sky says. "It's under Bill Cushing."

347

"Yes, your other party just arrived. Follow me."

I follow the hostess but lag behind Sky as I take in the breathtaking waterfront view. The ripple of the Puget Sound glistens like diamonds under the rose-colored hue of the evening sky. Boats drift lazily by, cutting the glassy water on their rendezvous with the Olympic Mountains. A dark outline of a bird catches my eye, and I watch the eagle dart in front of the carrot-ginger sun. It swoops down to bathe in the inlet of the Pacific Ocean and rises like a phoenix with a prize in its beak.

The sizzle of steaks seduces my ears while traces of garlic, onions, and sea salt perfume the air. I am aware of how underdressed I am seeing the diners in suits and cocktail attire. We approach a table by the window, and a man with curly gray hair stands up. His round glasses and the dark gray suit make him look polished, esteemed, and very professional. He smiles with the warmth of a cozy fire.

The gentleman shakes Sky's hand, and the two of them hug. "You're too thin." He reaches for my hand and gives it a gentle squeeze. "You must be Snow."

Sky pulls out my chair and introduces his friend. "Snow, this is Bill Cushing, a long-time friend of the family. He is with the *Seattle Times* newspaper."

"Let's enjoy some food and get to know each other a little before we talk business." Bill winks, and I immediately feel at ease with him. "I ordered a seafood platter to start. I hope you like oysters, scallops, king crab, and shrimp cocktail." He pours me champagne from a bottle of Dom Perignon, but I stop him.

"She's a lightweight," Sky explains. "A couple of sips and she'll be the same shade as the sunset."

Bill pours a generous amount of the light-amber liquid into Sky's flute. "You will find, Snow, that Ray's serves the best cuisines, offering flavors exclusive to the Pacific Northwest. They were the first local restaurant to purchase their own wholesale fish buyer's license, so they can buy directly from the fishermen. There is nothing better than fresh, wild-caught seafood. They also have an impressive beer and wine list."

Sky laughs. "Bill is a sales and marketing guy. He can sell you wool socks in the summer. She's not in the market to buy a restaurant."

"Maybe not now, but in the future when she is ready, she will remember me and know who to come to. You not only sell to the now but to the future. Have I taught you nothing, boy?"

It is heartwarming to see the two of them engage in an easygoing manner as if they are father and son who genuinely love and respect one another. I am curious about their relationship. "Bill, how you and Sky meet?"

Bill looks at Sky mischievously. "Well, he peed on me, you see."

Sky rolls his eyes and leans back in his chair. "Okay, here we go."

Bill takes a sip of his champagne. He rolls his neck and pretends to crack his fingers as if he is about to settle in for a night of storytelling. "Before Skyler was a twitch in his daddy's pants, Katrina and I were high school and college sweethearts. We were young, in love, and had the whole future ahead of us."

"But Bill was not ready for marriage," Sky says.

"I was stupid, but let's paint the picture in black and white," Bill says. "Katrina was in no hurry either. There were things we both wanted to do before we settled down and started a family."

"He wanted to be a journalist," Sky says, "and was very career-driven. He wanted to travel and see the world first."

"Yes," Bill says, "I wanted to move to the UK and work for the *London Star*. Katrina romanticized about moving to Paris and becoming a model. We were both twenty years old and had been together for almost five years. Our love was strong, and we thought it would last forever, but we were naïve."

Our waiter interrupts us by bringing out the appetizers. I have never seen prawns and scallops so large in my life and the oysters so small…and raw! The crab legs look intimidating, but it is the one I find most inviting.

"Ladies first," Bill says.

"I not used to ladies first," I say and place one of each, except the oyster, on my plate. "In my country, men always first."

"You will get used to it." Sky spoons a dollop of red sauce on my plate. "This is cocktail sauce for your shrimp. It's tangy. In the States, women have more rights and yield more power than they do in Vietnam. We, men, are smarter than we look. We know who truly holds the power." He laughs. I love it when Sky laughs. I know that at this moment, he is happy and not haunted by memories of the past.

Bill nods. "Women have a spell on us."

I watch with revulsion as Bill squeezes lemon juice on his oyster and slurps it down. I look away, unable to stop imagining the slimy mollusk slithering down his throat. He offers me one, and I politely decline. "Oysters are rich in zinc, which helps with testosterone production. They also boost dopamine, which is good for the libido, if you catch my drift." Bill winks at Sky. "I need all the help I can get."

In my attempt to distract myself from the gray, raw shellfish, I reel the conversation back to Katrina and Bill. "Bill, you and Katrina separate after college?"

"They parted ways right after ringing in the new year together," Sky says. "It was January 1945."

"I had these big dreams," Bill reflects. "I wanted to cover World War II from overseas and be in the middle of the action before it was over. The action was short-lived because months later, Germany surrendered, and Hitler killed himself. We bombed Japan and they, too, surrendered. I came back home for Christmas only to find Katrina married to Jean-Adrien. So tragic."

I sit dumbfounded and speechless. I sip my champagne and decide it is delicious. Bill is perceptive. He pours me more.

Sky finishes off his glass and refills. "I was a month old when he met me, and yes, I peed on him."

"Katrina had met Jean-Adrien at a museum. He seduced her with his Frenchy-French charms, his talks of travel, and his lifestyle of luxury and adventure!" Bill speaks sarcastically and twirls his pointer finger. "I was furious at him for moving in on my territory and heartbroken that Katrina allowed herself to be so vulnerable, but I soon realized I was the fool to have left. I chased my career when I should have chosen love. I felt I had this one chance to report for *The Star*. I didn't realize I also had only one chance with Katrina, and I blew it. She is a beautiful woman who had needs. Jean-Adrien gave her security and affection. He made her feel desirable and safe."

Our waiter comes back to check on us and takes our dinner order. Bill orders a bottle of Quilceda Creek Cabernet Sauvignon to go with our steaks. "Did you know, almost all wine grapes grown in Washington are grown on their own roots? This is special, you see, because most of the world's wine regions grow their grapes on grafted rootstock. A century ago, a louse ravaged vineyards, and the only solution was to graft new vines onto rootstocks that were resistant to the pest. There are a few vintners who still plant vines on their roots, but that's a gamble because they are susceptible to disease, especially if the soil is not resistant to the louse. For some reason, Washington has not had any problems. Own-rooted vines are old and deeply rooted, so they do not need as much fertilization and water, which makes them better equipped to survive harsh weather and resist diseases."

"That's Bill for you," Sky says affectionately. "The walking, talking, live encyclopedia."

"That's right, my boy," Bill jokes. "I've got the brains and the good looks."

I have no interest in wine and louse but every interest in the love triangle. "Tell me more about you and Katrina."

"Well, I went back to London and poured my heart into my work," Bill says. "I interviewed some of the world's greats like Bob Hope and Bing Crosby. I met the Glamour Girls, fashion models at the time. I was there to cover the royal wedding of Queen Elizabeth II and Prince Philip. I had my share of trysts to forget Katrina, but no one captured my heart. If you're lucky, you get one chance to find the great love of your life. You have a better chance of getting kicked to death by a horse while serving in the cavalry than finding your soulmate."

"You and Katrina remain friends?" I ask, already knowing the answer. I finish my champagne, and Bill pours me a little bit of the cabernet sauvignon in a fresh goblet.

"It was easy at first to harden my heart toward her," Bill says, "but then one day, Katrina and Jean-Adrien had a fight, and she called me. I wanted to be there for her as a friend, and since I still held a flame for her, I hoped she'd leave him and come back to me."

"But she stayed with him because of me," Sky says. "Although it's not like I'm still a child. She doesn't need to be tethered to him anymore. Don't get me wrong. I love my father, but he's a pompous, arrogant, narcissistic horse's ass who has no clue how to be a husband or father."

"You both deserved better," Bill says. "Anyway, leave the past where it belongs. It is the present we can control, and the future we can plan."

"Let's talk about you," Sky says. "You are much more interesting."

"Me?" I ask. "You know everything."

"Let's pretend you are on an interview," Bill says, "and Skyler and I are meeting you for the first time."

"Yes, Ms. Le, tell us about yourself." Sky grins and straightens his posture. He clears his throat and tries to look serious.

I play along, mostly for Bill's sake, and hope to impress him. "I from Vĩnh Bình in the Bạc Liêu Province of Việt Nam. I youngest of seven children. I was math teacher and bank teller, but after war, I sell medicine."

Bill clasps his hands and leans forward, resting his elbows on the table. He nods. "So you were in sales, and you are good with numbers. I like it. Go on."

"I have daughter. She seven year old, and her name Dolly."

"Tell me, Ms. Le," Sky says, "what is your dream job and why?"

I try not to laugh and mirror Sky's professionalism. "Mr. Herrington, my dream be like you and Mr. Cushing. I wish to be important and shaping our future's history. I believe in truth, and my dream job to story-tell the truth so people make right choice for themselves."

"How would you do this?" Bill asks. "Give me an example of when you were able to shape someone's future and help them make the right choice."

"I give two example." I hold up two fingers for a visual. "First, when I was in Sài Gòn, I shape my own future. I get communist soldier help me with license to sell dry foods. I able to go from my village to the city freely. I was friends with his mother, and after she die, I tell him she haunt him if he not help me. So I help him make right choice. I get license, and he sleep peaceful at night."

Bill roars with laughter. "That worked, huh?"

"Oh yes, the Vietnamese believe in ghosts," I say. "So many wars, so many deaths. Our country have many ghosts."

Bill frowns. "What is your second example?"

I smile and bring levity back to our conversation. "Every day, I help my daughter make right choice. For example, I make curry for dinner, but she no want to eat. She say yucky. I tell her people go hungry and die every day so she lucky, but I tell her she no have to eat the curry if she not want. So she go to bed with no dinner. In the morning, instead of Lucky Charms cereal for breakfast, I give her cold curry from yesterday. Oh, Mr. Bill, she cry, but she eat it all. Now, she eat anything I give her."

Sky and Bill burst out laughing. Bill claps his hands and wipes a tear from his eye. People in the restaurant look our way. Some smile, others look confused.

Sky raises his wine glass. "What did I tell you? Let's celebrate."

I raise my wine glass. "I get job?"

"You got the job, Snow." Bill clinks my glass with his. "Congratulations. You not only won our hearts but our respect."

"That fun," I say. "What else?"

"Bill," Sky says, "I don't think she understands what just happened. You better tell her."

"Snow," Bill says, "I am pleased to offer you a real job with the *Seattle Times*. We have a media coordinator position open that reports up to me, and it is yours if you want it."

"What?" I yell loudly. More heads turn, and one man gives me a demeaning stare, but I do not care. I lower my voice to a whisper. "Really?" They both nod. "What I have to do?"

We discuss the details of my job over dessert, and I agree to start the following week at $4.25 an hour. Sky insists on taking me car shopping and does not take no for an answer. I promise to pay back the loan from the Bank of Skyler.

10. THE THIRD WHEEL (OCTOBER 1981)

School is back in session, and Dolly is in second grade. In the morning, she walks one mile to Springbrook Elementary with Melissa, Jen, Jason, and Hùng. Because Jason is knock-kneed and because they always make a point to stop and pet the horses nearby on the way to school, the group leaves the apartment an hour before the first school bell rings.

Every day at eight in the morning, Hùng and Dolly meet outside and walk to pick up Melissa, then Jen, and finally, Jason. The five of them disperse once they are on school grounds and play with other classmates until it is time to line up, walk to class, and say the pledge of allegiance. By a quarter after four, the kids arrive back home.

It is a battle each morning to get my daughter ready for school. It can be raining, and she will refuse to carry an umbrella. It can be cold and forty degrees Fahrenheit outside, and she insists on not wearing a jacket. I tell her if she gets sick, the American tooth fairy will not visit for fear of germs. When Dolly disobeys me, I take a piece of paper out and write Santa Claus a letter. I never have to write more than "Dear Santa" before she consents to my requests. My child is not an accepting child and challenges my authority most of the time. Currently, she sports a short pixie haircut with a train of hair in the back that looks like a thick shoehorn. The Americans call this style a mullet. I want to cut the tail off, but she will not let me touch it.

This morning is like any other morning. I help Dolly with her backpack and give her a weather report. "I put an umbrella in your backpack. It is supposed to rain later. After school, I want you to come straight home. Do not open the door to anyone. You can watch cartoons for an hour, then cook two cups of rice like I showed you. Do your homework, and when I get home, I can help you."

"I know," Dolly says. "Can you buy more cereal after work?"

"Yes," I say. "I will be home a little after six o'clock. No playing outside, and no friends over. And no going to a friend's house."

"I know," she says.

I kiss her on the cheek. "Have a good day at school. I love you."

"I love you too."

###

My car is my confidante. I can talk to her or sing with her, and she does not judge. She is my partner in crime, always reliable when getting me to work, keeping me warm in traffic jams, and ensuring I get to the grocery store and home. What freedom and power to have at my fingertips! I slide into the seat of my silver, two-door, 1980 Honda Civic hatchback. As I wait for the engine to warm up and the windows to defrost, my thoughts drift to Tree. We used to be close. We used to rely on each other because life depended on it. And while I knew in my mind that he'd detach from me like Velcro one day, my heart is not ready. I miss him and look forward to talking to him later today.

It is foggy this morning. I push the cassette tape into the stereo and listen to Lionel Richie and Diana Ross proclaim their endless love. The drive to downtown Seattle is relaxing. There is little traffic since it is Friday. I pull up to the corner of John Street and Fairview Avenue to admire the three-story art deco building. I cannot believe I work here and wonder if Jean-Adrien would approve of the reinforced concrete and Indiana limestone office building. It was renovated two years ago and takes up the whole city block in the South Lake Union neighborhood.

I walk to the ornate aluminum gate, decorated with patterns of spirals, florals, and octagons. Above the main entrance, the newspaper's name is etched into the stone. I walk inside to the lobby, where the walls are made of tan Botticino marble and the floors are in a terrazzo pattern. I breathe in the scent of rubber, ink, and vanilla-scented paper. I am at home.

Bill sits in his office animatedly talking on the phone. He looks up and waves. I smile and wave back. I sit down at my desk, clean and clear except for a personal computer and phone. I stare at my new machine, an IBM PC with its sixteen-bit processor, sixteen

355

kilobytes of memory, two floppy drives, an attached dot matrix printer, and a 720x350 pixel green screen monitor. I turn it on. It beeps good morning to me. I am pleased to have fancy technology at my fingertips. While the machine boots up, I walk to the kitchen to get a cup of coffee.

Bill's assistant, Magdaleine, sits at one of the four-top tables, flipping through *The National Enquirer* newspaper. Her long auburn hair is swept up into a messy bun. She is twenty-four years old with a figure of a model and the emotional intelligence of a dolphin. She is extremely self-aware, knowing her strengths and limitations. As intelligent and perceptive as she is, I question her choice of reading material. Magdaleine is naturally beautiful without makeup but I cannot decide if her fashion sense is outdated or in vogue. Today she sports a chic, button-up, silk gray shirt, untucked over her mustard yellow capris, a tartan plaid print ascot, and burnt-orange loafers.

"Do Bill agree you read that newspaper?" I ask. "We work for *Seattle Times*."

Magdaleine rolls her eyes. "Oh, please. Snow, they are not even in the same league as us. I read for pure entertainment. Hey, do you watch *Dallas*?" I shake my head. "It's a soap opera. You'd like it. Do they have soap shows in Vietnam? Well, Victoria Principle is an actress in the show, and she's dating this singer, Andy Gibbs. Do you know who that is? He's a younger brother of the Bee Gees, only he's not one of the Bee Gees. Anyway, they just released a duet song…Victoria and Andy that is…called 'All I Have to Do Is Dream.' Well, they are going to get married! Imagine that. They are going to have beautiful babies. Andy is so dreamy. Why can't I meet someone like that, with perfect teeth, a sexy accent, and thick hair worthy of running my fingers through? And talent. Where are the men who have talent? I just want to run away to Los Angeles or New York City. Do you ever want to just run away?" I nod. "Me too. I want champagne and caviar, not a Mad Dog 20/20 and ramen life. You know what I mean? I need a raise—"

"Magdaleine," I interrupt her, "take a breath." I laugh. "You talk so fast. I understand half what you say."

She closes the magazine and sips her coffee. "Sorry. You're so easy to talk to. You're a great listener. I'm really glad you're here. We need some diversity around here. Your presence just makes the newspaper more cosmopolitan. How do you like the Pacific Northwest? How's your job going? Everyone treating you all right? You let me know if they're not. That's what I am here for, to straighten everyone out and run this operation like the little general that I am. Is Bill being good to you? I know he can be a hard man to work for, but it's only because he is so damn smart…sometimes too smart for his own good. His mind works faster than his mouth. When he is in meetings with big wigs, he trips over his words, only he's not a stutterer. Anyway, he needs strong women like us to tug at his ego strings and pull him down to earth."

Magdaleine takes another sip of her coffee, and I take the opportunity to speak while she swallows. "I need to find Jerry—"

"In accounting?" she asks. "He's on vaca—"

"No," I interrupt. "Jerry in advertising. He have new advertisements for Sunday's layout."

"Go see the creative team, and then find Allison's desk. I bet you'll find him there. He's been drooling over her. I swear he's going to find his heart in a blender. She is way out of his league. He's such a nice guy, but you know what they say. Nice guys come in last, but I swear, if I find out she's double-dipping here with both Jerry and Ted, I'm gonna—"

"Okay, thank you," I say and briskly walk away.

"Let's do lunch today," she calls out behind me.

"No can do," I call over my shoulder. "My nephew call me over lunch break." I wave over my head without looking back and leave her to the tabloid newspaper. I round the corner and bump into Bill.

"Good morning, Snow," Bill says. "Have you seen my secretary?"

"Magdaleine in kitchen," I respond. I walk slowly to my desk and hear Bill ask his assistant if she has purchased his ex-wife a birthday gift yet.

"I thought you were going to do it," Magdaleine says.

"If you've made that assumption," Bill says, "then you've already failed me. Please get her something nice."

"There's a new designer that just launched his women's label—"

"Fine. And get yourself something too…my birthday present to you."

The morning goes by quickly as I work on the promotional ads Jerry gave me. At three minutes to noon, my desk phone rings.

"*Seattle Times*," I answer. "Snow speaking."

"It is me." Tree's voice sounds breathy over the receiver.

"Are you well?" I ask. "Where are you?"

"You do not have to worry about me. I am not a child anymore."

"I do not think you were ever a child."

Tree laughs. "I just finished playing soccer with my friends in Renton. I have a job now, but I called in sick today to move into Chú Bình's house near Southcenter Mall. He is one of the people who comes and plays soccer with us. Poor man. His wife left him, and he is all alone."

"What is the job?" I ask.

"A mattress production company. I work in a warehouse and operate the machines that press the foam to make it firm, and then I stuff it by hand to make mattresses. It is nice. No more scraping bubble gum from school desks and walls for me. I make $3.35 an hour now and work only weekdays. I get the weekends to play. There is this Spectrum Nightclub in Kent that is nice. There are a lot of kids my age, all under twenty-one. You would not believe how many Blacks there are. They leave us alone though. It is funny because they are all so big, and my friends and I are small next to them. At school they bully us, but here we dance and play pool together like friendly cats and mice. Everyone has a good time. The club plays rap music and popular songs from Michael Jackson."

"Are you dating anyone?" I ask.

"Not really," he says. "There are always two or three girls who hang around and flirt with me, but I am not interested."

"Be careful," I say. "Your parents are not ready to be grandparents. You're the oldest, and they will expect you to choose wisely and marry properly."

"I know. How is Thủy-Tiên?"

I twirl the telephone cord around my finger and glance at the clock. Plenty of time. "She is very stubborn and independent, like you. She does not want to learn how to read Vietnamese and speaks to me in English. She has new friends at school. One of them is Jackie Osario. I am told she has black hair with bangs, lots of freckles, crooked buck teeth, and walks funny. Then there is Nadirah Ahmad from Saudi Arabia, who is tall and has a birthmark on her face. I tell you, Thủy-Tiên is becoming Americanized so fast, especially with this terrible hairstyle she has now. It is short like a boy's haircut but long in the back. I am going to cut it when she is asleep. It is not becoming of a proper girl."

Tree chuckles. "Aunt Eight, you are brave. She was born the year of the wood tiger. If you cut it, prepare to get scratched or bitten."

"Yes, I know. She wanted her hair to look like the mom on the *Brady Bunch* show. Did you know that July is the Leo zodiac? Not only was Thủy-Tiên born a wood Tiger but also a lion. The other day, I witnessed her taking a piece of Ex-Lax and selling it as chocolate for twenty-five cents to her friend Melissa. Imagine, selling a laxative as candy. She is ruthless taking advantage of her friends."

Tree laughs. "Auntie, she hustles like you. What is she doing with the money?"

"I do not know," I say.

"What name is she calling herself now?"

"Chris with a C-H."

"How funny," Tree says. "I better go now. I will call you after I get settled in at Chú Bình's."

We hang up, and I finish my work for the day. Bill has been in meetings all day. I rarely see him, but Magdaleine is good about letting me know when he has a little bit of free time. Before leaving work, she shows me the Saffiano leather wristlet she bought for herself with Bill's credit card. It is cute with its monogram MK design and gold emblem that says *MICHAEL KORS – EST. 1981.*

On my drive home, I stop at Safeway to buy cereal for Dolly. I still cannot get over how big the indoor grocery stores are and how wide the aisles. I pay with my food coupon and drive the two blocks home. As I pull into Homestead Apartments, I see my daughter wave to Jen and scramble up the stairs to our apartment. My face flushes red from the warm heat of anger brimming to the surface. She knows I do not want her playing outside after school when I am not home. I need to teach her a lesson and not be so lenient with disciplining her.

I get out of the Honda and step over the parking curb. The rain from this afternoon has left the sidewalk slick. I slip and fall to the ground, scrape my knee, and rip a hole in my pantyhose. There is a small scratch on my new black boots I purchased from Payless ShoeSource.

"Are you hurt, Mama?"

I look up to see Dolly looking down at me from the bedroom window. "I am not hurt."

Inside the apartment, I smell the aroma of white rice. Dolly runs to me and wraps her thin arms around me. She tells me to take off my shoes. I unzip my boots and kick them off. Dolly takes the plastic grocery bag and checks to see which cereal I brought home. "Oh, Cap'n Crunch. And there is a toy inside." She opens the box before I can stop her and drills her fist to the bottom of the bag to find the toy.

"Thank you for making the rice," I say. "What did you do today after school?"

Dolly crunches on her cereal and examines the tattoo sticker she dug out of the box. "I watched Scooby-Doo and cooked rice. I did my math and reading homework. I played with my Barbie doll and sewed her a new skirt."

"You did not go outside?" I ask. I narrow my eyes keenly and observe her face closely.

She looks at me and shakes her head with a smile. "No, you told me not to. Melissa and Jen wanted to play but I said I could not."

"Are you telling the truth?" I ask.

"Yes."

"I saw you run inside right before I came home. You were with Jen. You disobeyed me, and now you are lying to me." My daughter's lips quiver, but I hold firm. "What if you got hurt? Or kidnapped?" She shrugs her little shoulders. "Go get the yardstick."

Salty droplets bubble up in her eyes and shimmy down her cheeks. Her sobs get louder as she walks to the hallway closet to get the wooden stick. Dolly lies down on the floor on her stomach with her arms by her side. This is not the first time she has been spanked for being defiant or naughty. She clenches her butt cheeks. It pains me to discipline her this way, but this is what my parents and grandparents did when we were insolent kids. They believed a spoiled child would dishonor the family and become a menace to society. Perhaps that generation believed it was their job to rule by fear.

My father used to inflict pain on my brothers with a long, dried bull's penis, which was both sturdy and flexible. Brother Seven used to say the rod smelled like stale jungle water and stung like a colony of giant honeybees. The Việt Cộng used these Asian bees as weapons during the conflict, relocating hives to enemy trails and attaching firecrackers to the honeycombs.

I raise the yardstick above my head and give Dolly's bottom a hard whack. She shrieks in pain. The stick comes down a second time, and she yelps. I raise it a third time but cannot bear to inflict more pain on my child. She has been through so much already since the day she was born. Do American parents spank their children? I wonder. Why am I hurting my child? Am I crushing her spirit and hardening her heart by striking her? I make a vow to discipline her in other ways, to be fair, and to counter her rebelliousness with love.

I put the yardstick down and scoop her into my arms. "I think that is enough spanking. Did you learn your lesson?"

"Yes," she whispers. "I am sorry."

"Sorry for what?" I ask.

"For lying and not obeying you," she says. "I will be good. Please do not write to Santa."

I hug her tight and kiss her forehead. "I will not tell Santa. I am sorry for hurting you, and I think we both learned a lesson today."

I rock her in my arms until her sobs subside, and she exhales deeply.

My eyes are dry and itchy. I flutter my lids to alleviate the burning. I have not been sleeping well lately. Most nights I think about all the tasks waiting for me at work, and during the day I worry about how Tree and Dolly are adjusting to American life. I lie down on the couch and drape my forearm across my face, letting the push and pull of my hypnagogic thoughts battle between insomnia and slumber.

An image of Dolly walking down the aisle on her wedding day lures my conscious mind to enter the dream state. I lean in and fall weightlessly until I see the Galang Refugee Camp transformed into a botanical garden in the middle of an evergreen forest. A dusting of snow cascades softly to the ground. I am in Đà Lạt, but it is not the same city I remember when I was a math teacher there. This Đà Lạt is more like heaven because all my family and friends are there, smiling and happy. Thủy-Tiên is beautiful in her traditional red áo dài dress and gold lace robe. My American and Vietnamese families are all there as well as my family from trawler 93752 and the camp. I strain to see the face of Thủy-Tiên's groom. It eludes me at first but soon comes into focus. Minh-Hoàng! His smile is sinister. *"No!"* The reflection in his eyes is a self-portrait, and I stumble back, realizing it is me getting married. I look around the room. Minh-Hoàng's brother, Lopsided, and their she-Jekyll mother laugh at me. All the men who have loved me are there— Ommo, Tý, and Sam. They look sad, disappointed, and in pain. I run and trip on the train of my garment, only it is now a white wedding gown. Hands, hundreds of hands, grab, pull, and scratch me. Hải and Tâm wrap their arms around me. I cannot breathe. Cường, Dr. Nguyễn Văn Đức, his wife, and my neighbors in Vĩnh Bình are chasing after me. They want something from me. I cannot escape! I see my chicken and follow her, but I cannot catch her. I call out to her. "Mông Dơ!" Her little legs pick up speed, and she runs faster until her head falls off. It rolls to my feet. Her black beady eyes condemn me to hell.

I wake from the nightmare with a jolt; a residual tingle of electric currents sends shockwaves down my spine to my toes. I abandoned and betrayed them all. I failed them. I am here…free, alive, safe, and without hunger. How do I expiate this guilt?

Sleep comes in crumbs these past few days. My dreams intertwine like pretzels and I cannot make sense of them. I decide it is best to forget. I have an unhappy child at the moment who demands my sympathy.

The people here in America have a strange holiday custom on October 31. Children and adults dress in costume and demand candy from their neighbors, chanting, "Trick or treat. Smell my feet. Give me something good to eat." Last year, Dolly was too frail and scared to go out at night and knock on strangers' doors. It was cold, and I would not allow it. Instead, we stayed at home and handed out candy with Teddy and Catherine. This year, however, she has no fears about knocking on doors and asking for chocolates. No doubt, she will turn around and sell those to her friends at black market prices.

My daughter steps out of the bedroom in full costume, looking like a melting wax figure from a horror museum. "This mask is hot and sticky, and it smells bad."

"You chose it," I say. "It is plastic, so you will be hot, but it will feel better in the cold air outside." Her cheap, store-bought costume crinkles when she walks, and the Wonder Woman mask is grotesquely large over her small frame. "I offered to sew you something this year. I am getting better at it."

Dolly tugs at her mask. "But Melissa is going as Batgirl and Jen is going to be Supergirl."

We exit the warm apartment into the chill of October, crossing the threshold into another dimension where little princesses, superheroes, and goblins roam the streets. We knock on our neighbor's door.

Diệp opens the door. "Ah, alô Chị Tuyết."

My jaw drops. She is wearing a wiry orange wig, a big yellow pajama suit with sleeves, and knee-high socks in stripes of red and white. Her face is painted white and where her eyebrows should be, there are two thin black arches drawn in. Her nose is red and she has smeared bright red lipstick all over her mouth up to her cheeks.

I burst out laughing. "Diệp, why are you in costume?"

Dolly hums the McDonald's tune. "Baba bum bum bum."

"It is Halloween. Where is your costume?" Diệp asks. "I am the clown from McDonald's."

"I see that. Halloween is for children," I say.

"If you want to stay young, Sister, you need to do as the children do. Play, dress up, and use your imagination," she says. "I made this myself. Do you like it?"

"I love it," Dolly exclaims. "What is Hùng dressed as?"

Hearing his name, he jumps out from behind the door. He looks incredibly adorable. His costume complements his mother's.

"I am a Big Mac," Hùng says.

Dolly and he say in unison, "Two all-beef patties, special sauce, lettuce, cheese, pickles, onions, on a sesame seed bun." They giggle.

It dawns on me that McDonald's is my daughter's second brand recognition with 7-Up being the first. The four of us walk down the steps and pause to take in the scene. Under the bright moon, children and their parents jabber about which home to hit and who gives out the best candy.

We spot Donald and his son. I wave to them, and we walk toward one another. Donald looks handsome in his black suit and cape. I conclude he is a butler superhero. Little Jason is dressed in a shaggy carpet thing with a plastic mask that looks like an angry dog. His costume confuses me.

"Wow, that's a great costume," Donald says to my neighbor. He smiles and shows his fangs. Ah, you are Dracula!

I introduce Donald to Diệp, who gives him a big smile and sheepishly looks down, clearly shy and enamored by his vampire good looks. I giggle silently, thinking how ridiculous and hideous Diệp looks with her clown costume. The two of them stand awkwardly looking at each other, smiling and trying to communicate with one another in two different languages. Diệp just smiles and nods. I have seen this look before when there is a mutual attraction between two people.

"What is your costume, Jason?" Dolly asks.

"Chewbacca," he says. "You know, a Wookiee from *Star Wars*." He lifts his head as if to howl at the moon but instead lets out a low-pitched, moaning gurgle and tongue trill that sound like a wounded monster in distress. We all have a good laugh at his strange noises.

We head out together, going door to door, building to building. Every once in a while, Jason grunts and gurgles, and we are amused at how he stays in character.

I eavesdrop on Donald's and Diệp's conversation. I was going to offer to translate for them, but they seem to be doing fine on their own.

"So, Yip," Donald says, "Do you like America?"

Diệp smiles and nods. She answers in Vietnamese. "Amerrica đẹp quá nhưng không đẹp như bạn." *America is beautiful but not as beautiful as you.*

"Diệp," I say, "you are speaking so boldly."

She laughs at me. "He does not understand me, so what does it matter?"

"Do you understand what he is saying?" I ask.

"Only a little," she says. "Let me have my fun."

"Now I feel like the third wheel," Donald says. I give him a curious look. "Third wheel… it means I don't belong, like a bicycle that does not need an extra wheel."

"But three wheel safer. You here with us, make us safer."

Donald laughs. "Like a tricycle, which is a bicycle with three wheels."

We continue our trick-or-treating and along the way meet up with Melissa and Jen by the Cascade Apartments complex. The girls are chaperoned by Melissa's parents. Tony, Melissa's stepfather, has his thick, black hair tied back in a loose ponytail. His mustache is thick with a touch of gray. He wears jeans and a black leather jacket. A portion of his suncatcher tattoo peeks above his white crew neck cotton shirt. His smile lights up his eyes and twinkles under the street lamp.

Melissa's mother, Stephanie, is a slender woman with green eyes and the perfect cleavage, her firm bosom pushed together showing only an inch of smooth flesh above the V-neck sweater. She is fair. Her skin creamy vanilla and her hair strawberry blonde.

We walk behind them, and I take the opportunity to study them from behind. They walk with ease alongside one another. The two lovers hold hands and talk like best friends. They laugh and tease as if they are young teenagers in love.

Melissa holds her stepdad's hand. "Tony, once you adopt me, will that make me Cherokee too?"

"If you can master the Iroquoian language of the Tsalagi people, you will be more Cherokee than me, little Lissa."

"What's important," Stephanie adds, "is that we are a family, no matter what blood runs through our veins."

By eight-thirty a few droplets of water sprinkle from the sky, and we rush back to Homestead Apartments. Stephanie and Tony invite us to their apartment for hot chocolate. I decline, but the children beg to go, and even Diệp agrees wholeheartedly.

"If I did not know better," I say to Diệp, "I would think you are prolonging the evening to spend time with Donald."

Donald's ears perk up at the mention of his name. "Are you talking about me? That's not fair. Good things I hope."

Tony and Stephanie's apartment is spotless; everything is neatly arranged and color-coordinated in shades of teal and copper. The walls are adorned by both minimalistic artwork and avant-garde paintings, two styles that clash and yet work together to complement the décor, similar to how Stephanie and Tony seem to clash from outward appearances but work so symbiotically well together.

"Anyone want my peanut butter cups?" Dolly asks. "It is full size."

Hùng snatches her Reese's candy. "Me."

My daughter slaps his hand. "What will you trade?"

"My Gobstopper."

"What else?" she asks.

"What do you mean, 'what else'?" Hùng asks. "Gobstoppers last longer than chocolate and peanut butter cups."

My daughter ignores him. "Jen, do you want my peanut butter cups?"

Jen tosses her a Kit Kat, Whoppers, and Tootsie Pop. She takes Dolly's full-size candy. The two of them are satisfied with the trade, and poor Hùng is left wondering what just happened.

While the children sort and trade their sweet treasures, Donald and Diệp sit on the couch and duct tape words together to formulate a conversation. Tony and Stephanie are in the kitchen making hot chocolate and flirting. I feel like the third wheel now. My thoughts drift to Skyler and Tree, wondering how they are spending their night. I am in a room full of people yet feel lonely. Somewhere in Texas, Tý is probably enjoying Halloween festivities with his American wife and son. I wonder if he and Annette have more children and if he thinks of Thủy-Tiên and me.

"You're a million miles away." Stephanie hands me a cup of hot chocolate. "What were you thinking about?" She sits down on the carpet with me while Tony lies down on his side and props his head on his hand.

"Maybe the question is 'who are you thinking about'?" Tony says. "Where is Chris's father?"

"Chris?" I ask, temporarily forgetting that my daughter is going by that name at the moment. "Oh, you mean Dolly. Her father live in Texas. We separate in 1975. Long story."

We spend the next hour getting acquainted. I give everyone a synopsis of what brought us to Seattle and how we got here. By the end of the night, I did not feel like the third wheel anymore nor did I feel lonely. A new community is forming tonight in Tony's and Stephanie's living room.

11. PINKY PROMISE (NOVEMBER 1981)

Dear Eight,

It was good to receive your letter. I have to start by saying that Tâm is home! Little Sister, my poor Tâm has been through so much! She has been starved, beaten, humiliated, and shuffled around from one prison to another, but she crawled her way home. I did not even recognize her. Five years! It is as if she came back from the dead, frail, ghostly thin, with lesions, scars, and open wounds. She is missing teeth, fingernails, and hair, but worst of all, she has lost the light in her! My heart is at the bottom of the ocean floor.

It is bad here. People are still flocking to new lands and risking their lives to leave the country. I dare not think about their fate. The family is getting by. We do our best to oblige under the new regime and stay under the radar. Thắng and I are doing the best we can. Send money when you have a job. Maybe you can find a way to sponsor the children in America. I do not want them to grow up here. Brother Seven and Hiền were right to send Tree with you.

We started a money pool, and your brother-in-law and I are in charge of the hui. There are seven of us in the lending circle, including Thủy and Doctor Đức and our neighbors Tú and Vân. We each put in fifty-thousand đồng each month. Hiền was able to start her fabric shop with the 350,000đ hui money, and Brother Seven still drives his truck every morning. I wish you could see the dresses Hiền makes. They are almost as good as Thủy's!

The children are back at school, but I am not sure how much they learn. It is all propaganda. I know this because Trinh comes home singing praise to Hồ Chí Minh, and Tuấn believes Tâm and Hải were traitors because they spoke ill about the government and supported "the enemy." And no, I have not heard any news about Hải. It is best to forget him and move on. He would want you to. If he is not dead already, then he is nothing more than a worthless man begging to die. I know that sounds harsh, but a man who survives the re-education camp and loses everything will not feel like a man again.

Thủy and Doctor Đức are doing well and are pregnant! Can you believe it? They are going to have a baby, after all these years! What a miracle. Thủy's tailoring business has picked up. I hope to afford one of her tunics or áo dài one day, although Hiền is becoming quite the seamstress too. Doctor Đức's practice is also good, but his patients pay him with fruits and vegetables. He is still peddling his bananas on his cyclo and now peddles the other fruits he receives from his patients.

I am happy to hear Thủy-Tiên is doing well in school and making friends. I do not know how I feel about her speaking only English…maybe it is a good thing to immerse herself wholly into the new society so she can thrive. Do not be too harsh with her. America, not Việt Nam, is her home and the only one she will truly remember. You need to make America your home too. The Việt Nam we knew no longer exists. Do not give up on Tree. He is a good boy who is learning how to be a man without his father or his uncle to teach him. He is far from home, but give him time to figure things out, and he will come back to what matters most—family.

So you are learning how to cook? That must be a disaster, but sandwiches are a good start. Remember when Tâm brought home hot dogs and bacon for Christmas dinner? If that is American food, then you should have no problem learning to cook. Their food is not as delicious and delicate as ours. I heard a saying once from the Americans…You are what you eat. That makes us delicate and delicious and them greasy and stuffed with leftover, mashed up meat. Maybe that is the secret why Westerners are so big.

I hope your neighbor, Diệp, is a good friend and sister to you. Is she a good cook? In my mind, I imagine she has replaced me as your sister, but remember, I am still your favorite. It is good she and I are separated by land and water because I would sink her in a cooking competition. I hope this letter gets to you. I do not know how much the government regulates our mail, whether they check everyone or randomly. I will take my chances. I am testing a new recipe for egg noodle soup with char siu pork. Ingredients are hard to find and expensive when I am lucky enough to find them. When it is my turn to receive the hui money—I am last because I own the hui and since there are seven of us in it, I have to wait until the seventh month—I will open a small restaurant and serve egg noodle soup with pork or duck. It will be the only thing on the menu, but it will be the best.

One last thing. Tý has written. He sent us money. I gave him your address. Do not be mad. It is too late to be mad. What has happened, happened, and we cannot undo the past. I cannot glue the chicken's head back on after it has been chopped off any more than you can go back in time to save your soldier, Sam. Tý wants to take care of you and his daughter. Let him carry this burden for you.

Until better times, do not burn anything and stay safe. Promise with your pinky to me. Remember that I love you, little Eight. There, I said it.

Your favorite sister,

Six

###

The thought of Dolly's father having my address worries me. Will he try to combine our families? I am curious about his life with Annette. What would Dolly think if she knew she had a brother and stepmother? Will she want to live with them? I cannot let them into her life. I will wait to receive Tý's letter and tell him this.

I dial Sky and Katrina's number, waiting patiently for the rotary wheel to return to zero after each digit.

"Hello?" the voice on the other end says. I do not recognize the voice.

"Alô," I answer. "I speak to Skyler please."

"Bonjour, this is Jean-Adrien. Is this Snow?"

"Oui," I answer affirmatively in French, surprised it rolled off my tongue so effortlessly. I have not spoken French in over twenty years. I remember what Sky and Bill told me about Jean-Adrien, and his voice grates my patience into slivers.

"Vous parlez français," Jean-Adrien says. "How wonderful. Your French is perfect."

I frown. I said one word and he thinks my French is perfect. "I prefer English. I speak to Sky now?"

"Bien sûr." I hear the rustle of the phone being placed down and Jean-Adrien calling for Sky. While I wait, I think how rude of him to answer in French even after I tell him I prefer English. I hardly know the man, but his presence makes me feel like my shoes are on backward and I have shown up to a fancy dinner party in my pajamas.

The phone crackles, and Sky's familiar voice caresses my ear. "Hi."

"I receive letter from my sister," I say, not bothering to greet him first. "Dolly father write her. He know where I live. She give him my address. I not want him to come. I worry he and Annette take Dolly or claim me. I not want to be second wife and live with them. I—"

"Slow down," Sky says. "Listen, this is America. He does not own you and can't force you to live with him. Do you want me to come over and we can talk? I can use a friend to talk to right now too. You-know-who is driving me mad."

"Yes," I agree. "I see you soon."

###

I pour Sky a cup of green tea. He swirls the loose leaves in his cup and watches the tea settle to the bottom of the mug. He looks tired.

"Sky, you not sleep well?" I ask. I sit across from him and touch his hand.

"Where is Dolly?" he asks.

"She play with her friends next door," I answer. "Tell me, you okay?"

Sky sidesteps my question and volleys with his own. "How is your job? Bill treating you good?"

I sigh and give in to his questions. "I not see Bill much, but job and everything good. Bill assistant, Magdaleine, very nice. She help me a lot, and for young person, she very patient. Together, we manage database and make reports for managers and creative team, people in newsroom. They do advertising and circ…circu—"

"Circulation?" Sky asks. I nod. "Any interesting news the reporters are working on?"

"Sky, you not come here to talk about my job," I say. "If Dolly father write and he want to visit, what I do?"

Sky gulps his tea and helps himself to a vanilla wafer. I wait patiently for him to collect his thoughts and offer me advice. "Well, I think you need to face him. You cannot continue to run from him, and he is Dolly's father. He has the right to see her."

I shake my head vigorously. "No. He left us. He give away his rights."

"You let him go, Snow. He tried to take you both out of the country. It was your choice not to go with him." Sky squeezes my hand and lets his fingers linger on mine. "Was it wrong that he didn't tell you about his other wife? Yes. Should he have kept his secrets from you about his mob affiliations? Probably. Look, I know you feel betrayed, and you still harbor anger for him. But maybe this is a good time to start over and forgive him. Your resentment will weigh you down. Imagine how free you will feel if you let go. If he comes, I can be here with you to give you support."

"Words easy to swallow but not easy to digest," I say bitterly. "Maybe you should take advice and forgive Jean-Adrien." I remove my hand from underneath his and cross my arms over my chest. "He trying to be in your life. I see he has regrets."

Sky leans back into his chair. "That's different." His expression is cold and threatening. He purses his lips.

"How it different?" I ask. "You still angry with him. You feel he betray you. He not there for you when you grow up. He not protect you when you need him. He cheat on Katrina. How, Sky? How it different? He throw money at you both, like Dolly father throw money at us, but he still lie to us as Jean-Adrien lie to you."

"At least Ty wants to be in your life and is trying to make amends. He loves you."

"How you know, Sky? You talk to him? You know his heart and believe his stories?" I am angry now. Sky knows nothing.

"My dad is garbage. He's fake. Your husband at least fought for you and used his connections to get you exit visas."

I laugh. "Look at us. We fight for burn rice at bottom of pot. We so hungry for love, for attention. We throw away pride and take leftover of what Tý and Jean-Adrien give us."

"You're right. For a long time, we have accepted their crumbs because we didn't know better."

We sit in silence, each marinating in our own thoughts. Minutes tick by, and Sky is the first to break the silence. "Sometimes I feel like I'm walking between two planes of existence. Not quite dead but not alive either. My feelings get jumbled up like wet jeans spinning endlessly in a wad of bedsheets, trying to get dry but forever damp and rotten. Do you ever feel that way?" I nod. "When I want to laugh, it comes out as cries. When I want to cry, it comes out as laughter. I'm so fucked up. Where's the reset button when you need one? I want to be surrounded by people I love but withdraw because it is easier to be alone. Self-loathing becomes an addiction."

"But when you alone," I say, "the ghosts come to haunt you."

"Yes. And that is when I want more than anything to have someone there to get me through it all. I'm afraid the moment I find happiness, I'll sabotage myself. I shouldn't be alive and happy while Sam and others died a senseless death. You know?"

"What we do now?" I ask.

"I think you need to receive Ty when he writes and wants to visit. You can throw the burnt rice in his face and show him how strong you are, no thanks to him."

"You do same," I say. "You promise with pinky." I offer Sky my small pinky finger and wrap it around his.

"I pinky promise," he says.

"Good, you first. Before Thanksgiving. You make peace with Jean-Adrien. I be there for you if you want."

"I want," Sky says.

12. RETURNING VET'S SAGA (NOVEMBER 1981)

I drive up the familiar stretch of road to Katrina's house, admiring the Pacific dogwood trees that have dropped their leaves but still look regal with the last of their fall foliage. I round the circular driveway and notice the hanging flower baskets have lost their luster. Beneath them, rows of winter heathers catch the fallen petals and welcome the softness of purple pansies.

I turn off the engine and take a deep breath. I am here to support Sky today. It will be a difficult morning for all of us, but I expect it will be emotionally volatile for Sky. I feel drained and taxed already thinking about the conversation ahead. I check myself in the visor mirror to make sure I am presentable. My lips are dry, and my lipstick is cracked at the corners of my mouth. After reapplying a fresh coat of mauve moisturizing gloss, I step out onto the crunchy dirt. The biting Pacific Northwest air forces me to pull my scarf up over my ears and nose.

One more deep breath and I ring the doorbell. I wait, but no one answers the door. I knock hard on the door and wait again.

"Alô?" I open the door and step inside. "Sky? Katrina?" No answer. I feel strange intruding despite being invited. Sky said to come Saturday at ten for brunch. I glance at my watch. I am three minutes early. I hear a voice from the kitchen and follow the sound.

Sky looks up, startled. He is on the phone. "Wait for me in the reading nook," he whispers and points toward the hallway.

Inside my favorite room, I admire the books on the shelves and look to see if there are any new titles. I remind myself to read the book Sky gave me last year. A book catches my eye, and I take it down. *Black Beauty* by Anna Sewell. I thumb through the pages and discover folded sheets of paper tucked inside. Curiosity gets the best of me, and I unfold it carefully. It is a long poem written in cursive. At times the penmanship is artfully and legibly written, but

more often than not, the letters trail off. Some of the words slant
forward and the ink is smeared as if the poet was angry and crying. I
read it.

"Returning Vet's Saga"

On top of the world, I was and a once kind, gentle person was I.
Goals I had and dreams I had, of better things ahead.
No cares did I have and no problems were around,
I was enjoying a life of delight,
With destiny under my control, and me controlling my destiny.
Life was good and it was great to be alive.

Then, one day, a letter I received,
From the President of the U.S. of A. it was sent.
I did not want to go, you know.
In fact I once said, "I would never go!"
But what would I do, what could I do?
I could not say, "Hell, no, I won't go!" as many my age had already
made known.

Torn away from the life I had and the life I was building, all on my
own.
I went as I was asked, to serve for God, country, and apple pie back
home.
My president and government had asked me to go, and I could not say,
"No."
It was to protect my family, friends, and to defend my country that I
called home.
I was informed I would be fighting against a woeful aggressor
So his deeds would not come to haunt my home!

So I departed and went where I was ordered to go.
Lifelong goals and dreams now shattered they had become.
New ones I would be granted, but simple they would now become.
Exactly what would I be, where would I go, what would I do?
How long would I live and would I ever return?
Questions I had and no answers were there to be found,
I would have to wait to see what the future was for me!

Off to war I went, like so many before and after me.
Leaving family, friends, wives and lovers far behind me.

Young and innocent I was, returning I hoped, but dying I might.
Forgotten I became, unwanted I thought.

Off I went, young and innocent and hardened I became.
That kind, soft, gentle person that once was I,
Now became hard and abrasive and disillusioned was I.
A shell I built up, hard as a rock it became, for protection and sanity
it was made.

Before, life and dreams had surrounded me,
Now death, hurt, and sorrow are all around me.
If I sleep, would I live to wake? If I woke would I live to sleep?
Alone and helpless I felt, with destiny now dominating and controlling
me!

Fear, it became my constant companion and was always with me.
Will relief ever come to me?
Loneliness, so close we became.
Death, I stared it eye to eye, on many occasions, I thought I would say
bye!
Only I know how close I really came,
To this day I wonder why I survived, and others did not!
And now I wonder what significance my survival has really meant.

While serving in those foreign waters, a saying was heard over and
over:
"Mine was not to reason why, mine was just to do or die!"

While serving family, friends, God, and country in that war-torn land,
Letters I desired, but few I received.
Then one day a letter I received, and it was written to me,
"Dear John, another I have found."
And I thought, "Oh, if only I had stayed, that wouldn't have
happened to me."
And I wondered, "Does no one longer care to stick by my side?"

New friends I now gained and buddies we were called and mostly
nicknames we had.
Moose, Tiny, Slim, Shorty, Sweet-Pea, Ski, Chicago, Oly, Texas,
Buzzard, Doc, and much more.
But how close can I get to someone who is here today, but tomorrow is
gone.

How much loss can my mind endure?
How much sorrow can my heart now endure?

Up and awake for a day, two, three, or more, without sleep I went.
I had to stay awake and alert because others depended on me.
And then came their turn, awake and alert they had to be, and now I
depended on them.

At times the intenseness was great.
No noise dared I make, and no sound could I utter.
Quiet and still I had to remain, all to stay undetected and hidden from
those who were around.
This I had to do so another day I could return for more of the same!

A country that loved me I once departed. To countries that hated me I
arrived.
Un-liked I was, but never mistreated was I over there.
Then that day arrived, to return to a country that abhorred me back
here.
Un-liked, unwanted, and mistreated I now became over here.

Returned, I did and then left alone to recover from the death, hurt,
grief, and sorrow.
My stories of woe you did not want to hear.
When I returned, where was the handshake to welcome me back?
Where was the thank you for the job I had done?
Where was the encouragement to move on ahead?
Where was the hug to make me feel loved?

Where were the words, "You're okay and everything will be fine"?
Where were my friends, so many I once had?
Where was the thank you I needed to hear?
Where were the words, the kind words that would do so much good?
Where was the love I so desperately needed?

Where was the job I now needed even more than before?
Why was there no one that to me could say, "I am proud of you for
serving!"
And why did no one dare say, "I am glad you survived!"
And why did no one care to say, "I am glad you came back!"
And why was no one so kind to say, "Welcome back home, and we're
glad you're back alive!"

Hard it became because work there was none.
"Hire a vet" was the saying heard loud and clear throughout all the
land.
But country and men wanted those that had stayed,
But not those who had served in that war-torn land!

It caused me to wonder, "Where would I be, if only I had stayed?"
It made me think, "Where would I be, if served I had not?"
And then I began to ponder, "Who would I be, if only I had stayed?"
And the ringing in my mind became, "What would I be, if served I
had not?"

On returning back here, it was angry faces and voices that I found in
front of me.
"Baby killer, mother raper" words they scolded and screamed at me.
But such things I had never considered because that really wasn't me.
I only did as I was asked, so why are you scolding me?
Why all the anger that was directed at me?
Didn't they know that if they would have gone, they would be just like
me?
Didn't they know "I defended them, so they didn't have to go?"

The war was over for everyone but those that had gone and had fought
where they had been.
Give me a chance to forget where I've been.
But country and men would blame us for where we had been.
They blamed us for the problems they were in.

Where was the home I left so long ago? This is not the same as I
remember from before.
This was not the home I remember leaving when I went off to war.
Away from home I was taken, and never allowed to return to the home
I once knew.
I returned, but it was not to the gentle life I had known before.
Rather, I returned to be scorned and hated by those I had defended.

Then there were the cold sweats and nightmares, almost nightly for
many a year.
How do I explain what's happening to me? How do I forget what
happened to me?
The tears, will they ever stop, and they start for no reason at all?

Will anyone ever bother to gently wipe a tear from my eye?
Why is it so easy for them to bring tears to my eyes, and they don't
even notice?

Oh, if someone would just listen, oh, if someone would try to
understand
The hurt I feel, the losses I have endured.
If I talk, who will dare to listen?
If you hear my story of woe, will you kindly listen?
Or will you say, "We've heard that story before?"
And will you add, "You crybabies are all the same. You need to forget
and get on with your life."

Now, I need help.
Where is my government when I need them most of all?
I helped them when they needed it!
Who will defend me now, those I once defended?

The medals I wore over my heart while serving,
Have now become a burden my heart is bearing!

The frustration of war was bad,
The frustration of life after war is overwhelming!
Will I ever be taken off the battlefield?

In an instant, immediately I am back to where the danger was!
Reliving those life-threatening situations I once endured.
Again, so close to death I am,
Why am I here? What am I doing? Who cares about me?
No time to think. I must react.
Then the tears come,
And finally, I once again return to the present.

That war-torn, hardened shell, born for protection over there,
Now becomes harder and more battle scarred back here
Because of the war I now fight back over here.

On occasion, I now drift to the place in my mind, where solitude and
peace are all around!
A place I have made of what I would like it to be.
A place to retreat when I need comfort and rest!
Only to regretfully return to this place I am now in.

Will I ever recover, fully recover?
Will my hard, outer shell ever soften?
To let that kind, gentle person out,
That is hidden so well?

Will I ever again control my destiny?
Will I ever enjoy that life of bliss I once knew?
Will I ever recover, fully recover?

Will you remember me for what I once was? Or will you remember
what I have become?
Will you remember me for what I want to be? Or will you remember
what I have become?
Will you remember me for what I could have become? Or will you
remember what I have become?
Will you remember me for what I wanted to become?
Or will you remember me for what I really became?

"Snow, what are you doing?" Sky touches my shoulder and turns me around to face him. "You're crying."

My hand trembles as I give Sky the poem. "I sorry. You write poem?"

Sky shakes his head and sighs. "My friend Charlie Peters did." He sits down and stares at Charlie's handwriting. Sky smiles. "I never met anyone who talked as much as he did. His spelling and grammar are shit but man could he tell a story. And his jokes…" Sky chuckles. "So here's a joke he used to tell over and over." Sky puts the letter down. "So an American soldier and a Vietnamese soldier are in the trench together. Neither of them understands the other, so the Vietnamese soldier tries sign language." Sky laughs as he uses his arms to demonstrate. He holds his left forearm parallel to the floor across his chest. "The Vietnamese soldier asks, 'Are you a paratrooper?'" and with his right arm, Sky imitates a tree falling. "'Are you a field runner?'" He uses two fingers from his right hand to demonstrate legs running across the left forearm. "'A gun loader?'" Sky pokes his right pointer finger into a hole formed by his left hand. "'Or a lookout?'" Sky circles his fingers around both eyes like he's looking through binoculars. He slaps his knees. "The American soldier was so freaked out! He jumped out of the trench screaming, 'Help, help, there's a crazy Vietnamese soldier who said,

When the sun goes down and all the people start running, he's going to fuck me until my eyes blow out!'"

Sky roars with laughter. He leans back and lets out a loud howl. His breathing becomes shallow, and I worry he will choke on his spit. Sky bends forward and clutches my hips. He pulls me hard to him and buries his head into my stomach. He is no longer laughing but weeping uncontrollably. His cries of angst and pain leave me speechless. I wrap my arms around his head and hold him tight.

13. UNTETHERED (NOVEMBER 1981)

We wait for Katrina and Jean-Adrien to come home. Sky pours a glass of bourbon and offers me the drink. I decline. He swallows the shot in one gulp and switches over to scotch. I patiently wait for him to speak. In the past ten minutes, he has aged ten years in my eyes. The character lines on his face are simply wrinkles now. The tear tracks are remnants of the anguish he displayed earlier. His hair is tussled in different directions and is the only visible evidence of distress to the untrained eye. Will Jean-Adrien understand his son's sadness and offer to carry the weight of Skyler's burdens? Will he seek forgiveness for the pain he has caused? Will Katrina recognize her son's cry for help?

"I don't know what I'm going to say to him." Sky puts his scotch down after one sip. "Where do I even start?"

"Ask God be your voice," I say. "He be your eyes…your ears. You only need to ask."

The sound of tires rolling on dry leaves and pebbles signals they are home. The door opens. Katrina and Jean-Adrien laugh. A thud echoes from the hallway, and the sound of only one high-heel shoe clops on the hard flooring. We peek around the corner in time to see Katrina and Jean-Adrien fall to the floor. Their bodies squirm like snakes in heat. Katrina sinks her teeth into her husband's neck while he moans and lifts her skirt and fondles her behind.

Sky slaps his palm against the reading nook doorframe a couple of times. I catch a glimpse of his Adam's apple bobbing up and down. "Bloody hell you two!" He storms toward them and reaches them in four big strides. Katrina and Jean-Adrien scramble up and compose themselves. Sky takes a swing at his father and connects with Jean-Adrien's face.

Jean-Adrien rubs his jaw. "You son-of-a—"

"Careful, Dad," Sky warns him.

The two men lunge at each other like unwieldy dancers vying to lead. Katrina shrieks and tries to break up the fight. She pulls at Sky's arms to hold him back, but she might as well be a gnat pulling on shoelaces. She takes one of her plastic horses—the palomino one—and hits them both on the neck and shoulders.

"What is your problem?" Jean-Adrien yells.

"What is my problem?" Sky asks. "Seriously? You're my problem!" Sky takes another swing and misses. "You spread your butter over every goddamn muffin in town and you think Mom's just another piece of ass. You're a cheating, good for nothing—"

Jean-Adrien tackles Sky to the floor.

"Enough!" Katrina screams. "Both of you!"

The men ignore her plea. Katrina looks at me with helpless, pleading eyes.

I swing open the front door and scream, "Fire! Everyone, fire outside!"

I run outside and halt in front of my Honda Civic. Skyler runs outside with Jean-Adrien right behind him. The two of them look frantically for the smoke and flames. Katrina appears at the stoop, hands on her hips, looking satisfied.

"Where's the fire?" Sky asks. "Are the stables—"

"No fire," I say. "You both cool down outside."

"She's right," Jean-Adrien says. "Why don't we talk like mature men?"

"Yes," Katrina calls from the doorway, "like civilized adults, shall we?"

I take hold of Sky's hand and search for calmness in his eyes. "When I say you make peace with Jean-Adrien, I not mean like this. You pinky promise, remember?"

The muscles in Sky's jaw twitch. His face softens. "All right." He looks past me and points at his father. "You were never around for Mom and me. Instead, you left us with Uncle Dawson, that bastard."

"I was trying to build my career to support—"

"Cut the bullshit. I've had enough of your rotten excuses."

"Son, what my brother did to you—"

"—was my imagination…Yeah, that's what you said, and then you laughed at me for being foolish, as if I misinterpreted his intentions. He fucking had his hands on me for over a year. I was eight! And you…" Sky faces his mother and rolls his eyes. "You slapped me. I kept that secret for ten years, and when I finally told you both, you didn't believe me. That was the send-off I got before my tour. That was the care package I took with me overseas."

Katrina whimpers and covers her face with her hands. Jean-Adrien says nothing. He simply casts his eyes downward. Sky looks at his parents, but neither returns his gaze.

The November chill nips at my skin, and I shiver. Sky notices. He wraps his arm around me. "Let's go."

"No," I say. "You stay. Make peace with them. 'Remember that grit and tenacity will take you far in life, but love and forgiveness will carry you to the finish line.'"

"That's nice," Sky says. "Did you read that somewhere?"

I shrug. "Pastor George tell me. He say have strength."

"Did you have to look in the dictionary to see what 'grit' and 'tenacity' meant?" Sky asks. I nod. He gives me that wonderful smile that only he can radiate. "I'll call you later. Thanks for being here with me."

I leave Sky to tend to his family affairs. In the rearview mirror, I witness Katrina hugging her son.

###

Sky rings me two days later, but I miss his phone call. His message on my answering machine is brief. He will be gone for another meditation retreat. "You were right, Snow, about love and forgiveness. I need to learn how to love myself again before I have the strength to forgive my parents." I am not to expect him back until Christmas.

I dial Katrina a few times but always receive the same recording. "You've reached the Herrington's. Please leave a message."

I call Catherine and Teddy. After three rings, Teddy answers.

"Alô, Teddy," I say. "How everything?"

"We are having a great time. Toots and I are about to make some chocolate chip cookies with Dolly. Do you want to talk to her?"

Two blinks later, my daughter's voice greets me. We speak for a few minutes with her telling me how much fun she is having this weekend. They baked a pumpkin pie yesterday. She tells me about seeing rabbits in the backyard and how she wants a pet for Christmas.

Eventually, she hands the phone back to Teddy. "What are your plans for Thanksgiving?"

"Teddy?" I ask. "We not do Thanksgiving at Katrina house?"

"Oh." Silence. "I'm sorry. I thought Katrina or Catherine told you. Katrina canceled Thanksgiving. We would host, but Penny and Todd invited us down to Oregon. They had their baby, you know, so we're going to go meet our new grandson." Pause. More silence. "Want anything in Oregon? There's no retail tax there."

"No, thank you," I answer. "And Frances and Frank? They go to Oregon too?"

"Nah. They and the boys are staying in Wenatchee. Frank's family is traveling there for the holidays."

"Well," I say, feeling alone, "you and Catherine enjoy. I see you tomorrow. Please kiss Dolly for me and tell her I see her at church."

I collect my coat and knock on Diệp's door. "Diệp ơi, it is Tuyết."

Hùng opens the door. "Hello, Auntie."

I hear Diệp's laughter inside and a man's voice saying, "Open wide."

"You have guests?" I ask.

"Yes, Donald is here, and so is Jason. Mom invited them over for dinner."

"Are you their translator?" I ask. Hùng nods. "Have your mom come see me tomorrow."

It is a rare occasion for me to be alone without responsibilities. I do not know what to do with myself. It is too cold to take a walk as nightfall approaches. I can drive somewhere, but where would I go? I return to my apartment and cook a bowl of ramen noodles with poached eggs. Only the slapstick comedy of Lucille Ball and Desi Arnaz keep me from feeling lonely.

I think of Tree and wonder how he will spend the holidays. My mind meanders to Sam, and I remember I have a book to read. I crawl into bed and leaf through the first few pages of *A Separate Reality*. The photo of Sam and Sky bookmarks the Introduction page. On the back of the photo is a handwritten note: *Tuy Hoa, Vietnam 1971. Sergeant Skyler Herrington and Corporal Sam Hammond. US Army, 180th Assault Support Helicopter Company.*

I blink back the tears and read the first page of the book. I reread it two more times and take out a highlighter to mark the words I do not understand. *Yaqui, appellative, denote, fortuitous…* The list goes on and on.

This morning I wake to a November sky that promises sunshine instead of rain. Dressed in my favorite blue skirt with white polka dots and a cream-colored blouse, I float into the church feeling rested and untethered. I arrive in time to see my daughter head off to Bible study with Olivia, Opal, and Ocean. They all wave to me before disappearing behind a curtain.

"Good morning, Snow." Katrina's voice is easily recognizable, but the scent of her perfume is unforgettable— Chanel No. 5.

Katrina hugs me and hesitates to say more. She looks at the door as if expecting someone.

"You see Teddy and Catherine?" I ask.

"Not yet."

I scan the room in search of the Vanzwols but stop when I notice Jean-Adrien approaching us. His eyes lock onto mine. His startling good looks turn me into a mute.

"Good morning," he says. "You look lovely, Snow." I mumble a thank you. "After the service, will you join us for lunch? Kat and I want to clear the air."

"I have Dolly with me," I say.

Katrina waves her hand as if to swat an imaginary fly. "Of course Dolly is invited. Come, let's take our seats. I see Teddy and Catherine in the second row, and it looks like Pastor George is ready."

I sit between Teddy and Jean-Adrien, feeling like a pocketbook nestled between two great volumes of the *Encyclopedia Britannica*. Ten minutes ago I felt optimistic about the day. Now, I fear it will take just one raindrop from the heavens for me to unhinge.

I drift in and out between Pastor George's words, vaguely hearing something about a crushed spirit. "So as we let those words from Psalm 34:18 rest on our lips, let us savor the meaning, for the Lord is nigh unto them that are brokenhearted and saveth those whose spirit is contrite. Let us pray."

I say goodbye to Teddy and Catherine who are driving to Oregon after Pastor George's sermon. I follow behind Katrina and Jean-Adrien in my car, with Dolly begging from the back seat to sit in the front.

"When can I?" she asks.

"Maybe when you are ten years old," I say. "You have some growing to do."

"Can I have this car when I am old enough to drive?"

"Yes."

"Promise you will not sell it?"

"I promise."

I pull into a parking spot in front of a French bakery and take Dolly's hand. We follow Katrina and Jean-Adrien inside. The bakery is small and seats about a dozen patrons. The décor is in colors of blue, white, and red—colors of the French flag. Hanging on the walls are paintings from local artists. The smell of coffee and pastries seduces me to the display case where macarons, beignets, chou à la crèmes, and viennoiseries tempt me.

"I want the cream puffs, Mama." Dolly cannot contain her excitement. "And that." She points to the crème brûlée. "We can share."

"The maître pâtissier here is a friend of mine," Jean-Adrien says. "You both are in for a treat."

We sit down and order from the simple menu. I choose the crab bisque, Katrina orders a quiche, and Jean-Adrien opts for their charcuterie board. Dolly wants French fries, or steak frites, as they are called.

I dive into the heart of the conversation and skip the formalities. "Teddy tell me no Thanksgiving together this year. You cancel. Why?"

"After last week's incident, Sky took off to California for another silent retreat," Katrina answers. "He gave us a lot to think about and we've decided to do a couples retreat. We want to work on our marriage and be a family again."

Jean-Adrien looks at Katrina with genuine love and admiration. "It is going to take time to strip away all those years of grime...layers upon layers of selfishness and disillusionment."

"Snow," Katrina says, "we have you to thank for helping us realize we've been in a fog all these years, but we are starting to see now. After you left, Sky broke it down for us."

"And we listened," Jean-Adrien says. "He opened our eyes to his pain, his suicidal thoughts—"

Katrina wipes a tear from her eyes. "What kind of mother doesn't protect her son? He was always a loving child, wanting to help and please others. Even after the molestation incident, and even though he built this wall around him so others couldn't get in, he still offered himself to others. He has this innate desire to serve and give."

"He was the kid who helped carry in the groceries and said 'please' and 'thank you,'" Jean-Adrien says. "In some ways, the draft was a good thing for him. As Skyler got older, he engaged in self-destructive behavior, always angry and drinking to blackout mode. He'd get pissed off at the littlest things, punching holes in doors and walls. The army provided discipline and structure. The war though…it messed him up bad."

I take a sip of my coffee and am pleasantly surprised at how delicious and strong it is. "That good," I say.

Jean-Adrien and Katrina look offended. "The coffee so good, not the war." They nod and smile. "When I meet Sky first time in Tuy Hòa, he scare me. He so mad. A boy steal his gas can and windshield wipers from his truck. And he yell so much at the boy sleeping in his truck. He supposed to watch the truck so no one steal it."

Katrina smiles. "He told us that story. That's how we learned about you and your niece…and Sam."

A lump forms in my throat, and I swallow hard. I refuse to let the mention of Sam's name continue to affect me so deeply. It is the past. I steal a steak frite from Dolly's plate. She is content eating her fries and cream puff while coloring in her book.

"Sam's death was very hard on Sky," Jean-Adrien says. "What little joy Skyler had in his life died that day. And when he came back, he was worse than when he left. It didn't help that people spat on him and threw eggs at him. He took up LSD and heroine for a while but managed to quit cold turkey."

"That was rough." Katrina shudders at the memory. "Anyway, we all agreed to work on our dysfunctional selves so we can be a family again. We're going to get some counseling."

"And maybe Miss Cunningham here will shed her maiden name and be a Mrs. Herrington again," Jean-Adrien says. He winks at his wife and squeezes her hand.

"I believe," Katrina says, "that if Mr. Herrington can be faithful and true, I will let him be a Mr. Cunningham." She winks back.

The next hour goes by quickly as we share our opinions about food and culture. Dolly tells us that 7-Up is still her favorite soda but she likes hot chocolate too. This Christmas she is asking Santa for a pet, but she is not sure yet what she wants. She has to think about it.

14. LIFE CHOICES (SUMMER 1982)

Dolly plays with her friends in the living room while I fix them peanut butter and jam sandwiches. We have the television on in the background so that we can learn English.

Tree is here visiting with his new girlfriend, Ngọc. She is a sweet girl who grew up on the island of Phú Quốc. She spent her youth working to survive the war, helping her mother sell fruits, vegetables, and herbs at the market. The family was so poor that they sold her younger sister, Ann, to a husband and wife in a nearby hamlet. The husband and wife were childless, and the wife was disabled; she needed help cooking and cleaning around the house. The husband became a trader, like me, who sold items on the black market.

"After we lost our country, I ran to fetch my sister and steal her back," Ngọc says. "My mom did not want to leave without her. Ann had become attached to her new parents and I had to drag her home. It was traumatizing for both of us. She kicked and scratched and bit me most of the way. She cried and cried, would not speak to me for days except to scream how much she hated me."

"And now?" I ask.

"As long as we do not talk about it, we are fine," Ngọc says. "She lives in Everett now with her boyfriend."

Something on the television catches my attention. I hear the reporter say something about Green River. Can they be talking about my college where I take classes? Tree turns up the volume.

"The body of a young woman floating in the Green River was discovered on August 12 by Frank Linard. The remains of twenty-three-year-old Debra Lynn Bonner, a prostitute who disappeared on July 25, were found yards from a Kent slaughterhouse where Frank works. Further investigation links the Bonner killing to two other cases, that of Wendy Coffield and

Leann Wilcox, both known prostitutes. Police believe they have a serial killer on the loose targeting young women who are soliciting sex along the Pacific Highway. We will continue our coverage on the Green River Killer as new evidence arises."

"What is it?" Tree asks. I tell him about the murders. Tree and Ngọc urge me to quit my sewing and cooking classes at the college.

"The killer is targeting teenagers who are sex workers," I say.

"Aunt Eight, promise me you will drop your classes."

"He is right," Ngọc says. "Anything can happen. I heard there was another serial killer from here. His name is Ted Bundy, and he was arrested four years ago for raping and killing women. They were college students, not prostitutes."

"All right," I agree. "I will withdraw from Green River College. My newspaper is going to be busy covering this killer."

My response satisfies Tree and his girlfriend. We pack up the sandwiches and grab the sodas, potato chips, and fruits and head outside for a picnic. Behind our apartment is the community room where the neighborhood summer potluck takes place. Donald sets up a sprinkler system while his son Ricky, home from college for the summer, lays down a sixteen-foot Slip 'N Slide for the children to play. It is a glorious summer day—not a cloud in sight and nothing but blue sky above.

Ngọc spreads our blanket next to Donald's under a young cherry blossom tree. Jason runs over to join Dolly, Melissa, and Jen.

"Jason, sit next to me," my daughter commands.

I listen to Dolly boss her friends around and rip them off with the candy exchange. I do not know whether to be proud or concerned.

"Melissa, you owe me five cents," Dolly says.

"I do not."

"Yah hah, you do," Dolly says. "Remember? I gave you my Haw Flakes."

"But I gave you a turn on my big wheel," Melissa argues. "And I shared my popsicle with you."

I interrupt their childish argument. "It looks like Donald and Ricky are done setting up. Go play in the water."

Tree, Ngọc, and I content ourselves with watching the kids jump through the sprinklers and slide down the wet, plastic sheet. Donald and Ricky offer us some watermelon, and I offer them pears. Diệp is not with Donald and I wonder if their romance ended. I open my mouth to ask, but who should appear fifty yards away?

Diệp walks toward our group, her hips swaying back and forth to accentuate her figure. She wears a yellow one-piece bathing suit with green stars, looking like a moldy banana. Where does she buy her clothes? The large straw hat and brown sunglasses give her a Hollywood vibe if one can look past her neon green flip-flops and long tropical palm tree and flamingo-print shirt. She waves. Donald and I wave back. Hùng runs ahead and joins the children at the sprinklers. Diệp sits down and wedges herself between Donald and Ngọc.

"Why are you wearing a swimsuit?" I ask Diệp. "You are not joining the children, are you?"

She shrugs. "It looks fun." She dismisses me and analyzes Ngọc. "Who are you?"

"This is Ngọc," Tree says. "She—"

"Girlfriend?" Diệp asks.

Tree nods. "She lives in West Sea—"

"Where are your parents?" Diệp dismisses my nephew. "Any siblings?"

"Yes," Ngọc answers. "My sister lives in Everett and my parent—"

"Where are you from?"

"Phú Quốc."

"Island girl, I see," Diệp says. She squeezes Tree's cheeks as if he were a toddler. "And where have you been?"

Tree explains that he has been living with a man named Bình, whom he met on a soccer field, and whose wife left him.

"My mom and Mr. Bình are friends," Ngọc explains. "He came over to our house one day, and Tree was with him. It was fate for us to be together."

"Actually," Tree says. "it is your mom's egg rolls that draws me."

Ngọc playfully punches him and pouts, pretending to be offended.

While Diệp interrogates Tree and Ngọc, Donald strikes up a conversation with me. He scratches his head and asks, "How do you pronounce Tree's girlfriend's name?"

We have a good laugh over his attempt. He puffs his cheeks out to form the proper sound but the closest he comes is "nop."

Ngọc interjects. "You call me Kelly."

Donald looks relieved. "Good, because this old dog can't learn new tricks. I thought I'd have to avoid saying your name forever."

Tree tells us the two of them go to Spectrum Nightclub often. Apparently, according to Kelly, my nephew has a trail of admirers there.

"We plan on moving in together after he gets a job," Kelly says. "I can keep an eye on him every day."

"What happened to your mattress job?" I ask.

"The company moved, then work was slow, so they laid me off," Tree says. "If my English were better, maybe they would have kept me."

"You were fired?" I ask. "And your parents? Ngọc, are they fine with you two moving in together?"

Tree shifts his weight and takes a bite of his sandwich. He sits up straight and gazes at the children. Neither of them answers my question. Kelly takes a sip of her cola and jabs Tree in the arm.

"Well?" I ask.

Tree takes a deep breath. I have never seen him this nervous. "I asked her parents for her hand in marriage."

I stop chewing and stiffen my posture. Donald and Diệp make their escape and spring up to join the children in the sprinklers. I toss my pear down. "You are too young—" I stop myself and try not to lecture them. "What did your parents say?"

"My father does not agree to the marriage," Kelly says, "but my mother said it was up to me to choose my husband. She said I am to make my own life choices, and if I am either lucky or miserable, then it is my choice."

The rest of our afternoon is pleasant but a little awkward. I make a conscious effort not to impose my opinions and to be supportive. The last thing I want is to drive Tree away. Kelly's mom is right; they have to make their own life choices and handle the outcome of those choices. I cannot wait to write Brother Seven.

###

This summer has gone by slowly. Tree still checks in every once in awhile, but he and Kelly have not visited. Dolly spends most of her days playing outside and has a social network of friends. They spend a lot of time in the brush between the parking lot and the elementary school on the other side of the intersection, building forts and playing chase or cops and robbers. The blackberry thickets do not bother her. Bumps, scratches, and bruises are standard badges in her repertoire. Strangers who meet her mistake her for a boy. Her dark, dirt-smudged face and rigid way of walking make me feel like I have a son. Teddy says she is a tomboy and not to worry. I miss the sweet little daughter who liked cuddling with me and playing with my hair. She now has her own bedroom, having taken over Tree's old room, and spends a lot of time on the phone with Jen, gossiping about Melissa and Hùng being boyfriend and girlfriend.

Dolly sports a rat tail now, a hair trend worse than the mullet she had ten months ago. Gone are the frilly dresses and here to stay are T-shirts and shorts or jeans. Her dolls are put away in the closet and have been replaced by a skateboard. Tree's velvet posters of cobras and dragons remain on the walls. She says it makes her room feel like she's in the *Secret of NIMH* movie. Lately, the kids rotate houses to play in, deciding which house based on who is serving the best dinner that evening. Tony and Stephanie usually win. Dolly argues that Donald cannot cook, Diệp's food is stinky, and my cooking is weird. Oddly, she never says anything about Jen's parents, and I still have not met them. Jen is usually with my daughter and rarely home.

A new convenience store is being built across from the Safeway store. The children are happy they will be able to buy junk food at Circle K without crossing the street, but they are upset to lose the wooded area past the parking lot. Bulldozers are coming next weekend.

I take out my book, *A Separate Reality*, and pick up where I left off. Half the book is highlighted in yellow. There are too many words beyond my comprehension. I glance at the framed photo of Sam and Sky and wish I were in Sam's arms, listening to his voice. He had promised to read this to me.

After two pages of reading, highlighting, and referencing the dictionary, I give up. "Thủy-Tiên ơi?" I call out to Dolly, but she does not answer. I remember she is outside playing, but it is getting dark. The street lamps are lit. I open the window and call out to her. I hear a scream. My stomach somersaults to my throat. I recognize that scream.

Dolly runs out from behind the bushes. Hùng chases her. He is holding a stick with a snake draped around it. He flicks his wrist and sends the snake hurling at my daughter. It lands on her shoulder. She shrieks and brushes the serpent off her arm. She flails her arms and jerks her body like she has fire ants crawling up her legs. The snake falls to the ground but does not slither off. It is not alive. She kicks it for good measure.

"I hate you!" Dolly charges at Hùng. "I hate both of you!"

Hùng and Melissa laugh and run off together while holding hands. I call out to my daughter. She halts and looks at me, then runs to our apartment. I hear her bound up the stairs; urgent, heavy footsteps quickly spill into the hallway.

Dolly leaps onto my bed and into my arms. She buries her head into my breasts and sobs. "They are so mean to me."

I comfort my daughter and offer her ice cream to lift her spirits. We sit on the couch, and between spoonfuls of mint chocolate chip, she divulges what happened.

"I was chasing a grasshopper," she says and hiccups. "I saw them in the fort and saw them kiss." She hiccups again but declines my offer to get her water. "If I hold my breath, it will go away." She plugs her nose for five seconds and exhales. "They told me to leave and not tell anyone. And then Melissa threw dirt at me and stupid Hùng found that snake." She weeps. "I hate them, and I hate snakes!"

I rub her back and hold her. "Kids can be mean, even your friends. All your life, you will meet mean people or people who do stupid things. What is important is how you face them and handle the situation. Will your actions make you stronger and better? Will your decisions make that person or the situation better?"

"What if they are just mean and I cannot change them?" she asks.

I look at my daughter's face, still innocent and cute, despite the mullet-rat tail disaster that is on her head. "If they are just mean, then you have a choice to make. You can cut them out of your life until they change, or you show them love and compassion so that they learn how to be loving and compassionate. Do you understand what I am saying?"

"I think so," she says. "I love Hùng but he loves Melissa, so if I show him love, he will love me back."

That was not the answer I expected. My eyes open wide but she does not see my reaction. "You have a crush on Hùng?" My daughter nods. "Why do you think he likes her and not you?"

"Because she has pretty long blonde hair and green eyes," she says. "And she wears nice clothes and has a bike with a banana seat and a bell and a basket. She gives him candy and brings him presents."

I sympathize with her rationale. "She may have all those things, but let me tell you a secret about boys." Dolly sits up and locks her eyes with mine. She leans in to listen. I laugh. "Most boys are stupid and blind. They do not have the power like us girls do. They cannot see beyond the surface. Sometimes, they cannot even see what is right in front of them. And sometimes, they do not know what they want, so you have to tell them."

"I am going to grow my hair out," Dolly says. "You can cut my tail off when I am sleeping. He will see. I can be pretty."

My heart bobs with joy that she wants to cut the rat tail. Hallelujah. "Honey, grow your hair out if you want to, not because you think Hùng will like you more."

"I know," she says. "Melissa can have him. Who wants a dumb and blind boyfriend?"

I laugh and make a funny face. "That's my girl. Remember that you are worth a million times more than what you think you are. There is a better boy out there for you who will have the same powers as you and be your equal. He will appreciate your natural beauty and see how smart and funny you are. He is going to be so lucky because you're not like the other girls. You like sports, you are amazing at making money, and you have a good heart that has survived so much."

Dolly hugs me tight and kisses my cheek. "I love you."

"I love you too."

I stare at the envelope in my hand. The return address is from Humble, Texas. I do not have to look at the sender's name to know the handwriting is distinctly Tý's. My husband writes to me after all.

I suppress the urge to rip it open and devour his words. I remind myself I am not a young naïve girl hungry for love. Surviving the South China Sea and the refugee camp hardened me and made me wiser. I have a choice to make…open the letter or toss it in the garbage.

How many more slashes to my heart can I withstand before I run out of thread to mend it? What good would it do to have him in Thủy-Tiên's life when she already has a good life without him? I play several scenarios in my mind and decide there are too many unknowns and variables to risk tempting fate. I tear up the envelope and toss it in the trash.

The phone rings. I stare at it, fearing it is Tý on the other end, but the likelihood of him having my phone number is slim. I pick up the phone with trepidation. "Alô?"

"Hot damn, it's good to hear your voice." Sky's greeting drains the stress from my neck. He sounds happy and full of energy.

"Sky!" I exclaim. "How the retreat?"

"It was incredible," Sky says. "The longer I sat in silence and focused on my breathing, the more aware and alive I felt. All the pent-up feelings of despair and disgust eroded. I had no one to answer to but myself, and the alone time forced me to be truthful, to come to terms with the past. It was like with every inhale I sipped in healing powers and every exhale expunged the poison that has tormented me. I still have a ways to go but I experienced an epiphany—"

"What 'epiphany'?" I ask.

"It's like a realization," Sky says, "an 'ah-ha' moment where things become clear. What I learned was that my fears paralyzed me. My fears are not based on truth or reality. They are conjured by my wild imagination. The past few months…these sojourns…they have awakened in me a will to live and be happy."

"You deserve happiness," I say, thinking of Diệp's fear of the Americans after the massacre. "The core of you is survivor. Dark days of war and childhood over now."

He rambles on about his past three retreats since missing Thanksgiving last November. He has been to California, Tibet, and England and has sat in meditation and silence from fourteen days to as long as ninety days at each retreat. He went on reflective hikes and watched in awe how nature and nurture symbiotically work together, and how relationships unfold. He woke up early to catch the sunrise and witness the birds catch their breakfast. At night, he fasted and prayed with only the sounds of crickets to keep him company. Each time he finished a retreat, he came out on the other side feeling more buoyant than before. He became more in tune with nature, with the universe, and with his body.

I listen eagerly to his excitement, and although he speaks rapidly, I understand his enthusiasm and the successes of his experiences. "A tree that does not bend in the wind will break and die."

"Yes," Sky says, "an old proverb. We humans can be adaptable and thrive if we have the strength and willpower to do so."

The conversation swirling around his healing journey tapers off, and I take the opportunity to change topics. "How Katrina and Jean-Adrien?"

A waterfall of praise tumbles out of Sky's mouth. He is full of optimism about how his parents have stuck with counseling, taking trips to reconnect and fall in love again, and Sky feels he now lives with June and Ward Cleaver—references of people I have not yet met but hope to one day. They sound lovely.

In between breaths, Sky asks me about Dolly or Tree and how I am doing with work and my classes. I gossip about Donald courting Diệp, to which Sky declares we need to dine together soon so that he can finally meet my infamous neighbor.

"Anything else?" Sky asks. "Any news to catch me up on? What about your family?"

"I receive letter from my husband today," I say. "I throw away and not read it."

"Why?" Sky asks.

"I not want him in Dolly life or my life," I say. "Why, Sky? Why I let him back when he make choice already with first wife? Dolly and I do fine and do not need him."

"I think you are still very angry with him and need to make your peace with him. Mark Twain once said that anger is like acid that will do more harm to the vessel that holds it. And besides, you helped me make peace with my dad and to let go of the anger and pain…and guilt. You should do the same. It is liberating."

I give more thought to Sky's advice and before hanging up the phone, I tell Sky I will read the letter and make a choice about what to do next.

"Don't let anyone or anything have power over you." Sky's last words toss my thoughts around like a cyclone and for two weeks, I cannot think of anything but Tý. Dreams of him coming to claim Dolly and take her back to Texas drown me in night sweats. I have to face him.

<h2>15. TYPHOON SEASON (SEPTEMBER 1982)</h2>

My husband's letter, taped together like a macabre jigsaw puzzle, lies between two scarves in the top drawer of my dresser. I take it out and read it again for the one-hundredth time, searching for secret messages within his words. An infestation of paranoia creeps in. When I think about the truths he omitted and the danger he put us in, I shudder with disgust.

I remember back at the refugee camp when we had bed bugs. Tree and I noticed the tiny bloodstains on our sheets but did not question them. We simply accepted the condition of our squalor because at least we had a place to sleep. The darks spots on our pillows that were bug excrements were thought to be dirt stains, not fecal matter. The foul, musty odor of the bugs' glands blended in with the scent of tropical sewage. It was simply the stench of impending death.

Funny how thinking of Tý brings back memories of the bed bugs. Maybe he was the dark spot on my pillow, the shit on my life while I lived day to day not knowing any better. Old feelings of betrayal brew inside like a storm, and I say out loud, "You are less than a tick's dung to me now."

Tuyết,

Sister Six has been kind to write and give me your address. I want to see you and Thủy-Tiên. I cannot continue life while the guilt stacks higher and heavier. It will crush me to death unless you forgive me and I can atone for my mistakes.

I want you both to be a part of my life. I want us to be a family again. It has been seven years, my beloved wife. Your face haunts me every day, and at night your beauty haunts me in my dreams. I am not the same man you remember. Older, yes, but in this old heart there still burns a bright flame for

*Whether you read and answer my letter or not, I will be coming to
Seattle. I purchased my airplane ticket already. I understand now why Annette
only bought a one-way ticket to Việt Nam to find me. I thought she was crazy,
but look at me, doing the same thing now. I have many questions. I am sure you
do too. I want to get to know Thủy-Tiên and she needs to know her father.*

*I land in Seattle from the Houston airport at 10:10 a.m. on
Saturday, September 25, on a United Airlines flight. I hope you will pick me
up but if I do not see you, I will take a taxicab.*

*Please welcome me with a forgiving heart, and in case you do not
recognize me, I will be the beggar on my hands and knees, kissing your feet with
a forlorn heart.*

Always yours,
Tý

I collect my coat from the closet and Dolly's pink jacket
with the fake fur lining around the hood. She hates the coat and
thinks she looks like a big cotton candy with two sticks protruding
at the bottom. It is the only coat she has and it will have to do.
Outside, the rain falls sideways while the wind howls.

I place our coats on her bed and gently rouse her. "Time to
get ready. Your daddy is coming to see you today."

The past few days, all she could talk about was seeing Tý
and showing him her scar. She bragged to Melissa, Jen, Jason, and
Hùng that her father was traveling from far away and that he had
finally found us.

I had asked Tree if he wanted to come to the airport, but he
had said, "The reunion should be between Uncle and you only."

I asked Sky, also, to come with us, and reminded him that
he pinky promised, but he only parroted Tree's sentiments. "I'll be
there for you but not at the airport when you pick him up."

Dolly and I sit in the Honda Civic and let the car warm up.
The defroster blasts on high. It rains marbles; the pounding on the
car roof makes me nostalgic for Việt Nam. Sometimes it pummeled
so hard there that the raindrops were cacti needles on my face. I
cannot believe that in less than an hour, I will be face to face with
the man I once vowed to obey and love until the day I die.

I turn on the radio and scroll through all the stations. No
good songs are playing. I stop on KUBE 93 FM hoping to catch a
Lionel Richie song or a top forty hit I recognize. Nothing. Instead, I

hear a brief news update on Typhoon Ken, a tropical storm that has been punishing Japan the past week. I forgot it was typhoon season. I wonder how my family is faring with the tropical storms. The rainfall reminds me of the time Tree and I caught frogs for dinner. It was also the day Father died.

Before long, Dolly and I drive in circles up the spiral ramps to level four of the airport parking lot. I do not even remember getting on the interstate and taking the exit to the airport. I park, and we make our way through the sky bridge to the terminal. We find the gate and wait.

My stomach is in knots. Despite the cool air, my hands are clammy. I sit down for a couple of seconds only to spring back up again. I want to make sure I see him the moment he steps out of the gate. I check my reflection in the window. My hair is damp and flat. I run my fingers through them to give them volume. Will Tý still find me attractive? Have I changed in his eyes? I gained ten pounds since arriving in Seattle.

"Will Daddy know who I am?" Dolly asks. "I was a baby when he last saw me."

"You were only nine months old," I say, "but of course, he will recognize you."

"I am eight now," she says. "I have a scar on my chest now."

"Yes, but you are still his daughter," I say. "A daddy never forgets his daughter."

I look around and notice my reflection in the window. I comb my hair with my fingers and check my face for any smudges.

"You look pretty," Dolly says.

I smile warmly at my daughter. How far she has come, traveling through mosquito-infested jungles, sailing over ripples of a never-ending sea, and flying above freedom clouds made of hopes and dreams. She is alive, and I kept her alive, no thanks to my husband.

"He is here!" Dolly jumps out of her chair and runs to the window. She points at the Boeing 767 aircraft. I grimace, thinking Typhoon Tý has landed in the Pacific Northwest. What stories will he spin up this time? What lies will he use to shield himself from my prying lips?

The terminal gate opens. Passengers disembark and exit the jetway. It is a circus of clowns tumbling out of the narrow bridge. They wear expressions of delight, skepticism, or weariness on their faces. A young man in a naval uniform rushes to kiss his wife and hug his twin girls.

And then there is my husband.

He has not changed. It is as if he walked through a time machine from Sài Gòn 1975 to Seattle 1982. Still handsome and fit. Except for the ASICS running shoes on his feet, everything remains the same, from the lean muscles that show off his athletic build to the slight bow in his legs accentuated by tight blue jeans. His skin is tan and his teeth bright. I was expecting to hate him, but seeing the familiar face of the man I once loved, however briefly, makes my heart flutter. The happiness that descends on me catches me off guard. I let my defenses down; the curtain of insecurities pulls back. Tý swoops me into his arms and kisses my lips. I respond and cling to him.

"Hello, sweetheart," he says. The corners of his eyes brim with wetness. He drops his duffle bag and swings his daughter into his arms. Father and daughter hug. They both cry.

For our first dinner together since April 1975, I put out some stir-fried anchovies, barbecued chicken, pork chitlins, sautéed water spinach, pickled leeks, steamed rice, and winter melon soup.

Tý's eyes open wide. He cracks a smile and grunts. "Vietnamese soul food! Do you have any beer?" I pop the tab of a Rainier beer and place it on the table. I can hear Sam saying it was the only beer he drank because it was brewed here in Washington. "Where is yours? You have to *nhậu* with me and celebrate."

"You know I get drunk after a few sips," I say. It feels traitorous serving Sam's beer to my husband.

"Still a light-weight, I see, but now you can cook." Tý pinches a few anchovies with his chopsticks and pops them in his mouth.

"I have learned a few things since we separated," I say drily, finding how he chews his food annoying, lips parted and tongue slapping against the roof of his mouth. He does not even wait for his daughter and me to sit down. Typical man.

"Thủy-Tiên, honey, grab daddy some chili sauce," Tý says in English. "I like it spicy." He winks at her.

My daughter's ears perk up hearing her father speak perfect English. I see the look of pride and adoration in her face for him. It irritates me that he commands her to do his bidding and pulls her strings like a puppet. He has been absent from her life for seven years. He does not have the right to parent her. He should be groveling at my feet, begging for forgiveness, and selling his soul to the devil for a sliver of a chance to be in our lives.

I pull out my chair and sit down. I say a quick prayer and bless myself with the sign of the cross. "How long are you staying?"

"I just arrived, and you are already quick to send me away," he says. I do not know if the inflections in his voice are in jest and he is teasing me, or if he is being sarcastic and condescending. His words course through my veins like a thousand volts of electricity. I bite down and lock my jaw.

Dolly hands him two types of chili sauce and fresh red chili pepper. "Daddy, do you believe in Jesus?"

My husband slurps his soup before answering. "No, I'm an atheist or maybe agnostic. I don't believe in God, but there may, or may not, be a higher power out there. I don't know."

"Are you going to live with us?" Dolly asks.

I stop chewing and look at Tý. I hold my breath for his reply. He shrugs. "Depends on your mother."

I have no answer for them. My face feels flushed and my neck warm. My patience for Tý is a mudslide away from destroying our family reunion. He sits there at my table, in my home, uninvited, talking to my daughter, and resumes this pretend life as if time, war, and a failed marriage had never separated us.

"Mama says I was found in a garbage can," Dolly says. "Is that true?"

"All naughty children in Vietnam come from the dumpsters, honey. Are you a bad girl?"

"Not anymore."

"Make sure you stay a good girl. Otherwise, your mommy might throw you out with the trash, back in the dumpster, and the next person who fishes you out might be a mean mommy who will not feed you or buy you toys. Instead of candy, she will give you chores from sunrise to sunset."

"You need to speak to her in Vietnamese." It was all I could say without losing my temper.

"We are in America now," he says. "This is her home. There is no returning. Adapt or die."

His last three words are rusty nails impaled into the core of my beliefs. I do not want my daughter to forget her heritage. She must always remember where she came from and be proud of her roots. I bite my tongue. I do not want to argue in front of Dolly.

"Yeah, Mom," Dolly says. "It's stupid to talk in Vietnamese."

I glare at my daughter. She scowls back and challenges me. She straightens her posture and sets her fork down. If Tý were not here, I would claw at her false sense of security. Surely, she does not think that her father is her ally and his presence will protect her from punishment?

Tý defends me. "Do not disrespect your mother. Apologize, or back in the dumpster you go."

Dolly offers an apology and asks for forgiveness for talking back to me. I excuse her from the table and make her watch a documentary about birds.

Long after I have finished eating, Tý still picks at his morsels of food. Right when I think he is full and done eating, he picks up his chopsticks again to taste another anchovy or shovel more rice into his bowl. I try clearing the plate of water spinach, but he takes the dish from me and scrapes the last bits of garlic and leafy greens into his bowl. He finishes off the winter melons and reaches for the last drumstick. The only things left are three pickled leeks and fragments of chitterlings.

"Does Annette not feed you?" I ask. I am picking a fight tonight. All these years of pent-up disappointment and unfinished business are about to burst out of my mouth.

Tý ignores me. "You know what these chitlins remind me of? The L&M back in Sài Gòn." He pushes the fried pork chitterlings around like he's sifting through river sand for gold. "The restaurant was always full of black soldiers. They would sit and nhậu all day and order plates of chitlins at two-hundred *piastres* a dish. It was a brotherhood. They had this way of greeting each other, called the dap, and it was like a secret handshake. I later learned that 'dap' was an acronym for dignity and pride."

"How many children do you have other than Timothy?" I ask. My body temperature skyrockets. I am a tea kettle about to blow my steam.

"While we are on the topic of brotherhood," Tý continues, "how is my brother?" He pushes the chair away from the table and stands up. He clears the table and tells Dolly it is bedtime.

I help her get into her pajamas and watch her brush her teeth. She kisses us both and runs off to bed. In the kitchen, Tý lathers up a sponge and scrubs the dishes. I grab the sponge from him and throw it into the sink; a couple of soap suds splash onto his golden arm.

"Why are you here?" I scream. "All these years…why now? Are you dying? Do you need money? Did Annette leave you?"

He picks up the sponge and resumes washing the dishes. It infuriates me that I cannot get a rise out of him. If he does not engage, then I am only fighting with myself. I stare at my husband. I want to scratch his eyes out and tell him to go home to his precious American wife and children.

"I will answer your questions if you can calm yourself down and talk to me like a dutiful wife."

"You mean a sedated and mindless wife," I say. "What I would not give to have a bottle of Maotai right now. This time, I would not miss."

"Is that what you want? To split my skull open with a bottle of baijiu? Go ahead. You already trampled my heart when you did not get in that van. You could have spared yourself and our daughter a lot of suffering, but you let your pride get in the way."

He will never understand my position. How can he? He is a man. What did he have to lose? He will never feel the humiliation of being the second wife. He never had to worry about his next meal. He did not live his life perpetually tense, praying that the next man he sees is not the one who will rape him today. He will never understand the crippling fear a mother has of losing her only child.

"It is not like I can make more babies whenever I want," I say.

"What?" Tý asks. "You are not making any sense."

"Do not bother unpacking. You can sleep on the couch."

I sleep through my alarm. Feeling like a beached seal, I am too distressed to move. It is Sunday. Church service has already begun, and I am sure Sky will be anxious to know what happened. I hear sounds in the kitchen and decide I should be a good hostess and make coffee.

I drag my feet off the bed and shuffle out of the bedroom. Dolly stands in the hallway with a tray. Two bowls of cereal, two glasses of orange juice, and two spoons. "I made breakfast for you and Daddy."

"Where is Daddy?" I ask. Confused, she looks at my bedroom door. I rush past her into the living room. The couch had been slept on but is empty now. I walk into the kitchen, but Tý is not there. His duffle bag is gone and so are his shoes. I look for a note, but there is none. I take the tray from Dolly's hands and set it on the table. "Daddy is gone. He went back to Texas."

I hold my daughter and console her the best I can. This is my fault, but I convince myself it has to be this way.

It is better this way. Is it not?

16. THE CRUSH (DECEMBER 1982)

My daughter has been simmering in her thoughts the past month. I know her father's sudden appearance and disappearance crushed her. She has not been her usual hustling self, selling sticks of Juicy Fruit gum for five cents a stick or begging for sleepovers with friends. She has lost interest in Melissa and Hùng's relationship and declines invitations to play football or basketball with Jason and Jen. She spends her afternoons drawing, playing quietly by herself, reading, or watching cartoons. She assures me she is not sad and looks forward to another Christmas. She has not given up on a pet and has reminded Santa that she has been an extra good girl this year.

Teddy and Catherine have invited us over for a holiday party. "It's an ugly sweater party," Teddy announces, "and we are going to do a white elephant gift exchange." Teddy explains the concept of the white elephant game to me and the rules. "Be sure you each bring a wrapped gift of something you do not want."

If Tý were here, I would take him to the party as my white elephant, wrapped in paper with a bow on top. Someone else can have him. I giggle at my private joke.

Katrina, Jean-Adrien, and Skyler will be there. Pastor George and his family have RSVP'd as well. I am excited for them to meet Tree's girlfriend. The last time we were all under one roof was Christmas Eve two years ago. It is impolite to come empty-handed, so I make shrimp and pork fried rice to bring to the party.

I rummage through my closet and dirty clothes pile looking for the ugliest sweater I own. I have never been to an ugly sweater party and do not understand the purpose. Desperate, I tug at the orange and green crocheted cardigan. I found it at a thrift shop for fifty cents and have worn it twice. I hope it is ugly enough.

Then an idea strikes me. I dart out of the apartment and knock on Diệp's door. No answer. I rap louder and call out to her. "Diệp's ơi."

She opens the door. "What is the urgency?"

"I need to borrow a sweater for a party. Can I come in?" I push the door, but she stops it from swinging in. "Is something wrong?"

"It is not a good time," she says. "When do you need it?"

A man's voice calls from within. "Come back here, Yip."

"I need it now," I say. "Is that Donald?" My neighbor does not have to answer; it is written all over her flushed face. "Can I borrow one of your colorful sweaters…that one with the puffy sleeves and doily collar?" She returns in a flash and hands me her sweater. It is gaudy, loud, and ugly, with the cast of *Diff'rent Strokes* centered on the front. There are a few holes from moth bites and strands of yarn poking out by the armpit area. A pink stain runs down the center of it and dribbles over Philip Drummond's eyes, the dad from the sitcom. He resembles Donald, so of course, she had to have it. My audacious neighbor found it at a yard sale and negotiated with the seller down to ten cents; she would have paid a dollar for it. She wore the sweater proudly, even after she spilled juice on it.

"Perfect. Thank you," I say. "Tell Donald I say 'hello.'"

Two hours later we arrive at the Vanzwol house. It is a beautiful night despite the harsh winter air. It gnaws the warmth off my bones and sands down the traction on my shoes. One day I hope to acclimate to the Seattle weather and maybe then the cold, damp air will be inviting.

Dolly and I park thirty feet from the house. Cars fill the driveway and line the street. I wonder who else is here. As we approach the house, with its white lights clinging from the roofline, giving it a magical, winter wonderland touch, I slip and skate to my knees from the slick black ice on the sidewalk. I shiver in the night and exhale frost as the bowl of fried rice slips from my hands. Luckily it is salvageable. Dolly helps me right as the door opens. Holiday music spills out to the lawn and Sky stands in the doorway.

He looks me up and down. "Wow." He invites us in. "That sweater is…"

"Perfect?" I ask. "I borrow from neighbor."

"I was going to say ugly." Sky laughs. "It is obnoxious and hideous. Am I going to have to stare at his face all night?" He points to Philip Drummond's stained face.

"Do you like my sweater?" Dolly asks.

She wears an oversized purple sweater with a shiny, patent pink belt around her waist. It would swallow her whole if it was not cinched tightly.

"Very nice," Sky says. He stands before us in a V-neck sweater. Tinsel and a string of popcorn adorn his green pullover. Tiny ornaments cling to parts of the cloth, and a large gift-wrapped box covers his crotch. It is attached to his belt and hangs like a fanny pack.

I point at the box. "Present under tree?"

Sky grins. "For the naughty and not so nice."

Dolly runs inside and leaps into Teddy's arms. She kisses him on the cheek and strokes his beard. "Are you Santa's brother?"

Teddy puts his finger to his lips. "Shhhhhh." Dolly slides down and hugs Catherine before running off into the family room. Teddy whistles at me. "Snow, that sweater…"

My jaw drops. Teddy and Catherine are wearing similar sweaters, but his shirt has an image of a woman's breasts covered in a bikini top and Catherine has a fat man's hairy chest on hers. I laugh uncontrollably.

I offer Teddy the fried rice and go into the kitchen to help Catherine. The house smells of melted butter and sugary pies. Catherine hands me a glass of champagne. "Now, get!" She shoos me out of the kitchen and insists I enjoy myself in the family room.

I hear chatter and childish giggles in the next room, so I follow the sounds. To my astonishment, my boss is here and so is his assistant, Magdaleine. They are talking animatedly with Sky and laughing. I scan the room and see Jean-Adrien with Katrina, engaging in serious conversation with Pastor George and Dawn. Meanwhile, Opal, Ocean, Olivia, and Dolly sit on the floor by the fire. They play the Milton Bradley game of Operation. Opal picks up the tweezers and concentrates as she slowly removes the wishbone from Cavity Sam. The game buzzes and flashes red. The children giggle.

I walk toward Sky, preferring to join their lively conversation over Katrina's boring one, but I hear Dawn call my name. The women wave me over.

"Snow, perhaps you can settle a debate for us," Dawn says. "Nice sweater by the way."

Katrina pats the couch cushion and invites me to sit next to her. "Now, let me ask you this…If you got a vacuum cleaner as a present for Christmas from your husband, would you be excited?"

"But you complained about the old one and—" Jean-Adrien stops mid-sentence. Katrina covers his mouth with her hands.

Pastor George leans in. "It's the lastest, top-of-the-line, high-end, most expensive vacuum on the market, and it's on sale at Sears. Not to mention, it's compact and will save you a lot of time as it picks up everything."

"But giving your wife a vacuum is unromantic and sends the wrong message," Dawn argues. "Wouldn't you agree?"

"It's a thoughtful, functional, pragmatic gift," Pastor George says.

I glance at my watch and wonder when Tree and Kelly will arrive. Thank heavens Sky rescues me. He saunters over to our group and takes my hand. "I need your help in the kitchen."

I smile thinking I would never have heard those words back in Vĩnh Bình. Sister Six and Sister Seven protested sharply if I tried to help them cook. Sky and I join Teddy and Catherine around the kitchen bar.

Sky refills my champagne flute. "Your tolerance for alcohol is improving."

The three of us catch up on what has been happening in our world. Sky kicks it off. "The VA is phenomenal…at treating people terribly. Every time I see a doctor, there's someone new, and I have to tell my story over and over again." He recalls how he had major drug addictions after the war because he did not know how to be normal at home. "Normal was hunting for Charlie Company, watching your back so you didn't get killed, and protecting the locals. It was rushing into an ambushed area to save people and being in the crossfire, not knowing if the plastic bag on the side of the road was a bomb or simply trash."

My boss, Bill, joins our conversation. He pats Sky on the back. "Son, no country has ever historically taken care of their soldiers once the empire is at peacetime because no one wants to be reminded of how they got there. Soldiers become collateral damage."

"At the VA, you see guys sitting there, and they'll tell you they're waiting to die because no one talks to them or gives a flip about them. Some are missing limbs, some are homeless or jobless, others are hooked on crack." He tells us about a new treatment for people suffering from post-traumatic stress called stellate ganglion block injection. He had to write that down for me to comprehend what he was saying. It is a numbing medication for the nerves at the neck. The injection is used to treat chronic pain and has been shown to relieve the symptoms of PTS in as little as thirty minutes and can last for years. It essentially reboots the sympathetic nervous system to its pre-trauma state. The nerve bundles in the neck help regulate the body's fight or flight mechanism. Sky says the treatment is expensive.

"It sounds promising and too good to be true," Catherine says.

Sky scratches his head. "I'll try anything. The meditation is working. My friend Charlie deals with it by writing poems. Man, the stories you hear in therapy sessions. There was one girl in her twenties whose husband came back from Nam and stabbed her repeatedly. She was left on the ground bleeding to death and was able to call 9-1-1. There was another guy who served on a navy ship in Vietnam. They'd go through harbors and crush fishing boats and watch kids get eaten by sharks." Sky pauses and catches his breath. He blinks back tears.

Bill puts his arm around Sky's shoulders. "I sent him a letter almost every week while he was overseas."

"And I'd lie and tell him everything was fine so he wouldn't worry," Sky says. "The VA has well-intentioned angels who want to help veterans, but they're handcuffed by the government red tape. Restrictions, policies, funding, slow progression…it all lead to frustration and they quit. It's a revolving door of new faces, new names. I don't want to be the vet who tells the same story over and over, and all I have is that story." Sky looks at me with tenderness and squeezes my hand. "You and Sam were my story that I lived repeatedly in my mind."

"I have trauma stress like you," I say. "I have nightmare of Sam dying and worry Dolly father come back, make me live with him as husband and wife. In my dream, I sometime see my enemy want to kill me, and I see friends who die trying to escape communist. But Dolly and Tree…because of them, I keep going."

"That's because you have a purpose," Bill says. "We all need to find a purpose in life to keep us from giving up. We also have to recognize that we have the willpower to get through the adversities."

Sky snickers. "Like basic training. Everyone who went through basic training was quitting something, whether it be sugar, foods, cigarettes. Man, I was so miserable, but I made it, even the tear gas chamber training. You go in there, take off your helmet, and breathe in tear gas. Your eyes sting and so do your lungs and throat. Guys were coughing, drooling, and vomiting afterward…snot dripping everywhere, and because we had to shave every day, our skin was raw. We were all flapping our arms trying to escape it like a bunch of dumb, flightless birds. Anyway, sponsoring Snow here was my purpose, and now that we have Snow in Seattle, ensuring she thrives here is my purpose."

The layers of brick and historical rubble that have been crushing me these past few years suddenly lift. One look at Sky and I realize how much I love my friend. My angelic, handsome, and kind Skyler, who, despite suffering so much, can still be giving and selfless. Tears gush from both of us, and we do not hold back. I wrap my arms around Sky's waist and rest my cheek on his chest. He holds me tighter, and I hear the crunch of his fanny-pack box that covers his crotch.

We have a good laugh.

Tree and Kelly show up in time for dinner. Kelly apologizes profusely for being late, claiming they got lost, but Tree says she took too long getting ready. The two of them show up dressed like they are going to a wedding reception. Tree wears the same cobalt blue pants and matching jacket that Teddy and Catherine gave him two years ago. Kelly has a new perm and is wearing a burgundy *sườn xám*, a traditional Chinese cheongsam. The mandarin gown is made of velvet and has delicate white cherry blossoms running the length of her dress, from the high-collar neck down to her hemline at her ankle. The S-shaped design of the floral print forces admiring eyes to follow the curve of the female body. She looks magnificent.

She whispers in my ear, "I want to make a good first impression."

"You look stunning," I whisper back, feeling like a jungle monkey in my ugly sweater that has Philip Drummond's face on it.

Tonight's dinner party is perfect. Love and laughter fill the room, and peace fills my heart. Our conversation revolves around the new Vietnam Veterans Memorial Wall in Washington D.C. The black granite walls were brought in from India. The 144 panels list nearly 58,000 names of service members in the U.S. armed forces who fought and perished or are missing. I wonder if Sam Hammond's name is engraved on one of those slabs.

Jean-Adrien and Katrina present themselves as a new couple, smitten with one another once again. I wonder if Tý and I will ever feel that way about one another again. I catch Bill glancing in their direction every so often. If he feels jealous or forlorn, he hides it well. He is cordial to Jean-Adrien, and the two men keep the topic of their conversation light-hearted and high-level. Jean-Adrien shares with Bill that he used to work for John Graham & Company, the Seattle-based firm that designed Northgate, the Space Needle, and Southcenter Mall.

"What is mall?" I ask.

"What is a mall?" Magdaleine asks, flabbergasted. "It's a place to go shopping for clothes, shoes, and cosmetics. There are toys and gifts…just about everything you can imagine. I'll take you."

I ask Magdaleine to pass the salad dressing. While I have her brief attention, I inquire about the latest scandal on her favorite soap opera, *Dallas.*

Magdaleine's eyes light up. She shifts in her seat so that she can face me. "Okay, so they just aired episode ten. JR is getting married to Sue Ellen, again, and JR goes and does a mean-spirited thing. He invited Cliff to the wedding. Awkward! Sue Ellen and Cliff used to be a couple. Well, on the wedding day, Sue Ellen is walking down the aisle and sees Cliff, which is jarring, but what has my panties all in a bunch is the episode ends right in the middle of the wedding as Cliff stands up to protest the wedding. Oh, it is getting so good. You have to watch it."

"I will watch it," I say. "I watching *Dynasty* now and *Days of our Lives.*"

"It's nice to see you outside of work," Magdaleine says. "We never get a chance to do lunch because Bill keeps us all so busy, and you always scurry home after work. I understand why. Your daughter is quite a character. She's a rebel, that one. Do you know she tried to sell me fried rice? She said you were a good cook and that I could have a free sample tonight, and if I like it, I can buy more."

I laugh. "Me? A good cook?" To think my daughter is proud of me and boasts about my culinary skills makes me happy.

"She's endearing and hard to say no to," Magdaleine says. "Anyway, I'm so glad I'm here. I prefer the company of older, more mature people. My generation is boring, and they have nothing substantive to talk about."

"You and Bill dating?" I ask. It is an innocent question. Despite the big age difference, it is not out of the ordinary in my country for women to marry young, especially to older men who are established in their career and can provide for the family. My assumption, however, causes quite a reaction.

Magdaleine is quiet. Her face puckers like she just drank sour milk or ate a bug. She closes her eyes, bends forward, and covers her mouth. Her body shakes. She laughs hysterically and puts her hand on my knee. "Good God, Snow! You are a riot! No!"

"What's so funny?" Bill asks.

All conversation comes to a halt, and ten pairs of eyes turn to us. Magdaleine laughs so hard she chokes on her food and coughs.

Catherine clutches her pearl necklace. "Oh, dear."

Sky rises from his chair and rushes to Magdaleine. "Can you breathe?"

Magdaleine shakes her head. Sky steps behind her, bends her forward slightly, and wraps his arms around her waist. He makes a fist with one of his hands, grabs hold of it with his other hand, and repeatedly pushes into her abdomen inward and upward, thrusting her up and down, crushing her back against his chest. A crouton shoots out of her mouth. Biscuit quickly runs to claim his prize and licks up the cubed piece of dried bread.

Magdaleine gasps for air and seizes the back of her chair. She faces Skyler and thanks him. "Your Heimlich maneuver saved me."

"That's my son, the hero," Katrina says, "coming to the rescue." She applauds him, and we all join in clapping our hands.

Sky grins. "I feel like I need to give a speech now."

Jean-Adrien and Katrina chant, "Speech, speech!"

Sky takes his seat. "Instead of a speech, I've got a joke for you that my old buddy, Charlie Peters, used to tell. You're going to love this malapropism." He clears his throat, takes a sip of his wine, and begins. "Two rednecks are sitting at a bar. They see a woman choking at a nearby table. One of the rednecks springs to his feet. He spins the woman around, bends her forward, lifts up her skirt, pulls down her panties, and licks her bottom. The woman, shocked, spits out her food, slaps him, and storms off, humiliated. The other redneck says to his friend, 'Wow, that hind lick thing really works.'"

Teddy is the first to roar with laughter. I join in after Magdaleine explains the difference between hind-lick and Heimlich.

After dinner, we take our blueberry pie and ice cream downstairs to the second living room. Catherine explains the rules of the white elephant gift exchange. I tell them that in the Buddhist belief, white elephants are revered as good luck. The game becomes very competitive as we steal one another's prizes. Tree opens his wrapped gift from the center pile and shows his Fisher-Price Little People figures. Dolly steals them from Tree, Ocean steals them from Dolly, and I do the final steal from Ocean. Dolly bounces up and down with glee and hugs me so tightly I pretend to faint. Poor Tree ends up with a toilet seat as his take-home white elephant gift. There are great prizes tonight, and the most fought-over items are the Mickey Mouse and Pluto lunch box, a Lite-Brite game, and acid-washed button fly jeans. Dolly and I make a great team. She steals for me a Lionel Richie record, and although I do not own a turntable, I am determined to take the LP home with me. After all, it is Lionel on vinyl!

17. MY DATE (FEBRUARY 1983)

Christmas was a blur. Dolly and I were spoiled. We received a
record player and two albums: Michael Jackson's *Thriller* and Lionel
Richie's self-titled debut solo album. "You Are" is my favorite song
on the album and Dolly teases me when I try to sing along. Teddy
and Catherine got Dolly a beautiful Holy Bible, the New
International Version. It is a children's edition, engraved with her
name, Dolly Le, on the cover. The pages are filled with wonderful
pictures that bring the stories to life, and in the back are maps of
the exodus, world of the patriarchs, the empire of David and
Solomon, and travels of the apostles.

Her favorite, however, is the bicycle, blue with a banana
seat, training wheels, and a kickstand. She calls it the "mean
machine." It is a generous gift from Katrina and Jean-Adrien but
takes up a lot of space in her bedroom. It is also a burden to carry
the bike up and down the thirteen steps of our stairway.

Dolly also received roller skates that strap on to her running
shoes. She has been practicing all week rolling on the carpet and
using the walls to keep herself steady. Perhaps the most surprising
and most cherished gift, however, is the present from her father.

The package from Tý is wrapped in a brown paper bag, like
the one from the supermarket to hold our groceries. Dolly tears the
packaging tape away and rips open the brown paper. She can barely
contain her excitement since the package is addressed to her.

There is no letter from him. Oddly, it disappoints me that
he did not care to write or send me anything. I tell myself I do not
care and do not need anything from him.

"It's Connect Four and an Etch-A-Sketch!" she exclaims.
"And a picture of Daddy when he was a baby." She hands me the
photograph.

The picture is grainy and bent, warped from moisture. The baby is sitting on a red chair with a doll dressed in a yellow onesie. The black eyes in the photo staring back at me look like Tý, but it is not.

"This is you," I say, "when you were around nine months old at Ông Ngoại's house." Memories of Dolly's grandfather surface to the top of my memory bank. A fresh coat of sadness washes over me. I miss my parents deeply. Tý sent me a gift after all, a most priceless gift that I will take care to never lose. I wonder if he has any old photos of our life together. Did this photo stay close to his heart all these years? Does he have one of me?

I forgive my husband and commit to making peace with the past. We were young and thrown together during desperate times. Our arranged marriage was not unique, and our life together was brief. However, we had love between us for a time, and from our union came Thủy-Tiên. A new devotion and purpose blooms within me. To love again, I need to let compassion for him reside in my heart and allow forgiveness to dwell in my bones. I sit at the kitchen table and compose a letter to Tý.

Anh Tý,

Thủy-Tiên and I received your package. Your daughter loves her gifts. It warmed my heart seeing the photo of our daughter when she was a baby. She thought it was a picture of you. The resemblance is remarkable. You should be proud of how far our daughter has come and how brave she has been all these years. I do not know what I would have done if I had lost her…if we had lost her. I know she is your daughter too and of course, you should be in her life. We have already lost so much precious time. Forgive me. I have held onto this anger against you for so long but I am ready to let it go. In some ways, the wall I built around me has helped me survive and stay focused. I recognize now that the danger is over, that we are living a life of freedom, and the past is the past.

I stop to read my letter. My penmanship looks rushed, almost as if it is written in anger. My words slant forward, sometimes backward, and all the while, the letters are either round or jagged. He is going to think I wrote this letter while jostled on a tiny boat in the middle of an ocean storm. I am not sure how to sign the letter but decide on "your friend" in case his wife Annette sees the letter. I also do not want him to think there is a future for us.

If you would still like to be a part of our lives and want to visit again, you are welcome to come.

Your friend,
Tuyết

Dolly has been playful and endearing for the past few months. The holiday season was joyful, and now that it is February, we have the Lunar New Year to look forward to. This year is the year of the Water Pig and falls on Sunday, the thirteenth of February. I call Sky and ask if he is free this weekend to have dinner with Dolly and me to ring in the new year.

"Can I take a rain check?" he asks. "I have a date this weekend."

I cannot believe it. I am dying with curiosity to know who the woman is, how he met her, and where they are going. I tell him to give me all the details afterward. I ring my neighbor to see if she has plans for the new year, but Donald is taking Hùng and her to the San Juan Islands for the weekend. I sigh and summon my daughter into my bedroom. She runs out of the bathroom and jumps into my room. She startles me. Her face is painted with lipstick, blush, and eye shadow. Her fingernails have pink nail polish smeared on more than just her nails. From ten feet away, I can smell my new Gloria Vanderbilt perfume. She must have rolled in it because she is caked with the strong aromas of jasmine, pineapple, and cinnamon. My third grader is growing up.

"You look and smell delicious," I laugh. "Do you want to be my date this weekend? We can celebrate the lucky year of the pig, which represents good fortune and wealth."

Dolly agrees and asks if we can invite Bill from work and Mark Hartman, the new boy at school. "We can have a double date."

"No," I exclaim. "Bill is my boss, and you are too young to have a boyfriend."

She frowns and argues that she has a crush on Mark, but so does everyone else, and she wants to be his first friend. I learn he has blue eyes, thick brown hair, tan skin, and pretty teeth. Her friends at school, Nadirah and Jackie, have a bet to see who he will notice first, and Melissa recently dumped Hùng because she has her

416

eyes on him as well. I fear my little girl is growing up too fast, already noticing boys.

The workweek goes by quickly. To my surprise, Bill asks me over for a casual dinner, but I decline. "Sorry, Bill. I have date with my daughter. We go see *The Dark Crystal* and *Tootsie* movie at theater."

"Well, I don't suppose I can join you?" Bill asks.

It is hard to say no twice, so I agree. This upsets Dolly. She feels I betrayed her. I plead my case, saying it is not a date and bribe her with cotton candy, popcorn, and 7-Up. She agrees to the terms.

Dolly and I pull into the parking lot of the Cinerama in Seattle. It is raining cotton balls so light I mistake it for snow. Bill waves to us. He wears a black trench coat and fedora, making him look mysterious and dangerous but also dapper.

The Cinerama is a flurry of activity tonight. Teenagers huddle in groups, animatedly talking about school, sports, or the latest gossip. Their attention span is short, and they are easily distracted with people-watching. They googly-eye every person walking through the door as if they are expecting someone they know.

Bill is vigilant and leads us to the shortest line. "This one is moving fast." We fight over who is paying, but Bill's English is more succinct and authoritative than mine. The girl behind the register accepts Bill's cash. I thank him and insist on treating him next time. Dolly suggests I treat us to ice cream next time.

The movie is not what I expect it to be. While it is a children's movie, I find it dark and eerie. At times, it is scary with creepy characters. However, Dolly is engrossed and seems to enjoy it.

"I love scary movies," Dolly whispers. "I want to watch more."

When the credits roll and the lights come on, the three of us make our way to the lobby. Dolly yawns but insists she is not tired and is ready for the next movie. She is excited to do a doubleheader and stay up late.

After sitting for nearly two hours, we go outside for a breath of fresh air and stretch our legs. Once outside, however, the howling wind scares us back inside. It is a chilly forty-three degrees, too cold to stand outside. Instantly, I am awake and feel more alert than after having six cups of coffee.

While we wait for *Tootsie* to start, Bill opens up about life after Katrina. He had trysts with many women and two serious relationships that lasted three years each. He married one of them but admits it was a mistake. He never had children with any of his past relationships. He poured his devotion and energy into his work, and when he got the job at the *Seattle Times* as their executive director of marketing, he let his foot off the accelerator and has been coasting through life since.

"Even if Katrina and I had worked out and we had gotten married," Bill wonders, "would our marriage have lasted?"

"Why not?" I ask. "I think you find way."

"I was a workhorse, driven to climb the career ladder, and if Katrina and I married, my aspirations would eventually drive a wedge between us. I guess we will never really know." Bill rests his hand gently on mine. He looks at me tenderly like a loving father might on his daughter's wedding day. "The next time love comes, seize it, and make it work. Life is too short to be alone."

I rolodex through my past relationships, remembering how Sam, Hải, and Tý made me feel. I am indeed alone now, but am I lonely? Dolly keeps me busy. My community keeps me entertained. I have been broken-hearted enough times to believe I will be fine without another man in my life. Learning to cook and sew keeps me fulfilled, and my job is wonderful. I believe the year of the pig will bring me good fortune, and if a life partner is part of that, then I will be ready to receive it.

Soon after the second movie starts, Dolly falls asleep in her chair. Bill and I enjoy our movie, and before long, it is time to say goodbye. We hug and go our separate ways. While driving home, I think about Bill and wonder what his lips feel like and if he has chest hair. I quickly dismiss my thoughts. One thing at a time. I need to resolve my feelings for Dolly's father first and determine if there can be a future for Tý and me.

###

The following Sunday after church, Dolly enjoys a playdate with Ocean, Olivia, and Opal while I make my way to Southcenter Mall in Tukwila to meet Magdaleine. I park in one of the 7,200 stalls and hope I can find my little silver Civic later.

The 1.1-million-square-feet shopping center, with its 110 retail spaces, is the largest in the state and second biggest in the country, trailing second to Ala Moana Center in Honolulu, Hawaii. Inside the mall, the shiny terrazzo flooring gives the building a castle presence. A large chandelier, twenty-four feet in circumference, emits a warm amber light that reflects off six hundred bent and polished brass reflectors hanging from brass strings. I feel I have stepped into the house of nobility.

It is a bustle of activity with shoppers moseying in and out of stores. I stop briefly to admire the jewels at Ben Bridge Jewelers before making my way to Nordstrom. Magdaleine waves me to the perfume counter. She exposes her wrist so I can smell it.

"It smell funny," I say, "like spicy dirt."

Magdaleine laughs. "It's a men's cologne. Wait." She flags down a man in his late thirties or early forties and asks if he'd be her guinea pig. She spritzes a sample of the cologne on his neck and leans in for a whiff. "Now, you smell it, Snow."

"Oh, I cannot," I say. "That okay." Putting my nose next to the stranger's neck is rather bold and taboo. I would feel like I fondled him in public. However, the man gives me his permission and Magdaleine goads me to be wild and free. The salesman behind the counter winks and joins in on the coercion. I cave in and take a quick sniff. Lavender. Berries. Sandalwood. Citrus. I smile and give a thumbs up.

Magdaleine claps her hands. "Ding, ding, ding. We have a winner. I'll take it." The salesman rings up the bottle of Drakkar Noir. "I had the most wonderful date last weekend." She leads me to a bench outside the store entrance. "I know we're moving fast, but I feel I know him so well. He's thirteen years older than me, but that's what I like. He's mature and kind and, well, he's my hero." She pauses from boasting about her new love interest and looks at me playfully. "Any guesses?"

"Sky?" I ask.

She grins and nods. A strange sensation overcomes me. My stomach churns like it is in the spin cycle. I shake that brooding feeling that I have lost my friend Sky forever. I remind myself this is Magdaleine, my beautiful, smart, and kind friend. Of course, Sky and she deserve happiness together. She retells how after the holiday party, Sky called to check on her, even though he knew full well she was free and clear from the choking catastrophe. It was sweet, she says, and the two of them met up for coffee, which later turned to dinner, and finally led to buying a dog.

"You buy dog together?" I ask, surprised, and thinking they truly are progressing quickly.

Magdaleine clarifies that he helped her pick one at the pound. Her apartment was broken into last month, and Sky suggested a dog could keep her company and make her feel safer. The animal shelter was waiving adoption fees for the holidays through the end of January. It did not take long before she fell in love with Tank, a four-year-old, blue-nose Staffordshire Bull Terrier. The dog was jumping up and down when they approached his cell and tried to climb the chain-link gate. His eyes and smile hooked her, and his alert, perky ears won Sky over.

"I think maybe I go to shelter too for Dolly pet, but she have to wait ten months before Christmas come again," I say.

"You will have to come over," Magdaleine says. "We can watch *Dallas*, eat take-out, and you can meet Tank. He's a lovey and such a goofy dog!"

Feeling like kindred spirits, I keep our rapport dancing along by sharing with Magdaleine my story of going to the movies with Bill. I am quick to let her know it was a friendly outing between two business associates and that Dolly was present.

I enjoy my time with Magdaleine. Although I am twenty years older than she is, my youthful outlook on American life and her mature perspective on everything American helps us meet in the middle. We spend a couple of hours shopping—I mostly window shop—and then carpool to downtown Seattle to the Pike Place Market.

Magdaleine finds a lucky parking spot on First Avenue and Stewart Street. It is sunny today and comfortably fifty-one degrees. I have my scarf, gloves, and a knit cap to keep me warm, and with the sunshine on my face, I feel alive and in good spirits. I have never been to this open-air market before in downtown Seattle. What an amazing spectacle; it reminds me of the outdoor markets back in Việt Nam with people darting in and out of shops, selecting fresh fish, fruits, or vegetables to take home. A mix of ethnicities— Italians, Russians, Asians, Latinos—roam about all speaking their native tongues. I am delighted to see such diversity among the populace in this tiny corner of Seattle. Most of them are tourists, but even the locals appear lively and happy. Like me, they admire the fresh flowers for sale or the tantalizing bakery items on display. I decide that one day, I will live near Pike Place Market so I can be down here every day.

Beyond the market is the waterfront and view of Elliott Bay. There is a park nearby where families and lovers picnic; they enjoy the distant views of the Olympic National Forest, ferries, and Mount Rainier. A musician stands at a corner playing his guitar while a passerby drops money into his case. Magdaleine and I linger to listen to him sing and admire his talent. We each drop a dollar into his case before stepping into Starbucks Coffee to buy a pound of ground French pressed coffee.

"You are great tour guide," I say to Magdaleine, who is beaming with joy. "I love it here."

She whisks me to the Pike Place Fish Market. "You're going to love this, Snow." At the fish market, I watch fishmongers yell and throw fish to one another, quickly wrapping it before ringing up the purchase for the customer. I notice a sign that reads "Caution: Low Flying Fish" behind one of the fishmongers. Just then, a fish comes flying at me and hits me in the shoulder. Startled, I jump back.

Magdaleine laughs. "Not to worry. It's a foam fish." She whispers something in the salesman's ear and points to an albacore tuna resting on ice. She grabs my hand and pulls me toward Eric, our fishmonger. With a mischievous twinkle in his eyes, he drapes an apron around my neck and hands me a pair of latex gloves. Magdaleine shimmies a shower cap over my head, but it slips down over my eyes. They both have a good laugh at the folly. My protests and state of confusion go unnoticed and unanswered.

Eric grabs the tuna and yells, "Flying albacore tuna to the lady in purple." The two other fishermen repeat in unison. Eric launches the torpedo-looking fish at me. I have no time to think, just react, and to my surprise, it slips through my fingers. I catch it a foot from the ground. Everyone cheers. A rush of pride washes over me. Magdaleine buys the fish and has it divided in half for us both to take home.

"Eric," Magdaleine says, "please be a doll and keep this chilled for us. We are going to grab some food and drinks and be back to get our prize before you close." She gives him her name, phone number, and a flirtatious smile. "C'mon," she says to me.

We walk through Post Alley and stop in front of a pink door with no name, number, or address posted—no signage whatsoever to indicate if it is a residence or a business. She turns the knob, pushes the door in, and steps onto a small landing. I follow her down the stairs to a slightly musty restaurant, where the aromas of wine-soaked corks and cheeses tickle the senses.

"This is a small hidden gem," Magdaleine says. "You will find that Seattle has many of them. The restaurant is run by word of mouth. They do not run advertisements. A lot of Europeans dine here. I hope you like Italian food. I went on a date here once with a gorgeous Italian soccer player. The sex was yummy, but he was so shallow. Anyway, it's an intimate space, as you can see. I think the maximum capacity is like thirty or something."

The dining section is dimly lit, romantic if you are with someone you are enamored with…and I am quite enamored with Magdaleine. She is an enigma to me. Her femininity makes men fall at her feet and women clamor to learn from her. She is intelligent, kind, funny, and savvy, without the pretentiousness of most young adults trying to prove themselves to the world. I enjoy her company and stories very much and laugh at how she fawns over the show *Dallas*. In two hours, I learn a little about Seattle's history, about the Great Seattle Fire, and how the city was built on top of itself. I learn about the ghost tours and underground tours where we can see the old city below. Most mind-boggling are the stories of prohibition and how speakeasies came to fruition. She shares the secrets of Tavern Law, a small saloon in the Pioneer Inn, where behind a bank vault door is a private bar that seats twelve people. A phone will ring by the vault door, and if you know the password of the hour, you are admitted inside.

"You're escorted up a narrow staircase in the dark," Magdaleine says. "There is just enough light at the top for you to see the black and white portraits of nude models hanging on the wall. All tasteful pictures. There's soft lounge seating in one section and a few tables and chairs in another section. There's no drink menu. You tell the bartender what flavors and notes you like, and he'll design a drink for you."

"Magdaleine," I say, "this best date I be on!"

We leave the Pink Door in time to catch the sunset and retrieve our tuna from Eric as he packs up for the night. It has been a perfect day.

I pull into Pastor George's driveway to pick up Dolly and sense something is wrong. The lights are out, including the porch light. The windows are open. How strange, on a chilly February night, to have the windows ajar. I hear the girls scream and Pastor George laughing.

I do not think to knock or ring the doorbell. I burst into Pastor George's house and follow the sound of sinister laughter and a deep gurgling voice. Pastor George stands in front of the four girls, all huddled together with Dawn on the sofa, baring his teeth and curling his fingers above his head. He growls and lunges at them. I find the light switch and flick it on. All eyes turn to me. Dawn inhales deeply and clutches the children closer to her bosom.

Pastor George gasps. I step forward, ready to charge at him over the couch and beat him with my purse.

"Snow!" Pastor George exclaims. "You scared the nutsack right off my—" He stops abruptly and laughs.

Dawn looks embarrassed. "You gave us a good fright."

Dolly jumps out of Dawn's arms and runs to me. "Mama, I had so much fun. Can I sleepover? Please?"

"Another day," I say and watch the enthusiasm wax and wane from her face. "It is Sunday."

I have Dolly collect her belongings while Dawn gives me a recap of their day. They had fellowship and lunch at the church, then went to the video store down the street to rent a movie. The girls picked *Poltergeist*. They played at the house, baked cookies, and ate dinner before settling down for the movie. I had walked in as the movie ended to witness Pastor George capitalizing on their fear and relishing the moment.

18. A WEDDING TO PLAN (AUGUST 1983)

I put my cup of coffee down and snatch Dolly's spoon to use as a microphone. Lionel Richie is singing to me on the radio, and I serenade him back.

"You are you so," I sing, "you need not know, I love you so."

Dolly giggles.

My neighbor barges into my apartment and calls out my name. "Chị Tuyết ơi." She finds us at the table enjoying our brunch of canned sardines and rice, our staple diet back at the refugee camp.

Diệp crinkles her nose. "How can you eat that?"

"It is cheap and familiar," I say. "At least it is not dog food."

"Not that again," she says and laughs. Diệp sits down. "I have a dilemma…oh, oh…" She points to the radio. "Turn it up."

Dolly rushes to the stereo and cranks up the volume. The song "Puttin' on the Ritz" by Taco is airing on KUBE 93 FM. Diệp jumps to her feet and thrusts her hips side to side to the beat, looking like a broken robot short-circuiting. She reminds me of the robot Twiki from the show *Buck Rogers*. Diệp takes the spoon and sings into it. "If yoo is bloo, dunt no waa to go to, wai dunt yoo go, fa shoon seets… Pooty on da Rex." I sneak a peek at Dolly. She glances back at me. We exchange a smile and try to contain our laughter. "Diff'rent tips gorillas go pantz—"

I burst at the seams and cackle like an evil witch. I beg her to stop singing and dancing before she breaks something. She feigns sadness but perks up when I compliment her on learning English. "Has Donald been teaching you?"

She nods. "Donald's son, Ricky, is transferring from Washingon State to the University of Washington this September. His son is coming home for the summer, and Donald wants me to spend time with them so I can get to know Ricky. He wants me to go with them, too, when Ricky moves into his dormitory. Our relationship is getting serious."

"What is the dilemma then?" I ask.

"What if Ricky does not like me?" Diệp asks. "What if I cannot relate to him? What if he does not want me to help him settle into his new college?"

"Talk to Jason," Dolly says. "Ricky and Jason are best friends."

"That is a great idea," I say. "They are so close. Little Jason can tell you all about Ricky and offer suggestions. Honestly, though, Ricky seems like a sweet boy."

"If I pass this test," Diệp mutters, "maybe he will ask me to marry him."

"Is that what you want?" I ask.

"Yes, I am sure of it. He is the kindest man."

"Then he is not testing you," I say, "so stop thinking it is something you have to pass. Be yourself. Donald and Jason love you. Ricky will too. And if Hùng can accept Donald as a father and his kids as brothers, then you will be a family."

###

A week goes by. I have not spoken to Diệp but have seen her from afar getting in or out of Donald's car with both Ricky and Jason two steps behind. I suspect it will not be long before they marry. They are an odd couple but complement each other nicely, with her so quirky and him so patient, and she so animated while he subdued and conservative.

The phone rings. It is Tree on the line. "Aunt Eight…Ngọc is pregnant."

I panic. They are too young to start a family. "I hoped you would have a longer engagement. How do her parents feel about it?" I ask.

"Upset. Nervous. Excited."

Tree and I are at a loss for words and do not know what to say next. An asteroid of silence separates us. I am not sure what he expects or hopes to hear from me. Does he want advice or my blessing? Is he expecting me to get angry and yell at him? Perhaps he hopes I will help with the wedding and the baby expenses.

"I need to speak to her parents," I say. "Arrange for me to come. You make the introduction."

The next day, I drive with Dolly across the West Seattle Bridge and follow Tree's directions to the house. Dolly is my navigator and reads the directions from the notes I jotted down. At the end of the bridge, turn left onto Thirty-Fifth Avenue Southwest, then right at Southwest Graham Street.

Dolly points to the yellow house on the right. "That one."

The house is painted in a muted yellow with white trim. Two old chairs, pots filled with lush green weeds, and brown, dried-up flowers clutter the small porch. The front is partially fenced with white picket posts, stained green from moss and mildew. A big pile of fresh dog dung greets us at the threshold between the sidewalk and the lawn, overgrown with yellow foxtail grass and bright dandelions.

"Gross," Dolly says and steps around the pile of poop.

I look at the windows, half expecting to see a face staring out, spying on me. Instead, I see only two single-paned windows, one with a crack in it, and the other covered by bent and skewed blinds. The front yard is littered with car parts, a deflated basketball, one soiled sock, and a mess of glass and aluminum cans. I shudder and wonder what kind of people Kelly's parents are, but remind myself they raised a sweet daughter. After all, they were farmers on Phú Quốc and worked hard to survive, even if it meant they had to sell their youngest daughter to a childless couple. I respect honest people, hard-working people…survivors. At least they have a house, unlike me, sharing an apartment with hundreds of roaches.

I raise my hand to knock on the door when suddenly it swings open and a small woman with a round face and high-pitched, nasally voice greets me. She wears an *áo bà ba*, a traditional short shirt with long sleeves and buttons from the neck down to the stomach. The olive shirt is paired with black silk trousers. At once I am transported back to the countryside of Việt Nam, to the rice paddies and farmland of Vĩnh Bình.

"Sister Tuyết," Kelly's mother, Lan, says, ten decibels too loudly. "Come in." She ushers me inside and pats Dolly's head. "What a pretty girl you are." I realize this is her normal indoor voice. She is not shouting. If she and the laundromat had a humming competition, she would win. Perhaps she is hard of hearing.

"Thank you for having me over on short notice," I say softly.

"It is ridiculous that the kids have been dating for a year and we are only now meeting," she says. No, not hard of hearing—just a loud talker. Lan scurries down the hallway like a mouse on a mission to find cheese. "Ngọc's father will be home soon. I sent him to get coconut water for us." She steps over a shirt lying on the floor like it is a speck of dirt not worth noticing. I look around the room. They are Buddhist. There is a veneration table with eight pictures on the wall and a large handful of burnt, ashy incense sticks jammed into a tiny container of gray rice kernels. I assume they are pictures of parents and grandparents on both sides of the family. A large statue of Buddha and Lady Buddha sits prominently above the ancestral altar.

"Where are Ngọc and Tree?" I ask, admiring the pickled jalapenos, leeks, mustard greens, daikon, and carrots on her kitchen counter.

The front door creaks open. I hear six distinct voices down the hallway…four men and two women. Dolly runs out to the backyard and hops onto a rusty swing. It is fully fenced in the back, so I am not too worried she is out there by herself. A little Pomeranian trots out to greet Dolly but stops to eat a dry nugget of poop. I look away.

A parade of bodies filters into the room led by Tree. The only person I recognize is Kelly. Tree introduces me to Kelly's father, Toàn. He bows respectfully deep to me, bending at the waist and almost parallel to the floor. "Welcome to our home. Please sit and relax. Let me pour some coconut water for you."

Kelly's younger sister, Ann, greets me with the honorific title of Aunt Eight. "Cháo Cô Tám." She is a prettier, younger version of her sister but is not blessed with a straight and high-bridged nose; it rounds out wide at the bottom and reminds me of a pig's snout, albeit a cute one. Her boyfriend, Quang, does not greet me. He merely acknowledges my presence by looking at me and nodding, not in a respectful way but in an arrogant fashion. Ann walks into the kitchen to help her father, Toàn, bring out the iced coconut waters while Quang makes himself comfortable on a chair. He lights a cigarette and inhales deeply the Marlboro Reds. I can tell Ann is demurring and subservient in how she casts her eyes down, moves quietly, and looks for praise upon serving our drinks. Ann is like her father whereas Kelly is like her mother in terms of confidence, ease, and social skills.

I turn to the stranger behind Tree. He is the last to be introduced. Tree pulls a chair out, and the stranger sits down. He smiles at me. I smile back. He is attractive, although his top lip is thin and I have a superstition about people with thin lips—they are terrible kissers and not to be trusted. I quickly dismiss this delusional notion because I find him to be a good-looking Vietnamese man. His hair is thick and slicked back. He sits with a straight posture and clasps his hands comfortably on the table. Still, he says nothing, as if he is taking me in, bit by bit, just as I am dissecting him with my gaze, piece by piece. His polo shirt is clean and his pants wrinkle-free. He smells masculine, clean, and made of money. Who are you?

"Aunt Eight," Tree says, "this is Uncle Bình, the one I have been living with." Yes, of course, the man whose wife left him. I remember now. The man who plays soccer on the fields with men half his age. The man who lives in a house near Southcenter Mall and is friends with Lan.

Lan sits across from me and blurts out, "My daughter is pregnant." She states what we already know and the reason why we are together today for the first time. "Of course, we need to move up the wedding date. It needs to be this month."

Out of the corner of my eye, I see Quang roll his eyes and exhale with exaggeration. What is his problem? No one in the room speaks up. The men are unusually quiet. I gather this will be a conversation between Lan and me. That is a first—women doing all the talking and decision-making. Back home, I was used to the men making arrangements and managing everything.

"I am sure Pastor George can marry them in the church," I say.

"No, we are Buddhists, not Christians," Lan says. She is adamant that there not be a church wedding and we need a traditional Vietnamese wedding. I understand her point of view, but with short notice and limited resources, not to mention we do not know many people here, it would not be feasible to have a traditional one. Whomever we invite will likely gift the couple household items instead of money in red envelopes, and what good would that do them when they do not even have a house of their own? I argue there is no time, no temple, and no seamstress who can make an *áo nhật bình*, the elaborate and intricate wedding gown of our people.

Lan takes my argument under advisement. "We will have to do a hybrid wedding then, but we must seek counsel from a monk to determine the best date to marry based on their horoscope."

"Or a fortuneteller," I say. "Do you know any?

Tree interrupts us and questions which birth date we plan to use when we seek advice from the fortuneteller. That is a good question as it is important to be accurate.

"Your real birthday, of course," I say. "December 16, 1962, not '65."

At this juncture, Bình speaks up. "I know a fortuneteller and a seamstress, and if the kids do not get married in a church or a temple, why not a botanical garden?"

A man with ideas, connections, and solutions…My interest in this stranger and my curiosity over him spike. Lan and I fold him into our conversation and listen to what he has to say, giving him stock in our wedding planning venture but making it clear we have the final decision-making power.

Bình advises we must move quickly and be willing to pay extra to motivate the seamstress. We agree that he will arrange a meeting with the fortuneteller as soon as possible so that a wedding date can be pinpointed. I ask him to schedule a reading for me and Thủy-Tiên as well. We will get Kelly and Tree in with the seamstress as soon as possible to get measurements and pick out fabric. Lan and Toàn will plan the menu, Ann and Quang will find a venue, namely a park, and I will ask Pastor George to perform the ceremony. Tree and Kelly will manage flowers and the remaining details. Dolly, of course, will be the flower girl, as is customary in a Western wedding.

I leave the house excited for the wedding, where East meets West and the union of two souls will soon be witnessed. In eight months, Tree and Kelly's baby will be born and we will welcome the second generation of Vietnamese boat people. We will have a footprint in American civilization. It makes me happy knowing a legacy will be left from my generation's sacrifices. So begins the fusion of two souls, two families, and two cultures.

19. THE FORTUNETELLER (AUGUST 1983)

Tree, Kelly, and Bình are the first to arrive at the fortuneteller's home, immediately followed by Toàn and Lan. Dolly and I arrive twenty minutes late as I took a wrong turn, having never been to Federal Way before. I underestimated the time it would take to get here from Kent with I-5 traffic.

I pull into the government-subsidized trailer park for low-income immigrants and locate the mobile home that is rented out to Hồng Nhung, our fortuneteller. Many residents are outside tending to their tiny plots of land, pulling weeds, watering plants, putting down gravel, or lounging on the front porch. Everyone's face is brown, goldenrod, or cocoa…a rainbow of refugees. They all take great pride in their homes as the roads are clear from litter and junk and the homes immaculately landscaped and gardened. It must be nice not to have neighbors right next to you, sharing the same wall. I hope to upgrade to a mobile home of my own one day and start a flower and vegetable or herb garden.

Inside the single-wide home, the blinds are closed. Hồng Nhung limps to the big window with her walking stick and draws the extra curtains to block out sunlight. "We do not need any distractions or voyeurs."

She shares with us that she is sixty years old and that her cane was a gift of war. An explosion in her village left stubborn shrapnel in her thigh and she has learned to coexist with it the past ten years. Like most fortunetellers I have met, she is calm and patient, an oracle of wisdom and truth to those who believe.

"Spring arrived unexpectedly this year," Hồng Nhung says matter-of-factly. "My tulips noticed, but my daffodils are still hibernating." She invites Tree and Kelly to sit down at a small table with her. She takes Tree's hand and looks at his palm. "You were born on Sunday, December 16, 1962. A water tiger. Were you born at night or in the morning?"

"Morning," Tree says, "although I do not know what time." Tree looks to me, hoping I can provide the answer, but I do not recall the exact time.

Hồng Nhung studies the lines of his palm. "Your tiger sign shows that you are brave and take risks. You are smart, too, but street smart, not business smart. You are also the black sheep and will have many challenges ahead of you. Music will center you so you can make good decisions." She continues to tell him he is a born leader, a competitor, and not afraid to fight or overcome obstacles. He must be careful because he lives dangerously.

Our sage next reviews Kelly's hand but then takes out a deck of cards. She confesses to being self-taught but was a highly sought after practitioner of cartomancy back in Việt Nam because of her accuracy. Many who contemplated escaping the country by boat sought her advice, and if she predicted they'd make it, then they would go. If she said they'd get caught, sure as war and famine, they got caught. Even after the communist government banned readings, she had many Việt Cộng men come to her because they could not resist in times of uncertainty. After all, it is part of our heritage and custom. It is in our DNA and will forever be a part of our culture. They never arrested her because she dove deep into their fears and superstitions.

She asks Kelly to shuffle the cards and think about what she wants to know. She then lays out four columns of cards, each column with seven cards from the deck. She consults the cards quietly to herself before saying, "You two are quite compatible." This declaration makes Tree and Kelly look at each other lovingly and smile. "I see a lasting marriage and two, maybe three children. One of your children, the second one, may not live. Her life will be up to you."

"What do you mean?" Kelly asks.

Our spiritual counselor raises her hand to dismiss the question and continues. "You two will have many homes in different states. I suggest you see a geomancer when buying a house to ensure the chi flows positively. Any miscalculations will result in a life of suffering for you and the next three generations."

Kelly's eye twitches, and she shifts in her chair. "Suffering how?"

Again, our prophesier ignores her. Ultimately, our advisor tells them Thursday, August 25, is the best date for the wedding according to their astrological charts and zodiac signs.

We take a break following the readings with tea and coconut butter biscuits. To my surprise, Bình takes the lead and orchestrates who does what, by when, and how. He appoints himself as the wedding coordinator. Depending on which lens I have on, he can either be a charismatic, confident man who is marriage material or an attractive gay man who has done a great job hiding his true identity. Either way, I want to know him better and figure out how he identifies himself. At least he is beautiful to look at.

When it is my and Dolly's turn to have our fortunes read, I send everyone out and encourage them to go home. "This is a private matter, and whatever I learn, it will be my burden to bear."

They all protest except for Toàn, who is the ultimate introvert and happy to excuse himself from this nonsense. I bid them farewell and promise to give them a status update on Pastor George's availability on August 25.

After everyone leaves, my foreseer asks, "Who do you want me to read first?"

I decide on Dolly. I give Hồng Nhung Dolly's birth name, Lê Ngọc Thủy-Tiên, her birth date, and the time she was born. "Tuesday, July 30, 1974, at 11:53 p.m."

"Wood tiger," she says. "They like to be in charge. They are courageous and popular. Because she was born close to midnight, this makes her cunning. She will be successful, perhaps even famous and rich. Your daughter is charming and impulsive. She will have many admirers. She will need to lead a pious life or be thwarted into a life of instability. If she marries after age thirty-two, she will have a stable marriage. Her husband will love her very much, but if she marries before that, she will suffer greatly." Hồng Nhung pauses and frowns. "Your daughter was very sick." She points to the line of life on Dolly's hand. "See here how her lifeline starts out jagged, not deep and straight? But she grows stronger every day, so do not worry. She will live a long life and be lucky and prosperous." She frowns again. This is disconcerting. "I see Thủy-Tiên may have two husbands, three pregnancies, but only one birth." My look of alarm makes her quickly foretell the next thing she sees. "Tiger girls have strong personalities, but as mothers, they are very protective. You will have an important role as grandmother to provide a solid foundation for your grandchild."

The idea of being a grandma one day makes me happy. I hope Dolly will have a son to break the cycle of suffering women in my family inherited. Boys are more revered, more respected, and tend to have more freedom. I wish that for my grandson. Hồng Nhung finishes the reading and says to come back in a few years so she can read my daughter's chart again. I take a deep breath and give her my hand as it is now my turn, but she does not take it. Instead, I am asked to shuffle the deck of cards and think about what questions I want her to answer. I think about my family and whether they will be all right. I wonder about Tý and Hải and whether they will be in my life again. Finally, I wonder if I will find love again.

Hồng Nhung turns over the cards and arranges them in four columns. She hovers her hand over them and touches a few of them. She nods, umm-hmms and ahh-hahs several times before looking at me. "You said you were born on a Thursday?"

"Yes," I answer, "on April 13, 1939."

"The Earth Rabbit then," she says, "or Earth Cat depending on if you prefer the Vietnamese zodiac over the Chinese one."

I recall a conversation I had once with Dolly's father, who was born the year of the rat. Tý teased that it was me who chased him and was smitten with him first. "You are a cat," he had said, "and I am a mouse. Of course, you chased after me."

I told him if that were the case, I would have killed my mouse, not married it. I also clarified that he was a rotten street rat, not a cute mouse. He feigned being hurt and coaxed me into kissing him until he felt better. We made love that day and a part of him stayed with me. Eight months later, our daughter was born, prematurely with one hand clinging to life and the other to death.

I ask Hồng Nhung if identifying with a cat or a rabbit makes a difference in my reading. She says, "Not really," so I let her read my fortune at her discretion. She tells me my traits, for example, my thirst for knowledge and how I enjoy school more than work. She says I am an accepting person and do not like to argue. These are characteristics, perhaps flaws, I am acutely aware of.

"Because you are easy-going and do not quarrel or challenge others, many see you as timid. However, you have strong desires, and when you latch onto something, you will prove others wrong and contradict their beliefs." I ask her if I will love again. "You have many admirers and many lives. You have escaped death multiple times. I see two husbands in this lifetime, but as beautiful and kind as you are, you are very unlucky in love." She continues to tell me that my daughter and I will not live together, and we will not only be divided with our life choices but separated by state lines. She tells me to avoid a lot of travel as there will be complications. Additionally, while I will live to be an old woman, heaven will claim me shortly after I return from a trip.

I ask her if I will return to Việt Nam one day and if my family will be all right. She says yes to both. "Will I see Tý and Hải again?"

"Your husband will be in your life again," she says, "but his brother will not. You must forget him."

Hearing that saddens me. It can only mean Hải did not survive the re-education camps and will never come home. I did not tell her Hải and I became lovers after the war, but I did not need to. Hồng Nhung already knows and is legitimately the best fortuneteller I have ever met.

At the end of our session, I pay her and leave, feeling lighter and optimistic about the future, yet sad for Hải.

20. I DO (AUGUST 1983)

Chagrined by Ann and Quang's failure to find an affordable venue or a public park that could host a small wedding on short notice and specifically, on Thursday, August 25, I ask Sky if his parents would mind hosting the wedding on their property. Fortunately, the Herringtons come to the rescue and are delighted. As a matter of fact, Katrina and Jean-Adrien insist on it, which is a good thing, because I question whether Ann and Quang even tried to find a suitable locale. Both of them have been in foul moods leading up to the wedding day, see-sawing between hot-tempered arguments that flare up out of the blue to cold, uncomfortable silent treatments with stares that could turn Medusa and her Gorgon sisters into stone.

"I haven't been this excited since the Enumclaw auction when that stud of a cowboy, Judd, sold me Blazing Six Guns!" Katrina exclaims. She immediately takes action and prepares the property for the big day, making endless phone calls to a vast network of friends and associates. She takes the liberty of renting tents, tables, and chairs, purchasing party favors, and securing a live band. No detail is overlooked. She even orders fans and water misting stations to keep guests cool. I tell her it is too much and a simple ceremony will do. We plan to do a potluck reception afterward to keep things casual, but Katrina would not hear of it.

"This is our gift to Tree and Nop…er, Kelly," Katrina proclaims. "We are family."

The day finally arrives, and it is a clear day with nothing but powder blue skies. All morning, the house buzzes as Katrina, the caterers, Lan, Bình, and I finalize the little details. An hour before the guests arrive, we stand in the backyard to admire our work.

Folding chairs stand firm near the barn, split equally with twenty-five chairs on either side of the fifty-foot red-carpeted aisle.

White clusters of gardenias from Katrina's greenhouse adorn the first chair of each aisle on either side of the red carpet. At the front, a hedge of purple hydrangeas grows naturally and forms the perfect backdrop.

Between the stables and riding pen, a five-member band tunes their instruments to rehearse the first set in front of five empty banquet tables. Each table seats ten and is dressed in white linen with lavender centerpieces. The fenced, round pen has been transformed into a dance floor, and all around are white lights strung along poles to illuminate the area. Hitched in front of the stable are Katrina's two horses, Blazing Six Guns, the quarter horse she impulsively bought at the auction from Cowboy Judd, and a beautiful palomino named J'adore Champagne. Both beauties are hooked up to a carriage where guests can get their photos taken under the romantic sunset haze of summer sky. After the reception, J'adore Champagne and Blazing Six Guns will take the bride and groom around the nearby trails to a private yurt on the Herrington property. All these years, I never knew there was a small cabin, and Sky promises to show me sometime.

What was supposed to be an intimate affair with twenty people has now ballooned to fifty guests. It is still considered a small wedding, but I realize I do not know half the people coming.

Teddy and Catherine's daughters traveled in with their families yesterday from Oregon and Wenatchee. Tree invited our VOLAG representative, Joseph, who RSVP'd for two people and is bringing his wife. Sky and Magdaleine invited Bill, who surprised us all by saying he was bringing a date…a woman he met in May when the *Post-Intelligencer* and the *Times* entered into a joint operating agreement.

When I told Diệp about the pending nuptials two weeks ago, she invited herself, saying of course she will come and bring Donald and the boys. "I love weddings. Maybe Donald will get the hint."

All in all, between our guests and those on Kelly's side, there will be plenty of witnesses to celebrate the union of two people in love.

At last, we take our seats and wait for the bride entrance song to play. In front, Tree stands with Pastor George. Both men look handsome, Tree in his tuxedo and Pastor George in this linen suit. Tree gives a confident smile for the photographer but reverts to a nervous groom the moment the shutter closes. The band cues up the melody for "Here Comes the Sun" by the Beatles. All eyes turn to the back.

The back door of the house opens, and Dolly presents herself in a yellow A-line dress that Catherine worked tirelessly to sew, using the satin and tulle fabric she had on hand. My daughter walks hurriedly toward the front, tossing handfuls of white petals onto the red-carpeted aisle, no doubt nervous with all the faces focusing on her. A few people giggle, but I beam with pride.

I turn back and hold my breath for Kelly. I know what her red *áo nhật bình* looks like but have not seen the entire ensemble on her. She steps out, and we all stand. The wedding dress is made of red satin with intricately embroidered phoenix designs on the front. A gold robe drapes around her hourglass figure; the hems of her sleeves have five bands of colors, each representing the five elements of our culture: earth, metal, water, wood, and fire. Completing the outfit is a royal purple turban that frames her oval face. She is breathtaking.

Before Kelly reaches the front of the aisle to stand with Tree, Diệp bawls loudly and blows her nose into a handkerchief. Her cries become the catalyst for more tears as Lan wails with her. I stifle my outbreak and wipe the wetness from my eyes. Oh, Brother Seven, Sister Hiền, if you could see your son now.

Kelly hands her bouquet of hydrangeas to Dolly and takes her place next to Tree. The two join hands.

Pastor George invites everyone to sit. "Friends and family, today is a blessing that has been bestowed upon us. When two people find each other, as Tree and Kelly have, and love one another, we must commit to support this union and help them with their journey. When two become one…when the halves become whole…we all become family."

The ceremony goes by quickly. Pastor George finishes officiating the wedding and the lovebirds kiss after their "I Do's." Cheers and clapping erupt to send the newlyweds, walking hand in hand, back to the house. The band plays a lively Fleetwood Mac song, and the guests disperse. Some head to the banquet table to find their seat; others visit with the horses and get their picture taken in the carriage. Dolly and the other children run over to Penny and Todd to meet the baby, Andrew, who is now two years old.

Bình takes my elbow and asks if I would like something refreshing to drink. He leads me through a honeycomb of talking people, and we find the punch bowl with floating fruit. I take a sip and realize there is alcohol in it. I look at the sign. Sangria. I throw caution to the wind and fill my glass to the top. While we wait for Tree and Kelly to emerge, Bình and I take our seats at the reserved table where the bride and groom will join us shortly. Already at our table are Kelly's parents, her sister, Quang, Donald, and Diệp.

Quang and Ann are enjoying themselves and seem to have resolved their lovers' quarrel. They engage in boisterous conversation with the others, but it is Diệp and Quang who do most of the jibber-jabbering.

"You look like a sun goddess," Bình says to me. "Yellow looks radiant on you."

I blush and grasp for a compliment in return. "Thank you. You did a good job coordinating the wedding."

"All I did was get them to a fortuneteller and find a seamstress," he says. "Katrina relieved me of my other duties."

I laugh. "She did an amazing job. She should be a wedding planner."

Bình nods and asks casually whether I have given much thought to letting Dolly's father back into my life…and be a family again. His abrupt change in course puts a sour taste in my mouth. He does not know me well enough to ask about such intimate details of my life. I give him a stark look of annoyance and stiffen my body. "Why are you asking about him? It is a personal matter." I am not sure why, but Bình's inquiry about Tý strikes a nerve. The audacity!

"It is merely a question," Bình says. "Tree shared with me a little bit about your history and mentioned you two recently reconnected after all these years."

"You do not see me asking why your wife left you, do you?" I turn away and sip my sangria.

I can tell my comment stings more than my body language by the way he brusquely puts his drink down. "Are you still in love with him?"

I tell myself I have forgiven Tý. So what is the problem? Now, I am upset with myself for not knowing the reason behind my attitude. I dismiss Bình by turning my attention to Quang and Diệp, who are having a sprightly debate about the role of husband and wife after the wedding.

Bình deflects my standoffish behavior by pounding his drink and storming off to join Tree and Kelly, who have reemerged to greet their guests. Both bride and groom have shed the outer layer of their wedding attire; gone are the robe to Kelly's áo nhật bình and Tree's tuxedo jacket. The guests cheer as the two of them join hands and kiss.

"What do you think, Chị Tuyết?" Diệp taps my wrist. "You are kilometers away. Did you hear any of what I said?"

Something about the way my neighbor dresses and carries herself always makes me chuckle. She is an effervescent woman, and despite having gone through so much tragedy with the annihilation at Mỹ Lai, she chooses to live a life in color and optimism. I must learn to do the same. Today, Diệp is wearing a sleeveless, chartreuse green V-neck jumpsuit cinched at the waist with a gold braided curtain rope. The ensemble is couture-looking despite costing only three dollars at the local thrift store. Now that is the next level of refugee chic. I smile with endearment. "I heard you, Sister Diệp. And I agree with both of you. Quang makes a valid argument that after marriage, a wife must serve her husband and make him happy. She should nourish him with good food, keep the household orderly, raise the children to be well-mannered and productive. She should give her husband power."

Diệp's jaw drops, and Quang smirks smugly. I continue. "However, a husband, at least a smart one, knows that his powers come from his wife, and she can easily reduce him to a worthless man if he cannot make her proud and happy." I repeat this for Donald who has been left out of this conversation for the past twenty minutes.

"Aw, yes, happy wife, happy life," Donald replies. "The sooner he learns that the better off he'll be."

Quang stands firm with his masculine pride. "Women serve men. It has always been that way. We are stronger, faster, smarter, and have always been in charge. That is why boys are more valued than girls. We are providers and protectors."

The argument continues. Quang holds strong to his traditional beliefs and leans into the backlash from Ann, Donald, Diệp, and me. I admire Quang for not backing down and staking his claim on his convictions; however, the more we dig our heels into this topic, the more intense it becomes. By the time Tree and Kelly arrive at our table, we are shouting. The debate has turned into a sparring match. I have no doubt it would have escalated to a street brawl if the bride and groom had not shown up.

Quang stands and kicks the chair. "We are leaving." His eyes cast knives at Kelly before pulling Ann roughly out of her seat and dragging her to the front of the house. Ann looks apologetically at her sister and embarrassingly at us. She leaves with him and does not resist.

Lan and I chase after them. We yell at them to stop and not ruin the day for Tree and Kelly. Moments later, Kelly appears at my side.

"If you want to, leave," Kelly says, "but my sister is not going with you." She takes Ann's hand and pulls her to her side. Quang pulls her back. Lan grabs her daughter's arm, and poor Ann is jostled like a rag doll by grown children.

I try to remain calm and diffuse the situation with reasoning. I make a plea to Quang to be a better man and not make a scene. It is a stinging mistake. The piece of shit slaps me!

I am stunned by what just happened and slap him back. Quang advances one step forward, but before he can lay another hand on me, Sky grabs Quang by the neck, sweeps his leg, and pins him to the ground. I watch in horror as Quang's face goes from bright pink, flush with fury, to pale and cowering in fear. Sky's fist drills into Quang's face repeatedly and pulverizes his face to a bloody pulp. His skin shreds like it came out of a meat grinder. Sky towers over Quang and continues to beat him mercilessly as one by one, he flicks us off like annoying earwigs.

"Die, you commie bastard!" Sky screams.

Ann shrieks in terror and wails for Sky to stop. Teddy, Jean-Adrien, Bill, and Donald rush to Quang's aid. It takes the four of them to pull Sky off. This whole evening has turned into a debacle. Sky falls onto the grass and cries. I feel horrible for Quang, who despite being an egotistical and chauvinistic boar, did not deserve to have his face smashed in by a blender of fists and blades of revenge.

"Violence is not the answer," Bill says. "Don't let hatred be the virus that destroys us all."

Sky weeps and apologizes. "I don't know what came over me. Forgive me." Katrina holds her son and rocks him like a baby. She tells him he needs help and that his fight with war demons is not over. The resurgence of flashbacks and stress is hurting him still. Perhaps it is a quixotic notion to think we can control our demons before they completely control us.

I pity Ann and see myself in her…at least the old me. I used to be so accepting of everything that I was blind to what lay beneath the surface of things…the surface of people. It was old

Mrs. Trần back in Sài Gòn who taught me to be strong. She reminded me that my greatest artillery lies in the strength of my voice. Having a voice means having a choice. I tell myself that I can be Mrs. Trần for Ann.

Bình hoists Quang up to take him home. Ann follows them, but I hold her back. "Let him cool off. Your place right now is with your family. It is your sister's big day."

Ann frees herself from my grip and nips at me with her angry words. "My place is with him. This family," she points at her parents and sister, "sold me when I was a child." She sidesteps past me and yells at Toàn and Lan. "I had a new family, and you took me from them." Ann whips around to face Kelly. "And you, big sister, always have to steal whatever piece of happiness I have. First, you drag me to be sold like one of your fruit baskets at the market, and after I adopted a new life with my host parents, you drag me back and force me to come to this country. You should have left without me, forgotten me. Maybe my parents would still be alive if I were there to protect them! And now, look at you. You cannot be happy with one man. No, you have to steal mine too? His heart belongs to me. I will not share him." Ann's body shakes with rage.

"What are you talking about?" Kelly asks.

Ann impales her sister with a look of disgust. "Like you did not know. Quang loves you, but since he cannot have you, he settled for me. In time, he will love me, but not while you are around." She storms off and chases after Bình and Quang. The three of them disappear onto the main road in Bình's old Cadillac. I sigh in defeat and let the boulders roll off my shoulders.

It is Pastor George who breaks the spell and ropes us back to why we are gathered here today. Despite the heavy interruption and the shocking news of a twisted love triangle, we manage to get the celebration back on course. Even Sky manages to shake it off, perhaps for Magdaleine's sake. He puts on a brave face and mouths an "I'm sorry" to me before sitting with Magdaleine at the farthest table. The band rocks a high-tempo song, and the guests sit to devour their dinner. I admit we all drink more than our share of sangrias and whiskeys tonight. Alcohol is our bandage and the elixir to forgetfulness. As the night rolls on, the moon shines, and the music gets louder. Soon, I forget about the scuffle from earlier and enjoy the present moment.

I barely take two bites of my slice of lemon chiffon wedding cake when Bill asks me to dance. I look around for his date, confused.

"She left," Bill says. "Well, I sort of kicked her out. Seeing Skyler beat the crap out of that guy made her thirsty for a story. She wanted an article in the paper by tomorrow, 'Vietnam Vet Loses Control.'" He waves his hand in a semi-circle above him like it is a headlining title on a marquee sign.

We dance until my feet ache, and the stars drip into the pine trees. At midnight, Tree and Kelly ride off in the carriage pulled by Blazing Six Guns and J'adore Champagne. The remaining guests watch and wave as the couple disappears down the trail toward their yurt. As people leave I hear whispers of how the fusion wedding was the most exciting one they have been to and how the blending of cultures in today's matrimonial ceremony was a treat. People pay compliments to the hosts for the food, the wedding gown, the music, and the decorations, and when they run out of things to say, they marvel at the night sky and applaud the beautiful weather. No one dares bring up the sour discord that happened earlier in the day.

I offer to help Katrina and Jean-Adrien clean up, but they demand I take Dolly home. My daughter can barely keep her eyes open. I say my goodbyes; I hug the Herringtons and kiss the Vanzwols. Bill escorts me to my car and carries a sleepy Dolly in his arms. He slides her in the back seat of my small Honda Civic and buckles her seatbelt.

"What an interesting day," Bill says.

I nod. He removes a wisp of hair from my forehead and tucks it behind my earlobe. I blush at his touch. Bill strokes my cheek and follows the contour of my face until he reaches my parted lips. My heart is beating fast. Can he hear it? I dare not look into his eyes.

"You look beautiful." He bends down to kiss me, and I stand on my tiptoes, stretching my calves as long as they can go, to meet his mouth. Perhaps I am a little lightheaded from the alcohol. Perhaps it is the moonlight that has me bewitched. It does not matter. My body tingles. I melt into his arms and hungrily press my lips into his. I breathe in his scent of musk and whiskey and taste his lemon-tinged mouth. A million goosebumps ripple from my head to my toes and back up again, stopping at my womanhood. The curls and folds between my legs drip with desire. I cling to him, hungry for love, hungry for tenderness.

It has been a long time since the heat of desire has been awakened within me. I wrap my arms around Bill's waist and press my body into his hardness. I let out a moan and guide his hand to my breasts. We stand in each other's embrace, hungrily devouring each other's scent and taste. He offers one last lover's kiss before he abruptly pushes me away.

"You better take Dolly home," he says huskily.

I gaze into his eyes and search for clues to how he feels. My tongue is heavy and anchored down. I am too embarrassed to say anything.

His eyes are soft, yet I feel rejected. Does he pity me? Is he playing games with me? How can he turn his emotions on and off so easily? Maybe he will never love anyone because he still loves Katrina. Perhaps he feels guilty because he is my boss.

I take a step back, annoyed now. "Goodnight, Bill." I get in my car and drive down the driveway. I force myself not to look in the rearview mirror.

21. MOVE ON (JANUARY 1984)

Dolly is in fourth grade now, and Cabbage Patch Kids are all the craze with every child I know. I cannot change channels on TV without seeing a commercial about these dolls that come with a birth certificate and adoption papers. The retail stores have been selling them for thirty to fifty dollars, and the demand continues to skyrocket. I do not understand how a sixteen-inch doll with wool hair and a vinyl face can cost so much.

My daughter makes a plea and promises to get straight A's in all her classes if I buy her a doll. "Please, Mama, all my friends have one."

I give in to her nagging and sad face by pinky promising a doll in exchange for perfect attendance and perfect grades. In the pit of my stomach, I know I cannot afford to spend this frivolously on a toy. By June, if she accomplishes her side of the deal, I will have to take her to Sears or Toys "R" Us and buy a doll. Katrina says people have been fighting over these toys in the stores. It seems so long ago that my people fought over food, water, country, and home. They worried about how to live, not what presents to buy.

I will be lucky to find any "CPKs" as Dolly calls them. Both Katrina and Catherine vow to keep an eye out for me. If they find one, they will snatch one up. In the meantime, I have five months to budget and save a little from each paycheck. For once, I am hoping Dolly does not do well in school.

Ever since Tree and Kelly's wedding five months ago, I have been sorting through the cobwebs of that day and compartmentalizing the events. Kelly and her parents still pick apart that day like a scab. They cannot believe Quang was in love with Kelly and that he felt jilted by her. He had been harboring resentment and using Ann to get Kelly jealous. It backfired. Kelly only has eyes for Tree. Poor Ann fell for Quang's games and believes there is love between them to salvage. Perhaps in time, she can fuel that ember of love. Kelly and Tree are moving nine hundred miles away to San Jose, California, to start a new, independent life together. For the past four years, Tree has been in my care, and I watched him grow from a cuddly baby to a cunning teenager and now a resourceful and resilient young man. I could not be prouder of him than if I were his mother.

Kelly's parents have a family friend in San Jose and can give Tree a job in the sheet metal machinery industry. Kelly hopes that her distance from her sister will make Quang's love for Ann grow stronger. Her decision to leave Seattle opens my eyes to the great love she has for her little sister and the sacrifices she will make to give Ann a chance at happiness. This makes me miss Sister Six and the sacrifices she made for me. However, if I were in Ann's shoes and Sister Six were in Kelly's, my sister would chase Quang out of the village and punch me until the only bruise of love I had was hers. Yes, my Sister Six is a bully, but I mean that in the most cherished and loving way.

I have been thinking a lot about Bình as well. I owe him an apology for snapping at him. With Tree moving out and down to California, he will once again be alone. Had I chosen to receive his question at the wedding in a different light, I could have seen that he was merely making conversation. I could have opened up to him about my relationship with Dolly's father, and perhaps he would have shared what had happened with his wife. There are several sides to every story, and for all I know, maybe his wife did not leave him. Tree tells me he thinks Bình is infatuated with me. Since our first meeting, Bình asks a lot about me, and even after the episode at the wedding, he still inquires about my well-being.

I have been trying to reach Sky the past few days, but Jean-Adrien says Sky and Magdaleine are on a couples retreat. He describes the program as akin to oxygen and sunlight for relationships…therapy for couples to enhance their communication, build empathy for one another, strengthen their romance, and open doors to resolving conflicts.

"Sky is trying to be the best he can be for Magdaleine," Jean-Adrien says. "He's tired of self-sabotaging and he thinks this seminar will help."

"That good," I say. "You and Katrina prove it possible."

I mentally applaud my friend Sky for grinding at his fears like a mortar and pestle until those fears become fine specks of dust. Magdaleine will be the breeze that comes along to blow those "fear dusts" away. This makes me happy and hopeful for them both. I am one-hundred percent Team Skyler and Magdaleine and pray for them to make it together.

Sky has been through so much. He once told me about his addiction to opiates after he got back from the war. It was his way of forgetting, but he knew his self-destructive behavior was hurting those who cared about him, especially his mom, Bill, and Teddy.

"I decided to quit cold turkey," Sky had said. "Do you know what it's like? Your body goes through withdrawals, and it's like ripping your skin off. You're on fire, but you feel you deserve the pain because of what you've put others through." Sky lived recklessly and had a death wish, but he found purpose when he had the chance to sponsor Dolly, Tree, and me to the US. After we arrived, his purpose was to make sure we acclimated and thrived here. Now, it appears he has found another purpose, and that is to love Magdaleine the way she deserves to be loved. In doing so, he is learning to love himself again.

Will I find love again? I touch my lips and remember Bill's kiss. I know he is a kind and intelligent man—a living encyclopedia as Sky once called him. Bill is also financially established, achieving the pinnacle of success that he has wanted to achieve with his career…He says it is too late for him to have children and start a family but not too late to find love. I romanticize what life could be like with Bill, for us to grow old together and have his help raising Dolly. However, with our vast age difference, we may have only ten good years together before his mind and body deteriorates. I can see myself living another twenty years as a widow. One day when Dolly marries and has children of her own, will Bill have the energy to keep up with his grandchildren? I am getting ahead of myself. I mentally flush these ideas down the toilet, and at the same time, marvel how easy these Westerners have it with sanitation and plumbing. My days of squatting behind trees are long gone.

I bounce down the stairs, feeling jovial and free, to check yesterday's mail before heading into work. The elation quickly ends. My heart trips over itself. In my mailbox is a letter with a return address from Humble, Texas. It is not from Tý. The curlicue handwriting is round and flows poetically across the envelope. I say the name out loud just so I can hear it and know its truth. "Annette." I tear open the envelope.

Dear Tuyet,

I am not sure where to start except to say I am happy to know you and Thuy Tien are safely in Seattle. I wish you would have come with us all those years ago, but I understand why you did not. I suppose if I were in your situation, I would have taken my chances and made the same decision.

Life with Ty has been challenging. I love him with all my heart, but it is hard to know him. He has a lot of nightmares. His guilty conscience prevents him from being fully present with me and his children. He shuts us out and does not share with me his thoughts or feelings. During the holidays like Christmas or the children's birthdays, he never celebrates or buys presents for them…nor for me, for that matter.

I pause. How strange we know the same man, and yet he is not the same man to both of us. In Việt Nam, he always brought home gifts. Even now, he sent Dolly toys and me the photograph of our daughter as a baby. I continue reading the letter.

Ty and I have four children: Timothy, Theodore, Tessa, and Tina. Our youngest is two-and-a-half years old. Timothy is now thirteen. He was just five years old when Saigon fell and we left Vietnam. If I remember correctly, Thuy Tien is now nine years old? I am sure she is adjusting to life nicely. Children are so resilient, aren't they?

We have a good life together, nonetheless. Ty is studying to be a nutritionist or dietician and dreams of opening a wellness and supplements shop. I am a linguistics professor and author. I am sure you have certain notions about me, but I assure you, I am a devout Christian woman, educated, and devoted to my family. I am a good person.

I am aware that my husband's visit to Seattle did not go well. I was surprised to see him home so soon. I begged him not to go, but he is a man who sees only black and white and walks a linear path. I often think about what it would be like if we met. Do you? Sometimes I wonder if my children would like to know their half-sister, but then I play the scenarios in my mind, and it never works out. I believe in another time and place, you and I could have been great friends. I admire your strength and beauty and your devotion as a mother. Ty told me you have a university education and follow God. Yes, I should think we could have been the best of friends, but we should remain strangers. Wouldn't you agree?

Please respect my wishes as a mother, a wife, and a woman who wants to protect her family—do not contact my husband again. You should move on with your life and enjoy the freedoms this country has given you.

I wish you well.

Annette

I reread the letter two more times. *Four children? Best of friends? Enjoy my freedoms?* I hate to admit it, but Annette is right. I must move on and live my life. Enjoy the freedoms I have which include the liberty to choose my life partner and the best father for Dolly. I deserve to be loved, to be the sun and moon…and stars…in someone else's sky.

I crumple up the letter and throw it in the dumpster to dissuade myself from digging it out. Why reread it and torment myself? I try to remember what I wrote in my letter to Tý. Did Annette intercept the letter? Or did he hand it over so she could read it? I imagine her face flushing through the spectrums of red with doubt, fear, and fury before washing to a pale white, replacing the anger with cold composure.

As I pass the I-405 and I-5 interchange, I think of Tý and am not convinced he is out of my life for good. He has always been a strong-willed man who does what he wants. When he was a child, he intentionally left his home to live on the streets so that his mother would have one less mouth to feed. As he got older and the testosterone kicked in, he got stronger and learned how to fight. At first, it was to rebuff the store owners he stole food from, and then it was to protect those same vendors from street kids in exchange for daily meals and a percentage of their sales. Ultimately, he was recruited to fight with the Việt Minh against the French oppressors. He was fourteen. Somehow, he managed to continue his education. He attended classes during the day and did his lessons under the street lamps at night. He never shared with me what he did for the Việt Minh, but I imagine some wicked and gruesome things. How he loathed the French because they raped his mother and ruled Indochina for so long.

Despite his torrential life, he loved school and learning. He was the only student to have won fairly through hard work a scholarship to study abroad. The other five students were awarded that opportunity because of their family's station in life or their father's rank in the corrupt system. Tý took classes at the Milwaukee Institute of Technology, now called Milwaukee Technical College. No, my husband is a determined man, and if he wants to see us again, he will. Annette cannot stop him.

Stuck in traffic, my thoughts now drift to Bình. What do I know about him? Is he worth getting to know? I do not have many

Vietnamese friends here in Seattle. I have Diệp of course, with her eclectic fashion choices and fast-talking wit, but the tides of American life are taking her adrift, away from me and onto Donald's shores. Maybe Bình can be my shore, my safe harbor? He is only a few years older than I am, and he is Vietnamese. Therefore, he has the advantage of sharing a similar footing, history, and common ground with me. He is a good-looking man, with eyes that curve down, giving him that babyface charm. When he smiles, he looks like a cute boy who is both happy and sad at the same time. Tree admires him for his kindness and soccer athletics, and I trust my nephew. After all, Bình did offer my nephew room and board and treats him like a son. I admire his connections and networking abilities. He knew of a fortuneteller and a seamstress when we needed one, and he took charge of coordinating Tree's wedding. He also gracefully let Katrina take over the details and played the supporting role flawlessly. No Vietnamese man in my life has ever been as comfortable with gender-bending roles as Bình. He is not the typical Asian man I am accustomed to. In my village, to know one man was to know all men. They all thought the same way, disciplined their wives and children the same way, and stuck to the patriarchal ideals of society. When I think about how diplomatic Bình was in escorting Quang home after the fight with Sky, I wonder what he could have done to drive his wife away. I must learn more about this anomalous man.

###

KUBE FM is now playing a Michael Jackson song. The media refers to him as the "King of Pop," but I have yet to figure out why. Tree says pop is another word for soda. I saw him in a Pepsi commercial recently and the news coverage of his hair catching fire. Teddy says he is the first celebrity to get paid so handsomely, five million dollars, to endorse the beverage. Not only is the financial deal a mind-blowing marketing partnership, but it is significant because the singer is black.

"But Teddy," I argued, "he only half black. I think he mix like coffee and condensed milk. He look like *mỹ lai đen*, like the children in Việt Nam, half black left behind by soldiers. My sister say the war like boiling water, bubbling half Vietnamese babies all time."

Well, for five million dollars, I would not mind being labeled the king of soda either. Hearing Michael Jackson on the radio reminds me of two Christmases ago when Sky gifted Dolly the *Thriller* album. What a good man Skyler is. Had he not been drafted to war, had he not suffered so much, what kind of man would he have become? Katrina and Jean-Adrien said Sky was a good child and at the core of him was someone respectful, kind, and who served others. That loving, innocent little boy is still in there, begging to be found. I see glimpses of that boy. My wonderful friend, Skyler Herrington, could have been a confident and accomplished man, married with beautiful children, and changing the world for the better. I believe he can still be all these things. He had a challenging start on this jagged, crooked road of life with too many dangerous turns, but eventually, the curves will flatten out and the road will straighten. You will see, Sky…and then you will cruise the rest of the way until you grow wings and soar above everyone who pushed you down.

###

My car burps smoke and coughs as I pull into the parking lot. Without warning, it dies midway into the parking spot. A voice wafts through my window. It is Bình. "Do you want me to call the 'Big Toe' and have your car towed to a mechanic?"

"What are you doing here?" I ask. "Why are you at my work?"

"You will find out soon enough," he says. "Go on in. I'll take care of the car and can pick you up after work."

I thank him and make my way inside the *Seattle Times* building. The past few months have been a flurry of activity for the newspaper. President Reagan signed a bill two months ago creating Martin Luther King Jr. Day, and then five days later, a bomb exploded inside the United States Capitol. Meanwhile, technology has been advancing and our reporters have been covering Ameritech Mobile's introduction of a cellular network. A man by the name of Bill Gates introduced a system called Windows 1.0, and an Apple company showcased a new Macintosh computer. Teddy says it is revolutionary with the introduction of a mouse and "GUI." He says I will understand when I see it. I told him I did not understand how the gooey parts of mice can produce rainbow-colored apples. Teddy laughed at me. I suppose I will have to wait and see.

For the first time, I watched football this season. The Seattle Seahawks played in the AFC Championship game against the Raiders. Sadly, we lost. The Raiders went on to play the Washington Redskins in the Super Bowl. Teddy, Skyler, and Tree cheered on the Raiders, but I do not understand how they can cheer for a team that just defeated our Seahawks. Dolly convinced me to root for the Washington Redskins because "they are related to us, Mama. They are from Washington too." In any event, I could not cheer for a team that looked like pirates so the Redskins it was.

Amidst all this, there was leaked information about the ARPANET project in which the Department of Defense enabled all military computers to connect. Supercomputing centers at several universities were created and provide network interconnectivity. All of this, of course, is beyond my comprehension, and in my little media coordinator world, the daily routine of positioning advertisements is all I understand. At this juncture, I am tired of seeing Cabbage Patch Kids and Chubby and Tubby war-surplus ads. I want more responsibilities and a promotion.

I make a quick detour to Bill's office before settling in at my desk. Bill looks up with an expression of annoyance but quickly softens. "Snow, come in."

Seeing Bill in his office, concentrating on his work with his brows furrowing, makes me realize how aged he looks since we first met at Ray's Boathouse. I had told Magdaleine about the kiss, and she warned me not to play with fire. "Bill has unfinished business with his ex-wife, and he still has feelings for Katrina. Trust me, you do not want to open that Pandora's box." She filled me in on how Bill had tried to forget Katrina by marrying this woman, but it was a "rebound marriage" that went sour despite his good intentions.

I hesitate at the doorway. "Sorry to disturb. Magdaleine on retreat with Sky, and I…"

"It's all right," Bill says. "I can use a break."

I step past the threshold and close the door. The noise of the newsroom yields to quiet serenity. I have never sat in Bill's office before. I have been inside but always passing through to drop something off or pick something up, never to stay and soak in the smells and comforts of the room. It is well-lit with natural lighting coming in from the big windows. Today's view boasts clear skies with a sprinkle of telephone wires and a chance of good-luck pigeon poop falling on the window washer's head.

The leather chair smells of pine and chocolates. His desk is neat with everything in its place. In the corner is a photo of his ex-wife. She is, to put it bluntly, an ugly woman. Her blemished face is pale with dark sunspots orbiting around her left cheekbone. In her cream-colored wedding gown, she blends in nicely with the background. Even on such a special occasion as her wedding day, in full makeup and styled hairdo, she looks weathered. Her lips smile, but her eyes challenge me to a duel. I once watched Katrina use an iron pole to stoke a fire, and I now have the urge to use that pole to bring the picture to life.

"That's Rebecca," Bill says. "We're divorced, but I keep the picture to remind me what *not* to do ever again." He stifles a laugh.

Behind him are books, framed awards, and a painting of a cow. I point to the painting. "Why you have cow painting?"

Bill smiles. "You mean Barbara?" He swivels his chair around. We both gaze into Barbara's black eyes. "She was my favorite calf. She used to follow me everywhere."

"I have pet in Việt Nam too," I say. "A chicken. Her name *Mông Dơ*. It mean dirty butt, but she die. Communist come to our house, take her, and eat her."

"I'm sorry about your chicken," Bill says. He looks down at his clasped hands on the desk as if he were saying a silent prayer. "Listen, I owe you many apologies and…" His lips quiver, and his voice trails off. I wait patiently for him to speak again. "Snow, I took advantage of you that night. We were both drinking and love was in the air…It was the perfect night despite the blood bath Skyler gave Quang. It was wrong of me to kiss you."

I say nothing. I do not know how to respond. I did not want to admit I enjoyed the kiss—probably more than he did—but since we both came to the same conclusion, that it was not a good idea, there was no need to discuss it further. After a long pause, Bill asks me if I enjoy my job and if there is anything I need. I ask him for more responsibilities and a raise. I remind him my math skills are strong, and I can be persuasive in sales. I tell him I can be of value in accounting or be Jerry's assistant in advertising. Bill agrees I deserve a pay increase and promotion. He will talk to Jerry about transitioning me from media coordinator to advertising account manager. I like the sound of "manager" in my title.

I leave Bill's office and head to my desk. A large vase filled with gerbera daisies and baby's breath grace my workstation. I look around and catch Jerry's eye as he walks from the kitchen with a mug of coffee in his hand. He smiles and points to the flowers with a look of curiosity. I open the small envelope and read the card. *It is best to wash soiled linens at home. Think today and speak tomorrow. I am sorry. Bình.*

The old Vietnamese proverbs about thinking before speaking and not airing private matters for the world to judge has me appreciating Bình's method of apology. Once again, he is an anomaly. A man who surprises me with flowers and apologizes is a man worthy of my time. I will invite him over for dinner tomorrow.

###

Bình stands outside my apartment door soaking wet. "Do you have a dirty floor that needs mopping?" He grins with boyish charm and shakes his hair. Droplets of rainwater sprinkle onto the linoleum floor and on my face. His presence lifts my spirits more than I care to admit. He is like a ray of sunshine cutting through the drizzle of a winter's day. I let him in and offer him a towel.

He wipes his face with my pink washcloth that once was white but somehow snuck into a pile of red laundry. "The towel was for mopping the floors," I tease. "Where is your umbrella?"

He removes his wet shoes and leaves them by the doorway. "A true Seattle native does not use an umbrella, much less own one. I want to blend in like a local."

I take his coat and hang it over the bathtub. "That is absurd. Rain or shine, an umbrella is useful."

"In Việt Nam, maybe," he says, "but not here. The way I see it, the Americans worry more about fashion and trends, not functionality and purpose."

I agree he makes an interesting observation about the culture here. I tell him about Dolly's obsession with Cabbage Patch Kids and how people fight over them like it was their last piece of bread. Hearing my mention of these dolls, Dolly perks up. She tears her attention away from the television screen long enough to greet our guest and tell him she wants a preemie CPK doll.

"Can I help in the kitchen?" Bình asks as he washes his hands.

I decline his offer and invite him to sit with Dolly. They watch *Scooby-Doo* while I prepare a fruit platter. We graze on oranges, persimmons, and pomegranates while the chicken congee simmers to a finish.

Dolly takes her dinner on the couch, in front of the television, while Bình and I sit at the table. Over our meal, he updates me on the status of my car. It will be fixed and ready for pick up in two days. We share parts of ourselves that we remember with fondness, about the good times back home and the dreams we have for the future. Back in Việt Nam Bình's family had been involved with horseracing since the colonial days. His father and

453

grandfather were shrewd businessmen and used their relationships with French military officers to advance their horse breeding program. They belonged to the Saigon Horse Racing Association and owned a few prized ponies. Bình grew up loving horses and found racing thrilling. He admits he was not as savvy as his father or grandfather because he loved the animals too much and cared what happened to the jockeys. Some of the jockeys were as young as fourteen years old, and while they were lithe, they were often naïve about the industry, emotionally immature, and unreliable.

Bình met his wife at the racetrack. She was beautiful, charming, and sophisticated. She came from a wealthy family and was a descendant of the royal family, with a direct bloodline to emperors of the Nguyễn dynasty. She was also a communist, which he did not find out about until after the socialist government took over. Suddenly, racing became unlawful and gambling was prohibited. He had no way of making money.

His wife's family funded his business venture, and he turned to ceramics. He spent his days casting and firing molds of vases, elephants, and dragons, while his wife hand-painted the figures. They would have several kilns going at once, always painting, selling, and meeting the demands of the elite upper class. Their ceramic statues guarded entrances of grand hotels, homes, and buildings or stood over tombstones and graves, protecting the deceased as they passed over to the next realm. Their vases, filled with fresh flowers or silk floral arrangements adorned lobbies and tables of government officials or military officers. Life was good until his wife decided she was bored. She woke up one day feeling sorry for herself, married to a farmer who played with horses and tinkered with clay. She left him.

"When you love someone and then lose them," Bình says, "it is easy to close your heart off to everyone or find someone else to fill the empty void. For me though, I poured my energy into raising my two sons and daughter." Bình dips his *yàuhjagwái*, a fried Chinese doughnut, into the broth and sucks on the crispy exterior until it becomes chewy. "Did you know that the Cantonese word 'yàuhjagwái' means 'oil-fried devil'?" I shake my head. "It is delicious, which makes it evil." He pops the last morsel into his mouth and smacks his lips as he devours the last bit of this glutinous breadstick.

"And where are your children now?" I ladle more congee into his bowl. The steaming hot porridge is perfect for today's weather. Bình has a third serving of the congee and tells me all three of his kids live in the Bay Area of California. His oldest daughter, Thu, is his biggest joy. She is smart, pretty, and lives in San Jose with her boyfriend, Ken. His second child, Khoi, lives up to his name, which means handsome. He spends his time chasing girls and driving fast cars. He lives in San Francisco and is dating an aspiring Cambodian model named Linh. That leaves Phan, his youngest son, who lives with his mother in Oakland. Bình says Phan is a sweet kid but dull and slow.

"How can you say that about your youngest?" I ask, appalled he would describe his son as such.

"Well, it is true," he says. "Even I can see he is nothing like his older sister and brother. Sometimes I wonder if he is even mine."

My eyes and mouth open wide. "Do you really think so?"

Bình takes a toothpick and spears a piece of persimmon. "Thu and Khoi are good-looking people. They have personality, character, and ambition, even if Khoi's only ambition is to date the most attractive girls and drive the sportiest cars. Phan, on the other hand, has no motivation. His personality is lackluster. He can barely formulate two sentences without shying away. I cannot have a stimulating conversation with that boy. And the way he walks. It's like a gait of a camel, the way he bobs forward and back. It's unnatural. He was coddled too much and was held most of his childhood."

"Maybe I will meet them one day," I say. "After all, Tree and Ngọc are moving down to San Jose."

"Yes, it was my recommendation they go since I have connections there," Bình says. "Ngọc's parents also have a family friend in San Jose who is in the sheet metal industry."

"Tree mentioned he was going to learn machinery. You have many connections."

I share with Bình about my life in Việt Nam and how we came to Seattle. I find it easy to talk to him because he is a good listener. He expresses no judgment, even when I tell him about Sam and the love interests in my life; he does not think less of me. He admires my perseverance and wit. He applauds my resourcefulness. He thanks me for being made of flesh and blood, for having passion, and for not being afraid to love. Above all, he respects my devotion as a mother. He is full of compliments, and I am unabashedly reveling in his attention. I even brag about how I, a single mother with a dying daughter, managed to survive the war and make it this far.

We end our evening together playing the game Connect Four with Dolly. My little hustler suggests we play for money but we settle for candy instead. She is the big winner with fifty-three gummy bears while I come in second with twenty-nine gummies.

"Chú Bình," Dolly says, "do you want to know how I eat my gummy bears?" She sucks on the gelatin candy until it is shiny, then bites the legs off until it is just the head and arms left. She giggles. "Look, the arms look like boobies."

I give my daughter a stern glance and hold my breath for Bình's reaction. He must think my daughter is inappropriate and is second-guessing my aptitude as a mother.

He laughs and copies her. "These fruit bears taste better this way."

I watch Dolly and Bình interact with ease as if they are old friends and listen to them chat about candy and toys. In this new light, I think I can move on. Can I move on with Bình?

22. ROAD TRIP (SUMMER 1984)

I get home from work to find Dolly in tears. She is sprawled on the floor in front of our velour couch, which I have decided I do not like. As soon as I have extra money from my raise, I will buy a new used couch and donate this one. Diệp and her son Hùng need a sofa. Perhaps they will want this one. It is a comfortable couch, but the pattern is anything but calm. The repeating print of barns, pheasants, and daisies does not invite serenity and peace. Instead, it makes me think of the countryside chaos on a farm.

Dolly wails harder and thrashes her body on the floor, writhing like a sidewinder snake on our sand-colored carpet. In her hand is a piece of paper. I kneel beside her and ask her what is the matter. She answers with a moan and curls into a ball. She buries her face into the shag and shoots her hand in the air, waving the paper in my face. It is her report card with her final grades for the year. All A's and one B+ in social studies.

"I am sorry you did not get the straight A's you and I were both hoping for," I say, "but—"

Dolly rolls over and says softly, "It means I don't get my CPK doll." She sits up and hugs her knees, her cheek resting on top of them. One big teardrop makes its final tour down her cheek and stops at the top of her lip.

I clap my hands. "Encore!" She lifts her head and implores with her eyes to explain myself. "That was quite a performance you gave. Am I to feel sorry for you and buy you a doll anyway? Our deal was perfect attendance and perfect grades."

"Mama, I would have gotten straight A's, but—"

"But you did not," I say softly. I scoop her into my arms and hug her. "How much money have you saved from selling our candies and ramen cups to your friends?"

She leaps out of my arms and runs to her bedroom. A moment later she returns with a shoebox of money. She counts the coins. "Nineteen dollars and five cents."

"What were you saving the money for?" I ask.

She shrugs. "A sunny day, I guess, for when there is something good at the Circle K."

"How much is a Cabbage Patch Doll?"

She shrugs again. "Do I have enough to buy one?"

My turn to shrug. "It depends on which one you want. I think preemies are more expensive. Since it is not the Christmas season, maybe the prices are better or there is a sale. Do you want to go to Toys "R" Us and see?"

She perks up and gives me the biggest smile. "Can we go now?" I nod. "What if I don't have enough?"

"I will give you a loan, and you can pay me back with the money you earn from pulling my gray hairs and selling candy."

She eagerly accepts the offer. We grab our coats and make it to Tukwila two hours before the store closes.

###

Dolly and I are the new parents of an adopted CPK girl named Hycinthea Elaine. She has green eyes, brown hair, deep dimples, and a green signature stamp on the left butt cheek. She comes with a blue dress, adoption paperwork, and a birth certificate, which Dolly insists on framing. Jen and Melissa come over often to play "house," and they each mother their dolls like they are real children. It is the cutest thing to watch them feed and clothe the dolls, babysit each other's dolls, have playdates, and even discipline them for bad behavior.

"Hycinthea Elaine," Dolly scolds, "you apologize or get a spanking." She hugs her doll. "All right, I forgive you."

The phone rings. It is Tree. He and Kelly had their baby in April, a little girl they named Holly. They live in a one-bedroom apartment close to his work, so he bikes there every day. He tells me not to worry. They are managing fine, thanks to Bình's, Lan's, and Toàn's connections in the Bay Area.

They have met Bình's daughter, Thu, and her boyfriend, Ken. Both are nice people. "Aunt Eight, you have to meet them," Tree says. "Ken is Chinese. He looks like a movie star. He has thick black hair and is so tall. He is funny, too. Thu is more serious and conservative, but Ken brings out her playful side. They drive a BMW, live in a nice house in a pretty neighborhood, and have

Louis Vuitton everything. You need to come down. The weather here is so much better."

I ask about Kelly and the baby. Tree says both are happy, although Kelly wishes she had her mom and sister there to help out. Holly is an easy baby and only fusses when she is hungry or needs a diaper change. She sleeps a lot and laughs a lot. Tree is in love with his child and is amazed at how wonderful fatherhood can be.

"It makes me miss my parents and little brother even more," he says. "I hope we can go back to visit them one day."

"I received a letter from your Aunt Six," I say. "Our country is still at war, fighting the Chinese now at the northern border. China's encroachment to expand its power resulted in a death toll that surpassed six hundred soldiers on the first night of the invasion. It was a massive strike with artillery shells firing into several northern provinces."

Despite Việt Nam being a socialist republic and ruled by the very people I ran from, it does not make it any easier knowing people are still suffering and dying. Year after year of fighting takes its toll, and I worry one day the country will be lost forever. Every fiber, every cell, every neuron in my body yearns for a free and prosperous Việt Nam. I hope one day my country will be surrounded by allies, not enemies, and that the people can live in peace. I dream of the day when my people can recover economically and psychologically from decades of war, live in harmony, and not have to constantly defend our borders and ports.

"How is everyone doing back home?" Tree asks. "Any updates on Uncle Hải?"

Hearing Hải's name weakens my legs and sends a bullet to my gut. I plummet onto the chair and tell Tree that Hải is alive, but he suffered a stroke and is in a wheelchair. The tears fall. "Your father saw him in Sài Gòn on one of his deliveries. He could not believe it at first and thought he was seeing a ghost. They spoke briefly. Hải told him that imagination comes to life when you are in confinement. He saw things that were not there, heard screams that were not his. He tried to rationalize his existence. Oh, Tree, it is terrible. The Việt Cộng cracked him open like an egg and let his guts fry out in the hot jungle. They threw him for the wildlife to pick at. I cannot bear to think of how much he suffered."

I clutch my chest and swallow the lump of guilt and pain in my throat. I feel the knot making its way down into my stomach. The weight is so much to bear. I try to tell Tree more but the words will not come out. A guttural cry of anguish escapes my throat. I hate what they did to him. I hate that he sacrificed himself for my family. I hate that he loved me and made me happy. All this would not be so painful if I did not love him still.

"It was not your fault," Tree says. "You cannot blame yourself." Tree's words flow through me like a salve and soothe my conscience. I did not realize how much I needed to hear those words, that it was not my fault. Still, I wonder if Hải resents me. Years of rotting in a reeducation camp, imprisoned by his thoughts and tormented by dreams that are far out of reach. Eventually, it can break a man's spirit down and build it back up with resentment. Tree strategically steers my attention away from Hải and asks about Doctor Đức and his wife Thủy.

I inhale and breathe out slowly through my nostrils. I blink back the wetness around my eyes and sit back in the chair. I look to the ceiling as if it can give me the strength to speak. "They are well. Their son is three years old now. Your father still gets up at dawn and drives to the city. Your mom is managing her own little tailoring business out of the house. Your little brother is little no more. Tuấn is fifteen now, just a year younger than you when we left Vĩnh Bình."

"Has it been five years already since we left?" Tree asks. "I am almost twenty-two years old, legal to drink in the nightclubs."

I chuckle. "According to your papers though, you're only eighteen. Remember?"

"Oh no, that means I am not old enough to buy alcohol. Wait, that also means I have to work an extra three years before I can retire."

"I am afraid so," I say. We talk for another fifteen minutes about Sister Six and my brother-in-law and how they have been nursing Tâm back to health ever since she came home. Her younger sister, Trinh, has been helping Tâm recover and assimilate back into society. She has been reading to her big sister every day, brushing her hair, and taking her out for walks. Sometimes, they swing on the hammock together or pay their respects at their grandparents' tombstones. It has been a long and slow healing process for Tâm. Her physical scars are gone, and she has gained some healthy weight. There is some light in her eyes again but she does not trust her surroundings. Once in a while, she shares a memory that sparks joy like the time she and I went to the market and the sales lady ate a live cockroach to get a rise out of us.

Sister Six got her hui money and opened a food stand called Six's Kitchen. There is only one thing on the menu and she claims it is the best egg noodle soup in the province, served with your choice of char siu pork, duck, or shrimp wontons. In her letter, she said she will sell me her recipe for one-hundred US dollars. Knowing my sister, she is not joking.

Before hanging up with Tree, I promise to come down to San Jose and visit before Dolly starts the fifth grade.

###

I stare into my closet and realize most of my clothes are black, brown, or dark blue. I need more colors and prints, bold patterns, and vibrant designs. I can learn a few things from Diệp, Katrina, and Magdaleine about piecing outfits together. In two days, I am going to San Jose to see Tree and meet his baby. Instead of flying, we will do a road trip. It is cheaper and allows me the chance to see Oregon and northern California. Bình has offered to drive. He is anxious to see his children and for me to meet them. Dolly is excited for her first trip down the coast and plans to show Hycinthea Elaine the Pacific Ocean. We decide to take my Honda Civic since it gets good gas mileage and Teddy did a tune-up on it for me.

I dart across to Diệp's apartment to see if she will lend me a few blouses or dresses. Without hesitation, she pulls me into her bedroom and has me try on different outfits. I do a fashion show for her and humor her by putting on every outfit she picks, regardless of how hideous it looks on the hanger. We have a good laugh over the orange tutu dress and banana pants with suspenders and drawstring waist. The palm-print pants have bananas all over them and the way they fit on me, it looks like there is a banana coming out of my crotch. In the end, I settle on a giraffe-print halter jumpsuit in colors of cream and lilac, a yellow maxi dress, a pink V-neck blouse, and blue capri pants.

I ask Diệp if things are going well with Donald and how Hùng did in school this past year. She rolls her eyes and complains her son got B's and C's in his classes. "He has no interest in applying himself and only cares about sports." Donald promises to work with Hùng this summer on his subjects, particularly math.

Things are going extremely well with Donald. He is content to let her boss him around, and he caters to her every whim. His sons, Jason and Ricky, are used to having her in their life, and despite all their differences, they make a happy, blended family. She thinks it is only a matter of time before Donald proposes.

"This Halloween will be the third anniversary of when Dracula met Ronald McDonald," she proclaims. I laugh remembering that night. Donald was a vampire, Jason was Chewbacca, Diệp was in her handmade clown outfit, and Hùng was a hamburger.

"Please promise me your wedding will not be at McDonald's," I say. "What is your dream wedding?"

Diệp giggles. "Have you seen the new Rainbow Brite cartoons?" I shake my head. "You and Dolly have to watch it. I envision my wedding gown to be white like the Western gowns, only I want the train to be in rainbow colors. I cannot decide between a marine wedding or a mountain wedding."

"I admire your spunk and originality," I say. "You have an amazing zest for life."

"What do you think about a summer ceremony in a field of wildflowers near Mount Rainier with me riding a white horse?"

"Can you ride a horse?" I ask.

"Yes," she replies and laughs. "What about inside an aquarium with fish swimming around us, like the world below the waters of camp Kuku?"

"I love that idea," I say, "and that way you do not have to worry about the weather."

"I want to be surrounded by vibrant colors. For party favors, I will have Skittles and M&Ms. I want my cake to be bright and colorful too. Of course, Dolly has to be the flower girl and you my maid of honor."

It amazes me how a woman who survived the Mỹ Lai massacres can have such a positive outlook on life. I suppose the point is not to live in darkness but to seek the light and the rainbows. It is never too late to turn your life around or change your outlook on life, whether you have thirty minutes or thirty years left on Earth.

I thank Diệp for lending me her clothes and leave her in the bedroom daydreaming about her life with Donald. Back home, I pack a suitcase and get ready for the road trip down to San Jose.

###

By seven-thirty in the morning, Bình, Dolly, and I are on the road heading south on I-5. It takes thirteen hours to drive down to San Jose, but we decide to take the scenic route along the coastline. The three of us have never been to the beaches here and are excited to dip our toes into the Pacific Ocean.

We cut over to US-101 North and stop at a beach town called Ocean Shores. The coastal town sits on Point Brown Peninsula, bordered by the Pacific Ocean and Grays Harbor. It is a charming place, but at ten o'clock the sun is not at its peak yet, so the waterfront breeze is frigid. One toe-dip is all it takes for us to definitively decide the Pacific Ocean is not so hospitable. Dolly finds it amusing we cannot handle the cold water. She tortures us by kicking the salty waves at us and entertains herself by running along the shore looking for crabs and shells.

A few people on the beach fly kites, jog, or ride their horses. Watching the waves roll in brings back so many memories of Indonesia. Out in the distance where the sky meets the water, I imagine there is a tiny shrimp trawler bobbing up and down. Its identity number, 93752, is painted on the outside, but inside are forty-three refugees who fled their homes in search of freedom.

I want to wave the American flag so they can see this land where the colors of red, white, and blue fly high and proud. Today, I am standing on the shores of safety while thousands more are just beginning their journey. How many more will die at sea? How many will find their way to a new home? And how many will forever straddle the realm of life and death because while their heart beats on, their spirit died with the invasion of pirates, the tortures of prison camps, and the disappearance of loved ones?

My regrets are many. Every speck of sand on this beach represents every minute I have drifted through life. Sometimes I catch a good wave and ride it, but it always crashes. When will my life crash again?

The horizon is where both heaven and hell live. Out there, you are in limbo, half lucid, half hallucinating. The only thing you are sure of is the light that cuts through the glassy ripples and the image reflecting at you is not you at all. The face is unrecognizable because it is a mash-up of fear, hope, desperation, longing, and joy. It is a confusing, surreal period in which you see both your accomplishments and your failures. What is waiting on the other side of your escape is unknown.

My daughter runs and laughs with Bình. The two of them have fun outsmarting the sudsy surf. They squat on their haunches and watch a little crab scurry into a hole. I wonder if Dolly remembers much of our journey. I hope she only remembers the good parts of our adventure, like Ommo's kindness, playing the rebab under the coconut trees, and eating sweet sapodillas by the bonfire. I want her to appreciate every sunrise and every sunset because they represent the magic of life. May she look at the moon and the stars and realize so many people made sacrifices so that she can be alive today.

Dolly takes my hand. "What are you thinking about?"

I scoop her into my arms and nuzzle her neck. "I was thinking of how lucky I am and that you are my miracle."

We continue our journey down the coast, taking turns driving every couple of hours. The view from the Oregon Coast Highway is glorious. We see signs for sea caves and other tourist attractions like sand dunes and Crater Lake. Dolly looks for license plates from different states and takes a tally of how many California ones we see. By nightfall, we pull into a parking lot in front of a small motel. We are perhaps an hour's drive from the Oregon-California border. Bình and I get separate rooms for the night and agree to get back on the road early in the morning.

Dolly crawls into the bed and is fast asleep. I curl up next to her and let today's excursion slip quietly under the door and disappear into the night.

###

Four cups of coffee, two liters of soda, and three rest stops later, we turn into the bedroom community of San Jose in the Silicon Valley, at the southern tip of the San Francisco Bay. The street signs are hard to see in the dark, but we finally pull into the driveway of a two-story home. My back is tight, my legs are stiff, and my mood is questionable. The porch light turns on, and two figures emerge.

Bình's daughter, Thu, and her boyfriend, Ken, greet us in front of the garage. Thu helps me with my luggage while Ken carries a sleeping Dolly out of the car. For a tall man, he moves in and out of my Honda Civic like a ninja. One look at Thu, however, and I feel insignificant. I detect a glimmer of suspicion, probably wondering who her father has dragged in off the streets of Seattle. I am guessing her allegiance is to her mother first and her tolerance for her father is born out of necessity. I remind myself that I am her elder. It is she who needs to earn my respect and trust. I hold my head high with authoritative confidence despite feeling the rocks of travel on my fatigued body.

I forgive Thu's detached demeanor and cold reception of me. It is the dead of night at two-thirty in the morning, and everyone is tired. Tomorrow should be an interesting day. Tonight, however, I only care about blackout curtains and a soft bed.

23. SAN JOSE (SUMMER 1984)

I lift both eyelids to receive the glow of sunshine, but only one eye fully opens. It takes a moment to remember I am in Thu and Ken's house. I survey my room. The curtains are open, letting in all the natural light of the California sun. The walls are painted mint green, the décor and accents inside the room are white, and the bed frame, nightstands, and dressers are dark brown. I cannot help but feel I am inside a mint chocolate chip ice cream container. A large closet with floor to ceiling mirrors stands on the opposite side of the adjoining bathroom. The mirrors make my bedroom feel enormous. On the wall is a large painting of a tan horse with a silver-blonde mane and tail. A man stands beside the majestic beast, holding the reins, and squinting directly at me. It is a young Bình, looking proud, handsome, and aristocratic.

Laughter floats up the stairs. I press my ear against the bedroom door and hear Thu and Ken teasing one another. I smile. The young lovers playfully argue about what toppings are best on Taiwanese shaved ice.

"Strawberries and condensed milk," Ken says. "With lots of tapioca balls."

"No balls," Thu says, "just lots of exotic champagne mangoes."

"You like exotic?" Ken asks. "Nothing more exotic than Ken toppings." Thu squeals with laughter. "If you want me to stop tickling you, you have to declare Ken toppings with coconut cream is best."

"Durian is better." Thu's laughter gets louder as she runs up the stairs past my bedroom. Ken is right behind her. The door slams, and the giggles die down. The noise does not disturb Dolly as she slumbers soundly on the canopy bed that we shared last night. I open my bedroom door and peek out. I hear the lovers moan. The quiet creak of their bed testifies that they are enjoying each other's bodies.

Thoughts of the lovebirds entwined in one another's embrace send hot flashes of desire to my stomach and down between my legs. Bình's face from the painting sparks a light, electric tingle to my breasts. The longer I stare into those dark eyes, the more haunting those eyes become. I have seen those captive eyes before. I recognize how they can inflict fear one moment and show tenderness the next. I see Ommo's eyes looking back at me. Was I wrong not to write to him? What could I have said? I blew the flame out of his candle when I chose America over him. He must loathe me by now. He deserves a woman who is in love with him, who can give him children, and who will devote herself to making him happy.

A great sadness blankets me and smothers me with guilt as I remember Ommo's Adonis face and his minty kiss. Everything about him was primal and male. His athletic physique, his thick forearms, the way he gripped his AK-47, how his uniform sculpted his chest—these characteristics screamed danger—yet his music and smile whispered tenderness.

I miss the embrace of a man's hard arms. I want to feel safe again. I deserve love and need to give someone all my love. How do I open myself to it once more? It was easy with Sam and me. Despite being from different worlds, speaking different languages, having both an age and height difference, none of that mattered. We simply fit together. I swallow the lump in my throat and curl my toes as if that were the cure to my loneliness.

I walk into the bathroom and turn on the shower. The lukewarm water soothes my lamenting thoughts. I watch the stream of water circle the drain at my feet and disappear through the small holes. There goes another piece of Sam, another part of me, another morsel of remorse.

It is a new day. I am in a new place with new people. I must make different choices and live a charming version of my American dream. An exhilarating delight washes over me. I am a survivor. I am going to go after what I want.

What I want is Bình.

###

It is a beautiful day to explore. The five of us pile into Thu's BMW E28 with Ken behind the wheel and Bình in the front passenger seat. We meet Tree, Kelly, and baby Holly at the San Jose Flea Market at eleven. Thu is all smiles right now having conducted a little tête-à-tête this morning with Ken. She is polite, talkative, and curious. When she smiles, her two dimples make her look innocent. I conclude last night's uncomfortable encounter was due to the poor timing of our arrival. In time, I think we can be friends.

In the backseat, Dolly straps herself in the middle. Thu and Bình do most of the talking, catching up on family affairs, pointing out attractions along the way, and discussing Thu's wedding plans after she graduates from college. She will finish with a BS in economics and a masters in taxation. She and Ken will continue to support each other's aspirations while living under the same roof. The idea of them living together as an unmarried couple having pre-marital relations gives me pause. Of course, in Việt Nam, that is unthinkable and would bring dishonor to the family. Our reputation would be tainted and we would be treated as outcasts in our village. Heaven forbid if there is a pregnancy out of wedlock.

Thu's bold declaration that they will live together and marry after school is admirable. She has great strength which will serve her well. I wish I had that confidence when I was her age. Then again, we live in different times under more liberating and democratic circumstances. What surprises me most is how much Bình takes everything in stride without judgment or contrarian attitudes. I find this attribute in him pleasing and attractive. He is open-minded and supportive of his daughter's life choices. I hope I can be accepting when Dolly tells me one day that she is moving in with her non-Vietnamese boyfriend.

"What do you do?" I ask Ken.

Ken glances at me in the rearview mirror. Tree is right. He looks like a movie star straight out of a Chinese film. Before answering, he changes lanes to take the exit toward Berryessa Road. Ken downshifts to third gear and slowly comes to a stop at the traffic light. "I am a developer at Hewlett-Packard in Palo Alto. The company just introduced an inkjet and laser printer for the desktop computer. I develop the software for printing."

"Impressive," I say. "How long have you all been in California?"

Ken's great-great-grandfather was one of the Chinese immigrants who worked on the railroads in the 1860s. "He built the railroad between San Francisco and San Jose for twenty-seven dollars a month. I am generation five-point-oh, born right here in San Jose."

Thu explains that Bình was among the first wave of men to partake in the offshore pilot program hosted by the US Army and

US Air Force. They flew him to Fort Wolters, Texas along with a dozen or so of his fellow countrymen.

"We had intense English language training followed by classroom instructions on how to fly this piston-powered helicopter called the TH-55," Bình says, "and before I knew it, I was on a solo flight. It was the scariest thing I had ever done. It was confusing. They would draw a diagram on the chalkboard and show us how to complete a final approach, tell us where the take-off pad was, and ask us how to identify lane numbers and pad numbers. My English was mediocre, but luckily, I understood the mechanics of how it operated."

"After he came back to Vietnam," Thu says, "my father went through more training on the CH-34. He flew a lot of missions, and after the peace agreement was signed in Paris, the American troops withdrew, and Dad was one of the few who had the opportunity to resettle here."

"Of course, I could not leave without taking my family with me," Bình says. "I convinced my wife that a brighter future awaited us in California, and we could try to be a family again."

"That was 1973," Thu says. "A year later, as you know, the cease-fire was ignored, and war resumed in full force."

Hearing them retell their story makes me realize how many layers there are to Bình. He grew up as a farmer, his family rubbed elbows with the French military and bred racehorses, he married a wealthy woman descended from the Nguyễn dynasty, had ties with her communist family, and then flew dangerous missions into enemy territory for years fighting the Việt Cộng. On top of all this, his wife left him twice, but he still maintains a relationship with his children.

What different lives we lead. While he was making a new life for himself and his family here, I was getting married to Tý and mourning the loss of Sam. While Thu turned fourteen in the summer of 1974 and started high school, Dolly was born fighting for her life. Through all the pain and suffering I witnessed and with the nightmares and flashbacks I still have, I cannot fathom Bình being any less troubled than I am. I wonder if our relationship is already doomed before it even begins. And how in the world did he end up in Seattle?

###

We arrive at the flea market already bustling with pedestrians and eager to find some bargains, from used tires to emerging artwork. Dolly sees children carrying cheap, shiny, plastic toys, and begs to have one. Another child holds a melting ice cream cone with puddles of vanilla stuck to her shoes. My daughter begs for a cone too, and before I can answer, Ken scoops her up and says, "Of course."

The San Jose swap meet is like nothing I have seen before. Back home there are large blocks of open markets, alley after alley of vendors, all selling food, toys, fabric, and everything in between. This market takes it to another level and stretches so far in every direction that it can swallow a province. Each tent has something wonderful to offer, from enticing foods, electronics, and fashionable clothes, to bicycles, garden accessories, and home décor.

Almost immediately, I spot Tree and Kelly pushing a stroller in our direction. I wave to my nephew. Dolly runs to him and leaps into his arms. She misses her cousin who is more of a big brother than anything. Kelly and I hug. We all say our hellos to one another before Tree, Ken, and Bình take off down the first row of vendors. They agree to return to the hot dog and sno-cone area in an hour.

I squat to take a good look at baby Holly. "Let Great Auntie Eight take a good look at you." I smile at Holly and admire her flawless, pearly complexion. I stroke the damp wisps of hair that curl around her ears and notice the tiny stones in her earlobes. "Your ears are pierced." Holly smiles at me. I melt. "Your birthstone is a diamond, like mine." She smiles again as if she understands. I pick up Holly and gently hug her. "Ngọc, she is beautiful, a darling gem. She is smart, I can tell. Her eyes are alert. I am so happy for you."

We take turns coddling the baby before walking down the same path the men took ten minutes earlier. The market is alive with vendors seducing us with deals. We stop at a few booths and admire trinkets and souvenirs but buy nothing. Halfway down the third aisle, Thu stops at a booth selling ceramic vases and silk flowers. An Asian woman in a straw conical hat sits on a stool behind a small table arranging silk irises, magnolias, and dogwoods into a green foam base. Her helper is a young girl in her teens, half Cambodian, half European, with curly, sandy blonde hair and striking green eyes.

"Hello, Mother," Thu says. "Hi, Claudia."

The woman hovers a quick gaze at her daughter before droning over to me. She scans me like a bar code and makes me feel vulnerable. In just a few seconds, this woman probably knows everything she wants to know about me and has made up her mind whether I am worth her time or should be forgotten on a dusty shelf.

So this is Bình's ex-wife. I imagined her to be a beauty, full of grace and youth, but the woman before me has let herself go. She has weathered a great storm and has come out of it barely alive. There is distrust in her movements, contempt in her eyes, and a low growl in her voice. She makes it very clear I am not wanted here. She may have come from a royal bloodline, but the iron heart before me is bitter and cold.

I take my daughter's hand and steer her toward the booth two spots up where a man is selling volleyballs, basketballs, and other sports toys. Kelly follows us.

"Did you know that was Thu's mother?" I ask.

"No. I have never met her or seen a photograph of her before," Kelly says. "Not what I expected."

"What is her story?" I ask.

Dolly tugs at my shirt. "Can I have a volleyball?" She taps my bottom when I do not respond.

"Fine," I say to appease her. I motion to the salesman. "How much?"

The vendor holds up five fingers. I shake my head and show him two. He grins and dismisses me, refusing my counteroffer. I take a few steps toward another toy booth, and Dolly whimpers. The man calls me back and agrees to two dollars. That was easy. What a thrill to have the upper hand when entering a negotiating zone.

Kelly picks up right where we left off. "Thu looks nothing like her mother. She and Khoi look like Uncle Bình."

"Phan must look like her then," I denote. "I guess you cannot have everything in life. She may have had the wealth and status, but she did not have access to the fountain of youth and beauty."

Kelly nods. "I believe that if you are unfortunate in the first half of your life, you will be fortunate in the second half. I would rather suffer when I am young. What about you?"

I think of something wise to say, but Kelly does not give me an opportunity. She spots Tree and the other two men thirty feet ahead. She calls out to them, and they join us.

"Where is Thu?" Ken asks.

I answer Ken's question but look at Bình when I reply. "She is visiting with her mother."

Bình frowns. "So you met Trang."

"Not really," I say, "but we locked eyes."

Bình tells me they are on friendly terms, but they cannot tolerate more than thirty minutes together. Trang does not know anything about me other than I am the woman in Seattle he is interested in pursuing. Bình laughs when I look shocked. "Do not tease me. Of course, you suspected." I ask him how he ended up in Seattle. "I needed a change of scenery. My children do not need me. I had nothing anchoring me in California. I saw Seattle on TV one day, and it looked so majestic with the mountains and the lakes. Washington also has a lush rainforest and an arid desert. How marvelous to be so versatile and prosperous a state. So I made up my mind to move up there. Washington is also more receptive to the Vietnamese refugees. We are a burden to the Californians. One day I ran into Lan. We were classmates back in Việt Nam, so I took it as a sign that Seattle was meant to be home."

Bình and I split off from the group. Dolly goes with Ken and the others to get ice cream. We agree to meet back at the concession stands in twenty minutes and decide on what to do about lunch. Bình takes my hand, and I shy away at first, uncomfortable with the idea of publicly displaying affection. He reminds me this is the land of the free, and we can hold hands. He points to a couple laughing and hugging and another couple kissing. No one seems to mind they are openly loving. Not a person is staring at them except for me. I relax and feel his fingers dovetail with mine. We stroll up and down the next couple of rows and stop at a record store. People crowd around the tables and milk crates, thumbing through albums from all different genres. I immediately gravitate to Lionel Richie's new album, *Can't Slow Down*, and ask the salesman to play a song for me.

"No scratch?" I ask.

"New," he says. "No scratch."

The man puts on the A side and queues up the song "All Night Long." My hips sway, and I cha-cha to the chorus. Bình takes my hand and twirls me around. He cha-chas with me, and we move perfectly in rhythm back and forth. He takes it up a notch by spinning a full circle and resumes sidestepping the cha-cha without missing a beat. Our audience gets bigger, and another couple joins in. I let go of all insecurities, all pent-up fears of judgment, and focus on Bình's lead. The crowd cheers, and I collapse into his embrace.

"Is there anything you cannot do?" I ask. "You are full of surprises."

"So are you," he says. "Does this mean we are taking Mr. Richie home with us?" I nod, and Bình buys the album for me. He does not even haggle on the price. I object and try to strike a better bargain. Bình says I cannot put a price on something that makes me happy.

With the new album in hand, we meet up with everyone, including Thu, back at the food court. We enjoy a leisurely lunch at the flea market and show each other what we purchased. Tree and Kelly take Holly home for a nap and promise to come by the house for dinner later. Thu plans to extend the invite to her brothers, Phan and Khoi, and Khoi's girlfriend, Linh.

This should be interesting. I am curious about Phan.

In Thu's kitchen, I volunteer to be the sous chef and offer Dolly up as the prep cook. Thu glides around the kitchen with ease, and like all executive chefs, she barks her orders and wears her emotions on her sleeves. She is wound up tight today, and I think her mother may have something to do with it.

It does not matter that I am the elder and the guest in her home. Today, I am a crank turner. On one occasion, Thu catches herself from yelling and politely tells me to smash the garlic cloves, not mince them. She shows great restraint from pulling her hair out when Dolly spills the uncooked thread noodles all over the floor. At one point, while I wait for the water to boil, Thu rushes out of the kitchen and returns five minutes later, calmer, more poised, and wearing a different shirt. I notice the bait and switch and wonder if she has a twin I do not know about.

Immediately on her heels is Ken. His presence soothes her. He shows Dolly how to peel ginger and hands her the knife. Under his supervision and encouragement, she slices the knob into thin pieces, then cuts them into strips. My daughter smiles and looks at Ken adoringly. I have a feeling her crush on Mark Hartman at school has been replaced by a new crush on Ken.

We get into a new rhythm and despite having four bodies in the kitchen, we maneuver around each other without getting in one another's way or breaking anything. Before long, everything is cooked, and Thu shoos Dolly and me out of the kitchen so that she can put on the finishing touches. Ken stays back to tidy the kitchen and wash the pots and pans. It is good timing because the doorbell rings.

Bình opens the door. Tree and Kelly are the first to arrive. They look rested and have changed into something more formal. Tree is dressed in black from top to bottom, and Kelly wears a navy polka dot skirt and beige blouse. She compliments me on the giraffe-print halter jumpsuit and says the colors cream and purple suit me.

"I borrowed it from Diệp," I say. "Where is the baby?"

"With our neighbor and her daughter," Kelly says. "We both need a night out without her."

There is a knock at the door, but before Bình can answer it, a young man with slicked black hair walks in. He smiles and displays a pair of dimples identical to Thu's. He is in the middle of a debate with his Cambodian girlfriend and is talking faster than the vehicles on the autobahn. I understand now what Bình meant when he said Khoi is into fast cars and pretty girls. Whereas Thu has her mother's petite stature, Khoi is lanky and tall like his father. Same face, same smile, but with a burst of energy and effervescent youth.

Khoi walks toward me with a confident swagger. He greets me respectfully, "Chào Cô," and leans down to kiss me on the cheeks as if we are family, not strangers. I like him instantly and feel as if I have known him for years. He introduces me to Linh.

Shy and humble, Linh clasps her hands together and gives a slight bow. "Hello, Auntie Snow."

I cannot take my eyes off her. This young raven enchantress before me is a gorgeous femme fatale. I do not think she knows how aesthetically majestic she looks with her long slim legs, voluptuous figure, and full lips shaped like a heart. It is my turn to have a crush, if it is even possible for me to have one. The girl looks like she materialized from an unknown, exotic island.

"Dinner is ready," Thu calls out. We funnel into the dining room and encounter a beautifully set table with crystal stemware, fine china dinner plates, and thick cloth napkins. Even Dolly's place setting is arranged with the same expensive dinnerware.

"Wait," Ken says. "Where's Phan?"

Khoi pulls out a chair for Linh. "You know how he is. He'll be here when he gets here." Khoi drapes his arm across the back of Linh's chair. "Okay, sis, what did you make us?"

Thu proudly waves her hand over each dish and explains the cuisine before sitting down next to Ken. "Tonight we have Szechuan pork belly, braised in ginger, brown sugar, soy sauce, and green onions. This is a roasted duck with steamed hoisin baos. This is a fensi salad. And of course, we have jasmine rice cooked in a chicken stock then stir-fried in butter, garlic, and a pinch of sea salt. Last but not least, oyster sauce Chinese broccoli.”

“And the watermelon is to cleanse the palate?” I ask.

“Yes,” Thu says, “but it is also good with the rice.”

Impressive. We all dig in ravenously. No one says grace. I make the sign of the cross and partake in Thu’s culinary offerings. Every bite is divine. Dolly’s morsels of food get bigger and bigger with every reach. She is a greedy glutton tonight. I could not be happier to see her eat and am proud she is behaving like a proper young lady. She knows how special this is to be sitting at the adult table, dining with expensive dinnerware and stemware and being treated like an adult.

“You should open a restaurant,” Dolly says to Thu. “This is yum yum. What would you name it?”

“Well, I almost majored in hospitality,” Thu answers, “so that I could open a restaurant, but that is a lot of work. I don’t want to be a slave to it. That’s why I am getting a degree in economics and taxation. I want the business to work for me!” It is all jargon to Dolly. She repeats her question. Thu gives it some thought. “Well, I guess I would call it *Le Petit Gourmand* for the little greedy eater.”

Dolly puts her fork down and looks at Thu seriously. “That is French. You are not French. And all this food is Chinese.”

Khoi laughs. “Whoa, she told you!”

Thu cracks a smile. “You are too smart for your own good.” She playfully taps the tip of Dolly’s nose with her finger.

Like a reverberating earthquake, we rumble with amusement until someone lets out a ripple of flatulent noises. Dolly laughs nervously and says “rut-roh.” This amplifies our mirth, and an aftershock of laughter flows around the table.

We are so entertained and thoroughly enjoying our food that we do not notice the slinky figure looming by the archway. A shadow moves, and I turn to see if it is a ghost.

Bình’s youngest son, Phan, does not explain his tardiness or apologize for disrupting our dinner. He crosses the room, his head bobbing up and outward until he finds his seat on the far end between Bình and Khoi. He points to a sauce and makes a strange face to express his displeasure. Thu explains it is a hoisin and hot sauce combination for the baos. He waves at it as if to say goodbye.

Dolly leans over and whispers to me, “He reminds me of Willoughby. Do you know who that is, Mama?” I shake my head.

"He's a cartoon, a hound dog, and not a very smart one either. He is always chasing after something."

I observe him discreetly and try to figure him out. Bình had said he was shy, but he could just be socially awkward or have a neurological developmental disability. Whatever it is, he is not engaging with his surroundings or conversing with anyone at the table, not even with his siblings and father. It is as if he is sitting at this table alone and none of us exist. Our conversation, our laughter, our lips smacking, our silverware clanging are nonexistent to him.

His personality is uninspiring, and I feel a little guilty for thinking so. It must be challenging to be him. I am guessing he has been teased, bullied, and misunderstood all his life. If he did not look so much like his mother, perhaps I would find myself warming up to him or exercising more patience to get to know him. With only five days in San Jose, I decide it is not the time to take on that herculean project. I want to enjoy my vacation and explore as much of California as I can until our drive home. I will only be disappointed if I try to get him to like me.

As aloof as Phan is with everyone, he seems to be comfortable with Dolly. She is curious about him and is relentless with her questions. She eventually wears him down and bulldozes through his walls. As the evening crawls along, Phan is content to sit with my daughter and play go fish, slapjack, and war with a deck of cards.

Tree and Kelly are the first to leave. We say our goodbyes for the night and make plans to get together again before I return to Seattle. Phan is next to leave since he lost his game partner. Dolly yawns and can barely keep her eyes open. The heat of the day has worn her out, and the food in her belly hypnotizes her into dozing off. She hugs Phan and disappears upstairs to put herself to bed. If she likes him, then there must be more to him than meets the eye.

By midnight, the flow of alcohol slows down and only food crumbs remain, too small to be worth picking at. Khoi keeps us entertained with jokes and stories, and Linh comes out of her shell after two shots of Hennessey. Bình picks up a guitar and strums a song while Ken sings and Linh dances. Bình's talent with a musical instrument is yet another thing to add to his growing list of surprises. He seems too good to be true.

The party fizzles at one in the morning, and we all turn in for the night. Khoi and Linh are too inebriated to drive. They set up camp on the sofa bed.

I take one last look at Lionel Richie, propped up against the lamp on the nightstand, and then it is lights out.

###

I sleep well and feel energized by the bright sunshine. Dolly is asleep. I watch her little chest as it rises and falls. I am lucky to have her. I love her so much. I resist the urge to blip her lips and slither out of bed in search of coffee.

The house is quiet. I creep downstairs and find Linh and Khoi are gone. In the kitchen, there is a note from Thu. Ken is at work, and she has some business to tend to. I make coffee and sit on the back patio to enjoy the serenity of my surroundings. Today is another sunny day, and I hope to explore more of the Bay Area. My thoughts meander around Phan and how odd he is. He is not unkind, just distant. I will have to ask Dolly what the two of them talked about last night while playing cards.

The patio door opens, and Bình stands before me in his bathrobe and slippers, holding a mug of coffee, and wearing a boyish grin. "What do you want to do today?" He pulls out a lawn chair and sits beside me.

"I want to explore," I say. "Maybe San Francisco?"

"Yes," Bình says, "you will like San Fran. Also, if you are up to it, I want to take you to Orange County, but it is a six-hour drive south of here. A large community of Vietnamese refugees settled there. Being back in San Jose has made me realize how much I miss the weather, the food, and the bonds of family."

"I am up for the adventure," I say. "Tell me, was it hard for you to come here back in 1973? What was it like?"

A minute passes before Bình answers me. I almost think he did not hear my question, but he looks at me, grasping for words, deciding where to start his story. "The American War divided this country. So many were killed, missing in action, or became prisoners of war. The majority of Americans did not want us here. They feared we would take their jobs or dry up their welfare system. On top of that, unemployment rates were high, and the nation was in a recession. Like the American military who came home to hate and resentment, so did I. It was hard. We were called names, kicked at, spat on, and seen as diseased." Bình's voice trembles. He takes a long sip of his coffee.

I squeeze his hand. "Take your time."

"You know, we were at Camp Pendleton for a while before a VOLAG representative from Church World Service found us a sponsor to help us assimilate," Bình says.

"Did you have a good relationship with your sponsor?" I ask.

"Yes," he says, "in Santa Ana, but we were encouraged to be financially independent as soon as possible. Many of us took the first job we could find that did not require fluency in English. I did not want to burden my sponsors, so I took a low-paying job to ease their conscience. There was so much racism in the beginning. The Americans treated us as inferior because we are smaller than they are and do not speak the language or understand their laws and processes."

"Navigating that matrix must have been debilitating on one's confidence," I surmise.

"It did not help that the governor at the time publicly denounced us. Unlike Washington's governor, Dan Evans, who welcomed our people, Governor Jerry Brown tried to prevent planes carrying Vietnamese refugees from landing at Travis Air Force Base. Anyway, my first job was as a gas station attendant and I met other refugees over the years. We all sought each other out for unification and protection. Of all the pockets of refugees who came to the US, I think the solidarity in Orange County grew the fastest. Educated people who were businessmen, teachers, doctors, and lawyers somehow found one another and became resources for one another. A new extended family formed. Small restaurants and markets popped up, and now, it is beginning to look like a little Sài Gòn down in Orange County. Many of the small businesses got started because some families transferred their wealth to foreign banks before Sài Gòn fell, while others joined their trusted friends in a rotating credit system."

"Yes, the hui," I say. "My sister runs one, and she used the money to open Six's Kitchen. There is only one thing on the menu." I chuckle thinking of my sister giving a customer the evil stare and silent treatment if they ask for anything other than egg noodle soup. "So how did your family come to live in San Jose?"

"Thu got accepted into San Jose State University," Bình says. "She is my firstborn. I am protective of her. I also wanted the family to stay together, but my children became independent and more Americanized. They rebelled against our traditions and customs, which caused a divide between Trang and me. We took sides and developed different viewpoints. She was stuck in the old way of life, and because she did not work, she had no social connections or progressive views of American society."

"Do you miss our homeland?" I ask. "I get homesick all the time, and because we came here by boat and survived, I feel guilty. Too many people died escaping oppression, and they risked everything only to lose their life before they could taste freedom."

Bình says he misses his parents and sisters. He hopes to sponsor them over in the next year or two. He is saving money, and once he has nine thousand dollars, he will start the application. The government wants sponsors to prove they can take full financial responsibility for the sponsored family members. He needs a stable job and steady income. His deepest concern, however, is that there will be a huge culture shock for them, and without a thriving Vietnamese community, they will become depressed. Seattle is not exactly tropical weather, and chances are good that their world will be very small once they arrive. They do not know English and cannot drive, so they would be dependent on him. For these reasons, he has thought about moving back to California, to Westminster or Garden Grove.

"My parents are spry for their age. In our village, they are well-respected. There is nothing for them here in the US, but I cannot bear the thought of my parents living the rest of their life in Vietnam. My sisters bring little comfort because they are married and live with their husband's family."

It makes me nervous that Bình is entertaining the idea of moving back to California. I wonder if Seattle will become an enclave for the Vietnamese refugees. Will the community be able to thrive and sustain operations, or will it erode with each new generation and ultimately collapse? I suppose only time will tell. I enjoy our budding friendship. He is easy to talk to, and I know we have feelings for one another. If we dare to scratch harder past the surface and explore this companionship, will we find love or resentment? Bình has been through trials of his own and had his marriage fail twice. I have loved and lost as well and do not know if I can truly love again, even though I desperately want to believe I can.

Can we heal and build a strong foundation together? Can we trust again? Or are we both too damaged?

24. ORANGE COUNTY (SUMMER 1984)

Dionne Warwick's song, "Do you know the way to San Jose," plays
on the radio. Her demurring feminine voice coats my troubled mind
and cements the distress I have over Bình moving back to
California. If there is ever a more slap in the face sign, this is it. I
change the station so that any thoughts he may have of moving
away sink deep down into his psyche.

Yesterday's visit to San Francisco was amazing. Dolly, Bình,
and I walked around the waterfront to Fisherman's Wharf, visiting
the open markets similar to Seattle's Pike Place Market and seeing
the Golden Gate Bridge. We packed in so much activity, including a
visit to a botanical garden and a boat tour around the bay.

This morning's drive to Orange County has me straddling
the realms of excitement and dread. The sun siphoned a lot of my
energy yesterday. Bình drives so I can relax. The thought of
sightseeing the cities of Westminster, Huntington Beach, Anaheim,
Irvine, and Santa Ana has me strumming my fingers and tapping my
toes to the raspy sounds of Aerosmith and Bon Jovi. Their hard
rock sound reminds me a little of the '70s music in Việt Nam when
the American soldiers played their boomboxes.

We drive nonstop the 375 miles down to Westminster in six
hours, hitting a little bit of traffic on I-5 South near Los Angeles. By
the time we exit off the freeway onto Magnolia Street, my stomach
rumbles loudly.

"You know what sounds good?" I ask. "*Bánh mì* and iced
coffee with condensed milk. I miss this so much."

"If you want good bánh mì," Bình says, "wait until we get
back to San Jose. There is a place called Lee's Sandwiches on Santa
Clara Street that recently opened."

"I want *phở*," Dolly says, "with a lot of hoisin sauce and no vegetables."

"The herbs are good for you," Bình says. "I will get you a bowl of phở if you eat some of the green stuff."

Dolly agrees without arguing. If I try to strike a deal, she usually pushes back or negotiates. We turn onto Bolsa Avenue, and a surge of nostalgia wraps itself around my heart. On both sides of the street are storefronts and buildings with words written in Vietnamese. Hundreds of people from the Asian community, particularly the Chinese, Cambodians, Laotians, and Vietnamese ethnicities, congregate in small pockets to socialize, shop, and dine. It is incredible. I feel like an archaeologist who discovered an indigenous people living within the deep concrete jungle. My mouth waters. I roll down the window and take in the sounds and smells of Little Saigon.

I lean out the window when we stop for a traffic light and listen to the chatter at the intersection and crosswalks. It is music to my ears. I weed out the different dialects and tune in to the inflections of the Vietnamese language with its singsong diacritics of *ngang, sắc, huyền, hỏi, ngã,* and *nặng*—the six accents of my native tongue. I hear dialects from different regions: the proper north, the incomprehensible central, and the slang south.

The only thing missing is the blaring horn of a thousand scooters zipping in and out of traffic to dodge pedestrians, animals, and other riders. I point to a phở restaurant, and Bình signals to change lanes. We pull into the parking lot, and Dolly claps her hands. Unable to contain her excitement, she unbuckles her seatbelt before the engine turns off. Diệp once cooked us this traditional beef noodle soup, but other than that, I cannot remember the last time we had it. The one memory that stands out is my phở meal with my niece Tâm at the café in Tuy Hòa. That was thirteen years ago in 1971 when I first met Sky and Sam.

This restaurant is a cash-only establishment, which does not surprise me in the least. The place is a small hole in the wall and packed with patrons slurping their noodles and smoking their cigarettes. Just like Việt Nam. It feels like home. There are two groups before us waiting for a table, but we get seated first at a community table where three seats open up. Hearing everyone speak only Vietnamese fills me with an indescribable feeling of homesickness and pride. I have the urge to hug and talk to everyone like they are long lost brothers and sisters or old friends from a faraway land. The restaurant smells heavenly of beef, fish sauce, charred onions, and ginger. One table has iced coffee and *chè ba màu*, the three-colored dessert made of yellow mung beans, sweet red beans, and green jelly served over a slush of ice and bathed in rich and creamy coconut milk.

The menu is impressive. I have a hard time deciding as everything is delicious. I thought I wanted bánh mì, but the photos of classic dishes like *bánh hỏi* and soups like *bún bò Huế* vie for consideration.

"Oh heaven and earth, they even have *tiết canh*!" I exclaim. This northern Vietnamese cuisine is not for the faint of heart. It is blood soup made from freshly slaughtered duck. The blood is mixed with fish sauce and duck broth to prevent premature coagulation. It is then poured over thinly sliced, cooked duck meat and organs like gizzards. The chef will refrigerate it for a brief period so the blood coagulates to a pudding consistency. Crushed peanuts, lime juice, and herbs, such as mint, cilantro, and basil, top this dish for texture, zest, and flavor when it is ready to be consumed. I have had this once, but I am not adventurous enough to throw caution out the window a second time. I admit it is a popular and tasty dish with beer.

In the end, Dolly orders her phở, Bình gets a broken rice combo plate that comes with grilled pork, egg cake, shrimp, and pickled carrots and daikon, while I choose the delicate, steamed rice cakes called *bánh bèo*, topped with mung bean paste, toasted shrimp, and scallions. After our meal, we walk up and down Bolsa Avenue, exploring shops, food markets, and jewelry stores. Before long, it is dinner time, and we try another restaurant that also does not disappoint.

Tomorrow is Wednesday, and another adventure awaits us in Anaheim at a park called Disneyland. A part of me does not want to go back to Seattle as my people are here. However, I have a community in Seattle, and life would not be the same without Teddy, Catherine, Sky, and Katrina. And it definitely would be dull without Diệp.

###

Today's Disneyland adventure is expensive, overwhelming, and disappointing. Hundreds of people stand in long, unforgiving lines and wait to strap in on the rides. Dolly wants to buy, eat, and experience everything, but we find out there are height restrictions to some of the rides. The heat and crowded lines bring out the impatience in a lot of people despite this place touting to be the happiest place on Earth. Perhaps it is the happiest place for management and the owner because they are making a lot of money on the overpriced souvenirs and food. The best parts of the visit are the parade and fireworks above the Sleeping Beauty Castle. It is too bad I do not own a camera to take photos as these memories would be nice for us to reflect on one day.

Before we leave, I give in to Dolly's pleading for a Mickey Mouse hat with ears on it. While my daughter and Bình meander off to look at T-shirts, I head straight for the hats. The one I want is perched too high for me to reach. I stand on my toes and stretch but lose my balance and tip over. I bump into a man and immediately feel embarrassed.

"I very sorry," I say to him. "I try get—"

"Watch what yer doin'." The stranger looks down at me. His breath inches from my face. His caustic growl can melt my eyebrows. He takes a step closer to tower over me. I take several steps back. He means to intimidate me and disintegrate any wrought-iron resolve I may have. He is a good eighteen inches taller than I am. I stand dwarfed face-to-chest with him, staring at the red, curly hairs weeding out of his white tank top.

I cannot control the trembling in my body or my voice. "I sorry." My voice is so faint that even I question whether I actually said the words or merely thought them.

"Goddammit, ev'rywhere I turn there's 'nother one of ya. Why don't cha git the fuck outta my country? We don't want yer kind here. Don't ya have a country of yer own? Go home." He runs his fat, hairy fingers through his long periwig hair and mutters, "Damn gooks."

I want to cry but dare not make a scene or give him a reason to mock me again. The airway in my throat constricts. My vision narrows to a peephole view of my surroundings, and all I can see is this intimidating man.

He is a big, heavy-set man with tattoos all over his arms and neck. Everything about him is menacing, even his red mustache and thick sideburns. His nostrils flare, and I can see the thick hair follicles coming out of their cave to join the belittling party.

He points to the door and says, "Git, girl."

I feel like a dog who has chewed her master's favorite shoe.

"You deaf or something? Or just plain stupid?"

My fear of his condescension has me frozen.

He bends down, hunches over me, and grits his teeth. "What's the matta? Cat git yer tongue? Oh, wait, you no speaka Inglish?" He smiles and ridicules me some more. Spit flies out the corners of his mouth and erodes his disingenuous smile.

I am reduced to a child whose hand has been slapped for reaching into the candy jar. The man grabs my wrist and cackles. My fight or flight response kicks in.

Minh-Hoàng's face appears at the forefront of my mind. Remembering that two-faced bastard and what he did to me ignites my adrenaline. Minh-Hoàng had lured me into his good graces so I would trust and depend on him, only to try to collect on the debt when my guard was down. I feel dirty with this man's hand on me. I twist my wrist outward and break free of his grip. I dig my heel into his flip-flop hugging toes and punch him with all my might in his testicles. One punch, two punch. Right fist, left fist. I shudder at the touch of his groin. I cannot believe it. He is not wearing underwear beneath his shorts and his penis is salaciously hard. Is he turned on by the power he has over me? I punch him a third time for good measure.

"Son of a bitch," he bellows in excruciating pain.

"Big man so tough," I say loudly. "No baby for you!"

I scurry out of his reach, feeling half victorious and half terrified, like a Chihuahua who nearly got eaten by a big, bad wolf. I find Dolly and grab her hand. I dash out the door. Bình is right behind me. I look back. The man is not following me. Dolly is crying, no doubt scared, confused, and upset. Bình asks what is wrong. My jog slows to a brisk walk. I peer over my shoulder. Good, he is not chasing me.

I tell Bình what just happened. He wraps his arms around me, and I take comfort in his protective embrace.

Maybe Seattle is where I belong after all.

We are back in San Jose today. Bình remembers to take me to Lee's Sandwiches for a bánh mì. While waiting for our order, we chat with a fellow Vietnamese brother who turns out to be Henry Le, one of the co-owners of the sandwich shop. He tells us he is the second oldest of nine children. Like me, his family escaped the war on a boat. They settled in San Jose, and before too long, what started as a modest catering truck business soon became a permanent sandwich shop. His parents used the truck on the weekends to sell sandwiches near San Jose State University, and with the profits, they opened Lee's Sandwiches.

I ask him why there is an extra E in the name, and he says, "So people know how to pronounce it." He admits business is good, and in time, they hope to expand the store to offer a variety of comfort foods, desserts, and beverages. I am inspired by his family's success and the example they are setting for the Vietnamese community. Henry is a good man. In my brief interaction with him, I find him to be light-hearted, genuinely kind, respectful, and funny. I wish him much success with the business.

Binh picks up our food order and takes Dolly and me to a park. Today is our last day in California and we leave early in the morning to drive back to Seattle. Tree, Kelly, their baby Holly, and Thu join us for a picnic. Ken, unfortunately, has to work.

After lunch, we walk San Jose State's campus and make one last stop at the flea market, the last afternoon together before the vacation is over. I feel good leaving Tree here to fend for himself. He has a job, a devoted wife, a small network of people he can rely on, and a growing Vietnamese community in which to thrive.

25. COBWEBS AND HONEYCOMBS (MAY 1985)

I call Magdaleine to see if she wants to come over. I suggest we rent
a movie. "Dolly at Opal's birthday. They have sleepover at Pastor
George's house."

Magdaleine suggests we have a girls' night out instead. "I
want to see the new *Rambo* movie. Did you see the first one?" She
summarizes the storyline of the first movie, which was released in
theaters three years ago, of a US Army veteran soldier in the Special
Forces Green Berets who returned from the Vietnam War, became
a drifter, and faced animosity from deputies in Washington State.
The sequel is about John Rambo returning to Vietnam, and he
discovers there are still Americans being held prisoner in a remote
communist camp deep in the jungle.

I am hesitant to see the movie for fear of it triggering stress
and guilt for me. Magdaleine is desperate for me to join her. "Snow,
please, I feel like I need to see the movie so I can understand Sky
better. He still has episodes of depression and violence. Maybe this
movie can shed some light on what he's going through and how I
can support him."

"What you mean violence?" I ask. "Sky do something?"
Magdaleine is quiet at first and then I hear her crying.

"He was doing great after our couples retreat last year,
but…" She trails off and snuffles. I encourage her to continue.
"You don't know someone until you live with them. Lately, he has
been having nightmares. A couple of nights ago, he rolled over and
choked me in his sleep. I had to hit him on the head with the phone
to snap him out of it. I don't know what to do. Sometimes he yells
and screams orders in his sleep, and last month he took a swing at
me because I startled him."

She shares with me some of his stories that were discussed
during their counseling sessions. He does not talk about his time in

Vietnam unless she asks specific questions. He has mentioned comrades walking into traps, getting hammered with shrapnel, getting killed in front of him in a blink of an eye. Sky's depression can last hours to weeks, and he becomes withdrawn. "He goes into this dark place where he wants to be left alone, and it gets compounded with stress from work and house chores or family and co-workers." She admits Sky is on six different medications, for back pain, high blood pressure, anxiety, and insomnia. "But, Snow, he's been messing with the dosage and concocting his own remedy to balance himself out. Did you know he can't lift his arm for too long without it going numb? We sometimes have these big arguments, and I want to leave him, but I love him so much, and I know those are the times when he needs me the most. I don't want to give up on him, but…"

I soon drown her voice out and wrap my thoughts in a cocoon. Her frantic, high-pitched voice wearies me. The intermittent words of ambush, kill zone, and booby traps become morse code, dits and dahs for "I am scared."

Perhaps Sky is shutting down because he is finally happy and feels he does not deserve it. Maybe he loves Magdaleine so much that he is self-destructing and self-sabotaging so that she will leave him because he thinks she is better off with someone not as broken as he. It is his way of driving out the light so he can be alone in the dark without dragging loved ones with him. I believe this with all my heart because sometimes I feel this way too.

"Snow? You still there?" Magdaleine's curt voice intercepts my private sojourn.

"Yes," I say. "Magdaleine, the best gift you give to Sky is understand his military service not by choice and his goal was survive. Everything he do in Việt Nam, he do because he told to do. In war, we live minute to minute and worry hour by hour. We have no time to plan, just react and do, then regret later." As I say this, a tear escapes down my face. Will we ever be able to forget the atrocities? How can we self-soothe and heal from the pain?

I do not go with Magdaleine to see the new *Rambo: First Blood Part II* movie. I drive to the house she and Sky share in Renton, a city ten minutes north of where I live. I pull into the driveway. Magdaleine opens the front door and runs to my car before I put it into park and turn off the engine. The tear tracks still mar her beautifully sad face. We hug.

"He will be home soon," Magdaleine says. "Do you want me to stay or—?

"No." I cut her off. "Go see movie. I talk to Sky."

"Thank you," she says. "I know he will listen to you. You're his best friend. You can get through to him when no one else can."

Magdaleine puts on her sunglasses to shield her red puffy red eyes even though it is an overcast day. I wait until her car disappears down the road before letting myself into the house. Now, I wait.

Alone with my thoughts, I wonder what I will say to my dear friend. I want to believe he will be receptive to my presence and not see it as an invasion of his privacy, of me overstepping his boundaries.

I walk into the living room, and a stout, muscular dog with a rump as big as his head pounces on me. Magdaleine's dog, a Staffordshire Bull Terrier that she adopted at the shelter, jumps up and down, trying to reach my face. His tail wags wildly and smacks me in the calves, sending sharp stings down to my ankle. I bend down so he can give me canine kisses.

I rub Tank's square face and scratch his back. "Who cutest blue-nose? Huh, Tank? You the cutest staffy?" I give him belly rubs and look around for a toy or treat to give him.

On my way to the kitchen, I pass a few pictures hanging in the hallway and sitting on a console table. I notice there are no pieces of artwork, no eclectic sculptures, no avant-garde paintings, no mid-century modern collections of art anywhere in the house.

Framed photographs of family members, of Sky and Magdaleine as young kids and teenagers, and of Sky in his military uniform catch my attention. There are also two photos on the windowsill that take my breath away—one of Sky and Sam on the beach in Tuy Hòa with their uniform and rifle, and the other, a photo of Sam, Sky, and me. It was taken a month after we met when I bumped into them at my bank. An American reporter had taken our photograph and was writing an article for the publication on the blending of two cultures. The headline on the newspaper clipping says, "One War, Two Cultures, Three Friends." I had forgotten about that photo and never saw the printed work. I am tempted to take it out of the frame and read it. I touch Sam's face with my finger, desperately wishing I could feel his touch and willing him to come to life.

A door creaks open. Tank abandons me and runs down the hall. Sky is home. He calls out for Magdaleine. He stops when he sees me. His flushed face blossoms red. He looks gaunt. His eyes are sunken and hollow. Where is the light behind those kind eyes? Dressed in an oversized fawn-colored trench coat and brown hat, he looks like a southern black mouth cur, a breed of working dogs known for their protectiveness and intelligence. He has not shaved in a few days, and the dark bristles around his lips and chin give him a dangerous burglar vibe. We do not know what to say to break the awkward silence. He cocks his head to one side and asks what I am doing here.

"Forgive me, Sky," I say, "but I want to see you. I want talk alone with you. Magdaleine let me come, and she go see movie. Give us privacy."

"For what?" Sky asks. He takes off his coat and tosses it on the back of a chair. Sky strides to the wet bar and pours himself a drink. He offers me a glass, but I decline. "She told you, didn't she?"

"She worry for you," I say. "Me too. Magdaleine love you so much." Sky shoots his shot of whiskey and pours a double into his crystal whiskey glass. I put my hand gently on his before he lifts the glass to his lips. "I need you not drunk. Sky, you my best friend. I need you, and I think you need me too." I take his arm and lead him to the sofa.

I share my Disneyland story and the encounter I had with the red-haired stranger, hoping my story will invite him to open up. Together we can commiserate. I tell him it was the first time I felt unwanted here in America. Sky tells me the word for what I experienced is racism.

I tell Sky he is all I have, and I need him to pull himself together. For the first time in a long time, I am opening myself to the possibility of love and happiness with Bình. I remind him he has this with Magdaleine and that her gift of love is something he cannot throw away. "Remember what Bill say? If you lucky, you get one chance to find your great love in life. He say you have better chance getting kicked by horse than finding your soul's love."

"Soulmate," Sky says. "How do you remember these things?"

I shrug. "I thought counseling and the retreats go good for you. What happen?"

Sky remembers the glass of whiskey in his hand and takes a generous sip. "I guess I can't shake the compunction from—"

"What mean, 'com-pung-shun?'"

"Guilt," Sky says. "Snow, I destroyed a man's face at Tree's wedding."

"He heal," I say matter-of-factly, having no sympathy for Quang.

"But I reduced him from a man who stands with pride to a beast that slithers on his ass. I can't erase the look on his face and the terror in his eyes. I'm ashamed of how it made me feel, so powerful, and I liked it. Hell, I thirsted for it. I wanted him to die."

We agree that his actions further muddled the relationship between Kelly and Ann. The sisters will be challenged to close the divide between them. The familial rift will take time to bridge, but I tell him it would have happened sooner or later. "Sky, the truth alway come out."

"And I nearly killed Mags," Sky says softly. I cringe hearing Magdaleine's name shortened to something I find unflattering, but Sky does not notice. He stands up to pour another glass. "I can't erase the look of fear on her face. I felt like shit."

I look out the window and notice a dragonfly. Perfect timing for a much-needed sign. Dragonflies symbolize transformation and adaptability. I tell Sky this. "He here to remind us we need joy in our life."

"Yes, we do, but I'm a broken man."

"How broken?" I ask. "Like cobwebs or like honeycombs? Like glass or like horse?"

"What?" Sky asks. "I don't understand what you're getting at."

"Webs break but spiders spin more. Honeycombs break, but when they do, it for sharing. Make the honey sweeter when you can share with someone."

"So you are saying that if I share the broken parts of myself with people I love, the rewards will be sweeter?"

"Yes, Sky. Nothing ever really broken. Either it can be fixed or something new is created. A new version of Skyler Herrington can exist. A better version of you."

"And what about you?" Sky asks. "Are you broken?"

I smile. "Maybe."

"I don't see any cracks or broken pieces," Sky says. "Maybe yours are below the surface. Maybe in time or with more pressure, you'll break, but I see you as someone so put together despite the tragedies you've faced. How do you do it?"

"Vietnamese people good with secrets," I say. "Women learn to hide feelings and thoughts and not say anything to dishonor our family."

"Sometimes, I see things on the side of the street, like a plastic trash bag, and I tense up. My body temperature rises and so does my blood pressure. I question whether the bag is a bomb or if it's just garbage. I can't trust my judgment."

"Like you, I get nightmares," I say. "Beautiful sunsets make me cry because I thinking of floating in the sea. Sunrises make me miss my family."

"So what do we do?" Sky asks.

I pan over to the pictures and soak in the smiles on all the people in the photographs. I stare at Sam's face and try to commit it to memory. I yearn to kiss him, hold him, breathe in his scent, and laugh with him. I am pining over a man who is dead and will never come back to me in this life. It brings me overwhelming sadness and brief moments of joy.

I place the framed photos of Sam facedown. "I have idea." Sky implores me to elaborate. "We hurt ourselves with these pictures. We cannot bring Sam back. We cannot change the past. We look at them and we wish to go back in time. How we move forward if we alway look backward?"

"So you are suggesting we get rid of all the photos?" Sky asks.

"Put pictures of past away," I say. The more I think about the idea, the more I am convinced it will help. New energy and optimism surges within me. "Fill our home with new dreams, new inspire pictures."

Sky does not look convinced. He props the photos of Sam back up. He lets out a loud, heavy sigh. "Okay, fine." He gives in. "Let's do it before I change my mind."

We put the pictures in a shoebox and scavenge throughout the house for any trinkets, clothes or souvenirs that weigh Sky down with depression. Dog tags, a throw pillow, and mementos from Vietnam are put away in the attic. We go through photo albums and take out anything that reminds him of Uncle Dawson and the period of molestation in his life. In one of the holiday photos, there is a picture of a woman with long black hair who has her arm draped casually around Jean-Adrien's neck. Sky rips up the photo. It is a family friend who had an affair with Jean-Adrien for six months before Katrina found out.

It takes us nearly three hours to purge everything that brings Sky sadness or madness. We toast our good work with a glass of champagne.

"I feel like a dark cloud has lifted," Sky says. "I feel lighter and unburdened."

"Tomorrow," I say, "you go shop with Magdaleine and buy new, joyful things."

"You know what else I need?" Sky asks. "More photos of Mags."

I wince, and this time Sky notices. I tell him the nickname does not sound feminine and makes me think of a choking duck. I imitate a duck's quack by saying in a nasally voice, "Mags, mags."

Sky roars with laughter. There's the Sky I know, the Sky I want to see more of. I wrap my arms around his biceps and squeeze. He kisses the top of my head. All is right again despite the cobwebs and honeycombs in our lives.

26. LIFE IS GOOD (MAY 1986)

A year has passed since Sky and I had our discussion about
cobwebs, honeycombs, and "mags, mags." After I came home that
night, I took Sam's photo off the nightstand and put it in a shoebox
along with the book *A Separate Reality*. The hardest part was putting
away the emerald engagement ring that Sam surprised me with the
day he died. I said my goodbyes that night and cried myself to sleep.

Since then, every day has been one step closer to emotional
freedom as Sky and I learn to let go of our anxieties. We fill our
surroundings with people and things that bring us happiness. We
lean into God's teachings and have regular family gatherings. With
Bình by my side and Magdaleine by Skyler's, we've learned to hold
one another accountable for doing activities that swing the
pendulum of joy in the upward direction.

Sky continues to do his meditation retreats, and on
occasion, he tries writing poetry since it worked for his friend
Charlie Peters. He also started stellate ganglion block injections, and
the treatments have been working wonders for him. He is a
different man than he was a year ago with a more peaceful mind
and spirit.

As for me, I sometimes have setbacks in which I feel sorry
for myself or have disturbing dreams of the fall of Sài Gòn, the
communists and pirates, and the refugee camp. However, I no
longer let myself dwell on them. I joined the Family Fitness Center
and have discovered yoga again. Dolly and I often go to the gym to
swim in the pool, but when she is not with me, I exercise alone.

I made the mistake of taking Diệp once. She was too
disruptive, and I could not concentrate. While I showed up looking
Jane Fonda-esque in my matching leotard and tights, she looked like
a cross-dressed Richard Simmons wearing neon green high-cut
fitness thongs over her multi-colored spandex shorts. Of course, leg

warmers, a headband, wrist band, and hair scrunchie completed her outfit. She was a hot mess, sweating, grunting, and falling as she struggled to get into each yoga position. All hell broke loose in the last five minutes of class when the instructor turned off the light and let us relax in child's pose. Diệp was so exhausted and relaxed that she passed gas. Everyone heard it and laughed, but I was the only one who smelled it. It was the last time I took her as a guest.

Dolly is finishing sixth grade and is sad to leave Springbrook Elementary School. Some of her friends, including Nadirah Ahmad, Jackie Osario, and the on again-off again crush, Mark Hartman, will be going to different middle schools. Bình gave Dolly a Sony Walkman as a graduation gift, and she is excited to play it this week at sixth-grade camp. She and her classmates are off to Camp Walkawalka, located at the base of Mt. Si in North Bend, for some bonding with nature and storytelling around a firepit. It has been only two days, but I miss her dearly.

Bình has been courting me the old fashioned way, taking me to the park for picnics or a scenic drive through the Olympic National Forest. We have been to the beach a few times in Ocean Shores and Alki in West Seattle. We hold hands in public comfortably, and on occasion, I let him steal a peck on the cheeks or lips.

Today I call in sick, and Bill tells me not to worry. "Jerry can cover you." He reminds me that I report to Jerry now and should call him in the future when I am sick. I tell Bill he is the big boss, and I prefer to "cut out the middleman," a phrase I learned recently from Katrina, who started her wedding planning business and is in high demand this season. She turned away a high-profile client to squeeze in one important wedding, that of Diệp and Donald. I cannot wait to see how the fairytale wedding planning all comes together. Will it be a Rainbow Brite wedding with Diệp riding a horse or an aquarium wedding under the sea of brightly colored reef fish?

Bình is taking me to Mount Rainier today for a hike and picnic. We leave early in the morning in his Cadillac loaded with blankets and a cooler of food and white wine. During the drive, we listen to the radio until we lose reception and discuss everything from our favorite recipes to what I would do if King Kong climbs the Space Needle and throws up all over the *Seattle Times* building because he is afraid of heights.

He tells me he wants to test for citizenship and change his name from Bình Nguyễn to Ben Yuen. I tell him I like the name Benjamin better.

"If you become a US citizen," he asks, "would you change your name?"

I nod. "Yes, Liz, after Elizabeth Taylor."

"Liz Le sounds funny," Bình says. "Maybe Elizabeth Le is better." Bình slows down the car and pulls into a lookout spot. "Or better yet, how about Elizabeth Nguyễn?"

"Why would I—?"

Bình takes out a small jewelry box and pops it open. I open my mouth and admire the diamond ring. I look at him, excited and nervous at the same time. He takes the ring out of the box and reaches for my hand. "Tuyết, will you be my wife?"

Without hesitation, I say, "Yes!"

We spend a glorious day at Mount Rainier National Park taking in the stunning views of the lakes, groves, wildflowers, and wildlife. I am excited to plan our wedding and our life together. We daydream about the house we will have, the cars we will own, and the vacations we will take.

I tell Bình I want to go back to school. "There is a naturopathic medicine program at Bastyr University up in Kenmore. I want to get a doctorate in acupuncture and Oriental medicine." Bình encourages me to go for it, saying it is never too late. "I do not want to work at the *Seattle Times* forever."

As much as I adore Bill and am proud of the newspaper, I am not mentally stimulated. My boss Jerry is a little prejudiced toward non-white people and women. I tolerate him and perform my assigned tasks, but I have no passion to excel under his leadership. I doubt he would let me soar even if I wanted to climb the publication ladder.

We talk about what Bình wants to do. He thinks he will be good at real estate. I think it is perfect for him. He has a sales background and a business mindset. He also has connections and a knack for influencing others.

The only two questions that remain are where will we live and how do we tell Dolly about the marriage proposal and wedding?

With the exciting engagement news sitting big and bright on my ring finger, I take precautions not to show anyone until I can talk to my favorite person in the world.

My daughter steps off the yellow school bus and runs into my arms. She talks so rapidly I tell her to slow down. Funny how she used to ask me what people are saying and now it is me asking her this same question. The words slingshots from her mouth and ricochets off my ears. "I got to zip line from one tree to another. It was scary, but I did it, and it was so fun. And Jackie and I went canoeing, and she made us fall in because she stood up. But we had lifejackets, so we swam to a patch of dirt. The boys rescued us. I pretended we were on a deserted island. And at night we sang camp songs and told ghost stories. Nadirah didn't get to come because her mom and dad are super strict. I'm glad you're not that strict anymore and—"

Dolly abruptly stops and points to my finger. "What's that?"

I take a deep breath and tell her Bình asked me to marry him. "I said yes." I wait for her reaction. Will she be happy or upset? Will she fight me on this, or want to plan the wedding?

"Can I have a puppy?" Dolly asks.

"What? Why? Are you not happy for me? For us?"

"Sure," she says, "but I would be happier if we got a puppy. You promised to get me a pet."

"I did?" I ask. "When?"

"Well, you did," she says, and gives me the sweetest, undermining smile. That is my daughter, always looking for an opportunity or a profit. I do not say yes, but I do not say no either.

On the way home, we talk and laugh nonstop and share stories of what we did while we were apart. Life is good.

###

As I walk around downtown in Pioneer Square, new life springs under my feet. It is as if flora and fauna sprout out of the cobblestones and carry me from one block to the next so that I glide over the streets of Seattle. My walk takes me through Occidental Park down to the waterfront by Pier Forty Eight. Elliot Bay looks majestic in its sparkling splendor with the sun rays beaming bright and the breeze seducing boaters to stay awhile longer.

I look at my solitaire engagement ring and take comfort knowing someone loves me, wants me to succeed, and has no expectations in return. A light rain comes down and lasts less than ten minutes. A rainbow appears over the bay, and I think about what Pastor George once said about rainbows being God's covenant with man. In Genesis 9:13, after God sent the forty days and forty nights of rain, flooding the earth and destroying the wicked, he promised Noah that the rainbow would serve as a reminder he would never destroy mankind again.

Let this rainbow be a reminder, too, that I will never let anything destroy me. Let the vast oceans, lakes, and bodies of water no longer bring me sadness and guilt, but instead, be a badge of survival that carried me to the shores of freedom. I have her, the sea, to thank for giving me the strength to persevere and teaching me that I am strong.

For too long, I fought to survive. I kept my mind focused and my body tauter than a piano string. Now, I can relax, be carefree, take chances, and let love claim me. Bình could not have come at a better time when I least expected it but when I most needed it.

The breeze in my hair is now received eagerly as a caress rather than a threatening whisper. The gust of wind and the sideways rain is not here to stop me, but instead, carry me to the next best thing.

I am at peace and ready to rebuild, ready to thrive. Dolly, Tree, and I are safe. Our bellies are full, and our beds are warm.

27. THE RAINBOW BRIDE (OCTOBER 1986)

Seattle Supreme canters from behind the house and toward the wedding guests. She appears from the wet dirt trail that leads to Katrina's yurt. Yesterday it rained rocks, but like typical fall weather in Seattle, the clouds give way to the sun. Now the sky shines so brightly the autumn leaves glow like fire. We knew we were taking a chance with the weather having the wedding in October, but the fortuneteller, Hồng Nhung, assured us October 11 was the blessed date for Donald and Diệp to marry.

What a grand entrance Katrina and her horse make. The new Andalusian beast that Jean-Adrien gave to his wife on their do-over anniversary is tall and agile. Her white-gray coat is brushed and shiny for today's special occasion, and in the October glow, she looks like she is made of sterling silver. Cottonwood flurries run along with them as dandelion flakes swim through the air to guide both horse and rider to the ceremony that is about to start. Katrina slows her down to a four-beat gait and then halts in front of the barn door.

"Oh, Yip!" Katrina exclaims. "You are breathtaking."

Diệp gushes at the compliment. My dear friend is stunning in her ivory A-line wedding gown sheathed with gold silk organza. A rainbow gradient chiffon veil flows from the crown of her head down to the kitty heels of her shoes.

Jean-Adrien takes Diệp's hand. "Are you ready?"

She nods. Katrina gracefully slides off the horse and holds Seattle Supreme steady while Jean-Adrien gives Diệp a leg up. She has practiced getting on and off the horse many times, so today, Diệp hops on like a professional rider.

My dearest Diệp would not be Diệp, however, if she did not have something wacky up her sleeves. In this case, up her dress. As she swings her leg over the saddle, I catch a glimpse of multi-colored spandex shorts. I shake my head and smile to myself.

Pastor George drapes a colorful wreath made of fresh flowers around Seattle Supreme's long, muscular neck and steps back to admire this picture-perfect moment. "Now, I want a Rainbow Brite wedding!"

We all chuckle. Katrina takes the reins and leads our rainbow bride and the horse behind a curtain to shield them from view.

Dolly, Jason, and Hùng appear. Hùng hands his mother a bouquet of gladiolus—magnificent sword lilies in a spring mix of red, pink, white, yellow, and purple. My heart swells with happiness, and I dab the corners of my eyes to erase evidence of tears. The music plays. That is our signal.

Pastor George, as the officiant, walks first. Next is Donald, who steps out from the gazebo looking so dapper, Diệp will probably swoon when she sees him. Katrina and Jean-Adrien walk next and then it is the best man and maid of honor's turn. I take

Ricky's arm, and we walk toward Donald. Ricky's arm trembles. He has been as excited about his father's wedding day as Diệp. As we walk, I lock eyes with Bình, who winks at me. Teddy and Catherine are here. Tree, Kelly, and Holly are here. Our friends from Homestead Apartments are also here. I notice Kelly's family, Toàn, Lan, and Ann, but Quang is not with them. I am surprised to see a young man standing next to Ann with his arm around her waist. Good for you, Ann.

There are a few faces on Donald's side whom I do not know, but all in all, it pleases me to see so many of our community here to witness this magical union between two very different people who are made perfectly for one another. At the front of the altar, I turn to watch the ring bearer walk down proudly, the pillow held high at her chest. My daughter sashays along in her satin dress with an exaggerated thrust of her hips and shoulders. She is carrying the important treasures of two gold rings tied with a ribbon. She had insisted she be the ring bearer and Hùng and Jason be the flower boys. Surprisingly, they did not argue, and no one put up a fuss.

The guests giggle, and two people clap—Dolly's friend, Melissa, and her mother Stephanie. Tony sits between them taking in the entertainment that is my daughter. Hùng and Jason follow behind with baskets of flowers. They reach in, take clumps of rose petals in their hand, and throw them on the ground like they are casting Pop-Its.

We all rise and face the barn. The band changes melodies and plays a catchy beat from Daryl Hall and John Oates's song "You Make My Dreams." Seattle Supreme trots out and dances to the beat of the song. She moves playfully and gracefully like she is skipping, and changes her steps as the music changes. Everyone cheers and goes wild with applause. Diệp sits gallantly on top, smiling from ear to ear. I am in awe. She is full of surprises. When in the world did she learn dressage? How many hours of practice? And surely, the countless number of bruises before showtime! What a wonderful secret to keep from the guests.

I look over at Katrina, who is beyond elated and beaming with pride. Dolly tugs at my dress and says, "I want a horse like that one."

Seattle Supreme stops thirty feet from the last row of chairs, and Diệp slides off the horse. A handler takes the reins and leads the horse to the stables. My wonderful friend shimmies the rest of the way. What a character. High on endorphins and adrenaline, she throws her arms around Donald's neck and gives him a loud kiss on the lips.

"Not yet," Pastor George says.

We roar with laughter. Without warning my tears gush out. I cannot help it nor do I try to stop. They are tears of jubilation.

Everyone needs a Diệp in their life!

The band plays the same wedding entrance song to kick off the reception, only this time, with the lyrics to the popular Daryl and Oates song. Not a single person sits at their table. The tune is too upbeat not to get out on the dance floor. Bình tries to swing dance with me, but we look like two jiggly gelatins doing a hybrid cha-cha dance. We laugh at our folly and absorb the romance in the air.

"I cannot wait to start our life together," Bình says. "Imagine, me a real estate agent and you an Oriental medicine doctor practicing acupuncture. We will be rich." I like the idea of not worrying about money.

The music slows down and Bình holds me close. He draws in my scent and grazes my temple with his lips. Electricity runs down my back.

"I want to make love to you," Bình whispers. "Tonight."

I pull him in and close my eyes. His lips find mine and we kiss gingerly. We sway side to side and let the music carry our bodies. Bình's hardness pushes into my soft flesh and I let out a gasp. I clutch him tight and invite him to explore with his tongue. Our kiss is now deep and urgent. I am ready. For him, for peace, for change.

My mind drifts to the future. I cannot compete with Donald and Diệp's colorful wedding, but I know ours will be timeless and perfect.

I open my eyes and rest my head on Bình's shoulder. On the other side of the room, Sky and Magdaleine dance. Magdaleine's cheek rests on his shoulder. It will only be a matter of time before they get married too.

At the wine bar, Tree and Kelly talk to Toàn and Lan, while my daughter plays the auntie role to Holly. Ann and her new beau are enjoying each other's company, feeding bites of food to one another. Love is airborne tonight.

I scan the dance floor and watch Teddy, Jean-Adrien, and Pastor George enjoying their wives' company. Their interactions with their spouses look fluid and easy. Jealousy does not reside here tonight. No love triangles to fight over. No triggers that incite anger and fear. How the mattress flips between Tree's wedding three years ago and Diệp's wedding today.

"I want to move to California," I say to Bình, "after Thủy-Tiên finishes the school year." My words peter out and shock Bình. It surprises me, too, but I go with it. Up to this point, I have not given it much thought but seeing Tree makes me want to be together as a family. He has a daughter now, the second generation of our family. I want to be a part of raising Holly and watching her blossom into a young woman. "What do you think? I know you miss your children and the comforts of the Vietnamese way of life. The community in Orange County is growing, and our culture is there. And when you sponsor your parents and sisters over, they will have an easier transition. We will all be together."

"You would do that for me?" Bình asks. "That would make me very happy."

"Plus," I add, "I am sure we can find an acupuncture school down there. It does not have to be Bastyr University."

"But what about your sponsors and the friends you have here?"

I look affectionately in my fiancé's eyes and melt with love for him. "Blood is denser than water, right? I feel good leaving because everyone is in a good place. Family first."

"If you are sure, then California, here we come!"

In the cozy Herrington yurt reserved for lovers, Bình claims me as his. He takes his time exploring my body. It has been so long since I have been touched and tasted by another man. I want him now but my impatience amuses him.

The smells of evergreen trees and the cotton canvas has me feeling like a wild animal tonight. I dig my teeth into Bình's neck and my fingernails into his shoulder blades. I cannot take it any longer.

Bình lets out a groan and I reward him with a massage around his throbbing erection. Every inch of his manhood is mine. I spread my legs and wrap them around his hips, drawing him up until his virility finds my wetness. My body cannot get enough of him. With every thrust of his maleness, I hunger more for his strength and his tenderness.

I arch my back and offer myself to him, wanting him to go deeper. He teases me. His fingers caress the softness between my thighs, gently at first, until I squirm and cry out for more.

28. GOODBYE SEATTLE (JUNE 1987)

I share the news with Bill and Magdaleine at work that I am moving to San Jose and then later to Westminster. Magdaleine cries and promises to visit. She and Sky need a vacation. Bill takes me to lunch and his parting words are, "Go and do *you* in California."

On Sunday after the church service, Pastor George and Dawn host a farewell party for Dolly and me. My daughter and the girls, Olivia, Ocean, and Opal, are in tears. One by one, people seek me out to bid farewell and wish us luck. Word travels fast. My VOLAG agent, Joseph, is here as well. Katrina, Jean-Adrien, and Sky reminisce about my arrival in Seattle, and we laugh about how cold Tree and I were. We walk down memory lane of the times Dolly was in the hospital and how she came out of surgery like a champ. Now, she is healthier, stronger, and feistier than ever, and her command of the English language has surpassed mine. I share fond stories of my immersion into Western culture and divulge Diệp's misunderstanding of canned dog food. We have a good laugh over that one.

Saying goodbye to Teddy, Catherine, and Sky is the hardest. They have shepherded us from the beginning, and I owe them a debt of gratitude. I implore them to come down for a visit and promise to take them to Lee's Sandwiches and Little Saigon.

After the agonizing farewells at the church, Dolly and I come home to find the community clubhouse decorated with streamers and balloons. There stands Donald and Diệp with an army of Homestead Apartments residents, waving ribbons and blowing kazoos. Stephanie, Tony, and the neighborhood kids with their parents show up with platters of food and snacks for the party. Dolly, Melissa, Jason, Ricky, Hùng, and Jen play football and jump rope like it is another ordinary day. At the end of the day, after the food trays are empty and the juice has run out, the children embrace and cry their hearts out. Realization sets in. They make well-meaning promises to call and write often and never lose touch so they can go to each other's wedding one day.

And so another chapter closes, and my story in Seattle will soon come to an end.

Today is the last day of seventh grade. While Dolly is at school, I meet with a buyer and sell my Honda Civic to him at a fair price. I sign over the title and hand him the keys. My heart is heavy. I run my fingers over the hood of the car and give it a loving pat. This car gave me confidence and independence, took me to work, to California, to Canada, and all the roads in between. Dolly will be crushed when she finds out I sold the car. She has been wanting the Honda since the day I purchased it. The new owner backs the car out of the parking space and disappears down the street. I wave to her as if she is an old friend.

Toàn, Lan, and Ann arrive right as I turn to head back up the apartment stairs. They help Bình and me pack up the few remaining items and load up Bình's old Cadillac. We move like robots up and down the stairs of my apartment, dropping items on the sidewalk so that Bình can load our belongings like a game of Tetris into the trunk and backseat. We all keep busy and skirt around the inevitable, tearful goodbye.

Diệp and Donald stop in and offer to scrub the apartment clean so that I can get my security deposit back, even though technically, it was the church that paid my move-in fees seven years ago.

"Chị Tuyết," Diệp says, "you better get Thủy-Tiên from school and be on your way." She does not make eye contact with me for fear of losing control. Neither one of us wants to cry.

"This is not goodbye," I say. "This is 'see you later.'"

I wrap my arms around Diệp, and the walls crumble down. The waves crash in, and our sorrow drowns us. We stand for a long time, crying, shedding tears of pain and love and joy and hope. Diệp tells me a joke, but it makes no sense. In between my sniffles and hiccups and her bursts of wailing, we sound like two alien women about to go to battle, with her pounding my back and me suffocating her with my boa constrictor arms. Donald and Bình pry us apart, and we unwillingly accept what needs to happen next.

I hug Lan and Ann one last time. Bình shakes Toàn and Donald's hand, then opens the car door for me to slide in. I watch my friends wave from the rearview mirror as we drive away. The tears start up again and flood my vision.

"See you later," I mouth to myself.

###

Bình waits in the car while I walk to the front entrance of McKnight Middle School. A swarm of seventh and eighth graders runs out with smiles on their faces, happy that school is over and summer break has begun. Two girls holding hands walk slowly out of the building. Their eyes are moist from the rain pouring from their eyes. Dolly and her new best friend, Marina Ogawa, see me. They stop and hug. My daughter weeps louder.

Marina Ogawa, the girl from Japan who befriended my daughter on the first day of school and shared a bento box with her. Marina, who is a head taller than my daughter and looks sixteen, not thirteen, years old. Witnessing them hold each other tightly is like déjà vu with Diệp and me moments ago.

In nine short months, the girls formed a strong bond and did everything together. They giggled together, rolled their eyes about the same things, shared the latest gossip, and even crushed on the same teen heartthrob, John Stamos.

It is the saddest thing to watch, and I do not rush their farewell. The road to San Jose will still be there in five minutes or five days. When all the promises have been made and after all the exchanges of keepsakes and gifts have been passed, they wave a weak "Ciao, Bella" and go their separate ways.

Dolly wraps her arms around me and gushes another round of angry tears. "I don't want to go!"

I wipe the shimmer from her eyelashes. "My baby girl, you are the sunshine that makes the rivers sparkle. You will make new friends, and you will still have Marina and Opal, Olivia and Ocean, Melissa and Jen…and all your other friends."

Dolly sits down on the curb and hugs her knees. She buries her face and refuses to budge. We sit for a while. She is hurting so much, and there is nothing I can do or say to take the pain away. I cannot pick her up and carry her to the car. I cannot force her to come with me right now and drag her across the parking lot or threaten her to get in the car. I let it take its course.

I sit with her and hold her. I stroke her hair and soothe her with words of encouragement. Bình gets out of the car, but I shake

my head. He understands my unspoken cue and gets back in the
Cadillac to wait.

"What if I don't make any friends? What if Mr. Bình and I
don't get along, or I hate my new school? You are going to have a
new husband and new kids—"

"I am too old to have more children," I say.

"No, I mean sister Thu and brother Khoi and brother
Phan," she says. "I will have stepbrothers and a stepsister and you'll
not love me as much anymore."

I squeeze my daughter tight. "Honey, you will always be my
one and only. You are my miracle and my hero. You are my
number one, and I will always pick you over anyone else, even if
you lose your way and break my heart, even if you get jolly fat from
all the candies and chocolates." Dolly laughs. "It will always be you
and me."

"And our puppy," she says.
"And our puppy."
Dolly sits up straight. "Wait, really?"
"Yes, really."

THE END

Snow and Dolly (early 1980s)

Snow in Seattle (November 2015)

Dolly and Snow in Vietnam together, February 2008
(Twenty-nine years after their escape as refugees)

Dolly (Seattle, 1983)

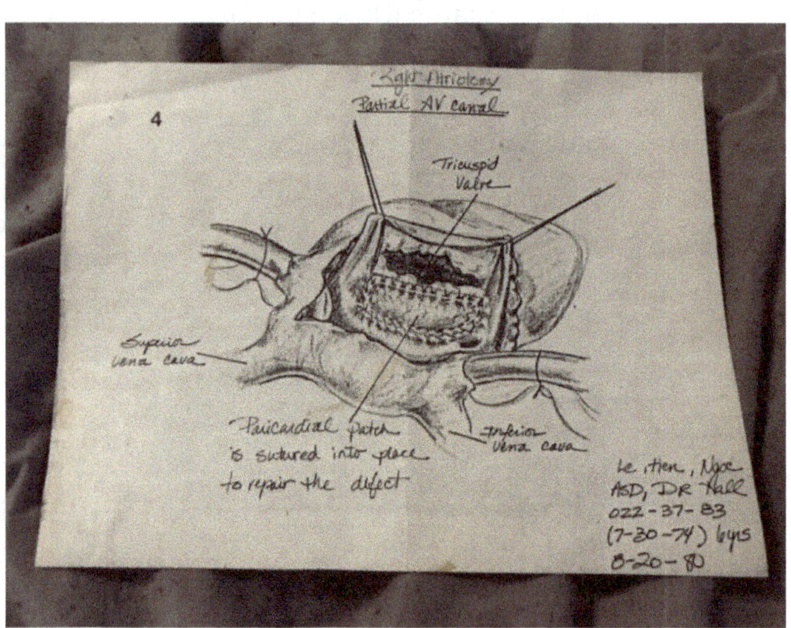

Drawings of Dolly's open-heart surgery
(Seattle Children's Hospital, August 1980)

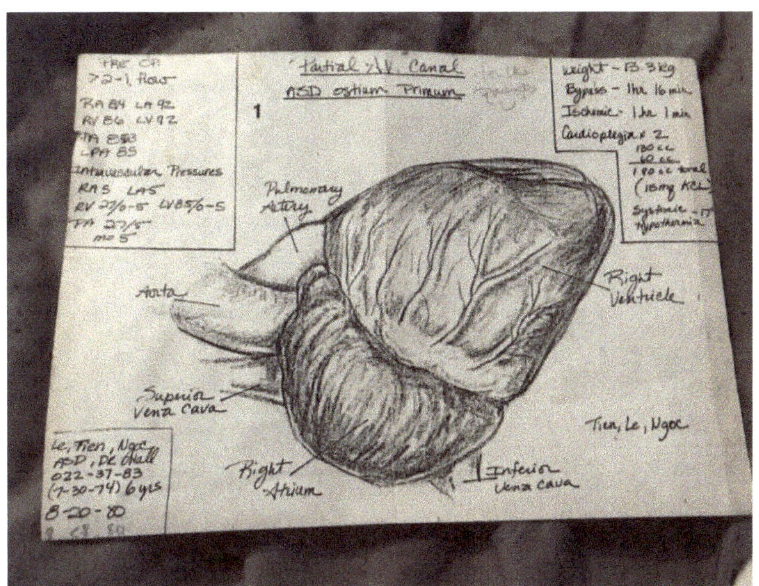

Drawings of Dolly's open-heart surgery
(Seattle Children's Hospital, August 1980)

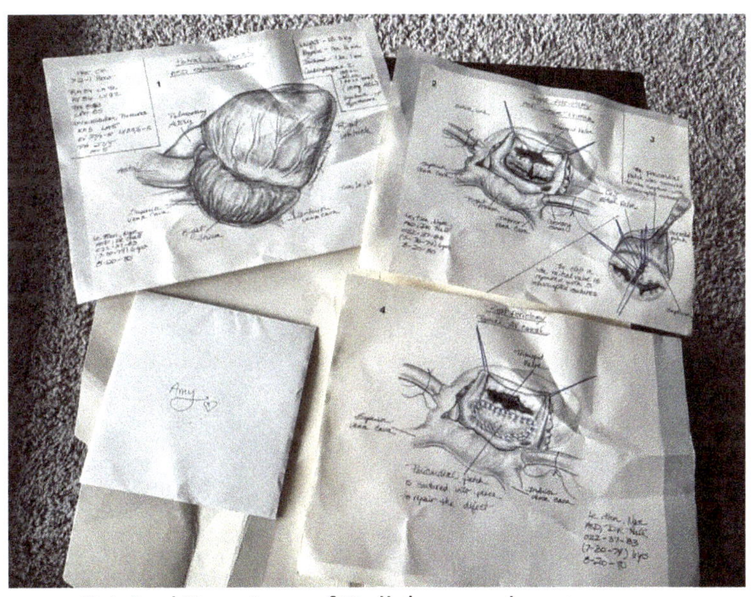

Original Drawings of Dolly's open-heart surgery
(Gifted in March 2021 from Dr. Dale Hall & Susan Russell Hall)

Snow (right) in Vietnam

T. Vuong (Dolly's Father)

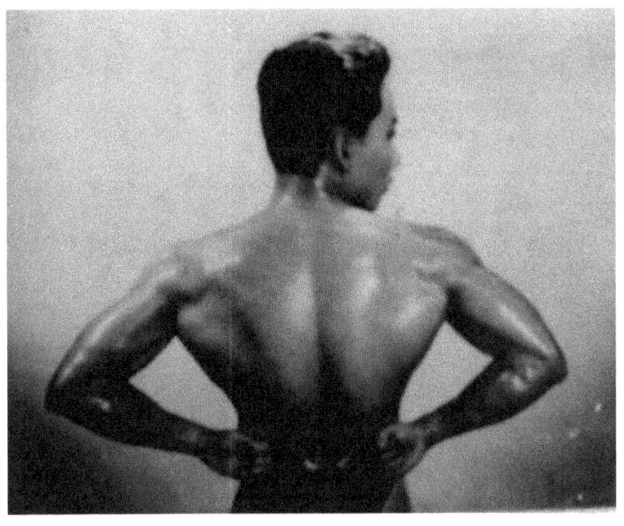

T. Vuong (Dolly's Father)

Dolly and her father reconciled in January 2018

"Tree" (November 1978, age 16)

"Tree" and Dolly (Age 67, Age 45 - Seattle, December 2019)

Henrietta & Gerrit Van Zwol aka "Toots & Bub" (1980s)

"Tree" (San Jose, early 1990s)

Dolly's childhood friend, Melissa

Dolly's friend, Jackie (1987)

Dolly and Snow (Seattle, 1980s)

Snow graduated with a Masters of Acupuncture and Oriental Medicine (California, March 1995)

Dolly's 7th-grade friend, Marina (Evergreen High, Prom 1991)

Snow and Sister Six (Vietnam, (February 2008 – Snow at age 68)

Foreground: Tree and his mother
Background: Sister Six and Tree's wife, Kelly
(Vietnam, February 2008 – Tree at age 45)

Brother Seven with his wife
(Tree's parents - Vietnam, February 2008)

Brother Seven and Brother Six (Vietnam, February 2008)

Foreground: Bình's father and mother
Background: Linh, Thu, Ken, Khoi, and Dolly
(San Jose, 1988 – Dolly at age 14)

Bình and Snow with their classic Citroen car (California, 1988)

Dolly's wedding day (Seattle, September 2008)
Left to Right: George & Tamara (Dolly's in-laws)
Joe (Dolly's husband) & Dolly (author/Amy M. Le)
Snow and T. Vuong (Dolly's father)

Tree and Kelly with their grandkids (Christmas 2014)

Left to Right: Joe (Dolly's husband), Kelly (Tree's wife),
Holly (Tree's daughter), Dolly (author), and Tree
(Vietnam, March 2015 – Dolly at age 40 & Tree at age 52)

Tree and Joe (Dolly's husband
(Vietnam, March 2015)

Tree and Dolly (San Jose, California, late 1980s)

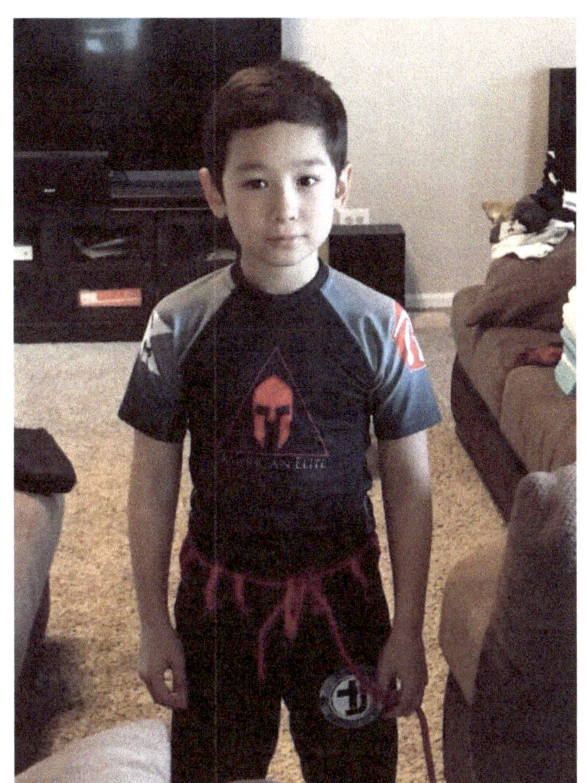

Dolly's son, Preston (11 years old, 2020)

Dolly's son, Preston (6 years old, April 2015)

Dolly reunited with Dr. Dale Hall (heart surgeon) & Susan Russell
Hall (medical illustrator, artist, and Dr. Hall's wife
Lotus Studios, Lakewood, WA - March 2021

AMY M. LE
SNOW'S KITCHEN
A NOVELLA AND COOKBOOK

INTRODUCTION

In 2017, I embarked on a life-changing journey of self-discovery. After my mama, Snow, passed from cancer, I quit my corporate job and never looked back.

To honor the brave and incredible woman who raised me, I wrote my debut, historical fiction novel, *Snow in Vietnam,* to share with the world our family's story of survival after the fall of Saigon. The sequel, *Snow in Seattle,* was my women's fiction novel of the Vietnamese diaspora and detailed our immigrant story of rebuilding and thriving in a new country while grappling with trauma and PTSD.

Snow's Kitchen is the final book in the *Snow* trilogy and was written in one month during NaNoWriMo 2020. It is dedicated to all the drifters and gourmands out there. I wanted to honor my mother's love for food by sharing with you some of her recipes. I also included some of my favorite recipes that I created or enhanced over the years.

Snow was born in Tra Vinh, Vietnam in 1939. She was the youngest of seven children and after the Vietnam War ended, she left her country in search of freedom. Like hundreds of thousands of refugees, my mother feared persecution, faced starvation and lost everything.

It was not until 1980 after my mother resettled in America that she took an interest in cooking. With one foot in the past and one in the present, she straddled the cultures of East and West and bounced between dystopia and utopia. Her flair for food represented the fusion of two worlds.

The first half of this book is a novella written from Dolly's perspective. Follow along as she navigates her way through adolescence experiencing a spectrum of emotions from love and pain to determination and self-discovery.

In the second half, I share with you our family recipes. Some of the foods are traditional but prepared with modern methods, while some recipes were borrowed and turned into something unique. I welcome you to Snow's kitchen and hope the foods inspire you, excite you, and introduce you to new flavors.

For my fans who could not wait for this book, I challenge you to try some recipes. Post pictures of your oopsies and hurrays on social media with **#SnowsKitchen**.

Enjoy and blessings to you all!

Amy M. Le aka Dolly

Liz Nguyen aka Snow

1. BOYS ARE STUPID (SUMMER 1988)

The first boy I ever kissed was named Dung. Let that marinate for a second. In Vietnamese, the name Dũng means heroic, but when you're a thirteen-year-old refugee boy living in Westminster, California, your name means shit, literally and figuratively. No way was I going to date a boy whose name translated to "poop."

In the summer of '88, I turned fourteen. My mom, Snow, and my stepdad, Binh, agreed to let me go to the carnival down the street. They gave me thirty dollars and a list of don'ts. Mom sent my cousin, Tree, to keep an eye on me, and Binh sent his son, Khoi, to spy on me. Unbeknownst to my parents, both Tree and Khoi each gave me ten dollars and told me to be home by ten.

Heroic-Poop and I were classmates at Johnson Middle School, where we had spent three months flirting from thirty feet away. Naturally, I fantasized about our first kiss. I used my last ride ticket on the Zipper and was determined to have that kiss.

"Dear God," I prayed, "may he be brave as his name implies and his kiss as explosive as fireworks. Oh, and please encourage him to change his name to something cool, like John Stamos or Rob Lowe."

Inside the steel carriage, I wondered how many times the padded cage had been wiped down over the years from all the vomit and sloppy wet kisses. Oh, if only the Zipper could talk. The fair attendant secured our straps and locked the gate. Dung and I held hands. We locked eyes. This was it.

While the world outside swirled in a blur, inside, we moved like two sloths finding our way to puckered lips. Then it happened. Our heads banged together from the G-force, and our lips skidded like two cars drifting around a bend. Saigon Drift.

I tasted wet, curdled chunks of pâté and bread. I screamed. Dung was mortified.

"I'm sorry," he said. "Christine, I'll buy you another shirt."

"You threw up on me," I yelled.

It took me months of flirting and two and a half minutes of being tossed around a metal crate to realize boys are stupid.

Dung was a turd after all.

###

I had moved from Seattle to San Jose the previous summer with my mom, Snow, and her fiancé, Binh. I was miserable. I didn't have my friends Nadirah, Marina, Jackie, Melissa, or Jen with me. I even missed knock-kneed Jason and stupid Hung, who threw a dead snake at me when we were in the second grade.

Right away my parents put me to work without pay. On the weekends, I went with Thu to the San Jose Flea Market where we had a booth and sold silk flower arrangements, ceramic vases, and ceramic elephants. During the week, Binh and Thu fired up the kilns to bake the clay molds. Mama and I hand-painting the elephants and tall vases. It was fun at first until it became a family business and making money was the priority. I dreaded the chore that it became.

My soon-to-be stepbrother, Khoi, understood my weary and lonely heart and surprised me with a gift.

"Tiên," Khoi said, "Linh and I have declared this Saturday 'Tiên Day.'"

Even though he broke my Vietnamese name Thủy-Tiên apart and shortened it to Tiên, I forgave him. I couldn't stay mad at charming, handsome, funny, and easygoing Khoi for long. He could have called me Richard, and I'd have been as happy as a soaring eagle. His girlfriend, Linh, was the perfect match for him. She was an aspiring model with gorgeous legs, sleek black hair, and heart-shaped lips. She was the kindest soul on Earth, and I wanted to be her.

"What do we do on Tien Day?" I asked.

"You'll see," he answered with a wink.

That Saturday Khoi excused me from flea market duty without consulting Thu. She threw a handful of paintbrushes at him and called him a lousy brother.

Khoi and Linh picked me up from the house and took me to a hair salon. Linh and I got our hair done while Khoi disappeared for an hour. He came back in time to see the drama unfold.

"Linh, why is she crying?" Khoi asked.

Linh panicked. "Christine, you look so cute!" She tried to

cheer me up, but it didn't work.

I had asked the stylist for a Princess Diana cut, but the moment his scissors assaulted my long, wavy hair, my eyes burned and leaked. Tendrils and snippets of wet black locks fell to the tile floor as I mourned the loss of my hair. I sank into my chair to sulk.

I gave the stylist a sharp stare. "I look diseased." In my mind, I thought I would look like the Princess of Wales, but the face staring back at me was a dark, sickly wannabe with small black eyes and the wrong shaped face.

Khoi paid for my haircut and tipped the man generously to make up for my embarrassing reaction.

"Why are boys so stupid?" I asked Linh. "If a girl had cut my hair, she would have gotten it right."

"Hey, now." Khoi raised his hand. "Boy present here."

"You're not a boy," I said. "You're Khoi."

Linh burst into giggles and playfully pinched Khoi's cheeks. "Ah, you hear that? You're my boy Khoi. Princess Christine said so."

We had a good laugh, and all was forgiven. The next stop was lunch. We visited Lee's Sandwiches for *bánh mì* and coffee, and I told them I was getting a puppy. My mama had promised I could have any dog under twenty-five pounds.

"It's still Tien Day," I said. "What's next?"

We drove to San Francisco, but before heading to the wharf, Khoi and Linh dropped by their apartment to get their sunglasses. Inside their small, cute home, I detected a faint urine odor. Linh and Khoi didn't seem to notice. They disappeared into the bathroom together, which was odd, but I concluded their sunglasses must be in there.

"What in the world?" I heard Khoi exclaim.

"Oh my!" Linh yelled out.

I darted to the bathroom and squeezed in between them. I shrieked.

Her eyes were small, round charcoal bits. Her coat was short and fawn-colored. Her ears drooped, and her small tail wagged fast. On a snowy Seattle day, she could have cleared all the roads in our neighborhood with her tail. I scooped the Chihuahua into my arms and kissed her. She was so excited she piddled on my shirt.

"A puppy!" I hugged Khoi and Linh. "What's her name?"

Khoi shrugged. "She's yours, Princess Tien. You decide."

Little Nikki and I were inseparable from that point on. I

loved that little dog wholeheartedly.

###

A few months before the end of eighth grade, I attended my first school dance. Feeling somewhat pretty in my refugee chic black ruffled skirt, white blouse, and goldenrod vest, I stood in the corner of the gymnasium pretending to hold the whole building up so that my schoolmates could have a good time. I hugged the wall, terrified of boys, especially the cute ones, content to watch the others dance to Madonna and Pet Shop Boys. Despite being the only girl at the dance with big calves and no pantyhose, I fit in with my sky-high Aqua Net hair and Cyndi Lauper punk makeup. Half the students at the school were Vietnamese refugees like me, grooving to new wave music and '80s rock. Like them, I was happiest listening to music and sneaking out of the house to get away from overbearing, overly protective, strict, paranoid, traditional parents.

An hour before the dance ended, a mysterious figure barged into the gym, pushing through the double doors like an army tank. His footsteps silenced the room, and all eyes stared at this encroaching intruder.

He grabbed my arm. "Time to go."

I pulled away and freed myself from his grip. "It's not over yet."

Binh froze. He scowled, and in a gruff whisper demanded we leave right that minute. My pride crushed, my insides hot and knotted, I stormed out, got into his Citroen Traction Avant, and slammed the door as hard as I could. A beautiful car for an ugly man.

I cried all the way home as my soon-to-be stepdad lectured. What was worse was he spoke to me in English to make sure I understood every nip of his tongue. *You are too young to be out this late. You are lucky your mom and I let you go to the dance. You must remain pious. You should not be loose around boys. Your makeup makes you look cheap. My daughter Thu was never disrespectful like you.* On and on he lashed with his fanatic insults. It took everything in me to bite my tongue and refrain from giving him a verbal beating of my own.

The following month, I cried from San Jose down to Westminster. We moved again, and I finished the last three months of eighth grade at Johnson Middle School. Yes, the school where I spent three months flirting with a boy name Dung, who ultimately regurgitated his banh mi in my mouth.

Things were about to get much worse. I felt powerless

531

living under my stepdad's thumb and more disconnected than ever from my mom. California taught me some harsh life lessons, and I wasn't prepared to grow up so fast.

2. YOUR MAMA IS BLIND (SUMMER 1988)

Our rental home in Westminster adjoined another house on the corner of Chestnut and Park Street across from Sigler Park. The fully fenced one-story property was quite spacious with three bedrooms, two bathrooms, and a large garage. The family who lived in the other house owned the property and were also Vietnamese. They had two daughters, Leena and Loanne, who welcomed me into their sisterhood with open arms and sticky fingers.

Leena was two years younger than I was, with round-rimmed glasses that made her look innocent even when she wasn't. She had the kind of smile that lit up her whole face. Her exuberance passed through her pores. While Leena looked like her father, Tung, her sister, Loanne, was a tiny spitfire and looked like her mother, Khanh. Despite being five years younger than me, I knew better than to question her. Loanne was wicked smart, a little sarcastic, and so darn adorable. I loved both sisters equally, and while Leena acted as our moral compass, Loanne conjured our fun. It was nearly impossible to be gloomy around Leena and Loanne, but on that last Saturday, before I entered my freshman year at Westminster High School, I sunk into depression.

Nothing could have lifted my spirits, not even a visit from my sponsors from Seattle, Mr. and Mrs. Vanzwol. As the marriage of my mama and Binh approached, I became apprehensive and sullen.

"Well, hot damn, Snow," Mr. Van howled. "The California sun went and colored your face!"

"Teddy," my mama said, "you still same. You so big and strong."

Mr. Van scooped her up and crushed her in a tight embrace. "Doesn't she look great, Toots?"

Mrs. Van nodded. "I can't believe we're here in California

for your wedding this Saturday. It seems like yesterday we were at Diep's wedding to Donald."

I poked my head into the kitchen and jumped on Mr. Van's back, covering his eyes with my cupped hands spreading my fingers so he could cheat. "Guess who?"

He played along. "Too heavy to be Dolly and too light to be Tree. Binh, is that you?"

Mrs. Van and Mama laughed, but Binh winced. I knew I was not behaving like a proper girl, and I was too old to be jumping on an old man's back. Still, this was Mr. Van, the man who had rescued our family from the refugee camp in Indonesia, the man who used to sing me songs while I fell asleep on his lap, the man I was convinced was Santa Claus when I caught him jingling bells outside his house one Christmas Eve.

"I'll give you a clue," I said. "I was born Thuy-Tien, grew up as Dolly, and am now…"

"Christine," Mr. Van said with confidence.

I slid off his back only to be jostled like a bag of rice. His left arm curled around my waist as he lifted me so that I was eye to eye with him. Without warning, Mr. Van brushed his rough, white beard up and down my cheeks until I begged for mercy. It was good to have them there, and I missed them more than I realized.

We gathered around the kitchen while Mama prepared spring rolls. I washed the basil, perilla leaves, lettuce, and mint while Mrs. Van offered to cut up the cucumbers and keep an eye on the vermicelli noodles cooking on the stove.

Mr. Van and Binh went to the dining room to enjoy some cognac. Binh was a big fan of Hennessy VSOP for its vanilla aroma and oaky, spicy taste with a fruity finish. He boasted it was the best and only cognac he served to special guests.

"Mr. Van is not a guest," I mumbled under my breath. "He's family."

"Catherine," my mama said, "please do not cook rice noodle all way. We want little bit chewy."

"Al dente," Mrs. Van said. "Got it."

"I so excited you come," Mama said as she ripped the heads off the prawns and peeled the shells. She threw the heads and shells into a pot of boiling water, then added salt and half an onion.

"Why do you put the shells in the pot?" I asked.

"The shell and onion add flavor and sweetness to shrimp," Mama answered. She spoke English for Mrs. Van's sake.

The three of us prepped the ingredients for the spring rolls and sat down with Binh and Mr. Van to enjoy a light dinner. With the wedding in four days, Mama didn't want to eat anything heavy or that would make her feel bloated.

Binh smacked his lips, chewed with his mouth open, and inhaled the food. Did he even taste it? My mama believed it was a compliment to the chef to eat like a pig, but I found it annoying. Mr. and Mrs. Van had well-mannered dining etiquette, and Mama was so dainty and graceful in her movements. I imagined us sitting at a candlelit dinner speaking proper English like the British royals while Binh the oinker slurped from his trough at the end of the table.

Binh leaned back and patted his stomach. "Very nice." He'd eaten five fat spring rolls in ten minutes.

I rolled my eyes. "I am barely done with my second roll."

"Eat slowly," Binh said. "You don't want to get fat."

To add insult to injury, Binh took my mama's roll, fed her a bite, then finished it for her.

"Dolly, I mean Christine," Mr. Van said, "has always been skin and bones. Remember, Toots, when we picked them up at the airport?" Mrs. Van dipped her spring roll in the hoisin sauce and took a bite just as Mr. Van posed the question. "Well, I remember it like it was yesterday. Lord have mercy, Tree was a pole, and Dolly looked like a real-life rag doll, so frail and tiny."

"And Snow was the most beautiful thing," Mrs. Van said. "I remember thinking your skin was so creamy, like milk."

My beautiful mother laughed. "I hide from sun. Too dark not pretty in Vietnamese culture. And sunspot too ugly." She pronounced "ugly" in three syllables uh-guh-lee. I smiled.

"Now, she's so tan," I said. "Must be all the hard work she has to do outside for the business."

I wondered if Binh noticed the little jab I made for making my mama work so hard on the ceramics. Mama dreamed of going to school to get her Oriental medical doctor (OMD) degree. She wanted to learn about herbal medicine and use acupressure and acupuncture to treat pain. Instead, she helped Binh build the family business. I don't know how he expected to make money when he gifted so much of it away. Each time he gave someone a vase to earn favor or climb the social ladder with someone influential, I cringed. There went a vase that I meticulously handpainted. Oh, and there went three-hundred dollars as he gave away an elephant statue that Mama painted.

My mama said you had to spend money to make money and

give away free samples to get free advertising. I had argued a potato chip was a free sample, not a whole bag of chips. Sometimes I thought she was blind because she was in love. She always had a reason or explanation, but to me, they sounded like excuses. Would I think this way if I were in love?

I went into the kitchen to clear my mind and took a break from Binh's loud "ah" each time he sipped his cognac. I came back with a few sodas the Vanzwols had brought over and offered them to our guests. "Would you like a Mountain Dew?"

My mama burst out laughing. We all looked confused. What was so funny?

"Má mày đui!" Mama chuckled.

I said, "Mountain Dew," and she heard, "Má mày đui," which meant "Your mama is blind." Neither of us could stop laughing. When I finally caught my breath, I explained to my sponsors. We laughed together, even Binh, and from that moment on, the green can was forever known as the "Your mama is blind" soda.

###

Mrs. Vanzwol's twin sister, Ms. Katrina, and her husband, Mr. Jean-Adrien, arrived early the next day while I slept. I dreamed of a man sitting under a tree on the beach playing a string instrument with his bow. His face was handsome and familiar. My cousin Tree swam in the ocean with the blue crabs.

I woke with a start at the sound of glass shattering in the kitchen and loud voices outside my bedroom door.

"Life with this minx has never been better."

I recognized the voice and accent. I knew only one Frenchman, and it was Mr. Jean-Adrien. I scurried out of my room to greet them, hoping they brought presents for me.

"Dolly!" Ms. Katrina exclaimed. She hugged me fiercely while I inhaled her intoxicating perfume, Chanel No. 5.

Glamorous as ever, Ms. Katrina wore a mauve summer dress with a thin fuchsia patent leather belt that accentuated her small waist and round hips. She colored her hair a warm copper blonde and wore it straight with blunt bangs. While most women had mall bangs, Ms. Katrina dared to be different with her bold fashion sense. Mr. Jean-Adrien's attire was always classic and masculine. He had grown his hair out since I last saw him and looked like the dashing actor, Roger Moore, in the James Bond movies.

"Is something broken?" I asked. "I heard glass breaking."

"Oui," Mr. Jean-Adrien confirmed. "Je te présente mon ami, Chef Tuan." He pointed to a Vietnamese gentleman in the kitchen standing next to my mama. He was a stout one, and I wasn't sure if he was built from fat or muscle.

"Chef Tuan is our wedding present to your mom and Binh," Ms. Katrina said. "Your mom was so excited she dropped a dish. Chef Tuan will be here for two weeks to cook for you and teach your mom some basics."

"Wow," I said. "That's a cool present."

The doorbell rang, and from the living room window, I saw a man and woman fussing over each other's hair. Mama flew to the front of the house and threw open the door.

"Sky!" Mama cried. "Magdaleine!"

"Snow!" They exclaimed in unison and embraced my mama with magnanimous joy.

"I thought you not come," Mama said. "Oh. My. Good. Nest. You having baby!" Mama touched Ms. Magdaleine's round stomach. "Why you not tell me? Shame on you. You have boy. I know. See? It round and high."

The adults spent the entire day catching up on life. Ms. Katrina got me a makeup kit and Uncle Skyler gave us smoked copper river salmon in a nice wooden box with tribal designs on the lid. Mr. and Mrs. Vanzwol came over minutes after Binh came home from work. It was one happy reunion while Chef Tuan slaved in the kitchen. I was his prep cook while the adults lounged and reminisced about Mr. Donald and Auntie Diep's colorful wedding two years ago.

"Are they coming to the wedding?" I asked. "Are they bringing Jason, Ricky, and Hung?"

My mama nodded. "They will be here tomorrow. They are driving down."

"Anyone else?" I asked. "What about your old boss, Mr. Cushing? What about Brother Tree and Sister Kelly? Is Sister Kelly's family coming?"

"Only your cousin, Tree, and his wife are coming," Binh answered. "And of course their daughters, Holly and Honey."

I wanted to tell Binh I wasn't asking him and my mama could answer for herself. Instead, I asked, "Did you not invite them?" My spiteful jab implied he was selfish and thoughtless. Binh ignored my question.

Maybe my teenage hormones took charge, but after he humiliated me at the school dance, I lost respect for him. The anger and embarrassment still lingered. Even when he was nice, I could not accept it at face value and believed he was manipulating me somehow. How could my mama not see he was wrong for her? For us?

"So are you going to be the flower girl?" Ms. Magdaleine asked me.

"I'm too old to be—"

"No, our neighbor's daughter, Loanne, is going to be the flower girl," Binh answered. "And one of my friend's sons will be the ring bearer."

"Then you must be your mom's maid of honor," Magdaleine said.

"There won't be—"

Binh cut me off again. "We are not going to have a best man or maid of honor. We are already married on paper. The reception is where we will formally present ourselves as husband and wife."

My jaw dropped. When had this happened? I could tell by the murmurs and raised eyebrows that everyone was equally stunned. Mama insisted it was a mutual decision since they both had been married before and did not want an elaborate wedding.

Everything about this approach was wrong to me. The contempt seeped in deeper and consumed me. My mother might be blind to his manipulations, but I would be her eyes. I was determined to expose him for the narcissistic fraud I believed him to be.

A motley crew of people spilled out of a Lincoln Town Car in front of our house and strolled up the driveway. One had her hair in pigtails and wore roller skates with pom poms on top. I could not believe my eyes. Before they rang the doorbell, I flung the door open.

Auntie Diep clutched Mr. Donald for dear life as he steadied her. She wore a green romper with knee-high socks and a gold, sequined fanny pack around her waist. Big sunglasses covered her small face and had slipped halfway down the bridge of her nose.

Auntie Diep reached for me. "Ơi, Thủy-Tiên, help me."

I laughed. "Hello, Auntie." Our Homestead Apartments neighbor hadn't changed one bit. I raised an eyebrow to Hung. "Why is your mom in skates?"

Hung smiled. He looked the same, only taller and thicker and with a deeper voice. "Mom thinks California is all about roller skating Santa Monica Pier, so she's been practicing."

Mr. Donald still looked like Phillip Drummond from the show *Diff'rent Strokes,* and his son Ricky hadn't changed other than some facial hair. Jason was still knock-kneed. Seeing them felt like home, and homesickness welled up in me like a fountain.

"Ói zòi oi!" Oh my God! Auntie Diep exclaimed when she saw my mama in the hallway.

"Trời đất ơi!" Oh heaven and Earth! My mama called back.

The two of them squealed and hugged tightly, swaying back and forth, talking animatedly as if on a mission to share every detail in five minutes. They Vietnamesed with each other as if none of us existed.

Shortly after their arrival, Brother Tree and his family arrived. All was right with the world in that brief moment. The next day was the wedding reception, and while I knew it would be egregious, I took comfort in knowing tomorrow was not today.

3. TWO'S COMPANY (SUMMER 1988)

Tree broke a teacup. He had one too many cognacs and a whole pack of cigarettes. Sister Kelly kept hitting him as if her little fists would magically make him sober up.

"It's not a party until something breaks," Mr. Van said.

Everyone but Sister Kelly roared and resumed eating, drinking, and karaokeing. It was good to see my mama laugh. She held court with Magdaleine, Ms. Katrina, Mrs. Van, Auntie Diep, and Sister Kelly. Men huddled in one area and women in the other. I entertained Jason, Hung, little Holly, and Honey, and my neighbors, Loanne and Leena, who came over for a few hours to play. I wanted to stay up late and partake in the fun, but Binh put his foot down, and Mama agreed. Both treated me like I was still in elementary school.

I stormed off to bed like a good little girl, but who could sleep with all the chatter and bad singing? Mama and Binh karaoked to the lyrics of "You're a Woman, I'm a Man" by Bad Boys Blue.

Brother Tree and Sister Kelly left first. Little Holly was four years old and had passed out long ago, but Honey, who was two, sat wide awake. She teetered between the dominions of cranky exhaustion and an energized high.

By morning, sunshine filtered into my bedroom, and its warm rays gently woke me. I listened for movement outside my room but heard nothing. I assumed all our out-of-town guests made it back to their hotels safely and nursed a hangover.

Soon, it was showtime, and I wanted the day to end before it even started.

Mama hummed the song "More Than I Can Say" in the kitchen. I scooped my dog, Nikki, into my arms and exited the room. She leaped out of my arms and scratched at the door.

"Good morning, Mama."

"How did you and Nikki sleep?" Mama asked.

I watched Nikki do her business in the backyard while I picked at the soggy egg rolls on the counter. "Not so good."

"I am sorry we were so loud. It was fun to see everyone." Mama hand-washed the glassware and let them drip-dry in the dishwasher.

I let Nikki inside and gave her the last morsel of my egg roll before serving her rice and kibble. "Is Binh passed out from all the Hennessy and Heineken?"

"He is running errands and checking on the restaurant for tonight's reception."

I opened a two-liter bottle of Mountain Dew and drank straight from the plastic mouthpiece.

"Má mày đui for breakfast?" Mama asked. We shared a giggle at her reference to Mountain Dew as "your mama is blind."

"Are you excited about the wedding reception today?" I asked.

Mama stopped wiping the counters and looked at me with a serious expression. "I want you to know he makes me happy, and I want you to try to get along with Bác Bình. I know you are not used to having a man in our lives, and you now have to compete for my time—"

"But he—"

I wanted to tell her it was he who should try to respect me and not treat me like a rotten child.

Mama held up her hand to silence me. "I want you to call him 'Dad' and—"

I took a step back and vehemently shook my head. "No way."

I picked up Nikki and held her close as if she needed my protection. In reality, she created a barrier between Mama and me. It was my heart that needed protection. All my life, it had been just the two of us. She always gave me one-hundred percent of herself. She doted on me, protected me, and saved me. I wanted nothing to change. She lived for me, and I lived for her. Couldn't she see that I was not ready for her to have a life where I was not the center of it? She didn't need anyone else to make her happy because I could do that. That was my job. I didn't want any man standing between us. I wanted to remain a child forever, and I missed the times when it was just Mama and me sharing stories and experiencing new adventures together.

My stomach churned, and my legs trembled. Mama had betrayed me. I suddenly hated California and our new beginnings there. I missed my friends back home. I planned to convince Mr. Van to take me back to Seattle with them after the reception. He had a soft spot for me and could never say no to his little Dolly. If that didn't work, I could hitch a ride back with Auntie Diep and Donald.

"Thuỷ-Tiên," Mama said, "you do not understand all the sacrifices I have made for us to be here, and I want nothing more than for us to be happy. Your cousin Tree has found his happiness, and it is our turn. We deserve it."

I clenched my fist and said under my breath, "My name is Christine now."

My mama sighed. She resumed wiping the counters but did not resume humming. I won the battle. She turned her back to me and collected the items to toss in the trash. I left her in the kitchen with her thoughts while I slammed the bedroom door and let the tears fall.

"I hate him!" I screamed. I hugged Nikki and pulled out my diary from underneath the mattress.

Diary, I can't stand him!!! Everything about him makes me want to smash his face, from the way he chews his food to the way he shoots his snot. I can see right through him, that narcissistic bastard. Today is their wedding. No, their reception. They fucking got married already without telling anyone. My mama has no clue. She is blinded by love. If I have to run away to free myself from his tyranny and strict, stupid rules, I will.

To know you is to swallow death.
I will not yield until my last breath.

To bow to you is a seal of doom.
I'll lie down for truth in my tomb.

I will not bend to the man that breaks.
His charms, his money, all but fakes.

Empty are his vessels in this harbor, this dock
For he is but a fucking cock-a-fucking-doodle-maniac-doo-doo!!!!!!!!!!

I HATE YOU!

Strangers who walked alongside one another in different realms…that was Mama and me that evening. She had never shone so beautifully as she did that night, and if my heart had not been rotten with malice and ill will, I would have found the evening breathtaking. Dressed in a stunning, currant berry red *áo dài*, speckled with luminous honey-colored paisley patterns, and adorned in eighteen-carat gold jewels, she graced the floor with poise, elegance, and glamour. She was exquisite. My stepdad looked sharp, I had to admit, in his dark blue suit. They went from table to table welcoming their guests and taking photos. When people clinked their glasses with the silverware, they obliged by kissing. Behind them Loanne wore her traditional Vietnamese dress, looking adorable as always. The ring bearer was a little boy I had never met, dressed in a male version of the áo dài. He was cute in an odd way, very pale and sickly-looking. He was maybe eight years old with an old man's face and youthful skin.

I chose to wear black on their special day. I was in mourning. I had lost my mama to someone else. Binh glared at me when he saw my dress. I had gotten a rise out of him and knew he was furious. My insolence and defiance, coupled with my chastising of his blue suede shoes, compounded the resentment in the air. I sat at the round table that seated eight people with Auntie Diep, Mr. Donald, their three boys, and the Vanzwols. Next to us were Ms. Katrina, Mr. Jean-Adrien, Uncle Skyler, Ms. Magdaleine, Brother Tree, Sister Kelly, and their girls. Love and family surrounded me, yet I had never felt more alone. I didn't know where I belonged anymore. Everyone had someone, and they were moving on with their lives. Not me. I didn't feel Vietnamese, and I didn't look American. My parents expected me to be the model minority student with straight A's and to play the piano, but instead, my last report card was riddled with B's and C's. I blamed it on moving two-thirds of the way into the school year and the disruption of the status quo. Soon, I would be a freshman in a new high school, and I feared being ostracized for my smallness.

I didn't want to be a doctor, a lawyer, or an engineer. I was certainly not a musical prodigy, and math was my weakest subject. English and history were my favorite subjects, but what did that matter? I failed my mama in every way. Why bother trying?

The night went by in a blur. I spent the evening stuffing my face so I didn't have to talk. The Chinese seafood restaurant they chose had amazing salt and pepper prawns and the best garlic onion crab. Each table had red envelopes filled with cash that Loanne received for the bride and groom in a lacquered box. Money was always given at weddings, funerals, and birthdays to help with expenses. When Mama and Binh arrived at our table, Mr. Van gave a speech.

"Snow, Binh," Mr. Van said. "You both have come a long way, and we are so happy for you both. Congratulations!"

Murmurs of "cheers" and "*vô*" escaped jovial lips as Auntie Diep initiated the glass clinking. The bride and groom indulged us and kissed. Mrs. Van dropped a wedding card in a white envelope into Loanne's box, and I noticed Binh's disapproval by the nanosecond of his frown. White was the color of death and reserved for funerals in the Vietnamese culture. Giving a white card was considered bad luck. Hopefully, there was a generous check in the envelope to counter the bad juju.

As the night wore on and the adults danced, I amused myself by laughing at the discord of the band and the uncoordinated movements of people swaying to the rhythms of tango and pop music. Hung, Ricky, and I stole a few swigs of champagne when no one was looking, and by the time my mama and stepdad danced their solo waltz, I felt loose and buoyant.

I grabbed a rose from the centerpiece and secured the stem with my teeth. I cha-chaed to the dance floor, wedged myself between them, and slide-stepped with my mama. She laughed and waltzed with me around the room, leaving Binh alone without a partner. The guests laughed.

"Everyone," Binh said, "please, come, join us on the floor."

From that point on, I had a ball. A little drunk and a little invincible, my inner fierce came out, and I focused on the music. The band took a break, and the sounds of Modern Talking stormed the speakers. Their songs "You're My Heart, You're My Soul" and "Brother Louie" got us all up on our feet. The moment Lynda Trang Đài's song "Daddy Joe" came on, people went wild. Auntie Diep and Donald were footloose and fancy-free. They jigged and gyrated while Auntie Diep's dress lit up and flashed like LED Christmas lights.

New wave music was very much alive and thriving in our refugee world.

I wanted to know how many red envelopes Mama received last night and if they received enough cash to cover the wedding expenses. I headed to the kitchen but paused when I heard Binh and her arguing.

Binh paced in front of the living room window. "She is so hostile toward me. Everything is so dramatic with her, from her makeup to her clothes to the way she stares at me."

I ducked into the hallway closet and crouched out of sight to eavesdrop.

Mama defended me. "She is a teenager going through some changes. Be patient and show her kindness. Show her love. She will come around."

"Do you think I should take her for a ride in the Citroen and spend some time with her?"

I held my breath. I hoped she'd insist he leave me alone and let me "come around" at my own pace and on my terms. Instead, she agreed to his idea. She failed me and disappointed me.

I slumped back on my bottom and bumped a box behind me. A stack of magazines slid onto my lap. There were photos of half-naked women on the covers. I surveyed one of them. *Hustler.* XXX-Star Spectacular. August 1988. The price was $4.50. I tossed it aside and picked up another magazine. *Playboy.* Entertainment for Men. The price was $4.00. My eyes flew open wider than my mouth as I flipped through the pages. I gathered the magazines to put back in the box. Inside, I found a few VHS cassettes with covers depicting more scantily dressed women.

"Maybe I can take her to Little Saigon, show her our shop at the Phước Lộc Thọ mall, and have lunch there." My stepdad's voice sounded closer. I froze and held my breath, not making a sound until the coast was clear.

The thought of spending the day with my least favorite person in the world at the Asian Garden Mall made me want to run away with the circus or slit my wrist. Unfortunately, it was settled, and within thirty minutes, we cruised along Bolsa Avenue, just him and me. Music filled the void. My thoughts wandered to the magazines and videos I found. I shuddered. I knew Binh's secret. What would I do with it? A Cheshire smile spread across my face.

"It is nice to see you smile for once," my stepdad said.

"I have something to smile about," I said.

"Good."

We pulled into the parking lot of the Asian Garden Mall, a large, two-story building with majestic pillars out front, a statue of a happy Buddha, and white marble statues of the gods, Phước, Lộc, and Thọ. The divinity of three represented happiness, prosperity, and longevity. The entire front of the building was covered in panels of glass. Splashes of red and green adorned the building and rooftops. Large banners on either side of the entrance promoted a night market where you could buy fruits, flowers, trinkets, delectable foods, fashionable clothes, and knock-off purses.

"I think Mr. and Mrs. Van and the others would enjoy the night market," I said. "We should bring Mama later tonight."

"She would like that, although everyone left town this morning."

I whipped my head and stared at him. My mouth flew agape. "Why didn't they say goodbye?"

"They did. Remember?" Binh asked. "Cô Điệp went to the Santa Monica Pier today, and then they were going to slowly make their way back to Seattle."

There went my plans to fly back with my sponsors or hitch a ride with my auntie and Donald. "I guess I was so tired last night."

"You mean drunk?" Binh stopped by the escalator and leaned in. "I know you had some alcohol at our reception."

I shrugged. "Mama lets me sip her beer and wine all the time." I stepped onto the escalator and rode up to signal that the conversation was over.

On the second floor of the mall, our ceramics shop nestled in the corner overlooking the parking lot. Prime real estate. Binh unlocked the doors and held one open for me. The bright natural light coming in from the large windows filled the room.

"Business must be good if we can afford this space," I commented.

Arranged neatly throughout the store on the floor were statues and large vases, all hand-painted by Binh, Mama, or me. Customers could choose from an assortment of silk flowers on display to arrange themselves, or for an extra fee, trust us to make the floral arrangements for them. I was getting good at sticking moss and plastic stems into green foam and presenting them as one-hundred-dollar centerpieces. We used all kinds of flowers, from birds of paradise to lotus blossoms, irises to magnolias, and tiger lilies to calla lilies. On the shelves were figurines, floral centerpieces, and smaller vases. I picked up one of the vases I had painted and admired my work.

"You have steady hands and a good eye for detail," Binh said.

On both sides of the vase were carvings of a bride and groom in their traditional wedding garments, holding hands and looking into each other's eyes. I lifted my vase and turned it over to see the bottom. My initials TT were painted underneath in thick, black paint. I should have signed it Christine.

"Do you love your mother?" Binh asked. I scoffed. What a stupid question. "I love your mom, and it is important to her that we get along. Do you think we can start over?"

"Stop treating me like a child," I said. "Don't be condescending, and stop making decisions for me. I have a brain and an opinion, you know."

"I will try," Binh said. "Do we have a deal?" I nodded. "I would like to be a father to you. Do you think you can call me 'Dad'?"

His question grated me. My back stiffened. I shut down and built up my wall again. "I don't even call my father 'Dad.' The day I call you father is the day the Berlin Wall comes crumbling down. You can be my mama's husband, but you will never be my dad. I don't need a father."

My stepdad crossed his arms over his chest. "Your tone is very disrespectful. Your mother would be ashamed of you speaking so rudely to your elders."

I pivoted on my heel and headed toward the mall exit. "Take me home."

Music filled the void again on the drive home. Binh gripped the steering wheel the entire way. I sat in the backseat and drilled holes in his head with my eyes. High school was around the corner, and I could not wait to free myself from him.

###

Diary, you won't believe this. I found porn in the closet. Of course, they belong to him. Who else would they belong to? What a dirty old man. He asked me to call him "Dad." No fucking way. I'll be cordial to him for my mama's sake. I'll even be respectful. Hell, I'll even be the perfect daughter and get straight A's this year. One way or another, though, I'm going back to Seattle, with or without Mama. I need a job first.

Hell hath no fury for the fury lies within me.
I hear, I know, I speak, I see.
Where two's company and THREE's an asshole.
And in this game of life where pain is the toll,
Only angels and devils sent down down down…
Only sewer rats and pennywise clowns clowns clowns…
They see the cloud with the silver-lined dagger
Disguised as prominent but soon the beggar.

4. A LESSON ON RACISM (FALL 1988)

Westminster High School (WHS) had a reputation for being a bad school with gangs and cretins. If you weren't Asian or Hispanic, you were in the bullied minority. To circumvent that you had to be a cheerleader or a jock. The rumor at rival schools in Orange County was that half of us at WHS were associated with the Triads, the Yakuzas, or the Black Dragons. The misconception that all Asians looked alike meant we could claim to be Chinese yesterday, Japanese today, and Vietnamese tomorrow. The other half of the school was Hispanic, which meant you were associated with one of the crazy brothers, Los Vatos Locos.

Racial slurs were part of everyday conversation. Spics, wetbacks, and lawn mowers versus gooks, dinks, and chinks. Over eighty percent of the students received free or reduced-price lunches. If you weren't a refugee imported from Southeast Asia or a Mexican who crossed the border, then surely you were with the Crips, Bloods, or KKK. These were the misconceptions I had as I entered my freshman year at Westminster High School.

I had a plan, though, to survive the first year and maximize my time away from home. I helped run the Vietnamese Student Association, was on the yearbook committee, took honors classes, joined the beginning band and played the trumpet, joined the Spanish Club, and made the badminton team. By the end of ninth grade, I had straights A's, was fairly popular, ranked number one in girls' doubles on my badminton team, and was initiated into the Pomona Boys, a street gang that wasn't nearly as organized as the Black Dragons but had street cred for being a menace to society.

I had a few hard lessons on racism in the first couple of months at school. My parents didn't get their act together in time for me to qualify for free or reduced-price lunches, so I brought my own. On day one I sat alone with my *thịt kho tàu*, a braised pork and egg dish simmered in a clay pot until caramelized and tender. It was typically served over rice. Chef Tuan helped my mama perfect this dish, and it was one of my favorites. I opened my lunchbox, and a sour odor assaulted my nose. I quickly put the lid back on, but it was too late.

"Gross," Mean Girl said. "What died in your lunch? Smells like feet."

Her friend laughed. "Probably chicken feet. It's what they eat."

She and her friends fled the area. They looked back and pointed at me as they joined another table. My mama had packed pickled cabbage and radishes in my lunch. The pungent smell of vinegar in the California heat nearly rotted my nasal cavity and liquefied my eyes. I starved that day and cried in the bathroom. I threw my whole lunch in the girls' restroom, hoping the smell would blend in with the usual bathroom smells.

A month later I had a hard time opening my locker. Flustered, I tried the combination half a dozen times before I gave up and kicked the locker next to mine.

"¿Cuál es su problema?" A short, pudgy girl leaned against the lockers and asked me what was my problem. She challenged me to answer. My eyes widened and I stared at the odd-looking person in front of me. She had long black hair, a cute face, and pretty legs, but the rest of her features didn't match. Somebody had "Mrs. Potato Headed" her wrong. Her torso made me think of an avocado trying to fit into a peanut shell. The jeans held her stomach in and made her waist small, yet she had more rolls on her than a King's Hawaiian bakery. Pudgy Potato Head looked me up and down and snickered. "Puta."

I knew enough Spanish from telenovelas to know she called me a whore. Thanks to Mrs. Swenson's Spanish class, I countered. "Estas loca en la cabeza." *You're crazy in the head.*

Pudgy Potato Head jabbed her pointer finger at my chest and touched the tip of my scar where I had open-heart surgery. "¿Qué?" She spewed angry words in Spanish that I struggled to comprehend. The only two phrases I understood were "come mierda" and "puta madre" meaning "eat shit" and "motherfucker."

Thankfully, her boyfriend rescued me. Nearly six feet tall and looking like the Spanish version of John Stamos and Rick Springfield, he cast his sexy smile my way and winked with his hazel eyes. He wrapped his arm around Potato Head's neck and leaned down to kiss her. He immediately pacified her anger, and together they walked away, leaving me to feel like an insignificant flea.

From that day on, I was obsessed with him. Being on the yearbook committee meant I had access to names and photos. I had the biggest crush on Julio the entire year, but his potato head girlfriend, Luz, was always in the way. Her name meant "light," but I called her "Loose."

I joined the Spanish Club with an ulterior motive of moving into Julio's circle, under the guise of wanting to practice Spanish. I was the only Asian person in the club, and by the second semester, I faded away unnoticed.

I unexpectedly found my niche when I joined the Vietnamese Student Association (VSA). In Seattle, I knew only one other Vietnamese kid, our neighbor's son, Hung. In Westminster, we were a colony of rabbits, but I was convinced they were not my kind of people. The girls had Aqua Net hair with towering bangs and dressed in black while the boys wore layered, new wave, punk clothes, and pointy shoes. Most of them spoke loudly with thick accents, and I didn't want to be associated with the FOB's, the Fresh Off the Boaters, who hadn't assimilated into American culture as I had.

I yearned to belong to something. I didn't talk like them or dress like them, but at least I looked like them. That first VSA meeting opened my eyes and taught me it was I who was racist.

"Welcome to the Vietnamese Student Association," Van said. "Here, fill this out."

She handed me a membership questionnaire asking for my name and phone number, what ideas I had for fundraisers, what activities and foods I enjoyed, and my favorite movie, song, artist, and sport. Through the VSA, I learned we all had the same frustrations with our parents, who coerced us to fit into a standard box where family traditions, culture, and beliefs were institutions of life. Meanwhile, we desperately wanted to experiment and compete to be individuals with our ideals and independence. It was the American way, and we were Americans. We liked Taco Bell, McDonald's, and Godfather's Pizza. We hated curfews, being seen but not heard, and getting scolded for public displays of affection with the opposite sex.

I came to understand that my fellow Asian-Americans were loud not because they were fresh off the boat country bumpkins but because they had fun. They laughed, they teased, they bantered, and they were great storytellers. I got caught up in the frenzy and found my niche. We liked the same music, enjoyed the same foods, laughed at the same jokes, and wrinkled our noses at our parents' old-world beliefs. In time, I was an important member of the VSA and helped Van lead the club through car washes, cultural fairs, potlucks, study groups, and social outings.

###

The school gazette advertised tryouts for a new badminton team. I poured over the blurb and failed to hear Mrs. Swenson call my name in Spanish class. Someone tapped my arm. It was Trina, a classmate.

"Christine," Mrs. Swenson said, "would you please kick us off in a song?"

The only song I had memorized in Spanish was "La Bamba," because it was repetitive and simple. Plus, I had recently watched the movie starring Lou Diamond Phillips as Ritchie Valens. Mrs.Swenson queued up the music and displayed the lyrics on the overhead transparency projector. The class sang one song after another for our Spanish lesson that day.

Trina and I quickly became friends. Like me, she was the only child of immigrant parents and put in the extra credits to get straight A's. She was smart, shy, and grounded. We were a good team and often partnered up in chemistry, science lab, and Spanish. I trusted her with my secrets. She knew I loathed my stepdad and crushed hard on Julio. We talked about everything and nothing. Many times, we walked home together and spent time in her bedroom listening to music or hanging out in my room playing with Nikki.

Like me, she was close to her mother and was raised without a strong father-figure in her life. Between the two of us, however, I was wilder, louder, and more social. I wore makeup and was not afraid to speak my mind or challenge authority. Trina and Van became my closest girlfriends, but my friendships with them were separate. With Van, I could be crass, foul-mouthed, vulgar, and boy-crazy. We loved '80s heavy metal and appreciated Skid Row and Poison. We lived day by day and acted foolishly and impulsively. I took risks when I was with Van. I was guarded when I was with Trina. She brought out the softer, more studious, well-mannered side of me. We listened to Madonna and Whitney Houston, strived for perfection on our homework, and dreamed of the future. I was two different people at times.

###

Too uncoordinated to try out for cheerleading and too small to play volleyball, I chose badminton thinking, how hard could it be? The school had never had a badminton team before. The new program had new coaches and competitive divisions for singles and doubles, junior varsity, and varsity. I walked into the gym and sat down with the other hopefuls. Coaches Marcelo and Zhang were easy on the eyes, and I knew I had to make the team. They went over the rules, history, and terminologies of the sport then demonstrated ways to serve, smash, and move within the tramlines. Their rally was impressive as I watched both coaches play a real men's singles game. The shuttlecock moved so fast at times I could not see it. Coach Marcelo scored the winning point with a kill to Zhang's body, and I pledged allegiance right then and there that I'd make badminton my sport.

Tryouts were tough. I rotated from court to court and played girls' singles, girls' doubles, and mixed doubles. Both coaches floated around the room with their clipboards, jotting down notes and nodding their approval or frowning their dismay.

When Marcelo shouted, "Drop shot," I finessed the shot and watched the birdie fall over the net into my opponent's court.

When Zhang screamed, "Drive," I sent the shuttlecock over the net like a bird shot out of a cannon and hit my opponent squarely in the neck.

I served when told to serve, and I flicked when told to flick. After two hours, I glistened and smelled like fish sauce.

The next day, I made the team and partnered up with Amy Chen to play girls' doubles. Amy was from Hong Kong. She had an older sister who looked nothing like her. Whereas Amy was petite with an athletic build and wore fashionable clothes from United Colors of Benetton, her sister, Mina, was overweight and introverted and preferred baggy and simple clothes. Amy and I quickly became friends and often surprised each other with gifts…new Yonex or Black Knight rackets or new feather shuttlecocks when ours fell apart. We restrung each other's rackets, and we coordinated our clothes so we'd look like twins.

During competitions, I'd yell, "Yours," or she'd say, "Mine," and when we scored, we high-fived with our rackets. We finished the season ranked number one in the girls' JV doubles division and earned a jacket.

All was falling into place, and my life was perfect until I met Jade, Mad Dog, and Juice. The Pomona Boys were anything but boys.

5. MISS THE BOAT (SPRING 1989)

She walked into my life like a fresh, inexplicable bruise, looking nebulous and mysterious. One day she wasn't there, and the next thing I knew, she appeared in beautiful swirls of blue, purple, and red. I never noticed her in my history class, but I suppose it was because I sat in the front row, right in front of Mr. Hamamoto's podium where a large poster of Clint Eastwood stared at me.

Mr. Hamamoto was a small Japanese man who didn't have much going for him in terms of looks. He was short, balding, and below-average looking. He was however intelligent and had an infectious sense of humor. He spoke to his students as if we were family, with respect, with compassion, with high expectations because he saw our potential, and he wasn't afraid to say "shit" in front of us. He was blessed with a beautiful wife who had blonde hair and was six inches taller than he was. He shared stories of their personal life and the crazy lessons they learned raising their baby daughter together. I was blessed to have fun teachers in ninth grade, which made school easy for me.

Mr. Hamamoto called students to the front of the classroom to give presentations on a historical event of our choice. "Jade, you're up next."

A Vietnamese girl from the back row slowly made her way to the front of the room and dramatically pivoted around to face the class. Her raven hair was long, jagged, layered, and thick like tar. Her black clothes, black nail polish, and thick black eyeliner made her look punk goth, but as dark and mysterious as she was, she had a light that shone through her eyes that reminded me of the grass jelly dessert of East Asia.

The rest of Jade's ensemble was full of color, from her eyeshadow and lipstick to her jewelry and Patrick Nagel pop art T-shirt peeking through her black jacket. I didn't know what to think of her. Part of me suspected she'd bomb her oral presentation, but the other part of me hoped she'd surprise us all and ace it.

"My presentation is in the form of poetry." Jade's voice was soothing and calm, almost hypnotic. Her poem was titled "Miss the Boat."

Gunfire screams and the roof collapses.
The sky ablaze with anger, I think I hear her.
Death. She comes to me. She's coming for you.
Death is but a prostitute. Pain is her pimp.
I run. My legs anchored in rot. I cannot miss the boat.

Headless soldiers stripped naked before me.
Limbless babes suckle and cling to Mother.
My sister, my brother, where are they?
Society crumbles. From ashes rise new power.
I must leave. I cannot miss the boat.

Where freedom has no footing
And truth swallows lies
I sit and wait and wait and sit
I puke and crap all over myself
Knowing I will miss the boat.

Bombs roil the air, they blind me.
Torpedoes light up the ocean floor.
Flames burn and smoke shields.
I wallow. I didn't take action, and now,
I've missed the fucking boat.

Jade stopped reading. Why had she stopped? I wanted more. I hung onto her words, hoping to catch every drip, thirsty to taste her message. I was drawn to her like a bewitched subject, afraid yet curious.

The class was quiet. I applauded. Jade looked at me, and if there was such a thing as humans imprinting on each other, then she imprinted on me. I was ready to draw a black dagger for her.

"Thank you, Jade," Mr. Hamamoto said. "What was your poem about?"

Jade gritted her teeth. "Um, it's about missing the fucking boat."

The class roared, and everyone talked over each other. Mr. Hamamoto did not appreciate her sarcasm. He shifted uneasily. He rang his cowbell, and we knew to shut up or spend an entire fifty minutes the next day writing on the chalkboard, "I will not disrupt Mr. Hamamoto's class."

"But," I said, "what part of history was this poem about?"

"Now you're missing the boat," Jade said. "It isn't about an event in time. It is time. It is history. It's every war, every missed opportunity, every time you skip dinner because you don't want to get fat. Wake up, people!"

Jade screamed the last part. She slammed her assignment on Mr. Hamamoto's podium, stormed down the aisle to the back row, and strode out the door. We still had twenty minutes left of class. Her temper escalated fast and left us stunned.

Jade didn't show up to class the next day, and then it was the weekend. For once, I stopped obsessing over Julio and let Jade's parasitic presence consume me.

Jade sat in the corner of the classroom and sulked like a child in timeout. I sauntered to her desk, trying to exude confidence and coolness. I wore black with a Patrick Nagel shirt underneath my faux leather jacket to impress her.

"I loved your boat poem," I said. "What inspired you to write it?"

She stared at me intensely and said, "Pomona."

"As in the city?" I asked.

"Hey, after class, you wanna get out of here?"

I shook my head, and before I could say no, Jade picked up her backpack and stood up.

"Wait," I said. "Where should I meet you after history class?"

"Taco Bell."

Mr. Hamamoto entered and blocked the doorway. "Jade, stay. Please." His eyes pleaded while his hand reached for the doorknob.

Jade stood stance to stance with Mr. Hamamoto and returned to her seat.

The hour ticked by slowly, and when the dismissal bell rang, Jade and I popped out of our seats. Instead of heading to my locker to get my lunch, I followed Jade to the parking lot.

A white Acura Integra with tinted windows and racing tires pulled up to the curb.

Jade opened the door. "You coming?"

Inside were two guys, one with pockmarks and the other with glasses.

I nodded and got in. "We're going to Taco Bell?"

No one said anything. I secured my seatbelt and held my breath. I wanted to play it cool and not act like a scared sissy, but truth be told, I silently prayed I would not get kidnapped and appear on the front of a milk carton as missing.

At Taco Bell Jade paid for my lunch since I did not have any money. The four of us sat down, and I dug into my Mexican pizza, pretending not to notice that the driver, the one with the glasses, stared at me.

"You going to introduce us?" Glasses guy asked.

Jade swallowed her taco. "Mad Dog. Juice." She waved her hand at both of them. Mad Dog was the one with glasses. He looked like the boy next door with his round face and kind eyes. I didn't dare ask him his real name or why he was called Mad Dog. Juice was the pockmark guy, lanky and quiet. He had scars on his forearm and a cobra tattoo on his neck. I wondered how old they were.

"Well, I'm Christine," I said. My voice trembled, but I tried to mask it by sitting up straight and following it with a peppy statement. "Thanks for inviting me to lunch."

I had never been off campus for lunch before. A lot of students did that, but I never had money to spend. Suddenly, I wished I were sitting with Trina or Van or Amy, talking about homework, rock bands, or badminton. It was the most awkward moment of my young life.

Mad Dog stood up and slid next to me. He helped himself to a slice of my Mexican pizza. "Why are you here?"

I wasn't sure what he was asking. "Um," I stammered. "Uh…Jade invited me. Well, she asked me to meet her here but—"

"You like Poison?" Mad Dog pointed at my heavy metal bracelet.

I blushed. "Yeah, Brett Michaels is amazing."

We talked about music, cars, fashion, and school while Jade and Juice ate silently. I found it easy to talk to Mad Dog and couldn't fathom how he got that nickname.

Before long, as the weeks passed, I spent less and less time eating lunch on campus and instead joined my new friends at Taco Bell. Mad Dog was charmingly intimidating. He opened doors for Jade and me but had no problem yelling at anyone who showed disrespect. He often paid for our meals but scoffed if we didn't eat it all. He showered me with compliments and made me feel smart, empowered, and pretty. With him, it was easy to be confident and speak my mind. He was the safety net that caught me if I messed up and the big brother to the rescue if anyone was disrespectful.

Juice warmed up to me, and I warmed up to him. He was scary to look at, but his scars and tattoos were simply expressions of individualism. I found out his pockmarks were caused by acne, not chickenpox.

Jade took on the role of big sister and stood up to bullies at school for me. She'd mischievously put drops of Visine in someone's lunch if they were mean to me or nonchalantly trip them if they said something degrading. We'd laugh when her victims scurried off to the bathroom or fell flat on their faces. Jade would ask if they had a nice trip. I took pleasure in the harmless fun and came up with ways to humiliate others. It made Jade laugh and I wanted her to like me.

After a month of darting off campus to meet them for lunch or to cruise around, they showed me their true colors. At first, they dared me to steal something small at the convenience store. Over time, I got more brazen and stole money right out of people's hands. I lived a secret life. At home, I stayed out of my stepdad's way and helped the family business. I cared for my dog, helped Mama in the kitchen, and pretended everything was fine. At school, I maintained my grades, joined club activities, and played badminton. I often lied to my mama that I had practice after school or a badminton competition. When I was with Mad Dog, Juice, and Jade, we were just four kids goofing off, pushing ourselves to the limit to see how far we could go without getting caught.

Mad Dog always talked about the Pomona Boys gang, how they cruised Little Saigon, gambled illegally, participated in drive-by shootings, sex-trafficking, and drug solicitations at nightclubs, but my naivete did not put two and two together. The same thugs he referenced were the same street gang members I ate lunch with at Taco Bell.

###

One Saturday morning, my mama and stepdad left early for the shop at the Asian Garden Mall. I promised I would weed the garden if they let me sleep in and stay home. A hard knock at the door startled me while I was feeding Nikki. I peeked through the side window to see Mad Dog waving at me.

I opened the door. "What are you doing here? How did you know where I lived?"

"Can I come in?" he asked.

I hesitated but opened the door wider. "My parents will be home soon."

"It's time you meet the Pomona Boys," he said. "But first…"

He advanced toward me with one swift stride and grabbed my wrist. My body slammed against his, and his hot mouth pressed against my lips. His tongue—wet, sloppy, rushed, invasive—dug deep. I pushed him away and stepped back, only to be pulled back into his arms. His fingers stabbed my back, and he towered over me.

"Stop!" I yelled. I kicked him in the shin. "What the hell is wrong with you?"

Mad Dog released me, stunned. His face softened. "I'm sorry."

I exhaled and let my guard down. Big mistake. He locked the front door and took off his shirt. My heart raced. The ceiling closed in and the room spun. I panicked. I swallowed the fear in my throat. My hands balled into a fist, and I stood defiant.

"You're a little Miss Vixen, aren't you?" Mad Dog asked. It was a rhetorical question. He lunged forward, and I ran in the only direction I could—down the hallway and straight into my room. I slammed the door shut, but he pried it open before I could lock it. I frantically looked around for a weapon. What good would a diary and stuffed animal do to halt him in his tracks? No lamp, no trophy, not even a picture frame to slow him down. *Why did I not run out of the back door?*

It was a cat and mouse game, and I lost. Mad Dog pinned me down on my bed and assaulted my lips until they were bruised. The weight of his body crushed me as he groped at my chest. *Dear God, please help me.*

His dry, calloused hand slid under my T-shirt and tugged at my bra. I froze. My body and will went limp. I opened my mouth to scream but nothing came out. I could not move even though I wanted to hurl his body out the window. His power over me was too strong, and I gave up.

I stared at the ceiling while he explored my neck with his mouth. A tear escaped the corner of my eye. His hand found the tiny bow on the front of my panties, and I closed my eyes. When I opened them again, the faces of Aerosmith stared back at me. The band's lead singer, Steven Tyler, told me to get up, to fight. *I can't.* Back and forth, I had this imaginary conversation with my poster. *You can,* he said.

Mad Dog slid off the bed and stood at the foot of it. He unbuttoned his jeans and pulled the zipper down. It was now or never. Before he could slide his pants off his ankles, I summoned all my willpower and sprang out of the room. I darted for the front door. He was two steps behind me and seized my waist. I stomped on his foot, but it didn't affect him. We pushed and pulled for control, falling to the floor. I clawed at his face and punched him in the throat. His shoulder slammed into the wall.

I leaped to my feet and crushed his crotch with all the force my ninety-five-pound body could muster. He cried out in pain, anger, and surprise. I ran out of the front door and did not stop until I was on the other side of Sigler Park. On the steps of the Blessed Sacrament Catholic Church, I watched from afar as Mad Dog got in his car and sped off. Inside the church, I slumped on the bathroom floor and cried.

That night, I thought long and hard about cutting my wrists. I wanted to die as I relived that event over and over. How could I have been so stupid, so trusting, so naïve? I was angry at Jade for befriending me. I was angry at Mad Dog for what he tried to do. I hated my stepdad for being overbearing. I resented my mama for not seeing how unhappy I was at home. I blamed myself for it all.

Jade tried to talk to me the following week, but I evaded her. One afternoon after badminton practice, Jade and Mad Dog cornered me in the parking lot near the gym.

"There's Miss Vixen," Mad Dog said. He acted as if nothing had happened and we were best friends. He swung his arm around my neck. "You're one of us now. C'mon, I'll introduce you to the rest of the Pomona Boys."

I slapped his arm off me. "Get away from me."

Jade pushed Mad Dog aside. "Leave her alone."

"What?" Mad Dog cried out. "Don't be mad. It was just a test. Vixen, you passed your initiation."

"Get out of my way, Jade," I said, "if that's even your real name."

"I wasn't going to do anything to hurt you, Christine," Mad Dog said. "I just wanted to make sure you could handle yourself."

Jade laughed. "And from what I heard, you did a number on him."

I swiveled around and screamed, "You think this is funny? I fucking hate you both. You tricked me. And to think, I liked you, Jade. Get the hell away from me."

Jade let out a nervous laugh. "Give her time. She'll get over it."

Mad Dog sneered. I knew his patience wore thin. "Get in the car."

I didn't wait to find out if he was talking to me or Jade. I ran back to the gym and prayed they would not chase me. Inside, Coaches Marcelo and Zhang were packing up. Two other players waited on them, getting ready to head out. I mumbled an excuse and asked if they had recommendations on where I could take my racket to have it strung at a higher tension.

As luck would have it, they all were heading to the Big 5 Sporting Goods near my house. We piled into coach Marcelo's car. I got my racket strung, and they dropped me off at home later.

Tomorrow was another day.

6. MY LIFELINE (SUMMER 1989)

School came to an end almost as quickly as it started. Jade dropped out a few weeks after the gym parking lot incident. Her last words to me before she disappeared were, "You're the one that got away, Christine. You're lucky. Watch your back."

I had so many questions. What was her initiation like? How did she get involved in the gang? Was Jade her real name? I could not find her on the yearbook roster. I wondered how Mad Dog and Juice got their names but was thankful I hadn't stuck around long enough to find out. And just like that, the beautiful bruise that was Jade, who had appeared out of nowhere one day, vanished.

I headed into summer relieved I never saw Mad Dog again or got tangled in their web. The experience gave me a new perspective on my life. I vowed to be a better daughter, give my relationship with my stepdad another chance, and never fall for bad boys again.

In the kitchen, Mama hummed a Lionel Richie song. She squatted on the floor with a meat cleaver in her hand, decimating a chicken. "Oh good, you are awake. I need you to cut the Chinese sausage for me and wash the bok choy."

I leaned down and kissed the top of her head. "What are you making?"

"Ba mày kêu," Mama said.

"My dad called?" I asked.

"He did?" Mama asked. "When? How did he get our number?"

I was confused. "No, Mama. You said my dad called. You sad 'Ba mày kêu.'"

Mama laughed. She tipped over from her squatting position and wiped her nose with her sleeve. She picked up the chicken head and bobbed it in front of my face like a hand puppet. She laughed so hard she could barely get the words out. "Ba mày kêu. Má mày đui!"

It dawned on me she was saying, "Barbecue. Mountain Dew."

She slapped my leg, amused at her cleverness for coining the words "barbecue" and "Mountain Dew" as "your father called" and "your mama is blind."

She had me in stitches. We would get serious for a few minutes, me cutting up sausage and her marinating the chicken in ginger soy sauce until one of us cracked a smile. Then it was over. Bouts of laughter rang through our kitchen and out the window.

During moments like these, she would strike with something serious. "I want you to learn Vietnamese and stick with it this time. You are Vietnamese. You must never forget that."

I rolled my eyes and sighed. "How can I forget? You remind me all the time."

"You speak broken Vietnamese like you are still six years old. I found you a school."

The last two times Mama found me a school, I was stuck in a classroom with children who were five and six years old. Two hours every Sunday, she'd push me into the classroom like a cat going into a carrier. I was humiliated. The little kids surpassed me each week in reading, writing, and memorizing songs. I was the only teen learning the alphabet and nursery rhymes. Both times I dropped out of Sunday Vietnamese school and refused to return.

"This is a different language school," Mama said. "The lessons are taught in English and Vietnamese, and the students are teenagers. You'll be with kids your age who are at the same skill level. It is like ESL, only it is VSL." Mama chuckled at the thought of a Vietnamese girl learning Vietnamese as a second language.

I hissed at her but agreed to go only if I did not have to work at the ceramics shop. We struck a deal, and off I went on Sundays to VSL. That summer, I learned the alphabet, how to write basic words, sentence structures, and sing the national anthem of the Republic of Vietnam. A dozen of us attended the summer class. Hormones flew like crazy as we teased, flirted, and played games with one another during breaks. I was thankful I knew the basics of pronunciation, the accent marks, and the inflections associated with them. I sounded out words like a toddler learning to read. Soon I read newspapers and magazines, but I still felt illiterate. Understanding what I read was a whole other issue, one that made

Mama and Binh laugh. At times I got frustrated, but then I'd hear how absurd I sounded and join in on the laughter.

My stepdad found the language school for teens, and for that I was grateful. The more I relaxed around him, the more playful he got. For my early fifteenth birthday present, Binh gave me two tickets to the Poison concert. They were on tour and came to the Long Beach Arena. I finally saw Brett Michaels live and took my friend, Van, with me. My stepdad promised I could stay for the entire concert and that he would not pull me out early. He even agreed to let me stay the night at Van's house that whole weekend since school was out. Fifteen was going to be a great year!

Everything about that concert was magical. The arena lights bounced off the walls and roof. People from all walks of life came in full makeup, ratted hair, and metal rags. I was most surprised to see men in their forties and fifties at the concert. I thought only young people in their teens and twenties enjoyed Poison. Mama gave me fifty dollars to spend on food, drinks, and a souvenir. Khoi and Tree gave me a little extra under the table as they always did, which was a good thing because the T-shirt I wanted was forty-nine dollars. After the concert, Van's cousin picked us up to take us back to her house where I would spend three nights engaging in girl talk, listening to heavy metal music, and lounging at the beach.

A little after midnight, a blue 1986 Toyota Supra pulled up in front of the arena. A young man with a short military haircut got out and gestured us over. New Wave music blared from his speakers the moment the door opened. The sounds of "Cheri, Cheri Lady" by Modern Talking lifted my spirits and revitalized my mood to keep the night going.

"That's my cousin," Van said. "Let's go."

My jaw dropped. The car shimmered under the moonlight and was bathed in the glow of concert lights. It was so waxed and buffed I could see Van's braces in the reflection when she smiled. I was afraid to touch the car, but I didn't have to. Van's cousin opened the door for me, and I climbed in the back. The car smelled nice—a swirl of musk and florals.

"What air freshener is that?" I asked.

"It's cologne," Ace said. "Obsession." Van's cousin popped in a new tape, and while we were stuck in concert traffic, the three of us absorbed the Euro-Italo Disco music of Bad Boys Blue.

"The grunion are supposed to be running this weekend," Ace said. "Want to go?"

"Now?" I asked. "It's after midnight. Aren't your parents—
"

"They're out of town," Van said. "My cousin just got out of the navy, and he's staying with us for a while."

"I get to babysit," Ace said.

"We're not babies," Van said. She whipped around and tossed me some Tic Tac breath mints. "We're fifteen."

"How old are you?" I asked Ace.

He was twenty years old. He had a younger brother, Tung, who went to college in Texas. His parents were still in Vietnam, and he hadn't seen them for over ten years. One day, he hoped to return to Vietnam and build his parents a nice house. His goal was to save thirty thousand dollars to buy them the land, materials, and labor needed to build a suitable home.

Ace's and Van's families were from a village in the north but migrated south during the conflict. After the fall of Saigon, they lost everything. His parents convinced Van's father to take Tung and Ace with them out of the country. They left on a rickety old boat that was not seaworthy at all, and like my family, they settled into a refugee camp.

The Songkhla Camp, located in Thailand on the beachfront far from civilization, housed over six thousand boat people. The camp was surrounded by barbed wire and controlled by the Thai army. Thanks to the charitable work by the United Nations High Commissioner for Refugees (UNHCR) and the personal humanitarian efforts led by Father Joe Devlin, the camp had a few wells to supply fresh water for cooking, huts and barracks for sleeping and schooling, and charcoal for heating.

Ace remembered fondly of talking to Father Joe and how much he loved the priest's compassion for the Vietnamese people. It was Father Joe who organized a sponsorship for the five of them to come to America. It was because of Father Joe that Ace became a Catholic.

By the time the three of us arrived at Long Beach, it was nearly two in the morning. The moon shone bright and the grunion flopped about on the sand. Hundreds of these fish came to shore to spawn during high tide twice a month from March through August. The females dug themselves into the sand and laid their eggs, then jumped out so the males could fertilize them.

The night was warm and my clothes stuck to my skin. In the distance, other people watched the grunion run. Ace peeled off his shirt and darted into the water. Van kicked off her shoes and bobbled in after him. The two of them splashed around and demanded I join them.

"But I'm watching the fish," I yelled.

Ace dove into the waves and swam to shore. He ran toward me, and I realized he meant to carry me into the water. I dodged him but lost my footing in the sand. He charged at me, threw me over his shoulder, and waded into the water.

Slung over his shoulder, I wrapped my arms around his hard, muscular torso. The faint smell of his cologne mixed with the salty air and made me lightheaded. My stomach fluttered, and my heart pounded against my chest as I tensed my body. Ace threw me in the ocean and adrenaline flooded my body. I was not a strong swimmer and scurried to stand up. We splashed around, and both Van and I charged at him.

Ace scooped me into his arms, and I punched him in the pecs, afraid he was going to dunk me again. Instead, he placed me gently on my feet and held me. It felt like minutes, but it was mere seconds. We locked eyes, and my gaze drifted to his full lips. I wanted to kiss him.

He released me. "Let's go. I better get you girls home."

Ace was the summer love and cure for boredom I desperately wanted. We had fun that summer, and even though he was five years older than me, we didn't analyze the fact that I was a minor and he an adult. Ace was my first love, and long after we parted, the magic was still there. He cast a spell on me that brought me total bliss, deep sorrow, and layers upon layers of regret. He carved his name into my heart so deeply, I could not breathe, could not function, could not think without him. He was my lifeline, and I was his.

7. BOUNDARIES (WINTER 1989-SPRING 1990)

Nineteen-eighty-nine was an historic year. I sat with Ace on the floor, tears streaming down my face, as we witnessed the Berlin Wall coming down on that November day. Every news channel and media outlet covered the event. The thirteen-foot-tall and ninety-six-foot-long wall was built after WWII to divide the eastern and western parts of the city. Anyone caught crossing it was shot down, no questions asked. Free passage from east to west was granted on November 9 and reunification of Germany was underway. Families who had been separated for twenty-eight years hugged and cried as relief and joy filled their spirits. They danced, drank, and celebrated throughout the night while tearing the concrete wall down.

Ace wrapped his arm around my waist and pulled me to him. "Communism will collapse for Vietnam one day."

I snuggled closer to him. "I hope so. I don't remember my family back home and hope to meet them. My mama misses her brother and sister, and I know my cousin wants to see his family again too. He hasn't seen them for almost eleven years."

"How can you two breathe?" Van asked. "There's like no air between the two of you." Ace and I snuggled closer with me on his lap. She handed me a bowl of popcorn and turned on the VCR. "What movie did you rent for us?"

I wrapped my arm around Ace's neck and kissed him on the temple. "Did you get the new *Nightmare on Elm Street?*"

"Did you go to Blockbuster or Hollywood Video?" Van asked.

Ace laughed. "Yes to all three." He ran his fingers through his hair. I knew my body heat was making him hot.

I moved to the couch to sit next to Van. Ace stood and removed his shirt. I gawked at his physique. I didn't think I would ever tire of looking at him. Every day he ran and did calisthenics to stay in shape. I loved watching him do his sets of squats, crunches, pushups, planks, and dips. Over time he got used to me being the creepy girlfriend who stared all the time. He grunted and sweated while doing his exercises, while I sat on the floor, guilt-free, eating my food and drooling. I had no shame.

Ace sat on the couch with us, and I immediately put my cold feet on his stomach to soak up all his warmth. The three of us watched the horror flick and stayed up late eating ramen, drinking pop, and helping ourselves to *chè*, a Vietnamese dessert soup that came in a variety of flavors, colors, and ingredients. Some chè were served warm while others were served with crushed ice. My favorite was *chè Thái*, a fruit cocktail made with jackfruit, longans, lychees, toddy palm seeds, pandan jelly, and coconut milk. Ace preferred *chè ba màu*, which was three layers of sweet yellow mung beans, sweet red kidney beans, and green pandan jelly nestled into a lot of crushed ice and bathed in sweet coconut cream. Van went for the *chè sâm bổ lượng*, a refreshing dessert made with kelp, lotus seeds, longans, pearl barley, and red dates.

As my sophomore year rolled on, I spent less and less time at home. I did my own thing, hung out with my friends, and continued to stay busy with badminton and club activities. During the first half of the school year, Ace waited for me in his Supra a block from my school. We didn't want anyone to know about our relationship, especially since he was five years older than I was. We stole moments together before my parents came home. Most of the time, we sat at the park and talked or he helped me with homework. If we weren't kissing, we were constantly touching, whether it was my head on his lap or his leg over mine. If our hands were not touching, then our shoulders were. We were so much a part of each other that being apart was physically painful. My stomach would knot or his head would throb until we saw each other again.

Ace made me laugh. With him I felt special, loved, and beautiful. We made plans for the future. That Valentine's Day, he had a bouquet of roses and a box of chocolates waiting for me in the car. I was so in love with him I could not imagine life without him.

"Happy Valentine's Day!" I leaned over and kissed him passionately. "I didn't get you anything."

"It's okay," he said. "I'm the one with the job."

"Do you want to come to the house?" I wanted to show him my room and where I hid his love notes. I wanted him to meet my dog and show him the scrapbook I made of us. I wanted to read my love poems, and most of all, I wanted to lie in his arms.

"I don't think that's a good idea," he said.

I pleaded and pouted. "We can cuddle…" I reminded him it was Valentine's Day, and he was supposed to spoil me.

Ace laughed and gave in. "All right, but no more than half an hour. The last thing I want is to get caught alone in your room in your parents' house when they come home."

"They're not due back until five," I said. "We'll easily have an hour."

Inside my room, we listened to music and ate Valentine's Day chocolates. We dreamed of our future together and planned to marry right after my eighteenth birthday. He wanted me to remain a virgin until then.

"And while you go to college," Ace said, "I'll work and save money for our house and children."

I giggled at the thought of us having babies. "How many do you want?"

"How many can you handle?" he teased.

I counted the numbers on my fingers. "Well, counting you…"

"Me?" Ace threw me on the bed and tickled me. "Trust me, I'm no child."

I laughed until I could not breathe. Ace let up and let me catch my breath. He tenderly stroked my hair and said the three words I had been waiting to hear.

"I love you too," I said.

We kissed and let our hands wander. I wanted to explore his body and see every inch of him, but he would not let me. It frustrated me. I felt rejected.

"We can't," he said. "I want to…but…you don't want me to go to jail, do you?"

"Three years is a long time to wait," I said. I straddled his hips and pinned his arms above his head. "If you love me…"

Ace rolled over and pushed himself away from me. He stood up and collected his keys. "If I love you, I won't ruin you. This summer, you'll turn sixteen, and I'll be twenty-one, and before you know it, you'll graduate high school and go off to college. I'm not going anywhere. We'll get married and do this the right way. We'll get both of our parents' blessings, because one day when the embargo is lifted and we can safely return to Vietnam, I want to introduce you to my family. Even though my family are northerners and yours are southerners, I want our families to get along."

"They'll get along," I said. "It's not like your family was Viet Cong. We fought on the same side."

"It's not that simple," Ace said. "Babe, I'm going to be here every step of the way to make sure you get your education. That's super important to me. We can't give them any reason not to give us their blessings. Besides, I want our daughters to be proud of us."

I raised my eyebrow. "Daughters, huh?"

A smile crept on his lips and lit up his face. "I want to be smothered with little girls. They are so cute."

"Well, I want boys," I said. "I can't handle little girls, and if they grow up to be anything like me…well, payback is a bitch."

Ace pulled me to my feet. He kissed me softly. "Happy Valentine's Day. I'll see you tomorrow after school."

###

Ace continued to come to my house after school for weeks. He taught me card games like *tiến lên*, also called the game of Thirteen, while we listened to music. Thirteen was popular in Vietnam. Players shed their cards in ranked order, with the two of hearts being the highest and three of spades being the lowest. As each player discarded, the last one left with cards was declared the loser and had to pay up. Stakes were often high when we played together with Van. The three of us were competitive and made up ridiculous penalties for the loser. Van once had to flash her breasts to the old neighbor across the street, who was nearsighted, but that didn't make it any less embarrassing. I often lost, and the nastiest thing I had to do was chew gum for five minutes after Ace and Van already had it in their mouths.

One particular Friday night, I slept over at Van's house, and Ace came over. We played Thirteen.

Van rubbed her hands together like she was warming them in front of a fire. "Okay, guys, if Ace loses, he has to teach us to drive his car."

Ace shook his head vehemently. I squeezed his arm and grinned, bobbing my head up and down. "And if Van or I win, then we'll teach you how to roller skate."

"Perfect!" Van exclaimed.

"Wait," Ace said. "Either way, I lose!"

"Perfect!" I said and dealt each of us thirteen cards. "Sorry, honey, it's two against one. Either you learn to skate, or we learn to drive."

Van picked up her cards and smiled mischievously. She rocked to and fro. "Yes, it's time we learned."

Now, tiến lên was not a challenging game to play, but it did require a little strategy. Although Van and I never admitted to ganging up on Ace or cheating, we did squeak out a win after six rounds. The following day, on the brightest California day of our young lives, Van and I learned to drive, and Ace nearly had a heart attack teaching us.

###

Spring break had arrived. Binh, Mama, and I came home from the Presbyterian church in Garden Grove and changed out of our Sunday clothes. Binh tended to the garden while my pup, Nikki, supervised. Mama and I busied ourselves in the kitchen.

"You have been happy lately," Mama said. "School is going well?"

I took the carrots out of the fridge and chopped them into one-inch pieces. "School is great. Trina and I have Spanish together again in Mrs. Swenson's class and we're partnering up in Ms. Phillips' English class to do a book report. Amy and I are partners again in badminton, but she mentioned she might be moving at the end of the school year."

Mama cut up the brisket. She was getting comfortable in the kitchen. The tutorial with Chef Tuan paid off. "Where is Amy moving to?"

"Back to Hong Kong," I said sadly. "Why can't people just stay in one place? I miss my friends in Seattle, especially Marina, and now I might lose Amy to Hong Kong!"

Mama sliced the onions and placed slivers behind her ears. "This is the trick to not crying when you cut them." Two minutes later, she sniffled and wiped her eyes with the back of her hand. "Maybe I am too close." She slid a step stool under her feet and then stood a foot higher.

I laughed at her. "Mama, I don't think that's the secret." I ran to my room and came back with sunglasses and Ace's bandana tied around the bottom half of my face. I slipped my hands through two plastic produce bags. "This is how you cut onions."

Mama placed her onion slices over my ears. "Extra safe."

I looked ridiculous but humored her for a while as we talked about school. "Van is not doing good in her classes. She doesn't understand things like I do."

"It is good you are helping her." Mama tossed me the parsley. "Chop these."

570

"Are you making *bò kho*?" I loved Vietnamese beef stew with sweet potatoes and French baguettes.

"No," Mama said. She scrubbed the mushrooms, and my curiosity peaked. "I am making a French dish. It is beef bougie ngon."

"Oh," I said. "You mean like a beef bouillon?"

"What booyon? I said bougie, like a bourgeois." She repeated "bougie ngon" louder, as if saying it again at a higher decibel would make me understand.

"Okay, Mama, I get it," I said. "I'm not deaf. You're making a fancy beef dish that is delicious. Ngon means delicious. I get it."

Mama shook her head. "Ói zòi oi! Trời đất ơi!" *Oh my God! Heaven and Earth!* She took out the spiral-bound journal that Chef Tuan gave her. Inside the pages were hand-written recipes. She flipped to page nineteen. Emphatically, she pointed at the recipe.

I read it out loud. "Boeuf Bourguignon."

"That's what I said."

At the end of that week, the Friday of spring break, Ace and I hung out in my room and did our usual thing while my mama and stepdad were at the Asian Garden Mall. Binh worked at the store selling ceramics while Mama studied for her citizenship exam in the back office.

"What time will they be home?" Ace asked. "We can go to the beach, and I'll have you back in plenty of time. They won't know you were gone."

I frowned. "I have to do some weeding, clean up the kitchen, and cook a pot of rice."

"I'll help you." He turned on the audiovisual system. "Wow, you have the latest episode of *Paris by Night*!" He popped in the VHS tape. "Thúy Nga Productions, video eighteen, season six."

My parents, like most Vietnamese families, had stacks of these *Paris by Night* videotapes. Each series was a variety show. Ace loved the slapstick comedy skits and Vietnamese folk songs called *cải lương*. I never appreciated these folk opera songs because they sounded so nasally and melodramatic. The comedy skits were over my head, and I didn't understand most of the humor. I enjoyed the performances of the pop and new wave singers who wore glitzy clothes and danced to choreographed movements with their sexy backup dancers.

Every time Lynda Trang Dai performed, I dropped everything and pretended I was her. Lynda was controversial because she wore skin-tight, lacy clothes and drank beer from a bottle. She sang in Vietnamese and English and was considered the Vietnamese Madonna. Others emulated her, but I considered them copycats of the OG, original gangster, of the new wave scene.

My mama had her favorite singers as well, like Huong Lan and Khanh Ha. Oddly enough, my stepdad liked Tuan Anh, who reminded me of Prince, Boy George, and Elton John all rolled into one with his outlandish style. His clothes were flashy, his shoes stilettoed or platformed, his hair a beehive mullet, and his face a bit odd with a mustache over heavy makeup. There was no denying it, however, he had solid vocals and was a talented artist.

Ace cooked the rice while I tidied up the kitchen. He washed the dishes and I arranged them neatly in the dishwasher to dry. We took a quick nibble break. Ace made us some condensed milk toast, which I had never had, but it was nirvana at first bite. Whereas Americans like their peanut butter and jelly sandwiches, the Vietnamese like their condensed milk and butter sandwiches, toasted, and enjoyed warm with strong jasmine or green tea. It gave us the little pep we needed to tackle the weeds together. After an hour in the hot sun, sweat poured down our face and our shoulders drooped.

"I need to shower," Ace said. "Want to join me?"

We had never seen each other naked before. I hesitated and cracked my neck. I inhaled deeply and smiled but did not advance toward him. The thought of seeing him bare-skinned and feeling the water cascade down our bodies excited me. My mouth was dry. I opened the fridge and grabbed a Mountain Dew. The brave and impulsive side of me was ready to make the leap for adventure and take our relationship to the next level. The innocent and apprehensive side of me was concerned the mystery and sexual tension between us would dissolve if I saw all of him.

"You shower first," I said. "Make it quick."

Ace laughed. He hopped into the shower while I put the weeds in the trash bin. I came back to the house and caught him by surprise, bare-chested and in his boxer briefs. My face flushed and I licked my lips. I looked past his shoulder to the imaginary poster behind him.

Ace tried to make me laugh and gyrated his hips. "Look at me. I'm an American gigolo."

I giggled. "Oh boy, Richard Gere, the American gigolo, in my home!"

Ace swaggered over to me and closed the distance between us. He caressed my cheek and bent down to find my parted lips. His skin felt like silk, and his body radiated so much heat that I wanted to take my shirt off to cool down. He carried me to my room and gently laid me down. The weight of his body on mine was comforting, and the more he rubbed his hips against mine, the more I wanted to open myself up and invite him in.

His warm breath in my ear sent tingles down to my toes. "You have to say 'stop' or else I won't be able to."

I felt his hardness against my thigh and his soft lips on my clavicle. "More." I arched my back and offered myself to him. "Don't stop."

Torn between passion and responsibility, we lay there kissing and exploring each other, touching every curve, every fold, every inch. His thumb caressed the raised part of my scar from my open-heart surgery and I guided his hand away from my scar. I held my breath. It was the one part of me that made me feel ugly, insecure, and unworthy of affection. I stopped kissing him and tried to sit up.

Ace stopped and looked at me. "That's the part I find the most beautiful." He lifted my shirt and kissed my surgical scar, all six inches of it from the top of my collarbone down to the end. "You're a warrior. It's your battle scar, and you cheated death."

I hugged him close and wrapped my legs around him. "How did I get so lucky?"

Two car doors slammed shut. Footsteps tapped the pavement. Keys jingled. Shit. Voices. I heard my parents. We had lost track of time. Thankfully, Ace's Supra was parked outside on the street in front of the nearby apartment complex. Ace scrambled to put his pants on but did not have time to get his shirt on. Heavy footsteps approached my bedroom. I threw the blanket over Ace and had him lie as flat and still as possible. My heart raced, and I crossed my hands involuntarily over my chest to keep my heart from bulleting through. The door opened. I froze. My stepdad popped his head in. He looked at me then closed my door.

"You better come here," Binh said. "Your daughter is hiding a boy in her room."

8. THE GOODBYE (SPRING 1990)

I stormed out of my room before Binh and my mama could come in. I was furious that my stepdad had barged into my room without knocking and without permission.

"You can't knock?" I screamed. "What if I were naked? I need privacy!"

My stepdad pounded his fist on the dinner table. "Not in my house you don't! Your door is to always remain open and unlocked. You cannot be trusted."

Mama sat down and bowed her head in shame. Wetness glistened around her eyes as she blinked to hold them back. "Is it true?" Disappointment and shame were written all over her face.

"Nothing happened," I argued.

"Then why was he in your room and your bed?" My stepdad was so angry he kicked Nikki. She flew across the rug and skidded on the kitchen floor. She yelped, and I ran to check on her.

Ace stepped into the room and bowed to my parents. "Please forgive—"

"Who the hell are you?" My stepdad said coldly. "What do you have to say for yourself, young man? Do you know she is only fifteen?"

"I love your daughter," Ace said. "I know she is young but—"

"Did you touch my daughter?" Mama asked.

"I am calling the police," Binh said.

"No!" I ran and stood next to Ace, holding a trembling Nikki in my arms. I hugged her close and patted her head. I was so pissed off that I lost my temper. "I fucking despise you. You're nothing but a demon." I grabbed the vase on the table and threw it at his feet.

"Do you see how she is talking to me?" Binh asked. "Control your daughter. She is a disrespectful little whore."

"She is anything but—" Ace didn't have the chance to finish.

My stepdad punched him in the jaw. "Shut up. You do not get to talk."

Tears ran down my mama's face. "Please, stop fighting. I'm tired of the two of you with this power struggle you have with one another. I just want peace for once in my life!"

My stepdad pointed at the door. "Young man, get out while you can. See what you made her do?"

Ace bowed deeply to my mama. "I am sorry. Please forgive me." He gave me an apologetic nod and headed to the door. I grabbed his wrist. "No, Christine, you stay here and make peace with them. I will see you later."

"No, you will not," my stepdad said. He escorted Ace to the door and slammed it shut. "While you live at my house—"

"It's not your house," I argued. "Mama lives here too. Or is she just another one of your possessions, like your car and your business and your garden? Everything is fucking yours. I thought marriage was a partnership. It should be 'ours,' not 'mine.'"

My stepdad bent down slowly and picked the vase off the floor. He placed it back on the table. It was eerie how methodical and calculated his movements were and how he suddenly was quiet. Was he premeditating my murder? Was he devising a plan to get rid of me? I braced myself for an explosion. I was ready to run if he threw the vase at me or put his hands on me.

My mama sat there and cried. She did not stand up to him. She did not defend me. She could not even look at me. I dishonored her. My beautiful, strong, gentle mother sat immobile. Was she frozen in fear? I wasn't going to live my life in fear. I wasn't going to let a man rob me of my spirit. I vowed I would never depend on a man for money or security.

I ran out the front door and looked for Ace, hoping to see his car still parked on the street. It was. I rapped frantically on the window and vaulted in the car with Nikki tucked close to my chest. Ace drove around aimlessly. We sat in silence. What now? I knew I could not go back, and somehow I needed to wake Mama up and convince her to leave him. Her life was too entwined with his. It was not going to be easy. He controlled everything and managed the finances…or should I say, mismanaged? He spent lavishly and liked to show off. He gave our products away freely to flatter people. In turn, they saw him as kind and generous and praised him as a shrewd businessman who had it all. He had a beautiful wife, a straight-A daughter, and a successful business.

I hated being Vietnamese then. Our society was built upon the stupid, patriarchal, male-chauvinistic belief that the man was in charge. A man could do no wrong and was the stronger of the two sexes. A woman's role was to be obedient, subservient, and cater to her husband. A child's job was to do, not think, and act, not speak. I denounced my ethnicity, my Vietnamese name, my language, and everything that was associated with the culture. In feeling that way, I also inadvertently denounced everything that Mama represented…everything that she was…and I hurt her more than I understood. Was I being insolent, selfish, and irresponsible? Was I insensitive?

I begged Ace to let me stay with him, but he insisted I go home. He lived with his two roommates and was not comfortable with me being there alone when he was at work. I couldn't live with Van. Her parents were dealing with personal issues at the time and could barely afford to pay the rent or feed themselves. I couldn't live with Amy and her sister, Mina. They were packing up to move to Hong Kong. Ace and I argued that night. It was our first fight, and I couldn't convince him to let me live with him. Why did he have to be so righteous?

Ace dropped me back off at home. "You have to swallow your pride and make up with your stepdad. If it were my daughter, I would be upset too, but they love you."

"He doesn't love me," I said.

"Well, your mom loves you, and she needs you." He kissed me, gave me some money in case I needed anything for the weekend, then drove away.

I quietly opened the door to the house and let Nikki inside. I tiptoed to my room, grabbed a thick sweatshirt, my purse, and slipped back into the night. Through Sigler Park and to the Catholic church I walked, engrossed in my self-pity and sadness. I wanted to disappear. I didn't care what happened to me. I wished someone would jump me and stab me to death. I let my imagination go dark and thought about finding Mad Dog, Jade, Juice, and the rest of the Pomona Boys.

I walked in a daze, entranced in a make-believe world where it was just Ace and me, living happy and stuck in time. Inside the church, a light was on. The glow illuminated the face of the Blessed

Virgin Mary on the stained glass windows. I curled my fingers around the door handle and pulled, only to discover it was locked. I walked to the side and back entrances, but those doors were locked as well. I knocked and waited, but nobody came.

I felt so alone. I was alone. I huddled behind the dumpster and slumped to the ground. A whimper became a demonic cry, and I released my troubled spirit into the night. Exhausted, I curled into a ball with my back against the unforgiving wall, and with one last sigh escaping my lips, I slept.

###

Saturday, I walked five miles to Van's house. The moment she opened the door, tears sprang from my eyes. I sobbed and told her the whole story.

"Go take a bath," Van said. "I'll get you some fresh clothes. You stink."

I didn't tell her I slept behind a dumpster. I ran a hot bubble bath and soaked in the soothing water. I didn't know how I was going to recover from this. Seeing Ace again would be forbidden. Existing without him in my life, without seeing him each day, was a death sentence.

Moving to California had been a big mistake. I had to find a way to return to Seattle. I sat numb and devoid of feelings. The world around me didn't matter anymore. Maybe everyone would be better without me. I didn't have anything to contribute. Ace would find another girlfriend eventually. He would soon tire of me and want a real woman.

What did I have to offer? I wasn't Vietnamese enough. I wasn't American enough. I wasn't smart enough, pretty enough, or talented enough. Was there anything worse than being ordinary? I got out of the tub and looked for a razor blade or something sharp. Girls slit their wrists every day. People committed suicide all the time. Mama didn't have to feel stuck in the middle anymore. I dragged her down, not Binh. She finally found love, and I ruined it for her. All these years, I was the rope around her wrists and the burden on her back. When she stumbled and fell, I wasn't there to catch her. When she needed to fly, I tethered her to the boulder. No more. *I'll set you free, Mama. I'll set both of us free.*

I found a shaving kit below the sink and took the razor out. Would it be sharp enough? I could try. I scraped the blades against my wrist. I didn't feel anything. Harder. You have to press harder. I dug the teeth deeper into my skin. Crisscross, like a tic tac toe. Again. Harder. Deeper.

At last, I drew blood and watched it drip. Fascinated, I sat back in the tub and zombied out. The haze of blood clouded the water and turned it a subdued red. I leaned back and closed my eyes. Everything would be okay.

###

Ace's face hovered inches from mine. The scent of his cologne carried me to a tropical island, and I ran along the shore. The sun beat down on me. I sat up but was pulled back by arms I recognized.

Ace's voice was soothing. "Close your eyes." I did as I was told. "I've got you, honey."

I smiled. I was in heaven. We were together.

"She's awake?"

Wait, why was Van in heaven too? I opened my eyes. Posters of Brett Michaels, Sebastian Bach, and Vince Neil hung on the walls. A large cross loomed above the headboard. I was in Van's bedroom and leaning against Ace's chest. My voice cracked when I spoke. "What happened?"

Van sat on the corner of the bed and squeezed my foot. "I called him." She nodded at Ace. "He came right away. I think you tried to kill yourself."

"You didn't call the ambulance?" I asked.

"No," Van said, "because you just fell asleep, that's all."

"You mean, I failed?" I didn't understand. I thought I was dying. "But I cut myself, and I was bleeding. I felt my life force and all the energy drain away."

"Honey," Ace said, "you had just walked five miles to get here. I'm sure you didn't sleep well last night either. I know I didn't." Ace handed me a can of cold *sữa đậu nành*. The sweetened soy milk tasted like the fountain of youth and rejuvenated me.

"What now?" I asked. "I don't want to go back home."

"I wish you could stay here with us, but—"

"It's okay, Van," I said. "I know things are tough with your dad losing his job. Maybe I can ask Trina and her mom. In three months, school will be out, and maybe things will be better."

"In the meantime," Ace said, "I'm getting you a beeper." Ace unclipped his beeper off his belt loop and showed it to me. "You can call my pager and punch in the number you're at. If it's an emergency just put 9-1-1 after it, and I'll call you back. And if it's not urgent or you just want to send me a message that you love me, put in 8-0-0-8."

Van laughed and slapped Ace on the shin. "Oh my God."

578

"Why 8-0-0-8?" I asked.

"My dumbass cousin wants you to spell 'BOOB.'"

I punched Ace playfully and gave him a charley horse. He feigned injury by hobbling out of bed and limping to the living room.

I called Trina that afternoon and asked if she'd talk to her mom about me staying with them for three months until school was out. I explained the situation at home but left out the part about having a boyfriend five years older than I was. We did not have to beg for Trina's mom, Auntie Chanh, to accept my request. They wanted me out of that volatile situation and believed I needed to feel safe and untroubled to finish the school year strong.

We agreed that on Monday after school, Trina would walk home with me to my house and help me gather my things. Trina's mom would pick us up and take us home.

I stayed with Van for the weekend and called home once to tell Mama I was safe. She was worried out of her mind and demanded I come home. I stood my ground and told her I'd be home Monday after school to collect my things.

My dear friend, Trina, sat on my bed and petted Nikki. It broke my heart to leave my dog behind, but I convinced myself it was temporary. Mama swore she would take good care of my pup. In the corner of the room was my duffle bag stuffed with my badminton rackets, team competition clothes, and birdies. Next to it was a trash bag of shoes and ten outfits to last me until laundry day. I wanted to be all packed before Mama got home. She was studying hard for her citizenship exam, and I urged her to take the time she needed. I promised I'd stay until she got home.

"I feel like I'm forgetting something," I said.

"Pajamas?" Trina asked.

"Got 'em. I've got underwear, bras, a jacket…"

"Toothbrush? Makeup?"

"Oh, yeah, I need my toothbrush and hairbrush."

After I finished, we sat and waited. Trina was an amazing friend. She was my cheerleader, always encouraging and supportive. She was not only studious but smart. I knew she'd be a doctor, lawyer, or engineer one day, which was what every Vietnamese family seemed to want for their children. My dearest friend was most comfortable when she was outside of the spotlight, behind the scenes, where it was safe and predictable. She had a pure heart. I teased her for her shyness and tried to bring her out of her shell.

She carried a little extra weight, and I guess that affected her confidence. She was soft-spoken with the cutest, childish laugh. When she was happy, her dimples came out in full glory, and I envied her dimples. The Vietnamese have a superstition about dimples being signs of good fortune and luck. In some ways, she was lucky. She had a mother who loved her whole-heartedly and protected her fiercely. Sadly, her mom couldn't protect her from everything or everyone. Her father had molested her, and that perhaps explained why she often turned away from the limelight, preferring to recoil inward rather than shine outward.

"Is your stepdad really an ass?" Trina asked. "I mean, he always seems so nice and gracious."

I was flabbergasted. "Don't play devil's advocate, Trina. I can't believe you just asked me that. You're usually on my side."

"I guess I don't know him as you do," she said.

"No, you don't." I debated whether to confess and tell her about Ace. Since our conversation went dry, I spilled the beans and told her everything.

"That explains why you hadn't been boy crazy over Julio!" Trina straightened her back and sat up taller. "I thought maybe you were seeing my neighbor, Tommy. He has a crush on you."

"What?" I put my hands to my cheeks and sat back against the wall. "Tommy? Tall, skinny 'I'm a slut' Tommy?"

We both laughed. Tommy was a flirt and always chased skirts. He thought of himself as a lady's man and made his move on anyone desperate enough for attention.

"He put his arm around me once, and I smacked him," Trina said.

"Good for you," I said. "He'd be a lot cuter if he plucked that caterpillar stache growing above his lips."

"Agreed," Trina said. "So…have you and Ace done it?"

"You mean had sex?" I asked.

"No." Trina rolled her eyes. "Study for the SATs. Of course, I mean sex. After all, it's unrealistic that you'd be a virgin for that long."

She was right. When we were together, we couldn't stop touching each other. It was always he who pulled away before we crossed the boundaries. How long would he be able to stay level-headed and in control?

Mama came home before I could confirm or deny. We came out of the bedroom and greeted her. She looked ten years older, haggard and disheveled in her appearance. I noticed she had two different colored socks on but didn't say anything. Dark smudges smeared her eyes, which drooped in solidarity with her mouth and cheeks. Her tanned skin no longer looked vibrant and youthful. Rather, the brown tinge showcased her age and the weathered expression on her face. Sadness sucker punched me in the gut, and guilt swallowed me whole.

Mama and I stood in the kitchen and talked while Trina waited in my room with Nikki. I let Mama start as I didn't know what to say.

Her eyes misted. "Thủy-Tiên ơi…Do you know how broken my heart is?" I shook my head and the tears I had held back quietly fell down my cheeks. Mama clutched her heart. "You tell me what to do. I want you to be happy, but I need to be happy too. You are growing up so fast, and you do not need your old mother like you used to."

I shook my head. "That is not true. I need you, truly I do, more than anything."

Mama patted my head and stroked my hair. "My entire life has been devoted to you, and I know it has always been just the two of us."

I knelt and grabbed her hand. I pressed her soft hands to my forehead, hands that once held me and fed me, hands that were once smooth and youthful but now wrinkled and spotted from cooking oil burns, and I begged for forgiveness.

"I'm sorry, Mama," I whispered. "I don't mean to be a bad daughter." It was hard to breathe. My nose was stuffy, and the more I sniffed, the harder I cried. I was such a disappointment. I knew this. Selfish, stupid, angry. And for what reason? Why did I feel so threatened by my stepdad, by this authority?

"For once," Mama said, "I am ashamed of you, but I cannot blame you. It is my fault for loving you and spoiling you too much, for holding on too tightly, because I was always afraid of losing you."

I wrapped my arms around her knees and pressed my head against her leg. "I'll do better. I'll try harder. I don't want to make you sad."

I lowered myself to the floor, still on my knees, and grabbed her ankles. I kissed Mama's feet. "I know I hurt you. I know I am an unworthy, ungrateful daughter. Please, forgive me. Please still love me. Don't give up on me. Please." The tears flowed. I hated myself. My bones ached and sorrow crushed my rib cage. I had no heart, no soul, to keep it from caving in.

Mama lowered herself to my level and sat on the floor with me. She wept. She cradled me in her arms and rocked me like a baby. I clung to her, but no matter how tightly I held onto her or how much I crushed her, desperately trying to be one with her, I could not get close enough. It left me drained, unfulfilled and wanting to disappear into her arms.

"Maybe this break will be good for us," Mama said. "It is only for three months. Miss Chánh is kind to take you in, and Trina is a good girl. Promise me you will not give them any trouble. Be respectful and dutiful, help around the house, do your schoolwork."

"Yes, Mama, I promise," I said. "Are you going to be all right?"

Mama lifted my chin. She kissed my forehead. "I will be all right for you if you be all right for me."

"And what about my boyfriend?" I asked. "His name is Ace. He loves me, and I love him."

"I know I cannot keep the two of you apart," Mama said. "Your stepdad and I will invite him over, and we will talk to him to understand his intentions."

"You will see," I said. "He is good." We sat in silence for a few minutes, respectful of each other's thoughts. "Mama, how is your studying going?"

"By August, I should be a naturalized citizen," Mama said, "and so will you."

That was news to me. "Do I have to take a test?"

"No, since you are under eighteen, you automatically become a citizen when I become one."

"Does this mean I can change my name and be legally any name I want?" I asked. Mama nodded. "Are you going to change your name?"

"I always liked Elizabeth Taylor, so I am thinking of changing it to Liz."

"I think I will stick with Christine, but maybe spell it with a K."

Trina's mom, Auntie Chanh, arrived. While she and my mama exchanged cordial conversation, I stood back and observed. Trina looked nothing like her mother, who was thin and rather homely looking. They shared the same nose and were both soft-spoken, but whereas Auntie Chanh had short, wavy locks, Trina had a long, straight mane with bangs that reached for the sky like vines held up by excessive Aqua Net hairspray.

I collect my bags, hugged Mama, and slowly walked away, determined not to cry. It was another difficult goodbye but far from my last. A few more farewells were to come.

9. TICKING TIME BOMB (SPRING-SUMMER 1990)

Sophomore life resumed as usual at Westminster High School, but now I laid my head at Trina's house instead of my mama's. The day I said goodbye to Amy and her sister Mina was the day I decided to change my name to Amy. What better way to celebrate our friendship and to honor the girl who had a profound impact on me in the short amount of time she was in my life? I was evolving away from the reckless Christine to a more aware and cosmopolitan Amy. She was everything I envisioned myself to be. She was well-traveled, athletic, funny, smart, and fashionable. She was respectful, outgoing, and accepting of everyone. She was competitive, but humble and gracious, and carried optimism around her shoulders like a warm shawl no matter the situation. In a few months, Mama and I would become citizens of the US and change our names to Liz and Amy.

I spent the Saturday before Mina and Amy left for Hong Kong with them and a couple of friends from school in Little Saigon. We shopped for trinkets, took silly pictures, and ate our way up and down Bolsa Avenue. We were teenagers on the loose, and it was a blast until we got to the Asian Garden Mall. I stopped in to say hello to my mama, but as I rode up the escalator and saw Ace's face come into view, my body stiffened. What were they talking about? How long had he been there? Why hadn't he told me he was meeting my parents at the shop? I remained calm. *It's good they're having an open dialogue.*

They abruptly stopped talking when they saw me with my friends. I stood next to Ace and slipped my hand into his. My stepdad's face grew stern, but he didn't say anything. I introduced my friends and told them to wait for me at the food court downstairs.

Ace was composed, respectful, and articulate when he spoke. "Your daughter's education is important to me. I would not stand in her way from graduating high school and going on to college."

"And how will you support her?" Mama asked.

I squeezed Ace's hand. "He's going to be an engineer, Mama."

"Yes." Ace squeezed my hand back. "I am a software engineer apprentice at IBM, but I want to go into sales."

"There is good money in sales." I looked at my stepdad for an approving nod, thinking he would appreciate and understand the world of sales. Instead, he looked at his fingernails and picked his nose.

"Right now I work with a team of developers and am learning software design, testing, and computing," Ace said.

My stepdad crossed his arms over his chest and leaned back in his chair. "Sales requires traveling. How are you going to protect her if you're gone for days or weeks at a time?"

Ace did not flinch or hesitate. "I don't have to travel domestically or internationally. I could stay local until Christine and I are ready for me to be more global. With all due respect, this will not happen overnight, so we have time to figure out the details of our future together."

"Let me remind you also that she is still a minor, and if you take her innocence away, I will be the first to visit you in jail and personally watch you rot in there." My stepdad's words were harsh.

Mama frowned, and my body temperature rose. I was ready to tell him exactly what I thought about his interrogation and threats.

Ace squeezed my hand tighter, and the veins in his neck stood out, but he remained collected. He took the high road and did not give my stepdad any ammunition. Ace nodded. "Understood."

"Then we agree," Mama said. "And since we are allowing you two to continue dating, maybe you should move back home." Mama looked at me while keeping one eye on Binh's reaction.

"Auntie Chanh has been very good to me," I said, "and I wouldn't feel right changing my mind back and forth. She went to great trouble to accommodate me with a bed and personal space for my things."

"It is better this way," Binh said, "because we have news to share."

I looked from him to Mama for answers. She smiled and looked thrilled.

"We are buying a house," Mama said. "We will be moving out of the rental house."

The news saddened me. I enjoyed being neighbors with Leena and Loanne. Although I did not see them often, it was comforting to know they were next door and could pop in anytime.

"Where is the new house?" I asked.

"Huntington Beach," Mama said excitedly. "By the time we get settled in, school will be out, and you can move back home. We will have a fresh start as a family."

I was not happy about moving to Huntington Beach. This meant a new school in a different district. I would be far from Trina and Van. Knowing that my days at Westminster High were numbered, I immediately went sour. My expression changed from hopeful to pessimistic. This annoyed my stepdad.

"This isn't about you," he said, "and you can't have everything you want in life."

"I know that," I said sarcastically. "I'm just absorbing the news. Can't you give me that basic right to have emotions and opinions?"

Now I had done it. He was angry. "I think we are done here. Go join your friends."

I hugged my mama and walked out with Ace, but before exiting, I glanced back and fired a disgruntled glare at Binh. I could not harness my emotions or swallow my tongue as Ace did. Not to speak my mind was to admit defeat. I did not want to pick my battles with my stepdad. I wanted to win every one of them. I knew I was starting a war, but I didn't care. I was confident I would win because, in the end, Mama always had my back. She always picked me. I was too strong-willed and would not bend so long as he continued to talk to me in a demeaning manner as if I were subhuman.

We joined my friends at the food court, and it took little convincing to let go of the grudge. The rest of the afternoon was about Amy and Mina. Ace bought us desserts, and we walked to a nearby park to throw a frisbee. We had so much fun I did not want the joy to end. By seven o'clock we were back in front of the mall. Amy and Mina's mom waited there to take them home. The three of us hugged and cried. We promised to write and send pictures. Saying goodbye to them was like saying goodbye to Marina, Jen, Melissa, and all my Seattle friends again.

I told Amy that by the time I started eleventh grade, I would be a citizen and my legal name would be Amy Le. Before they drove off, I said my farewell by quoting Anne Shirley from *Anne of Green Gables*, saying we'd be strangers living side by side. And with that, the other half of me departed to live her life in Hong Kong.

A few weeks after Amy and Mina moved, I walked to Mama's house after school to see how the packing was going. I was excited to see my dog, Nikki, and wanted to retrieve my diary from under my bed. I needed to collect a few things to carry me over until school let out for the summer. We were uprooting as a family and moving to Huntington Beach where I would start my junior year at Ocean View High School.

"I'm here," I called out. No answer. The door was unlocked, but neither Binh nor my mom was home. Perhaps they were next door visiting with Leena and Loanne's parents. "Nikki, where are you, little girl?" I walked into my room expecting to see my Chihuahua nestled on her doggie bed sleeping or wagging her tail. "Nikki?" She wasn't there and neither was her bed or toys.

I opened my closet, ran down the hall, looked in the bathrooms, and checked my parents' bedroom, but she was gone. Panic-stricken, I ran to the living room and out the back door to the yard and garden. She was nowhere in sight. Back in the kitchen, I opened the cupboard. Her dog food was not there. There was no trace of Nikki.

"What the hell did you do?" I said out loud. My thoughts immediately blamed my stepdad for her disappearance. My mind raced in circles. I was worried sick. My stomach rolled. My lunch crept up my throat but I suppressed it with a hard swallow. I sat down to calm myself but stood again, too agitated and restless. I couldn't wait for Binh to walk through the front door. I was firing on all cylinders and ready to harm him if he had given Nikki away or hurt her in some way.

I tramped to my room, huffing and grunting in anger, to get my Candies shoes, a pair of Jordache jeans, and my bomber jacket. I stuffed them into my badminton duffle bag. I lifted my mattress to get my diary, but it was not there. I lifted each corner of the mattress, but my journal had vanished. Had he found it? Had he read it? Oh, this was not good.

I sat on the couch in the living room, ready to confront him. The door swung open, and my stepdad walked in holding hands with a lady who was not my mom. They immediately let go when they saw me. I grew suspicious. The woman had features like my mom except she was taller, wore glasses, and had surgery on her eyelids to make them double-lidded. I could tell her eyes used to be monolidded by the puffiness around them and the bruising above the incision. I saw no reason to be cordial. I curtly asked about Nikki.

"Your dog was a nuisance," he said flatly. "I gave her away."

"What?" I yelled. "When? To whom?" I could not believe Mama let that happen.

"She is with a good family. Don't worry. It was too much to take care of her."

"You couldn't take care of a little five-pound dog?" I asked sarcastically. "That's a bunch of bullshit. You're an asshole. You've taken everything I love away from me. You're punishing me because I am not some docile girl you can control and bully. Do I scare you? Am I a competition?"

"Shut up!" he screamed. "I've had enough of your mouth."

"Where is my diary, huh?" I clenched my teeth and looked around for something to throw at him. We both reached for the heavy phone book on the table. I was faster and held it above my head, ready to chuck it at him as hard as I could. This time I was not aiming at his feet.

"Go ahead." He dared me and egged me on. "Know this though. You throw that at me, and I will make sure you end up in a wheelchair for the rest of your life. I will hunt you down and shoot you, not to kill you, no, to make sure you never live a meaningful life again. You will rot in that wheelchair, and your boyfriend can wipe the shit from your mouth and the drool from your ass."

I lowered the phone book. I believed his vile threat. "You do that, and you'll lose my mama forever."

"She is already slipping away from me because of you," he said coldly.

"You're a son of a bitch."

"How dare you insult my mother." Binh advanced in one swift stride and grabbed hold of the book. I gripped tighter with both hands and pulled as hard as I could. We tugged until I let go, and he stumbled back.

"You're a cheating bastard." I glanced at the woman he brought home. She stood horrified and speechless. "He's not worth it."

I ran for the door but was jerked back with tremendous force. Binh's lady friend gasped. I fell flat on my butt and a sharp pain shot up my spine. I winced and cried out. The woman tried to help me up, but I brushed her hand away.

"One way or another, I am getting rid of you," Binh said. "I read your diary and all the foul things you called me. If your mom knew what kind of child she raised and all your secrets, she'd send herself to the grave."

"First of all, do you think you have that much power over her that she'd kill herself because of you?" I laughed. "And you want to talk about secrets? Does Mama know about your porn magazines and tapes? Does she know you're sneaking behind her back? You're despicable."

"Get out!" Binh screamed, and both his friend and I flinched. His body shook, and he stormed to his room. I knew my stepdad had guns and rifles in the house. I ran out of the house as fast as I could and did not look back. I ran to the church and asked if I could make a phone call. I paged Ace with a 9-1-1 at the end. He called me back in under five minutes, but it felt like an eternity before the phone rang.

In twenty minutes, the Supra pulled up, and I threw myself into Ace's arms. I bawled and vomited the whole story. I begged Ace again to reconsider letting me live with him. I suggested he move out and find a cheaper place to live. I offered to get a job and help with utilities. My pleading fell on deaf ears, and this sparked another argument. I knew I was in a fragile and desperate state, but I didn't see any other options.

"Maybe Trina's mom will let you stay for another year so you can go to Westminster High for your junior year."

I nodded. "Do you think Auntie Chanh will agree? I can find an after-school job and help out."

"I can pitch in, too, to help with food," Ace said.

The world looked a little better with the possibility of me living at Trina's house. I held Ace tightly and showered him with kisses. "I guess you can't have a rainbow without the rain."

"You can't have a rainbow without the sun either." Ace kissed me tenderly. "There will be a lot of rainbows in your future, babe."

Mama was adamant I come home and not burden Auntie Chanh for another year. "Absolutely not. We agreed on three months until the end of the school year." She didn't understand how much I loathed my stepdad. I found it impossible to be in his presence. How would I tell Mama about the things I knew and the things he said? Would it make a difference? Surely it had to.

"Fine, I'll come home, but there are things you need to know."

I moved back in with my parents to our new Huntington Beach home. I expected a lovely home near the beach but was surprised when we rolled up to the gates of a mobile home park for residents fifty-five years old and above. Senior housing? Really? I would be living in a double-wide with the senior community? Mama was fifty-one, so Binh had to be fifty-five or older. I was ready to turn around and walk back out the gate.

In the first month, my interactions with Binh were minimal. We avoided each other like a virus and spoke only when necessary. Mama either didn't notice or pretended not to notice the strain between her husband and her daughter.

Ace and I saw each other less and less as his job with IBM became more involved. I resumed my summer VSL schooling at the church with other teenagers and improved on my language skills, mastering the accents and pronunciations of the Vietnamese words but still not understanding everything when they were strung together. I took a job helping the residents around the mobile park, doing light yard work, weeding, trimming, planting, and digging dirt. It didn't pay much, and my job was not steady, but it afforded me a little financial independence. Sometimes they tipped me with fresh baked cookies or extra servings of chili. Sometimes I worked for free just to get out of the house.

For my sixteenth birthday, my parents surprised me with a birthday party. I was allowed to invite one friend. It was a toss between inviting Van or Ace, but Ace decided for me.

"I have separate plans for us," Ace said. "You spend it with Van, and we will celebrate your birthday the following week."

"Not much of a party when it's just me and Van," I murmured.

"Cheer up," Ace said. "You also have your mom and stepdad."

I punched him. "Haha. Not funny."

We picked Van up from her house and drove north out of Westminster. The locale was kept hush-hush, so Van and I were excited.

"Do you think we're going to Six Flags Magic Mountain?" Van whispered.

"Maybe," I said, "but that's kind of far. Maybe Disneyland."

"Or Knott's Berry Farm," Van said. "I want to ride the Bigfoot Rapids."

"We are almost there," Binh said.

Van and I looked out the window, confused. Nothing but strip malls and car dealerships surrounded us.

"Maybe it's at a restaurant?" I asked Van. She shrugged.

We pulled into a large parking lot, and the only business that stood out was the Chuck E. Cheese restaurant.

"You've got to be kidding me." I slumped in the car seat and banged my head against the leather.

Van tried to sound upbeat and joyful. "Oh, are we going to Chuck E. Cheese? I love their pizzas."

Mama smiled. "We knew you'd like it here. They have games and pizza—"

"And an animatronic band that's creepy," I said dryly.

Van elbowed me and shot me a warning look. "Hey, it's where a kid can be a kid."

"Yup," I said, "because I'm still a kid."

"I think you will have fun," Mama said. "Binh reserved a party table for you."

"Of course he did," I said.

"And you get game tokens and cake," Mama said.

"That's great," I responded. "How thoughtful." My tone was sarcastic, but only Van picked it up. My stepdad was ten feet ahead of us and kept his distance.

We made the best of the situation, and for my mama's sake, I pretended to have fun. The two hours dragged on, and by the time the cake came out, I wanted to sink into quicksand. I stumbled out of the pizza joint feeling like I had been in a spin cycle with obnoxious kids running around, spitting and spilling fluids everywhere, screaming over games and toys, and touching every surface with their sticky hands.

###

The following weekend, Ace planned an evening picnic for us at Huntington Beach. He got my parents' permission to keep me out until midnight and told them where we would be. I wore a new summer dress for the occasion and took extra time getting ready. Mama got me a new Caboodles cosmetic case filled with lip gloss, sparkly eye shadow, blush, and all the makeup and accessories a girl on the go would need.

We arrived at the beach forty-five minutes before sunset and laid our blanket on the warm sand. The soft breeze and salty air encouraged me to relax and enjoy the moment. I watched couples stroll the beach, hand in hand, laughing and talking with ease, and I wondered what brought them together.

Seagulls squawked overhead while kites fluttered in the wind. Nearby, a bonfire blazed, and the smell of burning wood put me at ease. I kicked off my shoes and knelt before the picnic basket.

Ace spread out an array of food he had picked up at a local deli. He bought egg rolls, *hom baos*, shrimp toast, meat pies called *paté sô*, and my favorite, *bánh bèo*. These small, savory steamed rice cakes topped with mung beans, pork belly, toasted shrimp, fried scallions, and green onions were heaven in my mouth. The cakes were chewy while the meat provided some crunch. I loved soaking my bánh bèo in a lot of sweet chili fish sauce.

"I love street food," I exclaimed. "There is so much food though."

"And we have *bánh bông lan* for dessert," Ace said. "I figured a sponge cake would be less messy and can hold all the candles."

I laughed. "I'm sixteen, not sixty."

Ace chuckled. "I thought we'd celebrate our birthdays together. Mine is on August 15."

"Oh, that's less than two weeks away," I said.

He nodded. "So we need sixteen candles for you and twenty-one candles for me."

I looked at the sponge cake and shook my head. "I don't know, old man. I don't think this cake has room for all of your candles."

Ace pinned me to the blanket and stole a kiss. I felt his hardness against me and pushed him off before we lost ourselves in each other.

Ace sat up and cleared his throat. He poured cold water on his head and splashed a little on his crotch to cool down.

I laughed. "You peed your shorts."

He gave me a boyish grin. "Do you recognize this spot?"

I looked at the stretch of sand and the crashing waves and nodded. "This was where we went grunion running the first night we met after the Poison concert."

"That was over a year ago, and it was the night I fell in love with you," Ace said. "Your magic hit me hard. I felt it below the belt, and it ricocheted off my heart and into my gut. That was when I knew I belonged to you."

"You sure it wasn't the waves and the flippy floppy fish hitting you?" I teased.

"It probably was," he said with a smile, "but the moonlight disguised them as something more powerful, and it felt real."

We sat on the beach, ate our appetizers, and walked down nostalgia lane. We reminisced about the fun we had and daydreamed about the future. By nightfall, more bonfires were lit, and laughter drifted from every direction. Young lovers and best friends enjoyed one another's company, and West Coast hip hop music hit the beach scene. Ace and I danced and shared our food with a group of high schoolers. When it was time to blow out the candles on our cake, I wished that moment would last forever.

My wish did not come true. Two days after Ace's twenty-first birthday, my stepfather kicked me out of the house. My parents drove me seventy-five miles south of Huntington Beach and dumped me at a stranger's house.

My life unraveled, and overnight, my skin turned inside out. The agony of losing everything turned me into a ticking time bomb. No one was there to save me from exploding.

10. TWILIGHT ZONE (SUMMER 1990)

The following weekend after my beach birthday with Ace, Mama and I officially became naturalized citizens of the United States.

I proudly held my certificate of citizenship in my hand and read it out loud. "Be it known that Thuy Tien Ngoc Le, a.k.a. Amy Le, now residing at 6241 West Warner Avenue, Huntington Beach, California, having applied to the commissioner of Immigration and Naturalization for a certificate of citizenship pursuant to Section 341 of the Immigration and Nationality Act having proved to the satisfaction of the commissioner that she is now a citizen of the United States of America, became a citizen on August 10, 1990, and is now in the United States."

Gene McNary, the commissioner of the Immigration and Naturalization Service, signed it. I was proud of what Mama had accomplished. The path to citizenship had many requirements, including satisfactorily completing an interview, getting fingerprinted, undergoing a biometrics exam, and passing a civics test.

That evening we celebrated. I cut slabs of sirloin beef into bite-sized cubes while Mama prepared the vinaigrette. We made *bò lúc lắc*, a French-inspired beef cuisine shaken in a wok and served over a salad of lettuce, cucumbers, tomatoes, and onions.

"How do you say this word?" Mama took a brown bottle from the refrigerator. "Chef Tuấn gave this to me, but it has been used only once."

I shrugged my shoulders and sounded it out. "War...kester...sure? Worst...stir...shy...er. Hmm. I think it's wurster-sir." I put the Worcestershire sauce back in the fridge. "What do you use it for?"

"Chef Tuấn used the worsty-shir-shir thing on a steak." Mama stir-fried the beef and shook her butt while she shook the beef in the pan. "Beef shake shake."

She was so cute. I chuckled and shook my behind with her.

She flipped the meat over and shook both her butt and the pan. "Shake shake shake." She concentrated on shaking the meat lightly so that nothing flew out of the pan. When one of the pieces fell out, she picked the meat up with her chopsticks and threw it back in. It sizzled in protest. "Oh, still alive."

"Liz," I said.

Mama did not acknowledge me. I tested her name to see how it rolled off my tongue…tested to see if she knew her new name.

"Liz."

Nothing. She was in her zone, moving around the kitchen like a master chef. "Mama. Mom. Liz. Ma." I laughed. "Mẹ ơi!"

"What?" Mama froze. "Did I drop another piece?" She whirled around and looked on the floor.

I kissed her on the cheek. "Mama Liz, I am proud of you. You can cook and sew, and your English gets better year after year. Now you're a citizen. What is the next goal?"

Mama did not hesitate. "OMD. I want to practice acupuncture and be an Oriental medicine doctor."

"Oh, fancy," I exclaimed. "I guess someone has to be a doctor in the family. Ace is the engineer so I guess it's up to me to go into law. Do court reporters count?" I explained to Mama what a court reporter does and that there was a court reporting school not too far from where we lived. It sounded interesting to sit in courtrooms and record the proceedings.

"Typing is not lawyer work," Mama said. "You have to be a doctor, lawyer, or engineer."

Our conversation drifted to Ace and how things were going between us.

"We're behaving, Mama, I promise," I said. "Ace's birthday is on Wednesday. I'd like to do something special for him."

"Have him come over for dinner," Mama said.

"Can we not invite Binh?" I knew the answer…

Mama shook her head. "I thought you two were getting along better."

"We have a better understanding of each other now."

How could I tell her about the other woman? What would I say about his porn addiction? Where would I even begin? I didn't understand where all my anger stemmed from or how the distrust even began. Perhaps the genesis of my despair took root the night of my eighth-grade dance when he pulled me out of the gym and embarrassed me.

"Mama, why did you give my dog away? Brother Khoi and Linh gave Nikki to me as a gift and I can't believe you just gave her away without talking to me first."

"You were not home to take care of her, and both of us worked. It was not fair to leave her alone all the time. And she peed and pooped all over the house. She pooped in your stepdad's shoes, and he put his foot in it."

I laughed but caught myself. I gasped. No doubt my dog let him know in her not-so-subtle way what she thought of him. "Where is she now? Can I visit her?"

"Honestly, I do not know. Your stepdad had enough of her and gave her away the next day. I did not know until later that afternoon."

The lump in my throat settled in my chest and moved down to my stomach. Tears threatened to emerge, and I blinked them back.

Mama handed me four plates so I could set the table. "Four? Who is coming over?"

"A real estate friend of your stepdad's," Mama said. "Set the table and bring the pot of rice over."

"Are you lonely?" The question somersaulted out before I thought about it. "You don't have friends or family here. Brother Tree lives in San Jose and now that we live in Huntington Beach, you can't see our neighbors any time you want. You must miss Aunt Six and Uncle Seven terribly. And what about my dad? When was the last time you talked to him?"

"I have been too busy to think about it. Maybe this real estate friend of your stepdad's is nice and I can be friends with her."

I raised my eyebrows. "His friend is a woman?"

The door swung open with a creak, and my stepdad walked in. Our dinner guest stood behind him. The same two-lidded eyes, although no longer bruised and puffy, wearing the same glasses as last time. Her freshly permed and coiffed hair rose high above her forehead. She and I exchanged an uneasy glance. She lowered her eyes and looked away. I stared at her and pursed my lips. I mentally fired cannonballs at them. The audacity of this man. He had no shame.

"I don't feel well," I said. "I am going to lie down and rest and put some tiger balm ointment on my stomach."

"You are not going to eat?" Mama asked.

"Do not be rude," Binh said. "Say hello to Ms. Nga. You are going to join us for dinner. Your mom made all this nice food."

I mumbled a barely audible greeting, but no one pressed me to talk louder. Binh carried on as if he were entertaining royalty. He showed off his ceramics and bragged about his sales figures. He wrapped his arm around Mama and pecked her on the cheek, raved about her culinary skills, and then praised me for my dedication to VSL school.

"Christine also got perfect grades last year," Binh said, "and she is great with a racket."

"My name is Amy now." I gritted my teeth. Would he never say it right?

We sat down to eat, and with the first bite of Mama's beef, Nga sank in her chair and closed her eyes. "Mmm." She complimented Mama on the tenderness of the shaken beef and tanginess of the salad. "I must get your recipe."

Mama blushed and put more food on Nga's plate. "Did you have eye surgery?"

Our guest nodded. She accepted extra portions of the food. "I need to put some fat on my body, like you."

I swallowed my spit and leaned in. Did she just insult my mama?

"Who wants to be skin and bones? It is a sign you are poor and starving. I'm jealous you have the extra weight. It stretches and smooths out the skin."

I rolled my eyes. Was this seriously happening? My stepdad sat there with this floozy and pretended it was a regular dinner among old friends. He showered Mama with affection and let his girlfriend spoon-feed Mama a multitude of insulting compliments. My stomach revolted, and I wanted to throw up. I imagined heaving and gurgling until cow diarrhea shot out of my mouth and all over Binh and Nga. I gripped my chopsticks tight and sat sullen, disengaged. The more Nga talked, the more Binh smacked his lips, and the more Mama dished food on their plates, the more I wanted to scream, pull my hair out, and flip the table upside down.

"Everyone in California is skinny," Mama said. "I know back in our country being plump was good, but I need to lose weight. Too much sitting and cooking." She laughed, but it sounded like a nervous, insecure laugh. It trailed off and abruptly ended.

"Christine—"

"It's Amy, Stepfather," I said coldly. "For the last freaking time. Say it with me. Amy."

My stepdad wiped his lips with his napkin and threw it emphatically on the table. He pushed his chair back and walked briskly to the bedroom.

Was he going to get his shotgun? I told myself to run, but my legs would not move.

Mama and Nga looked at each other. Fear, concern, and curiosity marred their faces. The three of us waited silently for his return. I held my breath, afraid to exhale, believing if I remained still, time would also remain still.

Binh came back moments later and apologized. He did not explain his abrupt disappearing act. We moved on to dessert, and Binh poured some cognac. Mama made a beautiful caramel flan, but I did not trust myself to eat it. My body overheated, and my mind wandered down a dark path of violence. I imagined charging at Binh with a katana and piercing the sword between his eyes. I wanted to tear the fake eyelids off Nga and douse her hair with kerosene.

I stood up.

"Sit down," Binh said.

I kicked my chair back with one foot and pounded my knuckles on the table. I screamed at the top of my lungs. "Quỷ!" I called him a demon.

Mama jumped back. She clutched her necklace.

Nga's eyes opened wide and her lips quivered.

My stepdad calmly said, "Your daughter needs psychiatric help. She is out of control. She is dangerous. Do you see how she suddenly attacked me like that? Calling me a demon?"

"I am not crazy," I screamed. "You're the devil." I threw my chopsticks at him and when I missed, I picked up my plate and flicked it like a frisbee. "I hate you." I hurled my glass of Mountain Dew at his face. He dodged the tumbler, making me even angrier.

My stepdad smiled a wicked, evil smile. I knew then he had won. He wanted to get rid of me, and I gave him a solid reason to lock me up. The floodgates opened. Rivulets turned into a violent gush as tears streamed down my face, into my mouth, and along my jawline. My nose was stuffy, and the harder I sniffed to control the waterworks, the more I suffocated.

I was barely sixteen, and I'd had my first meltdown. Binh picked up the phone to call the police. Mama reached out to hug me, but rage burned within me, and I denounced her touch. The look of hurt and rejection on her face would haunt me for years. I was as angry with her as I was with Binh and Nga. I wanted nothing more than to die, to disappear, to vanish before their eyes.

I told myself I didn't need them. Who cared about good grades and living a pious life? Who could afford civility and humility? Wasn't life about "me" and what I could take, not give? I lost all hope. I did not feel human anymore. Like a caged tiger, I had paced back and forth far too long in my small cell. It was time to be free.

Mama hung up the phone before my stepdad could talk to the dispatcher. She slowly approached me and gingerly wrapped her arms around me. I let my pent-up anger and frustrations go. I howled and wailed. As my tears soaked her shirt, I dug my face harder into her shoulder.

"I'm sorry, Mama." I apologized over and over but my words did not make sense.

I don't recall when Nga left or when Binh went to the porch for a cigarette. I barely recall my mama tucking me into bed. I lay in my room shivering despite the heat and humidity outside. I called out to Ace in my mind and begged him to take me away. I prayed to God that he'd bring me home because I didn't want to live this life anymore. I begged Mr. and Mrs. Van to get me and take me back to Seattle. Even as I screamed in my mind, my voice box never opened, and I fell asleep, alone and hopeless.

###

Ace's birthday came and went. I feigned sickness and told him I'd make it up to him later. I harnessed all my energy to sound enthusiastic and wished him a happy birthday. I told him my mama wanted to invite him over for dinner to celebrate. My last words to him were, "I love you."

Friday afternoon, two days after Ace's birthday, I came home from helping Mrs. Poot Poot with her garden to find the house empty. Mrs. Poot Poot, an elderly woman who lived a few mobile homes down, got that nickname because she passed gas all the time. She was also hard of hearing and happily waved whenever anyone yelled out, "Good morning, Poot Poot."

I walked into the kitchen to get a glass of water and nearly tripped over a suitcase and two bags. I knelt and unzipped one of the bags. My LA Gears shoes, a couple of white-washed jeans, overalls…my clothes and belongings.

"Mama?" I called out, but she did not answer.

I pushed the door to her bedroom and saw her napping on the bed. I sat down and watched the rise and fall of her chest. I caressed her soft, smooth hand. She snored softly. I blipped her lips like she used to do when I was little but she didn't wake.

I snuggled up to her and lifted her arm around me like the old days when we slept together and I would curl up in her arms. More than anything I wanted to be six years old again and feel safe. I closed my eyes and thought of my cousin Tree. I missed him so much but he was living his life with his wife and children. I thought about Katrina and Mrs. Van showering me with Christmas gifts and Mr. Van reading me bedtime stories. I remembered how Uncle Skyler performed the Heimlich maneuver on Ms. Magdaleine to save her from choking. I wanted nothing more than to be back at Homestead Apartments with my friends and Auntie Diep. As ridiculous as she was, Auntie Diep was always cheerful and bright. She stood out like a turd in a swimming pool with her bright, mismatched clothes and loud, effervescent personality.

I closed my eyes and exhaled. I turned over and looked at my mama. She looked old to me. Being this close, I saw her facial lines and shockwaves of gray hair. The creases on her forehead and the character marks around her lips held secrets I'd never hear. I wondered if they were grooves of sorrow or joy. I counted the lines and wondered which ones were because of me. Did I bring her lines of pride or lines of shame?

My eyes misted, and I wiped them quickly to hide any trace of pity. I kissed Mama…not the American way with my lips, but the Vietnamese way, with my nose. I inhaled her essence and sniffed her cheeks, her skin, her bones. I nuzzled closer, and she stirred beside me. She stroked my hair and sang a song. I did not know the lyrics or the song, but the warm tone of her voice soothed me, and the melody wrapped me in peace.

"Thủy-Tiên," Mama said, "my daughter, listen to me carefully."

I nodded and pulled my mama's body closer to mine.

"I think we are destined to live apart."

I shook my head, unwilling to accept that.

"I once saw a fortune teller. She told me you were a wood tiger and that tiger girls have very strong personalities. They are more cunning than we give them credit for. My daughter, you are smarter and more strong-willed than me and you cannot thrive in the shadow of a weak boar."

My stepfather was born the year of the pig. I knew the boar referenced my stepdad.

"If we are to survive, we must live apart."

"What are you saying?" I searched her face for answers. "I saw the suitcase and bags. Are you sending me away?"

Mama's face turned pink and her eyes moistened. I wiped the wetness away.

"The Americans say if you love something, set it free. I am going to set you free."

"Where?" I asked. "I don't want to leave you."

"I have a plan," Mama said. "I am going to get my OMD so I can practice acupuncture and herbal medicine. When the timing is right, I am going to leave him."

I sat up and smiled. It was the best news ever.

"This will be two failed marriages for me. As a Catholic and a Vietnamese woman, you must understand how wrong and shameful this is. It means I can never marry again. No man will want me."

"Of course they will. Don't say that. You are beautiful and smart. You're funny and a good cook. You deserve someone who is not going to compete with you or feel inferior to you."

"I would not be worthy of another love if I cannot hold on to the ones I had."

"That's not true." I flung my arm around Mama's waist and rested my cheek on her bosom.

"Promise me you will graduate high school with honors and go to college. And I will promise to get my degree and become an acupuncturist. Then it will be the two of us again."

"What about Ace?" I asked. "Will I still get to see him?"

"That is up to you," Mama said.

"Where are you sending me?" I asked. "For how long?"

"My daughter," Mama said. "We leave soon. I cannot tell you but soon you will see." She kissed me on my head. "I know, sweet girl. I know."

"What do you know?" I asked.

"I know about your stepdad," Mama said. "I may not like conflict, but I am not stupid or blind."

"You mean you know about him and that lady, Nga? And the dirty magazines and videos?" I asked.

Mama nodded.

"Did you know he threatened to shoot me until I was paralyzed in a wheelchair?"

Mama did not answer. She pulled me into her embrace and squeezed tightly. I felt droplets of water slide down my forehead.

###

We drove in silence down to San Marcos, a suburb of San Diego, known for its pristine beachfront properties, close-knit communities, highly-rated schools, and blooming commerce.

I did not get to say goodbye to Ace. My stepdad tossed my belongings into the backseat, and then he and my mama whisked me away to southern California. My stepdad knew a woman who lived in San Marcos with her husband and two sons. He said she had always wanted a daughter and would love me the moment she saw me. Binh had known her back in Vietnam and attested she'd be the authoritarian I needed, both rigid in discipline and soft in compassion. She had the reputation back in Vietnam of turning corrupt men to reverent believers and unwieldy leeches to agreeable women. Her formula for love and punishment transformed even the vilest, rebellious souls into God-fearing, humble servants of all that was holy.

She sounded as scary as hell.

We pulled up to a large house in a gated community nestled in a quiet cul-de-sac. Healthy palm trees, birds of paradise, manicured hedges, and river rocks nestled in the lush garden along the cobblestone walkway.

The house was at least three thousand square feet, with two floors, a three-car garage, and a mailbox that came with keys. I was going to be living in style. My stepdad rang the doorbell and a petite woman with a high forehead and a tiny mouth opened the door. Everything about her was small, except for her forehead and hair. She looked odd with her tiny waist, high cheekbones, long manicured nails, and stiletto shoes. She was barely over five feet tall and without her shoes, I suspected she was four-foot nine inches tall. She wore a black jumpsuit and a white tennis visor. She smelled like lavender and lye. I guessed she was Binh's age or shy of sixty.

"Oh, it has been a long time." Her mousy voice squeaked like a violin that needed tweaking. She hugged my stepdad with a familiarity usually reserved for siblings. She embraced my mama with zeal and expressed how fortunate she was to finally meet her. One look at me and she nearly fainted with excitement. She clasped me tight and ushered me inside. She scurried along the hallway and fluttered into the kitchen, where she invited us to sit as she proceeded to make hot tea. I took note of my surroundings, impressed with the spotless kitchen, neatly arranged cookbooks in alphabetical order by title, and canned veggies in the cupboards, with the labels facing outward in order from artichoke to yams.

"This is Auntie Nhung," my stepdad said. "She will be taking care of you."

"And my husband Dan," she screeched. "He will be here soon with our sons Lộc and Hiếu. How was your drive here?" She peeled and sliced three cinnamon persimmons and arranged them neatly on a plate. One of the slices was thicker than the rest, so she took a thin sliver off to make them of equal width.

Mama chit-chatted about the weather and traffic. Binh helped himself to the persimmons and ate three slices before Mama finished one.

A man's voice called from the entryway and in came a tall, heavyset man with blue eyes and a red beard. He wore golfing shorts, a polo shirt, and a tweed flat cap. His lumbering walk made him look goofy, like a big buffoon. If ever there were an odd couple, these two took the trophy. Dan stood a good foot, three inches taller than his wife. Two Vietnamese men plodded behind him. One of them wore glasses, making his eyes look huge, like a tarsier. He had thin, receding hair. He wore Bermuda shorts and socks that rode up to his knees. He was a thick-built man with wide shoulders and rabbit teeth that protruded even when he closed his mouth. He looked thirty, but when he spoke, he sounded like a child. His eyes must have been bigger than his brain. I was introduced to Loc, Nhung's eldest son, who blushed and told me I was pretty.

The other man slothed behind Dan in his banana pants, Michael Jackson leather jacket, red bandana, and one white glove. He reminded me of Binh's youngest son, Phan. His face was narrow, hijacked with pimples, and his teeth took refuge behind metal braces. He had a small mouth like his mother and his narrow wombat eyes creeped me out. He had the same high forehead as Auntie Nhung and could have been her younger brother. His name was Hiếu, and he was going to be a junior in high school like me. Odd, because he looked twenty-five.

I had entered the twilight zone.

11. THE YELLOW JACKET (SUMMER-FALL 1990)

My farewell to Mama seared my heart. We both knew this would be difficult but necessary. We were on a mission to graduate from school and rendezvous back in Seattle. I wished Mama luck with acupuncture school and promised to stay on track with my education. She promised to give Ace my new address and Auntie Nhung's home phone number.

Mama gave me a dozen kisses, and with wetness in her eyes, she got in the car and disappeared down the road. I ran behind the car and watched it exit the gated community. I walked back to the house, where Auntie Nhung stood at the front entrance waiting for me. She opened her arms, and I melted into her tiny embrace. This stranger was all I had. I cried and let the fears, anger, and anxiety drain from my body. A sense of relief flowed through me as if a weight had been lifted.

Inside, Dan offered me a beverage, but I declined and thanked him. Loc and Hieu fawned over me like a shiny new toy. Loc, the eldest with bucked teeth, wanted to show me to my room. Hieu offered to help me unpack.

"Give her some space, boys," Dan said. "You're fighting over her like she's a puppy."

Auntie Nhung giggled and surprised me by speaking English fluently. "Lộc, you can show Christine to her room."

"Actually," I said, "you can call me Amy. I became a citizen and legally changed it to Amy."

"Oh, well, we registered you at the school under Christine," Dan said.

"You did?" I asked. "Wow, that was fast."

"It is too late and too much of a hassle to change it now," Auntie Nhung said. "School starts in less than three weeks."

"I'm sure it can be changed. I'll just talk to them—"

"I said it is too late." Auntie Nhung looked at me sternly and pulled her lips inward into a pucker.

Instinct told me to shut my mouth and drop the subject.

She smiled sweetly and put her arm around my waist. "It's just that we jumped through a lot of hoops to get you enrolled in school with short notice, and the administration office had been closed for the summer. Why don't you get settled in? The boys can show you around. The three of you will have to share the bathroom upstairs, so don't take too long in the morning. Use the timer in the bathroom. Each person gets fifteen minutes."

"We'll go over the ground rules and house chores over dinner," Dan said.

My stomach growled when Dan mentioned food. I pressed my tummy to quiet it down.

"Someone's hungry," Auntie Nhung said. "Since today is a special occasion with you joining our family, you can have seconds and dessert."

"Yay." Loc clapped his hand. "Dessert." His eyes opened wide, and his smile showed a lot of yellow teeth.

I smiled weakly. I supposed I should be grateful but thought it odd she would even say that. Food restrictions and portion control were never an issue after I came to the US. Mama, Tree, and I were blessed with government subsidies and homemade meals from our community of friends. We ate what we wanted, when we wanted, and as much as we wanted.

Hieu and Loc helped me with my bags, and I followed them up the stairs. The spacious and tidy home smelled of lemon and pine. My bedroom located above the garage with a window that overlooked the driveway was quaint and charming, although it befitted a little six-year-old princess more than a sixteen-year-old girl. The twin-size bed had two pillows covered in pink-and-white ruffled pillowcases, pink sheets, and a pink-and-white polka dot comforter. Stuffed animals rested in the center and claimed a third of the bed. A full-length mirror leaned against one of the walls, and a few framed posters of horses hung throughout the room. A family photo of Dan, Auntie Nhung, and their sons adorned the nightstand, and another family portrait rested on top of the dresser. Having pictures of them and none of my family and friends made me uneasy.

"Do you need help unpacking and putting things away?" Hieu asked. He unzipped my duffle bag, but I touched his hand to stop him. I did not want him going through my things. He quickly pulled his hand away as if my touch burned him and my closeness repelled him. He stepped back and paused before abruptly leaving the room. He ran down the stairs.

Loc followed him. "I better help set the table."

What oddlings. I dismissed their abrupt departure and took comfort in being alone for a few minutes to collect my thoughts and let reality set in. Memories of Seattle and my friends made me sad. Mama's and Ace's smiling faces filled my thoughts. I willed myself not to cry. Be strong. This was temporary, and I would see them again soon. I shoved my belongings in the drawers and hung up a couple of jackets. I stepped into the bathroom to freshen up and put my toiletries in the corner by the outlets. The smell of seasoned, grilled meat wafted up the stairs and beckoned me to come down.

Dan was in the kitchen wearing a frilly apron too small for his big frame. He wrapped his arm around Auntie Nhung and kissed her on the neck. He looked up and smiled at me. He had kind eyes and a simplicity to him that made me trust his genuine warmth. He carved the roast and placed each slice neatly on a platter of roasted vegetables.

Auntie Nhung orchestrated her sons' movements. "Get the green napkins. Take out the square bowl. No, make it the round, blue ones. Get the pitcher of water out of the fridge."

"Is there anything I can do to help?" I asked.

"You can help with the gravy," Dan said. "Over there. Just ladle it into the gravy boat, which is in that cupboard."

"Okay," Auntie Nhung said. "Come, come." She waved me over and patted the seat next to her. "Your place is next to me."

I sat down to her right at the round table and admired the setting and food. A bowl of minestrone, a beet and goat cheese salad, buttered rolls, and cranberry-orange relish filled the table. Dan placed the platter of beef and vegetables in the center and took his place on Auntie Nhung's left.

"Thank you, dear," Auntie Nhung said, "this looks delicious." Loc and Hieu chimed in with their thanks. I followed suit. "Now, each night, we like to go around the table and share one thing great and one thing bad about our day. We discuss it as a family over dinner. Christine, why don't you—"

"Could you call me Amy, please?" I asked. "Or my Vietnamese name, Thủy-Tiên?"

"Very well," she said. "Now, why don't you start and tell us—"

"I'm sorry, do you have any Mountain Dew or 7-Up?" I asked. "Any soda or juice?"

"We do not drink soda and juice in this house unless it's a holiday or someone's birthday. Too much sugar. Our body is a temple and we must take care of it." Auntie Nhung pursed her lips again and cut into her meat like she was tearing into a fresh kill.

"Do you say grace?" I asked.

"Say what?" Loc asked.

"A prayer?" I said. "Do you give thanks before you eat?"

"No," Auntie Nhung said. "We're Buddhists."

I looked at Dan. Was he Buddhist as well? He did not look up from his plate of food, and Auntie Nhung did not speak again, so I, too, kept my mouth shut. I made the sign of the cross like I had seen Mama do and said a silent prayer.

Dan cleared his throat. "Why don't I start?"

"Thank you, dear," Auntie Nhung said sweetly. "And boys, let's not interrupt Dad." She glanced at me briefly, but I caught the undertone of her message. I interrupted one too many times, and she was not amused. Another interruption would be a grave mistake.

Dan raised his glass of water. "I would like to make a toast to Amy. Her joining our family has been a great thing in my day. We hope you'll come to see us like family and enjoy your stay with us this year."

We all raised our glasses of water and clinked before sipping. The consensus around the table was that I was a welcomed surprise. I certainly felt like a novelty but wondered if that would quickly wear off. Dan talked about not getting a promotion at work. He was a graphic designer and ready to take on new projects as well as manage a team. Instead, he got an individual contributor raise and bonus but still reported to Gerald, a man he felt was not fit to manage people. Auntie Nhung praised him for putting his name in the hat for the promotion and agreed his company was blind for not seeing the talent Dan offered.

"Their loss, dear." Auntie Nhung offered her lips to Dan, and they kissed again.

Loc talked about gaining a pretty sister this year and was impressed that I played badminton. "I like sports and working out and staying fit." He flexed his muscles. I chuckled. He seemed so innocent. "No offense, Dad, but you work too much and are getting pudgy. You need to work out."

Dan pretended to be hurt and sucked in his stomach and cheeks. He was our comic relief, and I found him endearing. I could see how Auntie Nhung fell in love with him.

"I am down for playing badminton or volleyball or tennis any time," I said to Loc. "And you can show me some workouts. We can lift weights together."

"Oh, honey," Auntie Nhung said, "girls should not lift weights. You can do yoga or aerobics." I disagreed but did not push back. I winked at Loc when no one was looking. It was our little secret. He blushed and winked back.

"So what was the one bad thing that happened today?" I asked Loc.

"Nothing," he answered, "but I guess beets and goat cheese salads aren't my favorite. At least I can have seconds on everything else, plus dessert. I'm a growing boy." He flexed his muscles again.

I smiled. I loved that he found joy in the smallest things. Hieu shared his highlight of finishing his chores in record time, but his low point was scrubbing the toilets without gloves.

"What happened to your gloves?" Auntie Nhung asked. "Did you leave them in the backyard again? You know they are not garden gloves."

"But I like the way they fit," Hieu said. "and they are thick so the dirt doesn't soak through. The rubber ones are way better than the cloth ones."

Auntie Nhung let the topic of garden gloves versus cleaning gloves go. She asked me to share with the family my positive and negative points of the day. I struggled to pick one thing decent because I didn't see anything good about my day.

My hesitation irritated Auntie Nhung. She wiped her tiny lips with her napkin and threw it on her lap. "If you can't think of one good thing, let me remind you—"

"It's not that, Auntie Nhung." I interrupted her again. I had to think of something fast. "There have been a few good things today." I stalled to buy time and racked my brain. "Well, I am thankful to you all for your kindness in receiving me into your home and making me feel like a part of your family. And, um, I appreciate the care in getting my room ready for me, not to mention getting me enrolled in school."

Auntie Nhung nodded her approval. "We are excited you are here. It will be more balanced now having a girl at the house. These guys gang up on me."

Dan chuckled. "Don't believe her. She's the boss. She bullies us." Dan leaned over and gave his wife a peck on the lips. It was clear by the way Dan catered to her whims that he was whipped. He doted on her, kissed her often, and complimented her constantly. They must have magnets implanted in their lips because the two of them kissed all the time.

I yearned for Ace. "Can I have the house phone number and address?"

"What for?" Auntie Nhung asked.

"Um, in case there is an emergency?"

"Why don't we go over the rules and expectations?" Auntie Nhung handed her empty plate to Loc.

He stood and placed her plate in the dishwasher. He came back with apple pie.

"Now, on the refrigerator, there is a cleaning schedule. Each week the three of you will rotate so you're not doing the same thing. My boys will show you how to clean the bathrooms, the floors, and all the surfaces. We use specific products and materials for different things. Tomorrow is floor day. Chris…I mean, Amy…you will vacuum. One of the boys will sweep the outside, front and back, and the other will mop the floors inside the house."

"Once school starts," Dan said, "you need to do your homework right when you get home. You can have a snack first, but no food is allowed in the bedroom."

"We eat dinner together, and afterward, if you still have homework or need to prepare for an exam, then you can go back upstairs." Auntie Nhung cut the apple pie into eight equal pieces and handed Dan the first slice. "Television is a treat, and we watch together as a family. We don't want your brain to melt from the garbage on TV. You can read a book or do something creative."

"I lift weights," Loc said.

"What do you do, Hieu?" I asked.

"I like Legos," Hieu said. "I'm pretty good at building things. I'll show you my collection."

"In the mornings," Dan said, "there is a fifteen-minute limit in the bathroom on school days. Be sure to use the timer."

"Same goes with phone calls," Auntie Nhung said. "Fifteen minutes maximum. Anything else, dear?"

"One other thing," Dan said. "We have a penalty jar. No foul language allowed, and no backtalking. Each week you will get a ten-dollar allowance. Breaking a rule results in a hefty five-dollar fine. At the end of the month, one of you will get what is in the penalty jar, based on whomever we feel was exceptionally good or achieved something spectacular. The jar remains untouched if there is nothing worth rewarding that month."

My head reeled. I swallowed my tongue and refrained from scoffing at their rigid rules.

"I always win the jar," Hieu said. "He's always breaking rules."

That surprised me. I took Loc as the sweeter and more innocent one. I couldn't imagine him cussing, backtalking, or heaven forbid, using the wrong cleaning agent for the kitchen that was meant for the bathroom.

Auntie Nhung patted my knee. "We will not have any penalties for you the first week as you're learning, but after you are told once, we expect you to get it right the next time."

That night I dreamed about scrubbing toilets and getting locked in a room full of mice. My fairy godmother was Dan, and he brought me magic red ruby slippers. If I clicked my heels twice, the toilet sparkled, and my princess bed flew me home. It flew over Ace's Supra and kept going. I screamed for him, but I had no voice. I reached for him, but he did not see me. He was lost to me, and I could not get off the flying bed.

Then down the rabbit hole I tumbled and crashed with a thud on an underground nest of yellow jackets. The colony arose and swarmed around my head. I flailed my arms and struck the queen. Her yellow and black body charged at me and stung me repeatedly with her poison. I fell to the ground in pain, writhing in agony, withering to dust. Auntie Nhung hovered over me with her beady eyes and wasp-like wings and watched me die.

12. LOVECRAFTIAN (FALL 1990-WINTER 1991)

My first semester as a junior at San Marcos High School could be described in one word: Lovecraftian. Under the veneer of normal teenage life, where the jocks hung out with cheerleaders and the nerds hung out alone in a quiet, invisible corner of the school, bubbled a situation that changed my perception of mankind and taught me to trust my instincts. People were the same on the inside as they were on the outside if you looked closely enough and paid attention. Humans are flawed creatures, and vanity had a way of showing its true colors. I learned about vanity in San Marcos but lived with it at home.

In April 1986, the phenomenon of Halley's Comet had captured the attention of my sixth-grade class. Every store sold rubber balls with shiny streamers attached to them and every kid played with them at recess. When the Circle K convenience store down the street from Homestead Apartments began selling them, I saved my quarters and bought one. My friends and I tossed them high in the air and watched the shimmering tail as the ball came down and bounced off the ground.

In my art class, a girl named Carina resembled one of those rubber Halley's Comet balls, with her silky, long, blue, pink, and purple hair attached to a head as clueless as a rubber ball. Like me, she was Vietnamese. Her parents were refugees of the Vietnam War. She was rebellious like most teenagers and wild like some of the kids of my generation who didn't fit in with any culture. She appeared to be a loner like me, and we instantly connected and became friends. She introduced me to her circle of friends, Phuong, Lily, and Mary. The five of us banded together, ate lunch together, and enjoyed gossiping about others. I let them cheat off me in class whenever we had a test, and sometimes I did their assignments for them.

I desperately wanted to belong to a tribe, so I let my moral compass go south. I needed my new friends to survive the loneliness of being separated from those whom I loved. They needed me to pass their exams and get good grades to keep their parents off their backs. We had the perfect symbiotic relationship, although not a healthy one. Over time I became one of the mean girls who made fun of everyone and looked down on others. No teacher was safe from my snide remarks, and no student escaped my condescending, judgmental snickers. My tribe built an impenetrable force field around us, and we shielded each other from the ugly truth—that we were the true rejects and outcasts, not everyone else.

The sisterhood I had with Carina, Phuong, Lily, and Mary was tangible, strong, and believable while it lasted. The girls smoked cigarettes, skipped classes, and stole from their parents, and while I never succumbed to these habits, my heart marched in rhythm with theirs. Sometimes I gave in to their cajoling and peer pressure. I took a puff or two of a cigarette or skipped a class to prove I wasn't a prude.

We all hated our home life and thought we were better than our siblings. I did not have siblings, of course, but I knew I was smarter than Loc and Hieu. The adults in our lives were old-school, traditional as hell, overbearing, strict, embarrassing to be around, and did not understand that we wanted one simple thing—to be left alone. We sought refuge in music and fed off each other's sarcasm.

At home, life with Auntie Nhung was unbearable, but somehow I managed to stay on the other side of the line drawn in the sand. I stuck to the rules and held my tongue, lest I get punished and lose my allowance to the penalty jar.

Each time I paged Ace, he called me back, but Auntie Nhung yanked the phone away so that I never spoke to him. Why hadn't he visited? I worried he had stopped loving me and had forgotten about me. Had he moved on already? I resented him every time I thought he had given up. I still loved him with all my being and held on to what little hope I had left. Mama assured me she had given Ace the address where I lived. Auntie Nhung was so strict with phone usage that even with my mama, I was restricted to fifteen-minute conversations.

Auntie Nhung gave me just enough air to breathe but never enough to take full breaths. She gave me just enough rope to move about but never long enough to feel free. She fed me enough food I didn't starve, yet I never felt satisfied. Gluttony was a sin and gaining weight the ultimate disgrace to the body that served as our temple. I lived in a box that was not wide enough or tall enough. With my new family, I felt like the maid, the stepchild, the black swan, and the ugly duckling all rolled into one. Sometimes I felt like the prized possession perched on a pedestal in a curiosity shop, and other times I felt like a social experiment to see how thin my patience would grow before I snapped. Even I wondered how long Auntie Nhung could press me under her thumb before I collapsed.

She told me she had always wanted a daughter but under the same breath dropped matchmaking hints that I would make a great wife for one of her sons. I shuddered at the thought of being married to Brains or Brawns, nicknames I gave to Hieu and Loc. While the boys were nice to me, they were odd and mentally slow. Hieu looked at me with puppy love eyes and lust on his face. On several occasions, he rubbed up against me in the kitchen with a hard-on and acted like nothing was out of the ordinary. I dared not think about the fantasies he had of me when he was alone in his room or the shower. Loc only cared about bodybuilding and fitness. He spent every spare moment in the garage lifting weights. Girls did not exist to him.

I had my second meltdown while I was still sixteen. One day halfway through the school year, I skipped lunch and made a beeline for the only payphone on school grounds. I would page Ace and confront him. This time, there would be no auntie to rip the phone from me and no fifteen-minute time limit. I would skip my next class if necessary.

A girl on the payphone rambled about her favorite flavor of ice cream. I wanted her to hurry up with the call. I shifted my weight from one foot to the other. My palms sweated. I crossed my arms and tapped my foot. She looked at me and rolled her eyes. She resumed talking, so I tapped her shoulder. I was not going to be ignored.

She covered the receiver. "What?"

"Can you hurry up, please?" I asked. "I have an emergency."

She looked me up and down and rolled her eyes. She twirled the telephone cord and turned her back to me. I tapped her again, but she pretended I was not there. I waited only a split second before I ripped the phone from her hand and slammed it on the receiver.

"What the hell?" she yelled. "You've got some nerve, chink."

"I asked you politely," I said.

"Wait your turn."

She picked up the phone again and when I reached for it, she held it behind her. We scrambled and struggled for it until she clobbered me on the face with the phone. A sharp pain shot up my nose. Drops of red dripped from my face to the ground. All the pent-up anger, sadness, frustration, and self-control erupted. The she-hulk in me exploded out of my skin. I felt powerful and strong, invincible, and lawless.

I grabbed her hair and wrapped it around my fist. I slammed her face over and over and over into the side of the payphone. "I. Just. Want. My. Damn. Phone. Call."

She sat on the ground holding her face and whimpering.

Devoid of empathy, I made my call and waited for Ace to call me back. I kicked the girl now crumpled on the cement. "What's the matter?"

Her black eyeliner smeared around her eyes, and her face swelled.

The phone finally rang, and I quickly picked it up. "Honey?"

"Christine?" Ace sounded happy and relieved. "Baby, is that you? God, what happened? I've been trying to call you and find you but—"

"But what?" I asked. No answer. "Hello?" The phone went dead.

I was ready to punch the girl but froze. The cold eyes looking back at me belonged to Mrs. Jenkins, the school principal. I scanned my surroundings. An audience of faculty members and students stared back at me. The school nurse tended to my victim. Our blood mixed and covered everything—our clothes, our shoes, the phonebooth, the ground. I swallowed the dry lump of coal in my throat.

The principal had her finger on the receiver and hung up my call. "My office. Now."

Mrs. Jenkins grabbed my wrist and tugged at me to follow but I did not yield. I was done yielding. I was tired of authority.

I lost my senses and attacked her. "She started it." I pointed at the brunette whose nose was smashed and crooked. A massive hematoma developed on her forehead. She looked like a cosmic being, an alien from outer space. I laughed with delirium. "She hit me first."

Mrs. Jenkins did not care. To her, I was probably another Asian kid who didn't belong at her school much less her country. She was much taller and heavier than I was, but I was fast, feisty, and enraged. My arms and legs pounded away while my demons took control. Two people pulled me off and dragged me away like a wild monkey. My body drooped and became dead weight.

After that incident, Carina, Lily, Phuong, and Mary kept their distance. I was a powder keg, and once again, a ticking time bomb. The school suspended me indefinitely. Auntie Nhung flipped her lid, and I endured two long hours of her tongue lashing. No one rescued me. Loc and Hieu hid in their rooms. Dan wouldn't be home until eight o'clock.

"Do you know what I used to do to girls like you back in Vietnam?" Auntie Nhung asked. I said nothing, so she told me. "I threw them to the tigers of the jungle and let my thirsty comrades on the Ho Chi Minh Trail teach ungrateful shits like you a lesson."

I cringed. I lowered my eyes and stared at the carpet fibers beneath my feet. Her tiny frame loomed over me while I knelt on the floor with my head down and hands in my lap.

"That's right. I'd stand watch while my brothers raped those women. Their cries were their only salvation."

I lifted my head and stared at her. "You did what?"

"Shut up," she screamed. "You are really testing me, aren't you? We took you in and gave you a home. You've been ungrateful and need to be punished. Only then will you feel cleansed and free of guilt." She was a raving lunatic.

"You're mad," I said. "I have done everything you've asked of me. Every day I scrub your toilets, mop your floors, clean your windows. Not once did I complain. Not once did I break a rule."

"Is that so?" she said. "Don't think I didn't notice you watched television when you got home from school."

"Loc and Hieu told on me?"

"They didn't have to. I always leave the channel on seven and I'd find it on another channel when I got home. My boys know better, and they are good kids."

"You've got serious problems," I said. "And God will punish you for what you did to those women."

She slapped me. "That's where you are wrong. I have been rewarded. Look around you. What do you see? My big house. My doting husband. My two sons."

"Whom you've manipulated to serve you," I said. "Can't you see you're the one being punished, not rewarded, or has your vanity given you glaucoma? Your sons have the mental and emotional intelligence of rocks and your husband doesn't love you. He fears you."

She slapped me again. "You're jealous of me. You will never have this because you are too ruined to ever achieve greatness."

The sting of her hand invigorated me. I liked the pain and wanted more of it. I lunged at her and clawed at her throat. My fingernails dug into her face, and my teeth clamped down on her shoulder. We rivaled for dominance, rolling around on the floor and chasing after each other until I slipped on the freshly waxed floors.

Auntie Nhung snarled and cackled. Her laugh started as a low rumble from her belly and escalated into a high-pitched hyena's laugh from her throat. "Your mother is ashamed of you. Your father abandoned you. Even your boyfriend doesn't want you."

"Lies!" I threw the salt and pepper shakers at her. I knew what she was doing. Auntie Nhung chipped away at my armor and stripped my defenses.

Perhaps she was right. I was reckless, spoiled, disrespectful, and brought dishonor to my mama. My dad never fought for me. He didn't want me. He never called or wrote to me. I had always been a burden to my mama. I brought destruction and sadness. All those times of joy and peace in my life were because my mama and my cousin put me first in their life. I never did anything for them. I had been selfish to only think of myself. Gimme gimme gimme. Take take take.

I broke down in tears and sobbed. I did not want to fight. I wanted to disappear and not live that life anymore.

I returned to school after two weeks and would be expelled if I so much as looked at a teacher wrong. Auntie Nhung watched me like a salivating bear. One false move and she'd happily eat me alive. When I wasn't on my hands and knees scrubbing an imaginary smudge off the floors or polishing the silverware for the tenth time, I pulled clumps of soggy hair out of the drains and counted each grain of rice in a fifty-pound bag. She tormented me by making up ludicrous chores.

Dan felt sorry for me. He snuck me fashion magazines and art supplies to keep me sane. An article called for all artists and poets ages fourteen to eighteen to submit their projects in a statewide competition sponsored by the San Diego Chargers football team as part of their Hire-A-Youth program. I decided to enter both because I had nothing else to do.

I titled my poem "Redemption." It was about coming back from shame. I wrote several versions of it, but the one I sealed and gave to Dan never made it to the post office. It slipped out of his briefcase, and Auntie Nhung burned it. It was the first fight the couple had in the time I lived with them. Dan stood up to her and fought for me, but in the end, he lost the argument and slept on the couch for two nights.

Night after night after everyone went to bed, I did some stippling under the moon's watch as she shined her light through my window. Using the quill pen and ink that Dan slipped into my dresser, I dabbed hundreds of thousands of dots on an eleven-by-fourteen artist's pad of paper until the dots resembled actress Michelle Yeoh's beautiful face. The drawing took me a week to finish. Pride filled my chest over how detailed and intricate the jewels of her dress turned out, the density of the pigmentation in her hair, and the light shading of her skin. Dan sealed it carefully and did not address the packaging until he got to the post office.

I took the opportunity to write letters to Amy Chen in Hong Kong, to my seventh grade best friend Marina Ogawa in Renton, and Mr. and Mrs. Vanzwol in Kent. I never sent my letters to Amy and the Vanzwols because I didn't have their addresses. The only one I knew by heart was Marina's, and I told her not to write back. Writing the letters was therapeutic even though they'd never be answered.

It did not matter anyway. The only answer I wanted to receive was from God. Before I closed my eyes at night, I begged him to help me leave. I needed to find myself again. I needed to be happy. I wasn't thriving, and I so desperately wanted a second chance.

He told me to save my allowance and buy a one-way ticket to Seattle.

13. HELLO, MAMA (SPRING 1991)

Spring break arrived. I missed Mama and I begged her to drive down. I complained about the lonely winter break. The sunny, warm Christmas didn't have the magic of Seattle. I missed putting on my warm knit sweaters, gloves, and beanie and stepping out into the frost. I missed the snow and waking up to the glistening, white landscape of a true winter wonderland. I yearned to hear Mr. Van's deep voice as he jingled his bell and pretended he was Santa Claus. My heart ached for my childhood, and I wished I could relive those days again.

Hearing Mama's sweet voice was the balm my troubled soul needed. We spoke for seventeen minutes. I pushed my boundaries because I simply did not care anymore. I had survived the worst of Auntie Nhung and knew I could endure more. She was not my puppet master. I made that very clear.

Over spring break I kept my head down using the SAT and ACT exams as an excuse to stay home and study. Although I told myself it didn't matter whether I scored well on the exams or if I got into college, it went against my nature to be unprepared. While the family went to the zoo or SeaWorld, I humbly declined. Auntie Nhung was suspicious and did not like the idea of leaving me home unsupervised, but I gave her my most respectful and subservient promise. I encouraged Dan to spend time with his family and pointed out it would be one less ticket to buy and one less mouth to feed. He was reluctant, but financial planning was his love language.

I did not tell them about Mama's visit. Having her to myself was an exciting prospect I wanted to relish. The visit would be too awkward with Dan and Auntie Nhung hovering over us. I told Mama to come by herself. She didn't.

The doorbell rang. Excited and nervous, I ran to the door and swung it wide open. Mama stood there in a lovely yellow skirt and blouse. She had on a bonnet to keep the sun from scorching her light skin and giving her age spots. She had put on a lot of weight, and I was shocked. We embraced, and moisture leaked from our eyes.

"Hello, Mama."

"I know you told me to come alone, but…" Mama took my hand and led me outside.

My heart raced. I was unsure of what I would say to my stepdad or how I would react. His presence would put a damper on our visit, but at least Mama came. I reminded myself to be grateful for that. After all, all roses have thorns and sometimes you cannot have the beauty without the pain or the positives without the negatives.

I followed Mama to the driveway, and when I turned the corner, my knees buckled.

The Supra sat in the driveway.

Ace opened the door and held a bouquet in his hand. He scooped me up and held me tight. I breathed in his scent and squeezed him as hard as I could. The tears fell, and we stood there motionless for a long time. Neither one of us spoke. It was so unreal.

I finally broke away from our embrace. "I've dreamed so many times about this moment when I would see you again. I've missed you so much. You have no idea."

"I can't believe I'm here right now," Ace said. "We have your mom to thank for arranging this."

I turned to my mama and hugged her hard. I startled her by lifting her a couple of inches off the ground.

"Thank you, Mama!" A dozen kisses rained on her cheeks and hands. "I love you so much. Thank you!"

Joy and peace rose inside me at reuniting with the two people I loved most. I waved them into the house, and we sat down in the living room. I held both their hands and didn't let go for fear they'd disappear. My body floated, and my spirit soared.

"What time do you expect the family back?" Ace asked.

I wanted to kiss him so badly but didn't want Mama to feel awkward and disrespected. I held his hand and snuggled next to him on the loveseat. "I don't expect them home for another four or five hours."

"You look beautiful. You've lost some baby fat." He teased and kept his eyes on mine.

"Yes, I don't eat as much as I used to," I said. "Mama, you look lovely. Tell me everything."

Mama blushed and patted her thick arms. "I've gained too much weight as you can see."

"Too much good cooking in your kitchen?" I asked. "Any new recipes?"

"There is little time to cook now that I am enrolled in a naturopathic school," Mama said. "We dine out often. Sometimes your stepdad brings home food from the Asian Garden Mall. The studies keep me busy."

She rambled on about the qi flow of energy through the body and how each meridian was associated with an organ. She talked about how acupuncture and acupressure worked together and how fascinating the tiny needles pinpointed certain illnesses, stimulated relaxation, decreased pain, regulated blood flow, and brought peace to the brain.

"I practice on cadavers." She talked with great animation and passion.

It made me happy she had found something for herself. I wanted to know how things were between Binh and her but refrained from asking.

I summarized my school year for them, but I did not give them all the details because I did not want them to worry or stress out.

"I entered an art contest with the San Diego Chargers, and I've been studying for my ACT and SAT exams." I rested my hand on Ace's thigh. "I'm sorry our phone call ended so suddenly last time."

I told them about the altercation with the girl at the payphone but glossed over the broken nose and hematoma part. I wasn't sure how much Auntie Nhung had shared with my mama and stepdad, so I deviated down a less bumpy road.

I punched Ace's shoulder and gave him a charley horse. He jumped back in surprise. "What was that for?"

"Why didn't you rescue me from this hellhole?" I rubbed his shoulder like he was a wounded bird. "And what's the plan now?"

Mama and Ace didn't answer, so I bullied Ace to speak up. I pinched him.

"Ouch," Ace said. "You've gotten meaner, I see." He grinned, and I knew he was being playful. "I called your house a few times, but no one answered. Then I came to the house the following weekend, and your stepdad told me you were gone. I freaked out. He said you lived in San Diego and wouldn't give me your address or phone number. I prayed you'd page me so I could talk to you, and every time I returned the page, we got disconnected. Now, here we are eight months later."

"I counted on Mama to give you the address." I was confused. "They have me under surveillance here. I couldn't call collect to your beeper, and I didn't have Van's number memorized. But, Mama, you and I have spoken a few times, and you said nothing." I looked at Ace. "I thought you didn't love me anymore and had moved on."

"Honey, I never gave up." He kissed me tenderly on the forehead. "Your stepdad changed the phone number. I called one day, and there was a girl's voice on the answering machine. I was so excited thinking you came home, but I realized it wasn't your voice. And then your parents moved. I came to the mobile home, and it was for sale."

"What?" I said. "Mama, you moved? When? Where?"

"Business was not good," Mama said, "so we closed shop. I wanted to go to school so we moved back to Westminster northeast of the mall."

"And I went to the Phước Lộc Thọ mall to confront them, but the shop was a fabric store."

All these missed communications and passing ships. I shook my head. "So what is Binh doing now? Please tell me he's not doing real estate with Ms. Nga?"

Mama lowered her eyes, and I knew.

"Oh, Mama! This must be so hard for you." My anger flared, and I scowled. I stood and put my hands on my waist. "Oh, he's going to pay for this."

"Let it go, Thuỷ-Tiên," Mama said. "He is not worth it."

Unbelievable. How could she be so passive and laissez-faire about it all?

"Let him have his fun. Let him grow his real estate business and pay for my education. When the timing is right, I will divorce him and sue him for half his assets. Right now we have a marriage of convenience and perception. We sleep in separate beds and entertain together when we have to make an appearance. When the business went downhill—"

"That's because he's a poor businessman!" I said. "He gives everything away for free or at deep discounts so he can be popular."

It infuriated me that my mama endured all of this. She had been caged all this time in a deceptive marriage.

"I have made friends at acupuncture school." Mama perked up. "They are all Vietnamese, and they are all men except me and Liễu. Your stepdad is jealous, but there is nothing he can do about it. I torture him by telling him I have to stay late with my new friends to study."

"Just be careful," I said. "I don't trust him, and he can get violent."

"He will not hurt me," Mama said. "He's got holes in his mouth that retain nothing, only empty promises and casual threats. Trust me, he never follows where his mouth leads."

"School will be out in two months," I said. "I hate the idea of you living with him and putting on a show. What about our plan of leaving California and heading back to Seattle? We can do that once my junior year ends. We have some time to make plans. We can stay with Mr. and Mrs. Van, or what about Uncle Skyler or—"

"Your mom and I talked about this in the car," Ace said. "We ran into each other at the grocery store, and that's how we reconnected. We think you should go up there first—"

I looked at them. I couldn't believe what they suggested. "No, absolutely not." I shook my head wildly and crossed my arms. I pouted like a child throwing a tantrum. "We go together. Forget about suing Binh. There are acupuncture schools in Washington. We have family and friends up there."

"But I found a new community in Westminster, and I don't want to transfer," Mama said. "How would I even pay for school?"

"Get a loan," I said. "Jean-Adrien and Katrina are loaded. I'm sure they can lend you money."

"Absolutely not," Mama said. "I am too old to be starting over with everything and living off other people's generosity. I hate that I cannot support myself and am stuck with your stepdad. But we all have to make sacrifices. You have to go first."

"That's right, honey," Ace said. "Finish high school, get your Washington state residency, and then go to college as an in-state student. The tuition is less."

"You're going with me, right?" I asked him.

He shook his head.

"What do you mean?" I screamed at them both. "You both made these decisions about my life without me? You're treating me like a kid. I'll be seventeen this summer." Ace pulled me into his arms, but I pushed him away. "And where are you going?"

"I reenlisted with the Navy," he said.

"You what?" I punched his chest and paced back and forth. I pulled at my hair. "Where will you be stationed? For how long? Why?"

Things unraveled fast. I had not expected this reunion to go this way.

"I'll be in Corpus Christi in Texas," Ace said. "I'll be close to my brother."

I put my face in my hands and cried. "I'll move to Texas then. I'll live with your brother."

"You can't." Ace wrapped his arms around me, and I did not fight him. "I get out in two years."

"Two years?" I bawled. "No." I shoved him. "This is a shitty plan. Come up with something else."

"I'm sorry honey," Ace said, "but my hands were tied. "IBM laid me off and told me to get a degree. I lost hope of finding you, so I reenlisted. The Navy will pay for my education."

Why did he have to do things the proper way? I wanted him to get off his high horse and run away with me. We would figure things out as we went. He wanted to set us up for a bright future, a solid one where we didn't have to struggle and put stress on our relationship. I called him a coward and a few other names. I could not accept this change in plans.

I hit him in the chest. "We can get through anything if we loved each other. Don't you love me enough?"

"I love you more than you know," he said. "I know this is not easy, but we have our whole life ahead of us. You're almost seventeen, and I'll be twenty-two in August. We're still young."

Gloom pervaded the last couple of hours of our afternoon together. It would be a while before I'd see them both again. Mama promised to escort me to Seattle after school let out. I would stay with a family friend in Aberdeen, Washington. Mr. and Mrs. Van planned to move to Arizona and retire. Skyler, Magdaleine, Katrina, and Jean-Adrien traveled too often and could not host me. My cousin Tree would remain in San Jose and raise his three kids. Not even Auntie Diep and Donald could take me in. They had their cozy family of three boys and no room for another person to live with them.

Like a hot potato, I was being passed around from household to household. I stood ramrod and narrowed my eyes. I needed to survive one year in Aberdeen, then I'd be free. I'd be at a university, living an independent life, and would have no one to answer to but me.

I relented, and together we worked out the details. I gave Ace my friend Marina's address in Washington and told him I would always keep in touch with her. If he and I ever lost touch, he could write to her, and she would know how to find me.

Saying goodbye to Mama and Ace was difficult. I did not want to let go of either of them. I loved them deeply. Why did there have to be so many farewells in my life? We made promises to be strong, to stay safe, and to never give up. Two years was an eternity.

Mama pried me off Ace so he could get in the car. They had to leave before Auntie Nhung got home. With afternoon traffic, it would take them two hours to get back to Westminster.

I watched them drive away and went back inside to an empty, lonely, sparkling clean house that felt like a prison. This house was no Hanoi Hilton, and I was not a prisoner of war, thankfully, but it was still hell on Earth, and I had to break out. I had to be free. I could not live under the roof of a Viet Cong woman who stood guard while women were raped, who threw prisoners to the jungles of Vietnam to be slaughtered, and who freaking pursed her lips every single day because I was less significant to her than a dung beetle.

14. CONFESSION NIGHT (SPRING 1991)

My relationship with the Yellow Jacket remained tense. I lost all respect for Auntie Nhung knowing she was an accomplice to those violent crimes against women. It took all my willpower to be civil and respectful toward her. I knew not to bite the hand that fed me. I had a couple of months left of school, and the only way to endure it was to kill Auntie Nhung with kindness. I loathed her, but I would not turn into a monster like her. Hate would not consume me.

She did not forget my episodes of insubordination, but over time she swept them under the rug. The more polite and kind I was to Auntie Nhung, the more she accepted my theatrics. We both pretended nothing had happened, and because we were such convincing actors, I almost believed her kindness was genuine. I think she also almost believed I had converted from a child of damnation to one of salvation.

Loc and Hieu thought I had atoned for my transgressions and was back in their mother's good graces. The truth was I counted down the days to freedom. I focused my energy on ensuring I had no setbacks. Everything had to be smooth sailing or else I would never escape the cycle of mind control. Each day I did my chores and went the extra mile to help Loc and Hieu with their duties. The three of us made a pact that we would split the money in the penalty jar three ways no matter who won it.

Mama and Ace's visit gave me hope that I could set my course if I didn't allow little inconveniences to become major showstoppers. I saved all my allowance so that I could buy my plane ticket. I would prove to my naysayers, namely Binh and Auntie Nhung, that I was not a spoiled child who had lost her way. I could still be someone great and live the charmed life I deserved.

One spring evening we sat down as a family for dinner like we routinely did. It was confession night. The Yellow Jacket was in one of her rare benevolent moods and promised all topics were safe to discuss—there would be no judgment or punishment. She wanted to clear the air and start the month of May fresh, which meant leaving the worries and troubles behind with April. Having never participated in a confession night, I asked to go last. No one volunteered to go first, so Auntie Nhung voluntold her eldest son to go.

Loc cleared his throat and shifted in his seat. He stuttered as he confessed to watching television after school because he didn't want to miss an interview with Arnold Schwarzenegger. He changed the channel back to seven after he finished watching so that he wouldn't get caught. I held my breath for Auntie Nhung's reaction. Her boys were not so perfect after all.

"What did you learn from watching the interview?" Auntie Nhung took a small bite of her tenderloin and chewed slowly. I could tell she held back. She chewed the small piece of beef for what seemed like fifty times before she swallowed.

Meanwhile, Loc sweated. "Arnold is a seven-time Mr. Olympia champion. He holds the record of most wins, but Lee Haney may win his eighth one this year."

Auntie Nhung corrected Loc. "So he's tied. He doesn't hold the record if they both have seven titles."

He stuttered and fumbled his fork and knife. "I guess. Oh, and Arnold has a new movie coming out on July 3. It's Terminator Two. Can we go see it?"

"Did you learn anything else?" Auntie Nhung asked. "If you are going to break a rule, at least learn a life lesson or something valuable."

"Uh, well," Loc stammered. "Protein is the best for building muscle, like steak, chicken, fish, and eggs, and sugars make us fat, so I guess I'll skip dessert."

Loc came out of confession night alive. Who would get skinned next?

Dan volunteered. "So remember when Amy was going to enter that art and poetry contest?"

"Yes," Auntie Nhung said, "and I burned her poem because we do not reward bad behavior in this house by letting kids satisfy their itches."

"Well…" Dan said.

"What did you do, dear?" Auntie Nhung chewed her asparagus slowly and put her knife down.

"I sent in her drawing for the art competition," Dan said. "It was too good not to send in, and honestly, I did it for selfish reasons." Both the Yellow Jacket and I raised our eyebrows. What did he mean by selfish reasons? "First-prize winners in each category get cool stuff, including autographed Chargers memorabilia. Maybe she'll win, and I can convince her to give me the football swag."

"Wow, Dan." I pretended to be surprised. "Thank you for sending my picture in. Of course, I'll give you my Chargers gear if I win. I'm a Seahawks fan anyway. Kenny Easley and Walter Jones are my players."

Auntie Nhung let her husband off the hook with a disapproving look and said nothing. Hieu confessed next, but all he had was how he skimped on his chores by not spraying the tables down with Pledge cleaner. Instead, he used Pine-Sol. I gasped but Auntie Nhung was not amused. She went into a long soliloquy about why Pledge was best suited for the wood table because it was oil-free.

"It picks up all the dust while leaving a shiny luster." She compared the ingredients of Pledge and Pine-Sol and educated us on the chemicals in both products. "Pine-Sol is for degreasing and cleaning stubborn stains."

The woman even talked about how porous wood was compared to tiles. I was impressed with her knowledge of products and porous surfaces but equally annoyed with her rigid, duplicitous philosophy of what was proper and improper. How could a woman who ruled by fear instead of respect, who protected men's heinous acts of violence against women, and who manipulated the people around her, understand, much less educate others, on what was proper and improper?

I wondered what wrongdoing she would admit to that night. Maybe she would excuse herself from confession night because she was the queen and matriarch? Maybe it was an unspoken rule that she could do no wrong. I waited with bated breath.

"Amy, what do you have to confess?" Auntie Nhung asked.

"Oh," I said, "we haven't heard your confession yet. I'm going last, remember?"

Auntie Nhung dabbed the corners of her mouth with her napkin as if she were high society and proper. She folded the napkin and gently placed it across her lap. "I suppose it is my turn, isn't it?" She stalled a little by filling her glass of water to the top. She took a long sip and gently put the glass on the table. "Let me see."

I wondered if she would admit to slapping me. I didn't think she had told Dan about our kitchen feud where I threw the salt and pepper shakers at her, clawed at her throat, and bit her shoulder. Maybe it was because she lost that fight and didn't want to admit to losing to someone forty years her junior.

"Just admit it, Mom," Loc said. "You and Dad have sex all the time and you like it." Every jaw but Loc's dropped. Auntie Nhung's face turned crimson. "I hear you guys all the time, and you're always asking for more."

So Loc was not that innocent after all. He suddenly became my favorite. It took all my will power not to laugh. I shoveled food in my mouth like I hadn't eaten since the dawn of the Cenozoic Era. I kept my eyes down but my ears perked.

Auntie Nhung took another sip of water and dabbed her lips with her napkin. Dan broke the awkward silence by laughing. This embarrassed Auntie Nhung even more. She stood to clear the plates, even mine, though I was not done eating. I protested, saying I did not want to waste food, but she did not care.

Dan laughed so hard he triggered other emotions in his tiny hypothalamus. The tears leaked and he let out a fart. Loc and Hieu pointed at Dan and joined in the laughter. Without fail, flatulence always brought laughter, and the male species never seemed embarrassed. I giggled mainly because Dan was so nonchalant about passing gas at the table. All etiquette was out the window. We might as well have been laughing at Auntie Nhung, though, because she did not share the hilarity. She abhorred our juvenile behavior and feigned indifference.

The Yellow Jacket scooped up the salad bowl and grabbed Dan's plate. "Are you done?" He wasn't. She cleared the table anyway and put everything in the kitchen. "Lọc and Hiểu, load the dishwasher, and put the leftovers away."

We finished the night with a family movie called *Pretty Woman*. Auntie Nhung's mood changed as the night wore on. She let go of the embarrassment from earlier and dismissed the fact that both she and I got away with not spilling our beans. I was relieved because the only secret I had was Mama and Ace's visit while the family was out. I was not about to confess that and would have made up a story as absurd as Loc's and Hieu's.

The catfight between the two of us remained our little secret, and for the family's sake, we continued our charade. As far as everyone was concerned, my outburst at school and Auntie Nhung's scolding of my behavior was water under the bridge. I saw no reason to lift the veil and draw the curtains. The contempt lying beneath the surface remained concealed.

The Yellow Jacket and I moved forward with smiles and social graces. We behaved like mother and daughter instead of nemeses. Forty-five more days, I told myself. I had to survive long enough to finish my junior year of high school. Then I would be free of San Marcos High School, free of the Yellow Jacket, and free to be my true self.

15. THE MURPH (SPRING 1991)

A week before school got out, Dan handed me an envelope. It was from the Hire-A-Youth Program. I did not have high hopes. It was a statewide competition, and there must have been hundreds if not thousands of submissions. Dan shifted from foot to foot, but I stood motionless.

"C'mon, you can't leave me hanging," Dan said. "After all, I did send your entries in. I'm an accomplice now to your success."

"Entries?" I asked.

"Read it already, will you?"

I gently tore open the seal and took out the letter. I read it silently. I cocked my head to one side in confusion but a smile spread across my face as I continued reading. I frowned and scratched my forehead before handing the letter to Dan.

"Dear Amy," Dan read, "it is with great joy that we inform you of your placement in the statewide art and poetry competitions sponsored by the San Diego Chargers in partnership with Hire-A-Youth, a nonprofit organization that has been serving the young professionals of our nation since 1980. We received nearly three thousand submissions for both art and poetry contests. Your poetry submission of "Redemption" and your art entry of *Bliss* both placed in the top five in their respective categories. First, second, and third place winners will be announced at the annual televised Hire-A-Youth banquet on Saturday, June 15. Please join us for an evening of celebration. Poetry winners and honorable mentions will have the opportunity to read their poems at the dinner. You will meet potential employers, get inspired by our motivational speaker, and meet some of the San Diego Chargers players and cheerleaders. Please RSVP by May 30."

"I don't understand," I said. "My poetry submission never got sent in. I saw Auntie Nhung destroy it."

"So I have a confession," Dan said. "I took one of your crumpled versions of 'Redemption' and sent it off. I may have forged it and signed your name."

I opened my mouth to say thank you but closed them. Thanks weren't enough. My lips parted to try again, but I grasped for the right words to convey my sentiments. My eyes watered. Through all the endless days of darkness I had endured in San Marcos, Dan's light shone bright, yet he was content being in the shadows. No one had done anything so kind for me without any expectations in return. He genuinely believed in me and wanted me to succeed. I wrapped my arms around Dan and squeezed him with all my might.

"Thank you," I whispered. "Thank you for believing in me and truly seeing me, seeing my potential."

"You're a little songbird who has had her wings clipped," Dan said. "It's time you soar and sing again."

"Oh, Dan, what a poet you are," I said. "Are you sure you didn't write 'Redemption'?"

Dan gushed. "Want to check out the prizes?"

We sat down and poured over the details. Each nominee could bring two guests and pay extra for additional guests. The dinner would be held at "The Murph" with San Diego Charger's head coach, Dan Henning, giving the motivational speech. Prizes included a Chargers backpack full of football swag and autographed memorabilia, education credits toward art or writing classes at the local community college, a paid job placement for the summer, and tickets to NFL games. Other fun items like gift cards, trinkets, and interviews with the local TV channels were also included.

I called Mama and shared my good news. She shrieked and clapped her hands, saying she and Binh would come to the banquet. I told her I wanted only her to come but relented so that they could keep their façade of the happy couple. Dan sent in the RSVP letter and paid for his family of four to join me at the celebratory dinner.

The clouds finally gave way to a little sun haze. In two weeks, summer break would begin and so would my future. Mama would escort me up to Washington and get me settled into my new home in Aberdeen.

###

The Jack Murphy Stadium was transformed into a beautiful banquet hall under the cerulean sky. At one end of the field near the end zone was a large stage with a podium and projection screens all around. The band cranked out cover songs through the multimillion dollar audio-visual system. Cheerleaders walked around greeting the guests while television reporters pulled children and their parents aside to interview them. Waiters delivered trays of tapas and hors d'oeuvres and bartenders showed off their mixology talents by creating colorful cocktails. On the sidelines were photo booths and an 8'x8' step and repeat banner. The publicity backdrop had the San Diego Chargers lightning bolt logo and the Hire-A-Youth insignia. People were taking photos with the NFL players and cheerleaders and snapping photos in the booths.

Our group of seven found a round table at the fifty-yard line and settled in. We had one extra seat, and I wished Ace were there. Instead, he was on the naval station in Texas doing God only knew what.

"There are more people here than I expected," Auntie Nhung said.

I explained to her that there were subcategories within the art and poetry genres. Each subcategory had three placed winners and two honorable mentions. "In art, there's drawing, painting, photography, sculpting, carpentry, and mixed media. My stippling submission, Bliss, is under the drawing subcategory because it was done in ink."

"And here is your name under the poetry category," Mama exclaimed. "Our Vietnamese language is very poetic. It is good that you have poetry in your heart."

I looked at the program and saw the subcategories of haiku, ballad, free-verse, acrostic, sonnet, and epic. My "Redemption" poem was mentioned under acrostic. I explained to Mama that acrostic poems contain letters in each line that spell out a word or phrase. Typically, it is the first letter of each line that is used to spell out the message.

Arm in arm, I escorted Mama to the opposite sideline to the art display. The talent showcased on the field was impressive. The display included acrylics and watercolors, a piñata-looking sculpture of a big mouth titled *Speak Up*, and a photo within a photo within a few more photos that was titled *Reflections of Pain*. It reminded me of Bruce Lee's *Enter the Dragon* movie where he entered the hall of mirrors. The photo was in black and white, but the reflections of the girl in the red dress progressed from a vibrant scarlet to a dull raspberry. It spoke to me, and I understood the message. The pain never goes away. It will always be a part of us and makes us who we are, but in time, it gets diluted until it is not as bright and burning as in the beginning. We become different versions of ourselves in the healing process. I told Mama I bet *Reflections of Pain* would win first place in the photography subcategory.

"There is yours!" Mama squealed with excitement. "This my daughter drawing." She pointed to the 11x14 stippling portrait and bragged to anyone close enough to see my masterpiece. "My daughter, she draw that. That picture of me when I younger. Pretty then."

I didn't have the heart to tell her it was a portrait of an actress, so I let her believe it was her in her younger years when bliss lived in her heart.

We moved to the poetry section. Each framed entry rested on a stand. I pulled Mama to my poem. "I get to read this on the stage tonight in front of everyone. I'm so nervous."

"You should not be nervous," Mama said. "You are with winners. You should be nervous only if you had to read your last place poem next to the winning poem."

I laughed. "Way to put it in perspective, Mama."

She read one of the haiku poems and did not get it. "This is last place poem."

I giggled at her perspective and hoped the poet was not around to hear Mama. I had to admit I did not understand the underlying meaning within some of the poems but overall the verbal artistry was incredible and provocative.

By six o'clock, we all took our seats and enjoyed a four-course meal. Everyone was on their best behavior and dressed to impress in tropical casual attire. The fanciest thing I had was a mauve off-the-shoulder romper with a rose-colored velvet ribbon and nylon lace shawl.

Coach Dan Henning came to the stage and spoke about fighting for our dreams and that winners were not made overnight. He emphasized that we all were a part of the whole, a team, and to drive forward toward victory, every person had to do their part. He spoke about the fabric of our country was woven by the dreams of the young and shared success stories of players on his team who had big dreams. He reinforced how drive, perseverance, and a lot of stepping-stones would get us to where we aimed to go. He gave us a call to action to keep our eyes and ears open so that we might recognize opportunity, then keep our hands open so that we might seize the opportunity. When his motivational speech ended, I stood and applauded.

It was time for the award ceremony and one by one, poets climbed onto the stage to read the poem in their designated subcategories. Acrostic poems were read first. Coach Henning called my name. "Amy Le, reading her acrostic poem, 'Redemption.'"

I climbed the stairs and held my poem tightly, afraid it would blow away with the warm breeze. I stepped up to the microphone. "My poem is about living with shame but learning to fight back. It was written at a time when I felt I lost my voice."

> *"**R**estless is the heart that cannot find.*
> ***E**roded in memory our joy that binds.*
> ***D**are I scrub away the shame?*
> ***E**voked by you who scream and blame?*
> ***'M**orrow the lark sings my name.*
> ***P**etty and fear I play your game.*
> ***T**ethered around the same Life pole.*
> ***I** take back the me that you stole.*
> ***O**ver the clouds and rainbows, I rise.*
> ***N**ow and always, my warrior voice cries."*

I finished my poem and listened to the delayed applause. Were people processing the poem, or did my poem suck? Either way, I was happy to get off the stage and listen to the other contestants read their poems. One girl stumbled over her reading, and it was painful to watch. She was anything but eloquent. Another boy read his poem, and he was so dramatic I imagined him on a theatrical stage performing a monologue.

Finally, the time came to announce the winners of the acrostic poetry subcategory. "Redemption" came in third place. My hands shook as I received my ribbon and basket of gifts. I stepped off the stage to take photos with the winners and ran back to my table. Loc helped me open the gift basket to see what was inside. I gave Loc the Chargers T-shirt and Hieu the hat. There were gift cards, chocolates, and a voucher for a free class at the community college. I gave the chocolates to Auntie Nhung and the college voucher to Dan. I had no use for those things. The gift cards to Target and K-Mart would come in handy.

The night continued and when it was time to announce the winners of the art contest, I sat at the edge of my seat and squeezed Mama's hands. When my name was not called in the drawing subcategory for third or second place, my heart sank. I would have to be happy with an honorable mention.

"And first place goes to…" Coach Dan Henning paused for effect. "Amy Le, *Bliss*."

I could not believe it. Had he called my name? Had I won first place? I cried with joy and walked slowly to Mr. Henning's outstretched hand. I placed my small hand into his and shook it firmly. The band played music and camera lights flashed in our direction. We smiled for the photographers, and Coach Henning slipped a large San Diego Charger backpack over my shoulders. He congratulated me and patted my shoulder as I strutted off the stage. I floated over the carpet and stood in front of the step and repeat banner to be interviewed by a reporter.

"Amy, you just won first place in the drawing category for your piece titled '*Bliss*.' Tell us about your work."

I beamed with pride for the camera. Adrenaline and endorphins raced through me. "It was done with a quill pen and ink. The technique is called stippling. Using thousands of dots, I created this picture of my mama. She was the inspiration." The words petered out, and I didn't care to correct myself. Yes, the portrait was of Michelle Yeoh, but the world did not need to know that. Perhaps subconsciously I chose this drawing and this model because she reminded me of Mama when she was young, carefree, and happy. It started as a portrait of an actress but it became a portrait of my hero, the greatest woman in my life.

I darted back to my table and took everything out of the backpack. Loc and Hieu oohed and aahed over my swag—everything from a signed football to tickets to a game. I pulled out a five-hundred-dollar gift card in an envelope, some art supplies, a rally towel, candy, and an offer of employment at an art studio for the summer. I gave Dan everything Chargers-related, including the backpack. He especially coveted the autographed football. I was sad to miss out on the summer job, but I couldn't wait to leave San Marcos.

I was ready for Seattle. Was Seattle ready for me?

16. GOODBYE CALIFORNIA (SUMMER 1991)

On the last day of school, I emptied my locker and dumped everything in the trash. Unloading the year lifted a great invisible weight off my shoulders. My backpack was light and so was my spirit. While others signed yearbooks, took pictures, and cried, I watched a few boys chase skirts, some girls swoon over their friends' summer plans, and teachers rush to the lounge as fast as humanly possible.

The brunette whose face I smashed earlier in the year lingered by the vending machine as she twirled her hair and flirted with a boy I recognized from my social studies class. They made a cute couple. Carina, Lily, Mary, and Phuong huddled together signing each other's yearbooks. My friendship with them was nice while it lasted, but I had no regrets that it ended. The relationship was superficial, and we each got what we wanted from it. They cheated off me and felt better about themselves while I masqueraded my loneliness and pathetic existence by being a part of something for a little while.

I waited under the eaves of the administration building at the front of the school for Loc and Hieu to meet me. Loc exited the double doors of the south building first. He spotted me and waved. He was his jovial self, full of mirth and animation. He wished everyone a great summer and stopped to sign yearbooks. For a goofy guy who loved zipper pants and British Knights high-tops, he sure was popular. His bucked teeth, receding hairline, and big glasses made him too adorable to be the target of bullying. Picking on Loc would have been like picking on a baby, and no one rallied around that.

Together we waited for Hieu and made small talk. Loc showed me a rose a girl gave him and gushed about her pretty eyes and teeth. He said she liked his muscles and then flexed them for me. I squeezed his arm and agreed they were bigger than at the start of school.

"What was your favorite class this year?" I asked. "Don't say PE."

Loc shyly looked away and smiled. "Home economics."

"Really?" I asked. "Let me guess. The girl who gave you that rose was in your home ec class." Loc didn't answer, and I knew I pinned the tail on the donkey.

Hieu finally shuffled out of the building. He was in no hurry to go home. He wore a lazy, relaxed smile when he saw us.

"Walk faster," I yelled.

He picked up his pace but still snailed along. I laughed and ran to him. I looped my arm through his and locked elbows. I dragged him to where Loc stood. Hieu ran with me but struggled to keep his bag on his back and his pants up.

"What was your favorite class this year?" I asked.

"Computing," he said. "Mr. Moss let me work on his new Windows 3.0 computer, and the user interface is rad. It's fast too. The CPU speed is fifty megahertz. I'm going to ask for a computer for Christmas, one that has at least four megabytes of RAM and two-hundred megabytes of hard disk space."

I laughed. None of his jargon made sense to me. "Come on, Brains. Come on, Brawns. I see your dad's car. Let's go home."

"Are you coming to my graduation?" Loc asked.

"Of course," I said. "I wouldn't miss it. You're going to look handsome walking across the stage to get your diploma."

Balloons and streamers adorned the house. Cupcakes, coconut rum banana bread, cream puffs, and lemon cheesecake filled the kitchen counter. A buffet of chafing dishes invited us to peek under the lids and drool over the fried rice, egg rolls, shrimp toast, chicken skewers, and sautéed garlic pea vines. The fragrances of ginger, garlic, onions, and coriander seduced me to grab a plate and serve up.

Auntie Nhung hugged each of us and presented us with a gift. Her kind gesture touched me. She congratulated us for surviving the year, then also congratulated herself and Dan for surviving. She puckered her lips and lifted them to Dan, who obliged and swooped down for a kiss. He handed her a glass of champagne and she eagerly accepted his offering. I had never seen her drink alcohol before.

It was indeed a day to celebrate. Loc was graduating from high school, I was leaving their home for good, and Hieu was the last one in the house for another year.

"Can I open my present?" Hieu asked.

Dan nodded. Hieu tore open the wrapping paper and rocked back and forth when he saw his Sega Genesis gaming console and Sonic the Hedgehog cartridge. His hands went from rubbing his head to covering his mouth. He leaped up and buried his head in his parents' shoulders.

"I love my present. Thank you so much."

"You can only play on Saturdays," Auntie Nhung said.

"My turn," Loc said. He ripped apart the wrapper and shrieked. He hugged his yellow waterproof Sony Walkman Sports cassette player like it was a puppy.

"It comes with headphones," Auntie Nhung said.

"And we got you a C+C Music Factory tape," Dan said.

Loc put the cassette tape into the home stereo equipment and surprised me by rapping the lyrics to the song *Gonna Make You Sweat*. He started to breakdance and cut the rug with his dance moves. Who knew?

"Go Loc!" I clapped. "Let's get this party started." He entertained us until Auntie Nhung stopped him.

"You're going to break something," she said. "It's called break dancing because people break their necks and hips…or TVs." She laughed at her joke. "Anyhow, it's Amy's turn to open her gift."

The lightweight, twelve-inch box in my hand had one simple blue ribbon tied around it. Long and thin, it could have held a plane ticket or a quill pen. I shook the box and smelled the cardboard, wondering if there were traces of chocolate or something sweet. I untied the ribbon and lifted the lid to find tissue paper. With great anticipation, I removed the top layer and stared at my gift. My fingers trembled as I lifted three crisp one-hundred-dollar bills out of the box.

I had never been so excited to see a famous, dead man's face. "Benjamin Franklin never looked more handsome."

Dan laughed.

I unfolded the note tucked inside the box and read it out loud. "Amy, this year went by fast, and despite the ups and downs, you've proven to us that you are one smart and determined young lady. We know you will go far, and we hope this gift will help you get there. Don't forget us."

"That should be enough to get you from Santa Ana to Seattle," Auntie Nhung said.

The tears gushed. "This is very generous." I felt guilty for causing them trouble. Perhaps I misjudged Auntie Nhung. Perhaps I was too headstrong and willful—too wrapped up in my pain to appreciate what she tried to do for me. In some ways, I was like the Yellow Jacket herself, struggling for power and control, but in trying to put my life back on track, I spun other people's lives off track.

Auntie Nhung opened her arms to me, and I conceded. I wrapped my arms around her waist and hugged her.

"I'm sorry for everything. I am grateful to you both. Thank you. You taught me structure and discipline and that anything worth doing needed to be done right. I see that now. I know I was a brat wrapped in my cocoon of hate."

"We all make mistakes," Auntie Nhung said. "It is easy to hate and punish others when we are unhappy with ourselves. And when good comes into our lives, we don't always accept it. We reject it, we lose hope, and in doing so, we drive others away, especially people who care about us because they are the closest and easiest to hurt. I know I am guilty of this, and I work at being a better person every day. I used to hurt Dan and my kids because I didn't think I deserved their love. I know I hurt you too. I did things in my past that I regret. They still haunt me, but I know I am not the same person I used to be. Circumstances can harden your heart and make you do things you know are wrong."

Dan picked up both of us into his big arms. "You both are so tiny. You're two halves of the same person." He laughed and bounced us up and down. I heaved from his jostling and made a hurling sound.

"I have been spiteful and said terrible things," I said. "I've lost control and been mean. If I did not have people who loved me and didn't give up on me, I think I would have continued down a very dark and lonely path of destruction."

"Don't waste your life," Auntie Nhung said. "Visualize what you want in life, and go for it, one step at a time. You'll get there."

"That's right," Dan said. "Enjoy the journey, because before you know it, you'll be an old fuddy-duddy like me."

The five of us continued the celebrations into the night. We gorged on food, listened to Loc's new cassette tape, and played Sonic the Hedgehog on Hieu's new Sega Genesis system.

I reflected on the year with Dan and Auntie Nhung and saw events from a different perspective. Auntie Nhung taught me that if I were going to do something, I needed to do it properly, whether it be cleaning the bathrooms or preparing for college. A wild wood tiger like me needed a strong handler like Auntie Nhung who had the backbone to be the bad guy. Had my stepdad not sent me away, I might have lost my virginity to Ace and gotten pregnant. I might have dropped out of school and branched off in a life of struggles and suffering. I might have fallen back with the Pomona Boys and served time behind bars.

Perhaps I needed to re-examine my relationship with my stepdad, but I didn't think I could forgive him for cheating on Mama. Was it even my place to forgive him? He needed Mama's forgiveness, not mine.

My mama once told me it was good to struggle when we are younger and face our demons early. Only then could we enter the second half of our life with eyes open and weapons in hand. I was still young—about to turn seventeen the following month. I knew there would be more challenges and suffering in my future before I entered the charming half of my life, but on that day, nothing else mattered. I had not felt such love, peace, and relief in a long time.

Mama and Binh came down for Loc's graduation ceremony and an early dinner. I watched with pride as Loc strode across the stage and received his diploma. The future was as bright as he wanted it to be. He planned to attend community college for two years and continue living with his parents, much to Dan's chagrin and Auntie Nhung's excitement. She teased that she had looked forward to having one less mouth to feed but secretly loved having both of her boys home for another year or two.

Having Mama there was the best gift of all. With the allowance I had saved and the three-hundred-dollar gift I received, I had enough money to buy both Mama and me a ticket to Seattle, with hers being round-trip so she could come back and finish her OMD training. We made plans while cooking together in the kitchen. Auntie Nhung, Mama, and I made curry chicken and braised beef stew. We sent Dan and Binh on an errand to pick up French baguettes, Mountain Dew, and Courvoisier.

Mama reminisced about the time I refused to eat curry and she sent me to bed hungry. "You were seven years old. I cannot believe that was ten years ago."

"I was so sick of curry," I said. "You made it all the time."

"That was the one dish I knew how to make well," Mama said.

"Yeah, and I remember the next day, that same bowl of cold curry waited for me at the table." I stuck out my tongue and wrinkled my face. "You forced me to eat every bite for breakfast. It was so gross."

"But you love it now and you never turn down food," Mama said. "I taught you well."

"That's because I know better," I said. "Imagine if I complained about fish soup or fried crepes. You would have made me eat cold fish eyes or soggy crepes and limp bean sprouts. Yuck."

By the time Dan and my stepdad returned from the stores, the food was ready to be served. Auntie Nhung cooked a pot of rice to go with the curry and we toasted the bread for the beef stew. Over dinner, we talked about lighthearted topics like Auntie Diep. Mama described her friend as unforgettable, like seeing a man in a thong. I chimed in about her bright outfits and said she probably escaped from the Oompa Loompa sanctuary. Mama scowled so I took back my comment and apologized.

"So Amy, do you know what you want to study when you get to college?" Dan asked.

"I'm thinking about journalism," I said. "I want to be a news reporter or have a talk show. I'm nervous about college though. My stepsister, Thu, told me to be prepared to work harder than a two-legged dog in an agility competition."

Hieu found that hilarious and could not stop laughing. "Or a one-legged man in a river dancing competition."

Dan and I burst at the seams. The visual brought me to tears, and I laughed until my sides ached. Loc put it in motion and demonstrated his river dancing skills with one leg. It was impossible to take him seriously. He bent down and substituted one of his legs with his arm and tried again.

"Ingenious," I cried.

"Almost as hard as my mom trying to parallel park," Loc said.

Auntie Nhung tugged at her son's ear. "Why are you always picking on me?"

"I only speak the truth, Mom." Loc blew her a kiss. "We all know you are short and have depth-perception issues."

My stepdad put his spoon down and grabbed a toothpick. He finished his meal first as usual. "Delicious."

"You're done?" Dan asked. "Did you even taste the food?"

Binh picked at his teeth. "I tasted every bite, and see? Here is proof." He dug out a piece of beef and showed it to us. I crinkled my nose and looked away. I still found his eating habits repulsive and unrefined.

Mama poured more Courvoisier XO into her glass and raised it for a toast. "To our children. May they make us proud and give us all their money."

Auntie Nhung nodded. "And cheers to us. I say we grab our OG panties and holster, granny up, and show these kids we're not hillbillies from Vietnam."

"What does that even mean?" I laughed.

"Now wait a minute," Dan said, "if yer gunna git yer panties, we menfolk are gittin our tobacca and rifle, too, cuz we can still show these youngins a thang er two!"

The adults tossed back their cognac and poured again. Loc, Hieu, and I shook our heads. They were getting a good buzz on, and by the end of the evening, they were loud, crude, and rambunctious. Binh brought out his guitar and strummed a melody while Auntie Nhung sang. Dan put on the karaoke system, and suddenly, we teenagers didn't exist. Mama and Auntie Nhung fought over who would sing next and debated whether Hương Lan or Ý Lan was the better singer. They channeled their inner Lans and sang a duet. The adults let loose and acted like teenagers. They sure did show us a thing or two.

My stepdad drove Mama and me to John Wayne Airport. Mama packed enough clothes for two weeks in Seattle. She would help me settle in my new home in Aberdeen, Washington, a small town located two hours' drive west of Seattle. We didn't talk on the way to the airport. Instead, each of us sat inside our heads, deep in thought, playing a movie reel of what the future had in store for us.

Binh was unusually quiet. He changed lanes often. He sped up then slowed down. He gripped the steering wheel until his knuckles turned white. I wondered if they fought earlier. I welcomed his silence. He still grated me the wrong way. I simply did not trust him. We had too much bad blood between us, but we tolerated each other for Mama's sake. In my memory, he was still the bad guy who monopolized Mama's time and persuaded her to leave a great job to move to California. He was the jerk who kicked my dog and gave her away. He violated my privacy and trust by reading my diary and barging into my room the day Ace was there. He packed my bags and sent me away to San Marcos. His threats about paralyzing me and confining me to a wheelchair still angered me.

My stepdad parked the car and removed our suitcases from the trunk. He still did not say a single word. Mama didn't seem to notice or care about the silent treatment. She was as excited as I to return to Seattle. I could not wait to get on the airplane and say, "Goodbye, California."

Mama talked about her childhood friend, Tien. They were like sisters growing up. Mama said her mother took Auntie Tien in and raised her for a few years. I hadn't heard that story before.

"Your grandmother raised Tien as her own and the two of us grew up as sisters," Mama said. "You will like her. She and her husband have five children. Her two youngest are around your age."

"Are they girls?" I asked.

"Boys," Mama said. "They have three boys and two girls. The oldest son is in the military, the oldest girl works for Boeing, and the next daughter is in college at Western Washington University. Todd is your age and will be in twelfth grade. You'll be going to Hoquiam High School together. The youngest is Thomas and he'll be entering ninth grade."

"What happened to Auntie Tien's parents?" I asked. "Did they die in the war?"

Mama shook her head. "They were poor and struggled to take care of their children and aging parents. Tien was not an orphan but in some ways she was. My mother loved her and took it upon herself to foster Tien. She is younger than me and very pretty. She was lucky. She married for love. It was not an arranged marriage. Her husband is a handsome and good man. He played soccer in Vietnam. You will like him. You are to address them as Auntie and Uncle Four."

The three of us went through security, and Binh escorted us to the gate. Mama and I gabbed about the foods we missed and how much we looked forward to seeing our friends. I wanted to drive by Homestead Apartments and visit Springbrook Elementary School for old times' sake.

"Who should we visit first?" I asked. "Is anyone picking us up at the airport? Where are we staying until we get to Aberdeen?"

Mama laughed. "So many questions. Uncle Skyler and Miss Magdaleine will pick us up at the airport. They will let me borrow their extra car while we are in town. I cannot wait to see my dear friends. We will stay with them for a week and then go to Aberdeen for a week."

I wished Mama could stay longer. I hated the idea of her returning to California and Binh. I reminded myself sacrifices were necessary. We had to stick to the plan.

Suddenly my stepdad knelt at Mama's feet and broke down in tears. I distanced myself from him and gripped Mama's hand.

"You are leaving me," Binh cried. "You have no plans to come back. I know you do not love me." He looked at Mama's face and begged her to stay. "I am sorry for hurting you. I know I can be a better husband. Please tell me there is still a chance."

Mama was speechless. She looked around at the bystanders watching the tragic scene unfold. She hushed my stepdad and tried to pull him to his feet. Mama's face reddened. I gawked at Binh.

He kissed Mama's feet and clung to her ankles, throwing her off balance. I clutched her arm to steady her. I had never seen a grown man cry. If I had empathy for him, I would have softened my heart and forgiven him that instant. Instead, I regarded his pleas and emotional outburst as pathetic. I wished I believed him. I wanted to think he could make my mama happy and not resort to his old ways. However, people did not change overnight. How many months or years must she endure before he changed? By then, it would be too late.

"You are embarrassing us and yourself," I said.

Binh ignored me. "Please, Snow, promise me you will come back. Remember our first trip to California, how we danced at the flea market? Remember our trip to Mt. Rainier when I proposed to you? Remember the first time we were together after Diệp and Donald's wedding? I made you happy once. Let me be that person again. You deserve that. I beg of you. Please forgive me, and give me another chance to make you happy. I promised to take care of you."

His appeals were working. Mama's face softened. "Yes, you did promise, but taking care of me meant also taking care of Thủy-Tiên. My daughter is a part of me, and after we moved down, you stopped taking care of her. It was as if you used her to get to me. I remember you showered us both with affection and gifts. You used to play with her and spend time with her. But then you treated her as a nuisance and a burden. I think you owe her an apology as well."

Binh and I looked at each other. His expression changed from vulnerable to stern. His body stiffened, and his posture became stoic. I tried not to gloat and wiped the smile from my face.

Binh stood up. I knew he was conflicted. I expected him to say he was the adult and that it was not his duty to apologize to a child. Would his arrogance get in the way of apologizing to me? Would he risk losing his wife out of stubborn pride and old patriarchal beliefs that the man was never wrong?

I held my breath and waited. I thought about making it easy on him by apologizing first, but I was obstinate also. We were at a standstill. Who was more pigheaded out of the three of us?

My stepdad took a deep breath. "You have not been the easiest child to manage—"

"I didn't need you to manage me," I said. "I needed you to be my friend."

"Do not interrupt," Mama said. "Let him finish."

My stepdad crossed his arms over his chest and widened his stance. "Look, you are off to the next stage of your life, and I wish you success. I know I put a lot of pressure on you to be perfect, and I admit I compared you to my daughter, Thu, and that was unfair of me. You are two different people. I forget that you grew up without a father and I tried too hard to be a father. I thought that was what you needed, maybe even what you wanted. I guess I came on too strong and too fast—"

"Yes," I said, "you did."

"Stop doing that," Mama said.

"Sorry," I said.

"Can we agree that becoming an instant family was all new to us?" my stepdad asked.

I nodded. "We were definitely out of sync and out of touch with one another."

Mama wrapped her arms around both of us. "We made decisions in silos, and we need to discuss them as a family."

"I know I am a child, and you were raised in a culture where men held the power and parents had all the authority, but here, they value independence. Children are contributors, and they have a seat at the table. They leave the nest and go off to pursue their dreams."

"But the American children also disrespect their elders, talk back to adults, and put their aging parents in nursing homes to rot alone," Mama said. "They do not discipline their children and they spoil them too much. We do not want you to become that way."

"Mama, I would never do that to you," I said. "Not all of us are bad. We act badly because that is what is expected of us before we're even given a chance. And I think it is prejudice to think American kids all behave that way."

"We have been in the United States for eleven years now," Mama said. "We are also citizens. I guess the real lesson begins now on adapting to Western society."

I smiled. "We may be Americans, but we're still Vietnamese. After all, my broken Vietnamese is still perfect."

Mama laughed. "Well, we tried. No one can blame us for trying to teach you how to read and write."

"On the positive side," my stepdad said, "her Spanish is good. We can take a vacation to Mexico, and she can be the interpreter."

"¡Sí Señor!" I said. "Yo hablo español muy bien. ¿Dónde está el baño? Mi cumpleaños es mañana. Por favor, dame cien dolares. ¿Cuanto cuesta el sombrero? Mucho gusto. ¿Como se dice 'vacation' en español?" I laughed as I rambled in Spanish to show off my language bravado. "Maybe I'll work for the FBI one day and be a translator, or work for border patrol and interrogate suspicious people."

An attendant for Alaska Airlines called for us to board. Mama and I collected our belongings and stood in line. My stepdad wrapped his arm around my shoulder and kissed me on the head. He never did say he was sorry, but neither did I. I let it go and knew in my heart I would never see him again. My mama had to decide what she was going to do. I had my future to focus on and to do that, I had to let go of the past.

The only thing I was not willing to let go of was Ace. I knew we would be reunited again after he got out of the Navy. Until then, my job was to graduate high school and get into college.

Mama and Binh kissed. I teased them about the public display of affection. Mama blushed and Binh told her to ignore me. They both chuckled and gave one last embrace before separating. We waved to Binh before entering the terminal. How sad he looked to be left behind.

Goodbye, California. Thanks for the new wave music and grunion run. Thanks for the Poison concert and my first kiss. Take care of my dog and save me a bowl of pho.

EPILOGUE

In 1991, Aberdeen, a small mill town in Grays Harbor County, had a population of 16,565 people. Once called "The Hellhole of the Pacific," the town was sprinkled with seedy whorehouses, saloons, and casinos. The murder rate was high and the timber industry boomed until the late 1970s. The logging by Weyerhauser had siphoned all the resources in the area. One pulp mill still operated, and the smell of vanilla permeated the town. Situated close to the Pacific Ocean, the overcast seasons were long and the rainfall heavy.

In that depressing town, the only Asian people I crossed paths with were Auntie and Uncle Four's family. Thomas, Todd, and I were the minorities at Hoquiam High School. If I were a bloodsucking vampire, Grays Harbor County would have been the perfect home. However, I had grown accustomed to the sunshine and beaches of California, so Aberdeen was a lonely and boring existence. There was nowhere a teen could go to find trouble.

Every day I went to school, then straight home to do homework. I spent most of my time in my bedroom and did not interact much with my host family. I felt like an intruder and did not want to impose or inconvenience them in any way. I helped Auntie Four in the kitchen every night as I was the only girl in the home.

Mama was right—Auntie Four was beautiful. She had aged gracefully over the years. I envied her long, thick black hair and bangs, her dimples, and the way she commanded love and respect from her husband and two sons. She was a strong woman on the inside, soft on the outside, and a great role model for me. She laughed a lot and had a young girl's spirit.

Auntie Four worked as a waitress in the only Chinese restaurant in Ocean Shores, a beach town twenty-five miles west of Aberdeen. I got a job at the Lucky Dragon restaurant and bussed tables for her on the weekends. She split her tips with me, and I ate all the fortune cookies I wanted. The owner often fed us dinner before we drove home at night. I clutched the armrest as Auntie Four careened down dark, narrow, windy, two-lane roads. I imagined rolling down the cliff into the ocean. Auntie Four knew those roads like she knew the mannerisms of her children and always got us home safely.

Uncle Four used to work at the paper mill but was laid off. He loved watching soccer on TV and reminisced about the days in Vietnam when he played competitively. Uncle Four was handsome and fit. He had amazing legs and strong calves, a head full of hair, and a prominent jawline. He was quiet and reserved compared to Auntie Four. I don't think he knew what to do with me or how to act around me. I knew he loved me though from his small gestures of kindness, like giving me money just because or telling me about a scholarship I should apply to for free college tuition. Department of Social and Health Services had a dependent care program that provided cash assistance to families who needed help. We qualified and received four-hundred dollars each month. Uncle Four gave me three-hundred dollars each month and kept only a hundred to cover my room and board. By the end of my senior year, I had saved three-thousand dollars in my shoebox under the bed. I had no friends, no need for shopping, and no urgent expenses. I bought milkshakes or small gifts for the family during the holidays and birthdays with the money I made bussing tables at the Lucky Dragon.

I coasted through my senior year and graduated with honors. I was friendly with my classmates and got along nicely with Todd and Thomas, but never developed lifelong friendships or deep connections in Aberdeen, Hoquiam, and Ocean Shores. When I considered my university options, I decided I would go either to Western Washington University (WWU) or Washington State University (WSU), the two schools farthest away from Aberdeen but still within the state. WSU was a party school whereas WWU was close to the Canadian border, and the legal drinking age in Canada was nineteen. I chose WWU because Auntie Four's children went there, and Todd also got accepted to the university. Not to mention I won a scholarship to WWU and my first year was free.

Mama flew up, and together with Auntie and Uncle Four, we drove to Bellingham and settled into our dorms. It was a beautiful campus with grand brick buildings and a large water fountain in the center courtyard. The school was nestled in a charming coastal town with hiking trails and lakes on one side and beaches and scenic drives on the other. My four years there were the best years of my life. Dorm life and cafeteria food did not agree with me though. After one quarter, I wrote a letter to the board requesting a release of obligation from my residential contract, stating that the food didn't agree with me, and the loud parties obstructed my educational endeavors.

My roommate, Rina, was Cambodian and sad to see me go. She and I bonded and were inseparable. I often went home with her to Tacoma to visit her family and stock up on home-cooked meals. I missed authentic Asian foods and realized how much it defined me as a Vietnamese girl growing up in an American world. When I moved out of the dorm, I met Jane, my first Korean friend, who introduced me to bulgogi, onion pancakes, and kimchee. My housemates and I rented a townhome near campus and lived in the same complex as Todd and his roommates. James and Carrie were my roommates. I rarely saw James. He was a very tall black man with beautiful eyes and had served in the Marine Corp. He was working on an engineering degree. Carrie was a party animal, always late on her share of the rent, and the epitome of the ditzy blonde stereotype. We all stayed out of each other's way and circulated with peers who never hung out together.

I joined the Vietnamese Student Association (VSA) and found like-minded friends who loved potlucks and karaoke. Several times a week, we gathered for study sessions that turned into one hour of studying and two hours of eating and socializing. We ran the VSA club together, formed a volleyball team, and took trips to Vancouver, British Columbia, to eat and dance at the nightclubs. Richard's on Richards was our favorite night raver hotspot to flirt and lose our body to the beats of hip hop. College was a defining event in my life where I developed my political views and grew into my skin.

Mama and I spoke every Sunday morning and if I didn't call, she worried and gave me a lecture. Her life unraveled, and she took a break from school. Life with my stepdad was good for a while, but he continued to squander money. Mama said he was addicted to sex, something I didn't want to hear, and that he found attention elsewhere. She was miserable but she could not leave him yet. I encouraged her to get a financial loan to continue school, get a job, and move out. I offered to buy her a ticket to Seattle, but she was adamant that I focus on school. She would figure things out.

I had a job under a work-study program at Disabled Students Services and got paid to read textbooks into a cassette recorder for the visually impaired students. I also worked at Payless Shoe Source and while I was the top salesgirl each month, I admittedly spent my paychecks on shoes. I got a credit card and with my newfound freedom, I spent all my money shopping, eating out, partying, and buying books.

One sunny autumn day, I bundled up in my turtleneck sweater and knitted cap and took a walk outside to enjoy the beauty of the fall leaves on display. Washington had the best deciduous trees with foliage that turned from green to tones of gold, vermilion, amber, and apricot in late October. I checked the mailbox to see if there was anything fun. On occasion, James received letters from home, and Carrie received checks from her grandparents. All I ever got were junk mail, bills, and letters from Ed McMahon tempting me to join the Publishers Clearing House for a chance to win cash and prizes.

My breathing stopped and my heart skipped a beat when I recognized the handwriting on an envelope with a postmark from Oklahoma. I tore it open and caught a whiff of Ace's Obsession cologne. I put the letter to my nose and inhaled the scent. Tears of joy ran down my cheeks as I stood beneath the maple trees savoring the scent of his cologne and the romantic curves of his writing. My heart pounded. Was it bad news? I sat down on the viridian moss and counted the pages. Five. I turned straight to the end to see if he included a phone number. He had—one with a 405 area code.

He got out of the Navy in April 1993 and met a girl online named Trâm. He sold his Supra to his brother and moved to Oklahoma City in May. He bought a Nissan Maxima and was slowly modifying it, dropping the car to the ground, putting on low-profile tires, installing lights under the chassis, tinting the window, and putting on a new spoiler. In the fall, he started school at Oklahoma State University (OSU). He never stopped loving me and never stopped thinking of me. He thought all was lost, but then he found Marina's address and wrote to her. She wrote back and gave him my address in Bellingham. He was sure I had moved on, but if I still loved him, he would drop everything and come to me.

I read the letter a second time before I rushed to the townhouse and picked up the phone. My heart fluttered with excitement. Hearing from Ace was better than winning a Publishers Clearing House prize. I had dreamed of this day, and soon I would hear his voice. Two long years I had waited. I had so much to tell him and catch up on. With trembling hands, I made the long-distance phone call from my bedroom on my cheap, lip-shaped telephone that I purchased at Spencer's next to Payless Shoes Source at Bellis Fair Mall.

"Hello?" A girl answered.

"Hi," I said. "Can I talk to Ace?"

"Who's this?" she asked.

I wasn't sure whether to say Amy or Christine so I answered, "An old friend." She was quiet. I thought the call got disconnected. "Hello?"

"I'm still here," she said. "Is this Christine?"

I fumbled the phone and almost dropped the receiver. She knew who I was. "Anh Bé has talked about you." Who the hell was Anh Bé? "This is Trâm, his girlfriend."

"He mentioned you in his letter," I said. "Can I talk to him? Is he home?"

"No, he's not home," she said coldly. "He's at the restaurant helping my dad and learning the family business."

"Well, what time will he be home?" I asked. "I'll call back."

"No, you won't." Tram told me they had been dating for six months, that she loved Ace and was not giving him up without a fight. She said he had started school at OSU and needed to focus on his education. "We are happy together. If you want him to be happy and not distract him from his studies, I suggest you forget him and never call back." Apparently, all Ace ever talked about was me, his first love, his old flame, and the regrets he had. "I am tired of hearing about you, and I don't have the patience any longer to entertain his fantasies of reuniting with you." She hung up on me.

Oklahoma City was two hours ahead of Bellingham. I debated whether to call later that night but knew Tram would be monitoring the phone. I didn't call back that night or the following night.

On the third night, I could not take it anymore and resolved to talk to Ace. Tram was not going to dissuade me so easily. I dialed the number and the phone rang four times.

"Hello?"

My heart hammered inside my chest and somersaulted into my throat. It was my Ace.

"Christine, is that you?"

I nodded but could not speak. Finally, I whispered, "Yes."

"Oh honey," Ace said. "Oh baby, I can't believe I'm talking to you right now. Tram told me you called and we had a big fight. I was afraid she scared you off and you wouldn't call again. I threatened to drive to Washington if she pulled that again."

"Is she home?" I asked.

Ace laughed. "Yes, she's here next to me and planning my murder."

I had no ill feelings toward Tram. I empathized with her. I knew what it felt like to love Ace and how amazing it was to be loved by him. She was in a difficult situation. I was the ghost from the past that haunted them both.

"Well tell her I am back, and I'm reclaiming what I lost. You were mine long before you were hers."

Ace and I spoke for twelve hours straight. We had so much to say, and neither one of us wanted to hang up. We made plans for him to fly out and visit me after Christmas when the airfare was cheaper. We had waited for two years and would have to wait two more months. I came alive as I told him all about my life in San Marcos and Aberdeen. He talked about life in the Navy and how his younger brother married a redhead in Texas. Ace asked me if I had dated anyone after him, and I told him I had dated a college boy from Lopez Island but it did not last long. The islander boyfriend wanted to get married and move to Hawaii so he could be a geologist. I wasn't uprooting again and leaving Washington. Ace and I had a good laugh when I told him the ex-boyfriend stole all my seasonings during the breakup.

Ace and I finally hung up at six in the morning. I slept the entire day and woke up happier than ever.

###

I took the Greyhound bus down to Seattle and met Ace at the airport. The moment he stepped out from the tunnel, I jumped into his arms and kissed him fiercely. He looked the same except with longer hair. We held each other with my head buried in his chest for a long time. The moment was surreal. I did not let go for fear he'd vanish into thin air. We kissed and hugged, and just like in the movies, it felt like the world moved on without us. Time stood still. People came and went. Planes landed and took off. We didn't speak.

We pried ourselves apart and headed to baggage claim. Every few steps, we stopped and kissed again. It took us twice as long to get to the lower level to collect his suitcase. I didn't have a car and told him we'd have to take the Greyhound back to Bellingham. I took the bus everywhere and learned the route to get to work. If I needed groceries, I walked the mile down to Haggen and then back up the long hill with my bags of food. It was good exercise but exhausting.

"My poor baby," Ace said. "Let's find you a car while I'm here, something cheap for under a thousand dollars."

"How long are you here for?" I asked.

"Two weeks," he answered. "And I was thinking, if you want, I could apply to transfer to Western. If they accept me, which they will, I'll move here in June."

"And we can start school together in the fall!" I hopped like a bunny and squeezed his hand. "We can find our own place or maybe Carrie or James will move out by then."

We pulled Ace's luggage off the conveyor belt and took a taxi to a nearby hotel for the night. It was too late to catch a bus back to Western. Inside our hotel room, Ace and I cuddled and talked until our stomachs growled. We grabbed food at a diner and brought it back to the room. We started a movie and ate but soon abandoned the movie.

Ace looked at me with tenderness and desire in his eyes, and I knew it would be the best night of our lives. He turned off the light and opened the curtain a sliver to let the moonlight witness our lovemaking. I removed my clothes and helped him remove his. We stood naked. I traced his curves and lines with my eyes. His silky skin warmed my fingertips. I hungered for him, but he took his time and drove me crazy.

He flipped me over onto my stomach and gave me a massage with his lips and tongue. His touch fluttered from my neck down to the small of my back like a butterfly leaping from flower to flower. His hardness pressed against my legs, and I parted them slightly.

"Not yet," he whispered.

His tongue circled my earlobes as his hand found its way to my breasts and inner thighs. My body throbbed for him. I rolled onto my back and looked into his eyes just inches from mine, and I inhaled as he exhaled. One breath. One heartbeat. One body.

He caressed me and murmured he wanted to explore every inch of me. He mapped out my body with his eyes and lips, and the temptation was too much to bear. My body tingled under his light touch. His hair tickled my stomach when he moved down past my hips to the folds of my femininity. And when his hot breath landed on the pearl between my legs, I gasped. My toes curled and my body tensed. I shook and orgasmed for the first time. I dug my nails into his shoulders and pulled his head closer. His tongue enjoyed torturing me, and when his mouth found mine again, I took pleasure in returning the favor.

Ace and I made love for hours, releasing years of pent-up frustration, separation, and longing.

###

Ace bought me a white 1985 Honda Civic, four-speed manual transmission, for nine-hundred dollars. The base model hatchback had a solid engine and got me where I needed to go but not very fast. In the summer, he drove his Nissan from Oklahoma City to Bellingham and started school in the fall at WWU. Carrie and James did not move out, so we split the rent four ways with Ace and me taking over the master bedroom. Ace joined the VSA and life resumed with potlucks, karaoke, and trips to Vancouver.

We stayed together for four years. Ace got the sales engineer position at IBM and quickly received a promotion. He wore suits to work and took long trips to Amsterdam and other exotic places. Over time, we drifted apart. He worked a lot and spent more and more time at the casinos to decompress. On the night I planned to give him an ultimatum, I prepared a romantic evening picnic in our bedroom with candlelight and wine. I drew him a card and wrote him a poem. I turned on the music, slipped on a sexy black dress, and waited. Hour after hour, I ran to the bedroom window to see if the headlights belonged to the Maxima. It was never him. I drank the bottle of wine in under an hour and got drunk for the first time. The walls tilted, and the room spun. I laid down to rest my eyes and thought about our breakup.

Ace found me passed out on the bed, lying rigid on the mattress with my hands clasped on my stomach like a dead person. He cried, panicked that I had alcohol poisoning. He rubbed lemon juice on my palms and the bottoms of my feet—a superstitious belief that the citrus would absorb into my bloodstream and release the toxins. We did not break up that night but our relationship changed.

He hurt me deeply, but I loved him enough to part as friends after all we had been through. As our hearts healed, we became best friends and could laugh again. Ace left Washington, and I bought the Supra from his brother as a memento of our life together. I paid Tung to drop the transmission and put in a manual stick shift. I covered his travel expenses, and two months after Ace left Washington, the Supra arrived at my doorstep—the perfect part of Ace to keep close to my heart.

Ace and I kept in touch and dated other people. While there was some jealousy underneath our cool demeanors, we never interfered in each other's love lives. Ace dated a gal named Anna who was intimidated by me and insecure in her relationship with Ace. She was smart, nice, and came from a rich family. She was also plain looking with a big forehead and weak chin. It made me uncomfortable to watch her fuss over him. When I started dating Charlie, Ace admitted he wanted to smash Charlie's head into the window. He found Charlie too arrogant and thought he was a player.

The years passed and President Bill Clinton came into office. He appointed Ruth Bader Ginsburg to the Supreme Court as the second female Justice to hold that seat, and in 1994, he lifted a nineteen-year-old trade embargo with Vietnam. A year later, Mama got her OMD in acupuncture. She left Binh and never looked back. Mama was a fan of President Clinton until the extra-marital affair scandal came to light. She lost all respect for him so when I met him a decade later and told her I shook his hand, she asked me if his hands were dirty. I told her it was soft like butter with no callouses.

Mama found a small apartment in downtown Seattle on First Avenue and walked across Post Alley to get to the Pike Place Market every day for fresh seafood, meats, fruits, and vegetables. She adopted a black toy poodle and named her Bijoux. The two doted on each other and loved one another unconditionally. Mama and Bijoux took walks every day, and the vendors at the market knew them by name.

Once again Mama and I lived our best lives in Seattle with no drama or baggage to hold us back. Our most cherished moments were in the kitchen when I helped Mama prep and she cooked. We laughed over her mispronunciation of ingredients or clever renaming of cuisines. For example, sushi came to be called *xù xì* which meant shaggy, and cassoulet was "cá so lazy," which made no sense because *cá* meant fish. Fish so lazy was far from what the French coined a meat casserole.

In 2000, President Clinton visited Vietnam—the first president to travel there since the war. Mama and I held our breath as we tuned into the news to understand what his visit meant for us going back home and seeing our family. Another eight years passed before Mama, Tree, and I reunited with our mother country.

In between those years, I met a man I married but divorced after two years of abuse. Tree moved his family back to Seattle, and once again, we were together in the city that had welcomed us with open arms when we were poor refugees who knew nothing about life in a free nation.

By 2008, I worked for a great company called Microsoft, took home a six-figure income, owned two cars, paid off my student loans, and answered to no one. I had been dating a man ten years younger than me and married him that year. My father came to the wedding. Mama and my dad reconnected after she left Binh and returned to Seattle. He came to visit a few times, but I was too busy with work and travel to spend any time with him. Subsequently, I regarded him as an old friend from out of town who occasionally visited.

Nearly thirty years after escaping the clutches of communism on a rickety old shrimp trawler, Mama, Tree, and I flew home to our roots. Mama and her siblings picked up right where they left off in 1979, with tears of pain but hope for a brighter future. How sweet it was to get to know my aunties and uncles, to meet my cousins, and dote on their children. The family house still stood and continued to raise another generation of children.

I had left Vietnam a sick, frail child with an uncertain future and came back a healthy woman living the charmed life I dreamed of for myself. Mama and Tree were happy, healthy, and reaping the rewards that America afforded them. We spent a month in Vietnam getting reacquainted with the land, the people, the foods, and the traditions. I left there humbled, enriched, and fluent enough to think and dream in Vietnamese.

Ace later reunited with his parents in Vietnam and built them the house he promised. Mama and I never saw Binh again and Mama remained single until the day she passed. She lived life on her terms. Mr. and Mrs. Vanzwol retired to Arizona and the rest of our friends and family continued the rat race of living. We came full circle. We faced our fears, pushed through the pain, and found happiness within the strong bonds of love, forgiveness, and family.

Despite our busy lives, we made time for family. Food brought us together around Mama's kitchen or the family table. Tree's children and my son were the second generations to gather in the kitchen and feast on traditional dishes, such as braised catfish and spring rolls. We are now at generation 3.0. I hope our family will always remember the sacrifices of those before us and that our stories live on in the foods prepared in the kitchen and presented at the table.

To eat is to survive, but to cook is to live.

In memory of Snow

Tree, Snow, and Dolly – Vietnam 2008

Ace and Christine

Christine and Van

Amy Chen, a friend, and Christine at Asian Garden Mall

Vietnamese Student Association – Western Washington
University
(Amy aka Christine aka Dolly is in the center, red áo dài)

Dolly at the ceramic shop with dog Nikki
and the haircut that made her cry.

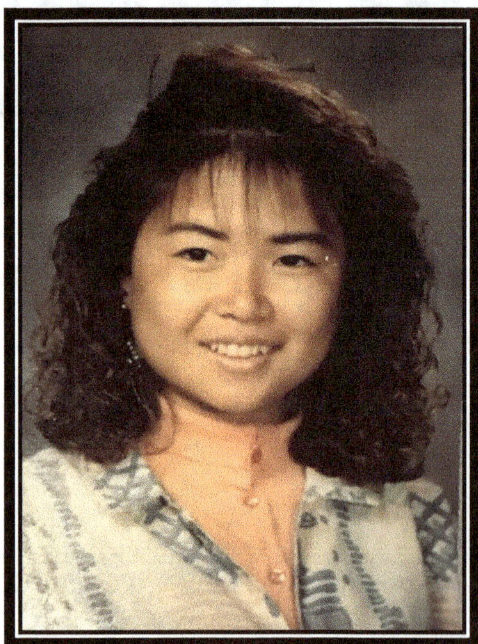

Amy Chen

Ace and Amy (aka Christine) in college

Ace and Amy (aka Christine) in college

Amy graduated from Hoquiam High School with honors

Amy and Snow on the first day at WWU campus

Snow graduated with OMD in acupuncture

Amy and Snow at a temple in Seattle,
dressed as queen and king

663

SNOW'S KITCHEN COOKBOOK

Dolly and Snow (August 2016)

Left to right: Derrick Adkins, Kristina Williams, Sarah "Too Sweet" Alpar

"I'm always more than happy to be Amy's guinea pig. She never disappoints! Even her experiments are tasty."
—Derrick "A-Game" Adkins, Raptor Jiu-Jitsu

"Amy is a true artist in the kitchen. Not only does her food look like a masterpiece it tastes like one as well!"
—Kristina "Warhorse" Williams, Professional MMA Fighter

"You can taste and smell what you're reading! Beautifully described and written."
—Sarah "Too Sweet" Alpar, UFC Fighter, Bantamweight

The rules are simple in Snow and Dolly's kitchen:

Rule #1: Always wash your hands.

Rule #2: Always be careful.

Rule #3: Always have a drink in your hand.

Cheers!

Contents

APPETIZERS & SIDES

Bánh Bao (Steamed Pork Buns)

Ingredients:

Dough:
1-16 ounce package Bột Bánh Bao (Steamed Dumpling Bun Flour)
*Follow the instructions on the package. You will need about 1/3
cup of sugar and water or milk to prepare the dough according to
the package.

Filling:
1.5 lbs ground pork
½ small sweet yellow onion (peeled & chopped)
½ cup dried wood ear mushrooms (softened in hot water, drained,
then chopped)
1 Chinese sausage (sliced thin diagonally into 10 pieces)
10+ quail eggs (hardboiled for 10 minutes, peeled)
*Substitute 2-3 hardboiled chicken eggs if you do not have quail
eggs. Cut each hardboiled egg into 3-4 wedges, enough for ten baos.

Marinade:
2 tablespoons oyster sauce
½ teaspoon sugar
½ teaspoon salt
¼ teaspoon ground black pepper

Other:
Steamer or a pot with a lid and flat-bottomed colander
Sheets of printer paper, cut into 10 circles, each about 3 inches wide
¼ cup flour for dusting the rolling pin and countertop
*If you do not have a rolling pin, use a highball drinking glass to
roll the dough. Whatever you do, don't use your beer can. Party
foul. That's for drinking, not rolling.

Directions:
1. Follow the instructions on the banh bao flour package and
    separate the dough into 10 equal balls, because seriously,
    who has time to make the dough from scratch?
2. Soak the wood ear mushrooms in a bowl of very hot water
    for 15 minutes. I like my water at 195 degrees F but you can
    eyeball it. (Kidding, don't stick your eyes into hot water.)
3. Drain and rinse the mushrooms, then chop into small
    pieces.

4. In a large bowl, combine ground pork, wood ear mushrooms, and chopped sweet yellow onions.

5. In a small bowl, mix the oyster sauce, sugar, salt, and black pepper. Taste the marinade and add more salt or sugar to your liking. (Now would be a good time to sip your wine or feel-good juice.)

6. Pour the marinade into the pork mixture and combine well. Separate the filling into 10 equal-sized balls.

7. Dust the countertop and rolling pin with flour. Roll each dough ball into a 4-inch circle.

8. For each dough circle, place pork, egg, and a slice of Chinese sausage in the center.

9. Gather up the edges of the dough to wrap the filling and twist the center point to seal the banh bao.

10. Place the banh bao onto a pre-cut sheet of paper.

11. Steam the banh bao in batches for 15-20 minutes. (This is a good time to have more wine.) If you do not have a steamer, bring a large pot of water to a boil. Place the baos in a flat colander and nestle it in a pot of water. Make sure the bottom of the colander is not sitting in water. Steam with the lid on.

12. The banh bao will almost double in size so do not crowd the steamer.

13. Carefully remove the baos and let them cool for a few minutes before eating. You must close your eyes when you eat these, so you don't see the calories or carbs you're consuming.

14. Wrap extra baos in plastic wrap and store in the fridge. When you're hankering for a bao, warm one up in the microwave or steamer.

Bánh Bèo (Steamed Rice Cakes)

Ingredients:

Dough:
1-12 ounce package Bột Bánh Bèo (Banh Beo Flour)

Toppings:
½ cup dried mung beans (soaked overnight then steamed until soft)
¼ cup dried shrimp (soaked in 2 cups hot water for 30 minutes, drain)
1 pound shrimp (deveined, chopped into small pieces, no shell)
½ pound pork belly (discard the skin & cut the pork into small pieces)
4 cloves garlic (minced)
4 shallots (minced)
½ cup green onions (chopped)
As needed: vegetable oil or bacon grease

Garnishes:
½ cup green onions (chopped)
¼ cup fried shallots/onions

Other:
10 ramekins or 15+ small ceramic saucers
Steamer or a pot with a lid and flat-bottomed colander
Pestle and mortar or food processor
Slotted spoon or ladle

Sweet Chili Fish Sauce:
¼ cup fish sauce
¾ cup coconut soda or water
¼ cup sugar
2 tablespoons lime juice
1 red chili pepper (minced) or 1 tablespoon chili sauce

Combine all the sauce ingredients into a bowl and mix. Taste the sweet chili fish sauce. It should be a balance between sweet and tangy. Add more sugar, fish sauce, or coconut soda if needed until the sauce reaches the flavor you desire.

Remember this recipe. Trust me, it's at the top of the V-ADED (Viet-All Day Ev'ry Day) food pyramid and a staple in Snow's Kitchen.

Directions:

1. STOP! Ask yourself. "Do I love them enough to make this for them?" This is a labor of love and if you answered no, find something else to make. If you answered yes, proceed.
2. Make sure you soak the dried mung beans overnight before starting.
3. Soak the dried shrimp in 2 cups of hot water for 30 minutes, then drain and grind up the dried shrimp in a food processor or with a pestle and mortar. Set aside in a bowl.
4. Drain and rinse the soaked mung beans then steam them until soft, about 20 minutes.
5. While the mung beans are in the steamer, prepare the sweet chili fish sauce by combining all the sauce ingredients into a bowl and mix.
6. Taste the sweet chili fish sauce. It should be a balance between sweet and tangy. Add more sugar, fish sauce, or coconut soda if needed until the sauce reaches the flavor you desire.
7. Ground the mung beans into a paste using a pestle and mortar or food processor. Set aside.
8. In a pan over medium-high heat, add a tablespoon of oil and stir-fry the pork belly pieces to render the fat.
9. Add minced garlic, minced shallots, and both dried and raw shrimp.
10. Stir-fry the shrimp and pork until both are cooked. Add additional vegetable oil or bacon fat if the pork belly does not render enough fat to fry the shrimp, onions, and garlic.
11. Add the ½ cup chopped green onions and mix well.
12. Using a slotted spoon or ladle remove the filling and set it aside in a bowl. You want the filling dry and crispy not oily and soggy.
13. Add the remainder of the green onions and shallots to the pan and fry in the greased pan for your garnish.
14. Prepare the steamed rice cakes according to the banh beo package. You will need to steam the cakes in batches.
15. Remove the steamed rice cakes and top each one with the shrimp and pork mixture. Sprinkle fried green onions and scallions on top to garnish.
16. Spoon the sweet chili fish sauce over the rice cakes and enjoy.

17. Reevaluate whether the people you fed these to are worthy of your efforts. If not, give them "MustGo" meals i.e. three-day-old leftovers in the fridge that must go.

676

Chả Giò (Egg Rolls)

Ingredients:

Wrappers:
1 package of egg roll wrappers (Each package comes with 25 sheets and can be found in the frozen section of most Asian grocery stores. Defrost for 15 minutes then ask your child to peel each wrapper into separate sheets.)
2 egg yolks, lightly beaten (Keep the whites for the filling.)

Filling:
1 pound lean ground pork or ground chicken
1 pound shrimp (peeled, deveined, lightly ground in a food processor)
(Substitute the meat and shrimp with fried tofu or portabella mushrooms for an alternative option.)
1 cup cabbage (chopped in a food processor)
1 cup carrots (chopped in a food processor)
Optional: 1 cup daikon (chopped in a food processor)
1 cup dried wood ear mushrooms or fresh mushrooms (soak the dried wood ear mushrooms in hot water for 15 minutes, then drain, and chop in a food processor)
2 egg whites
2 tablespoons pre-made sweet chili fish sauce (See page 137)
2 tablespoons granulated chicken flavor soup base mix (bouillon)
1 teaspoon ground black pepper
1 teaspoon salt

Dipping Sauces (optional to your preference):
pre-made sweet chili fish sauce or thick sweet chili dipping sauce
*To make your own sweet chili fish sauce, see the sauce ingredients for the Bánh Bèo (Steamed Rice Cakes) on page 137.

Oil:
peanut oil, avocado oil, sunflower oil, or any oil with a high smoke point. (You will need enough to fill a pot or pan 2 inches of oil to fry the egg rolls.)

Other:
silicone brush
food processor
paper towels

***Serve egg rolls with vermicelli noodles, other meats, veggies, and herbs for a nice meal. Be sure to drizzle sweet chili fish sauce on the noodles!**

Directions:

1. In a large bowl, combine all the filling ingredients EXCEPT the egg yolks. Set the yolks (not to be confused with yokes) aside in a small bowl.
2. Use your hands to mix the ingredients well, unless you're bougie and prefer a wooden spoon or spatula. My bougie meter depends on the length of my fingernails at the time of making these.
3. Place one egg roll wrapper on a plate and position the wrapper so that a corner is pointed at you in a diamond shape.
4. Spoon two tablespoons of the filling onto a sheet of egg roll wrapper an inch from the closest corner to you. Spread the filling out so it is two inches long, horizontally.
5. Roll the wrapper around the filling firmly by taking the corner closest to you and cover the filling. Roll and tuck the wrapper nice and tight to minimize air pockets.
6. Fold the side corners into the middle and continue rolling until you have an inch left at the end.
7. Use a silicone brush to moisten the end corner of the wrapper with a touch of the slightly beaten egg yolk wash. This will seal the egg roll. Use your finger if you're feeling like a Neanderthal.
8. It is super important you sip wine after each roll to celebrate your amazing accomplishment. After all the egg rolls have been rolled, you can fry them or freeze them in a plastic bag for later.
9. When you are ready to fry the egg rolls, heat the oil on medium heat in a pan or pot. The oil level should be two inches.
10. Once the oil is hot, fry the egg rolls in batches for 6-8 minutes until golden brown. Remove the egg rolls and let them rest on a plate lined with paper towels to soak up the excess oil.
11. Enjoy the egg rolls plain, with your choice of dipping sauces, or in a vermicelli noodle bowl with vegetables and herbs.

Chả Trứng (Egg Meatloaf)

Ingredients:

½ cup dried wood ear mushrooms (soaked in hot water for 15
minutes, then drained and chopped)
1 pound ground pork
½ pound shrimp (remove the shell, devein, and chop in a food
processor)
5 eggs (separate the yolks and whites)
4 shallots (minced)
1 carrot (chopped in a food processor)
3 cloves garlic (minced)
1 cup mung bean thread noodles (soaked in hot water for 15
minutes, then drained and cut into 1-inch pieces)
2 tablespoons fish sauce
1 tablespoon sugar
1 teaspoon salt
1 teaspoon ground black pepper

Other:
steamer or pot with a lid and flat-bottomed colander
parchment paper
silicone spatula
sweet chili fish sauce (See page 137)

Directions:
1. In a large bowl, mix all of the ingredients EXCEPT FOR <u>four</u> of the egg yolks.
2. Line a flat cake pan or deep plate with parchment paper – anything that will fit in the steamer.
3. Spread the meat evenly into the pan and smooth out the top surface.
4. Whisk the 4 egg yolks and pour them evenly over the meatloaf. Use a silicone spatula to spread the yolk so it covers all of the meat.
5. Place the meatloaf in a steamer. Cover and steam for 20 minutes.
6. Remove the lid making sure to not let the condensation drip onto the meatloaf. If you do, it's okay, just don't tell anyone.
7. Remove the steamed egg meatloaf and let it cool for 10 minutes before slicing into it.
8. Serve the meatloaf as a side to accompany rice and other meats and vegetables.
9. For extra flavor, drizzle sweet chili fish sauce on top. To make your own sweet chili fish sauce, refer to the sauce ingredients on page 137 under the Bánh Bèo (Steamed Rice Cakes) recipe.

Charcuterie Board

The possibilities are endless for this appetizer. Here are our favorites.

Ingredients:

Cheeses:
soft cheeses: triple cream brie, camembert, Couer de Chevre, Neufchatel
hard cheese: BellaVitano merlot, smoked gouda, cheddar, gruyere, manchego

Meats:
Peppered salami, pastrami, smoked salmon, pâté de foie gras, sausage

Nuts:
Cashews, macadamia, pistachios

Fruits:
champagne mangoes, kiwis, raspberries, blueberries, blackberries, strawberries, pineapples, persimmons, jackfruit, pears, mangosteens, pomegranates, apricots, figs, papayas, plums, sugar apples, lychees, grapes

Dips and Spreads:
hummus, garlic herb cream cheese, blackberry jam, cranberry orange relish, spinach and artichoke dip, pesto, avocado, orange marmalade, bruschetta, salmon dip

Crackers/Bread:
Kii Naturals Artisan Crisps, Triscuit crackers, Chicken in a Biskit, sourdough bread, French baguettes

Pickled:
green tomatoes, okra, peppers, olives, beets, jalapeno relish

Candy:
gummy bears, chocolate peanut butter cups, dark chocolates

Other:

mini pancakes topped with crème Fraiche and caviar (This is my son's favorite. I took him to a private caviar tasting experience when he was nine years old and there began his love affair with caviar.)

Chinese Barbecue Pork Hom Bao

Ingredients:

Dough:
1-16 ounce package Bột Bánh Bao (Steamed Dumpling Bun Flour)
*Follow the instructions on the package. You will need about 1/3
cup of sugar and water or milk to prepare the dough according to
the package.

Filling:
2-3 pounds pork shoulder, pork butt, or pork belly
¼ sweet yellow onion (diced)
2 cloves garlic (minced)
1 teaspoon salt
1 tablespoon olive oil or avocado oil

Marinade:
1 cup char siu sauce or char siu powder mix
2 tablespoon soy sauce
2 tablespoon oyster sauce
2 tablespoon honey
½ cup brown sugar
½ cup hoisin sauce
½ cup water
3 tablespoons cornstarch mixed with 2 tablespoons water

Other:
Steamer or a pot with a lid and flat-bottomed colander
Sheets of printer paper, cut into 10 circles, each about 3 inches wide
¼ cup flour for dusting the rolling pin and countertop
*If you do not have a rolling pin, use a highball drinking glass to
roll the dough.

Directions:
1. Follow the instructions on the banh bao flour package and
   separate the dough into 10 equal balls after the dough has
   risen.
2. While the dough rises, mix the first six ingredients of the
   marinade and taste. It should be sweet. Add more sugar or
   honey if you like a sweeter sauce.
3. Cut the pork into three sections and coat the pork in the
   marinade in a plastic bag for one hour.
4. Preheat the oven to 350 degrees.

5. Pour water into a roasting pan and put the pork onto a roasting rack. Place it in the pan, making sure the water level is below the pork.
6. Bake at 350 degrees F for 40 minutes.
7. In the meantime, spoon the residual marinade out of the bag and into a saucepan. Waste not, want not!
8. Add the last two ingredients in the marinade list (½ cup water and cornstarch/water mix) to the saucepan.
9. Bring the sauce to a boil then remove it from the heat and set it aside.
10. Once the pork in the oven is cooked, cut it into small bite-size cubes.
11. In a large saucepan, heat a tablespoon of oil and stir in the sweet yellow onion, garlic, and salt.
12. Add the marinade from the small saucepan to the large saucepan. Fold in the cubed pork and bring the sauce to a simmer until the meat is evenly coated and the sauce thickens to a jelly.
13. Set the pork aside to cool and continue thickening. You can put it in the freezer for 15 minutes to speed up the cooling.
14. Roll each dough ball into 4-inch circles. You can cover the dough with a cloth to keep it from drying out as you roll each ball.
15. Spoon the pork into the center of each circle and fold the dough up to the top. Pinch the peak with a twist to seal the hom bao.
16. Place the baos on a pre-cut sheet of paper and place the buns in the steamer or pot and flat-bottomed colander.
17. Steam for 10 minutes or until the dough is fluffy and cooked. Repeat until all the baos are cooked.
18. These freeze well. Wrap each bao in plastic wrap then aluminum foil and seal in a ziplock bag.
19. When you're feeling lazy to cook, take these out of the freezer, remove the aluminum foil, and microwave or steam them to eat. If you microwave them, drape a damp paper towel over the bao to lock in the moisture. A dry bao is an unhappy bao.

Gỏi Cuốn (Spring Rolls)

Spring rolls, like charcuterie boards, are versatile. What you roll in the rice paper is up to you! Here are our favorites. You cannot go wrong with any of the combinations from the list or make your own list.

Ingredients:

Meats:
pork butt or shoulder (marinated in your favorite seasonings, then
grilled)
*You can also boil the pork for a fresh, healthy option
shrimp (peeled, deveined, then boiled or grilled, and halved
lengthwise)
Chinese sausages (sliced into strips, then pan-fried)
pork belly (marinated in your favorite seasonings, then grilled)
cured ground pork a.k.a. nem nướng (See page 160 for a photo)
beef, chicken, or pork skewers (grilled)

Vegetables and herbs:
lettuce, cucumbers, pickled carrots and daikons, basil, bean sprouts,
mint, perilla, coriander, watercress, cilantro

Wrapper:
rice paper (I prefer square ones but round ones are good too.)

Sauces:
sweet chili fish sauce (See page 137. This is a V-ADED staple.)
Indonesian peanut salad dressing
hoisin sauce (diluted with water so it isn't so thick)
Sriracha sauce, chili peppers, or your favorite hot sauce for spiciness

Other:
Optional: fried egg roll wrappers for an extra crunch to your roll
(Take an egg roll wrapper, cut it into four squares, roll each square
into a cylinder, and then deep fry them. Make as many fried
wrapper rolls as you'd like for your spring rolls.)
vermicelli rice noodles (boil then drain the noodles as you would
with pasta according to package instructions)

Directions:

1. Boil, bake, or grill your favorite meats (or use meats from leftover "Must-Go" meals) and slice them into strips.
2. Wash your favorite herbs and slice your cucumbers into 4-6 inch strips.
3. Prepare the vermicelli rice noodles and fried egg roll wrappers if you're using them for your spring rolls.
4. Prepare a large bowl of hot water. This is for dunking the rice paper to soften it.
5. Dip a sheet of rice paper into the bowl of hot water and shake off the excess water. You do not want your rice paper soggy.
6. Place the wet rice paper onto a plate and add your veggies and meats, vermicelli noodles, and crunchy fried egg roll wrappers.
7. Once the rice paper is soft, roll your spring roll like a burrito and tuck in the sides.
8. Dip it into your favorite sauce. Enjoy!

Mango Couscous Salad

Ingredients:

1 cup large pearl couscous
2 tablespoons olive oil
2 garlic cloves (minced)
1 cup red onions (chopped)
Optional:1 bell pepper (chopped, seeds and ribs removed)
½ teaspoon salt
2 tablespoons lime juice
Optional: ½ cup raisins
Optional: 1 tomato (chopped)
½ cup basil, cilantro, or parsley (chopped)
Optional: vegetable broth
2 mangos (peeled, pitted, and cubed)
* I prefer champagne or honey mangos - they are sweet and not stringy

Directions:
1. Prepare the couscous according to the package directions. For a more flavorful couscous substitute the water with vegetable broth.
2. Heat the oil in a large pan and saute the garlic, onions, and bell peppers.
3. Sprinkle in the salt and lime juice.
4. Toss in the raisins, tomato, and cilantro, parsley, or basil.
5. Turn off the heat and fold in the mangos. Drain excess liquids.
6. Serve immediately.
7. So simple to make, you should have your child or partner do it so you can relax, drink your wine, or read a book.

Patê Sô (Vietnamese Meat Pies)

Ingredients:

Filling:
1.5 pounds lean ground pork
1 cup dried wood ear mushrooms
1 small onion (peeled and chopped)
2 tablespoons fish sauce
2 tablespoons garlic powder
2 tablespoons ground white pepper
1 teaspoon salt
Optional: sugar

Dough:
4 packages puff pastry (NOT phyllo dough. I repeat. Not phyllo dough.)
2-4 tablespoons oil (Olive, Avocado, Vegetable, or Coconut)
½ cup flour
2 eggs (lightly beaten)

Other:
baking sheet

Directions:
1. Defrost puff pastries for thirty minutes until the dough is soft.
2. Preheat oven to 400 degrees F.
3. In a medium-sized bowl filled halfway with water, microwave the water for two minutes or heat the water in a small pot on a stove.
4. Soak mushrooms in the hot water until soft, about 10 minutes.
5. Drain the water, rinse the mushrooms in cold water, and then chop the mushrooms into small pieces.
6. In a large mixing bowl, combine pork, mushrooms, onion, fish sauce, garlic powder, white pepper, and salt. Mix well.
7. Yippee, you get to do a taste test. Sauté a tablespoon of the filling in a frying pan and sample the flavor. If it is too salty, add a little sugar to the meat filling.
8. Roll the sheets of pastry puff dough onto a floured surface and cut the dough into 2-inch circles using a biscuit cutter or drinking glass.

9. Brush half of the dough circles with the lightly beaten egg wash. The other half of the dough circles will be the tops of the meat pies. The egg wash will make the pastry puff golden and extra flaky once baked.
10. Roll the filling into 1-inch balls and place each ball into the bottom halves of the dough circles.
11. Cover each meat pie with the other half of the dough circles.
12. Use a fork to seal the edges of the meat pies.
13. Brush the egg wash on the tops of each egg pie and put them onto a lightly oiled baking sheet. (I put parchment paper onto the baking sheet and coat it with oil.)
14. Bake at 400 degrees F for 20-25 minutes.
15. Enjoy the pies right away while they are warm and crispy. I like to toast the meat pies the next morning for breakfast with my coffee and pack them in my son and husband's lunch bag.

The perfect tailgate/stadium snack or lunch on the go!

Pork and Shrimp Wontons

Ingredients:

Filling:
1 package (14 ounces) cured ground pork for meatballs a.k.a. *nem mướng* and can be found in the frozen section of Asian markets. (You can make your own *nem mướng* if you're inclined. I go straight to the freezer section because I'm not getting any younger. Yep, the wrinkles are sagging as we speak.)
2 pounds shrimp (peeled, deveined, ground in a food processor)
1 cup dried wood ear mushrooms(soaked in hot water for 15 minutes until soft, then drained and chopped)
2 inches ginger (peeled and minced)
1 cup green onions (chopped)
2 tablespoons soy sauce
1 teaspoon of rice wine vinegar
2 teaspoons sesame oil
2 tablespoons cornstarch

Wrappers:
2 packages (16 ounces each) wonton wrappers (separated)
*Each package has around 85 wonton sheets. I prefer the yellow ones. This is a good job for the adult-in-training in your household.

Little child fingers are good at separating wrappers, but make sure those fingers are clean.

Other:
Optional: Peanut oil for deep frying the wontons (If you are steaming the wontons, no oil is needed.)
Optional: Steamer or pot with a lid and flat-bottomed colander

Directions:
1. Combine all the filling ingredients in a large bowl and mix well with a wooden spoon or your hands. (Are your fingernails trimmed?)
2. Put a cup of hot water into a mug. Don't drink it! The water is to seal the edges of the wonton wrappers.
3. Spoon a tablespoon of the filling into a wonton wrapper.
4. Using your finger or a silicone brush, wet the edges of the wonton wrapper with water to moisten edges.
5. Gather the edges together and press the sides together to seal the wontons. You can fold them like gyozas or be fancy and make stars.
6. Wontons can be steamed or deep-fried for 10 minutes and enjoyed in a noodle soup, as an appetizer, or as an accompaniment to rice and noodle bowls.
7. I freeze extra wontons to fry or steam later on those lazy days.
8. If you bite the wontons and notice the meat is pink, don't worry. The cured ground pork (*nem nướng*) has a tint of red due to the food coloring. But what are you biting it in half for? Pop the whole thing in your mouth already!

Salad Niçoise (French Summer Salad)

The French summer salad is traditionally made with tomatoes, hardboiled eggs, olives, and tuna. Feel free to add artichokes, capers, blanched green beans, radishes, potatoes, cucumbers, red onions, pickled okra, pinto beans, carrots, bell peppers, arugula or lettuce, and anything else you like.

Dressing:
¼ cup lemon juice or white wine vinegar
1 clove garlic (minced)
1 teaspoon Dijon mustard
¼ teaspoon of sea salt
¼ teaspoon ground black pepper
½ teaspoon honey
¼ cup olive oil
½ teaspoon fresh basil

Whisk together the dressing ingredients. Drizzle the vinaigrette over your perfect Niçoise.

MAIN COURSES

"I'm amazed by your culinary talent as much as by your writing. Your food posts are as intimate as your stories in your book."
—Hirut Negash, Instagrammer

Bánh Mì Sandwich (Vietnamese Baguette)

Ingredients:

French bread or baguette (toasted)
cucumber (sliced into thin strips)
cilantro (leaves and stem)
pâté
grilled pork or roasted chicken (I like the store-bought rotisserie chicken)
*See page 148 for a barbecue pork marinade from the Chinese Barbecue Pork Hom Bao recipe
soy sauce
optional: jalapenos or chili peppers, fresh or pickled (sliced thinly)
optional: hot sauce (e.g. Sriracha)
mayonnaise (regular or Vietnamese-style)
pickled carrots (shredded)
pickled daikons (shredded)

Vietnamese mayonnaise:
2 egg yolks
¾ cup vegetable oil
Pinch of salt

Directions for the mayonnaise:
1. Using a hand mixer, beat two egg yolks for one minute on medium-high speed.
2. Add one spoon of oil and continue beating for 30 seconds. Repeat this step until the oil is gone. You do not want the oil and eggs to separate.
3. Add a pinch of salt and mix in. This will yield a cup of fluffy, creamy mayonnaise, like whipped butter. Store in the fridge for up to 3 days.

Pickled carrots and daikons:
1 carrot, thinly sliced (peel and discard the skin)
1 daikon, thinly sliced (peel and discard the skin)
Vinegar
Sugar
Salt

Directions for pickling the carrots and daikons:
1. In a glass jar, put in the shredded carrots and daikon.
2. Fill the jar with distilled white vinegar.
3. Add equal amounts of salt and sugar, one teaspoon each at a time.
4. Stir and taste. Add more salt and sugar as needed until you get a tangy, sweet taste.
5. Seal the jar and refrigerate for a minimum of one hour before eating.

Assembling the sandwich:
1. Toast the baguette and slice it in half lengthwise.
2. Spread the mayonnaise on the top and bottom of the baguette. Don't be skimping on the mayonnaise now. Be generous.
3. Spread a thick layer of pâté on the bottom and work it into the bread like you're massaging the sandwich.
4. Drizzle some soy sauce on the top part of the sandwich. You have to give the top slice some love too. Balance is good.
5. Add slices of pork or chicken. If you're a glutton like me, you already added both. Yes, I see you.
6. Now comes the healthy stuff: cucumber slices, pickled carrots, and daikons. Don't forget the cilantro. Herbs need love too.
7. Finally, add some heat and do your hot chili/hot sauce dance.
8. Taste the nirvana in your mouth and say, "Hallelujah!"

Bánh Mì Bò Kho
(Braised Beef Stew with French Baguette)

Ingredients:

4 New York Steaks (cut into cubes)
French baguettes
2 tablespoons olive oil
4 cloves garlic (minced)
1 scallion (sliced)
2 carrots (peeled and cut 1-inch pieces)
1 large potato (peeled and cut into 1-inch pieces)
1 large sweet potato (peeled and cut into 1-inch pieces)

Marinade:
2 tablespoons soy sauce
2 tablespoons hoisin sauce
1 teaspoons salt
2 tablespoons Vietnamese Beef Stew Seasoning (Bột Bò Kho)

Broth:
32 ounces chicken broth (yes, chicken, even though this is beef stew)
1 12-fluid ounce can coconut soda
2 tablespoons tomato paste
1 tablespoon sweet soy sauce
1 medium yellow onion (peeled, cut in half)
2 inches ginger (peeled, minced)
2 stalks lemongrass (cut in half & tied together with string)
3 star anise
3 dried bay leaves

Garnishes (optional):
basil
cilantro (chopped)
red onions or scallions (sliced thin)
chili peppers (sliced)

Directions:
1. Crack open a bottle of beer or pop the cork. You're going to want to leisurely enjoy a beverage while making this.
2. Bring a pot of water to a boil and add the cubed New York Steaks. Boil for two minutes then drain and rinse the beef to remove the impurities. Don't be lazy and skip this step.

3. In a large bowl, whisk together soy sauce, hoisin sauce, salt, and beef stew seasoning. Taste and add more soy sauce or hoisin sauce according to your taste.
4. Toss in the cubed beef and marinate for thirty minutes.
5. In a large frying pan, heat the oil on medium-high heat. Add garlic and scallions. Stir-fry for ten seconds.
6. Add the marinated beef and its sauce. Reduce heat to medium.
7. Stir-fry the meat for 3-5 minutes. Meat should be evenly coated with the marinade and cooked to medium-well or well done.
8. Add chicken broth, coconut soda, tomato paste, sweet soy sauce, yellow onion, ginger, lemongrass, star anise, and bay leaves.
9. Increase temperature to medium-high and bring the broth to a boil. Once it begins to boil, cover the pot with a lid, and reduce the heat to low.
10. Simmer the broth for twenty minutes.
11. Add potatoes and carrots. Simmer, covered, for another 20 minutes.
12. Check the tenderness of the meat and vegetables. Simmer for another twenty minutes if you prefer more tenderness. Otherwise, turn off the stove.
13. Toast the French baguettes and serve on the side.
14. Spoon the stew into a bowl and garnish with cilantro, basil, and red onions or scallions.

"Can't get enough of Snow's Kitchen."
—Manuel Gonzales, General Sales Manager, RBDC

Bánh Xèo (Vietnamese Sizzling Crepes)

Ingredients:

¼ cup vegetable oil
sweet chili fish sauce (See page 137)

Batter:
2 green onions (thinly sliced)
1 package of bột bánh xèo flour mix (crepe flour mix)
*The flour mix will call for water but I do half and half of a
carbonated soda (e.g. club soda or coconut soda) and a light beer
(e.g. Bud Light).

*You can make your own batter by whisking together:
    1 cup rice flour
    1 tablespoon cornstarch
    1 teaspoon turmeric powder
    2 cups club soda or coconut soda
    1 cup light beer
    1/2 cup coconut milk
    1 teaspoon salt

Filling:
1 pound boneless country-style pork shoulder or pork belly (thinly
sliced)
1 pound medium-size shrimp (peeled, deveined)
1 small onion or scallion (peeled, halved, and thinly sliced)
2 cups bean sprouts

Sides:
mustard leaves, red-leaf lettuce, or romaine lettuce
1 cucumber (cut into 3-4 inch spears)
cilantro, mint, perilla, fish wort, and/or basil
chili peppers or hot sauce
rice paper (if you prefer to make it a crepe spring roll)

Other:
very good non-stick frying pan or cast-iron pan.
silicone brush

Directions:

1. Prepare the batter according to the instructions on the bánh xèo flour mix or make your batter from scratch if you're not lazy like me.
2. Add chopped green onions to the batter and refrigerate the batter uncovered for a minimum of 30 minutes.
3. Heat a good cast-iron pan or non-stick frying pan on medium-high heat. If your pan is not good, add a little oil to the pan.
4. Once the pan is hot, add one-fourth of the sliced pork. Reduce heat to medium-low and stir-fry the meat for three minutes.
5. Transfer the pork into a bowl and repeat stir-frying the rest of the meat in batches. Do not let the pan burn. Stir constantly.
6. Do not crowd the pan. You want each slice of meat to be crisp. Transfer all the cooked meat to a bowl.
7. Add the shrimp to the pan and stir-fry for another few minutes until cooked. Transfer the shrimp to a separate bowl.
8. Remove the batter from the refrigerator and whisk the batter until it is evenly mixed.
9. Turn the heat up to medium. Once the pan is hot, add a few pieces of onion slices (or scallions), a couple of pork pieces, a couple of shrimps, and a sprinkle of bean sprouts.
10. Ladle some batter into the frying pan and cover the pan evenly and thinly with the batter. (The thinner the better so that it is crispy.)
11. Cover the pan and let it sizzle for 2-3 minutes.
12. Once the edges start to lift and turn light brown, remove the lid.
13. Using a small silicone brush, brush the edges with vegetable oil and let some of the oil seep under the crepe batter.
14. Lower the heat a touch if you need to and pan-fry uncovered for another three minutes.
15. Fold the crepe in half with a spatula and transfer the crepe to a plate. It is best to eat one straight from the pan while the crepe is crunchy.
16. Repeat with the rest of the batter and filling until you run out. Make sure you stir and mix your batter each time as the flour settles to the bottom.

17. Serve the crepes with vegetables and herbs of your choice. Drizzle sweet chili fish sauce on top. (See page 137.)
18. If you prefer, you may roll your crepe in softened rice paper or lettuce and dip the roll into the sweet chili fish sauce like a spring roll.

Bò Bougie Ngon (Beouf Bourgignon)

Ingredients:

2 tablespoons olive oil or ghee
1 package bacon (cut into 2-inch strips)
3 pounds of beef brisket, sirloin, New York steak, or chuck roast
(cut into 2-inch cubes)
2 carrots (peeled, cut into bite-size pieces)
2 sweet yellow onions (minced) or 2 bags of pearl onions (remove
skin)
*You can use a combination of both sweet yellow onions and pearl
onions
2 tablespoons garlic (minced)
1 tablespoon salt
1 teaspoon ground black pepper
3 tablespoons flour
1 pound of mushrooms (sliced)
1 tablespoon butter

Broth:
2 bottles of red wine – although you'll only use 3 cups of it for the
broth. The rest is to keep you company while you cook and eat.
Burgundy wines are best. I prefer pinot noir and merlot wine in the
$15-20 range. Do not use cheap wines for this exquisite stew
otherwise, it will not be "bougie ngon."
32 ounces of beef broth
6 ounce can tomato paste
2 tablespoons beef bouillon (I prefer Better Than Bouillon
Premium Roasted Beef Base)
2 bay leaves

Garnish:
¼ cup fresh parsley (chopped)

Sides:
starchy foods like noodles, rice, mashed potatoes, baguettes, or
polenta

Other:
large pot or dutch oven
slotted spatula or spoon

Directions:

1. Heat the oil or ghee in the pot or dutch oven over medium-high heat and saute the bacon until crisp. Remove the bacon with a slotted spoon.
2. Sear the beef in the bacon grease for one minute on each side. Do this in batches. Do not crowd the pan. Remove the beef and set it aside with the bacon.
3. Saute the carrots, onions, and garlic in the same pot for 3 minutes. Add the beef and bacon back to the pot or dutch oven.
4. Sprinkle salt, black pepper, and flour onto the beef and stir fry.
5. Add 3 cups of wine, the beef broth, the tomato paste, and beef bouillon base to the pot.
6. Stir until the tomato paste is mixed evenly into the broth.
7. Add the bay leaves.
8. Bring to a boil and let it boil for 3-5 minutes.
9. Reduce heat to low, cover the pot, and let it simmer for two hours. This is when you enjoy the extra wine you purchased. Check the sauce after one hour. It should start to thicken. Sample the broth.
10. At the two hour mark, taste the broth and sample the beef. It should be tender and bursting with flavor.
11. In a pan, heat the butter and stir-fry the mushrooms for five minutes.
12. Add the mushrooms to the dutch oven. Cover with the lid. Turn off the heat and let it sit for five minutes.
13. Garnish with parsley and serve with your favorite starchy food.

Bò Lúc Lắc (Shaken Beef)

Ingredients:

1.5 pounds beef brisket or sirloin (cut into 1-inch cubes)
1 red onion (peeled, thinly sliced)
2 bunches of watercress or arugula
2 tomatoes (thinly sliced)
2 tablespoons cooking oil

Marinade:
4 cloves garlic (minced)
1.5 tablespoons sugar
2 tablespoons oyster sauce
1 tablespoon fish sauce
1 tablespoon sesame oil
1 teaspoon thick sweet soy sauce

Vinaigrette dressing:
½ cup rice vinegar
1.5 tablespoons sugar
½ tablespoon salt

Directions:
1. Prepare the marinade by mixing the six ingredients in a medium-size bowl.
2. Stir in the beef and coat the meat evenly in the marinade. Let it sit for a minimum of 30 minutes but ideally an hour.
3. Meanwhile, mix the vinaigrette dressing ingredients and taste. It should be a balance of sweet, salty, and tangy.
4. Pour half of the vinaigrette over the thinly sliced onions and let it sit for 30 minutes in the fridge, covered in plastic wrap, to pickle.
5. Prepare a bed of watercress or arugula on a serving plate and put slices of tomatoes on top. Cover and refrigerate until you are ready to serve the dish.
6. Heat a frying pan over medium-high heat with cooking oil. Once the oil is hot, add the beef in batches to the frying pan. Sear the beef for two minutes.
7. After two minutes, shake your bootie and the frying pan at the same time to sear the other sides of the beef for another two minutes.

8. If you do not shake your bootie, you're doing it wrong and your shaken beef will not turn out delicious. That is the secret.
9. Repeat steps 6 and 7 until all the beef is cooked to your desired doneness. I prefer medium-rare.
10. Spoon the beef onto the bed of tomatoes and watercress or arugula. You can toss the extra juice in the pan or drizzle it on top of the beef and salad. I drizzle the juice and a few tablespoons of the vinaigrette dressing on top of the beef!
11. Add the pickled onions on top and enjoy your shaken beef. I smother my salad in the vinaigrette dressing!

Bún Riêu Cua (Crab Vermicelli Soup)

Ingredients:

1 package rice vermicelli noodles
2 pounds pork spare ribs
1 - 3 ounce package dried shrimp
2 tsp salt
1 large lump rock sugar
¼ cup fish sauce
1 small whole onion (peeled, quartered)
12 jumbo prawns (peeled, deveined)
1 pound ground pork
4 cloves garlic
2 tablespoon mushroom seasoning powder
1 teaspoon ground black pepper
1 - 5.6 oz can minced prawn in spices (gia vị nấu bún riêu)
1 - 14 oz can minced crab in spices (riêu cua)
1+ lb crab meat
3 eggs beaten
1 - 20 ounce container fried tofu (cut in half)
6 large Roma tomatoes (quartered)

Herbs and Garnishes:
*Optional – pick and choose your favorite herbs
cilantro (chopped)
green onions (chopped)
perilla leaves (remove stems)
watercress (chopped into 1-inch pieces)
bean sprouts (rinsed)
lime (sliced into six wedges)

Other:
food processor

Directions:
1. Bring a large pot of water to a boil on high heat.
2. Add the pork spare ribs to the pot and bring to boil for 5 minutes.
3. Drain and rinse the pork.
4. Start a fresh pot of water, filled ¾ full, and add the pork back in along with dried shrimp.

5. Bring the water back to a boil, then lower the heat to medium to simmer.
6. Add salt, rock sugar, and fish sauce to the pot.
7. In a food processor, chop together the onion, prawns, and garlic.
8. In a large bowl, combine the ground pork with the prawns.
9. Sprinkle in the mushroom seasoning powder and black pepper to the bowl.
10. Add the entire can of minced prawn in spices, can of minced crab in spices, crab meat, and beaten eggs into the bowl.
11. Mix well, then spoon the pork, shrimp, and crab mixture into the pot of simmering water, pork ribs, and dried shrimp.
12. Let the broth simmer for twenty minutes without the lid.
13. Meanwhile, bring a fresh pot of water to a boil and cook the vermicelli noodles. Once it is cooked, drain the noodles and rinse.
14. Add the fried tofu and tomatoes into the simmering broth and let it simmer for another ten minutes.
15. Taste the broth. Add more salt if needed or a touch of sugar or another rock sugar if it is too salty. If the broth is a little on the salty side, it's okay, as it will balance out once you eat it with vermicelli noodles and lime.
16. To serve, put noodles into a bowl. Spoon the crab soup into the bowl. Garnish with your favorite herbs.
17. Squeeze a lime wedge into the broth and enjoy.

Cá Kho Tộ (Caramelized Braised Catfish)

Ingredients:

2 pounds catfish filets (bone-in, skin on)
3 tablespoons salt to clean the fish
3 tablespoons oil
6 cloves garlic (minced)
1 small onion (minced)
1 bunch green onions (chopped)
2 teaspoons salt
2 teaspoons ground black pepper
1 tablespoon thick caramelized soy sauce
3 tablespoons fish sauce
1 can coconut soda

Optional:
chili peppers (sliced) or flakes
large clay pot
*I use a large saucepan to braise the catfish, then transfer it to a clay pot once the fish and sauce reduces down and is cooked. It is traditional to cook and serve the braised catfish in a clay pot.

Sides:
cooked jasmine rice

Other:
Optional: clay pot, otherwise, a large saucepan works great

Directions:
1. Sprinkle 3 tablespoons of salt on the catfish filets and rub the salt all over the fish. Rinse in warm water and pat dry with a paper towel.
2. Marinate the catfish in salt, black pepper, fish sauce, and thick caramelized soy sauce for five minutes.
3. In a large saucepan, heat the oil on medium-high heat.
4. Open the windows and turn on the fan. It will smell pungent but I promise the braised catfish will be so delicious.
5. Stir-fry the garlic and onions for 2 minutes. Reduce the heat to medium.
6. Add the catfish filets to the saucepan. Do not crowd the pan.

7. Pour in the coconut soda and cover with a lid. Simmer for ten minutes.
8. If anyone asks what the smell is, blame it on them, your pet, child, or spouse.
9. Gently flip the catfish filets over and simmer another ten minutes with the lid on, over medium heat.
10. Taste the sauce. It should be a balance of sweet and salty. Add salt or sugar as needed.
11. Remove the lid and continue simmering. Spoon the sauce over the fish repeatedly for ten minutes.
12. Garnish with green onions. If you like it spicy, add chili peppers or chili flakes.
13. Turn off the heat, put the lid on, and let it continue to cook for another 5-10 minutes.
14. Optional – transfer the catfish and sauce to a clay pot.
15. Serve the catfish with a bed of jasmine rice.

"Food is AMAZING, packed full of flavor, and definitely made from love."
—Frances Moore, Foodie

Cà Ri Gà (Yellow Curry Chicken)

"Amy's sweet potato and chicken curry is like a warm hug on a cold rainy day! My favorite!"
—**Leah Dimino, Real Estate Agent**

Ingredients:

Marinade:
1 pound chicken breast tenders (cut into 1-inch pieces)
1 pound boneless chicken thighs (fat trimmed, cut into 1-inch pieces)
1 tablespoons salt
1 tablespoon sugar
1 teaspoon ground black pepper
2 tablespoons granulated chicken flavor soup base mix (or chicken bouillon)
2 tablespoons yellow curry powder or curry base
2 stalks lemongrass (mince 2 tablespoons of it and set aside for the marinade)

*You'll need **two stalks of lemongrass** total. Two tablespoons of minced lemongrass will go into the marinade and the remainder will go into the curry broth

Curry broth:
2 tablespoons olive oil
2 inches ginger (peeled and minced)
2 cloves garlic (peeled and minced)
1 small scallion or sweet onion (chopped)
32-ounce chicken broth
2-14.5 fluid ounce cans coconut cream/coconut milk
2 stalks lemongrass (with the remainder of the lemongrass, cut both stalks in half and smash the ends with a mortar and pestle to release the aroma and flavors. Tie the stalks together.)
2 tablespoons sugar
1 large sweet potato (peeled and cubed)
2 carrots (peeled and cubed)
2 large russet potatoes (peeled and cubed)

Optional garnish:
cilantro (chopped)

Sides:
French baguettes (toasted)
cooked jasmine rice (cooked)
rice noodles (cooked, drained)

Directions:

1. Mix the first eight ingredients and marinate for thirty minutes in the refrigerator.
2. In a wok or pot, heat olive oil on medium-high heat.
3. Add ginger, garlic, and scallions. Stir fry for two minutes.
4. Add marinated chicken. Lower heat to medium. Stir fry the chicken until it is cooked, about five minutes.
5. Add chicken broth, coconut cream, sugar, and stalks of lemongrass.
6. Increase heat to medium-high and cook for 10 minutes uncovered, stirring often.
7. Add sweet potatoes, carrots, and russet potatoes. Stir.
8. Lower the heat to medium.
9. Cover the pot with a lid and let it simmer for 20 minutes.
10. Taste the curry and add more salt or sugar according to taste.
11. Once the vegetables and chicken are tender, serve the curry in a bowl and garnish with cilantro.
12. Ladle a serving into a secret-stash container and hide this from everyone. The curry will go fast and when everyone is sad it is gone, you'll have your secret stash for the final meal! Worth the secret!
13. Serve with rice, rice noodles, or a toasted baguette. (I prefer dipping my warm, toasted baguette in the curry.)

Cháo Hải Sản (Seafood Congee)

Congee is also called rice porridge and is often cooked with chicken. The seafood congee is not as commonly known, but it is great comfort street food. I like mine with clams and shrimp.

Ingredients:

2-32 ounce box chicken broth
2 cups water
2 cups jasmine rice (washed and drained a few times until the water
is clear)
2 tablespoons olive oil
2 tablespoons scallions (peeled and minced)
2 cloves garlic (minced)
2 tablespoons ginger (peeled and minced)
1 pound large shrimp (peeled, deveined)
2-3 cups clam meat (cooked, no shell)*
¼ cup green onions (chopped)
¼ cup cilantro (chopped)
salt and black pepper to taste
2 tablespoons fried onions (optional)
2 tablespoons fried garlic (optional)

*If you can find clam meat without shells in the frozen section of
most grocery stores, that is best. Otherwise, steam your clams until
they are cooked. It is optional to leave the clams in the shells.

Directions:

1. Pour all the chicken broth and 2 cups water into a large pot
   and bring to a boil on medium-high heat.
2. Meanwhile, wash the jasmine rice to remove excess starch
   and drain. Repeat until the water runs clear.
3. Once the broth comes to a boil, add the jasmine rice to the
   pot and stir constantly so it does not stick.
4. Reduce heat to low, cover the pot with a lid, and let the rice
   simmer. Stir every ten minutes to make sure the rice is not
   burning or clumping together.
5. Heat the olive oil in a frying pan on medium heat.
6. Add the scallions, garlic, and ginger, and stir fry for two
   minutes to release the fragrance.
7. Add the shrimp and sauté for 3-5 minutes until the shrimp
   is no longer translucent.
8. Add the clams and stir-fry the ensemble for three minutes.
9. Turn off the stove and set the shrimp and clams aside.
10. Stir the rice every ten minutes to make sure the rice is not
    clumping or burning at the bottom.

11. Continue simmering with the lid on for an hour, checking every ten minutes.
12. After an hour, your congee is done. The rice should be broken and mushy like porridge. Add more water if you prefer your congee more brothy than thick.
13. Turn off the heat and fold the shrimp and clam mixture into the pot of congee, including the juices, garlic, onions, and ginger.
14. Add salt and pepper to taste.
15. Garnish with cilantro and green onions.
16. Optional garnishes: Top with fried onions and/or fried garlic for a little crunch.

"I always look forward to your food. Hands down the best! Hmmm!"

—Jeff Cole, Operations Manager, Red Bull Distribution Company

Chili

Ingredients:

Vegetables:
1 red bell pepper (minced)
1 orange bell pepper (minced)
2 stalks celery (minced)
1 onion (minced)
1 jalapeno pepper (minced with seeds)
3 cloves garlic (minced)

Canned/Bottled Ingredients:
2 tablespoons hot sauce
2 cans ranch style chili beans with the liquid
1 can red kidney beans (drained)
2 cans diced tomatoes with the liquid
1 small 6-ounce can tomato paste

Meats:
1 pound bacon (fried, save the bacon grease)
2-3 pounds lean ground beef
5 Italian sausages (cut into ½ inch pieces)

Seasonings:
3 tablespoons chili powder
1 tablespoon dried oregano
1 teaspoon cumin
1 teaspoon parsley (fresh or dried)
1 teaspoon basil (fresh or dried)
1 teaspoon garlic salt
1teaspoon black pepper
1 teaspoon cayenne pepper
1 teaspoon paprika
1 teaspoon red chili flakes
1 tablespoon sugar
1 tablespoon Worcestershire sauce (worsty-shir-shir thing)
2 tablespoons beef bouillon powder or concentrate

Garnishes/Toppings:
cilantro (chopped)
sour cream
cheddar cheese (shredded)
avocado (cubed)

cheddar cheese-flavored Fritos
bacon (crumbled)

Side:
Jiffy Corn Bread Muffin Mix or your favorite cornbread recipe

Directions:
1. Toss the first six vegetable ingredients into a food processor and chop on low until minced evenly. Dump it all into a large slow cooker, crockpot, or dutch oven.
2. Add the next five ingredients into the slow cooker, i.e., your favorite hot sauce, chili beans with liquids, kidney beans (drained), diced tomatoes with liquids, and tomato paste.
3. On medium-high heat, in a large frying pan, fry up all the bacon and set aside. Use paper towels to soak up the excess fat of the cooked bacon.
4. Reduce heat to medium, keeping the bacon grease in the pan.
5. Add the ground beef and Italian sausages to the pan. Use a blunt wooden spoon to break up the meat until it is cooked thoroughly and in small bits.
6. Use a slotted ladle or spoon and transfer the ground up meats into the slow cooker. Discard the excess fat and liquid in the pan.
7. Divide the cooked bacon in half and crumble the bacon into small pieces. Half will go into the slow cooker, half will be used as a garnish.
8. Add all the seasonings into the slow cooker, crockpot, or dutch oven.
9. Stir and mix the ingredients evenly. Cook on high for five hours in the slow cooker or simmer on low on the stove, with the lid on, for five hours. Check every hour if you are cooking the chili on the stovetop. Stir frequently to make sure the chili is not burnt or clumping at the bottom.
10. Serve the chili with your choice of toppings: cilantro, cheddar cheese, sour cream, avocado, bacon crumbles, and/or cheddar cheese-flavored Fritos.
11. Be prepared to enjoy this crack chili because it tastes better the next day!

Cơm Chiên (Fried Rice)

Ingredients:

2 cups uncooked jasmine rice
4 tablespoons bacon grease or vegetable oil
3 Chinese sausages (diced)
3 large eggs (lightly beaten)
3 cloves garlic (minced)
1 pound large shrimp (peeled, deveined)
½ cup carrots (peeled, diced)
2 tablespoons soy sauce seasoning (I use Maggi brand)
salt and pepper to taste

Other:
rice cooker
wok or large saucepan
colander
slotted spoon
wooden spoon or spatula

Directions:
1. Wash the rice in water and drain the water. Repeat until the water runs clear.
2. Put the jasmine rice into a rice cooker pot. Cook the rice **al dente**. Add fresh water to the pot and use your middle finger to measure the water level. With the tip of your finger resting on top of the rice, the water level should be below the first joint of your finger (about ¾ of your finger is submerged in water). **Note:** To make the perfect rice, fill the water to the first joint line of your finger, but for fried rice, cook al dente.
3. Once the rice is done, unplug the rice cooker and let it cool.
4. Once the rice is cool, use a spoon to stir up the rice. It should be on the dry side. Store the rice in the refrigerator for 4+ hours.
5. Spoon a tablespoon of oil or bacon grease (preferred) into a frying pan and heat the grease on medium-high heat.
6. Once the grease is hot, add the diced Chinese sausages and stir-fry for a few minutes until the sausage is cooked – about five minutes.
7. Using a slotted spoon, scoop out the cooked Chinese sausages into a large bowl. Reserve any excess grease in the frying pan.

8. Add another spoon of grease or oil to the pan and add the lightly beaten eggs. Hard-scramble the eggs with a wooden spoon or spatula.

9. Remove the eggs and add them to the same bowl as the Chinese sausages. Reserve any excess grease in the frying pan.

10. Spoon a tablespoon of the bacon grease or vegetable oil into the same frying pan and add the minced garlic cloves and shrimp. Sauté until the shrimp is almost cooked.

11. Add the diced carrots and continue sautéing until the shrimp is cooked and the carrots are soft.

12. Remove the carrots and shrimp and add them to the bowl with the sausages and eggs.

13. Add the last tablespoon of bacon grease or oil into the pan and add the cold rice by breaking it up with your hands. There should be no clumps. Crumble and separate the rice kernels.

14. Add soy sauce and continue stir-frying until the rice is evenly coated and uniform in color. Add more soy sauce if needed.

15. Sprinkle salt and pepper to the fried rice. Mix and taste. Add more according to your taste.

16. Drain any excess juices from your bowl of Chinese sausages, eggs, carrots, and shrimp through a colander so that it is dry.

17. Dump the bowl of sausages, eggs, carrots, and shrimp into the pan/wok.

18. Stir-fry and mix evenly, then turn off the heat. Let the rice cool down a little before serving.

Mì Sài Gòn (Saigonese Egg Noodle Soup)

Ingredients:

Chinese Barbecue Pork:
½ cup Chinese barbecue char siu seasoning mix
½ cup water
½ cup soy sauce
2 pounds pork loin

Broth:
2 pounds pork bones
½ package of dried squid
1-3 ounce package dried shrimp
1 sweet yellow onion
7 ounces sweet radish (about 4 pieces)
salt and sugar to taste

Other:
20 large prawns (peeled, deveined)
sesame oil
yellow egg noodles
baby bok choy (washed thoroughly)

Garnishes:
green onions (chopped)
basil
sawtooth herb (chopped)

Optional:
steamed pork and shrimp wontons (See page 159.)

Directions:
1. Preheat the oven to 370 degrees.
2. In a large bowl, whisk together the Chinese barbecue Char Siu seasoning mix, water, and soy sauce.
3. Add the pork loins to the mixture and marinate for 30 minutes.
4. Place the marinated pork loins on a non-stick baking sheet, roasting pan, or rectangular glass baking pan.
5. Pour the excess barbecue sauce on top of the pork.

6. Bake for 30 minutes. Turn the pork over and bake another 15 minutes. Turn off the oven and leave the pork in the oven for fifteen minutes.
7. Slice the pork into strips and set aside on a platter.
8. In a large pot, add pork bones, dried squid, dried shrimp, yellow onion, and sweet radishes.
9. Fill the pot with water leaving two inches at the top.
10. Bring the pot to a boil and remove the scum with a ladle.
11. Reduce heat to low and let the broth simmer for an hour uncovered. Continue removing the scum as needed until the broth looks clear.
12. Add salt and sugar to desired taste. The broth should be semi-sweet.
13. Bring a small pot of water to a boil and cook the prawns in the water for five minutes. Turn off the heat and let the prawns continue to cook in the hot water for five minutes.
14. Drain the shrimp into a colander and add them to the platter with the pork.
15. Fill a large pot half full with water and bring it to a boil.
16. Add a tablespoon of sesame oil to the water and the egg noodles.
17. Cook the noodles for 2-4 minutes, stirring constantly. Do not allow the noodles to stick. You will want the noodles **al dente**.
18. Drain the noodles and rinse under cool water.
19. Drizzle 1-2 tablespoons of sesame oil onto the noodles and toss to coat evenly.
20. Turn off the stove and cover the broth with a lid. Let it sit for 15 minutes.
21. Strain the broth through a colander into another large pot. Save the pork bones. Once the bones are cool to the touch, pick off the meat and add them to the platter with the prawns and barbecue pork.
22. Discard the onion, dried shrimp, dried squid, and sweet radishes.
23. Return the broth to the stove and let it simmer with the lid on.
24. Wash the baby bok choy then steam them for 10-15 minutes until tender.

25. Add the bok choy to the vegetable platter alongside the chopped green onions, chopped sawtooth herbs, and basil leaves.
26. Prepare your egg noodle soup bowl with egg noodles, pork, shrimp, wontons (optional), bok choy, and garnishes.
27. Ladle hot broth into the bowl and enjoy!

Phở (Vietnamese Beef Noodle Soup)

Phở broth is traditionally slow-simmered in a pot for hours but thanks to the instant pot, the same delicious broth can be done in less than three hours.

Broth:
½ pound beef bones with marrow
3 pounds oxtail (cut into 1 inch thick pieces)
2 inches ginger (peeled)
1 medium sweet yellow onion (peeled)
1 tablespoon salt
1 package pho seasoning (I use Pho Hoa Pasteur. It comes in a red
2 oz. box. Inside there are two packets. You will need only one.)
¾ cup fish sauce (I use Viet Huong fish sauce. It comes in a 24 fl.
oz. bottle with a pink label and a picture of three crabs.)

Meats (all optional to your preference):
1 pound ribeye beef (thinly sliced)
1 pound eye of round beef (thinly sliced)
oxtail from above in the broth section
tripe (cooked strips)
Vietnamese beef meatballs (bò viên)

Herbs and Garnishes (all optional to your preference):
soybean sprouts
peppermint or spearmint leaves
Thai basil leaves
fish wort
perilla leaves
cilantro
chili peppers
limes (cut into 6-8 wedges)

Condiments (all optional):
hoisin sauce (I use Lee Kum Kee hoisin sauce with a purple label.)
fresh chili peppers (sliced) or hot chili sauce (I use Sriracha.)

Noodles:
14 oz, package rice (pho) stick noodles (3 mm wide)

Other:
large 8 qt. Instant Pot
colander

Directions:

1. Fill a large pot half full with water and bring to a boil on high heat.
2. Add beef bones and oxtails to the pot.
3. Boil for five minutes to remove the impurities.
4. Drain into a large colander and wash the bones and oxtail in cold water.
5. In a large Instant Pot (or large pot if you do not have an Instant Pot) add the beef bones, oxtail, ginger, onion, salt, a package of pho seasoning (Pho Hoa Pasteur), fish sauce, and 16 cups of water.
   **I have an Instant Pot Ultra 8 quart multicooker.
   Set the Instant Pot to Pressure Cook on high for one hour.
   **It will take 30+ minutes for the Instant Pot to reach pressure cook temperature, plus one hour of pressure cooking.
   If you are cooking the broth the traditional method, in a pot on the stove, bring the broth to a boil on medium-high heat. Then reduce the heat to low and let simmer, covered, for 4-6 hours, until the oxtail meat is tender and falls off the bone.)
6. Cook the pho rice noodles according to the package by placing the noodles in a pot of boiling water for 6-8 minutes until cooked. Then drain and rinse in cold water.
7. Wash all your herbs and garnishes and set them aside on a platter.
8. Once the Instant Pot is done cooking, unplug it and let it rest for 45 minutes. Release the steam after 45 minutes of resting.
9. Bring a pot of water to a boil and flash cook your meats (thinly sliced ribeye beef, the eye of round, tripe, and meatballs) for 2-5 minutes.
10. Drain and rinse the meats. Set aside on a platter.
11. Assemble your pho bowl with noodles, meats, and garnishes.
12. Ladle hot pho broth into your bowl and squeeze a wedge of lime juice on top.
13. Add your desired condiments.

Spicy Red Curry Shrimp

Ingredients:

2 tablespoons butter
6 cloves garlic (minced)
3 tablespoons ginger (minced)
3 tablespoons red or yellow curry paste
2 teaspoons fish sauce
1 cup chicken broth
3 tablespoons sugar
1 can coconut cream
½ can tomato sauce
2 pounds pre-cooked shrimp
2 red, orange, or yellow bell peppers (chopped)
1 cup green onions (chopped)

Optional:
fresh chili peppers or dried chili flakes

Sides:
sourdough bread, French baguette, or rice

Directions:
1. In a saucepan, on medium-high heat, melt the butter.
2. Add minced garlic and ginger. Stir-fry for two minutes.
3. Add curry paste and fish sauce. Mix well.
4. Add chicken broth and sugar. Mix until the sugar dissolves evenly.
5. Pour in a whole can of coconut cream and half a can of tomato sauce. Don't be shy!
6. Taste the sauce and add a splash of fish sauce or teaspoon of sugar according to your taste.
7. If you'd like the sauce to be spicier, add the chili peppers or flakes.
8. Add the bell peppers and simmer for five minutes.
9. Add the shrimp and simmer for another five to ten minutes.
10. Stir in half of the green onions and reserve the other half to garnish.
11. Dip your bread in the curry or enjoy the curry over rice.

Thịt Kho Tàu (Caramelized Pork & Eggs)

Ingredients:

2 pounds boneless country-style pork shoulder or pork belly (cubed
into 1-inch pieces)
*You can do half shoulder and half pork belly
6 hard-boiled eggs (shell peeled)
2 tablespoons caramel cooking sauce or sweet soy sauce
½ cup fish sauce
12 fluid ounce can of coconut soda
2 teaspoons salt
2 teaspoons sugar
1 teaspoon ground black pepper

Garnish:
green onions (chopped)

Side:
jasmine rice (cooked)
pickled veggies (e.g. mustard greens)

Directions:
1. In a medium-size pot, bring 8 cups of water to a boil on
   high heat.
2. Add the eggs and boil for five minutes.
3. At the five minute mark, add the cubed pork and let the
   pork and eggs boil together for another five minutes.
4. Drain and rinse the eggs and pork in cold water until both
   are cool to the touch.
5. Peel the eggshells and set the hard-boiled eggs aside.
6. In another pot, add 8 cups of water and bring to a boil.
7. Add the cooked pork to the pot and reduce the heat to
   medium.
8. Add fish sauce, coconut soda, salt, sugar, and caramel
   cooking sauce.
9. Stir and reduce heat to a low. Taste the broth and add more
   salt or sugar according to your preference.
10. Simmer on low, uncovered, for twenty minutes.
11. Add the hard-boiled eggs and simmer for another 20
    minutes.
12. Taste the broth again and add more sugar or salt according
    to taste.

13. Simmer for 10 more minutes, then turn off the heat. The pork should be very tender.
14. Pour the caramelized pork and eggs into a large serving bowl, sprinkle black pepper on top, and garnish with green onions.
15. Serve with rice and pickled veggies.

Volcano Pizzas (Hawaiian & Italian)

These pizzas are called volcanos because they are spicy. You can adjust the spice level by moderating the amount of black pepper and chili paste in your sauce, as well as jalapenos on your pizza.

Crust:
3 1/3 cups flour plus ¼ cup for dusting
½ tablespoon salt
1 tablespoon honey
1 ¼ cup warm water, 100-110 degrees Fahrenheit
½ teaspoon active dry yeast
2 tablespoons olive oil

Directions for the crust:
1. In a small bowl, stir together water and honey.
2. Add yeast to the honey water and let it sit for five minutes, then stir together.
3. In a separate large bowl, combine flour and salt.
4. Slowly add the water mixture and fold in with a spatula.
5. Knead the dough with your hands for a few minutes. The dough will be sticky and so will your hands.
6. Cover the bowl with a plastic wrap and let it sit at room temperature for 5 hours. The dough will double in size.
7. While you're waiting for the dough to rise, prepare the pizza sauce and toppings.
8. When you are ready to roll the dough, preheat the oven to 400 degrees Fahrenheit.
9. Dust the countertop with flour and knead the dough, folding it 8-10 times.
10. Divide the dough in half to make two pizzas.
11. Use some of the flour to dust the rolling pin and roll each dough ball into a round crust about 12-14 inches.
12. Brush each crust with a tablespoon of oil.
13. Line two pizza pans with parchment paper and place the crusts on each pan.
14. Bake at 400 degrees for 8 minutes, then remove from the oven.

Sauce:
*This recipe will yield extra sauce for dipping if you serve pizza with breadsticks or freeze the sauce to make other pasta dishes such as spaghetti, lasagne, ravioli, or tortellini.

4-14.5 ounce cans fire-roasted tomatoes
4 cloves garlic (minced)
2 tablespoons Italian seasoning
1 teaspoon salt

1 tablespoon ground black pepper (be generous if you like it spicy)
1 cup basil (chopped)
 Optional: 1 tablespoon flour or corn starch for a thicker sauce.

Directions for the pizza sauce:
1. Put all the ingredients *except the basil and flour/ corn starch* into a blender and pulse on low for 30 seconds to a minute.
2. Taste the sauce and add more salt or black pepper according to your taste.
3. Pour the sauce into a saucepan and bring to a low boil on medium-high heat.
4. Reduce the heat and stir in flour or corn starch if you'd like a thicker sauce.
5. Simmer on low heat with the cover on for 10 minutes.
6. Turn off the stove and remove the pan from the heat.
7. Let the sauce sit for 5-10 minutes to thicken and cool.
8. Gently fold in the chopped basil.

Toppings:
For the Hawaiian pizza:
- slices of cooked ham
- pineapple chunks or slices, fresh or canned (drained)
- jalapeno peppers, thinly sliced
- mozzarella and parmesan cheese (shredded/grated)

For the Italian pizza:
- slices of peppered salami
- sliced pepperoncini peppers
- red onion (diced)
- grape tomatoes (halved lengthwise)
- jalapeno peppers, thinly sliced
- mozzarella and parmesan cheese (shredded/grated)

Assembly:
1. Preheat the oven to 400 degrees Fahrenheit.
2. Spread enough pizza sauce on each crust to cover the whole pizza.
3. Sprinkle a generous amount of mozzarella and parmesan cheese on top of the sauce and cover the whole pie.

4. Add the toppings. I usually start with the meats then finish with the fruits and veggies.
5. Bake for 10 minutes and remove the pizzas. Enjoy right away.

757

SWEET TREATS

"We hide Amy's food from the kids when she cooks for us.
Sorry. Not sorry."
—**Tricia and Blake Rutledge, Foodies**

Cà Phê Sữa (Vietnamese Coffee)

Ingredients:

3 tablespoons chicory ground coffee
(I prefer Café Du Monde or Trung Nguyen Premium Coffee)
1-3 tablespoons condensed milk (sweetness according to taste)
1-2 tablespoons creamer (optional if you want your coffee extra creamy)
6-8 ounces of hot water, around 194 degrees Fahrenheit, before boiling point.
1 cup crushed ice (optional if you want iced coffee)

Other:
6-ounce stainless steel coffee pot drip filter

Directions:
1. Spoon the condensed milk into an old-fashioned drinking glass.
2. Scoop 3 tablespoons of ground coffee into the stainless steel coffee pot drip filter. Do not pack the coffee down.
3. Assemble the filter gently in the stainless steel pot and turn it clockwise a couple of times. It should sit leveled and gently on the coffee grounds.
4. Place the coffee pot drip filter over the condensed milk, on top of the old-fashioned drinking glass.
5. Pour steaming hot water into the coffee pot drip filter and watch the coffee drip into the glass. It should drip nicely but not too fast.
6. If you do not like your coffee too strong, pour another 3-6 ounces of water into the coffee pot drip filter.
7. Once all the water has strained through the filter, remove the stainless steel coffee pot drip filter and place it on top of the stainless steel lid to catch excess liquids.
8. Mix the coffee and condensed milk with a spoon until evenly mixed.
9. Add more condensed milk if you like it sweeter.
10. Add creamer if you would like your coffee extra creamy.
11. If you prefer iced coffee, let your coffee cool down.
12. Fill a tall highball drinking glass with crushed ice.
13. Pour your French-Vietnamese coffee into the iced glass.

Chè Ba Màu (Three Color Dessert)

Ingredients:

Red layer:
1 can sweet red kidney beans (drained)

Yellow layer:
½ cup dried mung beans
3-4 tablespoons sugar
4 cups water

Green layer:
1 tablespoon agar agar powder
2 cups water
¼ teaspoon pandan extract or green food coloring
3 tablespoons sugar

Coconut cream:
1 can coconut milk
3 tablespoons sugar
1 teaspoon tapioca starch or cornstarch

Other:
3 cups shaved ice

Directions:
1. Soak the yellow mung beans in water for 4-5 hours or overnight, then drain the water.
2. In a pot over medium-high heat, cook the mung beans in four cups of water until the beans are soft. Stir frequently so the beans do not stick together or burn. Add more water as needed.
   **If you have a rice cooker, cook the mung beans in the rice cooker instead with ¾ cup of water on the regular rice setting.
3. Once the mung bean is cooked, mash the beans into a paste. Mix in 3 tablespoons of sugar and taste. Add another tablespoon of sugar if you prefer a sweeter mung bean paste. Set aside in the fridge to chill.
4. In a saucepan, bring 2 cups of water to a boil and stir in the agar agar powder until it dissolves.

5. Add the pandan extract or food coloring and turn off the heat. Stir the mixture evenly then pour into a glass container.
6. Let the pandan jelly cool down before chilling it in the fridge for 2-3 hours.
7. Once the jelly is thickened cut the pandan jelly into strips.
8. In a saucepan, whisk together the coconut milk, 3 tablespoons of sugar, and tapioca starch or cornstarch.
9. Heat the coconut cream on medium heat for 3+ minutes until it thickens. Remove from heat and let it cool down before putting it in the fridge to chill for an hour.
10. To assemble, put a layer of shaved ice on the bottom, then sweet red kidney beans, a thin layer of shaved ice, then mung beans, then pandan jelly. Top the dessert with more shaved ice and pour the sweet coconut cream on top.
11. Shovel the dessert in your mouth with a spoon and enjoy the chilled three-color dessert. It tastes better if you are in a hammock with a tropical breeze and a view of the beach!

Chè Thái (Thai Fruit Cocktail)

Ingredients:

Gelatin:
1 package coconut gelatin mix
1 package almond gelatin mix
½ package agar-agar powder (cook with 2 cups of water)
½ cup sugar

Directions for the gelatins:
1. Prepare the coconut gelatin and almond gelatin mixes according to the instructions on the package.
2. For the agar-agar, in a small pot with 2 cups of water, whisk in the agar-agar powder and sugar.
3. Bring it to a boil for 2 minutes then pour it into a glass container. Let it cool down before chilling it in the fridge for 2 hours.
4. Cut the agar-agar jelly, almond gelatin, & coconut gelatin into cubes.
5. Chill the gelatin mix in the fridge.

Imitation Pomegranate:
1 can water chestnuts, cut into small pieces
1 cup tapioca flour or cornstarch
2 drops red food color

Directions for the imitation pomegranate:
1. Put the chopped water chestnuts in a bowl and mix in 2 drops of red food coloring.
2. Add the red chestnuts to a ziplock bag. Pour in the tapioca flour and seal the bag. Shake it until all the chestnuts are coated in flour.
3. Pour the floured chestnuts into a colander and sift out the excess flour.
4. Prepare a bowl of cold water. You will be transferring your cooked chestnuts into a cold bath.
5. Bring a pot of water to a boil and then add the red, floured chestnuts. Let it boil for two minutes. When it floats to the top, it is ready.
6. Using a slotted ladle, transfer the chestnuts to your cold bath and let them soak in the cold water. Drain the water once the chestnuts are cool.
7. Chill the imitation pomegranate in the fridge.

Cream:
1 quart of half and half
1/3 cup condensed milk

Directions for the cream:
1. Mix the half and half with the condensed milk until smooth.
2. Chill in the fridge until ready for assembly.

Fruits:
2 cans longan with juice
1 can coconut meat (drained, cut into strips)
1 can coconut jelly and papaya (drained)
1 can jackfruit (drained, cut into strips)
1 can toddy palm seeds (drained, rinsed)

Directions for the fruits:
1. In a large bowl, combine all the canned fruits, making sure to drain all of the liquids except the longan. Keep the longan juice.
2. Cut the coconut meat and jackfruit into strips.
3. Chill the fruit bowl in the fridge until you're ready to assemble.

Assembling the fruit cocktail:
1. Remove the fruit bowl out of the fridge and pour in the gelatins, the imitation pomegranates, and the cream.
2. Ladle the fruit cocktail into a tall glass and enjoy. Feel free to add shaved ice to the glass but the cocktail should already be chilled.
3. Now, put on your sunglasses, regardless of the weather, because when you're this cool, the sun always shines.

Coconut Rum Banana Bread

Ingredients:

Bread:
2 cups flour
¾ teaspoon baking soda
½ teaspoon salt
1 cup granulated sugar
¼ cup butter, softened
2 eggs
5 very ripe bananas
¼ cup plain yogurt
1/3 cup of coconut rum
½ teaspoon vanilla extract
1 cup sweetened coconut flakes or shredded coconut

Glaze:
2 cups sweetened coconut flakes or shredded coconut
1 cup powdered sugar
1 tablespoon of fresh lemon juice or lemon curd
¼ cup coconut rum

Directions:
1. Preheat oven to 350 degrees Fahrenheit.
2. Combine the flour, baking soda, and salt in a bowl.
3. In a separate large bowl, combine the butter and sugar. Beat with a hand mixer until well-blended.
4. Add the eggs and continue beating until mixed well.
5. Add in the yogurt, bananas, rum, and vanilla extract.
6. Beat until blended, then add in the flour mixture. Beat on low until mixed. Stir in 1 cup of the coconut flakes.
7. Spoon the batter into a 9x5 inch loaf pan coated with oil.
8. Bake for one hour. Meanwhile, prepare the glaze.
9. In a bowl, combine powdered sugar, lemon juice or curd, coconut flakes, and coconut rum. Mix well and taste. If your tummy feels warm from the rum, it's okay. This is adulting. Want it sweeter? No problem, add more powdered sugar!
10. Once the bread is cooked, transfer it to a cooling rack for ten minutes.
11. Lather, don't drizzle, the tops of the warm banana bread with the coconut rum glaze.
12. Make it a party with some long island iced tea!

Cream Puffs

Ingredients:

Powdered sugar for dusting

Puff pastry:
1 cup water
½ cup butter, softened
1 cup flour
4 eggs

Directions for the puff pastries:
1. Preheat the oven to 400 degrees Fahrenheit.
2. Mix the water and butter and heat it in a saucepan on medium heat.
3. Lower the heat and stir in the flour vigorously until it forms a ball.
4. Beat in the eggs, one at a time, thoroughly.
5. Use a cookie scooper and drop a scoop of dough onto an ungreased baking sheet, three inches apart.
6. Bake for 40-45 minutes and let the puffs cool on a cooling rack.

Cream filling:
2 cups whole milk
1 teaspoon vanilla extract
1 cup sugar
½ cup flour
½ teaspoon salt
2 eggs, yolks separated
½ teaspoon lemon zest

Directions for the cream filling:
1. Bring the milk to a boil in a saucepan, then add the vanilla extract. Remove from heat but keep the stove on.
2. In a bowl, mix the egg yolks with only half of the sugar (i.e. ½ cup) and ½ teaspoon of salt.
3. Add half of the warm milk into the sugar and eggs bowl. Mix well.
4. Add the lemon zest, then pour the mixture into the warm milk in the saucepan.
5. Bring it to a boil while stirring until the filling thickens.

6. Remove the filling from the heat and pour it into a bowl or pan. Let it cool in a bed of ice.
7. While the filling cools, use a hand mixer to whip together on medium-high speed the egg whites and remaining ½ cup of sugar until a meringue with stiff peak forms.
8. Combine both mixtures of the beaten egg whites with the cooled cream filling.

Assembling the cream puffs:
1. Poke a small hole at the bottom of each puff pastry.
2. Pour the cream filling into a piping bag and fill each puff pastry with the custard.
3. Dust the tops of each cream puff.
4. Chill the pastries for an hour in the fridge before eating, if you can be patient!
5. I bet you can't eat just one!

Da Ua (Vietnamese Yogurt)

Ingredients:

1-14 ounce can sweetened condensed milk
1 ¼ cup boiling water
2 ½ cups whole milk (1% or 2% is fine)
1 ¼ cup plain yogurt (I prefer Greek yogurt)
Yogurt must contain active cultures
1 cup water

Other:
large Instant Pot preferred but not required.
7 – 8 ounce glass jars with lids (If no lid, use aluminum foil)
Any size and type of glass jars will do, such as mason jars or baby food jars.

Directions:
1. In a large bowl, whisk together condensed milk and boiled water until the condensed milk dissolves and well-mixed together.
2. Add cold milk straight from the refrigerator and mix well. The higher the milk fat, the creamier the yogurt. Adding cold milk ensures the mixture is below 130 degrees Fahrenheit. Active cultures will die if the temperature is above 130 degrees.
3. Add plain yogurt to the mixing bowl and whisk until smooth.
4. Pour the mixture into the glass jars and cover with a lid or aluminum foil.
5. Prepare the Instant Pot by adding one cup of water and placing the steaming trivet into the pot.
   **If you do not have an instant pot, place all the jars in the oven. Keep the oven off but the oven light on and incubate for 11 hours.
6. Place all the jars into the Instant Pot. It is alright to stack the jars.
7. Close the lid, ensure the vent is sealed, and select the "Yogurt" option on the Instant Pot.
8. Set the time to 11 hours and start the incubation. "Yogt" will display on the Instant Pot once the incubation is done.

9. Remove the jars and refrigerate for a couple of hours. The
    yogurt will keep for two weeks in the refrigerator – longer
    if you transfer to the freezer after two hours of
    refrigeration.
    **Enjoy frozen yogurt for a nice treat on a hot day.
10. Optional: Top yogurt with fruits or granola.

Dalgona (Whipped Coffee)

Ingredients:
4 tablespoons instant coffee
4 tablespoons sugar
4 tablespoons hot water
milk (your choice – 2%, almond, soy, coconut, whole, oat, etc)
ice cubes
Optional: Baileys Irish Cream or Grind coffee liqueur
Optional garnish: espresso beans

Directions:
1. Whisk together the instant coffee, sugar, and hot water until it thickens and peaks form. I start with a hand whisk then move to an electric hand mixer.
2. Don't give up. It will take some time to thicken and form majestic, caramel-colored peaks.
3. Fill a glass with ice. Add a teaspoon or an ounce of Baileys Irish Cream or Grind coffee liquor. It depends on how much of a good time we're having. Skip the Baileys or Grind if we're being good.
4. Add milk to the glass, leaving a half-inch available for the whipped coffee.
5. Spoon as much whipped coffee as you want on top and garnish with espresso beans if you're "bougie boozy."
6. Drink the dalgona with a straw or gently mix the whipped coffee into your milk and enjoy.

Flan/Purin (Caramel Pudding)

Ingredients:

Flan:
6 eggs
2 teaspoons vanilla extract
3 cups half and half
1 cup sugar

Directions for the flan:
1. Beat the eggs and vanilla together well then set aside.
2. Heat the sugar and half and half on medium heat until the sugar is melted and the color is caramel brown.
3. Pour the sweet milk into the eggs and vanilla mixture.
4. Strain the mixture so the batter is smooth and creamy.

Caramel:
1 cup sugar
4 tablespoons water

Directions for the caramel sauce:
1. Heat the sugar and water on the stove in a small pan until the sugar is melted and the color is a caramel brown color.
2. Evenly distribute the caramel into the ramekins or small tart pans. The caramel will harden quickly.

Other:
8 ramekins or 4 small pie tart pans
10"x14" baking pan
aluminum foil
strainer

Directions:
1. Preheat the oven to 300 degrees Fahrenheit.
2. Fill the baking pan with hot water to the level that is half the height of the ramekins or tart pans.
3. Place the pan of water in the oven while the oven is preheating.
4. Prepare the flan as directed above then make the caramel as noted above.
5. Pour the flan batter into the caramel-coated ramekins or tart pans.
6. Cover each with aluminum foil.

7. Place the ramekins or tart pans <u>carefully</u> into the hot water in the pan and bake for 40 minutes.
8. Remove the flans from the oven and let them cool for 30 minutes before putting them in the fridge to cool and set for about 3 hours.
9. To serve, put the ramekins or tart pans in a pan of very hot water. Let it sit for a few minutes to warm up the caramel.
10. Loosen the edges/sides of the flan with a butter knife or silicone spatula before flipping it over onto a flat plate.
11. Ring a bell. Your taste testers will come running.

Lemon Cheesecake

Ingredients:

Crust:
2 cups honey graham cracker crumbs
1/3 cup melted butter

Directions for the crust:
1. Crush the graham crackers into fine crumbles using a pestle and mortar.
2. Pour in the melted butter and combine evenly.

Filling:
4-8 ounce packages of cream cheese, softened
1 ½ cups sugar
4 tablespoons flour
1 teaspoons vanilla extract
1 teaspoon lemon extract
4 eggs (beaten)

Directions for the filling:
1. Using a hand mixer, mix the softened cream cheese and sugar evenly, then add the flour and continue mixing.
2. Add in the vanilla and eggs. Mix well to remove the lumps.

Lemon curd frosting:
4 lemons, zested and juiced
1 ½ cups sugar
1 stick of butter, softened
4 eggs
1 jar Dickinson's lemon curd or Trader Joe's lemon curd

Directions for the lemon curd:
1. Combine the lemon zest and sugar in a food processor. Pulse it until the combination is finely minced.
2. In a medium-sized bowl, cream together the butter and lemon zest.
3. Beat in the eggs, then add the lemon juice. Mix well.
4. Pour the lemon mixture into a saucepan and cook on medium heat until it thickens, stirring frequently.
5. Let the lemon curd cool, then add the store-bought jar of lemon curd to the homemade lemon curd. Mix evenly.
6. Cover it and put it in the fridge to chill for an hour.

Other:
food processor
pestle and mortar
cooking spray
springform pan
aluminum foil
spatula
large pie dish filled with water
electric hand mixer

Directions:
1. Preheat the oven to 350 degrees Fahrenheit.
2. Place a pie dish filled with water on the bottom rack and let the water heat up in the oven.
3. Line the bottom of the springform pan with aluminum foil.
4. Grease the bottom and sides of the pan with cooking oil.
5. Pour the graham cracker crumbles into the springform pan and press the crust out evenly and firmly.
6. Pour in the cheesecake filling (the batter) on top of the crust.
7. Place the springform pan on the rack directly above the hot water in the oven.
8. Bake for one hour then remove the springform pan out of the oven.
9. Drape a kitchen towel over the pan. Let it cool for 2 hours before putting it in the fridge to chill overnight. (Keep it in the pan.)
10. Prepare the lemon curd frosting per the directions above.
11. Remove the cheesecake from the springform pan and frost the top of the cheesecake with the lemon curd.

Mango Sticky Rice

Ingredients:

1.5 cups glutinous rice
19 fl. oz. can coconut cream
1/3 cup sugar
2 tablespoons sesame seeds (lightly toasted)
6 champagne or honey mangos

Directions:

1. Wash and rinse the rice a few times until the water runs clear.
2. Drain the rice into a sieve and steam the rice over a pot of boiling water with the lid on for 60-90 minutes. You can also cook it in a rice cooker like regular white rice. The rice should be sticky and moist.
3. In a small saucepan on high heat, bring the coconut cream to a boil.
4. Add the sugar to the coconut cream and stir until dissolved.
5. Remove the coconut cream from the heat and spoon 1 cup of it into a small bowl. Put the small bowl in the fridge to chill for 30 minutes.
6. Peel and cut up the mangos into cubes.
7. Once the rice is cooked, transfer it to a bowl and pour the coconut cream over the rice.
8. Mix the rice and coconut cream and let the rice soak in the cream for 30 minutes.
9. To serve, scoop the sticky rice into a serving bowl or plate, drizzle the chilled coconut cream on top, sprinkle some toasted sesame seeds on top, and spoon the cut mangos over the sticky rice.

Raspberry Lemon Cake

Ingredients:

Cake batter:
1 stick unsalted butter, softened
1 stick salted butter, softened
1 ½ cups sugar
¼ cup brown sugar
1 teaspoon lemon extract
1 teaspoon vanilla extract
1 lemon, zested and juiced
4 eggs
2 ½ cup cake flour
1 ½ teaspoon baking powder
½ teaspoon baking soda
½ cup milk (2% or whole)
½ cup sour cream
1 cup of raspberries

Directions for the batter:
1. In a large bowl, using an electric hand mixer on medium speed, combine the butter, sugars, extracts, and lemon zest and juice.
2. Add the eggs, one at a time, and continue mixing. Set aside.
3. In a separate bowl, whisk the cake flour, baking powder, and baking soda.
4. Add the dry mixture to the wet mixture and mix on low speed for a minute. It will be lumpy.
5. Add in the milk and sour cream. Use a spatula to fold the batter gently together and mix evenly but do not over mix otherwise your cake will be dry and dense. We want them fluffy and moist!
6. Fold in the fresh raspberries.

Filling:
1 jar of homemade or store-bought lemon curd

Frosting:
8 ounces cream cheese, softened
1 stick of salted butter, softened
3 cups powdered sugar
1 tablespoon lemon zest
1 tablespoon lemon juice

½ teaspoon lemon extract
3 tablespoons sour cream
Directions for the frosting:
1. In a large bowl, using an electric hand mixer on low speed beat the cream cheese and butter until it is fluffy.
2. Add in the powdered sugar and continue mixing on low speed.
3. Add the lemon zest, lemon juice, and lemon extract and mix until creamy.
4. Add the sour cream and increase the speed to medium. Continue mixing until the frosting is light and creamy.

Garnish:
3 cups fresh raspberries

Other:
cooking oil
2-9 inch cake pans
parchment paper, cut into two 9-inch circles for each cake pan
electric hand mixer
whisk
spatula
cooling racks

Directions:
1. Preheat the oven to 350 degrees Fahrenheit.
2. Coat the sides and bottoms of each cake pan with oil.
3. Place the parchment paper circles on the bottoms of each cake pan and coat the parchment paper with oil.
4. Pour the cake batter evenly into each cake pan and bake for 40 minutes. The tops should be firm and golden.
5. Test the cakes by inserting a toothpick or fork into them. If it pulls out dry, your cakes are done.
6. Let the cakes cool in the pan for ten minutes, then remove the cakes and allow them to cool completely on cooling racks.
7. Place one of the cakes on a plate or cake stand and spread a thin layer of lemon curd on top. Use the whole jar.
8. Spread the frosting all around the sides of the cake.
9. Gently place the second cake on top of the first one and press firmly down to seal the two cakes together with the layer of lemon curd.

10. Put the cake in the fridge to set for 20 minutes then resume frosting the rest of the cake, sides, and top.
11. Put the cake back in the fridge to chill for 20 minutes.
12. Now you are ready to decorate the cake with fresh strawberries.

"Get in my belly!"
—Jennifer Hwang, Escrow Officer

Joe Walls, my "will work for food" photographer

Amy supervising Joe, supervising Preston

Chloe, our quiet kitchen stalker, waiting for a treat

Ike, our kitchen cleaning crew

Follow Amy on social media!
#SnowinVietnam
#SnowinSeattle
#SnowsKitchen
#SnowTrilogy

https://www.facebook.com/authoramymle
https://www.facebook.com/quillhawkpublishing/
https://twitter.com/amy_m_le
https://twitter.com/hawk_quill
https://www.linkedin.com/in/amymle/
https://www.etsy.com/shop/QuillHawkPublishing
https://www.instagram.com/amy_m_le/
https://www.instagram.com/quillhawkpublishing/
https://www.amy-m-le.com

About the Author

Amy M. Le was born in Vietnam and immigrated to The United States in 1980 at the age of five with her mother and cousin. She graduated from Western Washington University with a degree in Sociology and worked in the telecommunications and technology sectors for twenty years. Amy calls the Pacific Northwest and Oklahoma her home. Her greatest joys are spending time with her family, cooking, and traveling.